M.W

AT THE TOSS OF A SIXPENCE

Also by Lynda Page

Evie
Annie
Josie
Peggie
And One For Luck
Just By Chance

AT THE
TOSS OF
A SIXPENCE

Lynda Page

HEADLINE

First published in 1997
by HEADLINE BOOK PUBLISHING

10 9 8 7 6 5 4 3 2 1

British Library Cataloguing in Publication Data

Page, Lynda
  At the toss of a sixpence
  I.Title
  823.9'14[F]

ISBN 0 7472 1804 8

Typeset by
Letterpart Limited, Reigate, Surrey

Printed and bound in Great Britain by
Mackays of Chatham PLC, Chatham, Kent

HEADLINE BOOK PUBLISHING
A division of Hodder Headline PLC
338 Euston Road
London NW1 3BH

For my mother – Edith Pearson

A mother is irreplaceable. No matter how old one grows a mother's love and wisdom is always needed. I wish you were still here to give me yours.

ACKNOWLEDGEMENTS

Clare Scott, Publicity Manager, Headline – and I thought publishing was supposed to be a serious business!

Annita Eddison – thank you for the 'three' words and the drunken scene. Neighbours do have their uses beyond providing cups of sugar and throwing candles over the garden fence during power cuts.

Uncle Ted (Edward Page) – how many authors can claim to have a beloved uncle who gets thrown out of a bookshop for pulling her books forward – apart from me? Please don't stop – I promise I'll bail you out of jail!

Chapter One

'Liar!'

Clarence Bailey gawped in surprise. Never in his fifty-five years of practising law had he been addressed in such a manner.

'Miss Listerman, really.' He whipped off his half-moon gold-rimmed spectacles and indicated with a gnarled arthritic finger the chair in front of his desk. 'Sit down,' he ordered, his voice cracked with age. 'You're upset. It's understandable in the circumstances. But let us try to discuss this matter in a civilised manner.'

The young woman who had addressed him so harshly turned and glared angrily. 'Upset! That word does not do justice to my feelings, Mr Bailey. I'm devastated, that's what I am.'

'Well, yes, as I said before, that's understandable. But hurling insults won't improve matters, will it?'

Albertina Victoriana Listerman took a deep breath. 'No, I suppose not.' Her large dark brown eyes flashed. 'But with the news you've just imparted, how can you expect me to react in a civilised manner? I came to see you thinking I was a wealthy woman, or at the very least comfortable. And now I'm led to believe I'm virtually penniless.'

Clarence stared at her for a moment before easing his aged body awkwardly from his red leather wing-backed chair. He slowly made his way across the highly polished floor towards the leaded-glass window, all the time conscious that his client was staring at him, waiting for his answer. Rivulets poured down the window, the beat of the rain against the glass ringing in his ears. He inhaled deeply. This situation really was dreadful. He turned and made his way back to his desk. 'I'm afraid that is the case, Miss Listerman,' he said, sitting down. 'But it depends on your interpretation of penniless. You surely have some money of your own? Your allowance . . .'

'Mr Bailey, my allowance hardly paid my dressmaker's bill. My half-brother was not over generous when it came to handing out money. There was none left for saving. Besides, the need never entered my head. Why should it have? I was never given an inkling we were heading for this situation.'

He eyed her thoughtfully. The seeds of this catastrophe had been sown years ago. And as he had suspected, Tobias Listerman had obviously kept the family's financial standing very much to himself. Despite Tobias's seeming co-operation on being questioned about his business dealings whenever Clarence himself had managed to force a meeting, he had never been able to shake the feeling that his client had been holding back far more than he was telling. Yes, Tobias Listerman had been a very secretive man.

A surge of pity for the young woman rose in him. The revelations of today were obviously a terrible shock to her. He had always prided himself on being a good judge of character and knew without a doubt that Albertina's angry outburst was just a cover for her true feelings. She was frightened – terrified – and she had every right to be.

Clarence mentally shook himself as he realised she was speaking.

'I don't believe a word of any of this, Mr Bailey. None of it makes sense. I don't know who exactly is behind this deceit but I intend to find out.'

Clarence clasped his hands together. 'Miss Listerman, every word I speak is the truth. Now if you'd care to sit down . . .'

'Stop patronising me! I'm no stupid girl without a brain in her head. I didn't spend all those years away at one of the best schools in London for nothing.' She stepped towards the desk, laid long slender hands on it, leaned over and looked Clarence straight in the eye. 'It's you, isn't it?' she accused. 'It has to be. You looked after the family business interests. You've embezzled the money. And like a good little girl, I'm supposed to swallow all this nonsense. Well, I won't! Now you tell me the truth – but be warned, I'm not going to let this matter lie. I shall fight you in the highest court and expose you for exactly what you are.'

Clarence's lined face reddened with indignation. He leaned back in his chair, his lips tight. 'I should have you marched out of here. Your accusations are slanderous. But I shall make allowances for your state of mind. The tragic death of your half-brother must have been a terrible shock. But that was ten weeks ago, Miss Listerman. In the meantime I've sent several letters and my clerk has been out to see you, imploring you for a meeting, but you chose to ignore this.'

She lowered her head in shame. How could she explain to Clarence Bailey that she had never had to deal with anything remotely like legal matters before? For the last ten weeks she had been struggling to get to grips with the running of the house while trying to accommodate constant demands from her future mother-in-law regarding the preparations for the wedding, as well as accompany her fiancé to the numerous social occasions they always seemed to be attending. In truth she hadn't had a moment to herself. Besides, she hadn't thought the visit to the lawyer was urgent. At the most she had thought her signature was required on documents to claim her inheritance. How wrong she had been! But how had she been expected to know otherwise? 'I was too busy,' she lied.

'Busy! Too busy to settle the estate?'

'Yes, I was,' she retorted. 'Besides, what estate? You're telling me there isn't one.'

'And I speak the truth. But matters still have to be settled. Now, I implore you, sit down so we can get this resolved once and for all. You need to understand your situation exactly.'

Albertina froze as the meaning of his words finally began to filter through. The elderly lawyer wasn't lying. He really was trying to explain to her as gently as possible her dire circumstances. A feeling of doom flooded over her. Groping for the chair, she lowered herself into it and fixed worried eyes on him. 'You are telling the truth, aren't you?' she whispered. 'But I don't understand . . . I mean, I know I never took much interest in the family affairs – I was never encouraged to. But I know they were extensive. The factory, the shops, all the property. They've been in the family for generations. What . . . what's happened to it all?'

Clarence Bailey ran a gnarled hand over his chin. Despite her unwarranted outburst he couldn't help but like her, just as he had liked both her parents, and he felt strongly she didn't deserve at her tender age, after a privileged upbringing, to be dealt such a dreadful unexpected blow. As a respected lawyer of long standing he had seen many tragic cases come through his office, but this young woman's was one of the worst. Through no fault of her own, she would soon have to face the harsh realities of life and he wondered how she would cope, considering she was so unprepared. Despite her boasts of a good education he doubted she had mastered much more than the art of catching a rich husband and the running of his household. Those skills would be of little use to her in the environment she would now have to enter.

From the way she had stood up to him, Albertina obviously possessed a very strong character, but would that strength be enough to see her through what faced her now? A flicker of a smile touched his lips. Despite her new circumstances she did have assets which would stand her in good stead. She was extremely pleasing on the eye. Even at his great age he still had a liking for a good figure. The pale blue fitted jacket she wore could not have complemented her shapely figure more, and although not a betting man, he would have put money on the fact that concealed inside high button boots beneath a long dark blue velvet skirt was a pair of very shapely ankles.

He forced his attention back to the matter in hand and straightened the pile of documents before him. In any case, her situation was not as dire as it could have been. She had said she was getting married. As things stood, that was the best thing for her. With a husband as provider many of the problems he'd worried she might face would be eliminated. He had no doubt the match would be a suitable one. He couldn't for the life of him see Albertina Victoriana Listerman marrying anyone beneath her.

He raised his eyes again. 'I cannot answer you regarding the money

3

that is unaccounted for. How your half-brother disposed of it I do not know. As for the assets – the factory was sold off not long after your parents died, the other properties gradually over a period of years. Of the three shops, only one remains and that's the Emporium on Humberstone Gate. But . . .'

'Then I'm not destitute as you said,' Albertina cut in quickly. 'I have the house and the shop. I could sell the shop and live on the proceeds.'

The old lawyer shook his head. 'My dear, selling it will not be easy. It could, in fact, take quite a while. As a going concern it would have been easier, but through bad management it was all but bankrupt when it was closed down a couple of years ago, so there is no goodwill. There is the added disadvantage that all the tenants were evicted from the rest of the building, so it has no trade at all. Whoever bought it would be starting from scratch.' He watched what was left of her colour drain from her face, and his own clouded with sympathy. 'The house has been sold to pay off debts. All the contents are to be auctioned.' He paused momentarily. 'The new owner takes possession tomorrow.'

'Sold? And all my mother's lovely things to be auctioned? But many of them are heirlooms. To me they are priceless. An auction!' She wrung her hands in distress. 'It sounds so sordid.' She shook her head in disbelief. 'Mr Bailey, please,' she begged, 'tell me that I misheard you?'

'I wish I could, my dear. If I had any other choice, Miss Listerman, don't you think I would have taken it? Despite your accusations, I cannot stress strongly enough that I do have your best interests at heart. But I had creditors demanding payment and thus had to take the first reasonable offer I got. That is why it was so urgent I saw you. I needed to prepare you for all this. But meeting or no meeting, the outcome would have been no different. The house would still have had to go. Be assured I got the best price I could. The monies gained from the sale and the auction combined should just about cover the debts.'

She gaped at him in horror. Not the house . . . the imposing gabled mansion set in rolling grounds . . . the house that had been in her family for generations, the place she'd been born and grown up in . . . must it really be sold? 'But why?' she uttered. 'How did we get into such debt? Why did my half-brother not tell me?' She frowned as a thought struck. 'And more to the point, Mr Bailey, fortunes are not lost overnight. As the family lawyer you must have seen what was going on. Why didn't you advise Tobias . . .'

'Advise?' he interrupted. 'Miss Listerman, you have put it in a nutshell. I am paid to advise and that is just what I did.' He leaned heavily on his desk and eyed her closely. 'My dear, I can advise until I'm blue in the face, but if the recipient does not want to listen . . .'

She frowned. 'Are you saying Tobias took no notice? That he let this all happen? I find it hard to believe that anyone in their right mind would

4

allow such a thing voluntarily.' She eyed him questioningly. 'Are you saying he wasn't of sound mind?'

'As far as I know your half-brother was as sane as you or I, Miss Listerman. But as matters stood when your parents died he had sole charge of administering the estate. He could do just as he wished until you came of age and inherited your share.'

'And when I come of age in two months' time what is my share of nothing, Mr Bailey? He has left me a worthy legacy, has he not? No wonder he took his own life!' She shook her head ruefully. 'His suicide makes sense to me now. He couldn't live with what he had done, squandering all the family's money. My birthday must have been marked on his calendar with a black cross because that was the day I would find out all this. But just what did he do with it all? That's what I want to know.'

'I would like a few questions answered myself, Miss Listerman. But as things stand the only person who could tell us is no longer around to do so.' Clarence took a deep breath. 'How well did you know Tobias?'

She looked at him quizzically for a moment then turned her head and stared hard at the wall opposite. It was lined with law books and for a fleeting moment it crossed her mind that Mr Bailey must be a very clever man indeed to practise and advise upon all the laws outlined in the numerous volumes. Momentarily she closed her eyes and pondered his question. She had hated Tobias. No, not hated. She had not known him well enough to hate him. But from the very start, despite her own efforts, Tobias had made no attempt whatsoever to know her. He had made it plain he found her presence irritating and had taken no pains to hide his feelings.

Albertina sighed heavily. She hadn't been aware of his existence until her parents died. She wondered if the old man sitting behind the desk could imagine what that had been like for an impressionable eleven year old who, prior to the terrible tragedy, had not a care in the world. They had been the most loving parents for whom a girl could have wished. Her life had been so perfect, cocooned by their protectiveness. To lose them both so unexpectedly . . .

She took a deep breath as memories of almost ten years ago surfaced and once again she was forced to endure the pain they brought. Pain she had learned to bury by sheer will-power.

The coastguards had still been searching for her parents' bodies when Tobias turned up and took control. His unexpected arrival had been such a shock. Although her father was much older than her mother Albertina had had no idea he had been married before, let alone had a son. It was something that had never occurred to her. They had all been so happy, such a complete family unit. Or so she had thought.

All these years later she still could not understand why the existence of Tobias had been kept such a secret. But the one question that had always

5

bothered her above all else was why her parents had been on that boat in the first place? They had told her they were going to attend to some business in town then pay a visit to friends, maybe stay overnight. They had wanted her to come with them, so why lie to her? If she hadn't sulked so much over having to miss her best friend's birthday party then she would not have been sitting here at all. She would have died with them.

She smoothed her cream cotton gloves distractedly over her knee. Tobias had had no idea of an eleven-year-old girl's needs. He had offered nothing in the way of comfort for her grief. She had just been packed off to boarding school, left to the mercies of the strict regime there. But, regardless, Tobias was the only family she had had and despite the fact that she did not like him, she tried very hard to have some sort of relationship with him. She wrote long letters but he hardly replied and she stopped going home during the holidays because he was never there. 'Away on business' was always his excuse. To all intents and purposes she might as well have been completely alone.

Regardless of her lack of feeling for Tobias, his suicide had shocked her greatly. Identifying his mangled remains had been the most terrible thing she had ever had to do. Not much had remained of him after the heavy goods train had rolled over him. He had wanted to die. Lying on the tracks voluntarily, having the iron monster bear down on him, was most definitely not the action of a man undecided as to what he wanted to achieve. Identification had only finally been made possible because of the envelope found at the side of the track, inside which Tobias had left his signet ring and a note.

Oh, that note! She shuddered to think of it. Tobias had not even apologised for his cowardly act nor had he given any reason for it. All he had written was: 'I don't want to live any more', and signed his name. But she knew now why he had done it and the word 'coward' seemed suddenly too tame to describe how she thought of him. But at this moment it was all she could think. How could he have done it? She, after all, was his half-sister, an innocent bystander, the person who would now have to suffer and shoulder the legacy he had left. And he hadn't even thought her worthy of a warning. If his note had held even a hint she might have been able to muster a little charity towards him.

A vision of him rose before her. He had been fat, clothes always straining hard against his bulk, a most unattractive man with small piggy eyes and hanging jowls. She had often wondered how a handsome, distinguished man like her father could possibly have sired him. Tobias had liked his drink. She hadn't been so innocent that she had not known that the broken red veins on his large bulbous nose were caused by alcohol. A rush of anger flooded through her. Was that where all the money had gone, on drink? But surely no one, not even Tobias, could drink away that much? So what had he done with it all?

Bewilderment was followed by anger and frustration at her worrying

6

situation. She raised her head and eyed the lawyer. 'If you'd done your job properly, Mr Bailey, then you would have known the situation between myself and my half-brother.'

'A lawyer only knows what a client confides, Miss Listerman. We have to deduce the rest.'

'And I suppose you have deduced that I am a spoiled female with no other interests apart from enjoying myself?' She smiled ironically. 'Well, Mr Bailey, you are probably right. But I have become what I am because I had no other avenues offered me, and at this moment in time I couldn't care less how people perceive me – you included.' She snatched up her gloves and rose. 'I'm going home, Mr Bailey. I shall be in touch in a couple of days. I need to think, formulate some plans.'

He raised his hand to stop her. 'Miss Listerman, please sit down. There are other matters I feel you ought to know . . .'

Her eyes flashed. 'Mr Bailey, with respect, I have learned enough for today. I don't think there is anything else of importance you have to relate to me.'

He stiffly rose and walked around his desk to face her. 'You can't go home, I'm afraid.'

'Can't?'

He shook his head. 'You can return to collect your own personal possessions but that is all, and my clerk, Mr Hubbard, will need to accompany you. Those are my instructions.'

'But that's preposterous! I have things to organise. I can't possibly be expected . . .'

'Miss Listerman, from today the house is no longer yours. Do you see now why it was so imperative we should meet? I even tried to arrange a visit myself, but how could I when you ignored my letters?' Pity for her situation filled him. He knew he shouldn't offer what he was about to but couldn't help himself. 'Look, why don't you come and stay with me and Mrs Bailey for a while? It'll give you time to adjust. I can arrange to have your possessions collected.'

It took all her strength not to dissolve into tears. She could not believe this was happening to her, that she would never again live at the house, feel the security of its familiar walls. But since her parents' deaths she had never cried in front of anyone and she was certainly not going to start now. Her crying would be done in privacy.

'I thank you for your offer,' she said stiffly, 'but I do have somewhere to go. My fiancé and his family will look after me, I have no doubt.' She pulled on her gloves. 'Do I still have the carriage at my disposal or am I expected to walk?' she asked sarcastically.

He ignored her jibe. 'I shall ask for it to be brought around.' He rang a bell on his desk and an elderly clerk entered. 'Please have Miss Listerman's carriage brought around and inform Hubbard we are ready for him.'

'Yes, sir,' came the reply.

Albertina made to leave then stopped. 'The servants, Mr Bailey. I'm concerned about them. If nothing else, will you please make sure they get their pay?'

He hid a smile. He knew he was right about her. Beneath the brittle surface was a very caring young woman. He wished that somehow he could have broken through her façade if only enough to help her handle the shock he had just dealt her. 'I'll do all I can,' he promised.

Albertina thrust out her hand. 'Good day, Mr Bailey.'

'What are your wishes regarding the Listerman building on Humberstone Gate?' he called after her.

She stopped and turned, replying without hesitation: 'What use have I for it? Do what you like. Give it away if necessary. As you are well aware I have no resources to finance any repairs or whatever else is entailed in its upkeep. If you need me to sign anything, I can be reached at the Williamson-Brown residence in Kibworth Harcourt.'

'But, Miss Listerman . . .'

His words fell on deaf ears. She had gone.

Clarence walked slowly round his desk and sat down, exhaustion sweeping over him. The interview had drained most of his strength. He picked up the documents and tied them tightly together with a piece of thin pink tape, then lifted his head and stared across at the closed wooden door. Albertina had learned only a part of what he really ought to have told her. And he was old; not many men lived to see the age he had reached. If he died she would never know. Only Clarence Bailey knew.

The door opened and he smiled a greeting at the middle-aged woman who entered carrying a laden tray.

'It's still throwing it down wi' rain. The yard's beginning ter flood,' she said, hobbling towards him. 'In all my born days I ain't never seen rain like it. Methinks someone up there forgot to turn the tap off.' She chuckled at her joke. 'There's talk that if it carries on the river'll bust its banks. There yer go.' She smiled. 'I thought yer could do wi' a cuppa tea before yer see yer next client.'

He nodded appreciatively. 'Thank you, Mrs Bell.'

The 'Mrs' was just a courtesy title afforded the woman during business hours. Agnes Bell had never married. Physical abuse at the hands of her father had killed any hope or desire she might once have had to spend her life with a man. His reign of brutal tyranny had left her with a badly disfigured nose and a pronounced limp. Her youth had not promised great beauty and these added handicaps had done her no favours.

She owed her employer her life. Clarence had gone to work earlier than usual one bitterly cold morning and found her huddled on his doorstep. She was barely fifteen years old but her face was so badly swollen her age at that time was indeterminate. Left much longer, the cold would have killed her. Without hesitation he had taken her in and he and his wife nursed her back to health, much to the misgivings of his friends and colleagues.

These misgivings proved to be unfounded. Agnes's gratitude knew no bounds. Once her outward injuries had healed sufficiently she repaid the kindness bestowed on her by becoming as trustworthy an employee as Clarence could have wished for. Her loyalty was fierce – so much so that he had no hesitation in offering her the post of housekeeper of his business premises, furnishing the attic room for her living accommodation. She had been with him now for thirty years.

He watched as she cleared a place on his desk and poured the tea.

'Agnes,' he said thoughtfully, 'do you think my clients see me as a cold man?'

Her head jerked up. 'What a question, Mr Bailey. 'Course they don't.'

He sighed heavily. 'I'm sure they do. But then, I have no choice. I have to appear impartial. If I am not, I cannot do my best for them. Oh, Agnes, I'm getting too old. I should have retired long ago. Let a younger man take over.'

She smiled as she continued her task. 'You retire, Mr Bailey? Never. They'll be carrying you outta 'ere clutching a sackload of case notes when yer pop yer clogs.' She handed him a china cup and inclined her head towards the door. 'Hard case, is it? I saw the young woman going down the stairs. She had a look of doom on 'er. Pretty thing, though.' She turned from him and made her way to the fire where she gave the coals a prod with the poker and put on several more lumps.

Clarence smiled distractedly. He would have liked nothing more than to discuss Albertina's case with Agnes, but would never dream of breaching a client's confidentiality. Neither his wife nor anyone else not directly concerned with business matters knew what went on behind his office door. He had always taken professional etiquette extremely seriously.

'Have we a drop of whisky, Agnes? A tot in my tea would go down very well.'

Straightening up, she turned to him and smiled warmly. 'I'll get some.'

As she went off in search of it, the junior clerk entered.

'Mr Sims is waiting. Bit agitated, sir.'

Clarence sighed heavily. He'd forgotten Mr Sims had an appointment – and he was not a favourite client. The man's business dealings were only just the right side of legal. One day, if he hadn't already, Clarence knew Sims would step over the line, then Clarence would have the excuse he wanted to withdraw his services. Until that time his client had to be suffered. 'Please apologise for the delay. I won't keep him much longer. I'll just finish my tea.'

'Right yer are, sir. And don't you worry, take yer time. Leave Mr Sims ter me.'

While he waited for Agnes's return Clarence sat back in his chair, his thoughts returning to Albertina. He really needed to see her again as soon as possible; felt strongly that he owed it to her and her dead parents to divulge what he knew. It was too late for Albertina to do much about what he had to tell her but, regardless, she had a right to know. He would leave it for a couple of weeks to let her accustom herself to matters and get settled at her fiancé's, then he would insist on an appointment.

Revived by a tot of whisky and the strong sweet tea, he turned all his thoughts to his next client and had him ushered in.

Chapter Two

Albertina glanced along the line of anxious faces. It suddenly struck her how little she knew of these people who had served her more than adequately, some of them all her life. If asked she would have had a job to recall their Christian names; she wouldn't be able to relate anything about their personal lives.

It hadn't always been this way. Albertina could vividly remember accompanying her mother down to the kitchen and sitting at the huge scrubbed pine table to partake of tea with Mrs Siddons, the cook, as they discussed menus and household events, she herself nibbling on a delicious assortment of home-made biscuits. The kitchen had always been warm, inviting, bustling with life. Now she couldn't remember the last time she had ventured down there. She felt a pang of inadequacy. Her mother had known all the Christian names of her employees and their respective families; had always enquired after their welfare. Praise had been readily given when it was due, and any chastisement had always been done behind closed doors so as not to cause the recipient further embarrassment. When was the last time she herself had bothered about these people? She couldn't remember that either.

Her years away at school and an unconscious desire to protect herself, in her youth and vulnerability, had distanced her from the staff, and when she had returned, try as she might to emulate what memories she held of her mother, she somehow could not carry it off. She wondered for a moment how her mother would have handled this situation. One thing was for certain: she would have put her employees at their ease as best she could and tried to allay their fears. But Albertina did not know how to do this. Her half-brother had always made it his business to deal with such matters, never failing to show his extreme annoyance should she trespass on what he saw as his territory – which in reality should have been hers. He had not been pleasant when angered and she had long ago stopped trying to assert herself and consequently life had become much easier. Now there was only one way she knew to handle this situation: give it to them straight and hope they understood.

She was conscious of Mr Hubbard standing behind her. His presence made her task even more difficult, knowing that what she said was bound to be relayed straight back to Clarence Bailey. Nevertheless she raised her

11

head high, wanting to get it over with.

'There is no easy way to tell you this, but the family money has all gone. It's as much of a shock to me as no doubt it will be to you all. To help pay the debtors the house has been sold.' She swallowed hard to rid herself of a lump of distress forming in her throat, fighting to keep her composure. It would not do for her to break down in front of the staff. She steeled herself and took another deep breath. 'The contents are to be auctioned. The new owner will be arriving tomorrow and I am to leave immediately. I can only wish you all well and thank you for your past service.'

She watched the expressions of horror and confusion settle on their faces, heard the murmurs of bewilderment and unease escape their lips.

Grudge, the butler, stepped forward. 'We knew summat were up, miss, when an official-looking chap arrived this morning after you'd gone out and instructed us ter tek down and crate some of the paintings. Went all round the 'ouse he did, demanding this and that. But we thought maybe you were getting the place redecorated ready fer when yer settled here after yer wedding. But when he told us ter pack yer trunks, well, we didn't know what ter think. But we had no idea of owt like this. It never entered our heads.' He eyed her worriedly. 'What's going to happen to yer, Miss Albertina? Where will yer go?'

Her eyes widened in surprise. She had expected an onslaught of questions about their own welfare, not hers. 'I will be going to the Williamson-Browns. Please don't concern yourselves on my account.'

'Oh, I see. Well, that's all right then.' Grudge shuffled nervously and cleared his throat. 'What about us then? What's going ter happen to all of us, Miss Albertina?'

Her heart went out to them. They were all good, loyal people and just like herself had been delivered a dreadful blow. She suddenly felt guilty. She had Lionel. Most of these people had been employed by the Listerman family for so long now they had nothing to fall back on. Looking after this house and its occupants was not only a job to them, it was their whole way of life. Her own situation was nowhere near as dire as theirs. 'I don't know,' she said flatly. 'I'm sorry, I can only hope that the new owner will need your service. I'm sure he will.'

She could see their expressions lengthen.

'Have yer put in a good word for us then?' Grudge asked hopefully.

'Er . . . that has not been possible. I haven't met the new owner and neither am I likely to.'

Their frowns of puzzlement deepened and she knew if she didn't escape now she would not do so without having to explain all the details of her own dire predicament. That she could not face, especially since she was still having terrible trouble accepting it herself.

She turned to face Mr Hubbard, knowing she could not leave without tackling one last task. 'I am just going to have a look around the house. I shall not keep you long.'

He stepped forward. 'I shall have to accompany you.'

Her face flushed with anger. 'I shall not steal anything if that is your concern,' she snapped.

He swallowed hard. 'No disrespect to yerself, miss. It's just me instructions.'

She was conscious that the servants were listening intently. Embarrassment filled her. She turned and headed for the sweeping staircase. As she ascended a vice-like pain tightened across her chest. Vivid patches where paintings had hung against the red flock wallpaper leaped out at her and she noted that a table on the half landing, on which there usually sat an ornate vase filled with fresh or dried flowers from the extensive gardens, had been removed. She had to grip the highly polished oak stair rail for support.

Albertina entered what had until that morning been her bedroom – a large room facing south, with views across the gardens towards rolling Leicestershire countryside. Across the years she had spent many hours inside this room; and shed tears of sorrow. It had been her one place of sanctuary. The only place Tobias had not had control of.

She stood just inside the door and gazed around. All her personal possessions had been removed. Her dressing table was empty. Its nakedness screamed out at her. Her eyes went to her bed, now cleared of the linen and tapestry bedspread that had covered it. She had lain in that bed this very morning and drunk the tea her maid had brought, waiting while the girl filled the bath. Albertina had taken her time dressing for her visit to the lawyer, fully expecting the appointment to be brief, and intending to go on to a viewing of items at Madam Delia's to add to her trousseau. Now she felt her legs buckle and caught hold of the door frame for support. Never again would she rise from that bed. Never again would she stare out of the window contemplating the view. But what cut the deepest was the realisation that she had taken all this for granted.

She froze as she heard the sound of the carriage being brought towards the front of the house, having now, she presumed, been loaded with her belongings. In a few moments she would be expected to board it and be carried away, never to return. Her whole body sagged. She couldn't bear it. This really was a living nightmare. She suddenly felt so alone, badly needed someone to put their arms around her and hug her tightly, tell her everything was going to be all right. Fighting her turmoil, she mentally shook herself. She was being silly. She wasn't alone. She had Lionel. She loved him with all her being and he in return loved her. And with Lionel came his family . . . a family that on her marriage would become her own. How vehemently she wished he was here, helping her through all this. His strength would have been her comfort.

She felt a hand on her arm.

'We really must be getting off, Miss Listerman. It'll be dark soon and it's a good distance to Kibworth Harcourt.'

She spun round to face Mr Hubbard, wrenching her arm away from his hand. How dare he manhandle her! Without a word she turned and strode out of the door and down the corridor.

The servants were still gathered in the hall. Hurriedly she said her goodbyes and climbed aboard the carriage, turning her head away from the house so no one could see the tears in her eyes.

The driver was just preparing to whip the horses into action when a thought suddenly struck her. Her mother's jewellery! How could she have forgotten that? After his arrival Tobias had collected it all up and put it in the safe, telling Albertina it would all become hers on her twenty-first birthday. Several of the pieces had been her grandmother's.

In her mind's eye she could still picture her mother wearing a large brooch made of rubies in the shape of an open rose. A single diamond like a dew drop sat on one of the petals. The brooch was unique, a specially made gift from Albertina's father in celebration of their first wedding anniversary. Amongst all the other fine pieces her mother had treasured that brooch above all else and suddenly it was important that Albertina should have it. They could have anything else to ensure the settlement of the family's debts, but the brooch must be hers in memory of her mother. It was in a box in the safe behind the painting in what had been her father's study.

For a fleeting moment she wondered if the old lawyer knew of the existence of the safe. She really should tell him. Then her eyes flashed. Maybe she would after she had done what she was about to.

She turned to Mr Hubbard. 'Stop the carriage!'

He jumped in surprise. 'Whatever . . .'

'Please do as I ask. Stop the carriage.'

Leaning out of the window, he shouted instructions to the driver then turned back to face her. 'Are you ill, Miss Listerman?'

'No, I'm not ill. I . . . er . . .' She stared at him. What plausible excuse could she use to go back inside the house? Her mind raced frantically. Of course, the most obvious one. She planted a look of embarrassment on her face. 'I'm very sorry but I do need the necessary room. It's a good hour's journey.'

Alighting from the carriage she felt her heart thump in trepidation at what she was about to do. The clerk seemed ready to follow her. She eyed him disdainfully. 'Well, really, Mr Hubbard. I can surely be trusted to attend to this on my own? I shall not be longer than two minutes.'

'But I'm . . .'

'. . . only doing your job,' she interrupted. 'Yes, I know. But that surely cannot include accompanying me to the necessary room? I shall be forced to speak to Mr Bailey about your conduct.'

She held her breath whilst he mulled the matter over in his mind, then anxiety got the better of her.

'Oh, for goodness' sake, I'm getting soaking wet standing here. I could have been there and back whilst you have been dithering.'

With that outburst she hurried up the steps towards the front door, praying he did not follow her.

Grudge, who was still standing just inside, eyed her in concern. 'Anything the matter, miss?'

'No,' she said, stamping her wet boots on the mat. 'I just need to make myself comfortable, that's all.'

He blushed. 'Oh, right yer are, Miss Albertina.'

Inside the door she paused. Thankfully all the other servants had dispersed, no doubt now gathered in the servants' hall to discuss their fate, but it wouldn't do for Grudge to spot her heading for the study. He might mention the fact at a later date. 'Oh, Grudge, just confirm the directions to Kibworth Harcourt to Mr Hubbard. It wouldn't do for us to get lost, especially on a night like this.'

He rubbed his chin. 'I ain't sure of the way, miss, I ain't never bin.'

'What! Oh . . . just . . . just tell him the directions to the main road then. Go on,' she demanded.

As he went down the steps towards the carriage Albertina spun round and swiftly headed for the study. She reached it unobserved and thankfully slipped inside. Shutting the door gently behind her, she headed for the mahogany bureau. Pulling open the front drawer, she thrust her hand inside and fiddled around. She found what she was looking for and heard a click. A side panel opened and she smiled. Tobias had not known she knew of this secret panel or that it was where he kept the safe key. Well, he wouldn't, he had been too preoccupied at the time doing something she could not see to notice her peering through the window. She had only been thirteen at the time and it had been a rare occasion when he had briefly returned home during a school holiday.

After Tobias's death she had on several occasions wanted to open the safe, take out the jewellery box and handle the contents. It would have been a comfort to be close to her mother in this way. On her twenty-first birthday they would all legally be hers and then she could wear the jewels openly. How she wished now she had not decided to wait!

Albertina suddenly became conscious time was wearing on. At least two minutes had passed since she had left the carriage. Panic rising, she grabbed the key, shut the secret door and headed for the wall where the Constable painting hung. Carefully unhooking it, she balanced it against the wall and thrust the key into the lock. She opened the safe door, extracting a large carved wooden box inlaid with mother of pearl. Carefully carrying it over to the desk, she gently set it down and slowly opened the lid. As she gazed inside her jaw dropped in shock.

The box was empty.

Chapter Three

Lavinia Williamson-Brown forced a smile of greeting as Albertina was shown by a gaunt, dim-witted maid into the drawing room of Meadowbank, a fourteen-bedroom red brick mansion house set in five acres of parkland on the outskirts of the village of Kibworth Harcourt.

Lavinia was a large matronly woman, greedy by nature. She loved her food, but more importantly loved money and what it would buy. After making a sensible marriage, her acquaintances, for she possessed no true friends, consisted of people whose names and bank balances were revered in the City. Lavinia was too full of her own self-importance to realise that these people only suffered her because she held the most lavish dinner parties in the county. She was legendary for them. Not to be invited to one was a terrible snub, social ostracism by the monied set. Therefore the wives of the gentry in the county bent over backwards to keep in favour with her; most hated themselves for it but unfortunately it was the way of things.

Just before Albertina arrived Lavinia had been staring into the fire, a worried frown creasing her fleshy forehead. She had a problem, a huge one, which was worsening by the week. But shortly everything was going to come right for the answer to her problem had just walked through the door.

'Why, Albertina, my dear, what a nice surprise. We didn't know whether to expect you as it's such a dreadful evening.' Her voice, like her dress sense, was loud. She indicated the settee opposite. 'Do sit down and warm yourself by the fire.' She cast her eyes over Albertina. 'Maybe you should change your clothes? You look quite damp. We don't want you catching something nasty, do we, my dear? Not with the wedding looming and still so much to do. Still, you are just in time for dinner. Fillet of venison followed by Queen of Puddings.' She clasped her fat hands together in delight. 'Oh, I do adore venison. Lionel is just dressing. He'll be down in a moment.' Her smile faded as she noticed the ashen colour of her visitor's face. 'Why, my dear, whatever's the matter?' Her glance settled on her son who had just entered the room. 'Lionel, get Albertina a glass of sherry,' she boomed. 'I do believe she's had a shock.'

He hurriedly complied and sat down next to his fiancée. He placed the sherry on a side table and took her hand. It felt cold to the touch and he stared at her in concern. 'Is Mother right, Ally? Have you had a shock?'

Her eyes brimmed with tears and the composure she had managed to sustain through sheer will-power disintegrated. 'Oh, Lionel, Mrs Williamson-Brown,' she wept, 'I *have* had a shock. A most dreadful shock. It really is most terrible.'

Lavinia sighed heavily. Disruption at mealtimes annoyed her. 'If it's so bad I'd better have a sherry too.' She reached for the bell push and pressed it hard. 'I hope it isn't anything to do with the wedding? I really could not bear that.' She eyed Albertina anxiously. 'It isn't anything to do with the wedding, is it?' Her beady grey eyes fixed on the maid hesitating just inside the doorway. 'Get me a glass of sherry,' she commanded, snapping her podgy fingers. 'A large one.'

The timid maid scuttled to obey her. As soon as she departed Lavinia tackled her son's fiancée head on. 'If it has nothing to do with the wedding, what is it to do with?'

'Mother, don't push her,' Lionel snapped. 'She will tell us in her own good time. Have a sip of sherry, Ally, it will calm you down.'

'Oh, Lionel, I'll need a decanter full for that! I am so distressed.'

The suspense was killing Lavinia who sniffed impatiently.

Ally wiped her eyes on her already sodden handkerchief and took a breath, lowering her head. 'It's my mother's jewellery,' she uttered. 'It's gone. Stolen. But it couldn't possibly be the servants. Apart from Tobias, I'm the only one who knew where the key to the safe was kept, I'm absolutely positive of that.'

'What!' blurted Lionel.

'It was worth a lot of money, wasn't it?' asked Lavinia.

She gulped on her drink and nodded. 'I expect so. Most of it was very old. But it's not what it was worth financially.' She raised red-rimmed eyes. 'To me that jewellery was priceless.'

'Who would do such a terrible thing?' Lavinia hissed, fingering the sapphire choker she wore round her neck. 'Have you any idea when it could have been stolen?'

Ally tightened her lips. There was only one person who could have taken it: Tobias. Despite the thought she shook her head. 'None.'

'Well, it's certainly a mystery,' Lavinia said, thinking that the truth of it must be that Ally herself had somehow misplaced it. 'Still, my dear, in two months' time you come of age and you'll be able to buy as much jewellery as you can possibly want.'

Ally gasped. 'That's just it, Mrs Williamson-Brown. I won't be able to buy anything. So, you see, my mother's jewellery is a double loss to me.'

Both Lavinia and Lionel stared at her quizzically.

'Don't be silly, my dear,' soothed Lavinia. 'You can't have forgotten you'll be coming into your inheritance? Get her another sherry, Lionel, she really is upset.'

Ally held her breath. Sherry on an empty stomach was making her feel nauseous. She jumped to her feet, hand clamped over her mouth as her stomach heaved. 'I'm going to be ill,' she gasped.

Lavinia stared in horror. 'Not on my Persian rug,' she hissed, thumping again on the bell push.

Ally almost knocked the maid out of the way as she ran through the door.

'Go with Miss Listerman to the wash room, and be quick about it,' Lavinia ordered the maid. Her eyes flew to Lionel hovering uneasily by the fireplace. 'What on earth's the matter with the girl? You would think someone in her position would be positively jumping for joy with all she's got coming to her.'

'Mother,' he scolded.

'I only speak the truth. Ah, Albertina dear, feeling better?'

She nodded as she re-entered the room and sat down. She eyed them both hesitantly, clasped her hands together in her lap and took a deep breath. 'It's not just the loss of the jewellery that's upset me. It's my inheritance.'

Lavinia eyed her sharply and scowled, confused. 'Your inheritance? What about your inheritance?'

Hands clasped tightly, Ally eyed them both anxiously. 'I haven't got one.'

They both stared in astonishment.

'What on earth are you talking about, child?' Lavinia scolded. 'Don't be silly, of course you have an inheritance. A large one. A very large one.'

She shook her head. 'No, I haven't. I don't know what Tobias did with it but it's all gone. Every penny. The house is sold – the new owner moves in tomorrow – and all the contents are to be auctioned to help clear the debts.' She sniffed miserably. 'It's all been such a shock, but at least I understand now why Tobias killed himself. He just couldn't face what he had done and took the easy way out.'

Lavinia gasped, astounded.

Lionel rushed to Ally, kneeled before her and took her hands. 'Oh, you poor darling. Well, don't you worry your pretty head about anything. We'll take care of you.' He glanced over at his mother. 'Won't we, Mother?' Then he turned back to Albertina. 'On our marriage I would have been taking care of you anyway, regardless of how much money you had.'

Her eyes filled with gratitude as she stared at the man she loved. He was so handsome, from his thick thatch of near jet black hair, which curled at his collar, to his long legs, muscular from riding.

Many hearts had been broken the day Lionel Williamson-Brown had proposed to Albertina Victoriana Listerman. But no one in their circle had really been surprised. The match was an ideal one.

Albertina raised her hand and ran it gently down his cheek. 'Oh, Lionel, are you sure this will not make any difference to us? I'm so frightened . . .'

'Don't be,' he commanded. 'I love you, Ally, whatever your means.'

The butler entered. 'Dinner is served, madam,' he announced grandly.

Lionel turned to his mother when she gave no response and frowned worriedly at the sight of her usually ruddy cheeks drained of all colour. 'Are you all right, Mother?'

Lavinia pulled herself together. 'Yes, I'm fine,' she snapped abruptly. 'You two go in to dinner. I'll follow shortly.'

He stared at her, shocked. His mother was always first in line when mealtimes were announced. Her response was most uncharacteristic. 'Are you sure you're all right?' he repeated.

'Oh, for goodness' sake, just go in, will you?'

Ally grabbed Lionel's arm. 'Would you mind if I gave dinner a miss? I really would just like to lie down for a while.'

'No, of course not. I'll have your things sent up.' He took her hands and kissed her cheek affectionately. 'You'll feel better after a rest. If you're hungry later, I can have a tray sent up.'

She smiled gratefully. 'Thank you, Lionel.' She looked over in the direction of her future mother-in-law who was staring distractedly into the fire, her fat fingers again absently stroking the sapphire choker adorning her neck. 'Shall I use the room I normally do, Mrs Williamson-Brown?'

'Huh? Mmmm? What? Yes, yes,' she uttered, waving her hand dismissively.

Albertina looked at Lionel enquiringly. He shrugged his shoulders, having no idea why his mother was acting so strangely. 'I'll find out what's troubling her. See you later,' he whispered, kissing her again on the cheek.

She left the room and Lionel turned to face Lavinia. 'Shall we go in, Mother? Or else our dinner will spoil.'

Her head jerked, eyes bulging in anger. 'Dinner! Is that all you can think of?'

'Well, yes. I am rather hungry. Aren't you?'

Lavinia's face reddened as her fury erupted. 'You stupid boy! You really have no idea, have you?'

He shrugged his shoulders helplessly. 'Idea? About what? Mother, what is wrong with you?'

'Wrong?' she boomed, struggling to lift her bulk from the chair. 'Just about everything, that's what.' She poked his shoulder. 'And all you can think about is your stomach! Just like your father. Always thinking of yourself.'

He took several steps back. 'Mother, I really don't understand . . .'

'No, you wouldn't, would you?' she jeered. 'Because what you do not realise, my dear son, is that I've tried to shield you from all this.'

19

His eyes filled with confusion. 'Shield me from what?'

'The truth,' she spat. 'The truth of our situation. This news is really the worst I could ever wish to hear. It could finish us, do you hear? Finish us!'

Albertina arrived outside her room. Her hand rested on the door knob. Her head was throbbing now and she felt the need for something to ease it or it would only get worse. Despite the pain she felt so much better now she had unburdened herself. Her initial fear for her future was rapidly evaporating. She should have known that this devastating turn of events would make not the slightest difference to Lionel. It wasn't as though he was marrying her for her money. His family had more than enough of their own.

She glanced up and down the corridor, hoping to catch sight of one of the servants to ask them to fetch something. No one was in sight. Reluctantly she retraced her steps and as she approached the bottom of the stairs, could hear a raised voice. Her future mother-in-law was shouting at someone angrily. Why? she wondered. Then it struck her the anger must be aimed at Lionel. Curiosity got the better of her. She made her way to the drawing-room door, which stood slightly ajar, and listened.

'What situation?' Lionel was asking. 'Mother, you really aren't making any sense.'

Lavinia grabbed him by his shoulders and shook him hard. 'We are broke, Lionel. Flat broke. If truth be told we are probably worse off at this moment than Albertina says she is. At least the sale of all her assets will hopefully clear the debts. In our case, I doubt it would cover half.' She thrust him from her and paced across the room, narrowly avoiding an occasional table on which sat several silver frames housing faded photographs of long dead family members. By the door she spun round and started back. 'For the last six months or so we have been living on credit.' She poked herself in her magnificent chest. 'Me, a Stibbing of Market Harborough, having to resort to credit. It's so humiliating.'

Lionel's mouth was opening wider by the second. 'Credit?'

'Is there something wrong with your hearing? Yes, I said credit. And not the usual trifling amounts. All in all we owe a small fortune. The only way I've staved matters off is by speaking of your forthcoming marriage. As Albertina's husband, you would have had control of her fortune and thus could have salvaged our situation. Why do you think I was so overjoyed by your engagement? Now . . .' she clenched her fists so tightly her knuckles shone white, '. . . I don't know what we're going to do.'

Lionel gazed at her, mystified. 'But how can we be broke? Father didn't exactly leave us destitute.'

20

'Well, that's where you're wrong, Lionel. Your father's investments were nowhere near as sound as he was led to believe. Several that were guaranteed to yield high returns actually sank without trace and lost their initial outlay. I can only deduce he was duped. Stupid man!'

'Mother!'

'Well, he was. Have you ever heard of the Canadian Red River Gold Mine?'

'No.'

'Neither had the stockbroker I talked to, and I don't suppose many Canadians had either. Your father was a fool and his dying so unexpectedly didn't help matters either. The death duties were enormous.'

'Mother, really. Don't speak about Father like that.'

She slammed her fists together in frustration. 'He had no business leaving us in such a precarious situation. If he had to play the stock market, he should not have taken such risks.'

Lionel raked his long fingers through his hair, mind whirling desperately. 'Well, we'll . . . er . . . we'll have to sell the house.' Ally's situation had afforded him that idea. 'Move into something smaller.' He didn't relish it one little bit but felt he had to offer something.

'I wish it were that easy,' barked Lavinia. 'But the house is mortgaged to the hilt. Selling it would gain us nothing by the time everything was settled. We'd have nothing left to buy anything else. Besides, I don't want to leave my home,' she added firmly.

Lionel froze in shock. 'Our situation is really that bad?'

'Have you not been listening to me? On your father's death eight years ago I was summoned to the lawyer's office. I felt such a fool, not suspecting any of it. But your father must have known what was happening. With hindsight it was probably what brought on his heart attack. I had no choice but to mortgage the house to keep up our lifestyle and see you through university.' She eyed him crossly. 'Which was a waste of time, wasn't it, Lionel dear? You left there knowing little more than you did before. So the prospect of your earning a decent living was just wishful thinking.'

'I'm not cut out for the academic life, Mother, you know that. Anyway you gave me no choice but to go to university. You paid for me to get in, remember, just so you could brag to your friends.'

'And what was the alternative? That you lazed around here? You've never had any inclination to achieve anything, and you know it.'

He bowed his head sulkily. 'Well, I didn't think I had to, I thought we were rich.' His eyes flashed angrily. 'That was your fault, Mother. You should have told me the situation.'

'And what difference would it have made?'

He shuffled his feet in frustration. 'I could have got a job . . .'

'You?' she scoffed. 'You don't get out of bed before noon. What kind of opportunities do you think are open with the kind of hours you like to keep? Keeping this house up and all else that goes with it, plus sending you to university and supporting your lifestyle, has drained us of every penny we possess. This marriage was to have been the making of you.'

Lionel scowled. 'Don't put all the blame on me, Mother. I didn't force you to go abroad for three months every winter. The only reason you haven't gone this year is because of my wedding. And what about all the dinner parties you throw? Each must have cost a small fortune. And recently you have had all those redecorations carried out, and in the grandest style. That must have cost a packet. Why go ahead with all that when you knew of our money situation?'

'Lionel, you know very well our English winters do not agree with me. I have to go abroad for my health. And I take it that you've not forgotten that on your wedding day several hundred people – the cream of society – would have been inside this house taking note of every possession we own? And don't look like that at me. Of course it matters. You have to look the part even if you're not. You and Albertina want the right invitations, don't you? To be seen in the very best of houses, you need to have one yourself plus all the trimmings.'

'Oh, rot!'

'Rot, is it? Listen, my boy, I've seen people shunned because they dared to have smoked trout, not smoked salmon, for luncheon. I didn't want that to happen to us . . . to you and Albertina.'

Lionel sank down in a chair and rubbed a hand distractedly over his chin. 'I know just how Albertina must have felt at the lawyer's this morning.'

'Not quite, dear. She thought she had us to fall back on. We haven't that luxury.'

He sighed loudly. 'Oh, Mother,' he pleaded despairingly, 'what are we going to do?'

'At this moment, I've no idea. But we'll have to do something quickly before Albertina's situation gets around. The creditors will soon come banging on our door. If we don't watch out we'll very quickly end up in the poorhouse, along with all the other misfortunates.'

'Oh, Mother, don't exaggerate!'

She narrowed her eyes and shook her head. 'You really have no idea, have you, Lionel, despite all I've told you? At this moment I haven't even the finances to settle the servants' wages. Though why I should be worried about them, I do not know. People like that are used to poverty – I'm not.'

Lionel gnawed his bottom lip anxiously. The thought of losing his privileged lifestyle did not appeal one little bit. Suddenly a brainwave struck. 'You could sell your jewellery. That would raise a tidy sum. I've a couple of rings myself I'm not too fond of. Doing that would buy us some time.'

'Oh, could I!' she erupted. 'Now why didn't I think of that? Take a closer look, my dear,' she snapped, pointing to her neck. 'Paste. Good paste, but paste nevertheless. My jewels went long ago. And it broke my heart, let me tell you.'

He groaned in even deeper despair. 'Oh, Mother, this is just too awful. If it all comes out, what are my friends going to say?'

Outside the door Ally flattened herself against the wall, her mind whirling, any guilt she may have felt for her eavesdropping overridden by the horror that filled her at what she had heard. Had her future mother-in-law really just proclaimed that she had only welcomed this marriage because with it came the Listerman inheritance? And Lionel . . . She couldn't blame him for his ignorance. Hadn't she herself been in just the same position due to her half-brother's silence? But all the same, all he seemed to care about was what his friends would say. She couldn't believe it. This wasn't the Lionel she knew and loved.

There was the sound of his voice addressing his mother again and she couldn't help but strain to hear.

'What are we going to do, Mother? I can't just sit around here waiting for the bailiffs to arrive.'

'The bailiffs will not enter this house. Over my dead body.' Lavinia's nostrils flared at the thought. That only happened to poor people, not those of her breeding. Though she knew that was not strictly true. Many people of their calibre had to throw themselves on the mercy of their relatives. But not Lavinia Williamson-Brown, a Stibbing of Market Harborough. She would sooner die than depend on others' charity. Eyes flashing, she fixed her gaze on her son. 'I know of one thing we're going to do, and without delay.'

He looked at her hopefully. 'Oh?'

'Put a stop to this wedding.'

He recoiled in shock, wondering if he had heard her right. 'I beg your pardon? You mean my wedding?'

'Of course I mean your wedding. Whose wedding did you think I was referring to?'

'But I won't! I can't . . . Besides, all the invitations have been sent out.'

'Well, we'll uninvite them all. We'll make up something. Better that than go ahead with this farce.'

'Farce? Mother, don't say things like that! I love Ally and we're getting married and that's the end of the matter.'

'Oh, and how are you going to live? She's no money and neither have you.'

'But everything's booked and paid for.'

'Booked, Lionel, not paid for. I was going to divulge all this after you were safely married. By then her money was as good as yours.'

23

He recoiled in shock. 'I never knew you were so mercenary, Mother.'

'That makes two of us then, doesn't it?'

'What do you mean?'

'You know exactly what I mean. Before Albertina came on the scene you were quite prepared to consider marrying Felicity Burginshaw, and before her Elinor Cravenhume. Elinor was dropped for Felicity and Felicity for Albertina. Each time because you realised the new girl's expectations were better than the old.'

'Mother, that's not true!'

'Of course it's true, and you know it. With Albertina's inheritance you saw the chance not only to go to the races but to own and train several horses. Well, it's all gone sour, my dear Lionel, because she hasn't a bean – all thanks to that imbecile of a half-brother of hers. Now tell me that you still love her?'

He gulped. 'I do,' he said weakly.

'Enough to give up everything? Because you'd have to. I know you, Lionel. You're no more prepared to give up all this than I am. Now we have to act fast. You'll tell Albertina tomorrow that the wedding is off. Tell her you're having second thoughts. She's penniless, Lionel. Considering her feelings does not come into it any more. And she'll have to park herself on someone else because we can't afford the expense of keeping her. And the sooner the better. That dealt with, you'll plan a chance meeting with Felicity. I know for a fact she still carries a torch for you. And if I'm not mistaken, her father was even more upset when your relationship ended than Felicity was. He badly wanted a union between our families. He'd do anything to gain the social contacts we take for granted. And that includes paying our debts.'

Lavinia smiled wickedly. 'Bertram Burginshaw made a fortune from buttons but, try as he might, his wealth never quite opened the right doors.' She pursed her lips disapprovingly. 'Mind you, what does he expect with a wife who addresses the servants by their Christian names and lets her daughters associate openly with the locals?'

'Mother, it was for exactly that reason you frowned on my courting Felicity. It wasn't I who wanted to end our relationship, it was you who made me do it.'

'Yes, well, things have changed somewhat since then. Now all you have to do is turn on that charm of yours and convince Felicity that your engagement has all been a mistake, that Albertina pushed you into it when it's really Felicity you've been in love with all along. That girl is so naive she'll believe anything.' She rubbed her chin, eyes glinting. 'She'll be far more easy to manipulate than Albertina. Have you got all that straight, Lionel?' she urged.

'But what if I don't want to marry her?' he said sulkily.

'What you want,' she erupted, 'does not come into it. It's your duty.'

24

'Was it your duty to marry Father? Come on, Mother, be honest. Did you marry him for his money?'

'Of course,' she replied matter-of-factly. 'But unfortunately your father did not have the business sense of his forebears. Hence the reason we have landed up in this situation.'

He sighed heavily. 'I'm not happy about this, Mother.'

'Happy! Let's see how happy you are if you don't go ahead with this and have to miss out on the Quorn because we can't pay for your mounts.' She watched the look of horror on his face. 'I take it you agree with me then?'

He nodded meekly. 'Yes, Mother.'

Outside the door Ally gasped with devastation. With all her heart she wished the floor would open and swallow her up. Never in her whole life had she felt so humiliated. She had thought Lionel truly loved her, and especially after her news of this morning and his seemingly loving reaction had had every reason to believe their feelings for each other would survive everything. She had never envisaged for a moment how fickle his love for her was. She was in such a quandary she didn't know what to do. She felt a presence nearby and jumped.

'Are you all right, Miss Listerman?'

Her eyes darted towards the maid she hadn't heard approach. 'Er . . . yes, yes. I'm . . . I'm quite well.'

The door to the drawing room opened and Lionel hurried out. His eyes bulged on spotting Albertina. It didn't take a genius to guess that, judging by her face, she had overheard practically everything. He reached for her arm. 'Ally, I . . .'

She stepped back, her hand raised in warning. 'Don't come near me, Lionel.' She fought with all her might to stem the flood of tears that threatened and to pull her thoughts into some sort of order. 'I really thought you loved me,' she whispered.

'I do,' he uttered. 'Ally, please believe me . . .'

'Don't lie,' she erupted. 'With all that's going on at the moment, I couldn't cope with you lying to me.' Her bottom lip trembled and her voice lowered to a whisper. 'Have you any idea how I feel at this moment, Lionel? I feel betrayed. By Tobias, your mother, but most of all by you. And that's what hurts the most. I think I could somehow have coped with everything else, but not this.'

He sprang towards her and grabbed her arm. 'You have to understand, Ally, the situation has come as a shock to me as well. I had no idea of any of this.'

'And you think I did? I felt such a fool at the lawyer's office. I said some unforgivable things to Mr Bailey and he was only trying to help. But all the way through, the only thing that kept me going was the thought that you would stand by me. How wrong I was, Lionel.'

She took a deep breath. 'I didn't think this day could get any worse. I was wrong about that too, wasn't I?' Her head pounded so badly she thought her temples would burst but she needed to get out of this house where she felt so unwanted. Where she would go she did not know, she just had to get away. She suddenly realised that the maid was still hovering and, worse, that she had overheard everything between herself and Lionel. She suddenly caught sight of Lavinia standing just inside the doorway; she too had been listening. Fighting to keep her dignity, Albertina turned to the maid. 'Would you please fetch my coat and have my belongings brought down?'

'Ally, please listen to me,' Lionel pleaded. 'I . . .'

'I don't think we have anything else to say to each other, Lionel,' she cut in. 'Do you think I could borrow the carriage?'

'We must talk, Ally. Please, just listen to me. Besides where will you go? It's a filthy night out there.'

'Tonight, tomorrow. What difference does it make where I go or what I do? You, Lionel, must concentrate your efforts on Felicity.' Her eyes darted to Lavinia. 'Isn't that right, Mrs Williamson-Brown?'

Lavinia showed not one trace of compassion or remorse. She just said tonelessly: 'Lionel, have the carriage brought round.'

His eyes darted to her. 'Mother!'

'If Albertina wants to leave then who are we to insist she stays?'

He nodded slowly. 'Yes, Mother.'

She froze, astounded. A little bit of her had hoped, despite all that had transpired, that Lionel would tell her he hadn't meant all she had heard, that he'd only said it to appease his mother, that he truly loved her and regardless of their desperate situation would face whatever lay in front of them together. That faint hope was now destroyed.

Her eyes strayed to her hand on which sat a solitaire engagement ring. The large diamond sparkled brilliantly in the light from the chandelier above. The night Lionel had given it to her flashed to mind. How happy she had been! Lavinia had thrown a lavish party, inviting all of society for miles around, and it had been a grand affair. Albertina's future had all been mapped out and every last detail had included Lionel. How could she ever have envisaged then that this was the way it would all end? Wrenching off the ring she thrust it at him. 'You'll be needing this, won't you?'

He reached to take it, then withdrew his hand. 'You keep it, Ally.'

She smiled frostily. 'I wouldn't dream of it. Besides, Felicity will expect a ring and it's not as though you can afford another, is it?'

Her sarcasm made him flinch.

Lavinia strode forward and snatched the ring from her. 'It is unfortunate how matters have turned out, Albertina, but I think you are wise to go without a fuss.' She eyed the maid sharply. 'Arrange for Miss Listerman's trunks to be loaded on the carriage and inform Bates he's to take her wherever she wishes to go.' She took Lionel's arm. 'You'll excuse us, won't you? Lionel, escort me in to dinner,' she ordered.

He eyed Albertina helplessly, then turned to Lavinia. 'Yes, Mother,' he said meekly.

As they turned from her and headed arm-in-arm towards the dining room, Albertina's already low spirits sank without trace.

Chapter Four

'Where to then, miss?'

Albertina stared blankly at the man addressing her through the carriage window, heavy rain bouncing off his waterproof cape. Although he had spoken politely, even in her preoccupied state she could not miss the spark of hostility in his eyes.

She shivered violently, turned her head and stared at the rain-splattered window and inky blackness beyond. This was no night to be travelling, let alone aimlessly. Still reeling from shock after all the day's events, her thoughts were numbed to such a point she couldn't remember even climbing into the carriage, let alone think of a destination. So where was she going to go?

She sighed heavily as an enormous tide of loneliness and desolation overwhelmed her. At this moment she felt she had no one in the world to turn to. Lionel's rejection had cut her to the very quick. So painful was it, it had pushed her financial situation into insignificance. As much as she tried she could not get out of her mind that vision of him turning his back and making his way towards the dining room, his mother's arm linked through his. She saw them both tucking in to their meal, discussing their plans regarding Felicity without a thought for herself and the pain they had caused her. That memory, she felt, would haunt her forever. How could he have done that after his many declarations of undying love, conveniently forgetting all the plans they had made for their future together? Regardless of his despicable treatment of her, though, life without the man she loved seemed unbearable, stretching endlessly. How was she going to bear it? Worst of all was the thought of him with Felicity: charming her, making the same plans with her as he had with Albertina herself. She hurt so much all she wanted to do was die.

'So, miss, where to?' The coachman spoke with harsh urgency. 'We really ought ter get going.'

Her head jerked and again she stared at him blankly. She still had no answer. Suddenly a face flashed before her. The full lips were smiling, large hazel eyes shining in welcome. Albertina's spirits lifted slightly. Of course! The one person she should have thought of instantly. The one person who despite this tragic turn of events would never, ever turn her back on her. Annabella. Her best friend.

Albertina and Annabella had been friends since the day as babies they had crawled across sweeping lawns, gurgling happily, whilst their respective mothers took tea together under a huge oak tree. As the years passed they spent idyllic long hot days in the summer house they had commandeered as their own, playing childish games. There had besides been horse riding, picnics, trips to the seaside, and all other manner of activities the wealthy affected. Winters, with only the intrusion of school hours, saw them closeted in each other's nurseries, occupying themselves with an abundance of toys and books under the watchful eyes of their nannies.

Advancing into their teenage years they had been allowed to attend their first grown-up balls followed by their first encounters with young men, every detail lovingly relayed to each other; all the things in fact that unworldly young women confided in the person they most trusted. Bella was the friend Ally had clung to on hearing of her parents' deaths; she would in fact have died with them if Bella's birthday had fallen on another date. She was the only person Ally had missed dreadfully when banished to boarding school, the first person she wanted to see when returning home.

It was only with her own growing attachment to Lionel that they seemed to spend less time together. Almost from their first meeting Lionel's demands on Albertina's time were exacting and he seemed to expect her constant attention. She suddenly frowned as realisation struck. Lionel had been jealous of her friendship with Bella. He had seen her as a threat, someone who could come between them. And suddenly Albertina knew why.

Without her loving parents to guide her, and in the face of Tobias's indifference, Bella was the only person who would have seen through the façade of his true motives for marrying her, egged on by his mother. Albertina herself had been blinded by love. Bella had not that hindrance. What a fool she had been! How could she have let herself be so easily manipulated? She closed her eyes tightly. This shocking realisation only added to her misery. She could only hope that Bella, once she was told the truth, could forgive her for pushing her aside to accommodate Lionel.

A surge of deep desire to see her friend filled her. 'Annabella's,' she blurted. 'Please take me to Annabella's.'

Harry Bates grimaced. 'Who, miss?'

'Annabella Langton. The Oaks, Countesthorpe.'

Blowing out his cheeks, he wiped rain from his forehead and shook it off his hand. 'It's quite a way across country to Countesthorpe, miss. I'm concerned about the state of the roads what wi' all this rain. Wouldn't it be better to wait 'til morning?'

The unworthiness of the roads was the least of her concerns but his reluctance to comply with her request was evident. She wasn't convinced either that their safety was uppermost in his mind. She strongly sensed the coachman did not want to make this journey. She couldn't blame him but nevertheless he was paid to do so. Her priority was to get as far away from this house as she could. At Annabella's she knew without question she would be made welcome – no, more than welcome. Arms would be thrown around her, enveloping her in love, and she would be listened to whilst she poured out her troubles. In return advice and help would be readily given. If she had to walk, dragging her trunks behind her, she would get there. She did not like the coachman's manner and if she hadn't felt so wretched would have chastised him.

'I'm sure you've driven in worse conditions. I'd like you to make an attempt at least,' she said curtly.

He fought to keep the anger from showing in his face. Harry Bates did not care a jot for the gentry even though he relied upon them for his livelihood. To his mind 'them upstairs' needed a lesson in manners. His parents had both served the Williamson-Browns – his father as under gardener, his mother as parlour maid. Both had died in their service and ever since he could remember Harry had worked his fingers to the bone for them, on call any time of day or night, for very little pay, spartan living conditions and never a thank you. As long as the stables and the gardens were kept in immaculate order they never looked in his direction, always seeming to begrudge the doling out of his pay at the end of the year. But woe betide him should a blade of grass be growing the wrong way! They noticed then and the words were harsh, the punishments severe.

Regardless of his feelings though he did uncharacteristically feel just a mite sorry for Miss Listerman who at the moment looked the epitome of misery, huddled in the corner of the carriage as though she carried every burden imaginable on her slender shoulders. He sniffed. Still, if she had half the troubles the lesser off had to contend with, she might not think her load so bad. In fairness, though, according to gossip, he supposed she had just cause. 'Her Majesty' it seemed had practically thrown her out of the house on hearing she no longer had her expectations. And as for that spineless fiancé of hers . . . well, none of the servants had been surprised at his reaction. Still, Harry mused wickedly, about time one of the gentry got their just deserts. It would be good to see how she coped now she hadn't the power of money to shield her. He hid a smile. Not easily, he'd wager.

Slyly he scanned his eyes across her. She really was a pretty woman, very pleasing to the eye. The good fit of her expensive clothes showed off her figure to perfection. Penniless or not, he thought Lionel a fool to throw this one over. Harry himself would sooner have his bed graced by a penniless looker than an ugly mug staring at him across a laden table. He wondered what her performance would be like beneath the sheets, compared to Cissie's. She, God love her, knew how to please a man. She always writhed in ecstasy as he hungrily ran his hands over her inviting body, fondled her firm breasts and sucked hard on her dark nipples. Always begged for more, did Cissie. She liked him to be rough. At these thoughts a stirring in his groin made him shudder. Harry tightened his lips. He'd always fancied his chances with a bit of class. It had been a fantasy of his since at the tender age of ten he had hidden in a pile of hay in a barn and watched a footman doing the honours to a visiting gentry friend of Mrs Williamson-Brown.

His lip curled. As an experienced man he saw that Albertina Listerman hadn't the wanton look in her eye of so many unsatisfied women. He knew that the only chance he had of having his way with the likes of her was to take it, but he wasn't desperate enough to run the risk. Besides he doubted she'd be worth it. She wouldn't be any comparison to Cissie, despite her fine attire and refined tone of voice. She was more than likely still a virgin, undressed in the dark, a peck on the lips enough to make her blush deep red, let alone anything else.

For that reason he couldn't blame the foppish Lionel for bringing his floozies to the stables, as he thought unobserved. Every red-blooded man needed servicing regularly. Harry hid a smile as he wondered if the young master had any inkling his exploits were no secret below stairs; that talk of his fumblings had enlivened many a dark evening when the older women servants had retired to bed.

He sniffed resignedly. Despite the fact that the young lady in the carriage was probably no better off than himself, 'Her Majesty' had given him an order and he would have to obey.

'I'll do me best, miss,' he replied sullenly.

Ally leaned over and stuck her face right up against the window when the gates of The Oaks loomed suddenly through the darkness. The journey had taken well over two hours during which time she had wondered if they would ever arrive safely as she felt the carriage wheels slipping over the wet clogging mud of the deserted country roads. Their arrival, she felt, was all due to the skill of the coachman. She would express her gratitude at the first opportunity. The rain, although abated, was still coming down in a fine drizzle from the dark clouds above and the roads they had passed along were beginning to flood in places.

The carriage slithered through the gates and proceeded down the gravel drive and Ally peered hard to see the house. She frowned. By now lights from the numerous windows should have been visible even on this dreadful night. For a moment she wondered if the coachman had got the wrong address. But then she knew he hadn't. She had passed through those gates on many occasions. There was no mistaking the stone griffins adorning the top of the pillars. Bella and she had spent many happy childhood hours throwing conkers and acorns at them.

The carriage drew to a halt and the next thing she knew the driver was addressing her.

'Is this the right place, miss, only it's all in darkness?'

Again she stared out of the window. It was very strange. Even if the whole family were out, some form of light would be evident. Suddenly the truth dawned and Ally clasped her hand to her forehead in dismay. Oh, what a fool I am, she inwardly groaned. How could she have forgotten that the family had gone on a long winter cruise down the Nile? Bella had been so excited about seeing the pyramids and ancient temples; sampling all the exotic foodstuffs. She could not wait to feel the sun's warmth on her skin. How could she have forgotten after Bella had done nothing but talk of her trip every time Ally could steal the time to see her?

Lowering her arm, fighting hard to keep her composure, she turned to him. 'I had forgotten that the family were all away. They won't be back for another month. Just in time for my . . .' Wedding she had been going to say. Renewed misery filled her being. How could I have forgotten? She thought again distractedly.

Harry fumed inwardly. Typical of the gentry! Not one word of apology for dragging him out on such a terrible night. 'What d'yer want me to do then, miss? Shall I take yer back?'

'No!' she erupted. Never, ever did she want to set foot inside that house again.

She clenched her fists tightly, face pinched and drawn. This really was the final straw. Her mind whirled frantically. She did have several other friends she could hope might take her in but their friendship was nothing in comparison to Bella's. The Williamson-Browns' reaction had made her see how fickle such relationships could be. Further humiliation she could not face.

She raised her head. There was only one more avenue she could see open to her: Clarence Bailey. She would just have to hope that after her rudeness towards him, his offer to open his house to her still stood. She had no idea where he lived but the housekeeper at his offices would tell her.

'How far is it to Leicester?' she enquired.

Harry pursed his lips. 'Fair distance, I'd say. Six or seven miles.' He frowned as realisation struck. Surely she was never going to ask him to drive her there? 'Why, miss?' he asked.

'Take me there, please.'

'But, miss . . .' His voice trailed off at the expression on her face. 'Right yer are, miss. Leicester it is.'

Angry now, he climbed aboard and coaxed the tired horse into action. Despite his own waterproof cape he was soaked to the skin, heavily fatigued and cold. He remembered the warm fire and half-eaten dinner he had hurriedly left on receiving a summons. Uppermost were the thoughts of the ripe, inviting body of Cissie Good, waiting for him in her bed in the servants' quarters high in the attics. He narrowed his eyes. One thing was certain: by the time he reached home tonight the remains of his dinner

32

would have been long ago thrown away, the fire burned out and Cissie fast asleep. But as much as he desired to turn about and head for home it was more than his job was worth.

The journey to Leicester progressed slowly, Harry growing more and more angry by the minute. His muscles strained to breaking point, eyes aching with having to concentrate so hard to keep the carriage on the road, visibility hampered by the blinding rain and the darkness of the night, he wondered ruefully if the woman he was ferrying realised what danger she was putting them both in.

Suddenly a sharp bend in the road loomed and he steadied the horse to negotiate it slowly. Persistent rain over five days had opened gaping pot holes. The one in the middle of the bend was large and deep and for all his skills he could not stop a carriage wheel slamming into it. The carriage tipped precariously. The horse's hooves slipped. Harry was jolted forward, only his years of experience keeping him in his seat. Inside the carriage Albertina was thrown around and on to the carriage floor, banging her head. As the carriage bounced out of the hole it swung sideways, the back end careering wildly before coming to rest in a ditch. The horse reared with fright.

Clambering down, Harry rushed round, grabbing its bridle, fighting frantically to calm it.

Inside the carriage Ally, still in a heap on the floor, rubbed the side of her head, dazed. Gathering her wits eventually she wrenched up her skirt and crawled her way to the door. Grabbing hold of the hand support, she pulled herself upright, opened the door and poked her head out.

'What happened?' she called anxiously.

Having successfully calmed the horse, he spun round to face her. Despite his subservience to this woman Harry was unable to control his emotions. 'Exactly what I tried to ter tell yer would happen, miss,' he retorted angrily. 'You near got us killed insisting we mek this journey tonight, that's what.'

Albertina's breath caught in her throat. Climbing out of the carriage, mindful of her footing on the slippery grass verge, she stepped across to him. Hands on hips, rain battering down on her, she stared at him haughtily. 'How dare you speak to me in that tone?'

His lip curled. 'I dare, miss, 'cos you're nowt now. You ain't no better than I am. So don't come yer airs and graces wi' me.'

She gasped in shock. Was this outburst the kind of treatment she would have to expect now? Wiping rivulets of water from her face, anger flooded through her. She would not be spoken to like that, by him or anyone. 'You impertinent man! I shall report you for this.'

'Oh, yeah? And who to? The mistress had you all but slung out. All she'll be concerned about is the damage to the carriage. I doubt your welfare or even mine would enter 'er head. And as for that cretin of a son of hers . . . don't think he's gonna come to yer aid. He's frying other fish now, ain't he? I heard he's got his eye back on Felicity Burginshaw. Someone should warn 'er what she's letting 'erself in for.'

His last words were slung at her mockingly. Albertina erupted in fury, all the terrible events of the day – her feelings of horror, rejection and humiliation – too much for her to bear. 'Your attitude is beneath contempt. Whatever you think of my status and how you believe you can treat me, you are wrong. Be warned, regardless of what you have seen, I have many friends in high places.' That last sentence was spoken before she could analyse the truth of it. But as she spoke it did cross her mind that many of her friends could not now be counted on. Maybe their reactions would mirror the Williamson-Browns' and this dreadful man's. Albertina thrust these thoughts aside. This man had insulted her, here and now, and she was adamant she wasn't going to let him get away with it. The rest she would face and deal with, if and when it presented itself. 'I can still get you sacked and make sure you find it hard to get another job. Now I suggest you get this carriage back on the road. Mrs Williamson-Brown ordered you to take me where I want to go, and I want to go to Leicester.'

They stood facing each other. The tension in the air was electric. For a moment, from the thunderous look on his face, she thought he was going to strike her. She hoped he did not realise that the stony look on her own face was one of terror: for being with this man in the middle of nowhere on such a terrible night, and for the fact he had so harshly brought home the realities of her situation. He was right. She no longer possessed the power of authority over him imbued by a wealthy background. That right had been stripped from her. Regardless, he was not going to intimidate her.

Immense relief flooded through her as he abruptly turned, marched towards the back of the carriage and stood sizing up the situation. Her words had obviously had their effect, either because he feared losing his job or because he believed her dubious claims to important connections. Albertina did not care why. She urgently needed to resume her journey.

'I'll need yer 'elp getting the carriage out the ditch,' shouted Harry abruptly.

'Me?' she responded, surprised. 'You want me to help you?'

'With respect, miss,' he said icily, 'I can't do it all meself.'

Stepping carefully, she made her way over. She was soaked through now, her woollen coat proving little protection against the extreme elements, her dainty patent and antelope boots clogged in mud, as was the bottom of her velvet skirt. She quickly saw that his statement was correct. The dislodging of the carriage could not be done single-handed. The added weight of her trunks would not help matters either.

'Do you think we could get help?' she asked. As soon as she spoke she knew her question to be a stupid one. They appeared to be in the middle of nowhere.

'We've two choices. Either we wait for God knows how long and hope someone comes along, or else you guide the horse while I lend me weight at the back. It's my opinion we ain't gonna see a soul tonight. So wadda you reckon, me lady?' His clipped tone held a hint of sarcasm.

He was right. The chance of anyone passing them was remote. She had no choice but to do as he suggested. Fighting a deep desire to smack his face for his condescending attitude, she plodded towards the horse and took hold of the bridle. She was used to horses, handling a frightened one did not perturb her. She ran her hand down the side of the animal's head and spoke softly to it. 'There, there,' she soothed. 'Good boy, good boy.'

Luckily the ditch wasn't deep, but nevertheless it took several strenuous attempts to get the carriage back safely on the road. Finally she clambered back inside, glad to be out of the driving rain. During the whole operation not one word had they spoken to each other, except for instructions from Harry. For herself Albertina would be more than glad when they finally parted company.

Her teeth chattered with cold and she wrapped her arms tightly around herself as the carriage lurched forward. It didn't seem they had travelled far when it was pulled to a halt and before she had time to wonder why, the coachman had opened the carriage door and poked his head through.

'We've arrived at an inn. I suggest we stop fer the night. We ain't gonna get much further and could end up stranded. In this weather that's asking fer trouble.'

Stopping for the night was the last thing Albertina wanted to do but she knew he was right and was far too cold, wet and weary to challenge his suggestion. The thought of a warm bed and something hot inside her outweighed everything else at this moment.

She nodded. 'I see the sense in that. But first thing in the morning we continue to Leicester.'

He tipped his forelock. 'As you wish, miss.'

The inn's lights beckoned welcomingly. Albertina sat in the coach whilst he went off to enquire about a vacancy. Several moments later he returned.

'They've a small room left. Seems other folks had the same idea.'

'Thank you.' Her show of gratitude had been difficult. Grabbing her vanity case which carried her toiletries, she alighted from the carriage. 'Would you please have the small trunk delivered to my room? The rest can stay on the coach.'

Ally was informed that the landlady was otherwise occupied and was shown to her room by a slovenly woman, nearly half of her large breasts bulging over the top of her grubby blouse. The room was small and far from warm.

'I can 'ave the fire lit, if yer want?' she reluctantly offered.

Ally nodded. 'Please do. And would you have a tray sent up?' She paused. 'What is on the menu?'

The woman sniffed. 'We don't 'ave a menu, me lady. There's some mutton stew left, I made it fresh yesterday, or I can do yer bread and cheese.'

The none too fresh mutton stew sounded disgusting and judging from the dirty appearance of this woman, Ally did not fancy it at all considering she had prepared it. 'Bread and cheese will be acceptable. And a pot of tea, please.'

'Right yer are, madam,' she said, lighting a spill from the oil lamp and placing it against the paper beneath the wood and coal in the tiny grate.

'Could I have a jug of hot water to freshen myself up?'

We call it scrubbing, the woman thought, but if you want to freshen, me lady, then being's you're paying, freshen it is. 'I'll have it sent up right away, madam.'

'Thank you. Oh, and could you have my clothes collected? They need a clean and press.'

Bloody stupid woman thinks this is the Grand Hotel. Those monied folks hadn't a clue. ''Fraid we don't do that, madam. No call, see. But give 'em a shake come morning and I'm sure they'll be as right as rain. Now I'll leave yer to it and go and see about yer supper.'

Ally eyed her, speechless. No valet service? That was ridiculous. What sort of establishment was this? It crossed her mind to go and search for the coachman, demand they find something more suitable, but then she chided herself, knowing she had not the strength at this moment to withstand his reaction. She should just count herself lucky they had come across this place when they had. It was only for one night and in this atrocious weather she couldn't be choosy.

Slowly she turned around and surveyed the tiny room. The walls were badly in need of a fresh coat of whitewash, the black beams supporting the low ceiling had cobwebs clinging to them. The curtains and bedding had seen better days as had the chipped basin and jug of ice cold water on top of the ancient tallboy. Neither the yellow chunk of soap in the dish at the side nor the towel hanging from a hook on the wall looked hygienic. She sighed. Thank goodness she had her own toiletries with her.

Gingerly she lowered her weary body down on the edge of the bed. Surprisingly it was very comfortable and at least the room was warming and more cheery now the fire had been lit. She looked expectantly towards the door, hoping that the woman would hurry up with her requirements and her trunk would arrive. She was desperate to get out of her wet clothes.

At the back of the inn, in the stables, Harry, having unbridled the horse, fed and watered it, and himself eaten a large helping of mutton stew – picking out the chunks of gristle and bone – settled back comfortably on a pile of straw and pulled sacks over himself. He grimaced. The sacks did not smell very pleasant and the odour would permeate his clothes but it was either that or freeze. As it was there was still a risk he'd catch pneumonia, having to sleep in his wet clothes.

He shut his eyes and for several moments listened to the sounds of snoring coming from several other coachmen in adjoining stalls. These sounds though did not drown out the renewed thrashing of the driving rain or the noise of a dozen or so horses shifting uneasily, nervous of the freak weather.

After a while he became accustomed to the sounds and his thoughts drifted to the woman he was ferrying. He was still smarting from her tongue-lashing and his anger rose at the thought of her housed in a warm room, lying on a soft bed, while he himself had to make do with a stable. Money dictated that. But then, this woman had no money according to gossip. In that respect this situation was unfair. She had no more right to the bed than he did. But then, he supposed, she might not have what the rich termed money but still had items at her disposal that she could sell. She could not be classed as anywhere near destitute, not if she was wise.

There were three large trunks and a smaller one still strapped on the carriage and for a moment he pondered on what they held. Mostly clothing, he mused. Rich velvets and brocades. Silks. Her blouses would not be the coarse cotton that Cissie had to make do with. He shifted his position. Those items would fetch a tidy sum if he haggled right at the pawnbrokers. He sniggered to himself as it struck him as a good possibility that Miss Listerman had never heard of the word 'pawnbroker', let alone knew what one was for.

She would also have some jewellery. A woman like her was bound to have a few bits and pieces which would tot up very nicely. He scratched himself where the straw was prickling. When all was said and done those trunks probably held a small fortune, one way or another.

Suddenly he sat bolt upright. Thinking of the trunks reminded him of the order to deliver the smaller one to her room. He had forgotten all about it. She wouldn't be pleased. He could picture her pacing about her room with impatience. Oh, sod her, he thought. Why should I bother? He was warm under the sacking, surprisingly comfortable on the thick layer of straw. Harry sighed loudly. Not to fulfil this task would be more than his job was worth. Despite his own thoughts on the matter, there could be an element of truth in what she had told him about her friends in high places.

Throwing off the sacking he rose, grabbed his damp jacket, hanging up to dry on a rusty hook in the wall, and made his way towards the carriage, giving the restless horse a reassuring pat as he passed. He made to climb up and unstrap the smaller trunk, but something stopped him and he stood and stared hard as his mind ticked over. An idea was forming. He stood for a moment in deep deliberation. It was a risky idea but one that could be his chance of bettering himself. One thing was for certain: he'd never get another opportunity like this again. The conditions were ideal. He'd be a fool to let this opportunity pass.

Taking a sly look round, satisfying himself that his companions were soundly asleep, he hitched the horse back to the coach and manoeuvred it out of the stables. As he climbed aboard a smug smile filled his face. Wouldn't she get a shock come morning? By which time he'd be long gone and extremely hard to trace, thanks to the weather. Serve her bloody well right! And not only her, Mrs Williamson-Brown to boot, because as soon as he sold the contents of the trunks, he'd sell the bloody coach as well. 'Her Majesty' would be furious when she finally found out, but by that time he'd be long gone and it wouldn't be hard for a man like himself to cover his tracks. Not with money in his pocket it wouldn't.

Clear of the inn he gave way to his stifled emotions and laughed out loud. At long last, after years of subservience, Harry had got his own back on the gentry and that feeling was better than anything he'd ever experienced with a woman.

Chapter Five

'Me lady. Come on, me lady. Wakey, wakey.'

Ally's eyes opened. 'What . . . what on earth's going on?' Still heavy with sleep, her eyes fixed on the grotesque apparition leaning over her. 'Who are you?' she demanded, trying to right herself as she rubbed her sore neck which had stiffened from the awkward position she had lain in. With difficulty she eased herself up and swung her legs over the side of the bed.

A woman of about her own age, dressed completely in black except for a white frill around her high-necked collar and on her leg-o'-mutton sleeves, straightened herself and placed her hands on her skinny hips. 'Me! I'm Maisie, miss. I'm the landlady's daughter,' she announced importantly. 'Me mam sent me up to see if you were all right. She were worried, see, being's you weren't up and about. Normally folks 'ave breakfasted and gone well before seven. But today most are still linger-ing, debating whether to risk the conditions or not. D'you know, I ain't never seen rain like this. Me mam sez it's freak weather. We've got barrels floating in the cellar. All the ale'll be ruined. Me mam's in a right tizzy.' She leaned forward, affording Ally a close up of her pimples. 'I keep out me mam's way when she's in a tizzy.'

Eyes still fixed on the woman, Ally fought to clear her fuddled mind. She had had the most terrible nightmare. It was so dreadful she couldn't bear to recall any of it. But slowly, very slowly, she was realising that it had been no nightmare. While asleep she had been reliving the events of yesterday.

Maisie went to the window and flung aside the faded curtains. It was so dismal outside the difference in light was negligible. She wiped conden-sation off the glass, peered out into the dark grey mist outside and shook her head. 'Too much water even fer the ducks, poor little sods.' She turned and looked hard at the paying guest. 'Me mam thought yer'd probably had a lie in, being's it's still thrashing it down outside, but as time wore on she thought it better to check, just in case.' She smiled, showing stained teeth. 'Wouldn't be the first death we've had by a long chalk. We nearly got closed down once 'cos we'd bin that full we'd let an old codger have the cubby 'ole right at the back and it were over a week 'til Betty the chambermaid remembered about him. The stench were worse than . . . Oh, me duck, a'yer feeling sick? Why, you've gone as green as winter cabbage.'

Hurriedly filling a glass with water from the wash jug, she thrust it at Ally. ''Ere, get that down yer neck. You know what your trouble is, don't yer?' she said knowingly, eyeing the tray still holding Ally's supper. 'You should never go to bed on an empty belly, it's asking fer trouble. You ain't touched a morsel of that food and me mam 'ates waste. Mind you, you must have bin tired being's you never bothered to undress.' She surveyed Ally for a moment. 'D'yer want me ter fetch someone to tek a look at yer? You don't look well, yer know.'

The woman's chatter was annoying Ally who shook her head. 'No, thank you. I'll be fine in a moment. I just feel a bit light-headed.' She desperately wanted to be left alone so she could gather her thoughts. More urgent was the need to get out of this dreadful place, arrive at Mr Bailey's and address some of the factors of her worrying situation. Thoughts of her uncertain future overwhelmed her and a terrible feeling of foreboding crept in.

Maisie sniffed. 'If yer sure.' She moved across to the door. 'What wi' this weather, I tek it you'll be wanting the room another night?'

'Another night? No, thank you. I'm only travelling as far as Leicester.'

'Leicester, London – take my word for it, in this weather you'll be lucky to mek the next village.'

Even in her preoccupied state Ally thought the landlady's daughter far too familiar for her station. 'I'll take that risk,' she said brusquely. 'Would you have a jug of hot water sent up for me, and a tray of tea? Oh, and please instruct my coachman to be ready to leave in forty minutes.' That's after I've given the man a piece of my mind for not bringing up the small trunk, she thought crossly then caught the perplexed look on Maisie's face. 'Is there something wrong?'

'Wrong! Oh . . . er . . . it's just that I didn't realise you had a coach-man. But then, you must have, mustn't yer? He's probably still sleeping. Drank too much ale last night perhaps. Keeps a good cellar does me mam – that's when it ain't in jeopardy of floating off to God knows where,' she said ruefully. 'I'll leave yer to it then. But it'd be appreciated if yer'd get a move on so we can clean the room. The stop-over coaches start arriving about five, that's if any get through a' course, and we like everything to be ready. Breakfast is past but I'm sure we can rustle up summat for yer. Yer tariff'll be waiting.'

She disappeared through the door and closed it behind her.

Eyes fixed on the closed door, a feeling of horror filled Ally. With so much else on her mind payment for her nightly lodging had never entered her head. Regardless, she couldn't pay it. She had no money.

Panic filled her. What on earth was she to do? Her mind raced frantically then she took a deep breath. There was only one course of action open to her. She would just have to hope that dreadful coachman

40

was carrying some money and ask for a loan until she reached Mr Bailey's offices. She shook her head. Belittling herself to the Williamson-Browns' employee was the last thing she felt like doing but she had no other choice.

Feeling slightly better after a strip wash and two cups of strong tea, Ally arrived downstairs and peered around. Apart from the large main room at the front the inn seemed to consist of a warren of black, tobacco-stained passageways, alcoves and tiny rooms. Every conceivable space housed dark wooden tables, stools, high-backed benches and wooden chairs. The floors were stone-flagged. The smoky, musty air bore the taint of stale food.

The hostelry was far from deserted. Frustrated travellers were sitting with eyes peeled on the windows for a sign of a break in the weather. Maisie was rushing around taking orders and clearing used crockery. Ally could not help but stare at her for a moment, impressed by the way she managed to balance so many plates, tankards and other dirty utensils all at once while still remembering the orders people were placing.

Across the room she spotted a hatch in the wall and presumed this was where she must settle her account. Unused to being in such a lowly establishment, one filled mostly with dubious-looking characters, several of whom were eyeing her suspiciously, she shuddered. She did not like this place, felt extremely uncomfortable in it, just wanted to leave.

She took a very deep breath before weaving her way through the room, all the time keeping an eye out for any sign of Harry Bates. There was none so she assumed he was waiting for her summons in the stable.

On top of the counter was a brass push bell and she pressed it hard. The loud noise it made startled her but not so much as the head that shot up, appearing from nowhere. She jumped back, shocked.

The head, which bore one of the ugliest faces that Ally had ever seen, was attached to a short rotund body and she had no trouble in guessing that this was the landlady as she dressed identically to her daughter except that all of her hair was scraped under a white mob cap.

'Yes?' the landlady bellowed. 'Oh, it's you, me lady,' she hurriedly apologised for her abrupt manner, spotting Ally's obvious displeasure. 'I thought yer were someone else. But I'm glad to see nothing has befell yer. I couldn't 'ave coped with the likes of that today. Ran off me feet, I am. I could have filled all me rooms thrice over. Reckon we had every Tom, Dick and Harry and his uncle in here last night. You were lucky to get a room when you did, another few minutes and you'd have bin sleeping on a bench like a lot of 'em did. Still, I shouldn't be grumbling. This weather ain't to everyone's taste but it's good fer business.' She placed her small hands flat on the counter. 'Breakfast is past but I could rustle you up some mutton stew? Maisie,' she shouted, 'clear a space fer the lady.'

'It's quite all right,' Ally insisted. 'I'll decline, if you don't mind.'

'Suit herself,' Edna Murkitt replied brusquely. She rummaged around under the counter then pushed a piece of paper towards her guest and smiled, showing even yellower teeth than her daughter's.

Ally glanced down at it. The amount was minimal but might as well have been several hundred pounds. Her financial predicament filled her with renewed embarrassment. Nevertheless, she raised her head proudly. 'Do you think you could have someone summon my coachman?'

Edna's beady brown eyes narrowed warily. 'Coachman, me lady?'

'Yes,' Albertina repeated sharply, wondering if this woman was hard of hearing. 'My coachman.'

Edna sniffed. 'Well, it's strange that because I was only saying to my Maisie that I wondered how you'd got here, what with you obviously being gentry an' all. Ethel, 'er what showed you up last night, wa' full of it. Gentry, she said. Fancy us 'aving one of the gentry staying 'ere. We don't get many gentry, you know. Well, not any really.'

I'm not surprised, thought Ally. The hint of sarcasm in the landlady's voice though was very apparent. Wondering why, Ally frowned. 'Is there some confusion about my coachman?' she asked.

'You might say that. It's the lack of, me lady.'

'Lack of?'

'That's right. All the coachmen 'ave been in and breakfasted and not one laid claim to being wi' you.' She ran her finger down the register. 'You are Miss Listerman, ain't yer?'

'Yes.'

'Oh, glad we've got that cleared up. But it still don't clear up the matter of this coachman you say you 'ave.'

Ally's hackles rose. 'Madam, I can assure you I arrived with a coachman, complete with coach, horse and trunks. Now, either you send someone to fetch him or I shall go myself.'

Before Ally had time to blink the landlady was standing in front of her, seeming to materialise from nowhere. She grabbed her arm and gripped it tightly. 'You ain't going anywhere, me lady. My name's Edna Murkitt, not Nelly No Brain. I know what your game is. I let you go and I don't see hide nor hair on you again. I've got caught just like this before. But not twice. Oh, no. Now just settle yer bill and you can go.'

Ally indignantly wrenched her arm away, conscious that several other guests were staring over. 'How dare you manhandle me? And I don't care for your accusations. Now I'm telling the truth – I arrived with a coachman.'

'All right, me lady, 'ave it yer own way. ''Orace,' she bellowed. 'Get out ter the stable and check what coachmen are there. What's 'is name?' she asked Ally.

'Name? Er . . .' Ally fought desperately to remember.

'You don't know it, do yer?' erupted Edna. 'Now why ain't I surprised at that? It's just as I thought. You people mek me sick! Come in 'ere acting all lah-di-dah when underneath you're just a con artist. Mek yer living outta fleecing good 'onest people. Well, if yer thought you could con me then you've another think coming. Let me tell yer summat fer nothing – a proper lady wouldn't be seen dead wearing crumpled clothes with mud on them, let alone spent the night in 'em. But I'll say this to yer credit: you speak the part. Got that off to a fine art. You should go on the stage, me duck.' Her eyes narrowed menacingly. 'Now pay up or I'll send 'Orace for the copper.'

Ally's mouth dropped open in shock.

A burly man arrived, a bushy grey beard matching the thick thatch of hair on his head. 'Trouble, Edna?'

'You can say that again, 'Orace. Trying ter get outta paying.'

Horace Murkitt looked Ally up and down. 'A' yer sure?'

'Trust me, I'm sure. Now go and check the stables and hurry up about it. I ain't got time to stand 'ere arguing the toss all day. I've a business to run.'

Horace departed.

'Will you listen to me?' Ally was fighting to keep her dignity, having difficulty believing she was actually being accused of theft. 'My name is Albertina Victoriana Listerman and the coachman who brought me here is employed by Mrs Williamson-Brown of Kibworth Harcourt. He will vouch for me.'

'If yer'd just settle your bill he'd have no need to vouch for yer, now would he? Do that, me lady, and you can be on your way.' She eyed Ally shrewdly. 'Now why should yer need the coachman to be 'ere to settle your bill?'

Ally froze then gulped hard. 'Because I can't settle my account. I . . . I left my purse behind. Silly thing to do, I know. I need the coachman to help me out until I reach my destination.'

The landlady laughed loudly. 'Well, I've heard it all now. Needing the coachman to bail you out and you such a lady? You honestly expect me to believe that?' She grabbed hold of Ally's vanity case and wrenched it from her. 'Let's see if there's anything worth owt in here.'

Ally gave a cry of distress. 'How dare you? That's my property. Hand it back.'

She made a grab for it but Edna was too quick for her.

'Oh, cut out the dramatics. You've been rumbled, lady,' Edna spat as she rummaged through Ally's belongings. 'Well, there's nowt worth owt in 'ere. Good quality stuff, mind.' She pulled out a bar of lavender soap and pushed her nose against it, sniffing hard. 'This 'as got a nice pong. I'll have that,' she said, slipping it into her pocket.

Before Ally had time to retaliate Horace returned. 'None of the coachmen owned up to being with 'er.'

43

'Then it's just as I thought,' Edna announced triumphantly. 'So just what do we do with you, eh?'

Two pairs of accusing eyes stared at her, and more of the guests were gathering round curiously. Ally felt the room spin. This situation was worse than her nightmare of yesterday. Why wouldn't this woman believe her, and where was that awful coachman?

The truth of the matter hit her like a thunderbolt and her legs buckled. He had gone, taking all her belongings with him. That could be the only answer. And how could the landlady be expected to believe her when, as she had quite rightly pointed out, Albertina looked such a dreadful sight? How was she going to make them listen to her? Her brain worked overtime. Then a thought struck her.

'Your employee who escorted me to my room last night . . . she saw him, my coachman. He enquired of her about a vacancy and she delivered a message to him in the stable requesting he bring up my small trunk. He never delivered it. But still, she met him and would remember. Ask her, please ask her,' she beseeched.

Edna scowled. 'I can't ask 'er, she ain't here.' She addressed her husband. 'The silly bugger decided to risk going 'ome, couldn't leave 'er kids. She's late for her morning shift an' all. I told 'er she'd be safer staying here and that her kids 'ud be all right, but would she listen?'

Horace wasn't listening either, he was weighing up Ally. He pulled his wife aside. 'I think this woman is telling the truth, Edna.'

She glared at him scornfully. ''Orace Murkitt, you're like all men. Put a pretty face in front of yer and you lose all reason. But then, what else can I expect? Your brain's controlled by what's in yer trousers.'

'Oh, shut it, Edna. All I'm saying is in my opinion she's telling the truth. And if she is, that coachman's absconded with all her belongings and we're doing her an injustice.'

Edna sniffed as she eyed their guest thoughtfully. 'Hmmm, I dunno.' She folded her arms and mulled it over for a moment. 'Regardless, there's still the matter of the unsettled bill. Maybe I'll forget fetching the bobby but I ain't gonna forget about *that*. I ain't a charity.' Her tiny brown eyes suddenly lit up. 'I'll make you a bargain, lady, and you either tek it or leave it. You can cover Ethel's shift. That way you can work the bill off. And I'm being lenient. A day's work elsewhere would nowhere near cover the two shillings you owe.'

'Seems fair ter me, Edna,' agreed Horace.

'Work?' uttered Ally, astounded. 'Doing what?'

'Come with me,' said Edna, grabbing her arm. 'And I'll show yer.'

Followed by Horace, she led a reluctant, bewildered Ally down several dark corridors until they came to a kitchen. Before they arrived the stench of rotting vegetables and grease met them and Ally's stomach churned. She was pushed inside. 'Yer can tackle that lot, and when you've finished I've plenty more that needs doing.' The landlady grinned, secretly enjoying the situation. 'I'd be thankful that Ethel couldn't make it in if I were you. Else you, me lady, would be facing jail.'

Albertina gulped as she stared at the mountain of greasy crockery piled in the huge pot sink, at further stacks of it to the sides and the dirty pans on the floor. She had never washed a dish in her life, did not know the first thing about it. The sight of it all frightened her witless – but not so much as the thought of going to jail.

Just then Maisie bustled in carrying even more dirty plates. 'We've no more clean pots, Mam. Ethel's still not arrived and we've food to prepare 'cos it don't look like those travellers are gonna budge today.'

Edna Murkitt grinned. 'Don't you fret now, our Maisie. The problem is just about to be remedied. That right, me lady? Me lady?'

Utterly defeated, Ally turned her head, stared at her blankly for a moment then slowly nodded.

Many hours later Edna folded her arms in satisfaction and stared around the kitchen. She nodded. 'Well, I never thought you'd do it, but I have to admit you've not done bad. Well, yer can get your travelling case and go.'

'Go?' uttered Ally. After being hurriedly shown what to do by Maisie she had scrubbed and rubbed until her delicate white hands were red raw and dried to the point of flaking after being immersed in greasy suds for so long. She had never felt so bone weary in all her life, wanting nothing more than to collapse in a heap on the nearest bed – and this woman was telling her to go. 'But it's getting dark and it's still raining so heavily.' She choked back a sob. 'And I've no idea where I am.'

'Me lady, I don't care. Despite what my husband sez, I ain't convinced of yer innocence. Now if I were you I'd get off while the going's good and count meself lucky. Maybe you'll think twice next time, eh?'

'Whatever you think, I wasn't . . .'

'Don't waste yer breath, lady. I meet all sorts in this game. I'm wise to everything. Now be off before I change me mind.'

'Eh up, our Edna,' challenged Horace who had just arrived in the kitchen. 'Don't yer think yer being a bit hard on the gel? You wouldn't send a dog out in that.'

She turned on him. 'And you can shurrup and get back behind the bar! You're losing us money.'

Wind so fierce it had uprooted trees whipped the torrential rain to a frenzy, battering the lone hunched figure as it struggled to travel down the pitch black muddy lane. Tightly gripping her vanity case, the only thing of any value left to her in the world, Ally was in such a state of shock from all that had happened to her in under thirty-six hours, she would not have raised one finger in protest should the devil himself have risen before her, sharp dagger held aloft ready to strike her dead. As she fought to concentrate her efforts on putting one foot in front of the other, each step forward a momentous achievement against the elements, death would have come as a more than blessed relief. She would have grabbed at it.

Weak to the point of exhaustion she stopped for a moment, panting heavily, fighting for her share of air against the strength of the wind. A sound registered and she strained her ears. Close by, no more than a few feet, water rushed past. A swollen stream – no, a river, a raging river.

Common sense struggled through the grey mist that had enveloped her mind since she had been all but thrown bodily out of the inn. It told her danger lurked. A foot in the wrong direction and her wish to die would be granted.

The sound of the water grew louder until it became deafening, drowning out all else. A sudden surge of desire to shut her eyes, walk towards it and throw herself in flooded over her. So strong was it, it overwhelmed her whole being. How easy it would be to end her life now, put a stop to her pain, her desolation, her feeling of unwantedness; slam the door on the dark void that was now her future. A future that until hours ago had been so bright.

Blindly, she turned off the path she had fought desperately to follow, taking several steps along the bank. She stopped and looked down. Through the darkness, only feet below, a torrent of water sped. No longer feeling the sting of the rain nor the stab of the wind she stared down at it, mesmerised, the urge to throw herself in overwhelming.

Without warning the sodden mud suddenly collapsed beneath her feet and as she tumbled down the bank the scream of sheer terror that erupted from her was carried away by the angry wind.

Chapter Six

Jack Fossett was an idiot, completely mad, insane. He was everything and more that his ma had called him. Well, he had to be, hadn't he, to risk his neck in the worst storm experienced for a decade and all for the sake of an old collie dog? But Sal was not just any old dog, she was as much a part of the family as any of them and the children were distraught at the thought that something had happened to her, despite the fact that their home and surrounding area was in danger of being engulfed by flood water. So against Ma's loud protests Jack had donned his coat, which had proved to be as much use to him as a boat full of holes in the middle of the ocean, and gone searching. He had been out well over an hour and was soaked to the skin, voice hoarse from shouting, near exhausted by his battle with the elements and angry in as much as he had a feeling on him that Sal, God bless her, was more than likely holed up somewhere quite safe.

He stopped for a moment and after shouting Sal's name several more times tried to get his bearings. He grimaced. He knew this area like the back of his hand yet hadn't a clue where he was now. He couldn't be that far from home yet not one sign of the familiar red brick streets was apparent. Mind you, he thought ruefully, he could have passed by the Almighty Himself and not seen Him due to the dreadful conditions.

His ears pricked and he strained to listen. He was near water and it was a lot of water by the noise of it. The River Soar . . . There had been warnings issued all day that it would burst its banks and by the sound of it, if it hadn't already, those warnings were in grave danger of coming true.

He really ought to get home. He had left Ma and the children struggling to carry the lighter bits they possessed up the stairs after he and a neighbour had done the honours with the heavier stuff. Not that they had much, but what they did they could not afford to risk. Ma's favourite chair, a rickety rocker, two spars at the back missing; the odd-legged wooden table; cracked dishes and old blackened pans – should they lose any of them, all would be nigh on impossible to replace.

He lifted his cloth cap just a fraction and wiped rivulets of rain from his eyes, then once again tried to fathom just where he was. But it was no good. All he knew was that he was somewhere near the river. Another turn in the wrong direction and he could wander aimlessly all night and if he didn't find himself shelter soon, considering the sodden state he was in, would go down with something terrible and then what use would he be to Ma and the kids? Despite this act of God, he could not afford to miss any time at work. A worker could be on his death bed but the bosses would still expect him to turn up and put in a full day's hard graft else face the consequences.

Jack thought rapidly. If he was near the river then boatsheds and huts were dotted thereabouts. But should he be lucky enough to come across one, considering the state of the river, he could be in more danger taking shelter than actually staying in the open and trying to make his way home. A blast of wind filled with driving rain nearly knocked him off his feet and his decision was quickly made. He would have one more try at finding Sal then find shelter on high ground if possible. Huts were made of wood, and if the worst happened, wood floated. He would just have to hope he did also.

Despite all his efforts there was still no sign of Sal. He would just have to pray that the old dog was safe somewhere, but when she finally did materialise he would certainly give her what for. Inwardly he smiled. Despite what she got up to no one could be mad with Sal for long. One gaze into her doleful brown eyes and she had you eating out of her paw.

He concentrated his efforts on finding shelter. His task was not an easy one, progress was slow, but thankfully he found what he was looking for – or more to the point it found him, as he stumbled straight into it, banging his head. Inching his way round, he found the door and fought to wrench it open. The wind blew him inside and he tripped on the floor. Hurriedly righting himself, he made a rush for the door and pulled it shut then dropped to his knees, panting heavily. After several moments he raised his head and peered around. Trust his luck, he thought, annoyed. Of all the huts and sheds in the area he had to stumble across one that appeared abandoned. He had been hoping for a lamp and maybe other items that might make his stay more comfortable but all he could make out was a pile of dirty sacks, several coils of old rope and pieces of rotting wood. Still, he had found shelter and he had to be grateful for that.

His eyes settled on the pile of sacks. He needed to strip off his wet things as quickly as possible. Those sacks would have to be his bed and his covering. He just hoped that the spiders and other creepy crawlies who had made their home inside didn't mind sharing until the storm blew out and he could leave them to it.

After his ordeal the sacks provided a surprisingly comfortable harbour for his weary body and, ignoring the smell of damp and must and the cloud of dust that rose when he spread them out, he settled down. Despite the pounding of the weather outside, his fear as to whether the hut could withstand the constant battering and the worry about struggling to arrive in time for work in the morning, he began to doze.

Just as the blissful release of sleep was about to envelop him, a noise outside startled him and his eyes opened and fixed on the door. Someone or something was outside. Fear filled him. He suddenly felt so vulnerable, lying naked between the sacks, and as the wind howled and the rain thrashed, his mind conjured up all sorts of visions of what lay behind that door. His eyes darted wildly, hoping to see something close at hand he could use as a weapon against an attacker. The pile of wood was just beyond his reach. He looked at the door then back to the wood. Slowly, and as quietly as possible, he manoeuvred himself just far enough to grab a length and pull it towards him. He snatched it up and ran his hand down it. His eyes shot back to the door as, heart thumping madly, he waited.

And waited.

Still rubbing his hand up and down the wood, he gnawed his bottom lip anxiously. Someone was outside. Why didn't they show themselves – get it over with?

Then the truth suddenly dawned and his fear flew from him, sending his heart soaring. Stupid man, he thought. He knew who was behind that door. It was Sal. From wherever she had been the old gel had smelled his scent and come after him.

A broad, relieved grin spread across his face. Dropping his weapon, he yanked aside the sacking, jumped up and leaped for the door.

'Sal!' he cried. 'Hold on, gel, I'm coming.'

He wrenched open the door, fully expecting the faithful old dog to leap at him. Instead the sight that met his eyes froze him rigid. So shocked was he, a cry of terror stuck in his throat.

From the muddy figure swaying before him a pair of terrified eyes locked on to his. The apparition let out one ear-splitting scream that drowned out the clamour of the storm, then collapsed to the ground in a heap.

Shaking violently, Jack stared down. It took him several long moments to calm himself, force his whirling thoughts into some semblance of order, then gradually it dawned on him that the heap on the ground was a woman and by the state of her something more than the storm had overtaken her. For a moment he wondered if she were dead. But whether she was or not, he needed to get her inside, and himself for that matter.

Jack grimaced in distaste as he pulled on his still sopping clothes. The wet material clung to his skin and he shuddered. He was annoyed to realise that in the early-morning darkness he had put on his shirt inside out. Stripping it off, he turned it the right way and pulled it back on again, then reached for his jacket.

As he laced up his boots his gaze settled on the woman in his makeshift bed. She seemed to be sleeping peacefully now, thank goodness, but it hadn't been that way for most of the night. As the storm had raged so had she, thrashing about, mumbling inaudibly, and he'd hardly had any sleep. Then, as the storm had gradually calmed, so had she. He wondered for a moment where she had come from, what she looked like, how old she was.

Indecision flooded through him. He really needed to be on his way but concern for the woman filled him. She appeared to be breathing easily, no sign of a fever or anything. But he hadn't time to linger. It must be getting on for five. He would have to rush in order to get home, calm Ma, then make his way to work – and not yet having poked his head outside, he had no idea what conditions faced him.

All his thoughts were suddenly with Ma and the kids and he prayed they were all right. An urgent desire to find out filled him and he abruptly made a grab for where he thought his other boot was. His hand hit the side of the shed and the sound echoed. The woman in the sacking sat upright, eyes wide in alarm.

'Who's there?' a frightened voice demanded.

'It's all right,' he hurriedly soothed her, stepping across. 'Don't be afraid, you're safe now. The storm's passed.'

Clutching the harsh sacking, a terrified Ally, still haunted by her nightmares, fought desperately to accustom her eyes to the darkness. All she could see was a large eerie shape looming over her and despite his reassurance she shrank back, afraid.

He sensed her fear. 'Please don't be frightened,' he repeated. 'You really are safe now. How d'yer feel?'

'Feel?' Ally suddenly became aware of how much her bruised body ached. She frowned, bewildered. Then like a thunderbolt her terrible ordeal of a few hours before flooded back to her. She had wanted to die. So strong had been the desire it overrode all else. But as the ground had unexpectedly collapsed and she had tumbled down the bank, her precious vanity case flying from her clutches towards the river, her beloved parents' faces had flashed before her and, confronted with the granting of her wish, her natural instinct for survival had surged.

She shut her eyes tightly as she relived her terror.

The iciness of the water almost took her breath away; the fight against the current was one she doubted she'd win, but resist to her utmost she had. With the storm raging around her, half submerged, strength fast ebbing, she had clawed at the saturated mud of the bank until her fingers had bled. To her dying day, she would never understand how she had managed to pull herself out. But she must have or she wouldn't be lying here now. How she had arrived at this place escaped her for the moment, all she could vaguely remember was a door opening and . . . something so shocking appearing she must have blacked out. But at this moment it didn't seem important; what kind of life she faced now wasn't important. The only thing that did matter to her was the fact that she was alive.

She opened her eyes and stared across at the man before her, features still obscured by the dim light. Her recent experiences of men – Tobias,

Lionel and the thieving coachman – meant she no longer trusted her judgement in that direction, but despite the fact that this man was obviously not of her class she did not sense any threat from him. Albertina took a deep breath. 'I think I am quite well,' she answered. But just to make sure drew her hand under the sacking and ran it over herself. Then froze in shock. 'I have no clothes on,' she blurted.

He looked surprised but his shock was not because of her observation. Judging by her bedraggled state, he had thought this woman to be a traveller or a gypsy but how could she be with such a cultured voice, tones the like of which he'd only ever heard coming from his brief encounters with the well-to-do? But her voice was not harsh or conde-scending like theirs had been. It was just . . . just music to his ears. He was fascinated by it. If her face was anything like her voice, then she had to be beautiful. But then again, knowing the ways of nature, she was probably as ugly as sin. He wanted her to speak again, willed it even, then realised she was waiting for his answer. 'Er . . . I . . . er . . . had to take them off,' he blurted. 'You were sopping. If I hadn't yer'd have risked pneumonia.'

'You . . . you took them off! But you're a man,' Ally cried, horrified.

In the darkness Jack smiled. 'Yes, for my sins. Look . . . er . . . don't be upset. It was so dark I never saw a thing. Besides, I was in too much of a hurry to get you warm to have any thought for anything else. Believe me, you've nothing to worry about.' He cleared his throat. If she was this distressed about the removal of her clothes, how would she react if she knew he had spent the night beside her in order to keep both of them warm, and that although they had been wrapped separately in the sacks, his own state of undress had been exactly the same as hers?

An uncomfortable silence stretched between them. On Jack's part, there were so many questions he wanted to ask. But time was rapidly wearing on, there was none to spare for explanations. Besides, what right did he have to ask? And did he really want to get involved?

He took a deep breath as a sudden desire to stay with this woman with the magical voice filled him. He felt responsible for her. After all, his action, whether she'd welcomed it or not, was probably the sole reason she was still breathing this morning.

As he wrestled with his conscience over whether to leave her or not, uppermost in Ally's mind was embarrassment that this man had stripped her naked. This act was all she could think of.

It was Jack who spoke first. 'I have to go.'

'Go?' Yes, please go, she thought. 'Yes, of course.' She paused for a moment. 'Thank you,' she whispered. Her expression of gratitude had been difficult to say. How could you thank someone for causing such embarrassment? But, regardless, it was probably warranted.

'Thank you?' he queried.

'Yes. For . . . for . . .'

51

'Oh, right.' He shrugged his shoulders. 'It was the least I could do.' A broad smile split his face. 'Thank you as well.'

'What for?'

'For nearly frightening me ter death! When I opened the door I got the shock of me life.'

Despite her predicament it was Ally's turn to smile. 'I looked that bad, did I?'

'You can say that again. I thought you were a demon.' He hesitated slightly. 'I . . . really have to go.'

Reluctantly he turned from her and headed for the door. Hand on the latch, he paused for a moment then turned back to face her. 'You'll be all right, will you?'

Inching herself upright, sacks under her chin, she nodded.

'Yes, thank you,' she said, with far more conviction than she actually felt. 'Though . . .'

'Yes?'

'Could you tell me where I am?'

'I wish I knew,' Jack answered helplessly. 'In a shed somewhere by the river. The only thing I am sure of is that we can't be far from the Aylestone Road.'

That fact meant nothing to her.

He pulled the door open. 'You'll be all right getting home?'

His simple question stabbed her painfully. 'Home?' she whispered distractedly. Then: 'Yes,' she replied firmly. 'I'll be all right getting home.'

He frowned. Something was not right somewhere. It was the way she had said 'home'. Then it dawned on him. For whatever reason, this woman hadn't a home. He was right, he knew he was. Jack rubbed the stubble on his chin, hoping he wasn't about to do something he'd regret. He knew Ma would go mad, but as matters stood he had no other choice. If he left the woman here and heard later something had happened to her, he wouldn't be able to live with himself. 'Come on,' he ordered.

'I beg your pardon?'

'Come on, I said. You're coming with me.'

'Oh, but I couldn't possibly . . .'

'Look, I ain't got time to argue and won't tek no for an answer. Besides, the bloke that owns this shed is bound to come soon,' he lied, in order to urge her to comply with his wishes. 'He won't take kindly to trespassers. So unless you fancy jail, I'd move yerself. I'll tek yer back to Ma's. At least you can wash some of that mud off. Come on now and hurry – unless you want me sacking on your conscience. Don't worry, while you dress I'll mek myself scarce.'

For Ally the mention of jail was enough. Thoughts of those terrible places she had heard of terrified her witless.

Chapter Seven

The head of a broom whacked Jack hard on the shoulder before he could duck.

'Jack, you bugger! Where yer bin? Oh, Jack, I thought you were dead.' Dropping the broom Florence Fossett threw herself at him, hugging him tightly. She held him at arm's length and scrutinised him. 'Look at the state of yer,' she scolded. 'Yer soaked to the skin.'

Rubbing his shoulder, Jack grinned. 'Well, it has been raining – just a bit.'

She scowled. 'Don't you be sarky wi' me, me lad. I ain't in the mood. I never slept a wink last night, what with one thing and another. And just look at this place! Bloody water everywhere. That new distemper you slapped on the walls to help kill the bugs was just a waste of time and good money. The water's stripping it off. The house was damp enough before all this – it'll tek a year of dry Sundays to make any impression now. And will that landlord show his face to see what he can do to help us? Like hell he will! Oh, but he'll be all right, won't he? Stuck nice and dry in his posh mansion with not a thought for how his tenants are faring. I doubt 'e'll be out of his bed before noon. Not like us, eh? Up before the crack of dawn, done a day's work while they're still snoring. Them monied folk are all the same.' She spat harshly. 'Only care about themselves, and that'll never change.'

'Ma, come on now, calm down. Even if the landlord had wanted to, I doubt he'd have got through. It'd bad out there. Worse than I can remember. I've had the devil's own job. The Aylestone Road is flowing faster than the river. People are using boats to get about.'

'Eh, don't you mek excuses for 'em. You got back here, didn't yer, on yer shanks's pony? Then I'm damned sure he could on his 'oss. Even if he'd just show his face it'd be summat. But mark my words, he'll mek sure his agent collects the rent, even if he has to swim, and there won't be any knocked off to help us put things right. Self-centred buggers, the lot of 'em.' She suddenly stopped in mid-flow and smiled sheepishly. 'Oh, don't mind me, Jack. I'm that het up I needed summat to have a go at and the landlord was the best thing I could think of.' She stuck her hands on her hips and grimaced deeply. 'But I don't tek back what I said. It's all true, the lot of it.'

Jack sighed. 'I suppose yer right. What about, Sal, Ma?' he asked to change the subject. 'She's back, ain't she?'

'Sal! Oh, she's all right. About the only one as is. Found her in my bed fast asleep not long after you'd gone. Mud all over the place. As if I hadn't enough to contend with. If I hadn't have bin that glad to see her, I'd have took the brush to her.' She eyed him, her eyes tender. 'But sod Sal. That dog is like a cat – got nine lives. What about you, Jack? Oh, I was so worried, I didn't know what to think.'

'I took shelter in an old boatshed. Seemed the only sensible thing to do. The storm was that bad, I'd no idea where I was.'

'I told yer, didn't I? I told yer not to risk it.'

'I know, I know, and as usual you were right, Ma.' He smiled at her fondly. 'But I'm back safe and sound and the only damage I've suffered is from the end of your broom.' He paused. This was a good time to tell her about the young woman but faced with it now he wasn't looking forward to it. He still didn't know the stranger's name and with it only just beginning to grow light, and her so bedraggled and caked in mud, had no proper idea what she looked like. Conversation on the hazardous journey home had been limited to his instructions as they had both had to concentrate hard on dealing with the aftermath of the terrible storm.

Jack hadn't been able to believe his eyes when he first ventured out of the shed. The rain may have abated for the time being, but the remains of the deluge were everywhere. Ma was right. The people who would suffer most were themselves, the folk right at the bottom. Those who had no resources to cope with unexpected catastrophes such as this. But they would have to cope as they always did. The daily grind of life did not stop because of a bit of rain.

'Ma, I have something to tell . . .'

'Is that Jack, Ma?' two voices shouted from upstairs, followed by a series of barks. 'Jack, Jack, is that you?'

'Yes, it is,' Flo bellowed. 'But don't you dare come down those stairs! If yer get wet again, I've nothing dry to put on yer. Give 'em a shout, Jack, to put their minds at rest.'

He waded to the bottom of the stairs. 'It's me,' he called. 'I'll be up ter see you in a minute. Just stay in bed where it's warm, and keep Sal up there too.'

'But we wanna help, Jack, and Ma won't let us.'

'And she's right. Down here is no place for kids. I shouldn't be in too much of a hurry, there'll be plenty to do once the water subsides.'

'And you think they'll want to help once that happens, do yer? It's the water that's attracting them,' Flo said haughtily. 'While I was doing me best to stop it coming in here last night, Eric was having a water fight with Tommy next-door. Emily – well, I have to admit she did try her best but she slipped over that many times she was more of a hindrance.' A broad smile of affection split her face. 'But that's kids for yer.'

Wading back Jack grinned also. 'Especially those two, eh? And you wouldn't be without 'em, would you, Ma?'

Her eyes flashed. 'Oh, Jack, did you have ter go and say that!' she erupted. 'Don't yer think I've enough worry at the moment without thinking about that?'

'Ma, I'm sorry. I didn't mean nothing by it.'

Her face softened and she patted him on the shoulder. 'No, I know yer didn't.' She sighed heavily and gazed around. 'I'm fighting a losing battle here. The water'll go when it's good and ready. I ought to get off ter work. I'm hours late already.'

'Ma, you can forget work. You won't get there.'

'I bloody will! I'm sure if I managed when we had snow up to our necks that year, then I can in this. As it is I've already lost money. If I don't go I won't be paid, then we won't eat, and Mr Sileby don't tek kindly to his workers teking time off willy-nilly.'

'I wouldn't call a situation like this willy-nilly, Ma.'

'Maybe you wouldn't but he just might and I daren't risk it. I need this job, Jack. I'll get there, you watch me. And you'd better get a move on too. I'll just pop . . .' She stopped and grinned. 'I mean, paddle down the road and see if Mrs Cox will have the kids, 'cos there's one thing I can be certain of and that's the school'll be shut whether it's flooded or not. Them teachers have the life of Riley.' She sighed heavily, her eyes darting around. 'Hopefully by the time I get back this afternoon the water will have subsided and we'll all set to then. Well, we can live in hope at any rate. Now go and get out of those wet clothes. Yer others will be damp, but better that than what yer wearing.'

'Ma, listen . . .'

'Oh, and I put the bread and dripping on me tallboy. And I tell yer, if that damn' dog has touched a crumb she'll have no fur left on 'er. Now just make sure you get something in yer stomach before you leave. I'll do me best to cook us something hot tonight.' She threw her arms around him again in a bear hug. 'Oh, Jack, I am that glad ter see yer.'

'Ma, listen . . .'

'What?' she snapped, releasing him abruptly from her embrace. 'Can't it wait? I've no time for . . .' She stopped in mid-flow, eyes darting over Jack's shoulder towards the tiny kitchen. 'Who's there?' Her gaze flashed back to him enquiringly. 'Jack, there's someone in my kitchen!'

He took a deep breath to prepare himself.

In the tiny sparsely furnished kitchen where Jack had whispered for her to wait, Ally had been listening to the proceedings in the next room, her already low spirits sinking further. She had heard the mother's views on the landlord and his kind. She herself was of that ilk and couldn't hide the fact. The truth would out the moment she opened her mouth and the woman would no doubt order her straight out of the house.

She gnawed her bottom lip, tears pricking her eyes as yet another blow struck her full force. She neither belonged amongst these people in their alien environment nor any longer in the privileged one she had been born into.

Lowering her gaze to the grey sludgy water lapping around her calves, she gulped in trepidation as she heard them approaching. What on earth was she to do? The thought of being treated in the same way as she had been at the inn was anathema to her. She needed to see Clarence Bailey. The need was imperative now. He was the only person who understood her predicament. The only one who would be able to help.

She became aware of a presence and raised her head to see a woman staring at her, hands on hips. Albertina's own eyes widened in surprise. Was this Ma? Her mental image had been of a small, rotund, severe kind of woman, well into her fifties, one she likened to Mrs Siddons, her former cook.

This woman could not possibly be the man's mother. She wasn't old enough. At the most in her mid-thirties. The man she now knew to be named Jack was, she guessed, about her own age, or maybe a little older. 'Ma' was tall, the shabby plain brown serge dress she wore showing a very shapely figure. To avoid the water the bottom of the dress had been pulled through her legs around her knees and secured in the band of a large sacking apron. She had a very good pair of legs. Her thick fair locks had been scooped up and tied on top of her head, loose tendrils framing an extremely attractive face. Albertina's eyes fixed on the pair of shrewd green ones scrutinising her now.

'Well, Jack's put me in the picture, told me as much as he knows about yer, and he didn't exaggerate, did he? You do look a sight, gel. As though you fell in the river and dragged half the mud back out with yer.'

Despite this reminder of her terrifying ordeal, of the dire state of her appearance and her total despair, Ally did manage a smile which cracked the dried mud on her face. 'Actually that's exactly what I did do.'

Astonishment flooded Flo's face. Abruptly she turned and pushed Jack, who was standing behind her, into the tiny back room and thrust her face into his. 'Who in God's name is that?' she hissed.

He shrugged his shoulders. 'I don't know,' he mouthed.

'What d'yer mean, you don't know? If you don't know, what the 'ell's she doing here?'

'Ma, keep yer voice down, she'll hear you.'

'I don't care, I'll say what I like in me own 'ouse. Is she a spy from the landlord?'

'Spy? 'Course she ain't a spy. Besides, why would the landlord go to all the trouble? The rent's paid up. You said yourself that's all he cares about. Look, Ma, last night she took shelter in the boatshed . . .'

'You spent the night with her!'

'Ma, it was nothing like that. We were both taking shelter, that's all.

And when it came time for me to leave . . . well . . . I couldn't leave her behind.'

'You couldn't leave her behind? What d'yer mean, you couldn't leave her behind? Why ever not?'

'I dunno, Ma. I just couldn't. I've an instinct about her.'

'Instinct? Men don't have instincts, only women have those.'

'Well, I have. I've a feeling on me about her.'

Flo frowned questioningly. 'What sorta feeling?'

'I dunno, just a feeling.' He grimaced thoughtfully. 'I don't think she's got anywhere to go, Ma.'

'And what makes you think that? Have you heard the way she speaks? As though she's a gob full of plums. People who speak like that have always got somewhere to go. She's gentry, she is. I can spot one a mile off.'

Jack exhaled scornfully. 'Just 'cos she speaks nice doesn't mean she's gentry. Look, Ma, I ain't asking you to adopt the woman, just let her get cleaned up. What harm would that do?'

Flo pursed her lips. 'None, I suppose. But I ain't happy about it, Jack. We've both ter get to work and that would mean leaving her here.'

'What difference would that make? It's not as though we've anything worth stealing.'

'Might not be worth stealing to some, but what I've got's precious to me. Anyway, what about the kids? She's a stranger. I couldn't leave 'em 'ere with a stranger.' Her eyes suddenly flashed with worry. 'Oh, Jack, what if she's . . .'

He eyed her sharply. 'Eh, you can stop thinking on those lines. We ain't bin in this house long enough for anyone to track us down.'

'No, no, we ain't. I s'pose yer right. But you know how I worry. I couldn't bear . . . Oh, Jack, you know I couldn't bear . . .'

'Ma,' he ordered, 'stop upsetting yerself unnecessarily. The woman happened upon the shed just like I did. Why she was out alone in the storm isn't really any of our business. Come on, Ma, what harm would it do to offer her a bit of charity?'

She eyed him suspiciously. 'You're taken with her, ain't yer?'

'No, I ain't taken with her,' he replied, offended, and scratched his chin exasperatedly. 'Oh, God, I wish I never offered to bring her back now. But, be honest, if she didn't speak so nicely, you'd have fell over yerself to help.'

Flo looked ashamed. 'Yes . . . yer right, I would have. Oh, Jack, I'm sorry. You've asked me to do this and I'll do it for you even though I still ain't completely happy about it.' She gave him a gentle push on his shoulder. 'Go and fetch her.'

Jack caught Ally paddling her way precariously down the yard, her already sodden skirt held as high as was dignified.

'Where yer going?' he called.

She stopped, took a breath and turned to face him. 'My presence is obviously not welcome. I thought it better to leave.'

His face fell in shame. 'Oh, I see, you heard then?'

'It was difficult not to.' She fought to quell the flood of tears that threatened. She suddenly wondered how much more she would bear, how much more her mind and body were expected to take. She took a deep breath. 'If you could just tell me which way to head for Leicester . . . I really do need to get there as soon as possible.'

He drew abreast of her and leaned forward to grab her arm, sharply aware of the musical voice that was sending shivers down his spine. 'Don't take any notice of Ma. She's a lot on her mind at the moment. She didn't mean half what she said.'

Ally sighed. 'Your mother has a right to her opinions. Now please, if you'll just be kind enough to point out the direction, I'll be on my way.'

Fear flooded through him, more urgent than it had been at the shed. For some unfathomable reason he did not want to let this woman go. He gave her arm a tug. 'Come on,' he insisted. 'Come and meet Ma properly. Then you can scrub away some of that mud and dry off a bit. There's a fire in the bedroom and I'm sure a hot drink will put some warmth back inside you. You'll need it if you're going to try and reach town today.'

His offer sounded so inviting she suddenly had no fight left in her to argue. 'Your generosity is most welcome. But only so long as you are sure it's all right with your mother?'

Jack looked down into the pair of deep brown eyes gazing into his. He saw the pain and weariness that filled them and compassion for this poor bedraggled soul surged through him. He felt the need to gather the unfortunate creature into his arms and hug away whatever was grieving her. Valiantly he fought this desire, knowing she might not welcome his actions. He smiled reassuringly. 'You won't be the first Ma's helped, nor I suspect the last. It's just that we hardly ever come across people who speak like you and she was suspicious. Believe me, she has her reasons. Now I don't know about you but I'm frozen so let's get . . .'

His name being loudly shouted interrupted him and Jack's head jerked to look past Ally towards the yard entry. A small rowing boat, badly patched with odd pieces of wood, blocked the entrance. A shabbily dressed man, half crouched inside, was struggling to hold on to the side of the gatepost.

'Oi, Jack,' he called again. 'I'm gonna attempt ter get into town. Does Mrs Fossett need anything?'

Hearing the shout, Flo came out to investigate. 'Did I hear yer say you were going into town, Mr Dimmin? 'Cos if yer are, I need a lift ter work.'

The threadbare middle-aged man in the ramshackle boat grinned at her. 'Attempt, Mrs Fossett. This is the first time I've rowed a boat fer years. But if you wanna tek the risk, yer welcome.'

Jack spun to face her. 'Ma, I ain't having you go in that old thing.'

'Oh, stop fussing, Jack. It floats, dunnit? I need to get to work and so, my lad, do you. We can't afford for your pay to be docked an' all. That old thing'll be quicker than wading.'

Jack could see the sense in that. He turned to eye the boat and its occupant then looked back at Flo. 'We're on low ground here,' he mused thoughtfully. 'The town's a bit higher so it might not be flooded. It's a possibility we won't be in the boat for long . . .'

'Well, a' yer coming or not?' asked an agitated voice.

'Give us two minutes, Mr Dimmin, and we'll be with yer. Come on, Jack, no time ter mess about.' Turning on her heel Flo started to hurry inside, the water rippling in her wake. She stopped suddenly. 'Oh,' she mouthed as she turned back, 'the kids. I forgot about the kids.' She eyed Ally warily, knowing she didn't have much choice. Jack seemed to feel this woman was all right or he wouldn't have brought her home, and Jack's judgement she trusted above anyone's. It was just a pity there wasn't more time to question the stranger. Flo didn't even know her name and there was no time to ask now. 'Look, er . . . I know it's an imposition . . . but I do have ter get to work and there's the kids, see. I just need to get them safely to Mrs Cox. She only lives down the street. The kids'll show yer. In return you can help yerself to soap and water . . .'

'A' yer coming or what?'

'Yes, we're coming,' Flo erupted. 'Will yer do it for me, please? I'd be ever so grateful.'

'Yes,' Jack piped up, eyes fixed on Ally. 'You'll be all right.' His eyes flashed to Flo. 'She'll be all right, she will, Ma.'

Ally needed to get into town herself. 'I . . .' she began.

'Oh, ta, me duck.' Flo turned and headed once more into the house. 'Just shut the door after yer when yer leave. I'll go and tell the kids what's happening. Come on, Jack, get a move on. Won't be a minute, Mr Dimmin,' she shouted after her.

Chapter Eight

Wiping a mud-caked hand across her mud-streaked face, Ally numbly watched the boat's precarious departure. Her eyes turned upward and scanned the sky. It was a heavy grey-black. More rain threatened. She really ought to be on her way as soon as possible. She had no idea how far she had yet to travel and must see Clarence Bailey today.

Taking a deep breath, she made her way into the tiny house and inside the flooded back room, took a moment to gaze around. Whatever had been inside had been removed and murky brown floodwater sloshed in the empty grate. Despite the damage the water was causing, Ally could still not help but feel appalled at the terrible conditions these people lived in. Poor people such as resided in this house, ones who dare not miss work despite the catastrophe that had befallen them, she had only ever come close to previously through her carriage window. Now here she was, not only having spent the night with one in a boatshed but having accepted their hospitality; also, albeit only for a short time, responsibility for their children.

Confusion filled her. She had always been told, been led to believe, lowly people were not to be trusted. They were all liars and thieves, the coachman had proved that. But could it be true of all his class? The man, Jack, had probably saved her life. She shuddered with embarrassment at what that act had entailed. He could have left her in the boatshed but he hadn't, and now his mother, although Ally knew she had not had much choice, was trusting her, a stranger, with everything she held dear. Could what she had always believed be true? Her confusion mounted, then revelation struck. The only two things the last forty-eight hours had proved to her were that thieves and liars came from all walks of life and that the lower classes mistrusted her own kind as much as they did them.

A loud bump from above startled her and her promise came to mind. Despite the fact she did not have a clue what to do, two little children were upstairs needing to be cared for and regardless of all the problems she had to contend with, all the confusion she was experiencing, the needs of those children must come first. Her own problems could be dealt with afterwards.

Tentatively she waded her way towards the door leading to a steep, bare-boarded staircase. The water had risen to cover the first tread. Just before she reached the top she let her sodden skirt drop. To either side of the landing well was a door. She took a breath and poked her head around the one to her right, facing the front of the house.

At first the small room appeared to be piled with junk until it dawned that the rickety furniture, ancient peg rugs and assortment of chipped crockery and blackened pans haphazardly thrown on the iron bedstead were the furnishings from below stairs.

Stepping back on to the square of landing she turned to face the other door, took another deep breath, pushed it open, stepped over the threshold and stared around. She was shocked at how tiny this room too was, even smaller than the other. She tried to comprehend how anyone could sleep in such cramped confines. This room would easily have slotted into one corner of the bedroom she had been used to. Against the sash window on the far wall hung an old net and a pair of faded beige twill curtains. A tawdry country scene print hung above the tiny mantel on which sat two white pot candle holders and an assortment of cheap fairground orna-ments. On the tallboy in the recess by a blue basin and jug was the remains of a loaf of bread, a chunk of something yellow and lump of something wrapped in greaseproof paper. There was a small sack and other odds and ends stacked to one side on the floor. The floor itself was bare and broken only by two colourful but faded peg rugs, one placed in front of the small fireplace and the other at the side of the bed.

Albertina's eyes strayed to the bed and she jumped in shock at the sight of the three pairs of eyes staring at her. She had been expecting two very young children. These children were not that young and no one had mentioned a dog. The boy was at least twelve or thirteen and the girl, arms around a mangy-looking black and white animal with large doleful eyes, was about ten.

After her initial surprise at Albertina's appearance the young girl suddenly started to giggle.

'Emily, stop that,' the boy said, nudging his sister. 'Ma sez it's rude to laugh at people.'

Ally frowned, shocked. 'You were laughing at me?' Then it dawned on her why. 'Well, yes, I can understand why. I must look an awful fright. But I'll look much more presentable once I get cleaned up.' Her shock turned to bewilderment at the look on the children's faces. 'Is there something the matter? I thought your mother had explained about me?'

The boy slipped his arm around his sister protectively. Neither spoke, just continued to stare at her.

'Well?' asked Ally again. 'What is it?'

There was a long silence before the boy, Eric, finally spoke.

'A' you one of them gentry?' This was not a question but an accusation.

She gasped, mortified. She was exactly what he accused her of being but how could she be truthful when these children were bound to share their mother's opinions? Then they would not trust her and she would not be able to honour her promise to Flo. But what could she do about it? Her thoughts raced for a plausible story that would appease them until she could get them safely to their neighbour, but nothing came to mind. Then she remembered the games she and Annabella had played in the nursery, and one in particular. It had been so much fun. Little had she known then how she would put that game to use one day. It would mean lying, but, she reasoned with herself, surely a lie in such circumstances would not matter? When she had cleaned herself up and delivered the children she would never see them again. She decided to go on with it.

'Yes, I must sound rather strange to you. But I don't belong to the gentry.' She took several steps towards the bed and clasped her dirty hands. Here goes, she thought. 'You see, when I was a little girl, a lot younger than you,' she said, smiling at Emily, 'my parents worked for a very rich family. They had a little girl of their own but she didn't have any companions.'

'Companions?' Emily queried.

'Oh, er . . . friends. Children of her own age to play with. So they asked my mother if I could be her comp— friend. And we became such good friends it was decided I would have lessons with her. So, you see, I spent so much time in her company, I began to speak the way she did.'

Emily was staring at her, engrossed. 'Where is she now, this friend? Why ain't yer still living with her?'

'Yeah?' asked a sceptical Eric. 'Why ain't yer?'

Ally froze. Her childish game had never proceeded as far as that. Nanny had always interrupted halfway through, announcing that tea was served. 'Oh, the . . . family moved away. Yes, that's right, far away, and I couldn't go with them.'

'Why not?' Emily asked.

''Cos rich folk don't really like poor folk, they only pretend to,' Eric said harshly. 'Well, that's what Ma sez. Did they chuck you out on yer ear then?'

'Pardon?'

'Them posh folk. Did they throw you out?'

Ally clenched her hands. 'Something like that.'

'And what about yer mam and dad? Where a' they?' Emily asked.

There was a long silence before Ally whispered, 'They are both dead.'

'Oh, that's sad. Ain't that sad, our Eric?' The shabby girl leaped off the bed, over to Ally, and threw her arms around her. 'A hug'll help yer feel better. Oh!' she grimaced, jumping back. 'Yer all soggy.' She spun round to face her brother. 'Ma said we were to get the lady the stuff for her wash. Get the pan on to heat and fetch the bath.'

'Fetch the bath? What, in here?' Ally exclaimed, horrified.

'Yeah.' Eric frowned. 'Yer can't have a scrub downstairs, it's all flooded.'

'You have no bathroom then?'

'Bathroom?' they both queried in unison, eyeing her in astonishment.

'I'm sorry,' uttered Ally, ashamed. 'I wasn't thinking. Of course you wouldn't have a bathroom.'

'Did you have one of them with the rich family?' Emily asked.

''Course she did,' answered Eric. 'And I bet you had yer own bedroom as well, didn't yer? I'd love me own bedroom. I have ter sleep wi' Jack and he takes all the room. He only moves up when I kick him.'

'I'd love me own room too,' said Emily wistfully. 'Ma snores and sometimes wakes me up.' Then her face broke into a grin. 'But she's lovely to cuddle into, is my ma. Eric, get that bath before the lady catches her death.' Emily began to rummage around for soap and a piece of cloth for Ally to dry herself on but suddenly stopped what she was doing and eyed her sharply. 'What's yer name?'

Automatically she replied: 'Albertina Victoriana . . .' and abruptly stopped at the look on Emily's face. 'Ally. My friends call me Ally. Ally List—' Oh, goodness, she thought. She could not give her proper surname. She could not take the chance that for any number of reasons it might be known to them. So what name could she give, one that would not arouse any kind of suspicion? 'Brown,' she blurted. 'Ally Brown.'

'Oh, that's pretty. I like that. Ally. I wish I was called that instead of just Emily. But what did you say before? Bettina summat, was it?'

'Oh! That . . . that's my Sunday name.'

'A Sunday name! I haven't got a Sunday name. My name's the same every day.' Emily resumed her task as her brother came through the door dragging behind him a battered tin bath. He proceeded to pour into it boiling water from the pan sitting precariously on the coals, then added some cold. 'I'm gonna ask Ma why I ain't got a Sunday name,' Emily muttered to herself, then addressed Ally. 'Maybe I'll get one. Gilly . . . I like that name. I've a rag dolly called Gilly. She got wet when I fell over in the water downstairs but Ma told me not ter worry she would soon dry her out.' Emily beamed. 'My ma can do anythin'. Eric, you go and wait in your'n and Jack's room while Ally has her scrub.'

'Ah, but it's freezing in there,' he wailed. 'And it's piled wi' stuff so there ain't no room. I'll turn me back . . .'

'You won't! You'll peep. Go on, skedaddle.'

Ally hid a smile as Eric sullenly departed. Emily was proving to be a very bossy little thing, at least where her elder brother was concerned. She suddenly realised she was warming to these two children Despite that she did not relish the thought of stripping off in front of the little girl and eyed her hesitantly.

'Will you be joining your brother whilst I bathe?'

'Eh? Bathe?'

'Have my bath.'

'What for? I can't help yer if I ain't here, can I? Ma likes me to help her. She likes me to scrub her back. I'll scrub your back for you. Now where's that brush?' She kneeled down and fiddled around under the bed then pulled out a large scrubbing brush. 'You'd better hurry or the water'll get cold.'

Ally stared in horror at the brush, then down into the inch or so of water in the bottom of the old bath, at Sal watching her dolefully, still sprawled on the bed, then at Emily poised at the ready. She sighed with resignation.

Despite the lack of privacy, consequential embarrassment and the sparseness of the water which by the time she had stripped out of her sodden clothing had grown tepid, a wave of pleasure flooded through Ally as she gingerly lowered her aching dirty body into the narrow rusting tin bath. Almost instantly Emily began her task and gradually, as the pore-deep mud washed away, the bruises and cuts covering Ally's smooth creamy skin emerged.

'Oh, I say,' Emily proclaimed. 'You ain't 'arf got some bashes on yer.'

Ally wasn't surprised, considering how she had been thrown about in the carriage then thrashed about in the river as she had struggled for her life. If bruises and a few abrasions were all she had suffered then even she considered herself lucky. Her clothes had been less so. Her coat and jacket might not be too bad once dried but her skirt was ripped in several places quite jaggedly.

'I fell in the river,' she said distantly.

'Yer never!' Emily replied, shocked. 'You're lucky yer dint drown. Ma meks us stay away from the river. She sez it's dangerous. Eric goes there sometimes, though. Oh, don't tell him I told yer, will yer, or Ma?'

Ally smiled. 'I won't say a word.'

Before she was completely clean the water had to be changed three times, the last lot being practically stone cold. As she dried herself down her skin tingled with freshness and she tried not to mind the alien smell of the strong carbolic soap. She wistfully remembered her own toiletries, the smell of lavender and camellia lost to her forever somewhere at the bottom of the river, and the bar of soap Edna Murkitt had slipped into her pocket.

Whilst she began on her hair, Emily rummaged around for some of her mother's clothing for Ally to put on whilst they tried to do something with her own. Hair washed, Ally cloth-dried it and ran her fingers through the tangles to tease free the natural wave that rippled through her chestnut tresses then tied them in a knot at the nape of her neck, fighting hard to dispel memories of the elaborate hair styles she had sported until recently, secured with tortoiseshell combs and pins of silver. She put on the brown twill dress of Flo's that Emily handed her. The fit was a little on the large side, the coarse material harsh against her skin, but after her own sodden attire it felt really comfortable. As she straightened up she caught sight of Emily staring at her.

'What is it, Emily?' she asked worriedly, wondering if she had grown another head or worse.

'Oh, er . . . it's just that you're so pretty, Ally. You are. You're really beautiful. Nearly as beautiful as Ma.'

Ally smiled warmly at the compliment. She reached over and cupped the young girl's chin. 'You're not so bad yourself.'

Emily's eyes lit up. 'D'yer think so? Really?'

Ally scrutinised the thatch of corn-coloured hair, chopped to chin length, and the tiny heart-shaped face it was framing. She saw the gangle of arms and legs that sprouted out of Emily's worn clothing and for a fleeting moment visualised the girl wearing decent clothes and sporting a proper hair cut. The transformation would be startling. But, regardless, there was no doubt this child would break a few hearts when she grew older.

Before she could reply there was a pounding on the bedroom door. 'Can I come in yet? I ain't 'arf cold.'

'Yes, please do, Eric,' she called.

He charged in and plonked himself in front of the fire, holding his hands out towards it. 'It's belting again,' he announced.

'Belting?' Ally queried.

'Wi' rain.'

Albertina grimaced. She had hoped the rain had stopped completely. It was proving a waste of time trying to dry off her clothes. A few minutes outside and they would be in the same state again and she really did want to arrive at the old solicitor's looking the best she could.

Emily ran to the window, moved aside the old piece of net and peered out. 'He's right.' She turned to Ally, her little face puckered in worry. 'What about Ma and Jack? What if they can't get back? Oh, what if summat happens to 'em?'

Ally rushed across to her and gently took her hands. 'Don't fret, child. They will both be back.' She wished she felt as convinced as she sounded. Dropping the girl's hands, she moved to the window and looked out. The rain began to batter against the glass and the child's fears were echoed in her, but the worst thing she could do was voice them. Her mind raced. Maybe she should get them to the neighbour's house. How far was it? From her recent experiences in weather like this, several yards could feel like several miles and before they reached the yard gate the children would be soaked through as would she. Oh, dear, she thought, suddenly feeling out of her depth. What would her long departed nanny have done? Nanny's shrill voice echoed in her head: 'Little minds need to be kept occupied.' That was all well and good, thought Albertina, when you knew how to do it. She didn't.

Eric broke into her thoughts.

'I'm starving,' he announced.

She suddenly felt very hungry herself and a vision of kedgeree, devilled kidneys and crispy bacon and eggs all laid out on hot dishes from which she could help herself rose before her.

'I'm famished too,' said Emily. 'I'll get the bread and dripping.'

The vision of the assortment of dishes filled with delicious food abruptly disappeared. 'Dripping? What's dripping?' Ally asked.

'You don't know what dripping is?' The little girl looked shocked. 'It's stuff that comes out of meat when yer cook it. Ma sometimes meks her own but the bit we've got now is from the butcher's 'cos we ain't had meat for a while. Oh, it's lovely. I like the brown jelly bit best wi' loads of salt sprinkled on it.'

Ally hid a grimace of disgust but watched closely as the young girl proceeded to cut a thick slice of bread and spread it sparingly with the brownish substance. After adding salt she handed the slice to Ally.

'Get tucked in,' she said, beaming.

Ally stared at it and gulped, it looked so unappetising, but it was obvious it was this or go hungry. And she was so very hungry. She suddenly realised she should be grateful that she was being offered a share in their meagre meal. She took a tentative bite, chewed slowly, then forced herself to swallow. Her eyes lit up in surprise. 'This is good,' she said, taking another bite.

'See, I told yer you'd like it,' said Emily matter-of-factly.

'Can I get another bit?' asked Eric.

Emily looked at the bread longingly for a moment, licking her lips. 'No,' she said firmly. 'You know we're only allowed one slice for breakfast, else there'll be nothing fer later.'

Ally stared, shocked. One slice of bread. Was that all? But their mother and brother both went to work so what did they do with all their money?

She remembered past conversations at hunt meetings and other social gatherings. Grim-faced employers had grumbled about their workers demanding higher wages and better conditions, how they were never satisfied with what they received and should be grateful for how well off they were. But it didn't take a genius to see that these people appeared to live very frugally.

Oh, it was all so confusing. She suddenly wished she knew more, understood better. She was beginning to realise how naive she was about life outside what had been her own social circle. She shuddered, the room growing chilly about her. 'Ought we to put some more fuel on?' she suggested.

Eric stared thoughtfully at the fire. 'Ma said we'd to be careful wi' the wood and coal. We can't get any more 'til payday on Friday.'

'So what do you do if you're cold?'

'Put another jumper on or go to bed.' Eric frowned. 'Ma sez the posh people never have ter go without food and coal. Is that right? You living with 'em, you would know, wouldn't yer?'

Ally shifted uncomfortably. From her own experience the children's mother was exactly right. 'I was only the friend so I didn't really notice.' How she hated lying to these children! She went across to the window and peered out. The rain didn't seem to be easing at all; if anything it was getting worse. The thought of venturing out in it again did not appeal one little bit, but she had to, she had things to do and couldn't abuse this hospitality any longer. She let the net drop and turned to face them. 'Maybe we should think about getting you to your neighbour's house? I really should be setting off.'

Emily's face fell. 'Do we have ter? I don't like Mrs Cox. She meks us sit in the corner and not move. And she shouts at us. We ain't told Ma 'cos she'd not be able to go to work else.' She raised tear-filled eyes. 'I wanna stay here.'

Eric put his arm around his sister and pulled her close. 'I'm old enough to look after us both.'

'Oh, but I couldn't go off and leave you alone. Your mother put you in my care and I must honour that obligation.'

Emily sniffed hard and two large tears spilled down her face. 'I ain't going. Please don't make me go.'

Ally clasped her hands. The sight of the child crying tore at her. What a dilemma she found herself in. If she insisted that these children went to their neighbour, what if their mother and brother were not able to get back? What if this woman was unwilling to keep the children for any length of time? But worst of all was the thought that they would be made to sit in the corner until such time as they were collected.

'You could stay with us,' sniffed Emily.

Ally sighed heavily. 'I can't, I'm afraid. I have to get into Leicester.'

'Why?' the girl demanded.

'Well . . . er . . . I have to see someone.'

'For a job?'

Ally stared at her thoughtfully. The child in her innocence had suddenly made her realise that she would now have to earn her living. Despite his kind offer, she couldn't expect Clarence Bailey to keep her for long. The shock of this realisation struck her forcefully and filled her with more worry. What kind of work was she qualified for? None that sprang to mind. 'Yes,' she said, swallowing hard. 'I have to see someone about a job. Please gather your things. I'll just quickly change and then we can be off.'

'But yer clothes are still wet.'

Yes, they were, they had hardly dried at all. But wet or not she would have to put them back on. She suddenly realised Eric was missing. She was just about to ask where he had gone when she heard him shout: 'The water's rising. You'd better come and look.'

Panic filled her. Emily following, they joined him on the tiny landing and peered down. The water had now risen above the second step.

'A' we gonna drown?' wailed Emily.

Ally grabbed her hand and squeezed it reassuringly. 'No, we're not going to drown.'

'Will we have ter climb on the roof?' asked Eric, quite happy at the thought of the adventure, not envisaging the danger.

'I sincerely hope not,' whispered Ally in trepidation as she wondered how much more rain would need to fall for them to consider that possibility.

As she stared down at the lapping water below Ally knew it would be foolish for her to attempt getting the children to the neighbour's and try to journey on her own to Leicester. The journey from the boatshed to the house had been dangerous enough. It would be worse now. She had no choice but to stay put for the time being.

A part of her was relieved. She did not really want to leave the children until their family was safely home, and after the kindness they had shown her it was the least she could do. Her meeting with Clarence Bailey could wait. Her dire situation would not change one bit in the meantime.

Still clutching Emily's hand, she took hold of Eric's arm. 'Come along, we'll risk putting a little more coal on the fire and I'll tell you some stories my old nanny used to tell me. Er . . . my friend's old nanny.'

'What's a nanny?' asked Emily, wiping her nose with the back of her hand.

Chapter Nine

Panting breathlessly, a horrified Flo stared at the expanse of water before her. She had run all the way through the deluged Leicester streets under a rapidly darkening sky until she had come to halfway down the Welford Road. There her route was blocked. The floodwater, engulfing a huge area of back-to-backs, shops, factories and the Royal Infirmary, appearing eerie and menacing in the twilight, had risen several inches since she and Jack had scrambled thankfully from the boat that morning.

Usually a strong-stomached woman, the journey had terrified her. Mr Dimmin was right when he had said she was taking a risk, she had been – with her life. It was only thanks to Jack that they had arrived safely. After the second time they had narrowly managed to avoid capsizing he had demanded control of the rotten oars and had painstakingly navigated them to safety. The memory of that journey was still fresh and she shuddered violently at the thought of how close the children had come to losing them both, and all because they had been so eager to work.

The sound of her name made her jump and she turned to see a figure heading towards her. Flo cried out in joy. It was Jack! Securing her brown paper parcel under her arm and hauling up her skirt, she ran to meet him, her feet sliding precariously on the mud. 'Oh, Jack, look, look! The water . . .'

'I can see it, Ma,' he interrupted her, staring at it gravely.

'The kids! Oh, Jack . . .'

'The kids will be fine with Mrs Cox,' he assured her.

'But, Jack,' she erupted, 'what if Mrs Cox wasn't able to have 'em? You know how temperamental she can be. And what if that woman's gone and left 'em on their own? Jack, what if . . .'

'Ma,' he snapped firmly, taking hold of her arms, 'she wouldn't do that.'

'But how do you know? What's one night in a boatshed? She could be a maniac, a murderer, she could be anyone, Jack. We don't even know her name.' She grabbed his sleeve and shook it angrily. 'Oh, how stupid I was. I should never have left them. I'll never forgive myself if owt's happened to 'em.'

'Ma, for God's sake, stop fretting unnecessarily. The kids will be fine. Either Mrs Cox will have them or the woman will still be with them. But anyway, give Eric some credit. He's quite capable of taking care of himself and Emily. And she, bless her, ain't as daft as she looks.'

Flo could not help but smile at Jack's remark. They both knew Emily to be a very intelligent little girl.

'Yeah, I know I'm being stupid. But whatever, I need ter get home. I only left 'em a bit of bread and dripping. They'll need a hot meal.'

'So do I,' Jack muttered. 'I'm bloody famished meself. Now just be quiet a moment while I think what's best to do.'

She smiled at him tenderly. If anyone could get them home it would be Jack. A thought suddenly struck her and she stared at him quizzically. 'It's early for you, ain't it?'

He frowned at her, annoyed. 'Ma, I'm trying to think straight.'

She looked ashamed.

Smiling, he shook his head. He never had been able to stay annoyed with her for long. 'Mr Green let all but two of his staff go early and those two were all right 'cos they only live around the corner.'

'He did? Oh, Jack, what a nice man Mr Green is. Which is more than I can say for that bastard I work for!'

'Ma!'

'Don't "Ma" me. I'm speaking the truth. He moaned like billyho 'cos we all turned up late. No thank you for actually getting there, no praise fer risking our necks, just told us to expect our pay to be docked for the hours he lost. The fresh delivery never got through, which didn't surprise us, so we hadn't much to do. But instead of letting us go he made us scrub the place from top to bottom then left us hanging around. He knows fine well we've all got families and were worried sick. Now tell me he ain't a bastard?'

Jack sighed. He agreed with her wholeheartedly, but all he said was, 'It's a job, Ma.'

She grunted. 'I suppose yer right. I should be grateful I've got it.' She took a despairing breath and turned her attention back to the water. 'I can't see owt else for it, Jack, we'll have to chance it.'

'Not likely! I'm not letting you wade in that. We know this road like the back of our hands, but not in these conditions. There's all sorts of hidden dangers under that lot. You'll stay here while I go for the boat. I just hope Mr Dimmin will let me borrow it – that is if it's still in one piece.'

'The boat!' she cried in alarm. 'If you think you'll ever get me in that old thing again then you've another think coming. Have you forgotten we nearly drowned? Not once but twice.'

'How could I forget, Ma? It was a nightmare. But we have no choice. Now you stay here while I fetch the boat.'

'Oh, I see, it's all right for you to face dangers but not me?'

'That's right, Ma.'

'Jack . . .'

70

'Ma!'

She sighed in resignation. Jack was right, it would be insane to insist she attempt such a task when she couldn't even swim. It was bad enough that Jack himself was adamant on making the effort. 'Just hurry, Jack.' She wagged a finger. 'And if you let anything happen to yer . . .'

'I know – you'll murder me.'

'I'll do worse than that. Now get off before I change me mind.'

'Tell us another story, Ally, please? Just one more,' Emily begged. 'Do the one again about the cripple boy and Scooge.'

'Scrooge,' Ally corrected. She stretched her weary body and stifled a yawn. It surprised her to see it was growing dark. She hadn't realised so much time had passed. Even more astonishing was that for those few hours she had been engrossed in relating the stories of several of her best loved childhood books to such a receptive audience, her worries had been temporarily forgotten. Now they reared again. She rose awkwardly from her huddled position by the low-burning fire and looked out of the window. It had stopped raining. Maybe if Jack and his mother returned soon there would still be time for her to make her journey. She sincerely hoped so. She really needed to begin sorting out her life.

Eric distracted her from her thoughts by announcing he was hungry.

'So am I,' agreed his sister. 'Me belly thinks me throat's bin cut.'

Staring at her, mystified, it took several moments for Ally to work out what the young girl had meant. Instinctively she chastised the child before she could stop herself. 'Emily, young ladies do not say things like that.'

'Why not? Me stomach *does* think me throat's bin cut.'

Ally froze, mortified. It had been wrong of her to speak out as she had. She would really have to watch what she said for the short time she was in the company of these people, who she was rapidly coming to realise were nothing like as bad as she had always been led to believe. How could this child know what was proper and what was not when she had not had the privilege of an education? 'You are right, Emily,' she said, smiling. 'My stomach thinks so too.'

They must be terribly hungry, she thought. All they had eaten was the slice of bread and dripping and that was several hours ago. She glanced across to where the remains of the loaf sat on the tallboy. Cut thinly and spread sparingly with the bit of dripping that was left, it would hardly satisfy Emily let alone Eric as well.

'What does your mother usually give you for supper?' she asked.

'She usually brings the dinner home with her,' Eric replied.

'Oh, but she must have a food stock in the larder, surely?'

They both looked at her blankly.

If their mother didn't have a stock in the larder, how did they manage?

71

Cook had always kept a well-stocked larder, prided herself on it, so Ally had thought every household did.

'We've some spuds left in the sack,' said Emily.

'Spuds?'

'Yeah, spuds. We could fry chips.'

Spuds and chips, Ally thought. What on earth were they?

'We ain't got no lard. Only marge,' piped up Eric.

Ally knew what lard was. It was some kind of fat. She remembered that Cook had rendered her own. What it was used for she hadn't a clue. And marge . . . Could that possibly be an abbreviation for margarine? She had read of margarine somewhere. It was the poor's substitute for butter. Margarine was a fat so whatever they were going to fry could be fried in that – couldn't it?

She suddenly felt so inadequate. How was it that she hadn't the first notion of how to cook a meal, how in fact to feed herself unless it was laid out on a plate in front of her. She wished so vehemently she had ignored Tobias's domineering ways and made even a little effort to notice what went on in the kitchen. As it was all she possessed were childhood memories. Apart from knowing that Mrs Siddons had kept a well-stocked larder and rendered her own lard – that fact only sticking in her mind because she had had some rubbed on her chest once while suffering from an extremely bad cold – she knew nothing else. Oh, she could order a meal in a first-class eating establishment, knew the difference in taste between a good leg of lamb and a fillet of venison, but nothing about spuds and certainly had never heard of chips.

She realised the children were looking at her expectantly and chewed her bottom lip. She just could not face the embarrassment of telling these children she didn't know how to feed them and the inevitable barrage of questions that would follow as to why not. She had told them enough lies already. An approach to this problem began to formulate in her mind and yes, she thought, it just might work and would also help to keep the children's minds occupied a while longer.

'Emily, fetch the . . . spuds.' First things first. Find out what spuds were and take it from there. She had to laugh when the unknown articles were produced from a sack. 'Oh, potatoes,' she exclaimed before she could stop herself. Before the children could question her again on her lack of knowledge she busied them both. 'Right then, Emily, Eric, I thought we could play a game.'

'Oh, yes.' Emily clapped her hands gleefully. 'I love playing games.'

'I don't,' muttered Eric. 'Games are for babies.'

'You play football, don't yer?' scolded Emily. 'That's a game, ain't it? Come on then, Ally. What game we gonna play?'

'It's called "cooking the supper". Now I'll ask you both questions, and from your answers I'll be able to see how much you know about cooking.'

'Sounds a stupid game to me,' mumbled Eric. But as there was nothing else to do while they were imprisoned in this cramped bedroom he decided to pass the time by joining in. He might as well, being's at the end of it he would get his stomach filled.

Half an hour later Emily had supervised the laying out of the plates and cutlery on a space on the floor. Eric had cut the remains of the bread into three equal thin slices. A chunk of margarine was melting in the smallest pan which had been wedged inside the grate over a sparingly stacked fire. Ally was concentrating hard on her task of peeling the potatoes, after being shown, via the game, by Emily.

'Eh up,' the girl suddenly cried. 'Yer teking too much off.'

Ally's hand jerked in shock, the knife slipping to catch her finger. It was only a tiny cut but nevertheless the blood flowed. Sucking her injury, she eyed Emily sharply. 'You made me jump. Why did you shout like that?'

'Because yer teking too much peel off. Ma'll go mad if she sees all that waste. Spuds don't grow on trees, yer know.'

'I know very well that potatoes don't grow on trees, thank you, Emily. I have to take this thickness of peel off as the potatoes are ... well, they're rotten.'

'No, they ain't,' snapped Eric. 'They've just got a few bad bits on 'em which you pick out after, that's all.' He attempted to snatch the knife. 'It's usually my job to peel the spuds. I'll do 'em.'

Ally snatched her hand away. 'I can manage, thank you, Eric.' After all, she thought, this was her opportunity to learn. 'Check to see if the fat has melted, please, and if you think it's hot enough. And be careful,' she warned.

Eric proceeded to do her bidding and Ally returned to her task. Now, she thought, the children had said that when the fat was hot enough the pieces of potato, which they called chips, were added and took about twenty minutes to cook. She smiled. This game was going rather well with no mishaps as yet. Except, of course, for her cut finger.

A little while later, the children sitting patiently on the floor in readiness, Ally lifted the chips from the pan with the serrated ladle and put them in the bowl. Looking at her efforts, she frowned. 'Er ... Emily?'

'Yes.'

'These chips. Are they supposed to be black?'

They both grimaced. 'Eh?' they said in unison.

She turned to face them. 'I asked if the chips were supposed to be black?'

'Black? Yer mean burned black?' asked Eric.

'No, not burned, just black.' She was no cook but knew the difference.

''Ere, let me look,' the boy offered, scrambling to his feet. His sister followed suit and all three gazed down into the bowl.

'Oo-er, they do look funny, don't they?' muttered Emily. 'They don't look like that when Ma cooks 'em.'

Sal, who had been watching the proceedings, launched herself off the bed, waddled over to the bowl, took a sniff, gave Ally a disgusted look – and settled back down on the bed.

Eric, who by now was absolutely ravenous, snatched up a chip and popped it in his mouth. 'Taste all right ter me,' he said.

His sister took one. 'Not like they usually do but they ain't that bad.'

Ally sighed, relieved. She squatted down and divided the chips, giving most of her share to the children, then sat back and watched, a wave of satisfaction filling her as they both tucked in. It was a new experience for her actually to have done something for others. She stared down at her own plate. Regardless of the children's enthusiasm for her efforts, the black chips appeared totally unappetising to her. Her stomach rumbled loudly, an occurrence which normally would have caused her acute embarrassment. Instead she smiled. Like Emily's, her stomach thought her throat had been cut! She picked up her fork, stabbed at a chip and was just about to put it in her mouth when a noise reached her ears. The children too heard it and all eyes darted towards the door.

It burst open and a sopping wet Flo loomed in the doorway. Ally wrinkled her nose as an overpowering smell reached her nostrils. Sal leaped off the bed, barking loudly, and bounded straight for Flo, leaping up at her and licking her face, tail wagging rapidly.

Catching her breath, Flo pushed her off. 'Get down, yer daft bugger.' Her eyes flew to the children. 'Oh!' she exclaimed. 'The pair on yer are all right. Oh, thank God.' Nearly tripping over Sal who was fussing around her ankles she dropped her soggy newspaper parcel and gathered them both to her, hugging them tightly. 'I've bin worried sick. I never thought we'd get home.'

'We were worried about you too,' sniffed Emily. 'I thought yer might have drowned.'

'Drowned! Me? Not on your nelly.' Flo's face split into a broad grin. 'You won't get rid of yer ma that easily.' She kissed them both on the cheek. She wasn't ever going to tell the children how nearly they had, though.

'Where's Jack?' asked Eric.

'He's just coming so I'd better get the dinner started.' Her eyes darted to Ally. 'Yer stayed then?'

The fishy smell was growing stronger. It appeared to be coming from the parcel but then Ally realised it was emanating from Flo herself. She reeked of it. She fought not to show her distaste and realised the woman was waiting for her answer. 'It seemed sensible, in the circumstances.'

'It did, oh, it did. I can't thank yer enough.' Releasing the children, Flo sat back on her haunches, eyeing Ally critically. 'Me clothes don't look bad on yer.'

'Oh, I hope you don't mind my borrowing them while my own dried?'

Flo smiled. 'It's little enough payment for watching me kids.' She looked expectantly towards the kettle. 'Oh, I could do wi' a bloody strong cuppa. Is there one brewed by any chance?' It was then she noticed the plates and what was on them and grimaced. 'What on earth are they?'

'Chips,' replied Emily.

'I can see that,' Flo snapped. 'But I ain't never seen chips that colour before.' Her eyes flashed to Ally accusingly. 'What on earth have yer done to 'em?'

Ally looked at the chips then guiltily at her accuser. 'Well, Mrs . . . er . . .'

'Just call me Flo. We don't stand on ceremony in this house.'

Before Ally could explain, Emily interrupted.

'Tell Ma how you lived in that gentry 'ouse, Ally? Go on, tell her how you was friends with the girl. And about the lessons and how you learned to talk posh.'

'Is this true?' asked Flo.

Ally gulped and fidgeted uncomfortably. 'Well, er . . .'

'Her mam and dad worked for the gentry, dint they, Ally? And they died, dint they, Ally? And, Ma, you'll never guess what – they slung her out when the family moved away. That's right, ain't it, Ally?' said Eric.

She could feel the heat of embarrassment creeping up her neck.

'Ally's only her weekday name,' Emily chipped in. 'Tell Ma yer Sunday name. Go on, Ally.'

Three pairs of eyes rested on her expectantly.

She gulped again. 'Albertina Victoriana.'

Flo stared at her for a moment then spluttered with mirth. 'My, that's some gob full, gel. Did yer mother have a thing for the old queen or what?'

Ally knew she had been named in memory of her mother's dead parents, but thought it better to let Flo think she was right. She nodded. 'Apparently so. I am usually called Ally. Ally . . . er . . . Brown.'

Flo smiled. 'That's easier on the tongue.'

'She's a nice name, ain't she, Ma?' Emily spoke in awe. Her hazel eyes looked puzzled. 'Why ain't I got a Sunday name? Can I have one?'

'There's nothing wrong with Emily,' snapped Flo. 'It's a nice name is Emily.' She folded her arms under her shapely bosom, pursed her lips and eyed Ally sharply. 'So Jack was right? He reckoned you had nowhere ter go.' Her eyes narrowed. 'Nothing surprises me concerning the bloody gentry. Use yer fer their own ends then get rid when they've finished. But fancy pushing you out in a storm like that! Want hanging, the lot of 'em.'

Ally flinched at her harsh tone.

'Who wants hanging?'

They all turned to see Jack just arriving. He shook himself down then raised his head to look across at them.

His gaze rested longest on Ally. Of all the ways he had visualised this woman he had never expected this.

She blushed scarlet when she realised she was staring back and fought to quell the surge of emotion that was racing through her. The tall, broad, flaxen-haired man standing in the doorway was the most handsome she had ever seen – and to think that, albeit in the dark, he had stripped her naked and wrapped her in sacking, then spent the night in the same room as herself! Her scarlet blush deepened to crimson.

Flo looked from one to the other, then addressed Jack sharply. 'What yer gawping at, lad?'

'Eh?'

'I said, what yer gawping at?'

'Oh, er . . . nothing, nothing.' How could he explain that seeing Ally properly for the first time had knocked the stuffing from him? Never in all his life had he seen such a beautiful woman. His whole body trembled.

'Why, yer shaking,' said Flo. She eyed him quizzically for a moment before adding, 'Clear a space by the fire, kids. Let Jack get a warm. Eric, put a few more lumps on, there's a good lad. Come on, Jack, stop standing there like summat from the asylum, get yerself a warm before yer catch yer death.' She snatched the plates from Emily and Eric, ignoring their wails of protest. 'What did yer cook the chips in?' she asked Ally.

'Just the fat.'

'The fat? But I had no lard, only . . .' She started to laugh. 'That explains it! Yer never fry in marge, gel. It burns if yer don't mix it one to three with lard. That's what turned the chips black. Didn't they teach yer nothing at that big house?' She thrust the plates at Emily. 'Chuck that lot away.'

'But, Ma, I'm starving,' erupted Eric.

'We're all starving,' she responded sharply. 'Now peel some spuds if there's any left and get me a pan of water. Thank God we pumped plenty before the flood took hold.'

Ally stood up. 'I'd better be going.'

Flo spun to face her. 'I wouldn't risk it tonight if I were you. We only got back home by the skin of our teeth.' She flashed a glance at Jack. 'You dare ever mention boats ter me again and I'll wallop you, big as you are. Now you, young lady, can stay put. The least I can do after you stayed with the kids is offer you a bed for the night. Well, that's as long as you don't mind squashing in with me and Emily? With a bit of luck the flood will have gone down enough by tomorrow morning.'

'But . . .'

Flo raised her hand. 'I'll hear no buts. My way of showing me gratitude.' She grinned at the kids. 'At least Ally being here saved yer going to the old battle-axe across the road, didn't it, eh? I get the feeling you don't really like 'er, but as she's the only one I know that doesn't work, I ain't got much option. Now, let's get cracking and get this meal on the go.'

Ally watched in fascination as Flo busied herself preparing a meal. Things she had never seen in their natural state before were thrown in the pan and before minutes had passed an appetising aroma began to fill the tiny room. Several times she caught Jack staring at her and after flashing a brief nervous smile at him, hurriedly averted her own gaze. Before long they were all being told to sit before the fire and bowls of something steaming hot were being thrust at them.

'Now eat up whilst it's hot,' ordered Flo, sitting next to Jack on the bed.

Raising her spoon, Ally stared down into her bowl. Chunks of things were floating in a puce liquid. She had just summoned enough courage to dip in her spoon when something rose to the surface of the bowl and she screamed loudly.

'What's wrong?' they all cried.

'There's . . . there's something looking at me.'

'Looking at yer?' Thrusting her own bowl at Jack, Flo leaped off the bed and peered down. 'Oh, for goodness sake, it won't bite yer, it's only a fish head. But then, what d'yer expect? It *is* fish soup.' She grabbed hold of the ladle and spooned it out. 'Yer soft 'aporth,' she laughed, sitting back on the bed. 'Now eat up afore it gets cold.'

Ally's stomach churned, the thought of eating the soup after such a dreadful shock nauseated her, but how could she be so rude as to refuse Flo's generosity? Now at least the stench emanating from her was accounted for. The parcel of fish must have leaked all over her on the journey home. Taking a deep breath, she gingerly dipped in her spoon, raised it to her lips and sipped tentatively. Her eyes widened in surprise for the second time that day and she took another spoonful.

'Good, ain't it?' said Flo.

'It is,' replied Ally sincerely. 'Very good.'

While the meal was in progress conversation flowed. First Flo described her day, then Jack, then the children. Ally listened with interest then her thoughts strayed to her own worrying situation. She did not have long to dwell on this as a sharp dig in the ribs jolted her.

'I beg your pardon?' she said, flustered.

Flo laughed. 'Hark at 'er! "I beg your pardon?" If I didn't know better I'd say you were taking the mickey. But, yer know, for all I've said about the gentry and the way they speak, I have to admit it does sound nice coming from you. Our Emily said you were looking for a job?'

'A job? Yes, I am. I have someone to see in Leicester.'

'You do? Well, that's all right then. I hope yer successful,' said Flo with a smile.

So do I, thought Ally.

Jack stared at her. If he wasn't careful this woman would just walk out of his life and suddenly the idea seemed unbearable. He took a breath. 'You'll have to ... er ... come and let us know how you get on.'

Ally was taken aback. For the first time since the reversal of her fortunes somebody was actually showing an interest in what happened to her. 'Yes, I will,' she replied warmly.

Chapter Ten

Ally stood outside the offices of Clarence Bailey and stared up at the windows. She frowned in confusion. They appeared closed. But surely solicitors' offices did not close on a Thursday?

A wave of exhaustion flooded over her. She had just spent the most dreadful night squashed on the edge of the hard lumpy mattress next to Emily and Flo. Emily was right, Flo did snore – but it was the scratching of the mice and scuttering of cockroaches that had kept her awake, terrifying her witless. When sleep had finally overtaken her, so deeply did she slumber that the house was empty by the time she awoke. A badly scribbled note propped up by the bowl and jug told her in Flo's words that thankfully the flood had subsided enough for the daily routine to resume. She was to help herself to whatever she needed and close the door behind her when she left. Flo also wished her all the best.

Having washed and dressed – dismayed at how dreadful her clothes looked – replenished herself with a slice of dry bread and a drink of cold water, as by now the fire had gone out, she replied to the note, thanking them profusely for their hospitality. After asking directions from a woman in the street, she had set off on the remainder of her journey.

It had not been easy. Beneath the remaining floodwater was a thick layer of squelching mud and trying to walk through it was hazardous and exhausting. Finding the street where Clarence Bailey's offices were situated took several attempts and, having finally arrived, to top it all not only did the offices appear devoid of life, but it had taken her so long to get there that night was drawing in and it was beginning to drizzle.

She pulled hard again on the bell and stepped back. The sound could be heard echoing around the large entrance hall but the door remained closed. Her heart began to pound. If Clarence Bailey was not at his offices, what was she going to do? She had pinned all her hopes on his offer of help.

'Yer can stand there all day, missus, but there ain't no one in.'

She swung round. 'I beg your pardon?'

The gnarled old man addressing her froze for a moment, not in the least expecting such a refined voice from such a shabby-looking woman. 'I said, there ain't no one in.' He dipped the leather with which he was cleaning the windows of the adjoining premises in his bucket on the cobbles and wrung it out. 'The old man's died.'

Ally stared at him blankly. 'Old man?' she uttered.

'Yeah, Mr Bailey. Unexpected it wa'. Copped it in his sleep the night afore last. Shame. He wa' a nice old gent. I've bin cleaning the windows round here for forty odd years and he always paid me prompt. Not like others I could name.'

Ally's hand flew to her mouth in shock. Mr Bailey was dead! Her one hope of salvation gone. This was all too much. She couldn't bear it. Then she was suddenly filled with shame for her selfish thoughts. From what little she had known of Clarence Bailey, he seemed a kind old man and a surge of remorse for her own attitude towards his well-intentioned attempts to help her filled Ally.

'One of his charity cases was yer, ducky?'

Momentarily forgetting her new status, she glared at the shabby window cleaner indignantly. 'I beg your pardon?'

'One of his charity cases. Doing a free one. Yer know, one of his good works.'

She frowned crossly. 'What my business is . . . was . . . with Mr Bailey is none of yours, my good man.'

The wizened old face screwed up menacingly. 'There's no need ter tek that attitude, yer haughty cow!' He flung his leather down into the bucket in temper. 'I was gonna tell yer that if yer were stuck, like, the geezer I'm cleaning winders for does charity cases too. But yer can piss off now. I wouldn't try to help yer if yer paid me.'

Ally's face fell. 'Look, I'm sorry, I . . .'

'Piss off out of it, I said. And I'd skedaddle quick if I were you before I chuck me bucket over yer, yer stuck up madam!'

Ally felt shocked. How dare the man speak to her like this? She made to retaliate but one glimpse of the window cleaner picking up his bucket was warning enough. She snatched up her skirt and fled, slipping precariously over the wet cobbles until she reached the corner of the street. Once out of sight she flattened herself against the wall, panting hard. Her head drooped and she shuddered, fighting tears of utter desolation. She hadn't thought her situation could possibly get any worse but it had and now she saw no way out, not even a glimmer of hope. At this very moment she wished she had never managed to claw her way out of the river.

'A' you all right, me duck?'

Ally jumped. 'I beg your pardon?'

A foul-smelling young woman dressed in rags pushed her face close and Ally recoiled at the dreadful stench emanating from her. 'I asked,' she repeated, lowering a heavy sack slowly to the ground, 'if yer were all right?'

Ally fought hard not to retch as she tried to skirt past the woman. 'Yes, thank you,' she uttered.

80

The woman was having none of it and blocked her path. 'Don't look it,' she said, shaking her head. 'If ever I've seen doom it's on you, gel. Well, don't you worry no more 'cos Martha's 'ere. Now as luck would 'ave it I'm off up the 'ouse early 'cos it wa' choc-a-bloc last night with this weather. You come wi' me, I'll look after yer. Got yer copper?'

'Pardon?'

'Yer copper. Penny.'

Ally stared at her, bewildered. A penny, a pound, she had neither. She had nothing and the thought filled her with terror. 'Why . . . why do I need a penny?' she asked worriedly.

Martha guffawed loudly. 'Where you bin hiding yerself, gel? You need a penny to gerra line fer the night in the poor house. Wha' did yer think yer needed a penny for? The lavvy!' She thrust out a calloused hand, chipped nails engrained with dirt. 'I've got mine, look. I'll be all right tonight. So 'ave yer got yours or what?'

A line. What on earth was a line? 'No, I haven't.'

'You ain't! Oh, yer in lumber then, gel. 'Cos if yer ain't got a penny yer won't get a space on the line, and if it rains as bad as it has done then you'll cop it fer sure if the 'enza gets yer. Goes straight fer the chest does 'enza. And once it's got yer chest, yer a gonna.' She grabbed Ally's arm and yanked her forward. 'Come on, I'll help yer get one. Oi, mister,' she shouted to a man passing by. 'Spare a penny fer a line.'

'No, really,' erupted an embarrassed Ally, wrenching herself free. 'I don't wish to get a . . . line. Really, I don't need one.'

The man side-stepped past and hurried on.

'Miserable old fucker!' Martha spat after him. She turned her attention to Ally and glared at her. 'Wa' did you do that for? He wa' good for a penny.' Her glare turned to a look of suspicion. 'How d'you get to speak like that?' She looked her up and down then made a grab for her skirt and fingered the material. 'Might be ripped and mucky but it's a good bit a' stuff. I know a good bit a' stuff when I see it.' She raised her head, eyes glinting. 'Who are yer, eh?'

Ally gulped, suddenly afraid. 'I'm nobody, really. I have to go. Please excuse me.'

The woman grabbed her arm and gripped it tightly. 'I asked who yer are, lady? You look like a nowt, but yer don't speak like one. Now, come on, answer me.'

'Now then, Martha. What's going on? Not spoiling for a fight, I hope?'

'Eh!' The grip on Ally's arm loosened and Martha spun round. 'Oh, 'ello, Constable Hickle. What are doin' round 'ere?'

'I should be asking you that question, Martha. Mill Lane's not your usual haunt, now is it? I hope you're not up to your usual trick of making a nuisance of yourself so you can have a night in jail, because if so you're out of luck. The jail's full tonight. Now I'd get a move on if I were you or you won't get a place on the line. Got your penny?'

81

Martha sniffed disdainfully. 'Yeah, I've got me penny,' she replied sulkily, picking up her sack and heaving it over her shoulder.

'Well, better be off before I start making enquiries as to where you got it from.'

'I'm goin', I'm goin'.'

She gave Ally a menacing glare before she turned and scuttled off.

Constable Hickle turned his full attention to Ally. 'Now, young lady, I haven't seen you before. What are you up to, eh?'

Ally's heart pounded painfully. She had never come face to face with a policeman before and although she was innocent of any crime, under his scrutiny felt obscurely guilty. A vision of him dragging her off to jail and her spending the rest of her days caged up filled her mind. Trembling, she raised her head, her eyes travelling slowly all the way up Constable Hickle's broad six foot three. Instead of the hostile accusing glare she expected, a pair of kindly green eyes looked at her expectantly as he waited for her answer. She realised her thoughts had been silly ones. She hadn't done anything wrong and he was only doing his job.

'I'm not up to anything, Constable,' she said, managing a smile. 'I came to see my solicitor and have learned that he has sadly passed away. That lady ... Martha ... mistook me for one of her friends, that's all. Thank you for your concern. Now, if you'll excuse me, I must be getting home.'

A dumbfounded Constable Hickle watched as Ally walked off down the street. He had not expected such an articulate response from someone he had assumed to be a down and out. Well, she certainly looked like one at any rate. But, as had just been proved to him, looks could certainly be deceptive.

As Ally disappeared from sight he shook his head. He had been pounding this beat for nearly twenty years and during the course of carrying out his duties had witnessed all there ever was and thought nothing would shock him again. Until tonight. That young woman had surprised him speechless.

An hour later Ally stood shivering inside a shop doorway. An icy wind had risen and the light rain that was falling was beginning to freeze. She rubbed her hands vigorously then dug them deep inside her pockets. Her coat was affording her little protection against the December elements. But then, when she had dressed herself two days ago for her visit to Mr Bailey's, never had she envisaged herself sheltering inside a deserted shop doorway with not a penny to her name, nowhere to go and not a friend she could turn to.

Thinking of friends made her thoughts turn to Bella. 'Oh, Bella,' she whispered desolately. If ever there was a time when she'd needed the support of her best friend it was now. But Bella was still away and would not be back for several long weeks. And when she returned? What would her reaction be when she saw to what level Ally had been reduced? Would she still choose to be her friend? No, she wouldn't, Ally thought tearfully. How could she? Their friendship had been forged when both were of a similar status. She had thought Lionel and his mother would stand by her. How wrong she had been! It would be quite wrong of her to put Bella in such a position.

Tears filled her eyes, blinding her as she made a momentous decision. It would be best all round if she kept her distance. That way Bella would be spared any embarrassment and she herself the pain of further humiliation.

Raising her head, she took a shuddering breath as she gazed around. She had told that kindly policeman she was going home. Of all the lies she had been forced to tell over the last couple of days, that was the most ironic. At the moment this grimy shop entrance with its peeling paint was the closest she had to a home. And to think she had been appalled at the tiny house and sparse facilities that Flo, Jack, Emily and Eric had welcomed her into, and had recoiled in horror from the fact they had no bathroom. What she would give now to be with them sharing their meagre dinner round the fire in the tiny bedroom. Just being a part of such a scene would help to lift the desolation that filled her very being.

A gust of icy wind blasted into the doorway and she shivered violently. She couldn't stay here. It was icy cold now and it was only early evening. She would have to find some proper shelter but where with no money? A vision of the boatshed came to mind and she forced away a feeling of repulsion at having to lower herself to that. But then, she thought, the boatshed was a step up from a doorway. She frowned deeply. Jack had mentioned the owner – not a nice man, he said. She didn't fancy coming face to face with him as she trespassed on his property nor the resulting jail sentence. She had heard that jails were terrible places and once inside you were extremely lucky ever to get out.

Oh, God, it was all so hopeless. Her whole situation was completely hopeless. She hadn't even the resources to secure herself a bed for the night in the paupers' lodging house. She raised tear-blinded eyes. 'Please, Lord,' she whispered, 'help me.'

Chapter Eleven

'Jack. JACK! For goodness' sake, man, it's not like you to stand daydreaming.'

His head jerked. 'Eh! Oh, Mr Green. I'm right sorry, Mr Green, really I am.'

'Ah, well, we'll let it pass this time. Now get a move on, lad, and finish meking up that order for Mrs Drabble. She's expecting it before four. At the rate you're going she'll be lucky to get it this side of tomorrow. And when yer've finished let Kenneth take over. I need you out front.'

Jack nodded. 'I'll be with you in a jiffy.'

Sidney Green smiled. 'D'yer know, it's the first time I've had to chastise you, me lad. I'll go so far as to say you're me best worker, and that's saying summat. I've had 'em come and go in this shop. In my experience most young 'uns never stick anything fer long. Always think there's summat grander over the road – only ter find they'd have bin better off staying put. But you, lad . . . I made a good choice when I took you on, dint I, eh?'

Jack smiled. 'I like to earn me money.'

'You certainly do that, Jack.' Sidney rubbed his chin and scanned him keenly. Jack obviously had something on his mind and Sidney wondered what it was. A sudden fear rose in him. Was Jack thinking of moving on? Had he found something better? He would have to think seriously about giving him a rise. Enough to stop him looking elsewhere. And, thought Sidney, eyeing Jack shrewdly, a man needed enough of a wage coming in to support a wife. His own daughter Lizzie had a strong fondness for his employee and at nineteen years of age it was about time she settled down.

Under normal circumstances he would never have encouraged a liaison between his precious daughter and a lowly employee, but Jack was different. Sidney had known it the moment the young man had entered his shop asking after work. Jack had been honest about the number of jobs he had had, saying it was because his mother had a thing about moving house. Sidney had had no qualms about taking him on. Better in his experience to employ a find like Jack for however long. And he had been proved right. The man was a natural born shopkeeper. Talents such as he possessed were not acquired, they were a gift. He instinctively knew where to place slow-moving stock lines to catch a customer's eye; could

84

add a long column of figures correctly; and sell – the man could sell a loaf of two-week-old bread to a woman with no teeth and make her go away happy. Not that Jack would – he actually cared about every customer who came into the shop. Sidney smiled inwardly. Yes, a match between Jack and his daughter would be most welcome. Then he could think about retiring. In Jack's hands his shop would be safer than gold in the Bank of England.

He pulled out his pocket watch and glanced at it. A quarter to four. Lizzie would be here soon to put her proposition to Jack. If he was the sensible lad Sidney knew him to be then he would grab at the offer and from then on his way would be smooth. Or so Sidney sincerely hoped.

He patted Jack's shoulder. 'I've bin thinking about giving yer a rise, lad. Let's see what position I'm in after Christmas and then we'll have a little chat.'

Jack's smile broadened. 'A rise, of however much, would be appreciated, Mr Green.' All the more, he was thinking, to add to his savings for the shop of his own he hoped to have one day. Not that he could save much, but the few coppers and odd shillings he kept in the box under his bed were slowly mounting. He had never voiced his dream to his employer, feeling it wouldn't do him any favours. Better for Mr Green to think he was an employee for life, not possible competition.

As Sidney went back to his customers, Jack resumed his task of parcelling the box of groceries for delivery but try as he might he could not stop his thoughts from drifting. The face that had filled his mind's eye since he had risen that morning rose before him again in its full glory. Those velvet brown eyes; the full sensuous mouth from which issued such a bewitching voice; the pert nose that crinkled when she smiled. And to top it all a figure that would stop a man of any age in his tracks. Jack had to smile as he remembered the state he had first seen her in, never for one moment visualising what loveliness lay beneath all that mud. But it wasn't just her physical attractions. There was something unfathomable about Ally that had captured Jack's very soul.

Silently he said an overdue thank you to Sal. Until the night of the storm the old dog's habit of wandering had been annoying, always happening at the most inconvenient times, but without Sal and her habit he would never have met Ally. He sighed heavily as he snapped a piece of string and reached over for a length of brown paper. Would he ever see her again? He sincerely hoped so, even if it was only to learn that she had fared well at her job interview.

'Hello, Jack.'

'Eh! Oh, hello, Miss Green.'

'You could look more pleased to see me.'

Jack inwardly groaned. Lizzie Green was the last person he felt like contending with. The boss's daughter was a nice enough woman, but not nice enough for him to risk his job over. He knew she had a liking for him, one that he didn't return, and didn't want to give her the slightest chance to misconstrue anything he said. Mr Green idolised his daughter, nothing was too good for her, and to upset her would upset his boss and then Jack's job would be in serious jeopardy. Ma's insistence on constantly moving house had forced several job changes upon him during his working life. He fully understood her reasons and supported her wholeheartedly but longed for the day when she would feel it safe to put down some roots. Apart from Lizzie's unwanted attentions, this job was the best he had ever had and Jack wanted to keep it for as long as he could.

He took a deep breath. 'It's always a pleasure to see you, Miss Green,' he said stiltedly, wrapping the string around the brown paper parcel and tying a knot. 'I hope you'll excuse me, but I've got to get this order finished then I'm needed out front.'

Lizzie took a deep breath. She wasn't normally a nervous person but whenever she was near Jack or even thought of him, which of late was practically all her waking hours, her body betrayed her. She fought hard now not to let him see she was trembling. She had fallen in love with her father's employee from the first moment she had set eyes on him standing behind the long wooden counter, a huge white apron like all the staff wore not drowning him like it did the others. She had thought, when her father first mentioned his new worker, that he would mirror the rest – not a redeeming quality to him and enough spots to send a chemist into raptures. But Jack had no spots and if 'sexual attraction' – which was something she had learned of from her best friend Iris – was an overwhelming need to get so close to someone you wanted to get inside their skin, then to her thinking Jack had enough to divide between a dozen. She had been steeling herself for ages to ask him a question and wasn't going to leave until she had done so. 'I need a partner, Jack, for the Grocers' Association Christmas dance.' There, it was out! She had finally done it. She clenched her hands, hazel eyes fixed on him intently as she waited for his response.

Jack froze. The moment he had dreaded had arrived. He would have to tread very carefully. He didn't want to hurt her. Besides, even if he had found her proposition inviting, he couldn't accept as he had nothing suitable to wear to the occasion. He smiled. 'I wouldn't have thought you'd have much trouble getting a partner, Miss Green.'

But she didn't want just any partner, she wanted him. 'It's a grand do, Jack. First there's a meal, with five courses, then the speeches and presentations. Then there's dancing.' She said the last bit dreamily, visualising herself crushed inside Jack's strong arms, pressed against his firm, lithe body. The very thought sent a quiver through her.

He nodded, eyes fixed firmly on the task in hand. 'I'm sure you'll have a fine time, Miss Green. Could you just excuse me?' he said, reaching by her for a box which he began to pack.

'It's more than a fine time, Jack,' she replied enthusiastically. 'This is the do of the year. All the dignitaries go. And I'm sure you . . .'

'Jack, you got that order ready? 'Cos we need yer out front. Oh, af'noon, Miss Green.'

Lizzie spun round. 'Hello, Mr Bott,' she said, seething. Of all the times to be interrupted! Could Kenneth Bott not have come in two minutes later?

Jack was elated at Kenneth's timely entrance and also saw his chance of defusing what for him was an extremely awkward situation. 'Kenneth,' he said, grabbing his arm, 'Miss Green hasn't a partner for the Grocers' Association Christmas dance.'

Kenneth looked at Lizzie Green in awe. He had always thought his boss's daughter a fine-looking woman, had often fantasised about her, but had never dreamed of actually getting the chance to accompany her anywhere. 'Ain't yer, Miss Green? Well, in that case I'd be delighted ter do the honour.'

Lizzie froze in horror, inwardly balking at the very idea of being seen out anywhere with the unattractive Kenneth Bott, let alone at such a prestigious do as the Grocers' Association Christmas dance which was held at the Bell Hotel. She would sooner not go at all than go with the likes of him. 'Mr Fossett misunderstood me,' she hissed. 'I have several offers to choose from.' Her heart sank at the knowledge that her ideal opportunity to start something with Jack had gone. She didn't know when she would get another one. 'Get out of the way,' she snapped, pushing past him.

A bewildered Sidney Green arrived in the stock room. He looked at Jack and Kenneth. 'What's with my Lizzie? She's just stormed out the shop looking like thunder.'

Both held their breath knowing it wouldn't do to admit to being a party to their boss's daughter's mood.

'I can't think,' said Jack casually. 'She was all right a minute ago. Was telling us how many offers she'd had to take her to the Grocers' dance.'

Sidney's jaw dropped. 'Really?' His eyes settled on Jack. 'She never asked . . . er . . .' He suddenly realised Kenneth was listening eagerly. 'Oh, never mind.' He had no doubt he would hear all when he got home that night and witness the floods of tears. 'That order ready yet?'

Jack grabbed the box. 'Just finished.'

As usual he was the last of the assistants to leave. He was pulling on his coat when Mr Green walked into the stock room, jangling his huge bunch of keys.

'Well, everything's secured so like you, lad, I think I'll get off home.' He rubbed his hand over his face and yawned. 'Mrs Green will be shocked ter see me so early but I'm quite tired tonight.' He grinned. 'Must be me age. I'll be sixty-five soon and I'm getting too old for such a long day.'

He gazed round the stock room at the neatly stacked shelves, picked up a tin of Nestlés condensed milk and studied the label. 'D'yer know, lad, me whole life's bin wrapped up in this place. I started as a delivery boy fer me dad. 'Course it were only a tiny shop then. We sold tobacco and sweets. It were my idea to expand. Quite a gamble it was in those days – the 1860s. Seems such a long time ago. I was nineteen. It was damned hard work but it's paid off all right. I've got a nice house, money in the bank . . . what more could a man ask for, eh?'

He turned and looked at Jack, thinking it would not hurt to push matters between his daughter and the object of her desire, and if he succeeded the trouble he faced at home tonight could be avoided. 'This will all come to Lizzie. The man she settles for will be set fer life. You know, Jack, I'd be right happy if it was someone like you. Lizzie would make a grand little wife, and with all this . . .' He swung his arm wide. 'Well, need I say any more?'

Jack swallowed hard. 'I'm sure your daughter would make someone a very good wife, Mr Green. For meself, well, it'll be many a long year before I can think of marriage. I have Ma and the kids to consider.'

Sidney's face filled with surprise. He had thought Jack would jump at his offer. 'Did yer not hear me right, lad? Marriage to my Lizzie means all this. Supporting your mother and brother and sister wouldn't be a problem.'

Jack never corrected anyone on their automatic assumption that Ma was his mother. It was easier to go along with than have to explain the truth. Secretly he was pleased. After all Flo was his mother in every way apart from the act of giving birth to him. He looked Mr Green straight in the eye.

'I heard you perfectly, Mr Green, and I'm flattered you think me worthy. But if I am to make anything of meself, then I do it my own way, not on the back of someone else's hard work. The same goes for when I marry. If and when I do take the plunge, it'll be to someone *I* choose and not for the sake of securing me future.'

So much, Jack thought, for trying to keep his job! His principles had probably just lost it for him. But regardless, if this was the way his employer's mind was working then it would be better to stem his train of thought now. 'If you'll excuse me, Mr Green, I need to get home. There's such a lot needs doing now the floods have almost gone.'

Mr Green followed him to the door. 'Look . . . er . . . Jack . . . er . . . I still think you should give some thought to what's bin said. Decisions made in haste, yer know . . .'

Jack tipped his forelock, then slapped on his cap. 'Goodnight, Mr Green.'

'Goodnight, lad.'

Deep in thought, Jack dug his hands deep down into his jacket pockets, shoulders hunched against the biting December wind. He sighed heavily.

What would Ma say if she had witnessed all that had just transpired? Would she call him a fool for dismissing such a lucrative offer? He frowned as a thought struck him. Mr Green hadn't intimated that if he did not comply with his wishes he would lose his job, but that was a fact Jack ought to consider.

A tram rumbled past. Jack jumped, startled, then grimaced. He had been so preoccupied that he'd missed his ride home. He stared down the deserted street. The next tram wasn't due for another twenty minutes. It was too cold to stand around so he might as well walk, and by doing so save his twopence. His journey wasn't far, Green's Provisions being situated at the top of Welford Road barely a mile down the hill from where they lived on Walnut Street off the Aylestone Road. But tonight a mile might as well have been six as Jack suddenly felt drained by his day. All he wanted to do was get home, sit in front of the fire with his dinner, then go to bed. But there would be clearing up to be done, and if Ma had managed to dry out the downstairs rooms sufficiently, the furniture to be shifted.

He hurried his pace. The sooner he got home, the sooner his chores would be done and he could go to bed. As he passed a shop doorway something caught his eye and he glanced inside. In a dark corner was a huddled figure, body heaving with sobs. He frowned in sympathy. The plight of the homeless was a terrible thing. He, Ma and the kids hadn't much but at least they had a roof. He didn't fancy that poor soul's chances if it dropped to below freezing tonight, which seemed very likely. He stopped and hesitated for a moment, fingering the saved fare in his pocket. It would buy a cup of tea and a space on the line for the night. What a way to sleep, he thought, hunched over a taut rope along with dozens of others. To be awakened by the slacking of the rope in the morning then herded out.

Jack retraced his steps. Inside the doorway he squatted on his haunches and held out his hand. 'Here, it's not much but yer welcome.'

The figure flinched, then the head lifted fractionally, eyes fixed on his outstretched hand. From the folds of its clothes a hand appeared. It hovered above Jack's then hurriedly withdrew. A choked voice said, 'Thank you for your kind offer but I couldn't possibly accept.'

Jack was stunned. That voice! He would know that voice anywhere. His heart soared. 'Ally,' he said, astounded, 'is that you?'

Her head jerked up, hand moving aside a curtain of hair. 'Who . . .'

'It's me,' he erupted. 'Ally, it's me, Jack. What on earth has happened to yer?'

Her head dropped, forehead coming to rest on her bent knees. 'Oh, Jack,' she sobbed. 'It's all so dreadful.'

He stared at her, sharing her distress. 'I take it you never got the job then?' he said gently.

'No,' she uttered. 'No, I never got the job.'

He rose abruptly, took hold of her elbow and lifted her to her feet. 'Come on,' he ordered.

'Come where?'

'Home, Ally. Where d'you think I would take yer?'

Eyes blinded by tears, she shook her head. 'I couldn't possibly. You haven't the room. I couldn't inflict myself on you again. It wouldn't be fair.'

'You'd prefer the alternative?'

'Alternative?'

'Ter freeze to death. 'Cos that's what'll happen to yer if yer stay here.'

She stared at him blankly. Yes, at this moment, that was exactly what she wanted. Not to wake up ever again and have to face the whole sorry mess that her life had become. Her red swollen eyes glazed over. She had read somewhere in her youth that freezing to death was a painless way to die. You just curled up and let the elements do the deed. Yes, that was exactly what she wanted. Just to go to sleep and never wake up. Twice in as many days she had felt a desire to end it all but this time the natural instinct for survival was well and truly buried and nothing would resurrect it.

She stepped back into the shadows and pressed her back hard against the shop door. 'Please leave me, Jack.'

This was not a request, it was an order. He stared at her. 'What! Is that what yer want, Ally? Really? Is yer life that bad? Well, it's a good job not everyone teks losing a job as hard as you else the streets would be full of bodies.' He reached over and grabbed her shoulders, pulled her forward to scan her face. It was difficult to see her features clearly in the darkness but regardless he knew that whatever was responsible for her misery was far more than just the disappointment of not getting a job. This woman had given up.

His whole being was flooded with concern for her. A desire to crush her in his arms and kiss away her pain was so strong it took all his will-power to release her and step away. But, just as in the boatshed, he could no more leave her than he could take his own life. But if she was so adamant, apart from forcibly dragging her, how could he get her to come with him? He sought for an answer. Then an idea came and he smiled inwardly.

'Are you a gambler, Ally?'

She eyed him quizzically. 'A gambler! Certainly not.'

He shrugged his shoulders. 'Well, that's a shame.'

'Why?'

'Because my conscience won't allow me ter leave you here in this bitter cold and you won't come with me. So I thought I could toss yer for it.'

'Toss me for it? I don't understand?'

He delved into his inside pocket and pulled out a well-worn leather wallet. Opening it, he felt inside and extracted something. He held it out towards her. 'Me lucky tanner. I've had it fer years. Now I flick it up and call heads or tails. If I win, you come home with me. If you win, I'll say my goodbyes and leave you in peace. That way my conscience will be clear and I can sleep peacefully. Is it a deal, Ally?'

There was silence for a moment. She thought his idea ludicrous, feeling he was playing devil's advocate with her life, but then he and his family had been so kind to her she couldn't have him wrestling with his conscience on her behalf. 'You'll promise to leave me in peace?'

'I faithfully promise.'

She sighed. Jack might be doing the deed with his lucky sixpence but her own luck had obviously run out or why had she suffered one terrible disaster after another, until there was absolutely nothing left? The quicker she got this over with, the quicker he would leave her, then she could go back to her huddled state in the doorway and wait for her blessed release. 'All right,' she reluctantly agreed.

'And if I win, you'll come quietly?'

'Yes,' she snapped, knowing that was not likely to happen. 'Please just get on with it.'

Jack carefully placed the sixpence between his thumb and forefinger. He gave it a flick with his thumb and the sixpence rose into the air. Despite the dim light he expertly caught it and slapped it down on the back of his left hand. He rubbed his fingers across it for a moment before he said: 'Tails.'

'Oh,' she exclaimed. 'I thought I was to choose?'

'No, it's my tanner so I get the honour.' He grinned at her. 'But if it makes you feel better, you can say heads if you like?'

'Oh, this is silly,' she fumed.

'No, it's not, Ally. It's quite serious. Now say heads.'

'Heads,' she cried.

Stepping out of the doorway he marched over to the nearest gas lamp, and standing under it, called: 'Come on. I want you to witness this. I don't want yer calling me a cheat.'

She did as he bade and both watched intently as he slowly lifted his hand. Suddenly she realised the enormity of the situation. Had she really agreed that her life was to be decided on the flip of a coin? Tails she lived, heads she died. Was it as simple as that? Despite the cold, beads of sweat appeared on her brow. But just as when the river bank collapsed, now she was actually faced with it, she didn't really want to die, not deep down she didn't. What she wanted was for her pain to go away and something to light the black tunnel she was in and give her a glimmer of hope for the future.

She caught her breath. God had answered her prayer! He had sent her Jack and she had been too wrapped up in self-pity to realise it. He was her last chance, and instead of grabbing at it, she had refused his offer.

She held her breath as the sixpence appeared between his hands, glinting in the light from the lamp. The wait for the outcome seemed to take an eternity.

He looked hard at the coin then slowly lifted his head and fixed his eyes on her. 'It's tails,' he announced triumphantly. 'I win.'

She did not show it but the relief that flooded through her was enormous.

Without waiting for a response, worried she would change her mind, he grabbed her arm. 'Come on.'

Chapter Twelve

Flo was busy mopping the last of the floodwater from the flagstones when Jack walked in.

'Ah, there yer are. I was beginning to wonder where you'd got to. Thought if you dallied long enough it'd all be done when you got home, eh? Well, you're outta luck, 'cos there's still loads ter be done before we can call this house anywhere near straight. Yer dinner's in the oven, hurry and get it down yer, then you can give me a hand. What a job I had to get the fire lit. Still, I managed it in the end.' It was then she spotted Ally standing just behind him. 'Oh, er . . . hello, me duck.' Her enquiring eyes flew to Jack.

'Can I have a word, Ma?'

She pursed her lips. 'Yes, I think you'd better.'

'In the other room.'

She sighed, her astute mind suddenly realising what was coming. 'Yeah, sure.' She glanced over at Ally. 'Help yerself to a cuppa, gel. You look froze to the marrow.'

Inside the tiny front room he shut the door. The room was icy cold and damp, the mark from the floodwater a slimy ring against the whitewash beginning to flake on the walls. Its starkness was accentuated by the lack of any furniture. Jack shivered.

'Well,' Flo demanded. 'What's so private?'

He took a deep breath. 'Ally never got the job, Ma.'

'Didn't she?' Flo replied matter-of-factly. She had already gathered that. 'Well, that's a shame. But I have ter admit, from the way she was speaking last night, she seemed to think she'd automatically get it. She'll have ter learn not to be so smug in future, won't she?' Flo eyed him sharply. 'What's her not getting the job to do with us?'

'She's nowhere to go and no money.'

'Spit it out, Jack. As if I don't know what's on yer mind.'

'Well, can she, Ma? Can she stay with us, just 'til she gets on her feet?'

'Stay here? Are you off yer head or summat? Where d'yer propose we put her?'

'You'll find somewhere, Ma.'

'Oh, I've no doubt I will. I could always move into the coalshed,' Flo said sarcastically. 'She ain't our problem, Jack. I've got enough of those without taking on any more. The answer's no.'

He eyed her in dismay. 'Ma, I found her crouched in a shop doorway. She's so down she was prepared to stay there and freeze to death.'

'Well, give her threepence for a bed in the workhouse.'

'Ah, come on, Ma. What's got into you? You're not usually so harsh.'

Her mouth snapped shut. Jack was right, she was being harsh. She wouldn't rest knowing Sal was out in that bitter cold, let alone a young girl who'd just had the stuffing knocked out of her. Under normal circumstances Flo would have welcomed the girl with open arms and done what she could to set her on the right road. But nothing about this situation was normal. There was nothing normal about the girl. All her instincts told her that there was far more to the stranger than she was letting on. But truth to tell none of that worried her overmuch. Everyone had secrets, herself more than most. It was Jack's interest that was the cause of Flo's disquiet.

Her eyes flashed at him knowingly. 'It's what's got into you that's concerning me.'

'Me? What are you talking about?'

'Don't play the innocent wi' me, Jack. You've taken a fancy to her,' Flo accused. 'A blind man would see it.' She poked him in the shoulder. 'Now you listen to me, and listen good. That girl is not one of us. Oh, according to her she might have been born one of us, but she ain't now. How can she be? She's been educated, been with people for whom money is no object. How is she ever gonna settle for the kind of life we have ter live after living like she has? Come on, Jack, use yer brain. You've seen for yerself what she did with those chips. She can't even cook. I think I should be congratulated because I never said a word about the waste of good food.' She sighed heavily and her eyes softened. 'Look, Jack, I can see what yer see in her. She's a fine-looking gel, and I never thought I'd hear meself say it but I could listen to her talk with that voice of hers all night. But if yer thinking along the lines I'm worried yer thinking on, then you heed what I say. The likes of her, however low she's come, will never look at you in the way you want her to.'

'Ma, stop it . . .'

'No, I won't. It's got ter be said. I think the world of yer, Jack. Your happiness and the kids' is all I'm concerned about. Fall for her hard and you'll get hurt. Badly hurt. And then it'll be up to me to pick up the pieces.'

'Ma, listen ter me, will you? I just feel sorry for her, that's all there is to it.' Who was he trying to fool? Jack knew his feelings for Ally were much more than sympathy. 'Ma, you wouldn't leave Sal outside in this weather. And you more than anyone should have sympathy for the way she's bin treated by those so-called . . .'

'All right, all right,' Flo erupted. 'Yer've made yer point, Jack. But say I agree to her stopping for a while? And it would only be until she got herself sorted. You tell me how we're gonna feed her and her with no money coming in? We just get by ourselves as it is. I can stretch our resources but not for long. I ain't a miracle worker.'

Jack's eyes filled with affection. 'Ma, you're more than a miracle worker. Like the kids always say: "Our ma can do anything." I'll give you extra.'

'Oh, yeah. And what about yer shop?'

Jack sighed. 'How many years have I bin saving for me shop? A while longer'll make no difference.'

Sighing heavily, she shook her head. 'Oh, Jack.' She eyed him searchingly. 'Well . . . if it's that important, we'll manage, I'm sure. But just take note of what I said. Yer promise me?'

'I will, Ma, and thanks.'

She paused thoughtfully. An idea that just might put a stop to this situation was forming in her mind. Deep down her natural instinct, as Jack had quite rightly pointed out, was to help anyone who required it. But this time she couldn't do it. Her beloved Jack's happiness was at stake. She raised her eyes to his. 'As for a job for her, I might just be able to help there.'

He gaped in disbelief. 'Ma, you're never thinking of . . .'

'Eh,' she cut in, 'if it's good enough fer me then it's certainly good enough for the likes of her. If she's desperate she'll take anything, like I have to do.' She grabbed his arm. 'Come on. Let's go and tell her the glad tidings.'

Chapter Thirteen

Ally, sharp knife poised, looked down in horror at the huge cod on the cold metal table gazing up at her from sightless eyes. She couldn't do this. There was no way she could stick the end of the knife they had given her into the grey scaly skin and slit it open, then pull out its insides and relieve it of its bones. From the corner of her eye she glanced apprehensively at Flo, working alongside her with two other women. Nattering ten to the dozen, Flo was gutting like she'd been born to the job, her pile of cleaned fish rising higher by the minute.

Albertina shuddered. The inside of the fish market was surely colder than the outside where it was just above freezing. She had only been here a little over two hours and her hands were so numb she felt her fingers would drop off. She had lost all sensation in her feet. She was dressed in an old brown hessian skirt and black blouse belonging to Flo, which were a size too big, and a huge black shawl, tucked tightly under her armpits. Flo had insisted on this, and much as Albertina had resisted, she was glad now she had relented.

Her lovely velvet suit, a sad semblance of its former glory, would have been most inappropriate should she have worn it and given her little protection against the penetrating cold. Besides, despite the state of her own clothes, the quality of the cloth was still very apparent and as Flo had quite rightly pointed out – something which had been upsetting at the time – the wearing of them would do her no favours in either getting the job or endearing herself to her colleagues.

The open-sided ornate iron framework holding up the plate-glass roof of the fish market was sectioned off to provide different areas for the numerous fishmongers who plied their trade, some just out of wooden boxes, some fortunate enough to afford an actual stall with a work area at the back. Boxes of fish, carted by wagons from the Great Central Railway Station, came from as far off as Galstone, near Yarmouth, Grimsby and Hull, and well before four in the morning the whole place was buzzing with activity. Despite her dismay and nausea at the terrible stench, Ally had at first been mesmerised, even a little overawed, by all the goings on – until, that was, it had actually sunk in that this was where she was expected to make her living.

Although she fought to prevent them her eyes travelled upwards. On large metal hooks suspended from runners hung unplucked chickens, their heads hanging limply. Next to these were rabbits of assorted colours, all waiting to be skinned. Skins fetched good money, so Mr Sileby had told her, and chicken feathers too. And when she had mastered fish cleaning, that was her next task.

The previous night, when the offer of hospitality was extended, Ally had been overwhelmingly grateful, and when Flo had mentioned the possibility of a job she had been overjoyed. At least this would help to restore her self-respect and allow her to contribute towards her keep. A job was a start, a definite step up from the position she had been in when Jack had found her in the deserted shop doorway. She had wondered what the job could possibly be but had felt it would be discourteous of her to enquire. She had gone to bed that night conjuring up all sorts of visions and had actually felt a flicker of excitement. Had she known what was actually in store she would never have slept.

It had still been the middle of the night when Flo had nudged her awake, thrusting a mug of weak tea at her. 'We start at four and it's a good walk to get there so rise and shine.'

Ally, when she had finally collected her senses, could not comprehend that anyone should be made to work such inhumane hours and had voiced the opinion, which at Flo's sharp response she'd instantly regretted. 'Tell that to the folks who like their fish nice and fresh, and there's work to be done to it before it can be sold.'

'Fish?' she had uttered, fully believing she had misheard.

'Yeah, I work at the fish market. And if luck's on your side, gel, so will you.' Flo had eyed her sharply. 'It's a job. You ain't in no position ter be choosy. Just be grateful, and thankful that Netty broke her leg in the floods or you'd have nothing ter be grateful for! Now get a hurry on 'cos there's no allowance fer being late. Oh, and whatever you do, let me do all the talking when we approach the gaffer. If he hears the way you talk, you'll never get the job.'

Whilst Flo had pleaded with Mr Sileby to give Ally a try she had hung her head in humiliation, hands clasped so tightly her knuckles had shone white. He had not been won over easily. Flo had practically had to go down on her hands and knees to him. The outcome was she had a week, one whole week, to master everything or she would be out and someone with experience would be hired.

She cast another glance in Flo's direction. Despite all she had gone through, how low she had sunk, she could not help but feel totally demeaned by what was expected of her. Misery filled her. Fish of any description she had only ever seen before covered in a creamy parsley sauce, accompanied by freshly cooked vegetables, all served on hot silver platters by maids dressed in black, their pinafores starched crisp and sparkling white. They had addressed her as 'miss'.

A deep longing for her old life surged through her. Oh, why? her mind screamed. As if all that had happened to her wasn't bad enough, now she was faced with this. She couldn't do it, she just couldn't do it. She fought the urge to drop the knife, gather her skirts and flee – but she couldn't do that either because where would she go and what would she do? Tears of distress pricked her eyes. She stole another glance at Flo and studied her. Whether she liked it or not she owed this woman and her family a huge debt of gratitude and the least she could do to try to repay some of that debt was tackle this job. It had never entered her head that getting work of any description would be so difficult, and it was only through Flo that she was getting this chance.

Just do it, Albertina, she told herself. Just raise the knife and after the first cut it will be bound to be easier. She took a deep breath, shut her eyes and made a tentative stab at the fish. Her knife rebounded and her eyes shot open. Her feeble attempt had not even made a mark.

Unbeknown to Ally, Flo had been secretly keeping an eye on her. She was pleased her plan seemed to be working. The girl wasn't getting on with the job at all. And if Flo was correct, any moment now, judging by the stricken look on her face, she would down tools and do a runner and that would be the end of the matter. Her Jack would then be spared the suffering Flo knew was facing him if this woman stayed around. She felt a surge of guilt rise up which she hurriedly quashed. She was protecting her own, wasn't she? Why should she feel guilty for that? She planted a smile on her face and turned to Ally, asking: 'All right there, gel?'

A watery smile crossed Ally's lips. 'Actually I'm not doing very well at all.'

Her words were more of a plea and the guilt Flo had just quashed returned, only much stronger. The acute aura of misery that surrounded this girl tugged at her conscience and before she could stop herself she asked: 'Want me ter show yer again, me duck?'

Ally's face flooded with gratitude. 'Would you be so kind?'

I don't know about kind, thought Flo. If I'd have been that kind I would have tried to get you work anywhere but in this hell hole. ''Course I will.' She moved across to Ally. 'Now you just watch me, and proper this time. It's easy, yer know, when yer get the knack. Just keep yer eyes peeled for Mr Sileby. If he catches me, he'll give me a rollicking.' She gave Ally a playful nudge. 'We all call him Cod Eyes. Don't yer reckon he resembles a cod?'

Albertina stared at Flo for a moment then a broad smile split her face and her eyes lit up with humour. 'Why, yes, now you come to mention it, actually he does.'

Both women fought to stifle giggles and for Ally this light-hearted moment was the turning point.

Much later that morning, Ada, one of her fellow gutters, pulled her aside. She leaned over and whispered in her ear: 'Flo's told us about yer.'

Ally stared at her, wondering just what Flo had said. 'She has?'

'Yeah, and you listen. I think yer've bin treated disgustingly. Just fancy them toffs bringing yer up as one of their own, then chucking you out when it suited 'em. Want hanging, the lot of 'em. I wouldn't trust any of 'em as far as I could throw 'em.'

Ally gulped. What would they say if they knew the truth? Her lies, told with such good intentions, were weighing heavily on her.

'But don't you worry,' Ada continued, 'we all think very highly of Flo, 'specially old Cod Eyes.' She sniffed disdainfully, glancing in Mr Sileby's direction, then turned back to Ally and smiled. 'And if Flo sez yer all right, then that's fair game wi' us too. We'll look out fer yer, gel, don't you fear.' She looked at Ally's efforts, pursed her lips and nodded approvingly. 'All things considered, you ain't doin' too badly.'

Ally stared at her dumbstruck, overwhelmed by all the kindness. 'Thank you,' she choked out and watched as Ada retook her position at the table and got stuck into her work. She suddenly felt privileged. These women had hardly anything yet during the morning she had caught them adding fish to her pile to make it appear she was getting on better than she actually was. And they were all paid piecework rates on the amount of fish they gutted.

A thought suddenly occurred to her and she narrowed her eyes. In her experience, her own kind would never even have considered such a thing, let alone carried it out. They wouldn't do anything for another person unless there was also something in it for themselves. Albertina suddenly felt wholeheartedly ashamed. To think she had dared to look down on these people, the kind who in her hour of need were the only ones to offer their help.

It was then that she finally accepted that her previous life was over. *This* was her life now. Instead of being waited on, she would be doing the waiting. As much as it repelled her, she would have to get used to it. It was not going to be easy, she would have a lot of new ways to learn and many old ones to forget. Or, she thought positively, perhaps in some cases she might be able to combine the two. Her spirits rose and the heaviness that had been weighing her down suddenly diminished. One thing was for certain: whatever happened to her now nothing would ever be as bad as what she had faced over the last few days. She made herself a promise that never again would she let things get her down to such an extent that she contemplated her own demise. She would rise above it all, just like these people seemed to do. A flicker of a smile touched her lips. Besides, whatever she had to tackle in the future to earn her living, nothing could ever be as awful as gutting fish.

'A' yer all right, Ally?' asked Flo, slinging a cleaned fish on to her pile.

'Oh, yes, thank you.' She smiled at the woman, a warm smile full of sincerity. 'I'm very well. Very well indeed.'

Flo's eyes widened in surprise. She leaned over and whispered, 'I'm glad ter hear that someone is, 'cos between you and me I hate this bloody job.'

Ally stared into the window of the little chemist's shop. Flo had just nipped into the grocer's to buy some soda crystals to help remove the ring of slime the floods had left on the walls. They were on their way home and Ally was having difficulty putting one foot in front of the other through sheer unaccustomed exhaustion. She reeked of fish and wouldn't care if she never saw another creature of the sea for as long as she lived; her hands, not so long ago perfectly manicured, were cut to shreds and raw red from the wet and cold, and the bottom of her skirt was soaking after she had accidentally tipped a bucket of cold water over as she had attempted to help the others with swilling down at the end of the day.

She was ravenously hungry but had a strong suspicion that in the newspaper parcel that Flo was carrying were several pieces of skate. At the thought her appetite started to wane. All she wanted to do was get home, wash the stench from her and crawl into bed. But despite all that there was a certain satisfaction in the thought that for the first time in her life she had actually earned some money. It wasn't much compared to what she had been used to, she had left more for a tip to a willing baggage handler at the railway station. Admittedly she had received help from her colleagues but she had still laboured hard. At this moment in time her wage seemed a fortune to her, and what made her feel even happier was the thought that she would earn even more tomorrow.

For a few moments everything was forgotten as she studied the scene in front of her. It was getting very close to Christmas and the shop staff had made the window inviting with a festive display. Her gaze travelled over the jars and bottles and settled on a bar of soap alongside a glass jar of matching bath crystals. She held out her hand, inside which was her wage. It amounted to two shillings and eightpence three-farthings. She eyed the soap and crystals again. She could just about afford both. Without a second thought she hurried into the shop, made her purchases and was out again before Flo rejoined her.

The older woman eyed her sharply. 'My, gel, you look like yer've lost a penny and found a shilling.'

Ally stared at her for a moment while she deciphered just what Flo meant. 'Oh, yes,' she laughed, hoping Flo had meant she looked pleased with herself. 'Well, I might have,' she said secretively.

Ally was just about on her knees by the time they arrived home. The children and Sal greeted them both joyously, Eric and Emily bombarding Ally with questions. While doing her best to answer, she sank down in a chair, expecting Flo to join her, but was astounded to notice that Flo's coat was no sooner off than her large sacking apron was tied around her and she was issuing orders.

'Emily, fetch the water. Eric, we need some more wood.' All this was said as she unwrapped the newspaper parcel and laid its contents on a plate. It was fish and Ally fought nausea at the sight as she jumped up and hovered uncertainly, feeling mortally inadequate, silently scolding herself. Who did she think was going to prepare the evening meal and tackle all the other tasks? There were no maids here. 'Can I . . . do anything?' she tentatively asked.

'There's plenty ter do,' Flo responded without lifting her eyes. 'As soon as Emily returns, I'll set you on.'

Her heart sank as she wondered how she was going to muster the energy. She hoped whatever it was, it wasn't too strenuous.

Emily returned lugging the full bucket, slopping some of the water on the floor. 'Careful, Emily,' Flo scolded as she wiped her hands on her apron. 'Those flags have seen enough water this week ter last a lifetime. Let's leave them dry for a little longer, eh?' She cuffed the girl playfully. 'Give the bucket to Ally then get the scrubbing brush from under the sink and soda crystals from me shopping bag. While I get the dinner, you two can make a start on the parlour.'

To Ally a parlour was a large room filled with comfortable furniture, occasional tables adorned with heirlooms and family photographs. On the flock-papered walls hung paintings; on the floor lay Chinese or Persian rugs. There would be a fire burning inside the grate of the Adam fireplace.

She stood inside the doorway of this room with its bare boards and her first thought was that the cupboard in her bedroom at home where she had stored her trunks was larger than this. Then for the second time that evening she scolded herself. Had she not made a promise to forget her old life while she fought to accustom herself to her new?

She glanced down at the bucket she was carrying and then at the scrubbing brush and box of soda crystals Emily was holding. Flo had requested the walls to be scrubbed. A simple task maybe, but difficult for someone who hadn't done it before. She turned to Emily. 'Well, how would you like to play our little game again?'

'Game?' She tilted her head and eyed Ally knowingly. 'Oh, the one where I show yer what to do, yer mean?'

Ally laughed. Emily was certainly a clever little girl. 'Yes, Emily, that one.'

She nodded as she entered the room. 'I heard Ma tell our Jack they obviously didn't teach you nowt of importance up at the posh 'ouse.' She turned and beamed at Ally cheekily. 'Ma was right, weren't she?'

Flo was just about to call Emily and Ally for their supper when Jack walked in. After giving Flo a peck on the cheek he rushed across to the fire and held out his hands. 'It's freezing out there. We could be in for snow. Oh, fish and chips! That looks good, Ma.' He turned and smiled at her. 'How did Ally get on then?' His eyes narrowed. 'By the way, where is she?'

Flo eyed him sharply as she placed plates on the table. Jack usually asked how the kids were and how her day had gone. But not tonight. All his thoughts were for Ally. 'She's in the parlour helping our Emily to scrub the walls.' Flo's astute eyes did not miss the look of relief that crossed his face. 'And she didn't do too badly today.'

Jack took the knives and forks from her and began to lay them out. 'You don't sound very happy about that, Ma.'

'Wadda you mean?'

He stopped what he was doing and looked across at her. 'Exactly what I said. You didn't sound very happy. I get the distinct impression you wanted her to fail. Did you, Ma?'

She sniffed disdainfully and continued busying herself with the pan full of frying fish. 'No, of course I didn't.' That statement would not have been true this morning, she thought. She had prayed that Ally would fail miserably, something for which she still felt guilty. But after her shaky start, even Flo had to admit that the girl deserved credit for the way she had got stuck in, which couldn't have been easy for someone who, since she had been adopted by the nobs while still very young, hadn't had to lift a finger for herself. She knew that, much as she didn't want to, she was warming to Ally. If it hadn't been for Jack's showing signs of taking a shine to her, and Flo's own deep reservations over what she thought the outcome would be, she would have been more than happy to extend her hospitality for as long as Ally wanted it. But now wasn't the time to discuss it. She began to lift the cooked fish out of the pan and put it on a warm tin dish. 'Yer know my feelings on the matter, Jack,' she said abruptly.

He walked around the table, placed his hands gently on her shoulders and turned her round to face him. 'Ma, I've told you, yer making something out of nothing.'

'Am I? Well, I'll reserve judgement, if yer don't mind. Now give everyone a shout, will yer, or this food'll go cold. Yer'll have ter bang on the wall for our Eric. He's next-door.'

Once they were seated around the table, Flo gave each of them a plate of fish and chips, except Ally. Flo gave a brief smile when she put a plate in front of her. 'I've given the fish a miss for you, gel, and done you an egg. Our Eric fetched it special for yer.' Her smile widened to a grin. 'I saw the look on yer face when I unwrapped the parcel. I thought you were gonna be sick. I have ter be honest, though, I couldn't eat fish fer ages after I started work there. We only have so much of it now 'cos I get it cheap.' She hurried around to her own chair and sat down, looking round at them all. 'Come on then, tuck in.'

Ally glanced down at her plate. Egg and chips. Not so long ago having such a simple meal put in front of her would have been cause for disgust. Now this offering seemed like a banquet. She smiled in appreciation. 'Thank you, Flo.'

★ ★ ★

102

Everyone had retired to bed for the night and Flo was just settling Sal on an old blanket in the kitchen. The dog usually occupied the space that Ally was now in and couldn't understand why she had been relegated to the cold kitchen.

'Now stay put, gel, or you'll spend the night in the coal 'ole,' Flo softly warned. She heard a movement nearby and spun round. 'Oh, yer gave me a fright,' she exclaimed. 'I thought you were in bed.'

Ally, dressed in a calico night shift of Flo's that was so threadbare she had considered it only suitable for use as cleaning cloths, hurriedly apologised. 'I'm sorry, I didn't mean to startle you.' She held out her hand. 'It isn't much, I'm afraid, but I just wanted to give you this as a token of my appreciation. Thank you for all you're doing for me, Flo.' With that she turned and left the room.

A dumbstruck Flo stared down at the package in her hand. Slowly she undid the wrapping and gazed at the contents. 'Oh, Sal,' she exclaimed, sinking down on a chair. 'Would you just look at these?' Lily-of-the-valley soap and matching bath crystals. Never in her life had she held such luxury in her hands. These must have cost a fortune. Nearly three bob at least.

Then it suddenly struck her that Ally must have used every single penny of her day's wage to buy them. She obviously hadn't realised that her pay was supposed to last her all through the next week because there'd be no more until the next Friday when she'd completed a full week. And, worse, Flo herself had been hoping to receive a good portion of it towards Ally's keep. She didn't know whether to laugh at what Ally had done, cry, or just accept the gift in the spirit it had been given. 'Oh, Ally,' she whispered. 'Why did yer have ter go and do that when I'm trying so hard not ter like yer?'

She leaned over and patted the old dog's head. 'What am I going to do, Sal? Come on, don't just lie there looking at me with those doleful eyes, I need yer advice. I'm really getting ter like that girl, but I'm worried fer Jack. I've seen the way they look at each other and it's only a matter of time before summat happens between 'em. What am I gonna do, eh, gel?'

She ruffled the dog's fur. 'It's our Jack I'm thinking of, Sal. I couldn't bear ter see him hurt. You know that, don't yer? You know I've only his best interests at heart.' She sighed loudly. 'Oh, hell,' she uttered. 'Hell and damnation.' And shook her head. 'It's all right, Sal, I know. Whatever I do, I can't win with this one. So we'll just have ter play it by ear and see what happens, eh?'

Much later that night Ally awoke with a start. The room was pitch black and for a moment she had trouble working out where she was, divorcing her dream from reality. Then Flo gave a loud snore and Emily turned over, flinging her arm heavily across her, and reality struck with force.

Flopping back against her lumpy flat pillow, Ally sighed heavily. Her dream had been so confusing. The place she had found herself in had been a combination of her old home and the Williamson-Browns', but every now and again she would find herself in Flo's parlour, an old rusty bucket in her hand full of fish with eyes staring up at her. They seemed to be mocking her. Lavinia had been sitting at a table. She had grabbed handfuls of the raw fish from the bucket and started ramming them into her mouth which was huge, taking up almost the whole of her face. Lionel had been hovering behind his mother, only it hadn't really been him because when she had looked into his face it had not been his.

Lionel, oh, Lionel, she thought with deep sadness. She wanted to hate him, despise him in the hope it might ease her pain, but as much as she tried hate would not come. The loss of him was like a bereavement. With all that had been going on, for the last few days she had managed to push her heartache to the back of her mind. Until the dream. Now the pain seared back. It was with a jolt she suddenly realised whose face she had seen instead of Lionel's. It had been Jack's.

Why should his face be replacing Lionel's?

She remembered an incident from earlier that evening when they had all sat around the table eating their meal. She had caught Jack looking at her and she had returned his smile. As their eyes locked a feeling of warmth spread through her body. For the rest of the evening she found her own eyes straying to him. She was perturbed, confused even, to realise that she liked what she saw. It was not just his physical attributes that were drawing her. It was everything about him.

'Can't yer sleep, Ally?'

She started in surprise. Across the bed, raised up on one elbow, Flo was looking at her. 'Oh . . . er . . . yes. I just had rather a bad dream, that's all.'

Flo gave a low laugh as she snuggled back under the covers. 'I get those all the time, me duck. Only in my case it ain't sleeping dreams, it's when I'm awake. I call 'em daymares.' She turned over and cuddled into Emily. 'Now get back to sleep, we've to get up shortly.'

A vision of the fish market flashed before Ally. It was so vivid she could even smell it. She shut her eyes. Flo was right. Working at the market was without question a living daymare.

Chapter Fourteen

Ally paused for a moment in the doorway, clasping the mug of water she had just poured herself, and surveyed the happy scene before her. Warmth flooded through her at the sight of Flo, Jack, Eric and Emily sitting around the table, laughing and chattering together. It was Christmas Day. Outside the weather was damp, misty and cold. Inside the tiny back room of the dilapidated terrace it was warm and, despite its sparseness, cheery and inviting. Around the walls hung newspaper chains the children had made, along with bundles of holly collected from nearby woods. Their finances not stretching to a proper tree, a bare branch had been stuck in an empty bottle and decorated with painted wooden cotton reels and colourful buttons.

After rising that morning they had all got stuck in and made a hurried fire, toast and tea, then presents had been opened. There had been a new rag doll for Emily, bartered for by Flo second hand from the market, along with a handmade dress sewn long into the night after the children had gone to bed. For Eric there was a boys' adventure story book, Flo hoping he did not notice the several pages that were missing, a shirt revamped from one of Jack's old ones and a pair of second hand knickerbockers. Both children also had an apple, an orange, and a small string bag full of silver-covered chocolate coins. They had both been thrilled with what they received and expressed their feelings with cries of delight.

Flo had knitted Jack a new pullover and he had bought her a thick pair of woollen stockings. She was overjoyed at having a pair for best and ones that had not been knitted by her own hands. Ally had bought them handkerchiefs, all her wages had allowed after she had paid her dues. A large white one each for Jack and Eric, a dainty embroidered one for Flo and Emily. In return she received a black hand-knitted shawl from Flo, and from the children a length of red ribbon to tie back her hair. She had been delighted with their thoughtfulness, knowing that their money hardly stretched to presents for themselves let alone their lodger. She had not expected anything from any of them but nevertheless had a job to hide her disappointment that Jack had not marked the occasion with anything for her.

The dinner they had just eaten had been made up from a box of groceries given by Jack's boss, plus the rabbit grudgingly donated to his employees by Mr Sileby, though because Ally had not long been employed she had received nothing. Flo, in private, voiced strong views on the 'miserable beggar'. Vegetables had been bought last minute from the market for cheapness. Flo had made her own plum pudding of suet and dried fruit enriched by a small bottle of sherry donated by Jack.

Ally's eyes glazed over as her thoughts wandered. How different this Christmas was from others she had spent, where money had been no object, the best of everything having automatically been provided. The only contribution expected of her had been the grace of her presence. As she watched the scene before her it shocked her greatly to realise that this Christmas Day was the happiest she could remember spending since her parents had died. Until she had become engaged to Lionel, most of her Christmases had been spent at Bella's. She could not deny those times had been very special. After the loss of her parents and Tobias's surly treatment of her, at times like Christmas she had needed to feel wanted, to share family life in what otherwise would have been a time of great loneliness for her. Bella and her family had striven to provide that comfort. At the thought of Bella, Ally realised how much she missed her dear friend and she wondered if Bella was enjoying this Christmas without her. Ally sighed and smiled because this special day, the one she had shared now, was even better than any she had spent previously. And Albertina knew why: because she had done so much towards it. She had helped Flo with the shopping, traipsing around for all the bargains; with the preparation of the food; with the cleaning of the house; and had willingly given what money she could spare from her meagre wage to help with the extras. And all this involvement had meant her enjoyment was so much more.

She eyed the gathering around the table thoughtfully. She had been privileged to lodge with this family now for just on three weeks and during that period had had little time to dwell on her past. This family between them had taught her so much. She still had far to go, much to learn, still needed time to adjust to her new way of life. But under their guidance she felt she wasn't getting on too badly for someone whose life had been devastated then turned completely upside down. By being with them she was managing to cope. How would her life be now, she suddenly wondered, if that sixpence had landed heads up? She shuddered and her gaze fell on Jack. Would he have walked away and left her as she had made him promise to do?

'Yer seem full of secrets.'

Ally looked at Flo in confusion. 'I'm sorry?'

'I said, gel, yer seem full of secrets.'

She gulped. She was. Two of them anyway. Her lie about the facts of her birth – something which was deepening the guilt she felt with every day spent in the company of these kindly people – and her feelings for

106

Jack. At first she had been confused about these. How could she be attracted to another man when she was still recovering from Lionel's betrayal? But however much she questioned herself, there was no doubt that she was.

She was filled with alarm. Flo was right. She was a woman with secrets and ones she could not possibly divulge to this particular audience for fear of the repercussions.

'Stop teasing her, Ma,' said Jack, giving Flo a nudge.

Flo grinned. 'It was only a bit of fun. But yer did look thoughtful, Ally. Not bad thoughts, I hope?'

'Bad thoughts?' she replied, joining them at the table. 'Oh, no. I was just thinking how fortunate I was to be here with you, that's all.' She shifted uncomfortably and turned to face Emily. 'Have you named your dolly yet?' she asked to change the subject.

'Yeah, I have. Vicbettina Albiana. Betty on a Sunday.'

They all burst out laughing, even Ally.

Just before nine that night, after singing carols around the fire until they were hoarse, even Sal joining in, then finally getting two exhausted children up to bed, Flo flopped down wearily into the armchair by the dying embers of the fire and stretched out her legs.

'D'yer fancy a nice cuppa, Ma?' Jack asked.

What she really wanted to do was to climb into bed and sleep for a week but that would mean leaving Ally and Jack by themselves and up until now she had managed to avoid doing that – without, she hoped, their both realising the fact. 'I'd love one, thanks, Jack,' she replied, trying to sound grateful.

'I'll help you,' offered Ally, rising from her seat.

'No, no,' said Flo, making to rise also, picturing the two of them closeted close together in the tiny kitchen. 'I'll help him.'

'Ma, stay where you are,' he ordered. 'All you've done all day is run after us lot. Now do as yer told and put yer feet up. It won't hurt me and Ally to make you a cuppa.' He smiled at her affectionately. 'It's the least we can do after the grand day you've given us.'

Flo sighed heavily. It was becoming extremely difficult to keep those two apart. Maybe she should just give up and let nature take its course. But she couldn't. She would do anything to avoid the possibility of Jack's getting hurt. Although what could possibly happen in the kitchen during the time it took to mash a pot of tea, and especially with herself in such close proximity? 'That'd be lovely, Jack, thanks. And you could drain the dregs of that bottle of sherry you got for the pudding into it? It's on the shelf near the bag of salt. Eh, and hurry up about it, the pair of yer,' she added.

Jack swung the kettle over the fire and went to join Ally in the kitchen, busy washing up the mugs. He began to dry them.

'Have you enjoyed yer day, Ally?'

107

She turned and smiled at him, her reply coming without hesitation. 'I've had the most enjoyable day I can ever remember.'

'Really?' he said, surprised. 'What, better than when yer lived with the posh lot?'

Her thoughts flew back once again. She pictured the huge Christmas trees, lavishly decorated, and all the expensive presents piled underneath. The endlessly laden tables full of the most sumptuous foodstuffs. The guests who had descended; the balls she had attended; the shooting and hunting – the utter extravagance of it all. Then she thought of the day she had just spent, of how it had all been put together from such scant resources. Two very different days, both planned minutely down to the last detail, the distinction being – quite apart from the financial aspect – that the one she had just spent had been planned and executed out of love.

It was ironic, she thought, that it had taken Tobias's selfish actions to make her realise how empty, for the most part, her former life really had been and how shallow most of the people in it. How far she had come in such a short space of time. She smiled inwardly. Maybe she did have something to thank Tobias for after all. She raised her eyes. 'Oh, yes, Jack, much better,' she said with deep sincerity. 'There really is no comparison. Did you enjoy it too?'

He had. Like her he thought it the best Christmas ever, but could not bring himself to tell her the reason. It was because she had been there.

'I did,' he said, turning from her to place the dried mugs on the battered tin tray. 'It's nice to spend a day not thinking of work.'

She laughed. 'I can appreciate that. I still have nightmares about the fish market – or daymares as Flo would call them. But as she would say, it's a job and I have to be thankful I've got it. And now I've got better at it, I'm hoping to earn a little more money.'

She made to pick up the tray to carry it through, but Jack stopped her. 'Ally, just . . . er . . . a minute.' As she raised her head and looked straight into his eyes, he nearly lost his nerve. He had been trying to get her alone for a few minutes for the best part of the day. Now he had finally managed it, he suddenly felt tongue tied. And what man in their right mind wouldn't, he thought, looking into such a lovely face? Even dressed in her second hand clothes, an ankle-length dark brown serge skirt and cream linen blouse, frayed at the edges, her lustrous chestnut hair tied back with the piece of red ribbon the children had bought her, she still looked a picture. He fought an incredibly strong urge to gather her into his arms and kiss her. 'I . . . look, Ally, I never got you anything for Christmas because . . .'

'Oh, Jack,' she interrupted, aghast. 'I never expected anything from you. You – all of you – have so much else to do with your money. I was gratified to receive what I did from the children and Flo. Please do not concern yourself.'

He smiled. 'It's nothing to do with money, Ally. It's just I had no idea what to get yer.' How could he tell her he had walked the whole of the Leicester town centre and surrounding shopping areas looking for something suitable? He had wanted to buy her something pretty. She was a woman who should, he felt, wear something pretty. A brooch, maybe, or a hat pin, although she hadn't a hat at the moment. She could have stuck it through her shawl. But everything he had wanted to buy had been too expensive. The only things he could afford were from the costume jewellery counter at the Home and Colonial, and a cheap trinket he would not settle for. Having set his heart on something special for her, nothing else would do. So he had decided on another idea and prayed she would accept. He was going to ask if she would like to go to the silent pictures with him. That was, if she gave him the opportunity of putting it across to her without butting in. 'I wondered if you'd like to . . .'

'Where's that tea? How long does it tek to make a ruddy cuppa? A woman could die of thirst, she could, waiting fer you two. Neither of yer'd last five minutes serving in a café.'

Two pairs of eyes darted across to Flo standing in the doorway. Jack's heart sank at her untimely entrance. Could she not have waited just another couple of minutes? He then knew exactly how Lizzie Green had felt a couple of weeks back. He should really see the funny side of how the tables had been turned on him, but all he felt was annoyed. When would he ever get the chance to ask Ally the question he wanted to, with Flo never leaving them on their own for more than two minutes at a time? She was becoming very obvious about it. He wondered if Ally had noticed.

'The tea is ready, Flo,' said Ally, picking up the tray, all the time wondering just what it was Jack was going to ask her, several possibilities running through her mind. She hoped he was going to ask to escort her somewhere. She would like that. 'I warmed the pot just like you said and put two heaped spoons of tea in. Shall I take it through?'

'Yeah, do that, Ally, me duck. 'Cos if yer don't mind, I'd like a few words with Jack.' She eyed Ally. 'Yer know, gel, family business like.'

'Oh! Oh, I see. I'll pull the door shut so you can talk in private.'

Once Ally had departed and the door was closed, Jack leaned against the pot sink. He folded his arms, tilted his head and eyed Flo, mouth tight. 'Come on then, Ma, what's so private?' As though he hadn't already guessed.

'You know,' she erupted, wagging a finger in annoyance. 'You were just about to ask her out.'

'I was? Read minds now, do yer, Ma?'

'Don't be bloody cheeky. I ain't stupid, Jack. I've seen the way you two have bin meking sheep's eyes at each other. Admit it, yer were going to ask her out?'

Jack's mouth tightened. 'So what if I was? What harm is there in that?'

'What harm? Jack, I've told yer, it'll all lead to heartache.'

'Oh, and you're the authority, are yer, Ma? You can see into the future, is that it?'

'In this case, yes, I can.' Her annoyance left her and her body sagged tiredly as she spoke. 'Look, Jack, I can't deny she's a lovely gel. I can't get over meself how hard she's working at fitting in, and none of it can be easy for her. And she's not a bit selfish. Look at the way she spent all her day's wage on that present for me when she could have spent it on herself. To be honest I thought she'd have upped and left by now, gone to live with people of her own kind, even if it's only in a working capacity.'

'You were wrong then, Ma, weren't yer?' Jack's grimace deepened. 'Just what are you saying? That the likes of me ain't good enough, is that it, eh?'

'We,' she said slowly, poking her own chest, 'are good enough fer anyone. The only difference between the nobs and us is that they have the money. Money buys, Jack. It buys good clothes and education and fine houses. And it buys respect. It opens doors that would otherwise remain closed.'

'Ma, you ain't telling me nothing I don't already know.'

'Well, if yer know so much what a' yer playing at? That's what I'm getting at. She's had a taste of money and all that goes with it, and once yer've had that taste, there's no going back. Come on, lad, be honest with yerself. Ally's at a low ebb just now and she's grateful to yer. Probably sees you as her knight in shining armour. She'll accept yer invitation. What gel wouldn't? Yer a good-looking man. But where do you tek her? Despite what she's had ter come down to, Jack, she ain't no Violet Hibbott, who'd be happy with a bag of chips and a walk round the block. So can you afford a fancy restaurant or a night at the theatre? And I don't mean the cheap seats at the Saturday afternoon matinee.

'Oh, Jack, I'm not saying Ally wouldn't enjoy it. This is all a novelty to her just now. But what happens later when she starts wanting more, which would only be natural in the circumstances? For God's sake, Jack, you're a shop assistant with a wage yer can hardly keep yerself on. You'll start using yer savings fer yer shop and when that runs out . . . Come on, be realistic. In the long run, what can you offer her?'

'In the long run! Ma, I was going to offer to take her out for a bit of enjoyment. You've us married off!'

'Jack, yer missing the point. I don't think it'd get anywhere near to marriage. Ally's a very pretty girl who's had a shock to her system. Once she gets on her feet and sorts herself out, she'll have time ter hanker after her old life and more than likely want it back. And she'll get it, mark my words. Look, all I'm trying to point out is the fact that it's not that you ain't good enough for Ally.' Her eyes scanned him. 'My God, Jack, you're good enough fer anybody. It's just that, given time, Ally won't *think* you are. And I'm not blaming her, it's all down to the life she's led. But you, my lad, will end up left in the lurch with a broken heart to boot.'

'So?' he said defiantly. 'Life has its good side as well as its bad. I'm nearly twenty-four, Ma, I can take care of meself.'

'Huh,' she grunted. 'Tek care of yerself, my foot! Yer heading fer a fall, Jack, and yer can't even see it.' She raised her chin, her mouth set firm, and folded her arms. 'I'm gonna make a stand 'cos I ain't never felt so strongly about summat fer a long time.'

His eyes hardened. 'Oh, and what's that? As if you haven't said enough already.'

'Yer leave me no choice, Jack. Make any advances towards her and I'll ask her to leave.'

'What?'

'You heard me.'

'But, Ma, that's ridiculous. Where would she go? You know she ain't the means at the moment.'

Flo shrugged her shoulders. 'Go back to her own kind, I expect. It's up to you, Jack. As I said, if I see anything developing between yer both, I ask her to go. And whether you realise it or not, I only have yer best interests at heart.'

'Really?' He looked her straight in the eye. 'If I didn't know better, I'd say you were acting jealous, Ma, seeing Ally as some sort of threat. Now excuse me,' he muttered, pushing past.

She spun round. 'Where yer going?'

'Ter bed. Or do I need your permission fer that too?'

'Jack, there's no need . . .'

But he had gone.

Ally was sitting in the next room, puzzled, wondering why Jack had practically ignored her as he had charged through and on up the stairs with a barely audible goodnight. She was feeling disappointed. He had been about to ask her something but that seemed to be forgotten about now. She was curious as to what had gone on in the kitchen between himself and his mother to cause this sudden mood change.

'Where's me tea?'

'Sorry?' Ally exclaimed, startled. She hadn't heard Flo enter. 'Oh, I was waiting for you before I poured it out. I hope it hasn't gone cold.' She raised her eyes to Flo as she passed over the mug of tea and frowned at the distracted look on the elder woman's face. 'Pardon me for asking, but is anything wrong between you and Jack?'

'Eh? Oh, er . . . we had a misunderstanding, that's all. It were nowt.'

Ally sighed, relieved. 'I was worried it was something I had done to upset him.'

111

Yes, it was you, Flo wanted to say. Our having words was all your doing. Then she silently scolded herself. None of this was Ally's fault, not really. She couldn't help being what she was. Flo eyed her sharply over the rim of her mug. Who or what *was* Ally? She wasn't anything really. She couldn't truthfully be classed a nob because she had no money; neither could she in reality be classed one of their own, not with her refined ways and tone of voice. Flo pursed her lips. She hadn't thought of that before. Suddenly pity rose within her for the girl's plight and she silently thanked the Lord she herself wasn't in such a predicament. At least she knew who she was. 'You? Oh, it was nothing to do with you, me duck, so put yer mind at rest.' She took a sip of her tea and forced a smile. 'Not bad, considering yer still learning.'

'I haven't quite mastered the art then?' Ally asked, dismayed.

'Eh? Oh! Not quite, me duck. Could have done with three more leaves in the pot. Then it would have bin just perfect.'

The girl looked at her for a moment, then laughed. 'Oh, Flo, you're having fun with me.'

'Yes, I am, the tea's just right.' Flo thrust her mug at her. 'Pour us another, then I'm off up ter bed.'

'Yes, I must admit I'm rather tired too.' She smiled warmly at Flo. 'Thank you for such a lovely day. I enjoyed it so much.'

'Really?'

'You sound surprised?'

'I . . . I suppose I am. I'd have thought it would have bin . . . well . . . not what yer used to, that's all.'

'Jack said that. Flo, let me assure you, this Christmas has been the best I have spent for a very long time.' She paused thoughtfully, her eyes growing misty. 'I know I keep repeating myself but I do have such a lot to thank you for. All of you. I hope you know how much I appreciate your taking me into your home? Jack too. If it wasn't for your son, I dread to think what would have become of me.'

'My son?'

Ally jumped at Flo's harsh tone and was shocked to see her face had drained of its colour. She frowned, bewildered. 'Your son Jack.'

'Jack is *not* my son,' she hissed. 'Whatever made you think he was?'

'Well, er . . . he shares your surname and he calls you Ma, so I automatically thought . . .'

'Well, yer thought wrong,' she erupted. 'I'm not old enough to have a son Jack's age.' She glared at Ally angrily. 'I'm only twelve years older than he is. You must never tell Jack what you thought. He'd be so ashamed.'

Ally reddened in embarrassment. She thought Flo's anger at her simple misunderstanding a little overdone. 'I'm most dreadfully sorry,' she uttered.

'I should think so. I don't know how you could have made a mistake like that. Jack was just a baby when his folks died of the dysentery and my mam and dad took him in 'cos there was no one else. And when they passed on, not long after, I took over. If I hadn't he'd have bin thrown in the workhouse. Since he could talk he's called me Ma. It's his name for me, that's all, and nothing more.' She rose abruptly. 'Now that's the end of the matter. I don't want this mentioning again, and 'specially not in front of Jack. Is that clear?'

'Yes, Flo, very.' Ally gulped. 'I'm . . . I'm so sorry. I really didn't mean to upset you.'

Flo clasped her hands, shut her eyes and sighed heavily, her whole body sagging. 'It's me that should be saying sorry. You weren't to know none of this. It's just that it brings back memories of awful times. Me mam and dad died when I was only fourteen. It was such a terrible loss and such a waste. I'll never forgive . . .' She stopped abruptly and took a deep breath. 'I don't want to talk about it. It upsets me too much. I'm off up to bed now. Can you settle everything down fer the night? Sal an' all.'

'Yes, of course.'

'Night then.'

'Goodnight, Flo.'

Ally thoughtfully stared after her. It had never crossed her mind that Flo had suffered the same sort of tragedy as she herself. They had both lost parents when very young. Her gaze travelled to a blurred sepia photograph on the mantel. Emily had told her that it was a photo of her father. He had died when she was just a baby. Ally rose, reached up and took hold of the frame and stared into the face of the man who had been Flo's husband. The photograph was not of good quality but from what she could make out he looked a handsome man and kindly, only to be expected when Flo herself was an attractive woman. It was a shame, though, that he had died so young, leaving a widow and two fatherless children, plus a young boy he had helped his wife take care of too.

Her heart saddened for a moment then filled with admiration. Flo deserved respect for what she had done and Ally felt she was wrong to think Jack would be ashamed if people thought she was his natural mother. If anything she felt he would be proud. The regard and love he held for Flo were readily apparent.

She replaced the photograph and stared down into the dying embers of the fire. It didn't make sense to her that Flo should be so angry about her misunderstanding. Albeit she had only known the woman for a short space of time, she would have staked her own life on Flo finding the mistake funny. But angry? It did not make sense.

She felt a movement by her feet and looked down to see Sal staring back up at her. She leaned over and stroked the old dog's head. 'Life's very strange, Sal. It holds many things I do not understand.' The old dog gave a low bark. 'You understand, don't you? I bet there's a lot you could tell me if you could talk.' She sighed softly and patted Sal's head again. 'Come on, old girl. Let's get you settled.'

'For goodness' sake, Eric, will yer settle down and go to sleep?'

Eric wrenched the eiderdown right up under his chin. 'How can I, with you tossing and turning so much? I can't get ter sleep 'cos you're keeping me awake.'

Jack sighed heavily. 'I'm sorry, lad. I don't know what's up with me tonight. I can't seem to get comfy.' That was a lie. He knew exactly what was wrong with him. He was still angry over Flo's outburst. She had no right to interfere between himself and Ally, despite her concern. It wasn't as though she was his mother. He sighed again as he fought with his conscience. Apart from actually giving birth to him, Flo was in every way his mother. In fact she had been more of a mother to him than most mothers would ever have been. He owed her much and his anger at what in truth was just her simply showing her love for him wasn't fair. He should at least have listened to her, then reasoned and maybe come to a compromise. As it was, his own stubbornness had caused her to issue an ultimatum.

But, regardless, his feelings for Ally were so strong. How could Ma, knowing how he felt, possibly expect him to live in the same house, so closely, and yet keep his distance? She was asking the impossible.

Jack had never bothered much with girls. Not that he wasn't interested, or they not interested in him. It was just that moving house so much, trying to save towards his dream of owning his own shop and helping Ma as much as he could, took most of his energies. He had had several light dalliances but nothing serious; no woman had interested him anywhere near as much as Ally had done. She was so different from any woman he had ever encountered and it had taken no effort at all for him to fall in love. She was without a doubt the one for him and he felt his feelings were returned. Not speaking out to her before this evening had taken all his self-control – and just as he had summoned up the courage Ma had arrived on the scene and stuck her oar in.

He folded his hands behind his head and stared up at the cracked ceiling, tracing the various shapes which damp had left on the plaster. As he did so the words Ma had spoken filled his mind and he pondered them anew. However much he fought against it, he had to admit she was right. What had he to offer a woman like Ally? A woman who, just as Ma had said, had tasted a totally different kind of life?

He sighed forlornly as good sense took over. Even if he did eventually achieve his dream and become master of his trade, it could be years, if ever, before he acquired the resources it would take to give Ally the kind of life she would want to return to. As Ma had pointed out, once you'd had a taste of something, no matter how hard you tried, the experience never left you. Had that not been exactly what had happened to him when Mr Green had left him in charge while he had taken to his sick bed? In that week Jack had tasted what it was like to be responsible, in control, looked up to by others, and the experience had been all it had taken to fuel a desire one day to own his own establishment. Since that time he had not been happy being just the assistant and the only thing that kept him going was his plan to better himself.

He groaned inwardly. Ma was right, confound her! Nothing but misery would come if he pursued his desire. Ally, like his plan for his shop, was a dream. But unlike his shop, which he knew he'd achieve if it took him a lifetime, a woman like her was out of his reach. She was everything he was not and he had no right even to be thinking she would ever settle for the likes of him. To stifle his feelings was going to be the most difficult thing he had ever had to do, but he had no choice, it had to be done. He would tell Ma tomorrow that he had taken her advice so she need worry no more.

Acute misery filled him, not only because of his reluctant decision but at the realisation that now he'd experienced and fallen for a woman like Ally, how could he ever settle for one of his own kind? He would be forever comparing.

'Oh, our Jack, that wa' sore,' cried Eric, diving under the bedclothes to rub his shin.

'What . . . what was sore?'

Eric resurfaced. 'That kick. A right belter yer gave me on me shin. I bet I'll have a bruise. Ma'll think I've bin fighting.'

'Oh, Eric, I'm sorry. I didn't know I'd done it. I've got such a lot on me mind. Don't worry. If Ma spots it, I'll square it with her.'

Eric sniffed. 'Is it yer shop?'

'What?'

'Yer shop. A' yer thinking about yer shop?'

Jack sighed. 'Yeah, that's right, I'm thinking about me shop.'

'Oh.'

Jack frowned in the darkness. 'What was that supposed to mean?'

'Nothing.'

'Don't nothing me, lad. Out with it.'

'I thought yer might've bin thinking about Ally.'

'Ally! Why would I be thinking of her?'

'Because yer like her, that's why. Emily reckons you'll get married.'

Jack froze. Had his feelings been so transparent that even young Emily had noticed? 'Oh, she does, does she? Well, you can just put our Emily right,' he hissed. 'I like Ally, 'course I do. We all like her. When people stay with yer, yer try and get on with 'em. Now that's all there is to it. Have you got that?'

115

'Yeah, Jack, all right, there ain't no need ter get mad wi' me. I'm only telling yer what our Emily said.'

'Well, our Emily has a big mouth, and big mouths can cause trouble. How embarrassed do yer think Ally would be if she got to hear? I shall be speaking to Emily in the morning. Now turn over and go to sleep.'

A subdued Eric turned on his side and snuggled into the covers. It was not long before his gentle snores filtered through the room. But it was a long time before Jack fell asleep, and what sleep he did get was not restful.

Chapter Fifteen

A rush of freezing February wind blasted in as Flo pushed through the door and kicked it shut behind her. 'Oh, it's bitter out,' she complained, then realised the tiny kitchen was empty. 'Where is everybody?' she called.

Sal waddled up, barking loudly, lifted her paws and planted them on Flo's chest, nearly overbalancing her. 'Get down, yer daft dog,' she scolded, prising off Sal's paws. The dog promptly fell back on to the stone flags with a thud. Flo bent over and patted her head affectionately. 'Jack'll tek you out when he comes home.'

'Hello, Flo. I was at the front door.' Ally arrived in the doorway. 'A woman called, enquiring . . .'

'Where are the kids?' Flo demanded, straightening up.

'The children are next-door.'

'A' yer sure?'

'Very sure. If you listen, you can hear them.'

Flo cocked her head. The noise three children were making, sounding like a dozen, filtered through the walls. 'Huh,' she grunted. 'As long as I know where they are.'

Ally had grown used to Flo's overprotectiveness of her children but even she, who prior to meeting Emily and Eric had had little knowledge of the younger generation, thought Flo went overboard at times. Generally children of the less well off seemed to roam freely, their parents glad of the peace and quiet. But not Flo. Apart from allowing them to play with Tommy next-door and to make the journey back and forth to school, with a stern warning of 'straight there and back', they were allowed no other freedom. Even Ally thought this unusual. But her peers had taught her to keep her opinions to herself unless asked for. On many occasions, such as now, she found that teaching hard to follow.

Flo lifted her head and sniffed. 'Summat smells good.'

'It's the evening meal.'

'Oh,' she mouthed, eyeing Ally warily.

'Don't worry, I couldn't possibly ruin sausages and mashed potatoes.'

'Couldn't yer?' Flo muttered, putting down her bag. 'We'll see.'

Ally grimaced. 'Though I do have to admit I'm not sure about the gravy. I was just about to fetch Emily to see what she thought.'

'What's wrong with the gravy?'

'I'm not sure. I did strain it well to get rid of the lumps but it's thin and very pale. I followed your instructions.'

Pale, thin gravy with lumps, thought Flo. Oh, well, at least she's tried. 'I'll take a look at it.'

Ally nodded, gratified. 'Did you get your errand done?'

Flo beamed. 'I did. But I'll have a warm first and a cuppa and then I'll tell you all about it.'

Ally eyed her, intrigued. Flo had been very secretive about the errand she wanted to do straight after work and for the second time that night frustration reared as she remembered it was impolite to probe. If a person wanted you to know something they would tell you about it in their own good time. She felt guilty for her own impatience. 'I've just made a pot of tea. I'll pour you a cup while you take off your outdoor attire.'

Outdoor attire, thought Flo. Why can't she just say coat?

Stripped of her outdoor clothing Flo followed Ally through and glanced over the pans on top of the range. The sausages, bursting out of their skins, looked an appetising golden brown; a fork poked in the spuds told her they were boiling away nicely. She glanced in the pan holding the gravy. It looked totally disgusting but she might be able to salvage it once she'd had her tea. She flopped down in her rocker and relaxed, stretched out her long legs and accepted the mug Ally passed to her.

'Don't worry about the gravy, me duck. I think I can do something with it.'

'You can? Oh, Flo, I was so worried. I know how you hate waste.'

'Ah, well, we all have ter learn, gel. I've burned a few pans in me time.'

'You have?'

Flo grinned. 'Don't look so surprised.' She took a sup of tea and eyed Ally searchingly. 'Them nobs that took you in did you no favours, gel, did they? When they chucked you out you weren't prepared at all to return to yer proper life, were yer?'

Ally cast down her eyes. 'No,' she whispered. 'No, I wasn't prepared at all.'

'Ah, well, yer getting there, gel. You can just about light a fire now and the sheets yer hung on the line on washday didn't blow away this time so that's an improvement. Mind you, yer need ter pay more attention when yer meking the beds. Me feet keep poking out the bottom, and in this weather, gel, that ain't funny. Just make sure you tuck 'em well under next time.'

Ally nodded. 'I will.'

Life was certainly unpredictable, she thought. Only months ago she would have laughed out loud if anyone had dared suggest that she, Albertina Victoriana Listerman, would be living in a house that in truth was unfit for human habitation; sharing a lumpy bed with two other people, tackling the washing, the cleaning, and everything else that needed to be done. And more astounding than anything was her job as a fish gutter. The very idea of her present life would have been absolutely preposterous then.

Regardless, though, one thing she would never get used to and that was taking her turn in the cleaning of the outside convenience or 'lavvy' as it was referred to. She had yet to prevent her stomach from heaving each time she ventured out armed with her bucket, Carbosil bleaching soda and scrubbing brush into the dark, dank outbuilding they shared with several other families. Insects of all varieties lurked there as well as mice. It was bad enough having no other choice but to use it, let alone clean it up after some of the disgusting habits the other families had. She knew that if she lived to be a hundred this was one job she would never grow used to.

But despite that she felt proud that not only was she tackling it all, now she was accepting her changed situation she was actually enjoying life. Her days were so full she hardly had time to dwell on her past.

She knew she had much to be grateful for and was in no doubt that the healing process was all down to this family she felt honoured to be a part of. She marvelled at their closeness, how they all pulled together, sharing every aspect of their lives. She doubted her wealthy acquaintances would ever begin to understand how she felt. But then, they had not faced the traumas she had suffered; neither had they experienced the warmth and sincerity of people they termed the dregs of society. She had done so herself, she thought, ashamed, until her harrowing experiences. In many respects, against all odds, her life had actually improved, she realised.

In all honesty she missed the financial security and all it had brought with it, but not, as she now knew, the shallowness of her previous existence. It was as though that life had belonged to someone else and she herself was now an onlooker.

It suddenly occurred to her that if she was given the choice of returning or staying as she was, even with her future so uncertain, the decision would be an extremely difficult one to make.

Without warning a profound thought struck and her feeling of well-being rapidly disintegrated. Tears pricked the back of her eyes, her head drooped and she gazed distractedly into her mug.

Flo meanwhile leaned back in her rocker and momentarily closed her eyes. How nice it was to come home to a warm room and the dinner on the go, even if part of it looked suspect. Now that her worries concerning Jack and Ally had ceased she had been able to relax and once again concentrate her efforts on their daily survival. She had been astounded when Jack had gruffly told her the very morning after her go at him that he agreed with all she had said and on that score she was not to worry any more. She knew by the look of pain in his eyes that his decision had been difficult, but regardless her opinion had not changed. A romantic attachment between those two would only lead to heartache.

She opened her eyes and secretly studied Ally over the rim of her mug. She had thought that having her around would be a hindrance, annoying, fully believing the girl's background would prohibit her from ever fitting in with their own contrasting lifestyle. She had been wrong. Never had she heard Ally complain about anything or caught her even once looking down her nose. Flo had fully expected her to and purposely kept an eye out for it in order to collect ammunition so she could have an excuse to ask her to leave. The girl had totally astounded her by how hard she'd worked at fitting in – basically just getting on with it.

And having her here did have its bonuses. Certainly the bit of extra money she brought in was making a difference, despite the costs of her mistakes, and it was nice to have another woman to talk to and share the chores which in turn meant that, as now, she could occasionally sit and have a cup of tea after her long day at work and not sup it on the hop, risking indigestion.

She smiled inwardly. Ally was certainly having an impact on all of them with her gentle ways and cultured tones. Flo had caught herself on more than one occasion using one of Ally's expressions or carefully pronouncing her words to sound more refined. In fact everyone's manners were steadily improving, especially the children's. They did not gobble their food so much; pleases and thank yous were more readily forthcoming, Emily's stomach no longer thought her throat had been cut – she was just hungry; and Ally was certainly opening all their minds to things that their previous ignorance had left them impervious to. Yes, she had to admit, having Ally around had been a good move and it suddenly struck her that she would be sad when the time did come for them to part company.

She smiled across at her fondly and frowned to see that Ally was gazing down into her empty mug. She looked very thoughtful. No, not thoughtful, she was upset about something.

'A' you all right, me duck?' Flo leaned forward. 'Ally, I asked if you were all right?'

Her head was slowly raised and a pair of eyes were fixed distractedly on Flo. 'I beg your pardon? Were you addressing me, Flo?'

Who the bloody hell did you think I was addressing? Flo thought in exasperation. 'I was. I asked if yer were all right?'

'Why, yes, thank you.'

Her tone told Flo all was far from right. 'No, you ain't, gel. Yer upset about summat, I can see. What is it?'

'It's nothing, really. I . . . I was just thinking, that's all.'

'You know what thought does, gel. It gives yer brainache. Come on, a problem shared . . . It ain't owt ter do with old Cod Eyes, is it? He ain't pestering you or . . .'

'Oh, no, Flo, really.' She smiled. 'Mr Sileby only has designs on you. I think the man is well and truly smitten. I'm sure he only agreed to give me a chance at the job to get into your good books.'

'I suspect yer right on that, gel, but he'll get nowhere.' Flo shuddered. 'The man meks my skin creep.'

'Yes, he does mine. But his appreciation of you comes as no surprise. You are a very attractive woman, Flo.'

Flo smiled, pleased at the compliment.

Ally studied her for a moment. Unusually for a hard-working woman of her age, Flo's skin still had the bloom of youth; her womanly figure was still firm for a mother of two, breasts still high. But most noticeable to Ally was that she carried herself straight and proud, so unlike the majority of her class who, through poor diet, lack of money and sheer exhaustion, usually stooped submissively whilst dragging their feet, dirty, undernourished children clinging to their skirts. As she gazed at her now Ally thought Flo positively beautiful as she sat before the fire, light from the embers and the oil lamp hanging from the ceiling to the side of her highlighting her natural blonde hair which she had piled up on her head, curly tendrils framing her face. Before she could stop herself Ally said: 'I am surprised you haven't married again.'

Flo raised her head and eyed her sharply. 'Again!'

Her abrupt tone startled Ally and she suddenly worried she had spoken out of turn. 'What I said was meant as a compliment. I meant no disrespect to your late husband,' she said apologetically.

'I'm sure yer didn't,' Flo snapped shortly. 'Now yer never told me what's upsetting yer so much?'

Ally stared, confused by her blatant changing of the subject. For a fleeting moment it crossed her mind that maybe Flo's marriage had not been as happy as Ally herself had assumed.

'Are yer missing your old life, is that it, Ally? After what you must have lived like, coming back down to this level must have bin a terrible shock.'

Ally flinched. Would her lie always keep surfacing? She clasped her hands. 'I had grown used to the kind of life I was living, so of course the changes I faced were hard to adjust to. There are some things I do still miss, I wouldn't be truthful if I said I did not. Though I'm being selfish, I suppose.' She did not want to say to Flo that she missed her silk underwear, her wardrobe full of beautiful clothes and having her hair done, to name just a few. 'I miss being able to buy good soap for my bath.'

Flo smiled. 'Yes, there is summat nice about pampering yerself with a nice smelly bit of soap. Still, carbolic washes just as clean. Personally I never hanker after what I can't have. I just content meself with what I've got.' She leaned forward and gazed into the fire. 'I have much to be thankful for. I've got the love of me family and me self-respect. Not much in some people's eyes, but it's enough fer me.'

Ally stared at her thoughtfully. She now knew to her cost that material possessions did not always bring happiness. Her eyes darted around the sparsely furnished room, marks from the flood on the whitewashed walls still apparent regardless of their having been thoroughly scrubbed several times. But despite the grimness of their living conditions, the poverty they had to contend with, this house was filled with so much love. Flo was right. The gift of true love, from man, woman or child, was far more precious than anything money could buy. A surge of envy rushed through her for what Flo so deservingly possessed. If ever she herself was lucky enough to be blessed with even a fraction of it, she would be more than happy.

'So, are yer gonna spit it out or what?' Flo fixed her eyes on Ally's. 'Look, lovey, I know when someone's got summat on their mind, and you have. I'm only trying ter help, yer know.'

She sighed. Flo was not going to give up. 'You are right. I am a little down. It . . . well . . . it's my birthday today.'

'Your birthday! Why didn't yer say summat?'

She shrugged her shoulders. 'I didn't feel it was important.' Besides, she thought, she had desperately tried to forget about the date. This was, after all, the day she'd been supposed to come into her inheritance, and also the day she'd been going to marry. All harrowing memories that she had hoped she could keep buried.

'Of course it's important,' Flo scolded. 'We always try to do summat special in this house on birthdays. How old are yer today?'

'I'm twenty-one.'

'Twenty-one? Oh, my Lord, that's worse. Twenty-one. Yer've come of age, gel, and that really should be celebrated. The kids'll be right disappointed and I know Jack would have wanted to mark the occasion as he always does with us.'

Ally lowered her head and gazed intently at her clasped hands. She could understand the children wanting to do something, they never hid their fondness for her. But Jack? Since Christmas night his approach towards her had changed drastically. It was readily apparent how he strove to avoid any contact between them. And she had been so positive he had been on the verge of instigating some sort of relationship. How wrong she had been. His total change of attitude towards her was thoroughly bewildering and hurtful, considering her own liking for him. It was the one thing that blighted her life more than her job at the fish market.

She realised Flo was talking. 'I beg your pardon? What were you saying.'

'I was just wondering out loud what I could do. It's too late to mek a cake or get you a present. Oh . . .' Her eyes suddenly sparkled. 'Maybe I do have a present for yer which I think you'll be chuffed with.' She noticed the look on Ally's face. 'Don't worry, gel, it didn't cost me owt.' She leaned forward, face wreathed in pleasure. 'What if I told yer that yer don't have ter work at the fish market no more? Neither of us does.'

Ally looked confused. 'I don't understand?'

Flo laughed gleefully. 'I've got us another job! That was me errand.'

'Another job?'

'That's what I said, gel. At Tyler's, the warehouse on Rutland Street. I heard they were teking on, and yer can't hang around when yer hear rumours like that. Not sure exactly what we'll be doing, more 'an likely packing boxes with boots and shoes. To be honest, I don't care so long as it ain't fish. We start at seven-thirty on Monday morning.'

'But they haven't even met me!'

'They ain't met Ada nor Betty neither.'

'What have Ada and Betty to do with it?'

'I got them jobs too.' Flo rubbed her hands excitedly. 'Oh, I wish I could see old Cod Eyes's face when none of us turns up on Monday.'

'Is it really true, Flo? We really needn't go to the fish market ever again?'

'That's right, gel. Not ever again. We got our pay today and I think me and you deserve a Sat'day off. I can't remember the last time I never worked on a Sat'day. Oh, what bliss!'

'Oh, Flo, Flo!' Ally cried ecstatically, clapping her hands together in delight. 'This news is really the best birthday present you could ever have given me. I can't believe it. We don't have to get up at three in the morning. And, oh, Flo, never to reek of fish again!'

'Yeah, won't that be a blessing? And I won't have ter put up with old Cod Eyes leering and meking his insinuating remarks.'

Ally looked worried. 'Shouldn't we give Mr Sileby some sort of warning?'

'I don't see why. We've all worked our guts out, and yeah, so he paid us what mingy bit it was for all we did – but he treated us worse than galley slaves. He never gave his workers consideration so why should we him?'

Ally stared at her thoughtfully. 'Yes, you are right, Flo,' she said gravely. 'Why should we indeed?' She raised her head and sniffed. 'The sausages . . . Flo, the sausages are burning.'

'Oh, my God,' she cried, springing up. 'So they is – are,' she corrected herself, grabbing the frying pan and looking at the contents grimly. She looked across at Ally and grinned wickedly. 'Not quite burned to a cinder, but when you cook it's what we expect.'

Ally's face fell, then she realised Flo was having fun with her and laughed along with her. They were still laughing when the children burst in.

'Tommy's mam told us ter come home, said she'd had enough of kids fer one day. Dinner's late tonight, Ma, ain't it?' Emily complained. 'I'm really hungry an' all.' She plonked herself at the table, looking at Flo and Ally expectantly.

123

Flo was doing her best to salvage the gravy while Ally was attempting to mash the potatoes which had practically boiled away to nothing.

'Don't yer mean yer stomach thinks yer throat's bin cut?' Flo replied, a twinkle in her eye as she stirred vigorously.

'No, I don't,' snapped Emily with conviction. 'Young ladies don't say things like that. That right, Ally?'

She looked across at the 'young lady'. Her fair hair was all tousled, the hem of her grey school dress coming down, the white pinafore over the top as grubby as if it hadn't been washed for at least a month when in fact it was clean on that morning, and she had obviously lost the elastic bands that held up her socks. She looked more of a street urchin than a young lady. Keeping her face straight was extremely difficult for Ally. 'That's correct, Emily,' she said matter-of-factly. 'Young ladies do wash their hands first, though, before they sit up at the table.'

'Since when 'as our Emily bin a young lady?' piped up Eric.

'We'll have less of that from you,' erupted Flo. 'And yer can get your hands washed an' all. By the looks on 'em, spuds could grow. What a' you and Tommy bin up to?'

'Nowt,' Eric replied sheepishly, sidling off into the kitchen.

Flo opened her mouth to question him further, but decided it best she didn't know.

They were all just about to sit down at the table when Jack popped his head around the door. 'Hello, Ma, kids.' He flashed a fleeting glance at Ally. 'Ally,' he acknowledged stiltedly.

Her happy mood abruptly vanished. Why is Jack so dismissive of me? she thought, sighing heavily, wishing she knew just what it was she had done to warrant his manner. Regardless, his appearance still made her heart thump madly and she hoped no one noticed.

Jack stood in the kitchen jostling alongside Emily and Eric for use of the sink. So distracted was he the children, splashing water everywhere, might as well not have been there. His decision and promise not to pursue a relationship with Ally was proving more difficult than he could ever have envisaged. He had thought he was strong enough to quash his feelings, bury them deep, but that was not so. If anything his liking for her was growing stronger. His burden would have been far easier to bear had he not had to face her daily, but equally the thought of never seeing her again was something he knew he could not cope with. He stood staring into space as he dried his hands, vehemently wishing he had never made his promise to Ma.

'Jack, Ma's talking to yer.'

'Eh? What was that, Emily?' His eyes went to the child staring back up at him.

'I said,' Flo bellowed, 'you're home early tonight?'

'Oh, yeah,' he called back. 'We had a couple of late orders that needed delivering and I volunteered. Mr Green said when I'd done them I could make an early night of it.'

'He's a nice man, is that Mr Green. You're really lucky, yer know, to have that job, our Jack.'

He absently shook his head knowing luck had nothing to do with it. Mr Green was being extra kind to him because he was still under the mistaken illusion that Jack was considering a liaison with his daughter. He sighed disconsolately. Maybe the answer to his problem was right under his nose. Marriage to Lizzie would put a stop to his pointless hankering after Ally. He rubbed his chin. Maybe he should give Mr Green's proposal some serious thought.

Making his way to the table he sat down and smiled appreciatively at Flo as she put a plate in front of him. 'This looks good, Ma.'

Flo winked secretively at Ally, then scanned her eyes across them all. 'Well, tuck in then before it gets cold.'

The usual babble of conversation was lacking that evening. They were all too hungry to ask and answer questions until they had eaten. Surprisingly the meal Ally had cooked with Flo's help was most palatable and her enjoyment of it was only marred by the tension she felt between Jack and her. It was painfully obvious as she covertly eyed him now and again that he was working hard at avoiding her eyes. His own looked everywhere but in her direction.

When all the plates were wiped clean, Flo sat back and eyed them each in turn. 'Well,' she demanded. 'What did yer think?'

All but Ally frowned quizzically.

'It was grand, Ma, as it usually is,' Jack answered. 'So why are yer asking?'

'Yeah, why, Ma?' the children echoed.

'I just wanted yer opinion 'cos, yer see, I never cooked it. Ally did.'

All eyes were on Ally.

'You did?' said the children in awe.

'It was very good,' Jack said blandly.

Ally blushed with pleasure. 'I'm glad you enjoyed it.' She did wish though that he had shown just a little more enthusiasm.

'Also,' Flo said, 'it's Ally's birthday today, so the meal is extra special 'cos, as you know, on birthdays in this house you get a day off from the chores.'

Emily jumped down from her chair at the table and rushed over to Ally and hugged her fiercely. 'Happy Birthday, Ally. I ain't got nowt for yer.'

Ally smiled. 'Your kiss is sufficient.'

Jack eyed her secretly. How he longed to mark the occasion in a special way. But he knew that, under the circumstances, even the suggestion to Ma was out of the question.

Flo had just suggested that they all sing 'Happy Birthday' when there was a loud thumping at the front door.

'Now who the hell can that be?' said Flo, scraping back her chair.

'Maybe it's the woman that called on Tommy's mam,' said Emily.

'What woman?' Flo called back as she headed out of the room.

Moments later she was back. 'Wrong house,' she muttered, annoyed, sitting down again. Folding her arms, she leaned them on the table and turned her full attention on Emily. 'Now what woman were you going on about?'

'She means the lady that called earlier,' replied Ally. 'I had just begun to tell you about her but we got on to something else and it slipped my mind.'

'What did this woman want?'

'She was after details about the children because . . .'

'Details! What sorta details!' Flo demanded, face paling alarmingly.

Ally frowned. There was a look on Flo's face that she couldn't fathom. She was conscious that Jack too was staring at her. 'Just their names and ages because . . .'

Eyes filling with terror, Flo sprang to her feet. 'What did yer tell her? Ally, what did yer tell her?'

'The truth. Have I done something wrong?'

The terror in Flo's eyes turned to sheer horror and her hand went to her mouth. 'Oh, my God!' She spun to face Jack. 'Jack! Oh, Jack . . .'

He jumped up to join her and grabbed hold of her arm. 'Ma, calm down . . .'

'Don't tell me ter calm down,' she cried, wrenching free from his grasp. 'This is just what I dreaded. I knew it! I knew one day . . .' She made a dash for the kitchen, grabbed her coat and yanked open the door. 'Start packing,' she ordered before disappearing through it.

Utterly bewildered, Ally turned to Jack. 'What on earth is going on?'

'Please don't ask me, Ally. Come on, kids, move yerselves. Eric, Emily, both mek a start on the bedrooms. And no fighting.'

'Ah, do we have ter, our Jack? We ain't long bin here. And we like it here, don't we, Emily?'

Tears filling her eyes, Emily sniffed and nodded.

Jack shrugged his shoulders helplessly. 'Now, kids, don't give me no arguments, you know the drill.' They both nodded reluctantly, got down from the table and ran up the stairs. He turned to Ally. 'Would you make a start on the kitchen? Just pack as best yer can. Then carry on in here. I'm off to get a handcart. Though God knows where I'll put me hands on one this late in the day.'

She caught his arm. 'But why, Jack?' she implored.

'Ally, I said no questions.'

His tone was sharp and final but regardless she ventured on: 'Where are we going?'

'Ma will tell us that as soon as she gets back.'

As she watched him rush away her thoughts raced frantically but however much she tried no plausible answer would come to warrant the blind terror she had witnessed in Flo caused simply by a woman calling at their door. It was however obvious that it had something to do with the children. What, though? What could possibly be so bad that they had to move from this house this very night? Then an even more worrying thought reared. Would she herself be asked to go with them? She was earning just about enough money now to afford a simple lodging for herself. But she didn't want that. She wanted to stay with this family who had come to mean so much to her.

Chapter Sixteen

Jack lit the lamp and stared in shock around the room of the dwelling Flo had guided them to. 'Ma, this place is dreadful. We can't possibly stay here.'

'We can and we will. And it ain't that bad,' she said defensively, placing an armful of possessions down on the earth floor. 'We've lived in worse.'

'That we ain't, Ma. There ain't nowhere on God's earth as bad as this.' Jack exhaled loudly. The single-storey, two-roomed cottage, situated off the Sanvey Gate, roughly half a mile from Leicester town, was one of a row of six engulfed by rows and rows of back-to-back terraces built in the 1820s. The cottages had been there a hundred years before that. They were riddled with damp, infested with bugs, and freezing wind whipped through the badly fitting window frames and rotting door. The people living in the terraces were amongst the poorest in the town. Poverty at its severest reigned among the five other families who resided in the adjoining dwellings. There wasn't the luxury of a privy, only a foul-smelling midden, and contaminated water was collected from an ancient rusting pump at the end of the row. As he gazed around Jack felt he had arrived in hell.

'You can put the stuff back on the handcart, Ma, we ain't staying here.'

Flo spun to face him, filled with alarm. 'We can't go back, Jack. I won't go back. I daren't risk it. It's only fer a couple of nights 'til I find summat else.'

'Ma, I couldn't stay one night in this place. And what about the kids?'

'The kids, Jack, as you well know, are the only reason we're here.' Her shoulders sagged despairingly. 'Look, I know it's bad, I was loath to take it meself, but I had no choice.' She forced a smile on to her drawn face. 'It won't look so bad when we've a fire lit, and once we get our bits and pieces sorted it'll seem quite cosy.'

Nothing they did, he thought, would ever make this place cosy. He looked across at Flo and a great surge of love for the woman who had cared for and raised him since before he could walk filled his being. She was the strongest woman he knew but also the most unselfish and what she had done tonight had been all because of her love for those two young children he regarded as his brother and sister. He strode towards her and gathered her to him, hugging her tightly. 'Don't worry, Ma. We'll mek the best of it.'

She rested her head wearily on his shoulder. 'Oh, Jack, thanks,' she whispered, sniffing back tears. 'I'm so sorry I've had to drag us all down to this.' She lifted her head and gazed around. 'It's terrible, ain't it? I pity the poor souls who have no chance of ever getting out. But . . .' she sniffed again, bringing her eyes back to his, '. . . you understand, don't yer?'

He took hold of her shoulders and held her at arm's length. 'I've understood all the other times we've moved, ain't I?' A twinkle lit his eyes. 'But this move has to go down as the quickest.'

'And the worst.'

He laughed. 'Most definitely.'

'First thing tomorrow, Jack, I promise yer, I'll be out looking, rest assured on that.'

He bent and kissed her forehead. 'You'd better.'

'I have me eye on summat. Have had for a while, in fact. I'll go and check it out first thing.'

'Always something up yer sleeve, eh, Ma? Well, let's get tonight over with first. I'll go and see what the others are up to, then I'll light a fire.'

Despite exhaustion Ally could not sleep. Her mind was too full, going over and over the unexpected events of the last few hours. She was also extremely uncomfortable and cold, drawing hardly any warmth from Emily or Flo squashed beside her. The mattress had been placed on the hard uneven earth floor, it being far too late in the evening to contemplate the task of bolting together the iron bedstead. That was still in pieces on the cart along with most of their other possessions, covered by tarpaulin and hidden out of sight. No explanation for the sudden move had been offered, she had just been herded along with the rest. What could not be balanced on the handcart had been carried. Alongside Emily and Eric, feeling grateful to be included, Ally had obediently followed Flo and Jack, he straining every muscle to push the heavily laden cart down the dark streets seemingly for miles, though in reality it could only have been around two before they reached their destination.

After their initial upset the children had taken matters in their stride and not said a word either way as just the essential items they needed for that night had been unloaded and carried in. Not so herself. She had stared in horror on seeing where Flo was expecting them to live. She had thought the little terrace on Walnut Street dreadful but now she knew that house had been luxury in comparison to this. It had taken great strength of will to force away her feeling of absolute revulsion, stifle all questions and help with the unloading.

How she wished she knew why Flo had done what she had but still nothing had been said to justify such stringent actions. She frowned deeply. She had seen another side of Flo tonight. A nervous Flo, strained and jumpy, completely different in fact from the woman she had come to like and respect, and this sudden change in her was of grave concern to Ally.

She felt a movement beside her. Flo was rising. She obviously couldn't sleep either. In the near pitch darkness Ally could just make out her shapely figure as she grabbed her coat off the bed, wrapped it around herself and made her way across the room.

Flo reached the window and peered out through the shredded piece of grimy sacking wafting eerily in the icy draughts which came through the rotting frame. She sighed desolately. She was terribly tired, desperate for sleep, but the terror she had experienced earlier was still hanging over her. So intense was it, it seemed to her to have seeped into every pore. No matter how hard she tried she could not rid her mind of the mental image of a stranger calling at their door asking for details of the children. During the last ten years, that had been her one dread. There could be only one reason for the woman to be asking those questions. And she knew who the woman was, had no doubt of her identity.

Flo clasped her hands and wrung them tightly. Despite her own evasive actions, what if the woman had managed to follow them? What if she was out there now, waiting? At the thoughts renewed panic rushed through her and she violently shuddered as her eyes scanned the dark courtyard. Suddenly her eyes fixed on an object and she gasped in terror. The woman was there! She was watching them!

At the sound of Flo's gasp, Ally sprang up from the mattress and across the room. She grabbed Flo's shoulders and pulled her around and was almost frozen rigid by the look of acute fear on the older woman's face.

'Flo, what is it? What on earth is wrong?'

She fought for breath, the sheer panic she was experiencing constricting her throat. 'It's . . . it's her,' she stuttered. 'It's . . . it's the woman.' Her trembling finger pointed at the window.

'Woman? What woman?' Ally released her and stared out, scanning her eyes across the courtyard. She turned back to face Flo. 'There's no one out there.'

'She is, I tell yer. Down by the last cottage. She's standing there watching us.'

Once again Ally looked out of the window. 'Flo, that's the pump.'

'The . . . the pump? Are yer sure?'

'Yes, I'm sure. Look for yourself.'

Tentatively Flo peered out, her eyes darting all ways. They settled on the water pump and she studied it hard, then her whole body sagged in relief. But despite her mistake she wasn't completely convinced and another wave of panic gripped her. 'Ally, I know she's out there, I just know it.'

Ally stared at her, bewildered. The older woman's fear was beginning to affect her also. 'Flo, listen to me. There is no one out there.'

Flo's voice rose hysterically. 'Ally, I can *feel* her. She's out there, I know it. We have to get out of here. Get away. And there's no time ter lose.'

Ally's mind whirled frantically. In all her life she had never witnessed such terror in a person. If she didn't do something quickly Flo would make herself ill. She grabbed Flo's arms and, using all her strength, pushed her down into her rocker. Placing her own hands firmly on the chair's arms, legs astride, she blocked Flo's exit. 'Now take a deep breath,' she commanded. 'Come on, Flo. That's it. Now another.' She thrust her face forward. 'Listen to me, there is no one watching you.'

'A' yer sure, Ally? Really sure?'

She nodded. 'Trust me, Flo. I'm sure.'

Her whole body slumped and she buried her face in her hands. 'Oh, God, dear God,' she groaned. 'I'm going mad, Ally. I'm imagining things now.'

Her obvious pain affected Ally deeply. Flashing a hurried glance across to Emily, who thankfully was still sound asleep, she felt her way across to the jug of water and poured out a mugful. She kneeled down before Flo. 'Sip this,' she whispered, taking one of Flo's hands and putting the mug into it. 'I'd have made you a cup of tea but the fire is out.'

As Flo followed her orders Ally watched her thoughtfully. It pained her greatly to see the woman who had been so kind to her in such dreadful anguish. This woman needed help. What help she could offer Ally was not at all sure, but she had to offer something. But before she could decide what kind of help was required, she would have to ask some questions.

She took a deep breath. 'Why are you so frightened of this woman, Flo? Just what is it she has done to you?'

Flo slowly lifted her head and stared at her blankly. 'Done ter me? She ain't done nothing ter me, Ally. It's what *I've* done to *her*.' She raised her hand and wiped away tears. Suddenly an overwhelming need to unburden herself to this young woman she had reluctantly come to admire and like overrode all else, and before she could remind herself of the consequences of doing so, she blurted: 'She's come for her children.'

Ally frowned, mystified. 'Come for her children? But I don't understand. What children are . . .' Her frown turned to shock as realisation struck her. 'Are you referring to Emily and Eric?'

Flo lowered her head, hands clasped tightly. 'I stole 'em, Ally.'

She gasped, completely astounded. 'Stole them!' she finally uttered. 'Why?'

Flo took several deep breaths. 'I had good reason. If you'll listen to me, I'll tell yer.'

Ally took her trembling hand and gripped it. Despite her own shock at this revelation, she instinctively knew that Flo's reasons for doing this

131

terrible thing would be valid. She knew her well enough to know that. 'I'm listening, Flo,' she whispered.

Flo's eyes grew misty as she stared distractedly across the dark room and began her harrowing story.

'It was eleven years ago or thereabouts. To be honest, it seems like forever. It seems those children have always bin mine. It's funny but it's the weather that sticks in me mind. It was the middle of July and it was so hot. Stifling hot. If it'd bin cold I doubt any of this would have happened. So I suppose if I wanted to blame anything, I could the weather.' She paused for a moment and smiled distantly. 'I was getting married in the August. Malcolm Carpenter his name was. Lovely man. Kind, considerate, all yer could want in a husband. And he looked on Jack as his own, was so good to the boy. He had his own butcher's shop in a village called Cosby.'

Ally knew the village, she had ridden through it on many occasions with Lionel. She remembered the village green complete with pond, ducks and swans, and the times they had dismounted and partaken of refreshment at the Cherry Tree Inn, sitting under the huge oak tree in front.

'It was a Sat'day afternoon,' Flo continued, 'and when Malcom had finished for the day he was taking us for a picnic. His mother was coming too. Nice woman, his mother. Treated me all right, she did, considering her son was about to marry a woman with a . . . young lad in tow. We lived in lodgings in Barwell because I worked for the Hinckley cottage hospital laundry. Hard work it was, but it was a job and just about kept me and Jack. I'd met Malcolm at Barwell village dance. I wasn't going ter go, but Mrs Kitchen, that were me landlady, said she'd mind Jack. So with a couple of other gels from work, I did meself up as best I could and off I trotted. Malcolm asked me ter dance soon after I got there and that were that.

'Me and Jack were looking forward to the picnic. Malcolm had promised to fish with Jack down by the river. He was so excited. He'd made a fishing pole, and right proud of it he was. Cosby was a few miles from where we lived and we could have paid for a ride on a cart, but I decided to walk. God knows why. It was far too hot for walking. But the fare I saved could be put towards a treat for Jack.

'We'd gone more than halfway when he complained he was thirsty. I was meself. I should have carried some water with us but I hadn't given it a thought. Me mind was too full of me forthcoming wedding. We passed by a track leading off through some trees. There was a plaque nailed on one of the trunks which read, "Lavender Cottage". It sounded so pretty and I thought the kindly old soul I imagined lived there would gladly part with a drop of water and maybe offer us a seat for a few minutes.'

Flo abruptly stopped her narrative as her face contorted in pain, her eyes filling with tears as memories she would sooner forget flooded back.

'Oh, Ally, I will never, ever forget the sight that met us as the track suddenly ended and we came to a clearing.'

'What was it?' she whispered, squeezing Flo's hand reassuringly but herself tensing in apprehension of what was to come.

'It wasn't an it, Ally,' she said, sniffing hard. 'It was everything. Despite what me eyes were seeing it was the smell that struck me first. I've never smelt owt like it and, believe me, working in a hospital laundry you got to smell all there was. Or so I thought. It was death, decay . . .' She shuddered violently. 'There was a cottage all right but if you think this place is bad, that was all but a ruin. There was hardly a roof and the walls were barely standing. The garden I'd imagined to be filled with pretty flowers was overgrown with weeds, some so tall they reached under the eaves. There was rubbish strewn everywhere. By the hedge at the side was a carcass – a dead dog, I think, it was difficult to tell. Big black birds were pecking at it and I could see rats lurking.' She shuddered again and her voice fell to a bare whisper. 'Then I saw him.' She paused again and took several deep choking breaths. 'There was a dog's collar around his neck, a thick chain running to the wall. He was stark naked and that filthy, caked in his own muck, no skin showing. He was just sitting, staring, a little skinny puppy nestled into his side. He was hardly more than a baby.'

Ally gasped, too shocked to speak. She knew Flo was speaking of Eric.

'Then I heard a noise and grabbed hold of Jack and pulled him close as a man appeared in the cottage doorway. He was drunk, Ally. He was that drunk he could hardly stand. He was ragged and dirty, with a mass of matted black hair and a straggling beard reaching down to his chest. He had a stone bottle in his hand and kept drinking from it. Then he shouted something and a woman staggered out. She was as filthy as him, and thin. I can remember thinking I had never seen such a thin woman. Her cheekbones protruded that much her eyes had sunk right into her head. She was carrying a gun. A long gun, the type farmers use. He snatched it from her. Then he grabbed her shoulder and pushed her forward. "Come on," he shouted. "We ain't got all day."

'As he stumbled off the step his boot caught the boy's leg and he started to whimper. He couldn't cry, Ally. He was too weak to cry . . .' Her voice trailed off.

'What happened then?' Ally gently urged.

'The man kicked him. He kicked him that hard his little body left the ground. And the puppy barked. So he kicked it too.'

'What did the woman do?'

'Nothing. She did nothing. I must have made a noise or summat then, or Jack did, because he looked across at us. "What d'you . . . effing want?" Nothing, nothing, I said. We'd just got lost. He raised his gun and pointed it straight at us.'

'He aimed at you!' Ally mouthed, stunned.

Flo nodded. ' "Well, eff off out of it. Go on, clear off." And he cocked the hammer. I grabbed Jack and we ran and hid behind a hedge in a field. I can't describe how I felt, Ally. What we'd seen was so bad I wondered if I'd imagined it all. It was only moments after that we heard the pair of 'em. They'd come into the field. They passed so close it's a wonder they didn't see us. Huddled in that hedge we sat and watched until they disappeared. Jack took me hand and looked at me. He read me mind. He knew I couldn't leave that little boy and neither could he. Without saying a word we went back. He was just lying there, curled up by the wall with the puppy. We were worried about them coming back and I couldn't get the collar off, I was shaking that much. Jack did it. I picked the boy up. Oh, Ally, he weighed nothing and I cuddled him to me and he held himself so stiffly and never made a sound. He'd never been cuddled before. Then I heard a noise coming from inside the cottage. I hesitated for a minute before I went to investigate. Oh, Ally, Ally . . .'

Flo groaned in anguish and gripped Ally's hand so tightly she nearly cried out in pain. 'There was a baby, only months old, a sparrow of a thing as dirty as the boy. It was lying in a box. Without a thought I gave the boy to Jack, found a piece of rag to cover it and grabbed it up. Then we ran. We ran as quick as we could and never stopped 'til I'd no more breath in me. It wasn't 'til we stopped I realised that Jack also had the puppy.'

'Sal?'

Flo nodded. 'Sal, bless her heart.' She released her grip on Ally's hand and rubbed her cheeks wearily. 'Now yer know why I did it. But I had no choice, had I? No self-respecting woman could have left those kids. But when all's said and done, I took a woman's children and no judge in the land would pardon me for that.'

'She did not deserve them, Flo,' Ally said icily, wiping tears of distress from her eyes.

'That's maybe so, but what I did amounts to kidnapping. The pair of them saw me and Jack, they know what we look like, and I've had the fear of God on me since that one day they'll find us. I don't regret what I did, Ally. I'd do it again. I'd risk jail. I'd go to hell and back fer the sake of those kids. But the dread I live with is them being forced ter go back to that life with those terrible people.' She sighed heavily. 'Not being able to settle in one place fer long ain't fair to the kids and it ain't fair to Jack but the alternative . . . well . . .'

Choked, Ally stroked Flo's hand. 'What you did was a wonderful thing, Flo. You have given those children a life. Do they know any of this?'

'Oh, no,' she said softly, gripping Ally's hand. 'And they mustn't. To them I'm their mother.'

'And a better mother they could never have.'

'I've tried me best.'

'What happened then, Flo, after you ran off with the children?'

Her mind flew back again. 'Well, I couldn't take 'em back to Mrs Kitchen's, for all she was a lovely landlady. She'd have questioned me about the sudden appearance of two poor little waifs. Jack told me about an abandoned old shed on the edge of the village where kids used ter play so we made our way there and took refuge. I despatched him ter Mrs Kitchen's to collect our stuff and tell her a cock and bull story that I'd had word from some distant relatives that needed us and we wouldn't be back.

'After I'd got as much milk as I could down 'em, the next task was washing. My God, Ally, that ground-in filth was hard to shift.' She gravely shook her head. 'It was what lay underneath that made me cry. The baby was covered in hideous sores, her little bottom red raw, hardly any skin on her from lying in her own muck. As for the boy, I don't think there was an inch on him that wasn't bruised or wealed. For the next three days all me and Jack's time was spent nursing those kids, trying to get some strength back in 'em. I thought we'd lose the baby, she was such a pitiful little thing. I sometimes wonder how they'd lived so long considering how starved they were and the brutality they suffered.' A smile lit her face. 'She survived. They both did, thank the Lord. We called them Eric and Emily. Emily was my mother's name. Jack chose Eric because he'd had a friend with that name and liked him. We obviously had to leave the area. I thought a town 'ud be best. People get swallowed up in a town. That's how we came to Leicester. I used the wedding money I'd saved to pay the rent on a squalid little place down by the canal, but once I'd cleaned it up it weren't too bad.' She cast her eyes around the room. 'It was better than this. I took any job I could get so long as it was nights, because of Jack's schooling, and we managed just about. The kids grew and thrived. But I was always afeared that the couple would come after us so to keep well ahead we kept moving house and I'd change jobs.' She sighed despairingly. 'And I thought I'd managed fine 'til tonight.'

'That woman who called, you thought it was her?'

'Who else could it be asking questions like that?'

'I can assure you it wasn't her, Flo. That woman was a representative from the Church. I did try to explain to you. After the damage the floods caused the hall was not fit to hold the children's Christmas party, but now it's all been rectified they've decided to organise it. She was making enquiries for numbers for the catering and also to help plan little presents for those who attend. She asked if you would be willing to contribute by way of some baking.'

Flo looked flabbergasted. 'Yer mean, I moved us to this hell hole fer no reason? Oh, God,' she groaned. Then suddenly a different fear filled her. For all these years she had kept this secret, now someone else knew. She eyed Ally worriedly. 'Now yer know all this, are yer . . .'

Ally raised her hand to stop her. 'Please do not concern yourself, Flo.

135

Your secret is safe with me. I think you are marvellous for what you have undertaken. Jack too.'

'You do?' she whispered, astonished.

'You are both to be admired. You have given up everything for the sake of those children and they in turn are a credit to you.'

Flo managed a smile. 'Yes, they are, ain't they? And I love 'em just as much as I would if I'd given birth to 'em. Jack has been wonderful. Without him I would never have managed. And never once 'as he complained over anything.'

'Well, I suppose he's repaying the kindness you showed him when he was very young. The circumstances are entirely different but . . .'

'Yes, I can see what yer getting at,' Flo snapped abruptly, much to Ally's astonishment. Then she smiled. 'I'm sorry, gel, I'm just so weary.' Then her face grew serious. 'You really ain't going to do anything about all this?'

'Flo, I feel honoured you have trusted me.'

Flo grabbed her hands and squeezed them tightly. 'You ain't a bit like the gentry, I'm glad ter say. And I mean that as a compliment.'

Ally eyed her quizzically. 'What exactly do you have against the gentry, Flo?'

Her face darkened. 'Let's just say I've me reasons, and good ones. But that's one story I'll never tell.' She rose awkwardly. 'I think I might be able to get some sleep now I know that woman's not lurking out there, and I've a lot to do in the morning.' Unexpectedly she leaned forward and kissed Ally affectionately on her cheek. 'Thanks fer listening to me and for yer understanding. I do feel bad that you've got the burden of this secret now. But, Ally, I also feel a little of the weight's bin lifted.'

A warm glow ran through Ally. It felt good that in some small way she had done something for this woman, even if it was only listening to her. She rose also and stretched her body which was aching painfully from spending so long on the floor. 'Bed sounds good to me too.' A question suddenly posed itself and Ally eyed Flo thoughtfully. 'Could I possibly ask one more thing?'

'What's that?'

'Malcolm, the man you were to marry, what happened about him?'

Flo sighed heavily. 'I struggled so hard with my conscience over Malcolm. He might have accepted me with Eric and Emily in tow, and understood why I did it, but I didn't feel it fair that he should carry such a burden. In the end I wrote him a note telling him that I'd changed me mind. I must have hurt him so badly. I still think of him, often. I loved him very much.' She smiled wanly. 'I hope he's found happiness. If anyone deserved happiness, Malcolm did.'

'The picture on the mantel in Walnut Street . . . it's of Malcolm, isn't it, Flo?'

She smiled and nodded. 'Yes, it's Malcolm,' she replied emotionally.

'When we get settled proper again I shall put it back in pride of place.'

His memory hurt, Ally could tell, and she watched thoughtfully as Flo felt her way over to the mattress, took off her coat which she laid on top then climbed inside, snuggling close to Emily. 'Come on, Ally,' she whispered. 'You'll catch yer death if yer ain't already.'

As Ally settled the covering around her, her heart filled with grief for Flo's plight. The woman had carried out a simple unselfish act of mercy. In all probability she had saved those children's lives yet even years later she was suffering greatly from her kind actions. That wasn't right. Ally felt strongly that Flo had enough to endure raising the children without the added possibility of that terrible couple searching for them and the aftermath should they succeed. But then Flo was right. Should any of this come to light, regardless of the reasons, she would be treated as a kidnapper and would face spending the rest of her life in jail. Ally shuddered at the thought.

Then a question posed itself and Ally frowned. What if the couple, for some reason, were not searching? She stared thoughtfully for several long moments. Then an idea began to form and a smile touched her lips. Maybe there was something she could do. She pondered for a moment, then nodded. It wasn't a bad idea, definitely one worth pursuing. Anything that would lead to the easing of Flo's burden was worth a try. She would embark on it first thing in the morning. She thought it best not to mention anything to Flo just in case her idea came to nothing.

Chapter Seventeen

Ally paused before the gate of the house. It appeared a neat place, the garden well-kept and come summer obviously full of colour. How different, she thought, to the dwelling she pictured nearby. On arriving at the entrance to the track Flo had described, she had lowered her head and hurried by. The faded sign was still nailed to the tree: 'Lavender Cottage'. Flo had been right, it did sound so pretty.

She had risen that morning before it was light as the rest of the family still slept soundly, and quietly as possible dressed herself as presentably as she could in the best clothes she possessed. Then, taking every penny she owned to pay for her fares and some breakfast, had hurriedly written a note on a scrap of paper she was lucky enough to find, telling Flo she had an errand to do and would be back later. She left the house and made straight for the railway station. There she had breakfasted on weak tea – all she could afford – and had boarded a train, travelling third-class, squashed on a hard wooden seat with a carriage full of other travellers. On reaching the nearest point to her destination, she had disembarked and walked three miles down a narrow rutted country lane until she had reached this house, which was the closest after the track leading to Lavender Cottage.

Normally she would be fatigued after such an early start, little sleep, the uncomfortable journey then a three-mile walk, but instead her heart thumped painfully at the thought of the act she was about to perform. She hoped she was up to it.

'Are you lost, my dear?'

Ally's head jerked around. In a corner of the garden stood a woman. She was extremely old and tiny and very rotund. She was dressed from head to toe in black, the only flash of colour being her iron-grey hair which was scraped back into a tight bun at the nape of her neck. She was smiling and had kindly eyes.

'Er . . . yes. Yes I am,' Ally said.

The woman tottered to the gate. 'Whereabouts are you looking for?' she asked, eyeing Ally keenly.

'Well, I am not exactly sure. A very close relative passed on recently and she always told me stories about where she grew up . . .'

'Oh, I see, dear,' the woman cut in. 'You're on a pilgrimage.'

'Er . . . yes, I suppose you could say that.'

'Well, you've stopped at the right gate because I've lived in this house all me married life and my husband's family before that. There isn't much concerning these parts that I don't know. My late husband, God rest his soul, was the local constable. So if there was anybody to be known, I'd know them.' She laughed, an infectious sound. 'And all about them.' She looked Ally up and down. 'You must be perished. Come inside and have a cuppa. I was just about to mash.'

'That is very kind of you.'

As she opened the gate Muriel Tittle smiled warmly. She hardly saw any visitors now and a natter with this pretty young woman would be most welcome. Muriel missed a good natter. As her friends had dwindled through death and her one daughter had moved quite a distance away through her husband's work, the days could stretch endlessly. A good natter over a cup of tea would brighten up this cold winter's day nicely.

Ally sat down in the comfortable armchair she was offered by the fire and loosened her coat. She had been right about the house. It was neat and clean and very homely. It seemed only moments before the old lady bustled through carrying a laden tray. 'I thought you could do justice to a couple of my scones. Made them fresh this morning. I must have known you were coming. Now then,' she said, sitting down opposite, 'tell me all about this grandmother of yours?'

'My grandmother? Oh, yes, my grandmother,' she repeated hurriedly realising the old lady had assumed that was the relative she'd talked of. As she accepted the cup of tea and scone, Ally felt a trace of guilt for deceiving this kindly woman, but then told herself it was all in a good cause. Putting Flo's mind at rest, if she achieved it, was a *very* good cause. 'My grandmother . . .'

'What was her name, dear?'

'I beg your pardon?'

'Her name. Your grandmother's?'

'Oh, Biddles.' She had chosen that name after seeing it over a shop as she had hurried by on her way to the station. 'Kathleen Biddles.'

Muriel pursed her lips thoughtfully. 'That name doesn't strike a bell. Can't remember any Biddleses living around these parts. Oh, there was . . . oh, no, that was Bunion. Any idea where she lived?'

'I remember her talking of a cottage, though the name escapes me. But it was a pretty-sounding name, a flower of some sort.' Ally paused slightly. 'Lavender Cottage maybe?'

Muriel's face fell. 'There's only one Lavender Cottage that I know of around here, though it can hardly be described as a cottage. It was built during Elizabethan times and a witch used to live there it is said.' She shuddered. 'Horrible place! It was derelict when I was a child. It's not fit to be occupied and never has been during my time. Oh, except of course by those dreadful people about twelve years ago. Pass me your cup, dear, I'll pour you another.'

'What . . . er . . . people were they?'

'Oh, you don't want to know about them, dear. Help yourself to sugar.'

But she *did* want to know about those people. 'Were they that dreadful?'

'Was what that dreadful?'

'Those people. Only from the way you spoke . . . I'm sorry, I was just intrigued.'

Muriel took the bait. She inched herself to the edge of her chair, eyes bright. 'Well, dreadful is not a strong enough word to describe those two, to my mind. Not that us locals hardly saw them. Kept very much to themselves. Where they came from is anyone's guess and how long they'd been living in the cottage no one was quite sure before John Talbot happened past. He got a gun aimed at him and profanities shouted that even he'd never heard, and him the landlord of the pub. So you can imagine, we all kept well clear. But let me tell you, my dear, I've never known filth like it. Gypsies have better habits. When the wind was blowing in the wrong direction, you could smell the stench a mile away so you can guess what it was like for me living so close. I just wish my Cyril had been alive. He'd have sorted them out. My Cyril wasn't frightened of anyone. He was a good copper was my Cyril. After all the trouble . . . Would you like another scone, I've plenty?'

'Thank you very much. They are very good.' She took a scone from the offered plate and placed it on her own. 'What trouble was that?'

Muriel frowned. 'Trouble, dear?'

'You were saying, after the trouble?'

'Oh, yes. The cottage was boarded up after the trouble. But it all started with the rumour of the child.'

Ally almost choked on her tea. 'Child?' she uttered.

'Yes, that's right, dear. It seems that some of the local lads used to go up to Lavender Cottage for a dare. Well, you know what children are like. School holidays stretching on and nothing to do. Well, one of the boys told his mother that he'd seen a child chained to the wall like a dog. Seen it several times, in fact. Well, at first she didn't believe him. Roland Makepeace had always been a liar. It's said the first words he ever spoke were "I didn't do it". Well, anyway, a couple of days later she was gossiping with another mother and she mentioned to Hetty Makepeace that her son had told her about a very young boy chained up like a dog at Lavender Cottage. Well, they told their husbands and you know how gossip spreads. Before the afternoon was out the whole village was up in arms about it.

'I remember the day like it was yesterday because of the weather. Isn't it funny, my dear, how little things can trigger a memory? Whenever it's unduly hot, I still think of that day. It was a Saturday and the weather was

140

stifling. You could have fried eggs on the cobbles. It was just after six and all of a sudden I heard the tramping of boots. I shot to my door and every one of the village men passed my gate, armed with pickaxes and shovels, anything they could get their hands on. They had murder in their eyes.

Muriel paused and eyed Ally in concern. 'Are you all right, dear, only you've gone white?'

'Yes, yes, thank you.' Tension was building inside her over what was coming. 'Please carry on,' she urged.

'They arrived at the cottage and all hell was let loose, I could hear it from here. Then I heard the gun go off. Twice.

'Apparently, when the men arrived at the clearing the couple were both slumped on the step. There were stone bottles lying everywhere. They were drunk, dear,' Muriel said disapprovingly. 'In the middle of the yard, amid piles of rubbish, Chad Makepeace spotted a sack out of the top of which poked the head of a dead pig. "Hey," he shouts, "that's my pig. The . . ." Well, he blasphemed then, dear, and it's not a nice word so I can't say it. Words to the effect of: "He's stolen my pig." At that this terrible man, who I think hadn't realised the village men were there, grabbed his gun, jumped up and ran towards them, aiming it at them. He was swearing something dreadful, words to the effect of "clear off". The woman then jumped up, waving her arms, screaming, "Don't shoot, Harry, don't shoot. They'll hang yer." He was in a right old rage by this time and spun round on her, shouting: "Will yer shut up, woman? You drive me mad." Then the gun goes off – bang, bang – and she drops down dead. The men overpowered him then and he was carted off to jail. When the trial came up he was sentenced to hang. It's a wonder you didn't read about it, it was in all the papers. But then, I suppose you'd have been too young.'

'Oh, my God,' gasped Ally.

'Yes, dreadful story, isn't it? And right on my own doorstep. We had nothing like it before and nothing since. When the place was cleared out, not one but four stills were found, all producing alcohol. There were piles of rotting potatoes and turnips.' She shuddered. 'And dead carcasses. Besides what they stole, it's reckoned they lived mostly off wild animals. Foxes and things. Ugh, disgusting!'

'And what of the rumours of the child?' asked a shocked Ally tentatively.

'Just rumours, dear. No sign of anything to do with there ever having been a child there. Mind you, there was the dog collar and chain the boys had described.' Muriel settled back in her chair, folding her arms under her full bosom. 'It's a blessing, if you ask me, that there were no offspring. Can you imagine what their lives would have been like? And after all, they'd have ended up in an orphanage. Yes, best there were none. You look better, dear, the colour's come back into your cheeks. Now how about I mash again?'

Ally did feel better. She felt positively jubilant. She had hoped to find out something to Flo's benefit, but had not dared hope for anything as momentous as this. She smiled warmly at her hostess. 'Thank you, but I really ought to be going. It's getting late and I have a train to catch.'

Muriel's face fell. 'Oh, but we haven't discussed your grandmother yet and after you making a special journey to visit where she used to live. I am sorry, taking up all time with that old story you maybe didn't want to hear.'

'That's quite all right, I found it interesting.' Ally rose and buttoned up her coat. 'With hindsight, I suppose I should really have armed myself with more facts before I embarked on this journey. For all I know I could be in completely the wrong area.' She held out her hand. 'Thank you so much for your hospitality. It has been a very pleasant afternoon.'

'For me too, dear. You make sure you come back, you'll find a welcome at my hearth any time.' Muriel suddenly frowned at her. 'Can I ask you something?'

'Yes, of course,' she replied tentatively.

'How did you come to speak so poshly?'

'Oh, er . . . my family's fortunes . . .'

'Oh, I see, dear,' Muriel interrupted. 'Family fell on hard times, did it?' She patted her arm. 'Happens to many, dear. Trouble is, the higher you are, the harder you fall. But you'll fare well, I can tell. I've a feeling you'll go far, dear. You really are such a pretty woman.'

Ally smiled warmly. 'Thank you.'

Muriel walked with her to the door. 'Take care now, my dear. Oh,' she cried, 'what time is it?' Leaving Ally standing bemused on the doorstep she disappeared back inside her house to reappear seconds later. 'It's just on four. Old Fred Houseman will be by any moment in his cart. Goes right to the station. He'll be glad to give you a lift.'

It was a weary Ally who walked into the near pitch black courtyard several hours later, but her tiredness was masked by overwhelming exhilaration. She could not wait to see Flo and divulge her news. Flo would be overjoyed that her fears were finally over and Ally felt so pleased that she had been able to do something, in a small way, to repay the kindness the woman had shown her. Part of her was sad for the stock the children came from, but Flo's stamp was set firmly on them now. They were all hers, showing nothing of their parentage, thank goodness. Now maybe they could settle in one place and build themselves a proper life.

As she arrived at the decaying cottage, she frowned. The place was in darkness. Surely they hadn't all retired to bed? She tried the door. It opened and she stepped inside where she stood for several moments accustoming her eyes, but even before she did all her instincts told her the place was empty. Her stomach lurched and she ran outside. The handcart that had been parked around the side of the cottage had gone. Slowly she retraced her steps and felt around, searching in case they had left her a note, anything, to say where they had gone. But she found nothing. Dread came over her and her eyes filled with tears.

Suddenly a presence filled the doorway. 'Ally, there you are,' Jack shouted joyfully. Before he could stop himself he came over and flung his arms around her, hugging her tightly. 'You had us all worried, we wondered where you were. I've bin back at least four times.'

She raised her eyes to his. 'Oh, Jack, I thought you'd all abandoned me.'

She looked so vulnerable, so beautiful, so inviting, his heart swelled with love and an overwhelming desire for her filled his being. He bent his head, intent on kissing her, but suddenly sprang back, shoving her from him. 'Ma's . . . er . . . kept yer dinner hot,' he blurted.

His voice was cold, emotionless, and Ally froze. 'That is very good of her,' she uttered, confused.

She lowered her head, sensing the tension between them, and for several moments they stood in awkward silence.

In Ally's mind was the fact that Jack had been so pleased to see her. His actions had not been those of a man who did not care. He'd been about to kiss her, she knew he had. So why, after his near display of affection, did he abruptly become so cold towards her? It didn't make sense.

Jack was struggling with his emotions, fighting to quash the sheer joy he felt over Ally's return. All day as he had laboured over his tasks her unexplained absence had worried him witless and he hadn't needed Ma's requests to keep returning to the cottage. Each time he found she hadn't come back, his heart had sunk lower, wondering all the time where she could have gone – had she, in fact, decided not to come back? Then this time, on finding her in the dwelling, he had been unable to control his emotions. Ally had felt so good against him, as though she belonged in his arms. Instinctively he had bent his head to kiss her – and as he had done so Ma's threat and his own promise had returned to him. Ma's threat was not an idle one and the thought of Ally's being banished was something he could not bear. Neither did Jack intentionally break his promises.

This situation must not happen again, he warned himself. In future he had to be stronger.

'We'd better get going,' he said coldly.

Ally stared at him, confused, before saying softly, 'Where to?'

'You'll see. I don't know what you'll make of it. It's different. Ma's certainly surprised us all this time. But,' he said critically, casting round his eyes, 'it's a vast improvement on this.'

Chapter Eighteen

'Where is this place, Jack?' Ally asked as he unlatched a wooden door inside a high brick wall, halfway down a long, dark alleyway, and ushered her inside. She knew they were somewhere near the centre of town but hadn't quite been able to get her bearings due to the speed at which Jack had hurried them along.

They had entered a big cobbled yard at the back of what appeared in the darkness of late evening to be a very large building. It looked empty. Dotted around the walled yard were several smaller buildings in varying states of repair; one was larger than the rest and had a proper tiled roof against the others' slates. She turned her attentions to Jack who was throwing across the bolts on the door and checking it was secure.

'Are you going to answer me, Jack?'

He turned to her and grinned mischievously, his abrupt, aloof manner seeming to have left him. 'I'll let Ma do the honours. Come on,' he ordered.

He led her across the yard in the direction of the largest of the buildings, opened the door and stood aside to allow her to enter.

Flo was kneeling on the floor unpacking a box and putting the items on the bottom shelf of a cupboard. As the door opened she turned her head and smiled with relief to see them. What she really wanted to do was jump up and throw her arms around the girl, telling her how worried she had been, how worried they had all been, and how glad they were to see her back. But she stopped herself. Actions like that would give Jack the impression she was giving him her seal of approval and she couldn't do that. Her own feelings towards Ally, especially after last night, had taken a turn for the better but even so she believed a relationship between two people from such differing backgrounds would never work, especially since one of those people had had such close connections with the gentry.

'So, yer back then?' she said, rising.

'Ma, I'm just off to take the handcart back. Shouldn't be more than an hour, but don't worry if I'm longer 'cos I might nip in for a pint.'

'Leave the cart 'til tomorrow, Jack. Yer've done enough fer one day without having ter trail that thing across Leicester.'

'I'd sooner do it tonight, Ma. Then tomorrow I can help yer finish getting straight in here.' What he really felt the need to do was get away from Ally and take a grip on his feelings. A walk in the cold would go some way towards achieving that.

'Suit yerself.' Flo turned to Ally. 'His boss weren't pleased he never went in today at such short notice. But he's an asset, is my Jack, and Mr Green knows that so I don't think there's any fear of him losing his job. But I couldn't have managed without him.' She frowned thoughtfully. 'Actually I've a feeling on me that summat's gone off at his work. Not quite sure what, but I know Jack'll come clean when he's ready.

'Well, what d'yer think?' she asked Ally, casting her arms wide. 'It's like a proper little house. It's got three rooms through there.' She pointed to a door at the back of the large room. 'They ain't that big but good enough for bedrooms. And a sink and range. Just look at the range, Ally. Ain't it something? It'll be luxury cooking on that instead of an open fire. It just needs a thorough clean and blackleading. And there's plenty of cupboards. I ain't never had proper cupboards before. Mind you, I haven't enough stuff ter fill 'em, but who cares? There's a privy outside. Proper brick-built too. And fancy not having to share! And we've our own pump. It's like a palace, ain't it, Ally? There's a school not far for the kids, and Rutland Street, where Tyler's is, is only up the road, five minutes away. Which means we don't have ter rise 'til six. Can't be bad, eh?'

'Is that Ally?' a voice shouted.

'Yes, Emily, it is,' Flo replied. 'You'd better pop through and say goodnight to the kids. They were tired to death after all the work they've done today, bless 'em, but they wouldn't go to bed 'cos they were worried about you. In the end I had to force them. Don't be long 'cos I'll put yer dinner on the table. It's only bought pie and peas, but as yer can see I was too busy fer cooking.'

Ally smiled, delighted to be asked to say goodnight to the children. The news she was impatient to divulge could wait a while longer. 'I could eat a horse, Flo. Pie and peas sounds most appetising.'

Flo laughed loudly. 'It's 'oss, Ally. Us common Leicester folks say 'oss. But you stick with 'orse, gel. The way you say it sounds more dignified.'

Ally was not sure whether Flo was poking fun at her or not, but regardless she laughed.

She went in to see Emily first. The young girl beamed with delight on seeing her. 'Oh, Ally,' she said, throwing her arms around her neck as she bent over the bed. 'We weren't half worried. Yer note said you were popping out on an errand, but you were gone hours.'

'My errand took longer than I anticipated.'

Emily frowned. 'Was it about a job, Ally? You ain't leaving us, are yer?'

'No, darling, I'm not. Not at the moment anyway.'

The relief on Emily's face sent a warm glow through Ally.

145

'Ma was bothered. She kept sending Jack up ter look for yer. Mind you, our Jack didn't need asking. He was out the door before Ma got a chance to finish asking him.'

'Was he? Oh.' Ally tried to sound indifferent but the fact pleased her. She wasn't mistaken about his concern for her after all. But there was still the question of why his manner had changed so abruptly?

'What d'yer think of this place then? It's nice, ain't it? I hated that last place. I'm glad we didn't stop. This is much better, innit?'

'I haven't had a chance to look around yet. But yes, I agree, it seems a vast improvement.' It suddenly struck her that the rent on this establishment must be more expensive than Flo was used to paying. Maybe that was why they were anxious for her return. They needed the money she contributed.

'There's another room through that door,' said Emily, pointing to a door on the left. 'It's only a tiny room but Ma was thinking you would like it for yer bedroom.'

'Really?' Ally turned and looked across at the closed door. She had grown used to sharing a bed with Emily and Flo but the thought of having her own room, and privacy again, was a welcome one. The only drawback was the lack of a bed. That was something she could not afford at the moment and she couldn't expect Flo to contribute towards one. She turned back to face Emily and sat down on the edge of the bed, taking the girl's hand. For a moment she studied her, remembering the story of the tiny scrap of a thing found in a box and the condition she was in. 'Oh, Emily,' she sighed.

'What's wrong?'

'Nothing, darling. Nothing at all.' She bent over and kissed her cheek. 'You get some sleep,' she said, rising. 'Goodnight, dear.'

Emily turned over and snuggled down. 'Night, night, Ally. I'm glad yer back safe,' she added.

Ally smiled. So am I, she thought.

She popped her head around the door of Eric and Jack's room. Eric appeared to be sound asleep. She tiptoed across to the bed and gazed down at the thatch of tousled fair hair that was poking out of the top of the eiderdown and again the memory of the children's terrible origins flooded back. A lump stuck in her throat as a picture of this boy, not much more than a baby, collar round his neck, being kicked by his brute of a drunken father, appeared before her. What other brutalities had he suffered apart from the ones related to her by Mrs Tittle? She shuddered, pushing the vision away. Thankfully they had been saved, spared by a lady who deserved gratitude and praise that could only be given by those who knew the harrowing tale – Jack and Ally. But in the interests of the children's well-being, never relating any of it seemed best. She leaned over and tenderly stroked the top of Eric's head before she quietly left the room.

Ten minutes later she pushed away her empty plate. 'Thank you, Flo. That was very nice.'

'I don't know about nice,' she replied, refilling Ally's mug from the cracked brown teapot. 'Yer never can be sure what's inside bought pies, but I suppose they fill a hole.'

Ally thanked Flo for the tea, then eyed her hesitantly. 'Have you a few minutes? I do need to talk to you.'

'Oh?'

'Please don't look so worried. I hope what I have to tell you will put an end to your worst problem.'

'Oh!' Flo sat back, folding her arms under her shapely bosom, and eyed Ally gravely as she imagined all sorts of possibilities. 'I'm listening.'

Ally steeled herself. 'I took it upon myself to do something today. The outcome was most satisfactory. My only concern is that you should not feel I have overstepped my position in your household.'

'Fer God's sake, Ally, yer worrying me summat silly. Will yer just spit it out?'

Ally cleared her throat and related the day's events from the beginning. Flo for once sat in silence. As the story unfolded of what had transpired after she had snatched the children, her jaw dropped wider and wider. When she had finished, Ally took a very deep breath.

'I hope you can see I had to do this for you, Flo. After what you told me last night, I had to try and do something that would afford you peace of mind. For obvious reasons you could not return to find out yourself, but there was nothing to stop me. No one knew me, would not connect me in any way to yourself or Jack. To all intents and purposes I was just a woman wanting to see where an ancestor lived, so I knew I posed no threat. Since you and Jack rescued Eric and Emily, the strain you must have endured would have broken most people. I did not have any idea what I would find out today, but I felt that either way, whether the children's parents were searching for you or not, whether in fact anyone was, at least you would know. Flo . . .'

Her voice trailed off as a groan sounded low in Flo's throat; her body began to tremble, her face crumpled and tears spilled down her cheeks. She doubled over, clutching her stomach, her head banging heavily on top of the table. Ally stared at her, horrified, as heart-rending sobs racked her whole body. Perhaps after all she had done the wrong thing? Dragging her chair across, she threw her arm around Flo's shoulder and pulled her close, Flo's head coming to rest on her chest. 'Flo. Oh, Flo,' she soothed her. 'I didn't mean to upset you. I only meant to help. I'm sorry. I'm so very sorry. Will you ever forgive me?'

Flo's head jerked up. 'Forgive yer? Ally, I should be kissing yer feet for what you've done for me.' She wiped her blotchy face on her sacking apron. 'I never thought this day would come. I prayed. Oh, Ally, I pledged me soul to the Lord for a miracle, but I never thought He'd answer me. But He has, ain't He? Somehow He heard me.' A shuddering sob passed through her body. 'I've never been a God-fearing woman, Ally. I've seen too much cruelty and had more than my share of sorrow. But like most I turn to Him in times of trouble. Tomorrow I'm going to church to say me thanks.'

She grabbed Ally's hand and gripped it tightly. 'I don't know how ter thank yer, gel. Yer've made me the happiest woman alive with this news. I can't believe that no more will I be looking over me shoulder or having to watch the kids like a hawk. We can live proper now, can't we? The only sadness I feel is for what those kids suffered before I took 'em.' A jubilant smile lit her face; her eyes, although still tearful, were bright with happiness. 'Me nightmare's all over now. Gone, finished. I can't wait ter tell Jack. He'll be over the moon.' She squeezed Ally's hand. 'Thank you,' she whispered emotionally. 'Thank you so much.'

A lump formed in Ally's throat at Flo's sincere gratitude, and tears stung her eyes. 'Please do not forget that I have much to thank you for too, Flo. You took me in when I knew you really did not want to. I dread to think what would have become of me without your generosity. So, you see, it's I who should really be thanking you.'

Flo blushed, embarrassed. It wasn't she to whom Ally should be addressing her gratitude but Jack. He, after all, was the one who had talked Flo into it. If it had been her decision Ally would never have crossed her doorstep, let alone become their lodger. 'Let's . . . er . . . just say we're quits, shall we, Ally? Now, there is one more thing you can do for me.'

'If it's in my power, Flo, I would be delighted.'

'I'm glad yer said that 'cos I could murder a cuppa. I couldn't attempt to mek it meself 'cos I'm still so shocked I don't think me legs'll hold me up. Mek it strong, gel, with plenty of sugar.'

Several moments later, supping from her mug of strong tea, Flo gazed around the room. The light from the oil lamp mingled with the fire, casting long shadows. She sighed, leaning back in her chair, still having difficulty believing that her fears for the children were finally at an end. Whilst Ally had made the tea her mind had gone over and over the shocking tale, and now more than ever, if that were possible, she was glad she had carried out her spontaneous act. 'It's a pity I didn't know sooner,' she said distractedly.

'I beg your pardon, Flo?'

'Eh! Oh, don't mind me, me duck, I was just thinking out loud. I was just thinking that in light of the wonderful news you brought me it was a pity we moved from Walnut Street in the first place, but then I suppose it's what brought it all to a head.'

Ally thought of the tiny two up, two down damp terrace, where it was hard to keep the bugs at bay, surrounded by hundreds exactly the same, all the tenants living just on or below the poverty line. She hadn't had a chance to take a good look around this place as yet but even with her limited knowledge, the terrace in Walnut Street could hardly compare.

Flo eyed her shrewdly. 'I know what yer thinking, gel. Yer thinking how the hell can I regret moving into this? I'm right, ain't I?'

'Well . . . yes.' Ally chose her next words very carefully. 'This is a much bigger house than Walnut Street.'

'What yer mean, Ally, is that this house ain't damp, there's no bugs or mice and yer can't hear the neighbours yelling at each other or their kids screaming. But you're too polite ter say it.' She sighed. 'It's true, though, this place is much better in every way. I'd love ter stay here.'

Ally frowned. 'Is there a reason why we can't, Flo?'

She paused, eyes flashing with worry. 'Oh, Ally, I'm gonna have ter come clean. You'll twig soon enough anyway.'

'Twig?'

'Find out.'

Her frown deepened. 'Find out what exactly?'

'That . . . look, first yer must promise not to tell Jack? I've got to keep it from him as long as I can. He'll go mad, though, when he does find out.'

'Flo, please tell me. I'm feeling quite agitated.'

She gulped. 'Well, er . . . yer see, we shouldn't be here. We're trespassing.'

Ally stared at her, having extreme difficulty in understanding Flo's announcement. 'Trespassing! You mean, you haven't asked permission or paid any rent?'

She nodded sheepishly. 'Yer didn't seriously think I could afford rent on a place like this, did yer?'

'It had crossed my mind. I thought maybe you had struck some sort of bargain.'

'Ally, I ain't in no position ter bargain. I couldn't afford any kind of rent at the moment. I spent the last I'd got on that hovel off Sanvey Gate. But after me scare of last night, thinking that woman was watching us, I had to move again. Besides, we couldn't have stayed there. We'd all have caught something nasty. I knew for a fact this place had been empty for ages and I was in such a quandary I just thought, what the hell? We could take a chance and move in and it might be weeks before anyone found out. And I know it's not honest but I thought the rent I got away with I could save up and put towards another place, and buy some bits and pieces for the kids.'

'Did you break in here, Flo?'

There was silence. 'Sort of,' she said finally. 'I scaled the wall and undid the bolts on the gate.'

The vision of Flo lifting her skirts to clamber up the high wall surrounding the enclosed yard was a comical one, but the situation was far too serious for Ally to show her amusement.

'I am going to have to get the lock on the front door replaced though,' Flo continued, eyeing her sheepishly.

'So you did break in?'

'All right, so I did,' she said sharply. 'I was desperate. You *know* how desperate I was. This place seemed ideal. It's not overlooked 'cos the building the other side of the alleyway has no windows facing out, and what with the main part being empty . . . well, yer can see me logic?'

Ally could, but at the moment preferred not to voice it. A few months ago she would have been horrified by what Flo had done. But now she wasn't quite sure how she felt. The only thought that did worry her was that if they were discovered they could be thrown in jail. She had suffered so many threats of jail recently she felt the law of averages was bound to come down on the wrong side of her at some time if she wasn't careful.

'How did you find out about this place, Flo?'

'I've known of it for years, only I kind of forgot about it. I was passing by once and the double gates facing Charles Street were open 'cos some stuff was being delivered and I had to wait while the cart manoeuvred in. I had a nosy inside. A woman was hanging some washing on a line at the side of this place and I remember thinking it strange that anyone would be living in a shop yard.'

'A shop? The building at the front used to be a shop, did it?'

Flo nodded. 'Part of it was. I used to do me shopping there. It was quite a shock to find it closed down. Happened really suddenly, it did. There was no warning it was shutting, just a sign stuck to the door. Mind you, things had been slipping for a while. Such a shame. Proper Aladdin's cave was Listerman's. You could get anything from candles to a dress pattern and the material. Not that I could ever afford to buy material. You could always rely on Listerman's for quality at a reasonable price, and if you couldn't afford what it was yer wanted they'd put it by and let you pay it off a few coppers a week.' Flo eyed Ally sharply. 'A' you all right, gel? Only you've gone all pale.'

She gulped. 'Er . . . yes, yes.' She rose abruptly. 'I need a glass of water.'

'Glass?' Flo scoffed good-humouredly. 'You'll find no glasses here, me duck. You'll have to make do with a tin mug like the rest of us.'

'I wasn't thinking, I'm sorry.'

Ally stood by the pot sink slowly sipping the water, her mind in a whirl. She felt sick. Would her lies never stop haunting her? Of all the shocks she had received in the last twenty-four hours, this one had to be the worst, but only because of the repercussions should any of it come to light. If the situation weren't so serious for herself, then it would be comical. Flo, in her innocence, had broken into and taken up residence in Ally's own property. With all that had transpired she had forgotten about

150

this place. Obviously, the solicitor who had taken over from Mr Bailey had not sold it – well, he couldn't without her signature on the documents – so it still belonged to her.

It was ironic, she thought. Here she was, a property owner without the means to get that property earning money. As it stood it was worthless to her unless of course sold, and from the way Mr Bailey had spoken it wasn't worth much, whatever 'much' meant in monetary terms. For a fleeting moment she wondered again why Tobias had not sold it along with everything else the Listermans had owned.

Her thoughts returned to her most immediate problem. The tables had now been turned. She was now Flo's landlady. But how could she tell her? That would mean confessing to her lie, and despite how close she felt she and Flo had grown, especially after the most recent happenings, she would not like to predict how Flo would react. At this moment keeping Flo's friendship and remaining as long as she could with this family was more important to her than anything. She was beginning to feel she belonged and welcomed that security.

Her mind whirled even faster. She needed to keep her secret and it was possible. Flo had no intention of staying here, only a matter of weeks at most. This place had been abandoned for a long time so the chance of discovery must be remote. She herself could keep reminding Flo that they would have to move, make sure they did not become too settled. Hopefully in the near future someone would purchase the building and out of the proceeds she could give some money to Flo, tell her she herself had come into some sort of inheritance. She was getting to be quite an expert at fabricating stories, a few more should not be hard for her. With the money, however little or much the amount, new and better lives could be forged. As she now knew, when you had nothing a few pounds could be a fortune used wisely. A warm feeling of pleasure spread through her. Doing something positive for these lovely people would give her a great deal of satisfaction. If that meant adding to her lies then in the circumstances she would live with it.

She sat down at the table. 'Flo?'

'Eh? Oh, I was miles away. Feeling better?'

'I was just thirsty. Listen, I have an idea.'

Flo eyed her keenly. 'As I'm out of ideas meself at the moment, I'm all ears, gel.'

'You are right, Flo. This place is going to waste, so why shouldn't we take advantage? If we are challenged we can say that we have been appointed caretakers. I doubt anyone will go so far as to check our credibility with the owners.' And if they did, she thought, that would not be a problem as *she* was the owner. 'And we'll only be here for a few weeks so it might not even come to that.'

Flo's eyes widened in surprise. 'Well, gel, I couldn't have come up with better meself. Caretakers. Of course.' She leaned over and slapped

Ally on the back. 'Perfect. Well done. Well, this calls for another cuppa and this time I'll mek it. Oh, Ally, what a day, eh?'

Ally smiled.

It was the next evening when Jack caught her on her own in the yard pumping water.

'We can never thank you enough for what you did, Ally. The difference this will make to us is . . . well, it's immeasurable.'

His voice was gruff and her back stiffened. Slowly she raised her head and looked into his eyes. His manner towards her was one thing but his eyes always told a different tale, one which she knew she hadn't mistaken. Jack cared for her – he cared very much. So why was he always so abrupt, sometimes even rude, towards her? It was all so confusing. They stood for several long moments staring at each other. Suddenly the nearness of him overwhelmed Ally and her throat constricted. All she could manage to say was, 'It was my pleasure. I'm just happy it all turned out so well.'

He hovered for several moments before he said, 'I'll carry that bucket in for yer.' Then snatched it up and marched away with it across the yard, leaving her staring in bewilderment after him.

Chapter Nineteen

Ally graciously accepted the coins and as soon as Mr Gideon, the gaffer, had moved to the next person down the line she opened her hand and counted the contents. Then she counted again.

'What's the matter?' whispered Flo, pushing her own pay into her pocket before lifting up several stacked boxes to load on to a trolley.

'It's as I thought. My pay . . . it's short again. One and sixpence three-farthings to be exact. Last week it was slightly less as I did not earn quite so much. It hasn't been right since I started to work here. Please cover for me, Flo.'

'Why? Where a' yer going?'

'To speak to Mr Gideon, of course. This cannot go on. Whoever calculates the pay isn't doing so correctly.'

Flo's eyes bulged in horror. She wanted to grab Ally's arm to stop her but was prohibited by the boxes she was holding. 'No, wait,' she whispered fiercely. 'Ally, wait.' But her plea landed on deaf ears. Ally was already addressing the gaffer.

'Could I have a word, please, Mr Gideon?'

'What d'yer want?' he growled at her. 'Can't yer see I'm busy? And,' he snapped, inclining his head towards her place on the line, 'them lot want packing and loading afore yer go tonight.'

'Do not concern yourself, Mr Gideon. They will be done. If you could just spare me a moment, I need to speak to you about my wage.'

He turned his squat body full towards her, his fat ruddy face scowling deeply. 'And what's wrong with yer wage?'

Flo, having abandoned her load, arrived at Ally's side and urgently tugged her arm. 'It's all right, Mr Gideon. She don't really want to speak to yer. Come on, Ally,' she hissed. 'Mr Gideon's a busy man. Can't yer see that?'

Ally pulled her arm free. 'What I have to say won't take a moment of Mr Gideon's time. My wage isn't right, you see, Mr Gideon. It's one and sixpence three-farthings short to be exact.'

A hush immediately fell around them and all eyes turned in Ally's direction.

Mr Gideon's face hardened. 'Is that right now?'

'It's all right, Mr Gideon,' Flo intervened, grabbing Ally's arm again and trying to steer her away. 'She's counted it wrong. She can't count, can't Miss Brown.'

Ally turned and glared at her. 'Of course I can count, Flo. What on earth is the matter with you? And please let go of my arm,' she snapped, wrenching herself free once again.

'Just what is it yer accusing me of?' he demanded icily.

'I'm not accusing you of anything. I am just pointing out that my wage is wrong. Whoever calculates it is not doing so correctly. It's been wrong since I started here.'

Flo's hands covered her face. 'Oh, no,' she groaned.

'Accusing me of thieving, are yer?' He turned and scanned his eyes over the onlookers. 'Anyone else want ter accuse me of thieving?' All eyes were turned downwards and, smiling smugly, he turned back to face Ally. 'Seems it's just you then.'

'I'm not accusing you of any such thing! All I'm . . .'

He grabbed hold of her shoulder, his face turning thunderous. 'As it's me that sorts out the pay, it's me yer accusing. And I take offence at being called a thief.'

'But . . .'

'Collect yer belongings and get out.'

Ally gasped in shock. 'I beg your pardon?'

'I beg your pardon?' he mimicked. 'A' yer deaf, lady? I told yer to get out.' He pushed his face close to hers. 'I don't know what the likes of you with yer airy-fairy ways is doing working here anyway. Now I'm sure you understood me, but if yer want it put plainer: get out, yer sacked.'

'Oh, Mr Gideon, sir,' Flo erupted. 'She didn't mean nowt, honest she . . .'

'And you can go with her,' he barked. 'Go on, both on yer. Bloody trouble mekers. And I shall pass word around about yer an' all. Mek sure no other bugger teks yer on. Now go on, get before I send for the owners.'

'Hello, Jack.'

Jack's head jerked up. He had been concentrating hard on the task of slicing ham from a large shank and hadn't heard anyone come into the shop. Usually ham was sliced on the machine but Jack knew some people preferred theirs cut by hand and whatever pleased the customer was important in his eyes. 'Evening, Miss Green. Mr Green is in the back. Would yer like me to fetch him?'

'No,' she replied, sauntering up to the counter. 'I'll go through in a moment.' She pulled off her gloves and laid them over her handbag. 'Mother sent me to make sure he gets home at a decent time tonight for dinner.'

That was a lie. Lizzie idolised her father, but the only reason she had come down to the shop on such a chilly evening was because she knew Jack would be there. She hadn't given up on her plan to land him.

She wanted Jack. He was the only man she would settle for and she did not care how low she had to stoop to get him. For a woman used to getting her own way, Jack's playing hard to get – for that was all she saw it as – only made him appear a far more attractive conquest. She had been throwing herself at him for ages now and was growing tired of coming up with ideas to initiate a relationship, one she had set her heart on lasting forever. But the latest plan she had concocted with the help of her father was bound to succeed. After all, what employee could refuse a request from his employer? Jack was no fool.

As he continued his task Jack was keenly aware of Lizzie's scrutiny. He had decided to give his boss's proposition more thought, but that was as far as he had got. Lizzie was a nice enough woman, and maybe if he hadn't met Ally he might be looking at her in a different light. But he *had* met Ally, and knew that until he had well and truly got her out of his system, which at the moment seemed beyond his capabilities no matter how hard he tried, considering another woman's charms was pointless, boss's daughter or not.

'Are you going to the St Valentine's dance?'

Oh, God, he thought, she's going to put me on the spot again and this time, Kenneth Bott's not around to interrupt. 'Er . . . I, er . . . didn't know there was one.'

'Oh, yes, it's . . .'

'Jack, before I forget, here's your pay,' Sidney Green said, bustling through the door at the back and handing Jack a brown envelope. He smiled on seeing his daughter. 'Hello, Lizzie love. Your mother's sent you to fetch me, I take it? Well, I won't be much longer.' He turned to Jack. 'Would you lock up for me tonight?'

'No problem, Mr Green.'

Sidney sensed the reason for his daughter's cross expression and flashed her a look telling her he'd got the message and all was in hand. 'Well, on second thoughts, why don't we lock up now? It's nearly time anyway. I doubt we'll get any stragglers tonight. To my knowledge all the regulars and a few others besides have already been in.'

Jack wiped his hands on his large white apron. 'I won't say no to an early night, Mr Green. I'll put this ham in the cold store and wash down the slab and knives, then I'm finished.'

'What's your mother done for our dinner tonight then, Lizzie? I'm famished so whatever it is I'll do it justice.'

'A joint of beef with all the trimmings.'

Sidney smacked his lips. 'Just the business. Your mother is a fine cook and no mistake.' He looked straight at Jack. 'Come back and have a bite of supper with us? If I know Mrs Green she's catered for twenty as usual and she'd be delighted if you'd join us.'

'Thanks for the offer but I can't. Ma will have my dinner ready waiting and she'll worry if I'm not back at my usual time.'

Sidney slapped him on the back. 'How old are yer, lad? Too old, I'd say, to be tied to yer mother's apron strings still. I'm sure she won't mind this once. Surely she can't object to your having supper with your boss and his family?'

'Ma would understand, Mr Green, but I've other arrangements that I can't break.' He did not like telling this lie but neither did he like being pressurised.

Sidney sensed his daughter's dismay and one thing he could not stand was seeing Lizzie upset. Suddenly he was fed up with playing this game with Jack; time to put his foot down. He jerked his head in Lizzie's direction. 'Go and wait in the back, I just want a private word with Jack.'

'Yes, Father,' she replied, quite happy to do his bidding.

Sidney squared his shoulders ready for battle. 'Now, Jack,' he demanded once she was out of earshot, 'what's all this nonsense?'

'Nonsense, sir?'

'Don't play games with me, lad. I'm on about you and my Lizzie. Just what has my daughter got to do?'

'I'm sorry, Mr Green, I still don't follow you?'

Sidney Green scowled. 'Oh, I know you do, lad. Now I've given you plenty of time to consider my proposition and I was lenient when you took the day off last Saturday without warning. If you'd care to look in your pay packet you'll see I ain't docked yer when I should have done.'

'That is very good of you, Mr Green,' Jack said sincerely.

'Good of me! I did it ter show yer just what it's like to be the boss. When you are, as long as things are running smoothly, yer can take time off to do whatever you please.' He took a deep breath. He was handling this all wrong and knew it. Jack wasn't the normal run-of-the-mill employee. This man had pride. Too much of it, in Sidney's opinion, for a man of his class. Regardless, he could not stop himself from emphasising to the young man just what he was about to pass up. Sidney decided to try a slightly different tack. 'Jack, you have to agree my Lizzie is a good catch. I've told yer, marry her and all this will be yours. Any other man in your position would have jumped at the opportunity to land her when she first batted her eyelashes. What's with yer, lad? Don't you think she's pretty?'

'Yes, Mr Green, I do.'

'And she's cultured. It cost me a fortune to get her educated. She's read all the classics, plays the piano, sings like an angel – and with all that comes a decent living. What more could any man ask for?'

Jack eyed him sharply. He was right. What more could any man want? But Lizzie Green, and all she brought with her, was not Ally. Ally was the only woman he wanted and he could not have her. Marriage to anyone else under these circumstances would not be fair. But none of those facts was really of importance to Jack except the glaring one: Sidney Green honestly thought that he would jump at a chance to marry Lizzie and better himself. A man in Jack's position, he had said. He had meant a man without a future unless he married one. In essence a man without honour. Well, Sidney Green had badly misjudged him and Jack was deeply offended. If and when he ever married it would be to someone of his own choosing, someone he respected and, most importantly, loved. He would not marry just to please others, he would sooner stay single. He had already told Mr Green this, the man had obviously not taken him seriously. The respect that Jack had always felt for his boss suddenly vanished.

'Look, Jack, if it's a partnership you're after . . .'

His eyes narrowed in anger. 'I'm not open to bribery, Mr Green,' he hissed.

'Bribery?'

'That's what it amounts to.'

'How dare you? Bribery indeed! I could take serious offence at that. All I'm trying to do is open your eyes to what's on offer. Now get yer coat, lad. Mrs Green will be waiting, and Mrs Green don't like mealtimes to be ignored.'

The furrow across Jack's brow deepened. 'Mrs Green is expecting me for dinner?'

'Er . . . well, I did intimate you might be coming.'

There was no 'might' about it, thought Jack. It had all been planned. His anger heightened. 'I'll get me coat, Mr Green, but I'll be putting it on to go home.'

Sidney Green's eyebrows rose in surprise. 'If yer do that, then don't bother coming back.' The instant the words left his mouth regret set in. Under no circumstances did he want to lose Jack as an employee.

'If that's the way you want it, I'll say my goodbyes.' Jack grabbed Sidney's hand and shook it. 'It's been a pleasure working for you, Mr Green. I'm sorry it's come to this but I hope you understand I'll not be pushed into doing something just to keep me job.'

'Now just a minute, Jack, let's not be hasty . . .'

But it was too late, Jack had already marched out of the door.

Lizzie appeared, looking around expectantly. 'Where's Jack gone, Father?'

A red-faced Sidney slowly turned to face his daughter. 'Er . . .'

'Flo, I'm so sorry.'

'Yer will be, ducky. Have yer seen the job queues lately? They stretch fer miles. I hope yer can live on fresh air, 'cos that's what we'll be eating shortly. You heard what he said. He's gonna spread word around about us. By the time he's finished we'll be lucky ter get a job rat catching.' She threw herself down into her rocker so forcefully it was only Ally's quick thinking in grabbing the back that saved her from tipping over.

'Ta,' muttered Flo grudgingly, leaning over to pull off her boots.

Ally eyed her anxiously as she moved around to stand in front of her. Flo had marched all the way back like a woman possessed, not uttering a word. On reaching home she had pushed open the door so violently it had bounced off the wall to come back and smack her in the face before she could stop it. The bruise on her forehead was darkening rapidly. This incident had not helped her mood.

Ally wrung her hands. 'I don't understand what I did wrong? I was only . . .'

Flo's head jerked up, eyes filled with anger. 'Committing a cardinal sin.'

'I was only questioning my wage.'

'And that's one thing yer don't do.' She sighed heavily. 'When totting up yer wage, you obviously forgot to account for the gaffer's dues.'

Ally frowned in confusion. 'Gaffer's dues! What are gaffer's dues?'

Flo groaned despairingly. 'Yer don't know what gaffer's dues are? Oh, my God, Ally, you really are naive. Them gentry did you no favours, did they, gel? They taught you nowt of importance. All gaffers skim the workers' pay. The owners know they do it but turn a blind eye.'

'They do? But we work so hard for what little we receive! That practice is not fair, Flo.'

'Fair? There's nothing in this life that's fair, Ally, it's about time you learned that.'

'My pay from the fish market was right.'

Flo laughed wryly. 'Like hell it was! Old Cod Eyes had the scales rigged. Did you not know? You were the only one then. They weighed at least half a pound light. He was fiddling us right, left and centre. But I can assure you, it's better to be fiddled than have nothing to be fiddled out of.' She rubbed her hands over her face. 'I don't know what the hell we're gonna do now. One of us outta work we might have been able to cope with, but the two on us . . .' She shook her head solemnly. 'And there was me thinking I'd been so clever in coming here. That I'd be able to put some money aside. Well, it's a good job we ain't got any rent ter pay, ain't it? Just let's hope we ain't caught, that's all I can say. Still, I suppose it could be worse. At least our Jack has a job.'

Tears of remorse pricked Ally's eyes. Oh, why, she silently screamed, why did she have to go and open her mouth to Mr Gideon? Why hadn't she spoken to Flo about it first? The results of her thoughtlessness were catastrophic. 'Would . . .' she gulped. 'Would it be best if I left?'

Flo looked at her but before she could answer the door shot open and the children bolted in.

'Ma,' Eric shouted, 'we can't find Sal.'

'There's no need ter shout, Eric, I ain't deaf. What d'yer mean, yer can't find Sal? I hope ter God she didn't get out of the yard door, you know how she likes to wander and there's no telling where she'll be. It's dark now so we've no hope of finding her.'

'She never got out the door, Ma. She was with us a while ago and then we suddenly realised she'd gone missing.'

Emily started to cry. 'Oh, Sal,' she wailed.

'Stop yer bawling, Emily. She can't be that far.'

'I'll come and help you find her,' offered Ally, glad of the prospect of getting out of Flo's way whilst hopefully she calmed down. She had not meant one word of her offer to leave but had felt obliged to say it. She sincerely hoped that Flo did not accept. 'Sal is probably asleep in one of the outbuildings,' she said.

'We've looked in all those,' replied Eric.

Ally smiled reassuringly. 'Well, we'll look again just to make sure.'

'There's no need for all of us to go looking, so I'll get cracking on the dinner. And, eh,' Flo said to Ally, 'don't go calling Sal too loudly 'cos we don't want to attract attention. You never know who's cutting through the alley.'

The yard was pitch black by now. Holding the oil lamp high, Ally, followed closely by Eric and Emily, began scouting around. Sal was nowhere to be found.

'There's only the dungeon left,' sniffed Emily.

'The dungeon?' questioned Ally.

'She means the horrible building down in the corner,' answered Eric. 'It's . . .'

'It's what?'

'Well, it's . . .'

'We don't like it,' said Emily. 'Sal won't be in there 'cos she don't like it either. And it smells.'

Ally turned and looked across at the small building they were referring to, looming eerily out of the darkness. She had not taken much notice of it before, it being at the back of the building where they had taken up residence, two of its walls being those of the boundary and dividing wall of the yard next-door. What it had been used for she had no idea. It was too small for anything she could think of. The children's description of it had unnerved her but she did not want to show them her apprehension. It was only because it was dark, she told herself. Many innocent things could appear sinister in the dark.

With her free hand she gathered up her skirt. 'Come on,' she said. 'We've checked everywhere else, so Sal must be in there.'

'I'll wait here,' both children said simultaneously.

Ally turned and glanced at them, then back towards the building. It surprised her that Eric was so unwilling to accompany her. Being a typical boy he was usually game for anything. A niggle of uneasiness flickered in her stomach, but not about to force the children to do anything against their wishes, there was only one thing for it: she would have to check by herself.

Taking a deep breath, she raised the lamp high and strode across. She arrived at the door which was fractionally ajar. 'Sal,' she called softly. 'Sal, are you there?' There was no response. She called again. 'Sal . . . come on, Sal, there's a good girl.' She stood for a moment and waited. Still nothing. She was about to retrace her steps when she thought better of it. What if Sal was trapped or injured and by not taking a look inside she herself caused the old dog further harm? She chided herself. It was silly of her to let the children's fear of this building unnerve her too. Without further ado she pushed open the door and stepped inside.

Instantly icy air thick with dust cloaked her, clamping her throat tightly like gripping fingers. Mingled with a strong smell of damp and must was something else, something nasty, like nothing she had smelled before. Long cobwebs, infested with dead insects, hung like curtains, wafting eerily in the draught from the doorway. The children were right, it was a horrible place. She shuddered violently, fighting a desperate urge to turn and run. But she couldn't, she had to check for Sal first.

Taking several further steps, she opened her mouth. 'Sal,' she uttered. 'Sal, are you here?'

A rustle coming from a corner of the building by the roof timbers terrified her rigid and before she could aim the lamp to see what it was, a black swirling mass surged out and was upon her. She screamed hysterically. Dropping the lantern, which crashed on to the hard ground, scattering chunks of glass, she spun around and with arms flailing wildly, fled for the door, yelling: 'Get off me! Get off me!'

Total mayhem erupted. Despite not having a clue as to what was wrong with Ally, Emily and Eric clung to each other, screaming in sympathy; Flo, hearing the commotion, came running out of the door, shouting: 'Who's being murdered?' Jack, who had just been about to unlatch the yard door, almost battered it down in his efforts to get inside. Once there his eyes darted around, trying to sort out the confusion that reigned. 'Stop that noise and get inside,' he ordered the children before he sprang over to Ally, caught hold of her arms and gripped them tightly. 'Ally, Ally, it's all right. It's me, Jack. What on earth a' yer bellowing like a banshee for?'

She fought to free her arms, wriggling frantically. 'Get them off me, Jack! Get them off me!'

He shook her. 'Get what off yer? Ally, get what off yer?'

'Them. I don't know what but there's one in my hair.'

He loosened his grip. 'Stand still, Ally, for God's sake. It's bad enough I can't see without you doing an Irish jig.'

Despite her painfully thumping heart and uncontrollable shaking, she somehow managed to do as she was bid.

Jack felt over the top of her head. 'There, I've got it,' he laughed. 'It's a bat.'

'A bat? Ahhhh!'

'Ally, shut up,' Flo hissed, joining them. 'You'll have the whole neighbourhood descending. What did I hear you say it was, Jack? A bat?'

'It is,' he replied, releasing the squealing offender and watching it fly off. He looked down at Ally, a twinkle in his eye. 'How did yer manage to get a bat in yer hair?'

Fighting to regain her dignity, Ally took several deep breaths. 'By looking for Sal in that building over there. There were lots of them. They all came at me.' She shuddered violently. 'It was horrible. Just horrible.' Suddenly a thought struck her and renewed terror filled her. 'I dropped the lamp,' she exclaimed. 'Jack, I dropped the lamp!'

They all spun towards the outbuilding, fully expecting to see it engulfed.

'It looks like we've bin lucky,' said Jack, relieved. 'When yer dropped it, the rush of air must have knocked the flame out.'

'Thank God for small mercies,' groaned Flo. 'Oh, but me lamp. That cost me nearly two bob, that did. I suppose it's beyond repair?'

Ally gulped, remembering the sound the lamp had made as it hit the floor. 'I'm so sorry, Flo,' she said remorsefully. 'I'll pay for the damage, of course.'

'Pay? And how, pray, do yer propose to pay me when yer've no wage coming in?'

'No wage?' Jack said, frowning. 'Did you not get your pay for some reason today?'

Flo eyed Ally scathingly. 'You tell him. I'm going inside before I catch me death.'

'That's a good idea, Ma. Come on,' he said, cupping Ally's elbow to steer her inside. 'You can tell me whatever it is over a cuppa.' And at the same time, he thought, there was news he had to break to Ma that he wasn't relishing telling her.

'You've bin sacked!' Jack exclaimed a short while later. 'The pair of yer?'

'Yes,' Ally said softly. 'It was all my fault.' She raised her eyes to Flo. 'I really am so dreadfully sorry.'

Flo gave the pan of scrag end stew a vigorous stir then turned to face Ally, placing her hands on her hips. 'If you say sorry ter me once more today, I'll . . . I'll . . .'

Ally gulped. 'I'm so sorry, Flo. I won't say it again, I promise.'

At the look of doom on Ally's face, Flo could not help but laugh. 'What am I gonna do with you, gel, eh? I'll say one thing – the Lord certainly does have His ways of testing us.' She scraped a hand through her hair which had escaped most of its pins. 'Don't look so stricken, we'll get summat. Even if we have to resort to emptying out middens.'

Ally's expression turned to one of sheer horror which sent Flo into gales of laughter. 'Oh, if yer could see your face, gel! But I ain't joking about cleaning middens. If it comes to it, that's what we'll have ter do, so you'd better get used to the idea.' She looked across at the children. 'You two can stop looking so miserable. If anyone's got the right to look

161

miserable it's me, with all that's happened today. Sal'll turn up. That dog knows where she's well off. Now mek yerselves useful by setting the table. Eh, and wash yer hands first.' She suddenly looked hard at Jack. 'You're home early again tonight?'

He raised his eyes to hers. He would have to come clean. He couldn't keep something like this from Ma for long. But suddenly his reason seemed so trivial. He had turned down the opportunity of a lifetime. Marriage to Lizzie would not have been so bad, and at least he would never have been out of a job and as a result would have been able to support Ma and the kids. He had been a fool to let pride get in his way. But if he was honest, the real reason behind his actions did not lie with his pride, it was the woman sitting in the chair opposite him – a woman who, since the moment he had met her, all caked in mud, had managed to turn his world upside down. He took a deep breath. 'I've . . . er . . . I've left me job, Ma.'

Flo and Ally stared at him blankly.

'Jack, I'm in no mood for jokes. And that one's in bad taste,' Flo scolded.

'It's no joke, Ma.'

'No joke?' she uttered. 'You mean you've walked out on a perfectly good job? Why, Jack? In God's name, why?'

Dreadful fear filled Flo as she pulled out a chair and sat down next to him. Her only comfort after today's disaster had been the thought that Jack was still employed. Now here he was telling her otherwise and she could not believe it.

'My job seemed to include marrying Mr Green's daughter. It was expected that I would.'

Ally froze, a vice-like pain gripping her heart. This was the first she had heard of Lizzie Green, and the thought of Jack being romantically attached to her or anyone chilled her.

Flo scowled deeply in disbelief. 'What?'

'Lizzie Green has been waylaying me for months and so far I've managed to avoid getting trapped. But tonight Mr Green openly propositioned me. I was angry, Ma, that he thought I could be bought with the promise that marriage to his daughter also meant getting my hands on the shop. As well as see Lizzie settled, he's desperate to start taking things easy and saw me as his answer. Thinking about it, though, maybe I should have gone along with it, especially now you've lost your jobs.'

Flo eyed him questioningly. 'Have yer feelings for Lizzie Green?'

Ally held her breath as she waited for his answer.

'She's nice enough, but no, not like that. Though I'm sure we'd have got along well enough. And you'd have bin set for life, Ma.' He placed his elbows on the table, rested his chin in his hands and groaned. 'I was a fool to turn this down. A complete and utter fool.'

'Oh, yer were, were yer? So yer'd saddle yerself for life, just to keep

162

bread on the table?' Flo banged down her fist. 'Well, if yer had, Jack, then yer'd not have been the man I thought yer was.'

He eyed her in surprise. 'You're not mad then, Ma?'

'Oh, I'm mad all right. But only against Mr Green. I've a damned good mind to go down and give him what for!'

'No, Ma,' Jack ordered. 'What's done is done.' He sighed heavily. 'I'll be out first thing tomorrow and won't come home 'til I get summat. I'll take anything.'

'That's the same as us then,' she said, eyeing Ally meaningfully. 'Now come on, the lot of yer, take that look off yer faces. We'll manage. We've bin in worse situations. We've got our health, strength and our week's pay. Eked out, we can make it stretch to three if necessary.'

Chapter Twenty

It was a very sombre group who rose just as dawn broke the next morning, and their mood was not helped by the fact that Sal still had not put in an appearance.

As Flo busied herself cutting slices of bread and spreading them sparingly with dripping, she thought of all the places she and Ally could try for a job. She hadn't been exaggerating when she had told Ally of the length of the job queues. Procuring those positions at Tyler's had been nothing short of a miracle and initially she had been incensed at the way Ally had lost them. Secretly, though, she agreed with her wholeheartedly. The skimming of the workers' wages by the gaffers was an abominable practice.

She wasn't too concerned about Jack. In his trade all sorts of outlets were constantly on the lookout for experienced men such as he. In that respect he should not have much trouble. Whether or not the manager was fair or Jack liked the place would be another matter.

As she filled the teapot with boiling water, Flo sighed heavily. She had always been a good manager, had had to be, but making their pay stretch until they all found something could prove very difficult. Still, she hadn't wanted to worry them all any more than was necessary. She just prayed that in the meantime whoever owned these premises did not discover their existence. They would surely be thrown out on the streets then. But far more worrying was the fact that trespassing carried a prison sentence.

'Cheer up, Emily,' she said as the young girl plonked herself down at the table, wiping sleep from her eyes. 'Sal'll turn up today, you'll see. In the meantime whilst me, Jack and Ally are out job hunting, you can make yerself busy by sweeping up in here. I want to keep this place looking nice.'

'All right, Ma,' came the reply.

Flo eyed her sharply. Usually Emily had a lot to say for herself. Sal's disappearance was obviously affecting her badly. 'Where's yer brother?' she asked.

'Out looking for Sal with Jack.'

'Oh, I didn't know they'd gone out? I thought they were both still in bed.'

'You and Ally were asleep when Jack popped his head round the door.

They've gone up Walnut Street in case Sal's gone back there.'

'Oh, well, we'll keep our fingers crossed that she has. Now eat yer breakfast. Hello, me duck,' she smiled as Ally walked through and sat down at the table. 'You tossed and turned a bit last night, but then I suppose it's understandable. I hope yer managed to get some sleep eventually?'

'I did, thank you. Any news of Sal?'

'Not yet,' Flo said matter-of-factly, flashing her a warning glance to show Emily was upset. 'The lads have gone up to Walnut Street ter see if she's found her way back there. They should be back soon. Emily, go and pump me some water, there's a duck.'

Without a word she got down from the table, grabbed the bucket and left.

'She's upset, bless her. They do love that dog. I hope the lads find her, really I do.'

'You love her yourself, don't you, Flo?'

'Yes, I do and that's a fact. She drives me to distraction sometimes, and feeding her – well, there are times I could do without it. But whenever I think of Sal, I see her as a pup nestled into Eric's side when he was . . . well, yer know.' Even now that vision of Eric chained to the wall horrified her. 'I like to think Sal was protecting him.'

'I think you are right, Flo. I fully believe she was.' And, thought Ally, she herself had a lot for which to thank the old dog. If Jack had not been searching for Sal that stormy night, Ally herself would not be sitting at this table now.

'Ma, Ma!'

Flo frowned, wiping her hands on her apron. 'What's with that child now? Wadda you want, Emily?'

She walked across to the door and peered out. Emily was standing at the pump, staring across at the huge building, part of which used to house Listerman's shop.

'I think I can hear Sal. I think she's in there.'

'In there?' Flo queried, advancing towards her. 'That place is all locked up. She couldn't possibly have got in there. Hold on, though, I think yer right . . . I'd know Sal's bark anywhere.'

The yard door opened and Jack and Eric entered. 'No luck, Ma,' Jack said glumly. 'We looked everywhere we could think of but we didn't see hide nor hair of her. We'll try again later.'

'Shush!' mouthed Flo.

Jack grimaced. 'What?'

'I said, shush. And you too, Eric.'

Ally came out to join them. 'What is going on?'

Jack shrugged his shoulders. 'Don't ask me.'

'Will you all shush?' ordered Flo.

In the early-dawn light, on a chilly spring morning, they all stood by the pump in the middle of the large cobbled yard, ears pricked.

'I can hear Sal barking,' Jack said after several seconds had elapsed.

'See, I was right, Ma,' erupted Emily. 'It is Sal. It is. She's in there.'

'Emily's right,' Ma said. 'But how she got inside is beyond me. That place is locked up tighter than the Tower of London, and I should know – I've checked every door. I'd have loved to have a butcher's inside. I had to get a box to climb on to see through the windows. I couldn't see owt, though, it were too dark inside.'

'I did that too, Ma,' said Jack. 'But like you, I couldn't see a thing.'

'So did we,' said the children.

Ally tightened her lips. She had been the only one of them who wasn't keen on seeing inside. The shop held too many childhood memories for her.

Jack lifted his cap and scratched his head. 'So how are we gonna get her out?'

They all looked at him in anticipation and waited.

Finally he said, 'We'll have to get the coppers . . .'

'Oh, no,' Flo erupted. 'We can't do that.'

'Whyever not?' he questioned her. 'They couldn't possibly arrest a dog for breaking and entering.'

'No, but they could us,' she blurted, before she could stop herself.

He narrowed his eyes. 'Ma, what's going on?'

Pressing her lips together, Flo flashed a glance at Ally.

'Flo, you will have to tell him,' she said.

'Tell me what?'

'I'll speak to you later . . .'

'Ma, you'll tell me now,' ordered Jack.

She turned to the children. 'Go inside.'

'Ah, Ma . . .'

'Do as I say.'

They spun on their heels and ran.

Flo flashed a glance at Ally, then settled her gaze on Jack, sighing reluctantly. 'You ain't gonna like what I have ter say.'

'Just tell me, Ma.'

She shrugged her shoulders. 'Well, you asked for it. We shouldn't be here, Jack. We're trespassing.'

'What!' He clamped a hand to his forehead. 'I don't believe it,' he groaned. 'Ma!'

'At the time I had no choice. And we've bin here nearly two weeks now and not been challenged.'

'Yes, but even so . . .'

'So,' she cut in, 'with a bit of luck we can stay here a few more. Now even you have ter admit it's a nice place, Jack. And no wailing neighbours.'

'Yes, but still, it ain't right. We must be risking . . .'

'You don't have ter tell me, Jack,' Flo erupted. 'I'm well aware of the risks. And it's me that's taking 'em, nobody else.'

Ally, who had been growing steadily more uneasy, decided it was time she intervened. 'Shouldn't we be trying to do something about Sal? She sounds to be in distress.' In fact, Sal did not sound distressed at all to Ally. Her barks were just to alert them to her location. If she wasn't rescued soon, though, Ally had no doubt the situation would be different.

They both looked at her.

'Ally's right,' said Jack, taking charge. 'We'll sort Sal out first. Then,' he added, glaring at Flo, 'we'll sort out this matter, Ma.' He turned his attention from her and looked across at the building. 'In the light of what you've just told me, I see we have no alternative but to break in. I don't like it one bit but I can't see what else to do. There must be a window we can lever up just enough for Eric to climb inside. If we're careful we shouldn't cause much damage.'

'Eric'll do no such thing. I'm not involving the children in this.' Flo eyed Jack sharply. 'Have you done this kinda thing before, 'cos you sound like an expert?'

'No, 'course I ain't. How could you even think such a thing?'

'I was only asking. Anyway, if anyone is to enter that building, it will have ter be one of us. We'll need a crowbar or summat. There must be something lying about in one of the outbuildings. Come on,' she ordered, 'there's no time to waste.'

A flat-ended length of metal was found by Jack in the privy, of all places. 'I wonder what it was used for?' he said as he examined it.

'As long as it does the job we want it to do now, it doesn't really matter, does it?' snapped an agitated Flo. Secretly she did not like the thought of what they were about to do one little bit and wanted to get it over with.

The three gathered around the window they thought would be the best one to tackle. It was a tight fit. Prising it up proved more difficult than Jack had envisaged. It took over fifteen minutes to get the sharp end of the bar between the frame and the wooden edge of the sash.

'Whoever fitted this knew their job all right,' grunted Jack, leaning all his weight on the end of the bar.

Fraction by fraction the window moved up until it came to a stop and would budge no more.

Jack frowned at it. 'I think there must be catches inside stopping it from going up any further. I expect it's a precaution against burglars. It's gonna be the devil's own job squeezing through that space.' He popped his head through the gap, then withdrew it. 'It's no good calling Sal. The door to this room is closed. I hope it ain't locked.' He turned and looked at Flo. 'I don't see no other option but to shove Eric through.'

'I said, we're not involving the children.'

'Well, what else do you suggest?'

Ally stared hard at the ground. Although she didn't want to, she knew she had no alternative but to offer to attempt it herself, being slimmer than Flo. 'Maybe I could get through it?' she offered half-heartedly. 'I could try.' After all, she thought, she could not be prosecuted for breaking into her own property.

'Yes,' piped up Flo. 'Eric's not far off Ally's size, so if you were thinking, Jack, that he could get through, I don't see why Ally couldn't.'

The only thought running through Jack's mind was the fact that Ally could hurt herself. He would feel the same about any woman but could not voice his concerns because he knew Ma would misinterpret this and resume her vigilant watch on Ally and him. It had been bad enough the last time without having to go through it again for no good reason.

He jumped off the box. 'I'll give you a leg up,' he addressed Ally. And then added gruffly, 'Just be careful.'

She nodded as she gathered her skirt and climbed on to the box.

Manoeuvring her head and shoulders through was relatively easy, it was her bottom half that caused the problem. Flo placed her hands firmly on Ally's posterior, pressing it down to help her through. Ally was glad that Jack could not see the crimson face caused by her acute embarrassment at the undignified situation. She knew without doubt that a good deal of her legs must be on show. But Flo's pushing and shoving and her own wriggling suddenly did the trick, and before she could stop herself she fell through the window, landing in a heap on the wooden floor below. She was dazed for a moment and sat rubbing her head.

'A' you all right, Ally?' Flo asked, her head poking through the window.

'I think so. I've scraped my leg and bumped my head but apart from that there's no other damage.' There was a scuttering sound from the corner of the room. Ally froze and gave a cry. 'There's mice in here!' She rose hurriedly and as she did so a cloud of dust swirled up which she waved away with her hand. 'It's very dusty too,' she said, coughing, and looked up at the window. 'You were right, Jack. There are metal catches stopping the sash from opening further. I'll find something to stand on and release them, then you'll both be able to join me.'

Acutely mindful of the resident rodents she quickly found a solid wooden chair close by, dragged it across to the window, stood on it and released the catches. Jack gave Flo a helping hand then climbed through himself. They all gazed around for a moment.

'I think this must have been the dispatch office,' said Jack.

'What's a dispatch office?' queried Ally.

'I'm not really bothered what it was or wasn't,' said Flo. 'I just want to find Sal and get out of here.'

'Yes, yer right,' replied Jack. 'Come on,' he said, crossing over to the door.

He grabbed at the handle and turned it, sighing in relief. 'Thank God for that! I didn't relish breaking this down to add to our list of crimes.'

'Jack!' Flo scolded.

'Sorry, Ma.'

The corridor they entered was dark and airless, and halfway down branched off in three different directions. They made their way down it huddled closely together. Arriving at the intersection they all peered up and down, wondering which way to go.

'Buildings like this are a warren of corridors,' Jack said knowingly. 'We could end up losing our bearings if we ain't careful.' He cocked his head. 'I can't hear Sal barking, she seems to have gone quiet. Sal,' he called softly. 'Come on, gel, where are yer? Eh, I think I can hear her. Down this way,' he said, pointing to the right.

''A' you sure, Jack?' Flo asked. 'I'm sure her bark came from that way,' she said, pointing ahead.

'I don't agree,' piped up Ally. 'I think it was that way.' She indicated the corridor to the left.

'This is getting us nowhere,' fumed Flo. 'Come on,' she said. 'She's down here somewhere, I know it. I might act a bit daft sometimes, but there's nowt wrong with me hearing.'

Shrugging his shoulders, Jack allowed Ally to pass and they both followed Flo, intermittently calling to Sal.

'Here, girl. Come on, Sal.'

They passed several rooms which they looked inside, noting the bits of discarded furniture, but still no sign of the dog. Eventually, after seeming to walk for miles down the zig-zagging route the corridor took, they arrived at the end wall which held yet another closed door.

'I told yer she weren't down this way,' moaned Jack.

Tight-lipped, Flo said, 'Tek a look inside that room first. If Sal's not in there, only then can you congratulate yerself on being right.'

Jack glared at her before he turned the door knob and stepped inside.

'God love me,' he gasped, gazing around. 'Would yer just look at this lot?'

Flo quickly joined him and she too gazed around in awe.

'What is it?' asked Ally, unable to see past Flo and Jack.

'It's a treasure trove, that's what it is,' uttered a shocked Flo.

She stepped aside to allow Ally a view.

Ally too stood still, her mouth wide open at the sight that met her eyes.

The large room they had entered was piled from floor to ceiling with all manner of items.

'It's the stock from the shop,' Jack said. 'It's got ter be.'

'But why abandon it all?' queried Flo. 'It don't mek sense.'

Jack scratched his head. 'No, it don't. This lot must add up to quite a sum.' He turned and looked at Flo. 'You used to do yer shopping here, Ma. Why was it closed down?'

'How should I know? I just came down one Sat'day morning and it were shut. The notice on the door didn't give a reason.'

Jack returned his gaze to the mountain of goods illuminated by the sun drifting feebly in at a row of grimy windows. There seemed to be everything here from tin baths to boxes upon boxes of candles.

Flo bent down and picked up an oil lamp. 'I could do with one of these. D'yer think anyone would notice if this went missing?' She glanced briefly at Ally. 'Mine got broke.'

'Put that back, Ma,' ordered Jack.

Running through Ally's mind was the fact that everything in this room must rightfully belong to her. But she could not lay claim to it. 'I'm sure no one would notice,' she said. 'After all, judging by the amount of dust, I'd say whoever left this lot has no intention of coming back for it.'

'Ally, I'm surprised at you,' gasped Jack, spinning round to face her. 'You're encouraging Ma to steal.'

'I ain't stealing, I'm borrowing it,' snapped Flo matter-of-factly. 'If we ever find out who the owners are, or the shop opens again, I'll mek sure I pay for it somehow. And while we're at it,' she said, bending down again and grabbing up a box of a dozen white candles, 'I'll borrow these an' all.' She turned and walked out of the room. 'Come on, this ain't finding Sal.'

Jack stared after her, then looked at Ally. Without meeting his eye she walked past him and followed Flo down the corridor.

'I think we're lost,' said Flo after they had walked for several more minutes. 'Oh,' she said, arriving at a set of double doors, 'I wonder what's through here?'

'Ma,' Jack scolded, 'we ain't supposed to be sightseeing, we're supposed to be looking for Sal.'

'Well, she could be in here,' replied Flo, hand on one of the door knobs. Before Jack could respond she had opened the door and poked round her head. 'Oh, I say, it's the shop. Oh, it don't half look big with nowt in it. Come and have a look, Ally.'

Ally did not really want to. She could vividly remember visiting the place on several occasions as a very young girl with her father. While he had conducted his business she had sat demurely on one of the chairs placed by the counter and spent a very pleasant time sucking on a twist of barley sugar given to her from one of the dozen or so sweetie jars displayed on shelves at the side of the long dark wooden counter.

She could picture her father so clearly, dressed smartly in his black morning suit and top hat. All of the staff, mostly men, had nodded their head respectfully to him. Despite her youth she had known her father was well liked – his employees had not appeared nervous or anxious in his company. They all smiled to see him and had been very nice to Ally herself.

'Eh up, Ally, yer looking all vacant. What's up?'

'Oh, I'm sorry, Flo, I was just thinking, that's all.'

'You'll give yerself brainache with all that thinking you do. Now come on, have a look. Might be the only chance you get.'

Ally sighed reluctantly. 'All right.'

She joined Jack and Flo behind the counter, looking across the huge expanse to the front of it. The deep wide-fronted windows had been covered in brown paper which was dusty and crisp with age. Not much light filtered through but enough to see by. The room's use as a shop was still very much in evidence. All it lacked was the stock to fill the shelves and the staff to sell it.

'Can you imagine what it would have been like to work here?' enthused Jack. 'Mr Listerman is still talked of in the trade, yer know. It's said he was a grand man ter work for, considering he was gentry.'

Ally opened her mouth to agree but quickly snapped it shut. 'I really think we should go,' she urged.

A noise to the front of the shop froze them all rigid and they stared across. A key was being inserted in the lock. Before any of them could move the door opened and two shadowy figures entered.

Chapter Twenty-One

'This is the part of the building that was used for . . .'

'I'm not interested in what it was used for,' the taller of the two men rudely interrupted. 'It's the commercial value that concerns the people I represent.' He gazed around him then nodded. 'It's got plenty of potential.'

The elder of the two men, his black suit decidedly shabby against the other man's smart attire, eyed him anxiously. 'May I ask, potential for what, Mr Clacker?'

'To be split up and sold off.' Mr Clacker smiled. 'Lots of money to be made doing that. This building could easily accommodate a dozen or so decent-sized offices and a couple of warehouses, possibly more. Maybe the Bell Hotel would be interested in expanding? A slice off the end incorporated into their premises would give them ten or more bedrooms.' He nodded his head. 'It's in good repair, considering it's been empty so long.' He rubbed his hands. 'Oh, yes, this building has certainly got potential, all right. Right, I've seen enough. Now let's clear up a few facts before we proceed any further. It's been empty for how long . . . two years?'

'Just over.'

'And during that time, has anyone made an offer?'

'Well, no. But then, it's only recently come on the market.'

'Don't play games with me, man. It was empty, and regardless of whether it was on the market or not, anyone interested in even a part of it would have made an approach.'

'Well, yes, I suppose that's true enough.'

'So if an offer is made, I understand your firm is empowered to sell it?'

'Yes, that's right.'

'Or give it away, if necessary. Is that correct?'

'How did you know that?'

'I have ways and means. But is that true?'

'Well . . . yes. Miss Listerman did give those instructions.'

'Then I'll make you an offer of five hundred guineas.'

The older man stared. 'You are joking, Mr Clacker?'

He narrowed his eyes. 'I never joke where money is concerned.'

'But this building is worth much more than that. Five thousand pounds at the very least.'

'My good man, a building is worth only what someone is prepared to pay for it. True?'

'Well, yes . . .'

'Well, then, do you accept my offer or not?' Clacker smiled slyly. 'I'll make it worth your while.'

'I beg your pardon?'

'You heard me correctly. You're a paltry little clerk in a law firm with a pittance of a wage. I bet you're nudging seventy with no money put by to live on in your dotage.'

'I have a little.'

'What's a little? Twenty pounds? How would you fancy several hundred, eh? Accept this offer and push it through and I'll make sure you're amply rewarded. Call it a thank you. Think about it before you answer.'

The motionless audience of three in the shadows at the back of the counter, all acutely conscious of their dire predicament, could not help but listen to the proceedings with interest.

The jail sentence that would surely be imposed should their existence be discovered was not at the forefront of Jack's mind.

So this was how the rich made their money, he was thinking. If only he had the means to strike such a bargain. Though he thought it criminal that this fine building, situated just off the town centre, should be carved up. It didn't seem right. This part had been planned and built for use as a shop, and to Jack, a born retailer, the property should remain unchanged, not have its interior walls knocked about to make way for a warehouse or whatever this man had in mind.

He thought of his savings, money painstakingly put by, copper by copper, week by week, year by year. It currently amounted to just over four pounds ten shillings and as soon as he reached the grand sum of twenty pounds his plan was to find a shop, something small with a reasonable rent, buy as much stock as he could and put his heart and soul into building up his own business. He did not mind if the premises he rented were ramshackle to start with. At least it *would* be a start, which with hard work and determination could only lead to better things. Oh, what wouldn't he give to be able to have this place? He grimaced. He wished the men would go and conduct the rest of their business elsewhere. His active mind was running over ideas that could not possibly come to anything and that knowledge was depressing him.

Flo, with the fear of God on her, wanted to sneeze. The dust of years all seemed to have gone up her nostrils and she was fighting with all her might to stem the onslaught that threatened. She silently wished, prayed, beseeched the Almighty Himself to cause something – anything – that would send these men away. Here she was again, she thought, calling on the Lord in time of trouble. For the first time since she had gathered up her skirt and clambered over the outer wall she wished she had never set eyes on the place. It hit her forcibly that all the money she was saving in unpaid rent was not worth the risk. As soon as they managed to get out of here, hopefully undetected, she would set everyone on packing up, she herself going off in urgent search of new accommodation. The need for them all to get some sort of work was paramount now. If she had to fork out rent, the money she had was not going to last long. Suddenly a vision of Sal came to mind and an awful thought struck. What would happen if she bounded in now?

At this moment the danger of being discovered and the lies she had told to Flo and Jack were not uppermost in Ally's mind. As she stood motionless behind the counter she was intent only on the conversation between the two men.

She could not believe what she was hearing. Was that shabby little man – who she assumed had been instructed by the successor to Mr Bailey's business – really going to sell her property for a fraction of what it was worth, and considering taking a backhander for his trouble?

It wasn't the amount of money being discussed that was incensing her. Five hundred guineas, less lawyers' fees, was a fortune to her at the moment, and considering her precarious financial status would make a world of difference. It was the whole principle of the matter. Her grandfather had had this property built and had started Listerman's Emporium. Until his death her own father had developed that business and further emblazoned the good name of Listerman far and wide. Tobias, her father's own son, had shut this place down. Why, she had no idea. And now here was a stranger about to profit from Tobias's actions, after she had suffered so severely from them.

Well, she wasn't going to allow it. She could not allow it, for the sake of her father and grandfather's memory.

Before she realised what she was doing or the possible consequences, she stepped towards the gap in the counter and walked through it.

Jack gasped, horrified.

Flo's face turned ashen. 'Ally, what the hell are yer doing?' she hissed.

Ally did not hear her.

'There will be no sale of this property. At least not to you, Mr Clacker.'

Both men stared at the shadowy figure in front of the counter.

'What the hell . . .' erupted a startled Mr Clacker.

The older man stepped forward, peering at her. 'Who . . .' His mouth dropped in shock. 'Miss Listerman!' He stepped further forward, scrutinising her. 'It *is* you, isn't it, Miss Listerman? But . . . but . . . what are you doing here?'

Ally did not hear the loud gasp from behind her, she was far too interested in Mr Hubbard, the man she had just recognised as Clarence Bailey's clerk, who she felt had treated her so badly. 'What I am doing here is none of your business, Mr Hubbard. I am quite at liberty to visit my own property whenever I choose. It's what you are in the process of doing that gravely concerns me.'

Mr Clacker joined them, eyeing Ally in astonishment. He turned to Mr Hubbard. 'Is this some sort of joke? Do you seriously expect me to believe that this . . .' he glanced scathingly at Ally, noting the cobwebs clinging to her brown serge skirt and coarse cotton blouse, '. . . woman is the owner of this property? You must think I'm a fool if you do.'

Ally's back stiffened indignantly. 'Well, Mr Hubbard, are you going to answer the man?'

Mr Hubbard gulped. 'It's true, Mr Clacker. This lady is indeed Miss Albertina Listerman.'

'I would be obliged if you'd leave, Mr Clacker,' she said icily.

'Let's not be hasty, my dear,' he replied patronisingly. 'Maybe we can do business . . .'

'I meant what I said. This building will not be sold to you at any price.'

He glared at her, his face darkening. He knew he was wasting his time. Acute anger filled him at the thought of the very profitable deal that had been whipped from his grasp. He turned and wagged a finger in Mr Hubbard's direction. 'You'll be hearing from me, Hubbard. I don't like having my time wasted.'

He marched towards the door, yanked it open and strode out.

Ally looked hard at the man cowering before her. 'I suggest you leave too, Mr Hubbard.'

'But . . .'

'Now.' She held out her hand. 'I'll relieve you of the keys to my property, if you please. And I would be obliged if you would inform your employer that I will not be requiring his services any longer. I will be placing my business elsewhere in future.'

'Oh!' Mr Hubbard gasped in alarm. 'But, Miss Listerman, I beseech you, I did my best to find you when Mr Clacker made his initial enquiry, but not a trace could be found. Please believe me, Miss Listerman. And, I implore you, whatever you think, I wasn't—'

'At this moment, Mr Hubbard, I am in no mood to listen to your excuses. What concerns me is how many other unsuspecting clients you have fleeced of their rightful dues.'

'None. Oh, none, I can assure you, Miss Listerman. I had no idea what was on Mr Clacker's mind. When he showed an interest in this building, I had every reason to believe he was going to offer a good price.'

'Really? And did that good price include your cut?' Her eyes narrowed angrily. 'When I think how you followed me around my home, just to make sure I did not steal anything I was not entitled to . . .' She filled her lungs with air. 'Please go, Mr Hubbard.'

'But . . .'

'Go,' she ordered.

Shoulders hunched in resignation, desperately wanting to question Ally on what she proposed to do about his fate, the old man turned and scuttled towards the door. Before he passed through, he paused and looked at her, eyes filled with shame, before he pulled it to behind him.

She stood for a moment staring at the closed door, having difficulty believing what had just transpired. A sense of pride flooded through her. She felt she had handled the situation well. What Mr Clacker had been proposing to do had been unjust, and his offer of a backhander to Mr Hubbard, surely illegal. Regardless she had put a stop to it, even if she had lost herself a sale.

Suddenly she became conscious of Flo and Jack standing behind her and the possible repercussions of her bravado dawned on her. Now was the time to explain her lies, something she had hoped she would never have to do. All she could hope was that Flo and Jack would understand her reasons and forgive her. Swallowing hard, she took a deep breath and turned to face them.

'Flo, I never meant to deceive you. You neither, Jack. I . . .'

Flo spun to face Jack. 'Come on, we've packing ter do.'

'Flo,' Ally gasped, deeply shocked by her reaction. 'There is no need for this. Please let me explain . . .'

'Explain! I've heard all the explaining I want to hear. Jack . . .'

A dumbfounded Jack just stared at Ally.

She darted through the gap in the counter and grabbed Flo's arm. 'Please listen to me. Please let me explain all this.'

Flo wrenched her arm free. 'You lied to us, Ally.'

Her words stung. 'Yes, I did. But I had no choice.'

'Yes, yer did. You could have told the truth.'

'No, I could not, Flo. By doing that I would have frightened the children and then I would never have been able to look after them as you asked me to.'

'But what about since? You've had ample opportunity to come clean.'

'Yes, I admit I have. But how could I? You've never hidden your dislike for . . .'

'People like you,' Flo interrupted. 'No, I ain't. If I had my way, they'd all be hanged.'

'Ma!' Jack gasped. 'There's no need . . .'

'Don't Ma me, Jack. She's gentry when all's said and done, and I'll have nothing to do with the gentry in any shape or form. I vowed that on me father's death bed and I'll not go back on that for anything. She's proved me right, ain't she? They're all liars.'

'Flo, please,' Ally beseeched. 'I do not know just what it is you have against the gentry . . .'

'I'll tell you then, shall I?' she spat, eyes prickling with tears as dreadful memories surfaced. 'Them so-called gentry, them what are supposed to lead us common lot by example, killed my parents, that's what the gentry did.' She pushed so forcibly past Ally that she nearly

176

knocked her over. 'Come on, Jack. I said, we've packing ter do.'

'Flo,' Ally cried, 'there's no need for you to leave.'

She stopped abruptly and spun round, face contorted in anger. 'Yes, there is. I'll not sit down at the table with a gentry, let alone have one living in my house. Oh, dear, I'm forgetting meself. It's your house, ain't it? Huh! No wonder you encouraged me to tek the lamp and the candles. Well, it weren't stealing, was it? 'Cos they were yours and you gave me permission.'

She headed for the door. 'I said, come on, Jack. We've work ter do.'

Outrage filled Ally's being. She was angry to think that Flo could be so dismissive of her, despite the friendship that had steadily been growing between them. Darting past the woman she stopped abruptly in the doorway, blocking her route. 'Your ideas of the gentry have been clouded by what happened to you, Flo. We are not all alike. Some of us are quite decent, caring people. I had nothing to do with what happened to your parents yet you are blaming and punishing me for it. I in turn could judge you by my experience. I was robbed of all I owned by a coachman. Therefore I could say all people of your class are thieves. Is that true, Flo? Are you and Jack thieves?'

Flo glared at her. 'You know we ain't,' she hissed, incensed.

'Yes, I do know that. But if I had not had the privilege of getting to know you, I could very easily have categorised you together with that thieving coachman. The least you can do is afford me the courtesy of listening to an explanation. If, after you have heard what I have to say, you still want nothing to do with me, then I'll accept that and I'll be the one to leave.

The women's eyes locked.

Shaken by what had transpired, Jack arrived at Flo's side. 'Ally's right, Ma. Listen to her. Just hear what she has to say. That can't hurt, can it?'

Her lips tightened. Jack was right. She was being unfair. Ally deserved the right to give her explanation. But regardless of what she had to say, nothing would change Flo's opinion, of that she was adamant. She hated the gentry. She folded her arms, tilted her head, face set grimly. 'Go on then, explain. But you'd better make it quick, I've things to do.'

Ally's eyes flashed. 'I'll make it as brief as I can.' She clasped her hands tightly, taking a deep breath. 'My parents were killed when I was eleven years old. Such . . .' She shuddered. 'Such a dreadful time.' Her eyes prickled with tears. 'I wish you could have known my parents, Flo. They were kind people, caring very much for all those around them. Despite knowing how you feel about the gentry, I'm sure you would have liked them.' She ignored Flo's grunt and carried on. 'The day after they died, Tobias arrived at the house. His arrival came as such a shock. Before then I had not known of his existence, of the fact that my father had been married before – nothing. I was soon to learn that Tobias was not a kind man, he cared nothing for me and took no pains to hide the fact. Consequently I was packed off to boarding school. I was lonely and frightened and it was a miserable time for me, but I tried my best. The only family life I had was thanks to my friend Annabella. For her kindness, and that of her family, I will be forever grateful.'

Her eyes glazed over. 'To . . . to have your life destroyed by someone else's actions is a terrible thing. My brother – half-brother, to be precise – did that to me. Why he did what he did I do not know, and never will now. He committed suicide and his reasons died with him. I was only to learn of his deeds unexpectedly through the family lawyer. I could not comprehend just what he was telling me. My family once owned factories, shops and other properties. When Tobias died everything had gone, every penny, except this.' Her eyes ranged around. 'Why he did not sell off this place with everything else is a mystery. Even the lawyer could not understand it. But the result was that I woke one morning under the mistaken illusion I was a wealthy woman, only to find out several hours later I had nothing except my clothes and a few personal possessions.'

'How come you never knew any of it?' asked a dumbfounded Jack.

'Tobias did not allow me to have any involvement in monetary affairs. In fact, I was not even allowed to run the household. He saw to everything.'

'That explains a lot.'

'Ma!' Jack scolded.

'Well, it does,' Flo protested. 'Anyway, get on with it,' she prompted. Nothing Ally had said as yet had been sufficient to change her opinion or excuse the telling and living of Ally's lie. 'This Annabella,' she asked bluntly. 'If her family were so good ter yer then why didn't they help yer when they found out yer were penniless?' She puffed out her chest. 'Didn't want ter know yer, was that it?' she added coldly.

'I never gave them the chance, Flo. I assumed, rightly or wrongly, that they would reject me after what my fiancé and his mother did.'

'Your fiancé?' uttered Jack.

Ally grimaced. 'I should have said my ex-fiancé. On learning of my predicament, he turned his back on me. I was being wed for my money.' She paused momentarily, her bottom lip trembling. 'Out of everything that has happened to me, the one thing I am glad of is that I found out the truth about Lionel.' She could not quite decipher the look on Jack's face. It was a mixture of bewilderment, disbelief, astonishment – but also of pity. It was the pity that hurt the most. She wanted to tell him not to pity her because it had not taken her long to realise that Lionel's rejection, as devastating as it was at the time, had turned out to be one of the best things that had happened to her.

She turned her attention back to Flo's stony stare. 'Annabella and her parents were out of the country when all this happened. But, regardless, I could not burden them. Anyway, then I had my possessions stolen by the coachman conveying me to Leicester. I had been hoping that my lawyer would help me out. He had offered to, and I had pinned all my hopes on that. But the coachman had other ideas. He abandoned me at an inn, taking everything I owned with him, and the proprietors thought me a thief because I couldn't pay my bill. After making me work off my account with them, they threw me out in that terrible storm.'

She wrung her hands. 'I wanted to die then, Flo. I had nothing to live for. I could not see a way out of my dreadful situation.' She gave a wan smile. 'You were right, I was not equipped to deal with anything. I knew nothing of fending for myself.' She took a deep breath. 'I cannot remember much of that night . . .' she shuddered '. . . except for my ordeal in the river and the struggle to get out. I cannot remember coming across the boatshed or how Jack found me. I just know that when he offered to take me with him the next morning, I could not refuse. I said I had a job offer to go to but in fact I had not. I went to see my lawyer to ask him if his offer of help still stood. It was not to be. Sadly he had passed away. I was devastated. Selfishly, all I could think was that his death meant the end for me too. That was when Jack came across me in the doorway, a broken woman.'

She paused, gaze fixed on Flo. 'The rest you know because you have seen and helped me through it. After hearing all you have, I hope now you can appreciate just how I felt at that time.' She looked at Jack and smiled. 'I am so glad you won the toss of your sixpence because my only hope of salvation was your taking me with you. I owe you all such a debt of gratitude. Without your help, I dread to think what would have become of me. You have been responsible for giving me back my self-respect and teaching me how to face the world I now live in.'

Returning her attention to Flo, she eyed her closely. 'I implore you, now you know the truth, please do not let this change matters between us. But whatever you decide, I do not regret my lie. I had no choice but to tell it at the time, and afterwards I could not tell the truth, knowing how you felt about the gentry. I am not ashamed to admit that I needed you, Flo. Needed all of you. I still do. I hope it has not been one-sided? I'd like to feel I have given something to you all in return. I meant what I said – if you want nothing to do with me now, I will be the one to leave. You can stay here rent-free until the building is sold, on that you have my word. And that offer is unconditional. Call it my way of repaying you. The decision is yours. Now I will return to the house and wait to hear what you have to say.'

Head high, she turned and walked out of the door.

The silence was deafening.

Jack looked hard at Flo. 'Ma . . .'

A hand was lifted to silence him. 'Don't say nothing, Jack.'

He stepped back, face troubled. By her tone he deduced that Flo had decided to carry out her threat and send Ally away. Such a decision would have a catastrophic effect, and not only on himself. The children had grown to love Ally so much she was considered nothing less than part of their family. Flo too liked having her around and would miss her dreadfully if she forced her to leave. He had learned to bury his need for her deep, had learned to cope with treating her as nothing more than a sister. If he was honest, though, part of him had longed for something to happen that would enable him to claim her. That longing had been cruelly smashed. In the light of today's revelations he now knew he could never hope or expect Ally to be his.

Still the thought of never being near her or in her company again was something he could not bear. He would sooner endure the pain of never having his desire fulfilled than not see her again. At least having her near he could keep a watchful eye on her, make sure no harm befell her, the same as he did with Ma and the kids. He could not do that if she went away.

His respect and love for Ma were far too great for him to challenge her with the fact that it would be wrong to send Ally away because of her own feelings towards the gentry. From what she had told him, Ma had suffered greatly at their hands. In that respect, as much as he did not want to, he understood why this news of Ally's had been met with so much anger. As much as he wanted to try to sway Ma, the decision was hers alone and whatever she decided he would have to stand by.

Flo turned her face away from Jack's so he could not witness her shame – a shame that was filling her whole being. That shame was only partly due to Ally's dreadful tale of suffering endured. Mostly it was for her own attitude. Ally was right: she did blame all the gentry for one particular person's deeds. Ally herself probably didn't even know the guilty family yet Flo was convicting her of their crimes. She knew for as long as she lived she could never forgive them but it occurred to her for the first time that she could not go on forever blaming the whole of monied society for the ills she had suffered.

She swallowed hard. In reality Ally had enriched all their lives. If she went away she would be greatly missed. Flo herself would miss her dreadfully. Whether she liked it or not, Ally was very much part of their family and it would be so wrong of Flo to sever what had grown between them for the sake of her own misguided hatred. Knowing Ally was true gentry need not change anything. She was still the same girl who had come to them all those months ago. No, that was not true. None of them was the same and never would be again.

Ally's arrival had without doubt changed many things, the most obvious being that without it Flo herself would still be living in fear over the plight of the children. That in itself more than compensated for any lie she had told. Flo took a deep breath. They could still live and work alongside each other. As Ally had unashamedly said, she needed them – probably as much now as she had done then. But was it not also true that they needed her?

Flo raised her head and looked at Jack out of the corner of her eye. He stared back, waiting for her response. Out of all of them, he would be the one to miss Ally the most if she went from them. Jack cared greatly for that girl. But, regardless, he had not for one instant gone back on his word and for that Flo admired him. For despite her soul searching and resultant change of heart over her feelings towards the gentry, nothing would change her opinion of a union between two people of such differing backgrounds.

'Come on, Jack, we'd better get back,' she said matter-of-factly. 'I'm just hoping Sal got out the way she got in. And the kids'll be wondering where we've got to.'

He eyed her sharply, unable to hide his grave concern. 'And what have yer decided, Ma?'

Heading for the door, she called, 'I've decided I need a cuppa. A good strong one. I bet you could do with one too?'

There was no need for them to climb out of the window as Ally had used her keys to unlock one of the doors. As they emerged Flo and Jack could not help but smile, relieved at the sight that met them. Eric and Emily were throwing a ball to each other, Sal waddling between them both, trying to catch it.

'Sal came out the window ages ago,' shouted Eric.

She came up to greet them and Flo bent to pat her head. 'You, gel,' she scolded, 'have a lot to answer for. 'Cos if it weren't for you going missing, today's revelations might never have come out.' And whether that would be a good or a bad thing, she thought, remained to be seen.

She paused inside the doorway of the building they now called home. A preoccupied Ally was sitting at the table nursing a mug of tea, a look of utter desolation clouding her lovely face. On sensing Flo's presence she placed down her mug and rose.

Ignoring Ally's questioning look, Flo eyed the teapot. 'Oh, good, yer've made a cuppa. Pour us one out, gel.' She pulled out a chair and sat down opposite Ally, accepted the mug then settled her gaze on the younger woman. 'I was just thinking,' she said matter-of-factly, 'that since you own this place, I don't think there's any rush for us to all go job hunting today. I reckon we can afford to leave it 'til Monday. What do you think, Ally, eh?'

Ally stared at her, stunned, for several long moments before a broad smile spread over her face. 'I agree wholeheartedly, Flo. I think we deserve a day or two of rest.'

Jack, hovering in the doorway, sighed with relief.

Chapter Twenty-Two

That afternoon as Ally came out to pump some water she observed Jack standing further down the yard, gazing intently up at the building. She smiled before abandoning the bucket and walking across to him.

'You could take the keys and have a good look round, if you would like to?'

He jumped, shocked, so engrossed in his thoughts he had not heard her approach. 'Eh! Oh, I'd love to, Ally. You don't mind?'

'Why should I?' She eyed him thoughtfully. His manner had held a trace of subservience. 'Jack, as I told Flo, what you know about me now changes nothing. I am still the same person you knew yesterday and I don't expect, or want, to be treated any differently.' She smiled. 'Flo certainly isn't doing so, or the children, so why should you? Now I'll go and fetch the keys and you can look around to your heart's content.'

'Thanks, Ally.'

Later she was sitting at the table preparing vegetables for the evening meal. Flo was kneading pastry. She pounded the dough as though she was beating it to death and Ally raised her eyes in concern.

'Is anything the matter, Flo?'

'Eh! Oh, I'm trying to work out a plan of campaign.'

'Campaign?'

'Yeah. Where best we could start our search for work. As my dad used ter say: "There's nowt gained by sitting around on yer arse." My dad talked a lot of sense so I reckoned it'd be best if we had a list of places we'd enquire at, instead of wandering around aimlessly.'

'That makes sense to me.' As Flo returned to her pounding, continuing her task, Ally watched her closely for several moments. There was something she wanted to ask the older woman and she felt now was as good a time as any. She risked a rebuff but was prepared for that. 'Flo?'

'Mmm?'

'Your father. You said he talked a lot of sense. What was he like?'

Flo abruptly stopped her task and eyed her sharply.

'Maybe I should not have asked,' Ally said worriedly.

Flo sighed, face relaxing. 'It's all right, me duck. Why shouldn't you?' She dropped the dough into a floured bowl and sat down. 'You said I would have liked your folks, Ally. I reckon in turn you'd have liked mine.

They were good people. My dad was a grafter. Little man, he was, wiry, on the thinnish side. Mam now, she was different. Plump and cuddly but little too. They reckoned I got my tallness from me great-grandmother's side. They were all tall apparently. Originally, back in the seventeen hundreds, the family moved down from Newcastle way for work. Somehow they landed up on Squire Belldon's estate near Matlock. Sprawling place it was. Acres and acres of land. Over forty tenants he had. He was a much feared man, was Squire Belldon, and mean with his tenants. But work was work, Ally, and mean or not, working for Squire Belldon gave them a living and a roof. And that was what was important.

'Me dad and his father before him were cattle men. I don't remember much of me grandad, but I often used to accompany me dad when he drove the cattle ter market. Mam wouldn't have anything to do with them, they frightened her to death, but me now, I didn't mind. We lived in one of a little row of four slate-roofed cottages with mud floors and a midden out the back. It was a hard life 'cos we never had much, but I was happy. Me mam had lost four babies before I came along so I was cherished. It used to get me down sometimes, but even I knew back then it was better to be fussed over than treated like some of the other kids on the estate.'

Resting her elbows on the table and her chin in her hands, listening intently, Ally asked: 'And Jack and his parents lived next-door to you?'

'Eh? Oh, yes, that's right. Next-door, 'til they died of dysentery and we took Jack in, that is.

Flo lapsed into a thoughtful silence.

'You . . . you said the Squire killed your parents, Flo?' Ally spoke softly. 'Was it by accident?'

Flo's mouth tightened and her eyes narrowed. 'It was no accident,' she said harshly. 'Although Squire Belldon never lifted a finger to strike them down, what he did was as good as.'

Ally was dismayed to see tears glistening in her eyes and suddenly wished she had never asked the question.

Flo's gaze rested on her, but it was not Ally she was seeing, it was the evil face of her family's former master, a man on whom they had depended for their very existence. Even all these years later she could still picture him vividly, eyes mocking, taunting them as he had had them turfed out. 'My father's crime was to challenge him, and as a result he turned us out.'

'Turned you out!' Ally exclaimed, astonished. 'What on earth did your father challenge the Squire over? It must have been something very serious to result in such a drastic action.'

Flo stiffened. 'Serious? Yes . . . it must have been,' she said abruptly. Serious, she thought, was not a strong enough word for what had happened. But she wouldn't think of that terrible time, she couldn't. It was all far too distressing for her. It was bad enough remembering the aftermath. And even now, all these years later, if the truth came out it could still destroy lives. 'I don't know what it was.'

Although she was too polite to probe further, Ally got the impression that Flo knew exactly what it had all been about.

'Didn't anybody try to do anything to stop it?' she asked.

Flo's head jerked. 'Such as, Ally? You must know by now that a master's word is law. And anyone siding with us would've been turfed out too. But he didn't just leave it there. Oh, no, Squire Belldon liked to do a thorough job. He spread word around about me father, told all sorts of lies about him. Consequently he couldn't get work of any kind.'

Ally was appalled. 'So what did you all do?'

'The only thing we could – we took to the road.' Flo shook her head ruefully. 'Life had been hard on the estate but nothing compared to living in the open. And we had the harshest winter for many a long year. I was sometimes that cold I thought me limbs would drop off. Me dad, a man who'd worked night and day all his life with nowt to show for all his hard labour, was reduced to stealing so his family could eat. But it wasn't the lack of food or the cold that killed him – he died 'cos that bastard broke his heart. Belldon took away his right to provide for his family.' Her eyes glinted. 'It was the most terrible thing, watching the life drain from me father, but can you begin to imagine what it was like for me mother? She idolised him. He was her life. When he went she just gave up. She couldn't live without him, see.' Her voice faltered. 'And it weren't a good death. She almost coughed her lungs up before she breathed her last while I stood helplessly by. There was nothing I could do for her. Not a thing.'

'Oh, Flo,' Ally whispered. 'I'm so sorry.'

'Yes, so am I. I still miss 'em, even now.' She took a deep breath, fighting to control her emotions. 'So there I was, Ally, barely fourteen, left on me own with Jack to care for. And it wasn't easy getting any kind of work with a youngster in tow, but I was determined I wasn't going to have us both land in the workhouse. Even when we were starving hungry and frozen with cold, me dad stood firm against that and died for his convictions. Once in the workhouse you never get out, and while he was breathing me father wouldn't hear of it.' Her voice fell to a hushed whisper. 'Maybe if he hadn't bin so proud they would still both be alive.'

Her voice trailed off and she paused for several long moments. 'It was very hard for me but I took any work I could get. Spud and fruit picking, skivvying, you name it. Sometimes I was reduced to begging so Jack could have food. They were bad times, Ally, terrible. That's why, to me, having bin through all that, the hovel off Sanvey Gate didn't seem so bad. Me saving grace was landing the job in the hospital laundry and finding lodgings at Mrs Kitchen's. She watched Jack for me while I went to work. I had to bung her extra for it, mind. She was a kind lady, was Mrs Kitchen, and good to Jack, and I hated leaving her the way I did. But then, I had no choice, had I?'

'No, you didn't.' Ally sighed softly. 'You have had a hard time of it, Flo. I thought life was bad enough for me when my parents were lost at sea, but I cannot compare what I had to endure to what you have gone through.'

'Well . . . best not to dwell on that, eh, gel? What you were born into has caused enough trouble between us.' She wiped a hand over her wet eyes, then flashed a wan smile. 'D'yer know, that's the first time I've really talked about all that? I feel better for it an' all. But I have to put it all to the back of me. It happened over twenty years ago, and as I nearly learned to me cost, yer can't carry grudges forever.' She studied Ally for a moment. 'Do you carry one against that half-brother of yours?'

'Tobias?' Ally stared at her thoughtfully. 'There are so many questions that remain unanswered, and I'd dearly like the answers. But I suppose I've been too busy trying to build a life for myself to harbour grudges. I am angry, I will say that. Angry at the state of affairs he left me in.'

'And yer've every right to be. I'd bloody want some answers too! He must have squandered a fortune, from what you've told us?'

Ally nodded. 'Yes,' she said absently. 'A fortune. But as he's dead . . .'

Their attention was diverted as Jack strode in. They could not help but notice that his eyes were shining with excitement.

'What you bin up to?' asked Flo.

'I've just been having a good look around the building. Ally, what a' yer going to do with all the stock?'

'Stock? Oh. I . . . er . . . haven't given it any thought. I presume it will go with the building when it's sold.'

Flo eyed Jack quizzically. 'What's on yer mind?'

He grinned. 'Can't fool you, can I, Ma?' He sat down at the table, fixing keen eyes on Ally. 'Have yer thought about selling it?'

'Selling it? Who to?'

'Anyone who'll buy it. There's a lot of stuff there, Ally. I had a good poke through it and there's all sorts.'

She frowned. 'I wouldn't know the first thing about how to do it.'

'You, gel, knew nothing about fish gutting 'till someone showed yer. But Jack knows plenty about selling, don't yer, our Jack? Come on,' Flo ordered, 'spit out what's on yer mind.'

He placed his hands flat on the table. 'Well, there's the shop, sitting empty. Then there's the stock gathering dust. Why don't you open the shop as a temporary thing, Ally, and sell it all? It'd bring in a tidy sum. Better than someone else having it. You'd probably lose on the deal quite heftily if the stock were sold as a job lot with the building.'

Ally stared at him, her mind in a whirl. 'Open up Listerman's?' she whispered, and looked at him quizzically. 'Is that possible?'

''Course it's possible. It's your shop. Your stock. There's nothing to stop yer.'

'He's right, Ally,' Flo erupted. 'My God, he's right.'

'Yes, he is, isn't he?' she replied thoughtfully. 'If we managed to sell the stock it would bring us in much needed money. It would be all profit, wouldn't it? Mmmm.'

Flo smiled warmly. Ally had said 'us', not me. 'Us'.

She ran her hand over her chin. 'I'm still not convinced opening Listerman's is the right thing to do, though. Could I lose a buyer if the shop was trading for however long it took to sell the stock? I was told the building was practically worthless. I would hate to devalue it any more.'

'Opening it up wouldn't do any harm as I can see,' replied Jack.

'Neither can I,' agreed Flo. 'Surely a building being used would be far more interesting to someone than one lying empty? And don't look so surprised, our Jack, I ain't completely brainless, yer know. I do know about some things.'

'I can see that,' he said, grinning.

'Cheeky bugger,' she responded. 'Anyway,' she continued, 'that bloke earlier offered five hundred guineas. The old man said it was worth at least five thousand. You can't turn your nose up at either sum, and you could live for the rest of yer life on five thousand guineas. To my mind you ain't got nothing to lose by sticking out for a good price.'

'Yes, you are right, Flo. I have nothing to lose by holding out for the right buyer, because in the meantime we can carry on living here.'

'There's always the possibility,' said Jack, his mind working overtime, 'that if things go well, you might want to keep it going.'

I doubt that, Ally thought. If they managed to sell part of the stock to bring in some cash she would consider they had done all right.

They both looked at her keenly. 'Well?'

Thoughtfully she rose and headed out of the door to stand in the yard, staring across at the building. My goodness, she thought. Opening up Listerman's. What would she be getting herself into? But as they had both said, what had she to lose? At the moment none of them had any income coming in. That state of affairs was a very worrying one.

Jack arrived at her side. 'Have yer made your decision?'

She turned and faced him. His blue eyes bored deep into hers and a tide of emotion ran through her. Oh, Jack, she thought, all thoughts of the shop momentarily flying from her, if only you could care for me as I do you. But during the last few weeks it had pained her gradually to realise that her feelings for him were not returned. He treated her as nothing more than a sister. She fought to concentrate all her efforts on her immediate problem and returned her attention to the building. 'I still don't know what to do, Jack. Common sense tells me to do it but . . .'

'Something's holding you back?'

'Yes, something, but I don't know what. Fear, I expect, in case it all goes horribly wrong.'

'I wouldn't be encouraging you to do this, Ally, if I thought anything could go wrong.'

186

She looked up into his eyes. 'No, Jack, I know you wouldn't.'

He could contain himself no longer. 'I tell you what, I'll toss you for it.' He delved into his inside jacket pocket and pulled out his battered leather wallet, extracting a coin.

'Is that the sixpence?' she asked.

'Me lucky one. Yes, it is.' His eyes twinkled brightly. 'I wouldn't trust such an important decision on any old tanner, yer know.'

She laughed, then grew serious. Jack was right. She hadn't realised until now that opening the shop could be another turning point in her life; even if it only brought in a few pounds, that money could change their lives.

'Go on then. Tails we open the shop, heads we don't.'

'No, it doesn't work like that. I flick it first, then we decide.' The coin flew upwards. He caught it and slapped his hand over the top.

A thrill of anticipation ran through Ally and she stared, transfixed, at Jack's hand, his fingers lightly passing backward and forward across the coin. He was grinning and if Ally had not known better she would have said his expression was a mischievous one. But then she knew Jack took this as seriously as she did.

Her impatience to know the outcome spilled over. 'Jack!' she scolded.

'All right, calm down. You women have no patience. I say tails we open, heads we don't.'

Ally frowned. 'Is that not what I said?'

'Was it? Oh! In that case we agreed, then.' He lifted his hand and his whole face lit up. 'We open the shop, Ally,' he erupted excitedly. 'It's tails.'

Mixed emotions raced through her: of excitement and fear. At that moment she didn't know which was the stronger. Suddenly she gasped, eyeing Jack in confusion. 'How did you know the outcome without looking at the coin?'

'Eh? Don't be daft, Ally, 'course I looked at the coin. If I could do tricks like that, I'd mek a fortune on the stage.' He grabbed her arm. 'Come on, let's go and tell Ma the good news.'

She stared after him agog. She could have sworn he hadn't looked at that coin. Still, his enthusiasm was so infectious she couldn't help but feel swept along by it. She sighed. Once again a major decision had been decided on the flick of Jack's lucky sixpence. Oh, well, she thought resignedly, she could not go back on it now. Besides, it had turned out to be a lucky flick of the sixpence for her the last time. She would just have to hope this one was also.

Chapter Twenty-Three

'Eric,' Flo scolded as she stopped her counting of the numerous metal lamps spread before her and wagged a finger at the boy, 'dent that bath and we won't be able to sell it without knocking down the price. Drag it carefully.'

He reddened. 'Sorry, Ma.'

This had all been a game to him and Emily, helping to clean up all the stuff that was piled in this room and then take it through to the shop at the front. Well, it had started out as fun but both children had been quick to realise that what they were doing was to be taken very seriously. As he dragged the dusted bath, one of many, along the corridor he thought for the umpteenth time how exciting it was to learn that Ally was the owner of this enormous building. She must be rich, he thought. Well, if she wasn't now, she would be when all this stuff was sold.

Emily, in her element, met him at the door. 'Stack it with the others,' she ordered. 'By the far wall. And do it properly,' she added. 'So they don't all fall down.'

'I am doing it properly,' he bellowed back. 'And yer can stop being so bossy. You ain't in charge, yer know.'

'Oi, you two,' intervened Jack from his position up a ladder, 'cut it out and just get on with it. We ain't got time for arguing, there's too much to be done if we're going to open on Friday.'

They both mumbled something then hurriedly continued their tasks.

Not for the first time Jack asked himself how all this stock had come to be abandoned. Considering how much it was all worth, it did not make sense. Still, he thought, best to count that as their good fortune and not dwell on it. Although he knew Ally did. The mystery puzzled her greatly.

He took a moment to look around. The shop was coming on well and he was glad he had insisted they set it out properly. No point, he had said, just dumping it all and letting potential customers rummage through. No good sales could be made that way. His eyes fell on the dozen or so bolts of material they had found stacked behind five mangles. Ma had been struck speechless on discovering the mangles and had quickly claimed one for their own use, to which Ally had readily agreed. Having the luxury of a mangle, they had argued, would

188

make all the difference to their washdays, leaving them more time to help in the shop.

The material, dress fabric as well as for soft furnishings, still wrapped in its protective covers, was a find indeed. Ma had tried to claim a bolt of that too, but there Jack had put his foot down. She could have it if it wasn't sold. If he hadn't made a stand, Flo and Ally between them would have commandeered much for themselves, sadly depleting their stock. He did not care if they thought him unfair. Apart from in a way fulfilling his dream, the scheme they were pursuing was meant to bring in as much money as possible. They hadn't taken kindly to what he had said but eventually saw his reasoning.

Flo arrived, armed with a mug of tea and a plate holding a noggin of bread and lump of cheese. 'Take a minute to eat this, Jack. Don't want you fading away with hunger.' She put them on the counter and gazed around. 'It's looking good, ain't it? Just like a proper shop.'

'It is a proper shop, Ma,' he laughed, climbing down from the ladder.

'Oh, I didn't know that we had any of these,' she said, walking across to a stack of carpet beaters and picking one up.

'Put it down, Ma. You don't need one of those, we ain't got any carpets.'

'I know, but I might have one day.'

'When that day comes you can have one. Not until.'

'You're a hard man, our Jack,' she scolded, but there was a twinkle in her eye. She put the beater down. 'I've counted those lamps. There's three different sorts. Twenty-nine in all. What price were you thinking of charging?'

'Half a crown and three bob. The smaller one . . . I dunno, I'll have to check.'

'How?'

'By visiting other shops and checking their prices, then putting ours a bit lower.'

'I could do that. You've plenty to keep you occupied here. Won't take me long to pop round a few shops and I won't be so conspicuous as you. Women go from shop to shop checking prices all the time. They have to, don't they? I'll go now.' Glancing around, she blew out her cheeks and exhaled loudly. 'Do yer think we'll be ready to open on Friday? There's still so much to do. We ain't sorted out half the stock yet.'

'With luck, and plenty more hard work.'

He hoped Ma could not detect his own apprehension. They had reached a stage in the proceedings where the thrill and excitement of any new venture had settled sufficiently for worry over what they had tackled to creep in. His concern was not for their eventual success, he had enough faith in their combined abilities not to be worried over that. It was whether they would be ready to open in time that bothered him. Everything had to be just right. Start as you mean to go on.

189

He was vehemently hoping that things went so well that Ally would want to keep the shop going and let him manage it for her. As this week had progressed it had become glaringly obvious to him that it would be years before he could ever afford his own business, and then years more, if he ever managed it, to build it up to the kind of establishment he had in mind. And he would never ever get the chance of a magnificent place like this. If he were lucky a corner shop on a back street was what he would have to settle for. He gave a deep sigh. Running this place would fulfil a great need in him and also, God willing, provide a decent living for all of them.

'Where's Ally and the kids?' he asked lightly in order to change the subject.

'The kids are stuffing their faces like they've not eaten for weeks, and Ally . . . well, she's around somewhere. Last time I saw her she was disappearing down the corridor with a pile of brooms. I thought she was heading in here.'

Ally had taken what she had intended to be a minute's break, having like all of them worked without stopping since before dawn had broken. She knew Flo had gone to prepare some food and had said she would join her after she had finished her inventory of the assortment of brushes. Left alone she had suddenly remembered that with all they had to do, she had not found the time to investigate the rest of the building beyond the part used for the shop. Now she thought it was about time she took a proper look around.

The rest of the building had been partitioned from the shop and could only be reached from inside via a door at the end of a long corridor, each of the separate units having their own front doors and yards. It took several attempts using different keys from the large bunch she had taken from Mr Hubbard before she found the right one. The door was stiff and unyielding and she had to push against it hard to get it to open.

As she wandered around she was amazed not only by the sheer size of the place but the grandeur of the building. Her grandfather had spared no expense in its creation. She had an eye for architecture and was thrilled to discover the ornate ceiling complete with mouldings. In what she assumed must be the centre of the building was a wide sweeping staircase with a broad mahogany banister, topped with a thick layer of dust and curtain of cobwebs. From her position at the bottom of the stairs, as she gazed up to the small glass dome in the roof, it struck her that the building had not originally been designed to accommodate offices, the partition had been done after, and she wondered what her grandfather had originally had in mind for it.

Maybe, she thought, her grandfather had planned the shop to be much larger than it was now but for some reason had changed his mind? Leicester after all, although expanding rapidly, was a small market town then and probably there had not been the need for such a large shop. She suddenly felt a desire to know more of her family's history, but as things were, all she could do was guess. It was a pity, she thought, that Mr Bailey had passed on. He could have told her much, filled in many gaps.

She moved on. The number of businesses it had held before closing astonished her. Names still painted on doors and in dusty brass panels on walls told her that lawyers, coal and corn merchants, spice importers, to name but a few, had carried out their businesses from the Listerman premises. The rents they had paid must have brought in a very considerable income besides the Emporium's. Renewed anger filled her at the thought of the paltry sum Mr Clacker had had the nerve to offer. Regardless of whether their venture worked or not she was glad she had not accepted it and had sent him away.

More confused than ever as to why Tobias had had the premises emptied, she made her way back, locking the connecting door firmly.

So engrossed was she, she did not hear Jack's footsteps approaching around the corner. They bumped into one another so hard that Ally stumbled backwards, tumbling awkwardly on to the hard floor and yelling with pain.

Shocked for a moment, Jack hurriedly gathered his wits, threw himself down beside her and, before he could realise what he was doing, gathered her into his arms. 'Ally, oh, Ally,' he uttered. 'A' you all right?'

She felt no pain from the bump on her head or the throbbing of the bruise forming on her backside; all she could feel was Jack's strong arms around her, his closeness to her. She lifted her head, gazing deeply into his eyes. 'Yes, Jack,' she whispered. 'I'm fine.'

He scanned her face closely. 'Thank God. I thought at the very least you'd broken something.'

He could feel her, smell her, and passion overwhelmed him. How long he had willed this moment to happen, dreamed of it, prayed for it, and now it was here.

All reason left him and his lips came down on hers.

She responded willingly. Their kiss was a hungry one, needful, full of emotion – neither wanting it to end.

Suddenly he sprang away from her, face filled with shock. 'Ally, I'm . . . I'm so sorry. Forgive me. I didn't realise what I was doing.'

From her position on the floor, she stared at him, mystified, as he took several steps away from her.

'Jack, please,' she uttered. 'It's all right . . .'

'No, it's not,' he erupted. 'I took such a liberty. It . . . it . . . was wrong of me. It will not happen again, that I promise.'

Before she could stop him he had turned and gone.

Tears sprang to her eyes. How long she had dreamed of being crushed in his arms, the taste of his lips upon hers. She had finally got her wish and then had repelled him. Her bottom lip trembled as deep anguish filled her. She must have done or why had he sprung away from her as if she had burned him, his face filled with horror? He had not wanted to kiss her. Somehow, she must have forced him. The distress filling her was unbearable. She had been wrong all along. That look he always gave her, the strong sensations she felt whenever he was close – had been all in her mind.

Intense pain stabbed her to the heart. Jack did not want her. And to find that out after she had given herself to him so willingly! How was she ever going to face him again when all she wanted to do was pick herself up and run?

But she could not do that. They were all reliant on one another for this venture to succeed, as they were desperate for it to do. This situation had to be faced. It was going to be very hard but she had no choice. As soon as the stock was sold she would go. She did not want to leave the people to whom she had grown so close but how could she stay, having to face him every day, knowing what she now knew?

Fat tears flooded her cheeks. The humiliation of it all, the utter grief of his rejection. She had felt the same over Lionel, only somehow this was worse, because suddenly she realised that she loved Jack Fossett, loved him as she'd never loved before.

She shut her eyes tightly. What was she to do? How would she handle it? Then it came to her. She would have to pretend their intimacy had never happened. Force the incident away. She would have to. It was the only way to cope until she could leave.

Jack, only feet away around the corner, collapsed against the wall and groaned silently in despair. How could he have done what he had after promising Flo not to? And what must Ally think of him? He shut his eyes tightly. He could still feel her in his arms, still taste her on his lips. That kiss – one that should never have happened – had reawakened and forged an even greater longing for her.

His head flopped forward and he buried his face in his hands as realisation struck him. He loved her. Had loved her for a long time. He knew now his feelings for her had started the moment they first met and her magical voice had drawn him to her, despite the mud that covered her. Against the odds, he had recognised her qualities even then.

Ally was different, special, one of a kind. His fascination with her had developed and grown as he had watched her struggle to become accustomed to her predicament. And it was only recently that he'd fully realised how much of a struggle that must have been, when he had learned of her true origins.

His love for her was not just a superficial affection for a pretty face, but a deep love, an enduring love, one to last a lifetime. But how futile. Ally was out of his reach; even more so now he knew the truth about her. Someone of his class had no right to hope or expect a person of her calibre ever to consider the likes of him.

Whilst he had still been under the mistaken illusion that she had just been adopted by the 'toffs', his hope that one day they might come together had seemed reasonable. But now even that was shattered.

But how did he control such deep emotions when all he wanted to do was gather her in his arms and run away with her, cherish and protect her to the end of his days?

His whole body sagged and he shook his head despairingly. Surely, somehow, he must have done some terrible misdemeanour for whoever it was up there to punish him so severely? But whatever that terrible deed, his immediate problem was how to face Ally again after his impulsive actions.

He gazed intently at the brown-painted wall opposite. His only choice was to act as though it had never happened, pretend to himself that it had just been one of his dreams. Force it out of his mind. Hope Ally could find it within herself to forgive his inexcusable behaviour.

Righting himself, he took a deep breath and dragged his feet down the corridor.

Much later that night, gratefully resting her aching legs on the fender at the front of the range while she sewed herself a shop apron, Flo eyed Ally first then flashed a glance at Jack, who was poring over ledger books he was preparing for use in the shop. She grimaced thoughtfully. Something was wrong between them, but she could not put her finger on quite what it was. But there was definitely an atmosphere, strong enough to cut with a knife.

Since she had returned from her task of price-checking in several shops she had felt the tension between them. So what could have caused it? she thought.

She flashed another glance at them both and her expression changed to one of worry as a thought struck. She hoped that Jack had not started all that nonsense again, especially since she had had every reason to believe he was keeping to his promise. No, it couldn't be that. Jack had too much sense, especially now he knew Ally's true background. That in itself should convince him that any pursuit of Ally would be doomed to failure.

She stifled a loud yawn, then inwardly smiled as a thought struck. That was it! They were tired, bone weary. Their quietness was all due to that. And it wasn't surprising, after all the work they had tackled. It was just her own fatigue causing her mind to run riot, seeing problems that were not there. And apart from the work, they were all worried over the outcome. The little pot of money they had was dwindling rapidly, despite being augmented by Jack's precious savings. Regardless of making do as much as they could, items needed to open the shop had had to be purchased. The white material for their aprons, for instance. Fancy finding all those bolts of material and not one of them white! And they all had to eat.

Flo yawned again. She would have done anything to set aside her sewing and make her way to bed, but she couldn't. Just two days to go and still so much to do. As she resumed her task fear filled her. This venture had to work. It just had to.

Chapter Twenty-Four

Gripped with anxiety, Ally paced up and down behind the counter. It was fifteen minutes to their planned opening time and every last detail that could go wrong was racing through her mind.

She stopped her pacing and eyed Jack who was busy making a last-minute check around. 'Do you think anyone will come?'

He turned to face her. 'Ally, for the hundredth time, trust me they'll come. Even if it's only to have a good nosy, they will.'

'But nobody knows we are opening, and . . .'

'Ally, I've already told yer, when I was cleaning the windows several old biddies stopped and asked me what was going on. Believe me, old women's gossip is the best advertisement we could get. And remember, gossip is free and in my opinion pays far higher dividends than billboards or the papers.' He paused and looked hard at her. He suspected the last few days had been more of a strain for Ally than for the rest of them. He deduced that this venture had far greater implications for her. This must be bringing back painful memories. The building was not just any old building, it was part of her past, a past that was far removed from the life she was living now. Being here and doing what they were could not be easy for her. He understood completely why she had shown initial reluctance.

He wanted to go to her and hug away her concerns and worries but that was the one thing he could not do. The one good thing about all this hard work was that the incident in the corridor had been forgotten. The tension between them immediately afterwards had been so strong Jack marvelled that Ma had failed to notice it. Thank goodness she hadn't. Facing her questions and rebukes with everything else that was going on and his own dreadful feeling of remorse was something he could not have done. The only thing he did sometimes wonder was how Ally felt about the incident. From her attitude he could not tell whether she was angry or not. But one thing he did know: she had responded willingly to his kiss, had enjoyed it as much as he had. He wasn't so daft that he didn't know that. But, regardless, the answer to his question must not weigh on his mind. In their circumstances it hardly mattered.

'Are yer all set?' he asked Ally.

'Sorry? Oh, yes, I think so. I'm having difficulty remembering all you've taught me.'

'Don't worry, Ally, it will all come back when they swarm through the doors. If yer get stuck, just give me a nudge and I'll help you out. You'll soon get the knack of it.'

'I hope you are right. I've a terrible feeling I am going to make a dreadful mess of things.'

Flo appeared in the doorway behind the counter, straightening her apron. She eyed them both, rubbing her hands together. 'Well, that's us ready. If anything needs packing, me and Emily will do it. Eric'll be through in a minute. He's just dashed to the lavvy once again. I keep telling him it's only nerves.' She puckered her lips. 'Yer do think he'll be all right out here, Jack?'

'Ma, he'll be fine. I'm just glad it's the school spring holiday 'cos we wouldn't have managed without him and Emily. Ah, here he is. All set, Eric?'

The boy was quaking inside but tried not to show it. 'I think so, Jack.' He looked towards the door, frowning. 'What's that noise?'

'Yeah, what is that noise?' frowned Flo. 'Sounds like bedlam outside. 'As summat happened, do yer reckon?'

They all stared across as Jack went to investigate. Paper blinds, ready to be pulled up at opening time, covered the display windows and door. Gingerly he poked aside the one on the door and peeked through. The sight that met his eyes made him gasp. 'Oh, my God!' he exclaimed.

'What, Jack? What's happened?' Flo erupted.

He spun to face them. 'A bloody miracle, that's what.' He beckoned them over. 'Come and see for yerselves.'

Gathered by the door, they peeked through. A queue stretched further than they could see. It was of chattering women armed with their shopping bags and, hopefully, their purses.

'Get these doors open now, Jack. Come on,' Flo ordered. 'If them ladies want serving, let's serve 'em before they go somewhere else.'

Chapter Twenty-Five

Three equal piles of coins sat on the table in front of Ally. Smiling warmly, she pushed one towards Jack and one towards Flo.

Both stared at them in bewilderment.

'What's this?' asked Flo.

'Your share,' she replied.

'Our share?' said Jack. 'But we didn't expect a share, Ally. Just a wage.'

'A wage? Surely not, after all the effort you have both put in? Oh,' she exclaimed, 'how remiss of me, I have forgotten the children. They should be rewarded for their efforts too.'

'Give over, Ally,' scolded Flo. 'What you have given me is more than I've ever earned in a month, let alone two days. I'll sort out the kids' payment. But yer right, they deserve paying. They've worked harder than galley slaves, bless 'em.'

'A' you sure about this money?' said Jack. 'I still don't think it's right. I'd have bin quite happy with a wage.'

'So would I,' agreed Flo. 'I never expected this, Ally.'

'Didn't you? Oh. I thought this was a joint effort between us.'

'So it is to some extent,' said Jack. 'But after all, Ally, it's your building and your stock, so it wouldn't be fair to call us equal.'

She smiled at him. 'Yes, I know it's my shop and stock. But a shop that would still be lying empty waiting for a buyer, and stock gathering more dust, had it not been for your idea. And let's face it, Jack, without your expertise I doubt we would have so much money to divide. And as for you, Flo, a paid employee would not have worked half as hard as you have. Not only did you parcel everything that required it, you also managed to keep us fed as well. I do not know how you managed it.'

'And what about you, Ally?' said a blushing Flo. 'For someone who's never served behind a counter before, you did a pretty good job of it.'

She laughed. 'Maybe in the end. I have to admit I was terrified at first. For a start I hardly expected the shop to be so well patronised, and with Jack kept so busy, I had no choice but to get on with it. I had some scary moments, especially when I was asked if we stocked a lump hammer. But thanks to Jack, I now know what that is.' Her eyes sparkled. 'Oh, it was so much fun. I really enjoyed myself helping people choose what they

197

wanted and being careful not to be pushy. Just like you taught me, Jack.'

Leaning on the table, he eyed her keenly. 'Did you enjoy it enough to keep it going?'

'Keep it going? What, the shop, you mean?'

'I do. You have to admit it beats working for someone else?'

Ally eyed him thoughtfully. This escapade had been fun, but to consider it as a serious future for them all . . . it was a huge undertaking. Although they were halfway set, already having the building and the fitments, so many other things would need to be considered.

She clasped her hands and studied the table top hard. Even though Jack and she had managed to work together amicably since the incident in the corridor, so much so she had often wondered if she had imagined it, hadn't she been planning to leave once the stock was sold? But when she had made that promise to herself, she had not taken into consideration what she would do then. She would have to find lodgings, and cheap lodgings at that as the money she had made was not a fortune. And, as Jack had said, she would have to get a job eventually. The thought of working for people like Mr Sileby and Mr Gideon, now she had had a taste of being her own boss, was not an appealing one. Even worse were the jobs Flo had suggested, rat catching and midden clearing.

But her main concern was not for her finances, nor was it a fear of branching out on her own. In truth she did not want to leave the family to whom she had grown so close. The thought was unbearable. But if she did not leave, that would mean seeing Jack day in, day out, and not only would they be living in close proximity, they would also be working together as well. Could she cope? Could she keep up the difficult pretence that nothing had happened between them; keep acting as though she cared no more for him than she would have a brother?

She pondered carefully. If it meant staying with them, surely she could continue the effort, and as time passed it would become easier. The worst thing she would have to face was when Jack met a woman. She would have to be prepared for that to happen. Because he would. A good-looking man like Jack would meet and marry someone eventually. For a moment she considered Lizzie Green and wondered painfully whether Lizzie was a serious contender. Despite her wish for Jack to find happiness, she hoped it would not be with Lizzie.

She stole a glance at him under her lashes. His thatch of fair hair needed a cut. It was curling over his shirt collar, and a long strand fell over his brow and brushed his long lashes. She fought to quell an impulse to reach over and gently move it from his eyes. She must never do that, never again think of anything like that. If she was going to consider his proposal then the first thing she must do was harden herself to such an extent that actions such as that never entered her mind again, starting right now.

Inhaling deeply, she forced her thoughts to a more businesslike course. Jack was right. This was a wonderful opportunity to do something, make something of themselves, a chance that might never come again if she decided against it. Maybe in hindsight Tobias's dreadful deeds had not left her in such a catastrophic situation as she had at first thought. His selfish actions had forced many things. She had had to learn to look hard at herself, adjust to her new surroundings, value what was really important, see life as it really was. It was up to her now to forge a future for herself. She would be a fool not to go ahead. If it failed, she could still do as she'd originally intended: sell the building and split the proceeds with Flo and Jack. But with hard work and luck, maybe it would not come to that.

She took a very deep breath and raised her head. 'Jack, if we did proceed with your idea, how would we go about it? I know we already have the premises and the fixtures and fittings. What else is involved?'

His face lit up. 'You are considering it then?'

'Jack,' scolded Flo. 'Stop pushing her.'

'I ain't, Ma. I just want Ally to understand what a great opportunity this is.'

'I understand, Jack. But I would like to hear the answer to those questions before I make my final decision.'

'Oh, right. Well, the first thing we need to do is to put all the money that was made back into a pot, then work out the bare minimum we need to survive on. What's left needs to be put into replenishing the stock, possibly diversifying.'

'What d'yer mean by that, our Jack? Stop using words I don't understand.'

He grinned wickedly. 'I thought you said you weren't brainless, Ma?'

Flo reached out and cuffed him round his head. 'Yer cheeky beggar.'

He yelped playfully and Ally smiled.

'Jack means sell other things,' she said.

'Such as?' asked Flo.

'I dunno,' he replied. 'But anything of quality we can afford that people want is worth considering. It's just a thought, Ma. But the more different things we sell, the wider the clientele we'll bring in. We just have to work hard at finding ourselves good suppliers and build up links with them.'

Ally eyed him in admiration. He certainly knew his trade all right. She would never have thought of selling anything other than the range of items that Listerman's had previously offered.

'I used ter get really frustrated with Mr Green,' Jack continued. 'He was so narrow in his business views, just stuck with suppliers he had dealt with for years, never giving new ones a chance. You have to take chances in this game or you stagnate. And that means, Ma, you don't progress.'

'I know what stagnate means,' she snapped. 'I fell in a pond once that was stagnated. Full of slimy green water. Ugh!' she shuddered. 'I was covered in the stuff.'

Jack and Ally stared at her, both fighting to control an eruption of mirth.

'So . . . er . . . Jack,' Ally hurriedly changed the subject, 'you make it all sound so simple?'

'It is when it boils down to it. Although I can't deny that it's going to be very hard work for us all. But what have we to lose? If it fails, at least we've had a go. But I can't see it failing.'

She digested his words and turned to face Flo. 'And what about you? What are your feelings on all this?'

'Me? Oh, I'll go along with what you both decide.'

Ally eyed her in surprise. Flo's answer was most uncharacteristic. 'I really would like to hear your opinion,' she said. 'Your views are as important as Jack's and mine.'

'Really? Oh, in that case, I agree with Jack. What have we to lose? Meking a go of the shop beats cleaning middens any day. I don't mind hard work, I've had to work all me life so that part don't worry me. And I ain't worried about scrimping on money. I've done that all me life as well. So I'm willing if you two are. And you can rest assured, I'll put me all into it.'

Ally smiled. 'I've no doubt of that, Flo. You neither, Jack. And I hope you know I will too.' She paused, eyeing them both for several long moments as she weighed everything up. 'All right,' she said finally. 'I agree too. Let's go ahead.'

'Oh, Ally,' Jack blurted. 'You won't regret this. I know yer . . .'

'Just a moment,' she interrupted him. 'You never let me finish. We proceed on two conditions.'

His face fell and Flo frowned.

'What's them?' asked a wary Jack.

'Well, we go ahead on the understanding that it is a proper threeway equal partnership. I insist upon that.'

They both stared in shock.

'You really mean that, Ally?' Jack whispered.

She smiled. 'It is the only fair way to do it.'

'Oh, Ally,' said Flo. 'I can't take it in. Really I can't.'

'You said two conditions,' said Jack. 'What's the other?'

'That we change the name of the shop. After all, it isn't really Listerman's Emporium any more, is it? I may still be a Listerman but you two are not and if we are to be equal partners the name should reflect that.'

They were both speechless. This was just too much for them to take in.

'What . . . er . . . name were you thinking of?' Jack finally asked.

'As we are partners now, I think we should all decide. But as a suggestion what about . . . Listerman and Fossett?'

'Listerman and Fossett?' Flo repeated in awe. 'My name above the door. Oh, Ally, really?'

She nodded. 'I rather like the sound of it myself.'

'So do I,' Flo erupted. 'So do I. Wadda you think, Jack?'

He nodded vigorously. 'Sounds grand to me too. Listerman and Fossett,' he mouthed excitedly.

Chapter Twenty-Six

Laden with bags, a hot and thirsty Ally dodged across the busy street. It was her turn to do the shopping and for the last hour she had jostled amongst the crowds in the market, and haggled – as she had been painstakingly taught by Flo – over the foodstuffs she now carried inside three heavy hessian bags. Although she was more than willing to take her turn with the chores, food shopping gave her the least satisfaction. The whole process was so time consuming. Now Listerman and Fossett was beginning to take off, her time could surely be put to much better use? But then, she thought, someone had to do it. She stopped for a moment to position the bags more comfortably, and not for the first time thought it a pity they did not sell foodstuffs themselves. Not only would they be free to take their pick, it would also save this daily grind.

She set off again and in order to take a short cut through to Humberstone Gate, turned into a narrow side street congested with an assortment of ancient, higgledy-piggledy buildings, a remnant of Elizabethan times. Halfway down her route was blocked by a loaded handcart and as she approached a loud argument coming from the dilapidated building beside it reached her ears.

As she inched her way with difficulty past the cart a man stumbled out of the doorway, landing against the cart with a thud, followed closely by a young woman of no more than sixteen years, her pale face furious with anger. She grabbed two of the bags from the loaded cart and heaved them towards her.

Mesmerised, Ally stopped and stared.

'Wadda yer think yer doing?' the man shouted.

'Teking back what's mine,' she responded frenziedly.

Righting himself, the man flew at her, trying to grab the bags, but the girl was too quick for him. Swiftly turning from him, with a strength seemingly impossible in such a thin frame, she hauled the bags back inside the building then blocked his route with her body. 'You'll 'ave ter kill me first,' she threatened.

The man's face darkened thunderously. 'I paid fer those. They're mine. Now if yer know what's good for yer, yer'll hand 'em back.'

Her head reared back defiantly. 'You paid half the agreed rate, so you only get half.'

'I paid what the work's worth.'

'In your opinion, not mine. Yer a thieving bastard, Wilf Milner, that's what yer are!'

'I'd watch yer mouth, Nelly,' he hissed threateningly. 'I could have yer for slander.'

'Slander, is it? And what you're saying about our work ain't? Substandard, you said.' Hands on hips, she glared at him. 'There's nowt substandard about our work, and you know it.' Grabbing hold of one of the bags remaining on the cart, she wrenched it open and pulled out a handful of knitted stockings, waving them towards Ally. 'Oi, you there, missus?'

Ally hurriedly glanced around before looking back at the young woman. 'Me?' she asked.

'Yeah, you,' she replied, skirting round to her. 'Would yer say these were substandard? Would yer, eh?'

Bemused, Ally put down her bags, accepted the garments that were being thrust at her and examined them closely.

'Well?' Nelly snapped.

'I would say they are of excellent quality.'

'See,' Nelly spat triumphantly. 'Excellent, she said, so how come you reckon they're substandard? Go on, explain yerself?'

'What would she know?' he erupted, looking at Ally with a nasty glint in his eye.

Her own flashed warningly. 'Actually, I know quite a lot about hosiery and I appreciate quality when I see it. And these, my good man, are quality.'

Nelly wagged an angry finger at him. 'See, yer thieving bastard! I'm sick of you lining yer own pockets at our expense. You won't be 'appy 'til we work fer you for nothin'. Well, I'm not standing fer it no more. Now ged off out of it and don't show yer face round 'ere again. A' you listening?'

Wilf Milner's shifty face contorted dangerously. 'You'll regret this, Nelly Bramble,' he hissed.

'Regret?' she erupted. 'The only regret I've got is being taken in by the likes of you in the first place. I'd sooner starve than have owt more to do with yer.'

'And starve yer will,' he spat. ''Cos regardless of what she says, that work's shoddy and no other bugger's gonna take it off yer hands for any more than the price I'm offering. I wa' doing you a favour, I wa'. Well, if this is all the thanks I get . . .'

'Thanks!' Nelly cried, astounded. 'You've got a bloody nerve, you 'ave, Wilf Milner. Oh, bugger off before I wallop yer one!'

Wilf shot round to the back of the cart and grabbed the handles. Before he pushed it off he turned to Nelly. 'Mark my words, you'll be crawling back ter me before the day's out.' He put all his strength behind the cart and as it lurched into motion, eyed Ally menacingly. 'If I see your face again, you'll be sorry, you interfering cow!' He gave the cart an angry shove, purposely causing it to tilt slightly and a sharp protruding piece of wood above the wheel caught her hip. She cried out in pain. 'Serves yer bloody right fer being so nosy,' he laughed. Shoving the cart hard, he ran off with it down the short street and disappeared around the corner.

Nelly spun round to face Ally, eyeing her in concern. 'A' you all right, missus?'

She rubbed her hip. 'A scratch, I think, no serious damage. Who was that man?'

'Him? Just the biggest bastard that's ever bin born, that's who.' Her shoulders suddenly sagged. 'Oh, I'm sorry, I'm just so mad. But wouldn't you be if yer'd slaved nineteen hours a day to get an order finished, then not been paid proper for it?'

'Yes, I would. I would be very annoyed,' Ally agreed. 'What exactly do you mean, he's not paying you properly?'

'He agreed a price like 'e always does for a dozen gross of assorted stockings. Then when it came to paying up time, he hummed and hah-ed and med excuses to offer us less. That's usual, but this time he went too far. Halved his price, he did, and we only get twopence a dozen as it is. *And* we have to buy all the yarn *and* pay the repairs on the loom. Then we 'ave ter eat, to say nowt of the rent. How we s'posed ter do all that, eh, on a penny a dozen?'

Ally stared at her, astounded. 'I do not know,' she replied.

'No, neither do I.'

'But it's scandalous, as you say. Those stockings sell in the shops for at least eightpence a pair, I know for a fact. You produced them and sold them to Mr Milner for twopence a dozen and now he's offering you a penny!' Shaking her head, Ally grimaced. 'Someone is making a lot of money somewhere.'

'Yeah, and it ain't us.' Nelly suddenly froze and stared at Ally in horror. 'Oh, me lady,' she uttered, giving a slight bob. 'In me anger I didn't realise who you was. Please forgive me.'

'I beg your pardon?' she said, wondering who this girl had mistaken her for. 'Oh!' she exclaimed as the truth dawned. 'Please do not curtsey like that. I cannot help the way I speak.'

Nelly swallowed hard, still staring at her in awe. 'Oh, but you've a lovely voice, missus.' She eyed Ally up and down, noting that although her clothes were of a much better quality than the threadbare assortment she herself was wearing, Ally's could not be classed as anything like the garments the wealthy wore. 'I was mistaken about yer being posh, it was yer voice that did it.' She frowned quizzically. 'How come you speak like that?'

Heartily tired of continually having to answer the same question, Ally did not do so this time because her thoughts were elsewhere. An idea was forming and as it developed a feeling of excitement mounted. 'Er . . . Nelly, is it?'

She frowned. 'That's right, missus. Nelly Bramble.'

Ally held out her hand. 'Albertina Listerman. I'm very pleased to meet you.'

Warily, first wiping her hand down her coarse sacking apron, Nelly accepted Ally's and shook it. 'Likewise, I'm sure. But why are yer pleased ter meet me?'

'Because I think we can help each other. Look, Nelly, what do you propose to do with the rest of those stockings?'

Nelly turned and eyed the bags blocking her doorway, then looked back at Ally, sighing despairingly. 'There's only one thing I can do and that's go crawling back to Wilf Milner. I'll 'ave ter else we won't eat.'

'Maybe that is not your only answer. Would you sell the stockings to me?'

'Sell them to you? And what would you be wanting wi' eight hundred and sixty-four pairs of stockings? All in different sizes,' she added.

Ally grimaced. 'I can appreciate your confusion. That sounds an awful lot of stockings.' She laughed. 'Far too many for me ever to get through in my lifetime. But, you see, I have a shop. Well, I'm a partner in a shop. Listerman and Fossett's.'

Nelly gaped again. 'Listerman and Fossett! You're that Listerman?'

Ally smiled. 'Yes, I am.'

'Oo-er. Nice shop that. I can't afford to go there, though.'

'Oh? But our prices are very competitive.'

'Don't make no difference to me what yer prices are, I still couldn't afford ter shop there. Most of what we have gets give us or I go down the pawn to see what they've got. Anyway, I thought it was more a hardware kinda shop nowadays?'

'Yes, we have tended to concentrate on that end of the market, but we do also stock limited lines on other household items. But your predicament, Nelly, has given me an idea.'

''As it? Oh!'

Several people passed by and Ally glanced around. 'Is there anywhere we can talk business?'

'Talk business? Well, er . . . yer can come in, if yer like? Well, yer'll need to meet me granddad if it's business yer want to talk.' She eyed Ally warily. 'But I'll warn yer, I ain't about to be fleeced again.'

'No, no,' Ally hurriedly reassured her. 'I'm sure the arrangement I have in mind will benefit us both.' And, she thought, I should not be attempting this at all without discussing it first with Jack and Flo. But, she argued with herself, as she gathered her bags and followed Nelly inside the dwelling, time spent in discussion with her partners could delay this opportunity.

Ally had been utterly horrified by the conditions in the tumbledown dwelling in Sanvey Gate; she was mortified to see the dire conditions into which she was being led now. Discoloured plaster had come off the walls in huge chunks in places, exposing the ancient framework of the wattle walls of the narrow dark passageway she was being led along. The ceiling was low and Ally, at five foot five, had to bend her head to get through the doorway.

The room they entered was small and sparsely furnished. A blackened pan hung over the fire, whatever was inside bubbling furiously – it smelled to Ally similar to the mutton bone soup Flo had many a time prepared when money was tighter than it usually was. The table in the centre of the room held an oil lamp with a cracked funnel, two age-stained chipped mugs, a tin jug half full of milk covered by a ragged piece of muslin, and on a plate was the remains of a loaf of bread. In one corner of the room stood a pot sink, inside it an old bucket which Ally presumed was for collecting water from a pump somewhere outside. By the fireplace were two uncomfortable-looking wooden chairs, the leg of one propped up by a block of wood. To either side of the room, up against the walls, were two threadbare, moth-eaten straw shakedowns. There were no adornments of any kind to alleviate the room's starkness.

From somewhere close by the steady rhythm of metal against wood vibrated.

Nelly indicated one of the chairs and spoke loudly over the noise. 'If yer'd like to sit down, I'll fetch Granddad. 'E don't like ter be disturbed when 'e's working but I'm sure 'e'll want to 'ear what yer've got ter say. This business with Wilf Milner 'as upset 'im badly and I know 'e's worried about 'ow we're going ter manage on even less than we normally get. The workroom's next-door. I won't be a minute.'

Ally smiled as she put down her bag and sat. It was several moments before the noise stopped and several more before a gnarled old man hobbled in, followed by Nelly.

'This is Miss Listerman, Granddad.'

A pair of shrewd hazel eyes scanned her closely then he nodded a greeting.

'Good morning,' Ally responded.

She waited patiently whilst the old man slowly and painfully lowered himself into the chair opposite, settled, then leaned forward and eyed her keenly. 'Nelly sez yer interested in our stockings?'

'Yes, that is correct. If we can come to an amicable agreement, I would like to purchase them.'

He pursed his lips and stared at her thoughtfully for several moments, then turned to Nelly who was standing to the side of him. 'Mek a cuppa, gel. We can't discuss business wi' dry throats.' He leaned back in his chair. 'Nelly tells me that yer one of them Listermans that 'ave the shop on the corner of Humberstone Gate?'

'Yes, that is correct, Mr . . . Bramble?'

He gave a toothless smile. 'That's me. Martin Bramble.' He paused, studying her thoroughly. It was some moments before he said, 'I dint realise Listerman's 'ad opened up again 'til Nelly just told me. I don't get out much nowadays. I'm either at the loom or sitting in this chair. That right, Nelly?'

Leaning over the fire to swop the pan for a kettle, she smiled fondly at him. 'That's right, Granddad.'

'Listerman's was a landmark when I wa' a lad. Me and me pals used ter sit on the wall opposite and watch gentry carts being loaded wi' the orders. Me mam used ter clout me round the ear for idling when I should have been helping me dad wind the bobbins. It were the 'osses, yer see, that fascinated me. I used to scrump apples so I could feed 'em. Oh, it were a sad day when I heard the place 'ad shut down. Still, I'm glad to 'ear it's opened again.

'Listerman himself cut a fine figure and it was said he was a fair and just man, qualities yer don't come across very often in the likes of the wealthy. You sure you're the daughter? Yer might speak nice but yer don't look wealthy ter me.' This was not a question, more of an accusation.

'The Listermans are no longer a wealthy family, Mr Bramble. I have to work for my living. But, I can assure you, I am the daughter of Robert Listerman and would like to think I have inherited his fair and just ways.'

Martin pursed his lips. 'That remains to be seen. Well, as it's stockings yer want to talk about, let's talk about 'em. Yer won't get better quality than off my loom. I tek pride in me work, not like some I could mention. I use good yarn, not inferior stuff, and I get the work finished when I say I will. I'm one of only a handful of homeworkers left now. All the rest 'ave gave up and gone into the factories. Too old I am for a factory, but I still 'ave ter earn a living.' He smiled affectionately at his granddaughter who, having filled the tin teapot with boiling water, was adding milk to two mugs. 'Well, me and Nelly do it between us, don't we, our Nelly? I don't know 'ow I'd manage wi'out 'er.'

'Oh, ged away, Granddad. You do all the 'ard work at the loom. Me, I just seam the stockings and wind the bobbins.'

It all sounded extremely hard but very skilled work to Ally, and she was most impressed. During her lifetime she had worn and ruined many pairs of stockings, woollen as well as silk, and never given a thought to how or who produced them.

'Yer tea, Miss Listerman,' Nelly said, handing her a mug. 'I'm sorry we ain't got any sugar.'

'That's quite all right,' Ally replied. She detested tea without sugar but would not be so impolite as to say so. She sipped tentatively on the sour weak liquid, trying not to show her distaste. 'Mr Bramble, Nelly told me that you are usually paid twopence a dozen for your stockings.'

'That's usually right, miss. I couldn't believe it when Milner welched on his deal and offered us a penny. A deal's a deal in my book.' His wizened face scowled deeply. ''E's a cheating so and so is that Milner, so 'e is.'

'Are you obliged to sell to him?' Ally asked.

'I can sell me stockings to whoever I like. I'm not tied to anybody,' he said proudly. 'We deal with Wilf Milner 'cos 'e's the only putter out who operates now around 'ere.'

'Putter out?' queried Ally.

'Fancy name for a middleman. 'E sells our stockings on to the warehouses, who in turn sell 'em on to the shops and suchlike.'

'Oh, I see.'

''Is days must be numbered, what wi' all the factory-made stuff these days. In 'is case that might be a good thing, 'cos 'e's nowt but a bloody crook!'

'Granddad,' Nelly scolded, squatting down beside his chair. 'Mind yer manners in front of Miss Listerman.' She had the grace to blush, considering the language she herself had used when dealing with Wilf Milner.

'Oh, I agree wholeheartedly with your grandfather, Nelly. Mr Milner does indeed seem like a . . . bloody crook. And from what I observed of him, he deserves everything he gets.'

Martin grinned. 'You've got 'is measure all right, gel. I think I like you.' He passed Nelly his empty mug. 'You can 'ave your tea now, I've finished wi' my mug, gel.' He rubbed his hands together and eyed Ally keenly. 'Right, I think I might be interested in what yer've got ter say, so let's 'ear it.'

Chapter Twenty-Seven

Ally burst through the gate, nearly dropping the bags, hardly able to contain the excitement she felt. She could not wait to tell Jack and Flo of the deal she had struck and hoped they would be as pleased with it as she was. Most importantly today's incident had formed an idea that did not have to begin and end with just stockings. The principle could be applied to many sorts of goods, which would not only bring in ample profit for themselves but would also give poor outworkers a much improved return for their efforts. There must be many people like the Brambles who produced quality goods in and around Leicestershire. All they themselves had to do was seek them out and put a proposition to them. That was, of course, providing Jack and Flo agreed.

Ally's arrival woke Flo who had fallen asleep in her old rocker which she had dragged out into the warm summer sunshine. She'd intended to rest her legs for just a few moments after a hectic few hours in the shop before she began on the dinner preparations.

'Oh, my God,' she cried. 'Where the 'ell am I?'

Ally rushed to her side, put down her bags and laid a calming hand on her arm. 'It's all right, Flo. You must have dozed off.'

She rubbed her eyes. 'I didn't mean to. I only meant to snatch a quick sit down.' She gave a loud yawn and stretched herself. 'Oh, d'yer know, Ally, I dreamed I was living in a cottage in the country, with roses around the door and pretty flowers in the garden. I could even smell it.' She glanced across to the cobbled space between their house and the small brick outbuilding by the far wall where Ally had been attacked by bats. 'It's a shame we ain't got a bit of ground where we could grow some flowers. I've always hankered after a bit of a garden. Still, I ain't complaining.' She raised her head and eyed Ally sharply. 'Where you bin? I was getting worried.'

'Oh, Flo, I have some wonderful news to tell you! But I would prefer to tell you and Jack together.'

'News? Oh, Ally, what is it? It ain't awful, I hope? Oh, go on, tell me?' she pleaded. 'Yer've got to tell me? Oh!' She clasped her hand to her mouth. 'Jack. I've left him with only that new 'prentice to help and I ain't even made a start on the dinner. Well, I couldn't do that, could I?' she said scathingly. 'It's in those bags.' She scrambled to her feet and straightened her apron. 'What time is it?' she demanded.

'I'd guess nearly noon. For goodness' sake, calm down, Flo. Take a minute to come to yourself. I'm sure Jack would have sent for you if he wasn't managing. And as for the meal, it won't hurt us to eat later for once. The children won't mind bread and cheese when they come home from school.'

Flo eyed her thoughtfully. 'No, I s'pose not.' She grinned broadly. 'Oh, it's grand being yer own boss, ain't it, Ally?'

She nodded. 'Most definitely. The only one that can sack you is yourself.'

It was after their evening meal when Ally finally managed to get Flo and Jack together to tell them her news. She need not have worried, both were extremely impressed.

'It's a good deal all round, Ally,' praised Jack. 'I must say, I couldn't have done better meself, buying those stockings at eightpence a dozen. Even if we sell them at sixpence a pair we still make a handsome profit. And you were right to act straight away. Deals can be lost by dithering. A chap desperate to make some money came into Green's shop once and offered to supply them with all the produce out of his allotment. First-class stuff it was an' all. Green dithered, worried about upsetting his wholesaler, so the bloke struck a deal elsewhere.'

'That was more or less what I thought. I was worried that character Wilf Milner would return and somehow force the Brambles to continue doing business with him. It's too late now, of course. They were speechless when I made the offer.'

'I expect the old chap nearly had a heart attack, didn't he?'

Ally smiled. 'He nearly did, Flo. But the joy on their faces, I could not describe. Oh, Flo, you should have seen how they lived. We live like royalty in comparison.'

'I've done it myself,' she replied gravely. 'I don't have to imagine.'

'I do like your idea of opening up the section next-door and turning it into a haberdashery,' mused Jack. 'It'll need some alterations, though, shelving and whatnot. And we'll need more staff. A new senior and a junior will be the least we can get away with.' His eyes grew wide with excitement. 'And why stop at haberdashery? We could open more sections, making separate shops selling greengroceries, foodstuffs, meat and fish. And what about furniture and shoes? And then there's . . .'

Ally raised her hand. 'One moment, Jack. You're getting carried away. I only meant that plan for the haberdashery if the stockings do well.'

'Jack's right, though, Ally. You have the space here to do whatever you want.'

' "We", Flo,' Ally affirmed. ' "We" have the space.' She leaned on the table and paused thoughtfully. 'Yes, Jack is right. Why stop at hardware and haberdashery?'

An idea suddenly occurred to her and she gasped.

'What? What is it, Ally?' Both Flo and Jack asked, worried.

'Oh! Oh, I . . . why, that's it! That's what we must do. That's what my grandfather originally intended when he had this building constructed, only the timing was not right. I am positive I am correct.'

'What?' they both cried. 'Positive about what?'

'Don't you see?'

They shook their heads. 'No.'

'Not separate individual shops, just one. One big one, selling everything anyone could want. The big cities in America and Canada have operated this practice for years. Indeed, if I remember correctly an American gentleman, Mr . . . oh, what is his name? Selfridge, Harry Selfridge, is in the process of building a store in London. Only I believe he has problems with his partner. Which may, of course, have been rectified by now. It is many months since I have been able to afford to buy *The Times* where I read of this.' Her gaze misted over. 'I have shopped many a time in Knightsbridge and Oxford Street. The shops in London are wonderful . . .'

'Oi,' interrupted Flo. 'This is Leicester. Not many of us have the kind of money yer need to shop in London, yer know.'

Ally blushed, ashamed. 'I do apologise, Flo. But regardless, there are people in this vicinity who do have the money. And, Flo, if our business is successful, so will you eventually.'

'Oh,' she mouthed at the prospect. Since the age of fourteen her life had been filled with the worry of providing the most basic necessities. Though this had been somewhat alleviated during the last few months, life-long fears did not fade easily. Regardless of not having to find rent, she still worried whether the shop's profits would leave enough to provide for them after all the bills were paid, and now they had the apprentice's wage to take into consideration.

Taking on the young lad had been discussed at great length but was felt to be unavoidable. And as the business grew, Jack had pointed out, more staff would be needed to cope. Flo glanced at Jack and Ally. It seemed only days since they had all sat around this table, as they were now, and planned to open the shop just long enough to sell the discarded stock. Now here they were planning to have what seemed to Flo the biggest shop for miles around, selling everything. The thought suddenly frightened her. How were two simple lower-class working folk and a remnant of the gentry going to handle all that entailed? She shook herself mentally. Well, there was nowt gained by not trying. And why not have big plans? You only got one such chance during a lifetime, so why not grab it? And why shouldn't they succeed? Others had.

Her mind flew back to the vision Ally had conjured up. Having the means to be able to buy all she wanted. 'Oh,' she mouthed again. 'I would love a suit like the one you were wearing when we first met. In pale blue with black braiding. Without the mud and rips, 'course.'

They both looked at her, bemused.

'I beg your pardon?' said Ally.

Flo gave a guilty laugh. 'Oh, don't mind me, me duck. I was just thinking out loud. Now what were yer saying?'

'We were just saying, Ma, that it'd be best to go slowly, expand as we go along. The last thing we want is to go bankrupt.'

'Oh, yes, I agree,' she said seriously. 'That's the last thing we want to happen. 'Cos I don't know about you two, but I'd sooner stay just as we are than have ter work for someone else again and go back to living as we were.' Her eyes sparkled merrily. 'Oh, but ain't the thought of all this exciting?'

Yes, it was, but also daunting.

Ally caught up with Jack in the yard as they were about to open up the next morning.

'Do you think it possible to create a little garden for Ma?' she asked him.

Jack withdrew the key from the lock of the shop and glanced around. 'A bit of a garden for Ma, eh? Why, yes, she'd like that. Anything's possible, Ally. Where d'you have in mind?'

They both stared back across the large cobbled yard and at the scattered outbuildings around it.

'Well, there is only one suitable place. The piece between the house and the back wall. Although that small building . . .' she shuddered at the memory of her ordeal with the bats '. . . could block some of the light needed. But still, it's worth a try. It would be so pleasurable for Ma, for all of us really, and the children could lend a hand in tending it.'

'I agree. The only work needed would be to lift the cobbles and give a good dig to the earth underneath. We could . . .' He paused.

'We could what?'

'I was just thinking, we could always knock down that small shed. We don't use it for owt. It wouldn't take much effort. It's falling down as it is. We have all the storage space we'll ever need with the rest of the outbuildings.' He grinned down at her. 'You hate that place, don't yer? In fact, none of us has been near it since that night.'

She shuddered again. 'I don't mind admitting I loathe the place, Jack. There's something about it . . . I am most likely being silly, but I wouldn't be sorry to see the place go. And the whole yard would benefit from that area being filled with flowers and shrubs.' A picture of the view from her old bedroom window flooded to mind; the gardens and their sweeping lawns. To Ally a garden of any size afforded peace and tranquillity, a place to think in. She smiled. 'We could even plant a tree.'

'You'll be wanting an orchard next.'

She missed the twinkle in his eyes. 'There's hardly the space for that, Jack. But as I see it, moving is out of the question for a very long time whilst we concentrate on building up the business. We might as well make our stay here as pleasurable as possible, using what resources we have.'

'All right, Ally, yer've convinced me. I'll mek a start on Sunday after we've done our cleaning and stock-taking in the shop. But let's keep this to ourselves 'til we make a start. You know what Ma's like. She'll go on and on about it.'

'Yes. And thank you, Jack.' Ally bent down and patted Sal's head affectionately. While they had been talking she had waddled up to greet them. 'You can't come with us, you know that, Sal. Back you go.'

Flo arrived, trying on her apron. 'What a' yer two still doing out here? That shop should be open by now. What yer bin doing?'

'Nothing,' they both answered cagily. 'Nothing at all.'

Chapter Twenty-Eight

'Stack them bricks up neatly, Eric. And you, Emily, get out his way before you come a cropper.'

Emily glared over at Jack. 'I'm only trying to help.'

'I know that, but there's helping and helping. You're being a hindrance. Why don't you give Ally a hand . . . Eric, I said neatly! Oh, God, I knew it,' groaned Jack as the pile of bricks Eric had haphazardly stacked against a larger outbuilding toppled over.

Flo appeared in the doorway. 'What's all the noise? It's Sunday, fer God's sake.' She advanced across to them and surveyed their handiwork. 'It's coming on, ain't it?' she beamed, and eyed Jack guiltily. 'Shouldn't you be resting, though, after working so hard all week in the shop?'

'Ma, we said we were making a bit of a garden for yer and that's what you'll have. Besides, I find this work kinda relaxing.'

'Yer do?' She grimaced. 'Don't look it ter me.'

'It's a change from the shop, that's what I meant. Eric, stack 'em in rows of four like I showed yer, then they won't fall over. Now what's that damned dog doing?' he cried in exasperation, leaning heavily on the long-handled lump hammer he was using to knock down the building. 'A while ago she was standing at the shed door, barking her head off. Now she's scratching up the earth. Sal, get out of it, come on.'

Flo laughed loudly. 'And you say this is relaxing!' She turned and looked at Ally, who on all fours, hands covered by an old pair of woollen gloves, seemingly oblivious to the rumpus all around her, was painstakingly scraping out the cobbles by the wall. 'How yer getting on, Ally?' shouted Flo.

Her head jerked up. 'Sorry? Oh, very well, Flo, thank you.' She sat back on her haunches and surveyed her handiwork. 'I've managed six so far,' she said, proud of her efforts.

Flo scanned the area they had planned to make into a garden. There were at least three hundred cobbles. She had better give Ally a hand after she had cleared away the pots else this garden would never start growing – not this year at any rate. 'I'm just putting the roast spuds in so dinner'll be about another hour,' she announced.

Before she turned back inside she took another look at the tiny space Ally had cleared and began to visualise the colour the tiny garden would bring. It would be their sanctuary, somewhere to sit and enjoy after a hard day in the shop. A little bit of the country in their own back yard.

She smiled contentedly. A rambling rose would look lovely just there, climbing up the wall. Yes, a red one. And next to it honeysuckle. Their fragrance would be heavenly. Oh, wasn't her surprise a wonderful one? She was indeed a fortunate woman, having people around her who cared enough to give up their limited spare time to tackle such a hard task primarily for her benefit. Thinking of that, the least she could do whilst they laboured was make sure they were fed. She hurried back inside the house.

A while later, just before she was about to serve up, she glanced down to see Sal at her feet, wagging her tail. 'Hello, gel ... oh, goodness, Sal!' she cried. 'Just look at all the mud you've trailed in on me clean flags.' She frowned. 'What's that you've got in yer mouth? Give it here.' She leaned over, intending to take the offending object from the old dog's mouth, but Sal was not going to give up her prize easily. She tried to make a run for it but Flo grabbed her, straddled her, leaned forward and forced the object out of her mouth. Sal barked in protest.

'You can bark all you like, you old bugger, but I won't have you bringing ... What is this?' she said, examining the object closely. 'Ugh, Sal, it's an old bone. Where the hell did you dig this up from? Well, I'll tell you where this is headed,' she said, opening up the range door and throwing the bone into the fire. Slamming the doors, she stood back and nodded. 'Best place for it.' She turned to Sal and could swear blind the dog was glaring back at her angrily. 'You needn't look like that. You'd mek yerself ill, gnawing on that old thing. I've got a bone for you and it's got a lot more meat on it than that one had, so just be patient. Now, out me way while I get dished up.'

It was late in the afternoon before Jack finally called a halt. He was pleased with his efforts. The roof of the building had been removed, though first he'd had to coax out the bats, a task he hadn't relished. Then the bricks from just over a quarter of the two freestanding walls were removed and stacked neatly along with the slates and roof timbers. The timbers were only good enough to burn but the slates and bricks were in reasonable condition and suitable for repairs should they ever need them.

'I think we've done enough for one day,' he called to the others. 'Next Sunday, weather permitting, should see all of it down.'

Ally stretched her aching body and also admired her work. 'About fifty cobbles would you say, Flo?'

She nodded. 'At least.'

215

'I did three,' pouted Emily, worried she was not going to be given any praise.

'Yes, you did. You have been a great help, and so have you, Eric. Thank you both,' said Ally. 'They look tired, Flo. I hope we haven't worked them too hard?'

'Hard work don't kill yer.' She yawned loudly. 'They ain't the only ones who are tired. I'm dead beat. I think it's bath and bed for them, and I won't be long following.' She raised herself, wiping a mud-streaked hand over her forehead. 'Come on then, you lot,' she ordered. 'I need some water pumping.' And hiding a smile she added: 'Who's going ter volunteer?'

It was exactly a week later and they were all preparing to resume their work on the garden when Jack, having gone out ahead, burst back through the door, his face grim, and pulled Flo aside.

'Keep everyone in here, Ma,' he ordered. 'I'm off to fetch the police.'

'Fetch the bobbies?' she gasped, worry filling her. 'Whatever for?'

'Ma,' he hissed, 'just do as I ask. Don't let none of them outside.'

Flo eyed him sharply. Jack was upset. He was shaking. She had never seen him like this before. She grabbed his arm. 'What is it? What's happened? Fer God's sake, you'll tell me what it is?'

As he pulled on his coat, he glanced quickly across at the others. Fortunately they were too engrossed in their own concerns to be interested in him and Ma. He inclined his head towards the door and Flo followed him outside.

The August sun was beating down and she squinted as she looked at him. 'Well?' she demanded.

He took several deep breaths. 'I'm not quite sure, Ma, but I think there's something buried in the shed we're demolishing.'

She looked astounded. 'Something buried? What d'yer mean, Jack?'

'I reckon it must have been Sal . . .'

'Sal? What's she got to do with it?'

'She must have dug the hole.'

'What hole! Jack, you ain't making sense. You're confusing me.'

He shuddered. 'Oh, Ma, when I went to mek a start just now I noticed a deep hole in the earth floor. I automatically looked down into it . . .' He shuddered again, violently this time. 'There was a bone sticking out.'

'Bone?' She tutted. 'Yer daft bugger, our Jack. Years ago, before the shed was built, it was probably where someone buried their rubbish.'

'Ma, I know an animal bone when I see it.'

Her mouth dropped open. 'And . . . Oh, Jack, yer saying this one ain't?' she uttered.

'I ain't saying nothing 'til I fetch the police. Now use whatever excuse yer can, but keep them all inside.'

★　★　★

216

Sergeant English was a tall man, and solidly built. His presence seemed to fill the large room. It was a week after the gruesome discovery. An autopsy had revealed that the bones were definitely human and were the remains of a man and a woman. How long they had been buried under the outbuilding could not be pinpointed exactly, but it was no less than nine years and no more than fourteen. Their deaths had not been due to natural causes.

Sergeant English was investigating two murders. The skull of the male had been crushed, obviously hit with such force it was deduced the blow had killed him outright. How the female had died it was not possible to tell after all this time.

He glanced in turn at each of the three people staring up at him expectantly. After lengthy questioning he and his superiors were satisfied they were in no way involved, although a question mark had at first hung over the younger woman, which was quickly dispelled. She was a Listerman and the bodies had been found on Listerman property. But when the murdered people had met their grisly untimely end she would have been just a child and could not possibly have been involved.

All that remained now was for him to express his thanks for their co-operation and take his leave. He took a deep breath. The people looked tired, haggard. All this had upset them badly. When the news had broken it had spread like wildfire and hordes of sightseers had descended. The newspapers had loved it, squeezing the story for all it was worth, and it had reached the nationals. Up and down the country people from all walks of life had read and discussed, accused and acquitted. It was a shame, he thought, that these innocent people had had their lives disrupted. But then, that was the way of things. In his own experience it was always the innocent who suffered the most where crime was concerned.

'So, Sergeant English, the police don't know who they are?' asked Jack.

The sergeant gravely shook his head. 'Nope. We've come up blank. Exhausted all the possibilities.'

'So what happens now?' asked Flo.

'The bodies will be given a burial and the case'll be shut. Then all the fuss'll die down and you'll be left in peace.'

'Thank God,' muttered Flo. 'It's bin a nightmare. The only ones who have enjoyed all this are the kids,' she said, ashamed. 'They've revelled in it. Eric reckons he ain't never been so popular at school.'

Sergeant English smiled. 'That's kids for yer, Mrs Fossett. Like everything else, it'll be a nine-day wonder. The newspapers and kids alike will soon be on to something else.' He picked up his helmet. 'Right, I'd better tek me leave. All that remains is ter thank you for your co-operation. And . . .' he shrugged his broad shoulders '. . . if anything should strike yer or . . . well, I dunno. Maybe you might unearth something else. Inform us straight away if so.'

'Don't worry, Sergeant. I can assure you we'll not be knocking down or digging up anything for the foreseeable future,' said Jack.

He rose to see the sergeant out and Flo turned to Ally.

'You're quiet, gel? All right, are yer?'

She exhaled. 'This has all been so distressing, I'm glad it's over. But I can't help wondering who those poor people were and what they did to deserve such a terrible end. And why whoever did it picked on Listerman property to hide his deed.'

Flo shrugged her shoulders. 'Ours not to reason why. It's over now.' Her eyes glinted mischievously. 'And it ain't bin all that bad, 'cos the takings have trebled.'

Ally nodded. 'Yes, they have. The publicity this has given the shop could never have been achieved without spending a fortune on advertising. It wasn't a nice way to get publicity but, well . . .'

'We had no control over it, Ally, so stop feeling guilty.'

She smiled wanly. 'You are right, Flo. Let us hope that after all this dies down, people will still continue to shop with us. Maybe it's wrong but I cannot help but feel pleased at the fact that we can afford to expand a little. Without all this we wouldn't have been able to do that yet for a while.'

'Out of bad comes good, eh? And the other good thing is that the police have dug up practically all the space we intended for the garden. Now that were good of 'em, weren't it?'

'Flo!' Ally scolded.

'Well, it was,' she responded haughtily.

Ally paused thoughtfully. 'We should plant a rose or something where the bodies were found, as a mark of respect. Oh, hello, Sergeant, did you forget something?'

Striding back in, Jack following, Sergeant English removed his helmet. 'I did, as a matter of fact. It's just a formality but I was asked to see if any of you recognised this? You won't, I'm sure, but you appreciate I have to do me job?'

'What is it, Sergeant?' Flo asked.

Carefully unwrapping a folded piece of paper, he displayed the contents. Flo grimaced. 'Never seen it before. It's pretty though, ain't it?'

She made to pick it up but the sergeant reprimanded her. 'Don't touch police evidence, Mrs Fossett.'

'Oh, I'm sorry,' she quavered, rapidly withdrawing her hand.

'What about you, Miss Listerman?' he said, thrusting his hand towards her.

She peered at the contents. All eyes were upon her as a gasp escaped her lips.

'Where did you say this was found, Sergeant?' she asked.

He frowned, eyeing her in concern, not failing to notice that her face had drained of colour. 'Well, I didn't, miss. But it was found clutched inside the hand of the female.' He leaned towards her, all his policeman's instincts brought to bear. 'Do you recognise the brooch, miss?'

Her hands clenched tightly, her head drooped over and she nodded, slowly. 'I do,' she whispered, chokingly. 'The rose brooch belonged to my mother.'

Chapter Twenty-Nine

'Drink this up, Ally.'

She shook her head. 'I can't.'

'Yes, yer can, and you will. You ain't hardly drunk or ate for nearly a week. What yer trying ter do to yourself?'

Ally's ashen face was slowly raised. 'You don't understand, Flo. You can't possibly know how I feel. It's as if my parents have died all over again. And now to find out after all this time that their deaths were no accident, and that they have been lying under . . . Oh, Flo, it's all so dreadful. It really is too much to bear.'

Flo eyed the pale, drawn face of the girl she had grown so fond of and her heart went out to her. But the worst thing she felt she could do was to cry along with her, smother her with sympathy. It was that she wanted to do, but acting that way would not be in Ally's best interests, would go no way towards aiding her recovery. Detachment and strength, something the others were finding extremely difficult, were Flo's ways of coping.

Although there was one thing worrying her: she did pray she was managing to hide her guilt for the innocent action she had performed three Sundays ago when she had thrown the bone Sal had dug up into the fire. She had never mentioned this to anyone, not even the police, and could not bring herself to do so. Until her dying day she would never know whether she had unintentionally destroyed part of the remains of one of Ally's parents and felt it was certainly best that Ally herself should never know. Wasn't she suffering enough without that knowledge, true or not, adding to her grief?

She took a deep breath. 'Come on now, Ally, you'll have ter chivvy yerself. I hate ter say this but I don't know how much longer we can cope in the shop without yer.'

'Oh, Flo, I couldn't . . .'

'Now look here, Ally,' she blurted. 'I know you're bereaved and I sympathise, I really do. We all do. But life has ter go on. We've a business to run and we need yer. And what you need is something to occupy yer mind. It ain't doing you no good sitting here, moping and dwelling.'

'Flo, you're heartless. How can you expect me to smile and be pleasant with the customers when I feel like this?'

She inhaled sharply. 'Oh, I see. Well, I might have known. That's just typical, that is.'

'Typical! Of what?'

'You gentry. If this had happened to one of us working-class folk we wouldn't have bin given any time to grieve. Oh, no, straight back to work. But you gentry, you can take to your beds and wallow in it.'

'Flo, that is uncalled for.'

'Is it? My mother lost four children. It broke her heart, but she weren't allowed no time to recover. She was expected in the kitchen the very next morning. You've had a week, Ally. How much longer do you want? Me, Jack, the 'prentice and the kids have coped, but we can't cope no more. Equal partnership, you said. Well, we can't carry you forever.'

Suddenly she felt guilty for what she was saying. It was true, all of it, but in Ally's case maybe she was being a little harsh. She perched on the edge of the bed and took Ally's hand. 'We know you're hurting and we'll mek allowances for that, 'cos I know as well as any that this kind of pain don't fade easily. But you ain't helping yerself lying here.'

Ally eyed her for a moment. 'No,' she whispered. 'I know I'm not.'

'So you'll come back to work?'

She sighed. 'Do I have any choice?'

Flo shook her head. 'No, yer don't.' She leaned over and kissed Ally affectionately on her cheek. 'I didn't mean any of that, yer know.'

'Didn't you?'

'No. Well, maybe I did, but it was gentry in general I was talking about.' She rose. 'We'll expect you in the shop tomorrow then.'

Ally nodded.

'Good. Well, mek sure you eat all yer dinner tonight 'cos yer'll need yer strength to cope with the crowds.'

Chapter Thirty

One of the double entrance doors to the shop shot open and a woman strode in and stared around. She was short, bordering on the plump side, her fair hair neatly styled in a roll held in place with diamond-studded pins. She wore an expensively tailored light green ankle-length afternoon dress; draped across her shoulders was a mink stole. Her whole being proclaimed just what she was: the well-bred daughter of a wealthy family.

Eyes still darting, she stepped forward. Finally she spotted what she was looking for and gathered up her skirt just high enough to totter as fast as she could on her high-heeled brown boots, crying: 'Albertina! Oh, Albertina!'

Ally spun around, eyes wide in shock as recognition of the voice struck, but before she could respond the woman was upon her, hugging her fiercely.

'Oh, Albertina, Albertina, where have you been? We have been so dreadfully worried. Is it true what the papers are saying? Oh, my poor darling, what you must be suffering.' She pulled back, scanning Ally up and down. 'Let me see. Oh, just look at you! What on earth are you wearing? And your hair . . . oh, darling, what has become of you? Well, never you mind, I am here to fetch you. You are coming home with me. Get that white thing you are wearing off, we are getting out of here.'

Stunned by the unexpected arrival of her very dear friend, someone she had thought would never acknowledge her again, and not knowing which of her barrage of questions to answer first, Ally could only say sincerely: 'Oh, Bella, it is so good to see you.'

Bella fell upon her again, hugging her tightly. 'And you, darling. Oh, Ally, I've missed you so much. I was distraught when I returned from Europe and heard what had happened.' She shuddered in distress. 'I could not believe how badly off Tobias left you financially, then how Lionel and his mother treated you, and now all this. Is it true what the newspapers are saying about the bodies? Oh, Ally, are they your parents?'

Tears sprang to Ally's eyes and she swallowed hard to rid herself of a lump that was forming in her throat. While she threw herself into her work she was for the most part able to stem her misery over the discovery of her parents' bodies. Now the surprise arrival of her dearest friend with these searching questions brought the torment back.

'The police are as positive as they can be,' she said quietly.

The pain her friend was suffering filled Bella's being. 'Oh, Ally,' she whispered, and suddenly grabbed her arm, conscious that several shoppers were listening to their conversation with interest. 'Let's get out of here.'

'I can't, Bella. I can't leave the shop . . .'

'Of course you can, you silly thing,' she interrupted. 'I'm sure your staff are quite capable of carrying on in your absence. I'm surprised you are actually working behind the counter. Shouldn't you be in the office or somewhere, doing what owners do?'

Ally became aware of Jack staring across at them from the far end of the counter. She took Bella's arm and pulled her close. 'Please keep your voice down. This . . . this set up is not what you think. I am not the full owner, only a partner. And I have a responsibility to my other partners to pull my weight.'

'Pull your weight? What kind of talk is that? You sound positively common, my dear. And a partner? I don't understand. The papers said . . .'

'I know what the papers said. Half of it they concocted themselves. Listerman "heiress" indeed, who had reopened the Emporium to make ends meet. They made me out to be a deeply wronged poor little orphan. I have been deeply wronged, but I am not the defenceless creature the papers make out. I'm a woman who is quite capable of standing on her own two feet.'

Bella eyed her, astounded. 'My goodness, Ally,' she gasped, 'you have changed.'

'Yes, I have. For the better. And I have been taught and nurtured by the most wonderful people you could ever wish to meet. Without them, Bella, I dread to think what would have become of me. Now come through to our living accommodation and I will explain it all.'

'You live here!'

'Yes,' she answered, head erect. 'We have made our home in a building in the back yard.'

'Oh, I see.' Bella did not like the sound of it. 'Er . . . I, er . . . thought we could go to the Grand for tea before we made the journey back home.' She glanced again at Ally's shop attire. 'On second thoughts, maybe the Bell, that's nearer. The tea there isn't so good, I'm told, but it will suffice.'

Ally hid a smile. 'Annabella Langton,' she scolded, 'are you ashamed of my second hand clothes?'

'Second hand! Your clothes have been worn before? Oh!'

Ally hid her amusement. 'Oh, Bella, you gave me such a shock with your unexpected arrival, but I can see I have shocked you much more. Come on,' she said, hooking her arm through her friend's. 'I want to introduce you to Jack and Flo and the children, who will be home from school shortly.' As she guided Bella across to meet Jack, she smiled warmly. 'Oh, Bella, it is good to see you.'

This tea is quite palatable, Ally,' Bella said, surprised. 'I wouldn't know the first thing about making it.'

'Well, maybe it's about time you learned. I would hate you ever to be in the position I found myself in.'

'Oh, God forbid,' cried Bella, mortified at the very thought. She put down her cup. 'I do admire you, Ally. I know for a fact I could not have survived what you have gone through.' She glanced around. 'This place . . . it's . . . er . . . quite cosy, isn't it?'

Ally knew Bella hated it, felt uncomfortable, was having difficulty imagining how Ally, Jack, Flo and the children all managed to live amicably in what was to Bella such a tiny space, but she was glad her friend was too polite to voice her true feelings. 'We like it, Bella.' Her eyes twinkled mischievously. 'I wish you could have seen the dwelling in Sanvey Gate.'

'Oh, no, thank you,' she replied, shuddering. 'Your description of it was quite enough for me.' She eyed her friend searchingly. 'Ally, can I not persuade you to return home with me? Mother will be so upset, knowing you are living like this. She felt your coming to us was the least she could do for your mother, her dear departed friend. Ally, you do not belong here,' she beseeched. 'Look, you could still manage the shop if you felt the need. But you wouldn't have to. Father and Mother have both agreed that we'll take care of you financially. After all, it will only be a matter of time before you meet a suitable man and settle down. So you won't need any of this. Please, Ally, do reconsider?'

'Bella, I have already explained and was hoping you'd understand. This is where I belong now. I am happy here. I enjoy all this.'

'Really?'

'I know you are having difficulty believing it, but yes, I do. I have a purpose in life now, something I did not realise was lacking before. Oh, Bella, I do appreciate all you have offered. And you will still be my friend, won't you? My circumstances will not alter that, will they?'

'Of course not. How could you even think it? If only you knew how upset I was when I found you had disappeared. We tried everything to find you. But nothing, not a trace. And, Ally, I would like to point out that we are not all like Lionel and Lavinia Williamson-Brown. Their treatment of you was deplorable. It was Mrs Gibbs, our housekeeper, who told my mother. The servants were full of it. So degrading for you, darling. But then, you know what servants are. You cannot stop them gossiping.'

Ally clasped her hands tightly. There was a question she wanted to ask but had difficulty getting out. 'Bella, have you . . . have you heard anything of . . . of Lionel?'

Her eyes glinted harshly. 'After all he's done to you, do you really want to know? Ally, I hope you are not still carrying a torch for him?'

'No,' she replied with conviction. 'I can assure you, I am not.'

Bella sighed with relief. 'I'm glad to hear it. For obvious reasons I have nothing to do with Lionel but I have heard he is about to get himself engaged to Felicity Burginshaw. Silly girl! Someone should warn her. I've also heard Felicity's father has given him a job. Can you imagine Lionel actually working?'

Ally made no comment.

The hint of a smile touched the corners of Bella's mouth. 'Nathaniel Bunting-Smythe always enquires after you. He has always liked you, you know, and his family are so well connected. Not the handsomest of men and he's a bit soppy sometimes, but you could do a lot worse . . .'

'Bella!'

'All right, Ally. I will return your regards, though, just in case.' She rose. 'I really must be going. Are you sure you won't change your mind and come home with me?'

Rising also, Ally smiled, placing her hands on Bella's shoulders. 'Don't let's go through that again.'

Bella sighed. 'All right, but the offer remains open.' She pulled on light green kid gloves, smoothing them over her hands. 'You will come and visit?'

'Of course. Whenever I can, business permitting.'

Bella began to make for the door but stopped, turned, and eyed Ally pleadingly. 'Are you sure there is nothing I can do for you? Do you need any money or . . .'

'Bella, I'm well, really. Now please stop worrying. Though actually there is something you can do . . .'

'Oh?'

'Please ask your mother, and she in turn all her friends and acquaintances, to give Listerman and Fossett a trial at supplying whatever we are able for their household needs. Will you do that for me, Bella?'

'Of course I will. I should be delighted to do anything.' Her eyes twinkled merrily. 'I would have anyway.'

Ally kissed her warmly on the cheek. 'Thank you. Business of that volume coming our way would really help to establish us.' She took Bella's arm. 'Come on, I'll walk you to the door and wait with you while Albert summons you a cab.'

'Albert?'

'Our apprentice. A nice enough young lad, but his manners need improving somewhat towards the customers. Jack is training him well, though, and he shows promise. Well, that's what Jack says. I'm still learning myself.' She laughed. 'I hope he thinks that *I* show promise. Anyway, Albert is soon to be joined by another lad if business keeps growing the way it is.'

'I do hope so, Ally. Really I do. You deserve it. Well, I feel so much better now I know you are all right. I'm glad I met your partners. You are right, you have been in good hands so I need not have worried so much.

Florence is nice for a . . . She's a nice lady.'

Ally had to think for a moment who Florence was. Then the penny dropped. She had never heard Flo called by her full Christian name before. 'Bella, shame on you,' she scolded. 'You were going to say "nice for a working-class woman"', weren't you? Your attitude will have to change if you are going to become the frequent visitor I hope you are.'

Bella had the grace to blush. 'Jack is a handsome man, isn't he?' she said to change the subject, then felt Ally stiffen and eyed her quizzically. 'Have I said something wrong?'

'No, not at all,' she replied sharply.

How come, Bella thought, as they made their way back through the shop and out into the street, that her innocent remark had somehow touched a raw nerve with Ally? Bella had always been astute and knew instinctively, even from just those few short words, that there was more here than met the eye. As she journeyed home, mulling over all she had seen and heard, the possible romantic feelings that Ally harboured for Jack Fossett were the ones she pondered over the longest. She hoped she was wrong. Ally and Jack were of different social classes and no matter what the Fossetts had come to mean to Ally, how fond she had grown of them, romantic liaisons between people of such differing backgrounds never worked. Bella would have to keep her eye on that situation. Ally had suffered more in the last year than some people did in a lifetime. She deserved some peace and happiness now.

But it was a tearful Ally who returned to the shop.

'Has yer friend gone?' Jack asked as she resumed her place behind the counter.

Since his introduction to Bella a feeling of doom had settled over him. He felt Ally's past had come to reclaim her. Ma had warned him that this would happen and she had been right. As Ally rekindled this relationship, how long would it be, he thought worriedly, before she felt the need to return to her former way of life?

'Is everything all right, Jack?' Ally asked, concerned at the distressed look that had settled upon his face.

'What? Yes . . . 'course it is,' he stammered. 'It's just been busy, that's all.' That being the first excuse he could think of. 'I'm just glad to see yer back after being run off my feet. Maybe next time you could give me warning then I can rearrange the staff?'

'Oh,' she gasped guiltily, then grimaced. Jack was being unreasonable. She had never before left to spend time with a friend. 'The situation will not occur again, Jack. When Bella calls, or I take time to visit her, be assured I will give you plenty of warning,' she snapped angrily.

Chapter Thirty-One

Bella was not the only surprise visitor Ally received that week. Two days later found her in the kitchen clearing away the dishes. It was Wednesday half day closing; the children had just been packed off back to school, Flo was taking her turn with the daily shopping, and Jack had gone out also to visit a possible supplier in connection with their new venture into haberdashery. Ally had not let him know that she was actually acquainted with the manufacturer of buttons and trimmings, Bertram Burginshaw, whose daughter Felicity, she assumed, was now engaged to Lionel. She did not want to remind Jack of her former social standing and, besides, felt this knowledge could hinder his negotiations or, worse, he might have suggested she accompany him which was the last thing she wanted to do. There could be a chance of bumping into Lionel. That was a situation she did not want to put herself into.

She was feeling pleased with herself and hummed tunefully as she tidied up. The meal she had cooked had been a success. It was her first attempt at suet dumplings and they'd been nearly as good as Flo's. Well, they should have been, Flo had instructed her on the making of them clearly enough. Plates had been scraped clean. Ally preferred to think that this was due to the quality of the food she had prepared and not the fact that they were all so hungry they would have demolished anything that was placed before them.

The September sun was still warm and once she had finished her chores she planned to take a chair outside and read a book she had picked up from a second hand shop.

Sal fussed around her feet and she bent over to pat the old dog's head. 'Are you trying to tell me you are hungry, Sal? Well, come along, I have your dinner all ready.' She retrieved the dish of scraps she had collected, and before she had placed it on the floor Sal's head was in the bowl. Ally laughed. 'My word, you are hungry, old girl. When you've finished you can join me outside. You can have a nice nap in the warm sunshine while I relax with my book.'

The discreet clearing of a throat alerted her to a visitor and she spun around to see a figure standing in the doorway.

'Hello, Albertina, my dear. I was told I would find you in here by a little girl coming out of the yard entrance. Oh, my dear, I hope I didn't startle you? You look as though you have seen a ghost.'

Ally thought she *had* seen a ghost and the shock was causing her to tremble.

The old man in the doorway advanced further inside, his face creased in concern. 'Sit down,' he ordered. 'I'll get you a glass of water.'

Still deeply shocked, she sank down into a chair and automatically accepted the cup of water that was thrust at her. She gulped it down.

'Do you feel any better now?' he asked.

She nodded. 'Yes, thank you. I'm so sorry, I . . . I . . . well, I was told that you were . . .'

'Were what, my dear?'

'Well, that you had passed away.'

'Really? Oh, the confusion must lie with my father.'

'Your father! Oh, Mr Bailey, I do apologise. Please forgive me.'

Clarence Bailey smiled. 'I understand your perplexity. At my advanced age I was fortunate still to have my father. His recent death shocked me greatly but he had lived a good life. He was ninety-six, and until the day he passed over still came to the office. He was such a character! You would have liked him, my dear. It's a pity you never met. His going made me take stock. I decided it was time I handed the practice over and enjoyed retirement. Mrs Bailey deserved some of my time too. She has spent all our married life not knowing what time I would be home and with me at people's beck and call at all times of the day and night. It is amazing how people think they own their lawyers. She has been very understanding but there came a time when even I realised that enough was enough. Anyway, Albertina, it is not myself I have come to talk about, but you. I was so distressed when I read about all this terrible business in the paper and journeyed to see you as soon as I could. I live in the Derbyshire countryside now. It is peaceful but unfortunately not an easy location to travel far from.'

All the time he was speaking Ally was wondering why Clarence Bailey should make all this effort to come and speak to her. What could he possibly want to talk to her about? She jumped up. 'I am forgetting myself, Mr Bailey. Can I offer you some refreshment? Tea?'

'Tea would be most welcome, my dear.'

'And something to eat?'

'Thank you, but I have already eaten quite a substantial lunch at the Imperial Hotel.'

For a few minutes she busied herself with the making of a pot of tea. As she set the tray on the table she eyed him apologetically. 'We have no china, Mr Bailey. I do hope you will not mind taking your tea in pottery mugs?'

'I do not mind what you serve it in, my dear.' Smiling, he stared around him. 'You have made this place very comfortable. It is good to see it being lived in again. It used to be the housekeeper's cottage.'

'You have cleared up a puzzling question, Mr Bailey. We could not work out just what its previous use had been.'

Armed with her own cup, she sat down again.

'I have to say, Albertina, that I am most impressed with what you are achieving with the shop. Your father would have been so proud of you.'

'I like to think so.'

'Do you think I could take a look around later?'

'I'd be happy to show you.'

He smiled, then eyed her critically. 'You look very well, Albertina. Happy in fact. I did not know what to expect when I set out on my journey. I am glad I came now. I feel satisfied. I was horrified when I read of the discovery of the bodies. The police are sure that they are your parents, by the way, I have been to see them.'

'You have?'

'I needed to before I came to you today. I had to clear up several matters before I talked to you. But firstly, my dear, please accept my condolences. This is all terrible for you. You have been through so much, and now to face this. Oh, if only you could have been spared it! But deep down I always suspected something . . . I did not know what but I was never convinced, you see, by the business of the boat. It was all so out of character. Your father, I knew, did not like water. So why hire a boat to sail around the coast? And it was all so convenient . . .'

'Convenient? I am sorry, Mr Bailey, I do not follow you?'

He drained his cup and placed it on the table. 'Albertina, do you remember the day you came to my office and I had to explain to you about your inheritance?'

Of course she remembered. How could she ever forget? Nor could she forget her rude treatment of this kindly man. She nodded.

'I said to you then that I had something I needed to tell you, but you were upset and left. I tried to contact you afterwards but you were untraceable until now. That is why I am here, my dear. What I have to tell you is not pleasant but it needs to be said. It may also help you to understand matters better. Do you think that first I could have another cup of your delicious tea?'

'Of course.'

The tea poured and several sips taken he eased himself more comfortably into his chair and settled kindly eyes upon her. 'As you know, Albertina, your father's marriage to your mother was not his first. Previously he was married to Jennifer Addington, who originally hailed from Bath. Her family were merchant bankers. The marriage was a happy one and produced a son, Tobias.'

Fear was building inside Ally. Trepidation for what the old lawyer was about to tell her. But she could not stop him. Whatever he had to relate, he obviously felt it was important enough for him to make the long journey from Derby.

At the look on her face, he leaned forward in concern. 'Are you all right, my dear?'

Hands clasped tightly, she nodded. 'Yes. Please go on, Mr Bailey.'

He took a deep breath. 'Right from birth Tobias was a difficult child. Nannies came and went but none could control him. As he grew, despite every effort they made, he was indifferent towards his parents, rude to the servants, insolent with his tutors, and retained no friends thanks to his bullying nature. At the age of ten it was decided therefore to send him away to a strict boarding school. His mother took this decision badly, but was fully aware that there was no other choice. The decision seemed a good one. When they visited the boy and he returned home for holidays he appeared much changed. Years went by, then came a summons to see the headmaster.'

Clarence sadly shook his head. 'Your father and Tobias's mother received the greatest shock. It appears that he and several other senior boys, all from prominent families, ran a gambling school which had been going on for a very long time. Between them the boys had won or lost quite large sums of money. As the truth emerged it transpired that their flow of stake money came from the percentage they took off a number of other boys' allowances. A worried parent raised the alarm initially. Could not understand, you see, why her son kept asking for more money. It was thought the school was to blame. At great cost the authorities were kept out of it all. Although Tobias pleaded his innocence, said he'd been forced into it by the other guilty parties, he was not believed and they were all expelled.

'This was a dreadful time for the Listermans. The stigma attached should any of this get out could have done your father great damage. That was not his main concern, of course. Despite everything he cared deeply for his son and strove to do what he felt was best for him. But Tobias was very soon disrupting the household again and his mother's health began to suffer. Your father knew he had to do something so he visited many schools up and down the country but was satisfied with none. He decided to hire another tutor but this time it was one with a difference. Isaiah Brennan had a military background and had built himself a reputation for dealing with boys like Tobias. His services came at great cost but that was not a consideration. Your father purchased a house on New Walk in Leicester and Tobias, Brennan, and a no-nonsense housekeeper by the name of Mrs Thunder were installed.

'Again everything seemed to go well. Your father visited regularly and after a time it was felt that Tobias could come home for short stays. As the family's lawyer I visited the house quite regularly for social calls as well as on business and I encountered Tobias on quite a few occasions. I have to say I was impressed with the change in him. Isaiah Brennan seemed to know his job. Your father was even discussing Tobias's joining the family business. Then, most unexpectedly, after a visit home Tobias

230

disappeared – but not before he had rifled your father's safe, taking with him a substantial amount of money. He was seventeen.'

Ally gasped.

'Do you wish me to continue, my dear?'

She nodded.

'Then a terrible incident occurred.' Clarence Bailey paused for several long moments. 'Your father had been away all day on business and did not arrive home until late. He knew something was wrong when his carriage drove up the drive and he saw the doctor's carriage parked outside. His wife, it seems, had taken a fall down the stairs. Her neck was broken. There were no witnesses to the accident as at the time all the servants were having their dinner in the servants' hall.'

'Poor Father,' Ally uttered.

Clarence nodded. 'He was beside himself. He loved his wife very much. It was several weeks later before he could bring himself to go through her things. That was when he made the discovery – all her jewellery was missing.'

Ally frowned deeply as a memory stirred. 'Was it discovered who had taken it?'

'Not precisely. The police put it all down to an unknown intruder, and guessed they may have contributed to Mrs Listerman's fall.'

'You do not know this, Mr Bailey, but when I returned to the house after my last visit to you I . . . felt there was a piece of jewellery belonging to my mother I wanted to have. When I went to retrieve it, I found all her other jewellery had gone.'

Clarence's eyes flashed. 'Really? Oh, my dear, you should have reported that.'

'Mr Bailey, at the time I was in no fit state to think clearly.'

'No, no, maybe not. Who did you think had taken it?'

'There was only one person who could have.'

He nodded. 'It fits in very well with what I have to tell you next. It was a while after that that a jeweller friend of your father's paid him a visit. Pieces of his wife's jewellery had turned up. It seems they had originally been sold on the continent and had found their way back to England. Discreet enquiries revealed that a young man answering the description of Tobias had sold them in Paris, under an assumed name of course.' He sighed heavily. 'Your father did not pursue the matter. He was deeply distressed by his wife's death, and of course this news of his son. He tried his best to put it all behind him and carry on. He was approaching his fortieth birthday when he met your mother.

'Albertina, I saw the light come back into his eyes. He'd never thought to find happiness again but he was being given a second chance. Your mother was a lovely creature, lively as well as intelligent. She was the only child of aged parents who welcomed the match despite your father's tragic past. The age difference did not seem to concern them. Your mother and father adored each other. When you were born they were both overjoyed. Life was good for them. They were a popular couple. Content with his life, Robert concentrated on the family businesses which flourished under his expert guidance.'

He stopped abruptly and shook his head. 'You were eleven years of age when Tobias came back on the scene. He turned up one night out of the blue, demanding a private audience with his father. Tobias had fallen foul of some very nasty people, owed them a great deal of money. He pleaded with your father to settle his account, saying his life was at stake. On being tackled about his mother's jewellery and her accident, Tobias emphatically denied all knowledge of it, said he could prove he wasn't even in the area at the time. He admitted stealing the money from his father's safe previously, his excuse being that Isaiah Brennan was a tyrant and that his own life was miserable. Feeling his father would not believe him, his only option had been to steal the money and disappear.

'Despite Tobias's insistence he was telling the truth, your father was not convinced. He felt he had no choice but to settle Tobias's debt but that was all he would do. Tobias was to be cut out of his will and Robert wanted no more to do with him. He was deeply saddened finally to admit that his son was a thoroughly bad lot.

'He came to see me the very next day, updating me on the latest developments and instructing me to draw up a new will which he would sign as soon as it was ready. As his lawyer and friend I had seen your father through some trying times, Albertina, but I had never seen him cry before. His decision distressed him greatly but he had you and your mother to consider and did not want anything to jeopardise your future.'

Ally was crying herself now as the pain her father had endured because of his son flooded through her. She remembered her father as a loving man, kind and considerate, and knew Mr Bailey was right when he said that the situation would have pained him deeply.

Clarence Bailey reached over and took her hand. 'Before I had a chance to inform your father that the new will was ready for his signature, I learned of their deaths and had Tobias strolling into my office demanding his rights as executor. There was nothing I could do, Albertina. He had the law on his side. The only thing I was glad about was that he sent you away to school. I know you must have resented being thrust amongst strangers at such a dreadful time, but at least you were largely out of his clutches. I tried my best to protect what should rightfully have been yours but I was just the family lawyer. All I could do was stand by and watch as Tobias systematically sold off all the family assets, except of course the shop which we now know the reason for.'

Ally sobbed quietly into her handkerchief. This fresh knowledge of her half-brother was almost unbearable. How could a man possessing such qualities as her father sire such a devil? Then a thought struck her, one even more dreadful than she could begin to contemplate. Dabbing her eyes, she slowly raised her head, locking shocked eyes on Clarence Bailey's. 'You . . . you think Tobias killed my parents, don't you?'

His answer came without hesitation. 'I have no doubt whatsoever, Albertina.'

A shrill, strangled cry burst from her. 'Oh, no, Mr Bailey! No, no. Please say you are mistaken?' she pleaded hysterically.

He gravely shook his head. 'I wish I could. Tobias did this terrible deed, I know he did. He needed the money, Albertina, to finance his lifestyle. It was for no other reason than that. Men such as he have no regard for human life. Their own greed overrides all other reasoning. I have no doubt either why he shut the shop so suddenly. I have done some investigating and found out that the manager who was running the shop for him was pressing Tobias to enlarge the stabling. That would have meant the demolition of the small outbuilding and a possible discovery of his terrible deed.' His voice trailed off. The distress he was causing this young woman was great, but she had to know, had to understand; could not live the rest of her life not knowing. And as he himself was the only one privileged to have all the facts then he must be the one to inform her.

He momentarily shut his eyes, feeling his age. This deed he was performing distressed him too. He had admired Robert Listerman greatly and could see many of his qualities in his daughter. She was still a young woman but a fine one. He knew once she had put all of the past behind her, she would strive for greater heights. He knew without doubt her parents would have been proud of her. It was just such a great pity they were not here to witness her achievements.

He took a deep breath. 'To pull off what Tobias did would have been relatively simple for a man such as himself – to hire a boat in his father's name then pay some unscrupulous person to wreck it on the rocks. Your father was in the habit of driving his own carriage. Tobias would have known that fact and I suspect your parents were ambushed in a lonely spot after they left the house that fateful Saturday morning. No one saw them after they left the house. And what better place to hide the bodies than here? Somewhere he knew they could never be discovered because Tobias himself had control of it. If it was Tobias who . . .' he paused, not wanting to say 'murdered' '. . . actually killed your parents or whether he got someone else to do it we will never know, but he was responsible. He was determined to get his inheritance at any cost.'

'Why?' Ally sobbed. 'Why if he had all the family money and was not concerned about his deed being discovered did he kill himself, Mr Bailey?'

A grim frown crossed his face. 'I have pondered that question deeply, my dear. And I came up with several answers, all possibilities. It was known that the company he kept included many criminals. Very dangerous people. He could have got himself into trouble with them or may have been blackmailed by any accomplices to his misdemeanours. Or else

233

he did away with himself simply because he had gone through all his money and with nothing else available to him did not relish living a poor life. And of course, my dear, you yourself were about to come of age and questions would have been raised which he would have had to answer and face the consequences of.'

She shook her head in bewilderment. 'I am having trouble accepting all this. I did not like my half-brother, Mr Bailey, but to believe him capable of such terrible things is beyond me.'

'I know, child, I appreciate your difficulties. Please believe me when I say that if I could have avoided divulging any of this, I would have. But I felt strongly that to face your life with so many unanswered questions hanging over you was not fair to you when I had most of the answers.'

She nodded miserably. 'I understand, Mr Bailey. I know you had a great respect for my family and are only doing what you think best.'

'I'm grateful you see that. You have come far, my dear, and what you have to do now is put all this behind you and face your future.'

'At this moment, Mr Bailey, I do not know if I have it in me.'

'Oh, yes, you do. For a woman who had lost everything, just look what you have achieved already. If you gave up now Tobias would have won. Don't let him, Albertina. It would have given him a great deal of satisfaction. Strive to go forward, not just for yourself but also for your parents.'

She stared at him hard. 'You are right, Mr Bailey. If not for myself, I will do it for my parents. I also owe a debt of gratitude to people who have stood by me through all of this. I cannot give up now. Before you depart I would be proud to introduce you to the Fossetts. You will like them, I know, and they you.'

Smiling warmly, he leaned forward and patted her hand. 'I would be delighted to meet them. Now show me around this shop. I want to see what you have done so far, and hear all your plans for the future.'

Chapter Thirty-Two

'So, we're all in agreement on the next steps we take? Greengrocery, grocery provisions and meat?'

Ally and Flo simultaneously nodded.

'I think it's a grand idea,' said Flo, and nudged Ally in the ribs. 'Save us doing the bloody shopping, won't it, eh, gel?'

Ally laughed. 'Yes, that is one chore I will not be sorry to see the back of. Well, for the most part. We will still have to shop for some of our own needs but diversifying into provisions does seem a logical next step.' A proud smile lit her face. 'Two more sections to add to our growing list.'

She eyed fondly the two people sitting with her at the table. The first three months of the last year had been extremely difficult for her to cope with as she had striven to come to terms with the revelations Clarence Bailey had delivered. During the days she had functioned automatically – carried along by Flo and Jack, both fully conversant with what the old lawyer had told her – and so the daylight hours had been just about bearable. It was the nights she found the hardest to endure, as she tossed and turned in the darkness, fighting to accept all that had transpired. Despite everyone's encouragement and help it had taken all her resilience to stop dwelling on the past and begin to get on with her life.

The future now looked bright. She felt her ordeal had brought forth a far better person, one able to cope with the life she now lived. She also understood and tolerated people of all walks of life, accepting them for what they were and not what they appeared to be. She had the shop and she was so lucky to have her friends, Bella as well as the Fossetts. And the best day's work she felt she had ever done was to make Flo and Jack her partners – better she could never have wished for. They were both so enthusiastic, both so willing, and for the most part easy to get along and live with.

The shop was flourishing, several significant factors all playing their part. Customers, their patronage at first due to a macabre interest in the newspaper coverage of her parents' deaths, had liked the service they received and the quality of goods they bought and continued their custom. And Bella came up trumps. Not only did she insist her family buy only from Listerman's, her mother told all her friends and acquaintances and now they did too. Word spread and snowballed and shortly

235

much larger quantities of goods had to be purchased to keep pace with their customers, and larger orders meant more profit.

The only people not pleased about their growing success were the other shopowners who quite rightly saw Listerman and Fossett as a threat. But they could not do much about it. Listerman and Fossett held a trump card which the other shopowners did not. As business developed they had the capacity to keep on expanding at minimal cost, due to the size of their building.

Now Ally's gaze settled on Flo. Although most of the profits for the foreseeable future were being ploughed back into the business, they had allowed themselves to take a little more money. For the women that meant buying some decent clothes. Ally had taken great delight in accompanying Flo on a shopping trip. And what fun they had had, being kitted out by experts in stylish clothing that suited them. Today Flo looked a picture in her smart burgundy skirt and crisp cotton blouse with its high neck, frills and leg-o'-mutton sleeves. Her blonde hair was piled up into a bun on the top of her head, curly tendrils falling round her still attractive face. She had yet to buy the longed for blue velvet suit and often playfully complained that it would be out of fashion by the time she had sufficient funds to purchase it. But that suit was no longer an impossible dream; they all knew that if business continued the way it was, then achieving it was only a matter of time. Ally often thought that the only thing lacking from Flo's life was the love of a good man and felt it a terrible pity there was no one in the offing. Now many of her burdens had been lifted, Flo had much to offer a suitable partner.

Ally's former vision of Emily dressed in a pretty dress, new boots, her fair hair cut properly, had now become a reality and it seemed certain that when she was older she would break many a man's heart. Emily was now twelve years old and showed great promise. She was still bossy, still a little tomboy, but good schooling and the advice of Flo and Ally would one day produce a lovely young lady.

Eric was now a permanent member of staff, apprenticed to Jack. At first the title 'apprentice' had not sat well with him. He'd thought it an insult to be treated as what he saw as a glorified runabout. His family owned the business, didn't they? As such he should have some sort of status. Jack had severely told him the 'status' would come when he had earned it and not before. He had sulked for a while then gradually begun to realise that he did have much to learn and decided it best to knuckle down and get stuck in. He did not relish being an apprentice forever which Jack had told him would happen if he was not prepared to learn the trade properly.

Along with Eric there were now four other apprentices, apart from Eric, all living in the attics in what had always been intended to be apprentices' rooms. Seven new assistants and three juniors had also been hired.

For the three partners, the working arrangements in the shop had changed. Jack presided over its day-to-day running and much of the hiring and firing; decided what stock was needed and what new lines to try. Ally had taken more of a back room role. Taught by Jack, she now took care of all the paperwork, along with Mr Trumper, the office clerk, and Brenda Beam, his assistant. Ally and Jack between them visited and negotiated with new suppliers. She was proud of the fact that she was getting quite proficient at striking fair deals. Flo, with the help of a daily, looked after the apprentices as well as the family, and when they were busy would willingly lend a hand whenever she was needed.

They still resided in the building at the back of the yard. It made sense and with the aid of some good quality second hand furniture and other household adornments, their lives were now far more comfortable.

None of the Fossetts ever said as much but each knew that the day Albertina Victoriana Listerman had walked into their lives had been the day things had looked up for them, and they were all secretly grateful.

'Ally, a' you listening to me?' Flo snapped, giving her a nudge.

'I beg your pardon? Oh, I'm sorry, I was lost in thought.'

Flo tutted. 'Bloody day dreaming. I dunno.' She winked at Jack. 'I'll have ter speak to the management about this.' Then she guffawed at her own joke. 'What I was saying was, I'm a bit worried about the meat side of things. Jack knows all there is to know about the greengrocery and provisions trade, but meat . . .' Her voice trailed off and Ally noticed a faraway look in her eyes which she rapidly disguised. 'Well, I know a nice bit of neck end when I see it, but not much else. And I definitely wouldn't know the first thing about carving up a side of beef.'

'What yer trying to say, Ma, is that we need to hire a butcher.'

She flashed her eyes in Jack's direction. 'Don't you be so cocky.' She sniffed haughtily. 'Still, I s'pose that's what I do mean.'

'Mmm,' mused Ally thoughtfully. 'I might have an idea there.'

They both looked at her.

'I'll make enquiries and discuss my findings with you,' she said secretively. 'So, just to recap, I will ask Frapp the builder to give us a price to do the next stage of the alterations. And while he is at it, I do feel it would be a good idea to expand the size of the haberdashery department. If we intend to sell more materials and a wider range of trimmings, we will need more room. In fact, this might be the ideal opportunity to change all the departments around. I feel the food side would be better situated all together where the hardware is now. We will need all that space if it's not to become congested. Leave haberdashery where it is but knock down the wall at the back and enlarge into the room behind. Then put the hardware in the next sections the builders knock into.' She eyed them with sudden concern. 'It's only an idea.'

'A damned good one, Ally,' Jack said, impressed. 'What d'you think, Ma?'

'Yeah, definitely. I'm in agreement.'

Ally smiled. 'The only concern I have is that when we next expand, we will be in the middle of the building and will have to consider the sweeping staircase. We could make it a feature or leave it hidden behind a wall for the time being.'

'We'd have to leave it hidden, wouldn't we?' said Flo thoughtfully. 'Yer can't have stairs leading nowhere.'

'They wouldn't lead nowhere, Ma,' Jack replied, his eyes twinkling. 'They would take shoppers up to the next floor.'

'What for?'

'Ma,' he scolded, 'to buy whatever it is we happen to be selling up there. That's what for.'

'Oh, our Jack. Upstairs indeed. You're getting too big fer yer boots, you are.'

'Jack has a point, Flo. When we have expanded as much as we can widthways, the only way is up. Clothes . . . that's what we should be thinking of next, and the rooms upstairs, suitably altered, would make the perfect setting.'

'Oh,' Flo mouthed in awe.

Jack cast a glance in Ally's direction. Some of her ideas were astounding. She never ceased to amaze him in her drive to see Listerman and Fossett the biggest and best shop for miles around. She was patient too. More so than he was. She only agreed to expansion when the idea was a sound one and money allowed. She wanted it all to work too much to gamble unnecessarily. A smile touched his lips. She certainly looked lovely today . . . but then, to him she looked lovely every day. How he hid his feelings for her he would never know, but he had become an expert at it. Without warning he suddenly felt the old ache in the pit of his stomach and fought hard to suppress a longing to leap around the table, take her in his arms and kiss her until she begged for breath. He thought of what Ma's reaction would be if he did just that, then thought of his nest egg slowly mounting in the bank. He had spent some of his earnings on two good suits, shirts and ties, and a decent pair of shoes, feeling it important to look the part when in the shop, but most of his money he put away.

Ma's main argument against a relationship between Ally and him had been their different social standing. Well, he was doing something about that. Secretly, two nights a week he attended night school classes in English which would go some way towards bettering his education and allow him to converse more easily on Ally's level. He felt his social standing was the same as hers – they were after all partners in the business. So all he needed now was a good bank balance. When he achieved that Ma's disagreements would be null and void. All he had to pray for was that Ally did not meet anyone during the time it took him to reach his goal. That would break his heart. The thought of it worried him constantly. 'Right,' he said abruptly, 'is this meeting finished only I have to get back?'

'Yer've time for a cuppa,' said Flo. 'It won't take me a minute to mash one.'

He rose. 'Maybe later, Ma.'

'I wonder what's bitten him,' she said as he went out of the door.

I wonder too, thought Ally as she gathered together the notes she had made of the meeting. She tried hard not to think of Jack and his attitude towards her, which she found totally confusing. The incident in the dark corridor when he had kissed her so passionately seemed oddly distant. Now, when she allowed herself to dwell on it, she wondered if she had imagined his desire. Yet despite his seeming indifference on a personal level, she would still catch him looking at her oddly from time to time. There was something in his eyes she could not fathom. Like just now at the table. If she did not know better she would have said the look he'd given her was one of longing. But she *did* know better. Oh, Jack, she sighed inwardly, wishing she could bury her love for him. She had managed to live with her grief for her parents; the shock of Tobias's evil deeds; Lionel's rejection – so why could she not manage to overcome her feelings for Jack?

'Ally, a' you deaf or what?'

'Sorry?'

'Do yer want tea or not? I ain't got all day, yer know. I'm busy an' all.'

'Er . . . no, thank you, Flo. I have things to do in the office.'

She tutted disdainfully. What was wrong with her bloody tea, that neither of them wanted it? 'Suit yerself,' she muttered.

Ally was halfway down the dimly lit corridor, making her way towards the office area, when a figure appeared from nowhere and nearly knocked her flying.

'Albert Farthing, what has Mr Fossett told you about running in the corridors?' she scolded as she grabbed him by his collar, pulling him to a halt. 'You could have caused a serious accident. Please remember to walk, there's a good lad.'

'I'm sorry, Miss Listerman,' he spluttered breathlessly. 'Only some old geezer's fell over and bumped his head.'

She released her grip on him. 'Old geezer?' she queried.

'Bloke. Some old bloke. He don't look well. I've been sent to fetch Mrs Fossett.'

'Oh, Oh, I see. Well, hurry then. I'll go ahead and see if there's anything I can do.'

The old man did not look well at all. By the time Ally arrived in the shop, Jack had him sitting on a chair. His head was bent and he was clutching a battered brown case. A crowd had gathered around. She took Jack aside. 'Do you think we should call a doctor?'

Jack grimaced. 'Might be wise.'

Flo arrived, kneeled by the old man, took his hand and felt his forehead. 'He don't feel hot or owt. I reckon he's just shocked.' She addressed the old man. 'How yer feeling, me duck? Do you want us to fetch a doctor?'

He looked at her blankly.

'Doctor. D'yer want us to get you a doctor?'

'Eh? No, no doctor. I . . . er . . . could I sit here for a minute to catch me breath? I'm so sorry about all this.'

Flo straightened up and turned to Jack. 'This crowd can't be doing him any good. Give me a hand to get him through the back. I'll mek him a cuppa tea and he can rest there 'til he comes to himself.'

'You're needed here, Jack,' Ally said. 'I'll help Flo.'

Between them they supported the old man through to the house in the yard and seated him comfortably before the range. Flo handed him a mug of sweet tea which, with a shaking hand, he gratefully accepted.

Glad me tea is appreciated by someone, Flo thought as she sat in her rocker opposite. 'You get back if yer want, Ally. I can manage here.'

But taking a chair from beside the table, Ally dragged it across beside Flo and sat down. 'I had better stay for a moment in case you do need a doctor. And I wouldn't mind a cup of tea now.'

'Oh.' Flo eyed her scathingly. 'You'd like one now, would yer?'

Ally did not take the bait. 'Yes, please.'

Flo folded her arms. 'Well, pour it yerself. You know where the teapot is.' She eyed the old man in concern. 'How yer feeling now? Bit better?'

He nodded. 'Yes, a bit, thank you. Silly fool that I am. I don't know what happened. One minute I was walking across the floor, next I was flat out on it.'

Flo leaned over and patted his knee. 'Well, these things happen when yer getting on a bit. You sit there for as long as you like.'

He smiled gratefully. 'You are so kind . . . so kind.' Suddenly his faded grey eyes filled with tears which rolled unashamedly down his cheeks. Ally and Flo looked on, horrified. 'I'm so sorry,' he blubbered. 'I really am so sorry.'

'You cry if yer want to. We don't mind, do we, Ally?'

'No, no. Not at all.'

Ally took the cup from his shaking hand, refilled it and placed it on the floor close by him.

They both sat looking at him helplessly.

Presently he wiped his eyes on a large threadbare handkerchief. 'Please forgive me,' he uttered. 'You ladies have been so kind.' He made to rise. 'I'd better go.'

Flo leaned over and gently pushed him back. 'You'll stay there 'til you've come to yerself. It's no bother to us.' She eyed him for a moment. 'D'yer want to talk about it?' she asked softly.

'Talk?' He gulped. 'You ladies don't want to hear my troubles.'

'Yes, we do, if it'd mek you feel better. We do, don't we?' she said, looking at Ally.

Ally really needed to get back to the office but in the circumstances felt it wouldn't be right to leave. 'They say a trouble shared helps to ease a burdened heart.'

'Do they?' Flo said, frowning at her. 'I ain't never heard that one.'

'Well, it's something like that,' she whispered.

The old man blew loudly into the handkerchief, wiped his nose and dabbed his eyes. 'I lost my wife a few weeks ago. We'd been married forty years.'

'Forty years?' Flo gasped.

He nodded. 'It's a long time to be with someone, and I miss her so dreadfully. We never had any family of our own. Just me and Edna. Always it was me and Edna, right from when we were kids.' He sighed heavily. 'She'd been ill for a long time, ten years almost, and I gave up me business to nurse her 'til she went. The neighbours offered but I couldn't bear anyone else doing for my Edna. I managed to keep us going by working as best I could from home. But you know how it is, the bills soon mounted and by the time she . . .' his voice faltered '. . . died, I had hardly a penny. That's what brought me here to Leicester.'

'I didn't think you came from these parts,' Flo said gently.

'I'm a Londoner. A true cockney at that. I was born only a stone's throw from Bow.'

'Ah, that's what Londoners sound like, is it?'

'Flo,' Ally scolded.

The old man smiled. 'I admire a woman who speaks her mind.'

'Flo does that all right. Don't you, Flo?'

She grimaced and ignored Ally's comment. 'You were telling us what brought you to Leicester?'

'Well, not just Leicester. I've travelled all over. I'm a jeweller, you see. I was fortunate to learn my trade from an old Russian Jew. What a man he was! Huge, quite frightening to look at, but with a heart of gold. The stories he used to tell of his life growing up in Russia . . .' He sadly shook his head. 'My parents were so poor when I was young that sometimes four of us had to share a bowl of soup. But that was nothing compared to some poor Russians. Boris's family were often reduced to eating grass. When he told me that I felt really humble. I was a skinny kid when I first met him. I broke one of his windows. It was an accident but luckily for me he didn't tell the authorities, nor my parents. Instead he offered me a job as a runabout and before I knew it he was teaching me all he knew. It was a sad day for me when he passed away. Eighty-three he was. He left me his tools and I took over the rent of his tiny backstreet shop in Bethnal Green and we lived in the back.

241

'I never made a fortune, just enough to keep me and Edna. Then she took ill and steadily got worse. I worked as much as I could but it was difficult because Edna needed constant care. After she died, for a while I couldn't bring meself to do anything. It was as if I'd died too. By the time I pulled meself together it was all too late. The landlord showed no mercy. I owed weeks of back rent. I begged him to allow me some time to make and sell a few pieces but he couldn't care less. As I was thrown out, someone moved in – a cobbler. My little shop that I'd worked in all me life was turned into a cobbler's. Boris Rashinski would have turned in his grave if he'd known. Edna too, God bless her.'

Both Flo and Ally felt acute sadness for the old man's grief.

Flo swallowed hard to rid herself of the lump forming in her throat. Having suffered so much hardship and grief herself she thought she would be hardened to the plight of others but that was not so. 'So what did yer do then?' she asked.

'The only thing I could. I took to the road in search of work. But not many people want an old jeweller.'

'No,' Ally whispered. 'I suppose not.'

He gave a brief smile. 'You've got a lovely shop. Big too. You sell lots of different things.' He eyed them both keenly. 'Have you considered . . . would you ever . . . er . . . what I'm trying to say is, have you ever thought of selling jewellery? I'm really good at what I do. Look, I'll show you.' He grabbed up his battered suitcase, placed it on his knees, flicked open the locks and began to search through it.

Ally and Flo looked at each other then back at the old man.

He pulled out a black parcel of silky material, closed the lid of the suitcase and laid it on top. Carefully he unfolded it. 'I had to sell most pieces I had in order to live. These three are all I have left.' He smiled proudly at the contents. 'Come take a look.'

Both Ally and Flo rose, walked over and peered down at the pieces of jewellery twinkling brightly against the blackness of the silk.

'Oh, I say,' Flo mouthed, gently picking up a brooch. It was in the shape of a butterfly, its wings fashioned in gold filigree. Delicate rubies lay the length of its body and two minute diamonds were placed at the ends of its antennae. 'Look at this, Ally. It's beautiful. You made this, you say?'

He nodded. 'Every bit with me own fair hands.'

Ally knew a good piece of jewellery when she saw it. This man was indeed a true craftsman.

Flo carefully put the piece back with the others and eyed Ally meaningfully.

She leaned closer and whispered, 'Are you thinking on the lines that I am?'

Flo nodded. 'I very well could be. He's such a sweet old man too. Surely we could do something for him?'

Thoughts racing through her mind, Ally watched the old man as he carefully stowed away his precious belongings. A solution to his immediate problems quickly occurred to her, and if it worked it would also benefit them too. She pulled Flo aside and whispered to her hurriedly.

Flo beamed. 'It's a grand idea, Ally. Put it to him.'

'Mr . . .' she began.

'Arnold. Roy Arnold.' He held out a gnarled hand which Ally shook.

She smiled. 'I am pleased to meet you, Mr Arnold. We do not sell jewellery in our shop. That is not to say we won't in the future. But at the moment we haven't the means to support a venture of that nature.' She saw a crestfallen look cross his face. 'But,' she added hurriedly, 'that does not mean to say we could not help you in some way.'

'Anything. I'd accept anything,' he replied eagerly.

'Well, we would of course have to clear matters with our other partner first but what we propose is that we should advance you enough to purchase adequate raw materials to get you started; give you a place to work and a room to sleep in the attics with the apprentices for as long as you need it.' The delighted expression spreading across his face was not lost on her. 'We could set up a small display of your wares in the shop, and if we sell any take a small percentage. If it all works out, we can reconsider the situation. Of course, as I explained at the beginning, this will all depend on the agreement of our other partner.'

'Oh, I can't tell you what I feel! I'd just about reached the stage when I thought I'd see me days out in the workhouse. I'll not let you down. You'll see, you'll be glad you gave me this chance. You ladies are truly angels.'

Flo grinned. 'I've bin called some things in my time but never an angel.'

Ally leaned over and whispered in her ear, 'Knowing what I do of you, Flo, I think his description fits you perfectly.' Once more she addressed Roy Arnold. 'If you would like to wait here for a few moments, we will go and speak to Mr Fossett and if he likes the idea we'll bring him back to meet you.'

'I'll be waiting,' Roy Arnold excitedly agreed.

Jack was sceptical but agreed to meet the jeweller and inspect his wares. Although extremely impressed at the man's ability he was a little concerned at taking such a gamble with their hard-earned profits, albeit the proposed outlay was not a large one. But he quickly decided that the women were right. This old man needed help and who was he to refuse? Gambles sometimes paid off.

After considering several possibilities for a workroom, ones that would not hinder the planned alterations, Roy asked if he might have something at the far end of the building. His craft required peace and quiet. The three partners thought it strange that the old man should wish to be so isolated, but readily accepted his need for solitude. If it produced such fine quality craftsmanship, then who were they to question it?

It was three pleased partners who retired to their beds late that night. The arrival of Roy Arnold might just prove to be another rung up the steep ladder of success for Listerman and Fossett.

Chapter Thirty-Three

The bell on the butcher's door in the tiny village of Cosby clanged loudly as Ally entered the shop. The burly, grey-haired, pleasant-faced man standing behind the butcher's table was in the process of taking off his stained white apron. He stared across at her, surprised.

'Oh, I'm sorry, me dear. I thought I'd locked the door. I was just about to have me dinner.' He hurriedly began to retie his apron.

'Would you like me to call back later?' she offered.

'No, no, not at all. For a pretty customer like you, the dinner can wait. I take it you're the new teacher? Settling in all right, are you? I'm sure you'll like living in the village. Now what can I tempt you with? A nice pork chop, or what about a bit of stewing steak?'

'Oh, dear, this is most awkward. I should have written. I do apologise. My name is Albertina Listerman and I have journeyed here today to discuss business with you, but I can see my timing is most inopportune. When would it be convenient for us to talk?'

He looked perplexed. 'Er . . . business, is it? Oh, me dear, I'm sorry, the shop is already sold.'

'The shop is sold? You are giving up the business?'

'My young assistant and his new wife are having it. It was only right that they had first refusal.' He smiled. 'I'm going to travel. See the world before it's too late. Now my mother has died there's nothing left in this village for me.' He eyed her in concern. 'Have you come far?'

'From Leicester.'

'Oh, that far? Good eight miles, I'd say. Well, I'm sorry your journey's been wasted. Look . . . er . . . come through. The least I can do is offer you a cuppa.'

'Thank you but I could not possibly intrude. You were about to have your dinner.'

'Oh, it's only bread and cheese. Since Mam died I don't bother much. Well, seems pointless going to a lot of trouble just for one. Stupid of me, I know, but . . .' He smiled. 'I'll let you in on a secret – I can't cook. I'm hopeless at it. I can boil a kettle, though. So come on through,' he ordered, pulling off his apron. 'I can't let you travel all that way back without something in your stomach.'

Without waiting for Ally to respond he hurriedly locked the outer door and led her through to a small room at the back. It was comfortably furnished and spotlessly clean. A large fire burned in the grate. He indicated a chair at the table. 'Take your coat off and sit yourself down, the kettle won't be long. Could I offer you some bread and cheese?'

Ally eyed the fresh crusty loaf sitting on a plate and the tasty-looking piece of cheese inside a dish on the snow white tablecloth. Suddenly she felt very hungry and the simple meal he was offering looked very tempting. 'That would be most welcome. Thank you.'

'It's my pleasure. I don't often get company.'

'You live here alone, do you?' she asked carefully.

'Yes, quite alone.' His tone was wistful. 'It was always me and Mam. These past four years it's been just me.'

They lapsed into silence while he busied himself and as she watched, not for the first time since she had begun her journey, Ally wondered whether she was doing the right thing in coming here. Her good intentions could be completely misconstrued and ultimately, if matters did not turn out the way she hoped, she could face Flo's wrath and even possibly lose her friendship. But as she studied this kindly man she could see why Flo had fallen in love with him all those years ago and even now still harboured feelings for him. Ally herself had only known him a matter of minutes but had immediately liked him, sensing his kindness and sincerity. And one major question had already been answered: he was not married. But then, he had said he had plans to travel. Maybe she was just too late, after all.

She accepted the noggin of bread and lump of cheese and tucked in gratefully. She must ask him, she thought, who made the cheese. It was delicious.

As they ate Malcolm Carpenter studied his visitor. 'Was you making enquiries for your husband?' he asked.

'I beg your pardon, Mr Carpenter?'

'The shop. Your husband's a butcher, is he?' He gave a loud laugh. 'I hope you don't mind me saying, but you don't seem to me to be the butcher's wife type.'

'Don't I?' Ally's eyes twinkled with amusement. She knew by his tone he had not meant to be offensive. 'You are right, Mr Carpenter, I am not a butcher's wife. It was not the shop I came to talk to you about.'

'It wasn't?'

'No. I am a partner in a shop in Leicester and we are in the process of expanding. We are going to be selling all kinds of foodstuffs as well as fresh meat.'

He nodded. 'It sounds interesting. So why are you here?'

'Our aim is to sell the best quality local produce we can find. We hope to build our reputation on it. We will only take factory goods if there is no other option. I came to ask your advice on the purchase of quality meat,

246

and also finding a butcher to work for us.'

He eyed her quizzically. 'Why me? Why come all this way when there are plenty of butchers in Leicester who'd have been happy to help?'

This was it. The time had come. Should she take a chance and be honest with him or abandon the whole idea?

'You look troubled. What's wrong?' he asked.

She clasped her hands tightly. 'I am troubled to some extent, Mr Carpenter. I haven't as yet told you everything. You see . . .' She paused. Well, here goes, she thought. 'I believe many years ago you were going to be married?'

He looked shocked, this question being the last one he would have expected. His face darkened. 'How do you know about that?' he snapped.

Ally gulped. 'I know all about it, Mr Carpenter, and the reasons why the marriage never took place.'

Stunned, he glared at her. 'How?'

She took a deep breath. 'Because Flo Fossett is a very dear friend of mine.'

'Flo?' he uttered. 'You know Flo?' His face suddenly paled, his broad shoulders sagging as all the pain of his old loss suddenly flooded through him again. 'How is she?' he asked.

Ally smiled. The question proved to her that Malcolm Carpenter still cared for Flo. 'I am glad to say she is very well.'

'But you didn't come all this way just to tell me that?'

'No, I didn't. To be honest, Mr Carpenter, I am not sure why I came. I did not know what I would find. For all I knew, you could have been happily married.'

'Is Flo?' he asked quickly.

'No, she has never married.'

He looked relieved. 'I should have thought she would be, a woman like her. For years after she disappeared the thought of her with another man drove me nearly insane. It's took me a long time to live with her going.' He stared at her questioningly. 'Why have you come here after all these years? Did . . . did Flo send you? Is there something wrong? Does she need help? Is it the lad – Jack?'

'No, Mr Carpenter. There is nothing wrong with Jack. And, as I said, Flo is fine.' She paused. 'Mr Carpenter, Flo does not know I'm here.'

'She didn't send you then? Well, why are you here? And what purpose have you for raking all this up? Do you not know how painful this is for me? I loved that woman. It's took me years to get over her. Why? Why are you doing this?'

Ally gnawed her bottom lip anxiously. 'Because, Mr Carpenter, I know Flo still loves you and wanted to find out if you still loved her. And if you do then I feel it's a shameful waste that two people who still care so much for each other should remain apart. I care very much for Flo and want to try and do something for her. You see, her leaving had nothing to do with not loving you, or falling for another man.'

'Then why did she go? What was so dreadful she could not talk to me about it? I would have understood. I would have helped. She knew that.' He shook his head, bewildered. 'You say she still loves me? Well, to my way of thinking she can't or she wouldn't have walked away without so much as a word.'

'I wish I could explain why, Mr Carpenter, but I am not at liberty to do so. Flo is the only one who can do that. But please take my word for it, her reasons were valid.'

He narrowed his eyes, face darkening in anger. 'You sit there at my table, eating my food, telling me the only woman I've ever loved still loves me – but you can't tell me why she decided just to disappear without a proper explanation?'

At his outburst she jumped up from the table. 'Oh, I'm so sorry, Mr Carpenter, I should not have come. I understand your anger but please believe me when I say that what happened to cause Flo's departure was nothing to do with her feelings for you. I was hoping by coming here today . . . I don't know . . . maybe I felt if you were still free that . . .'

'No, you shouldn't have come,' he erupted. 'I had just about accepted all this, managed to make decisions on what to do with the rest of my life. Now you come here on a whim and bring it all back.' Scraping back his chair, he sprang up, slapping his large hands flat on the table. 'Get out! Get out and leave me alone.'

Grabbing her coat, Ally fled for the door. She was past the village boundaries before she stopped for breath. Slumping against a stile she covered her face with her hands. Oh, why had she taken it upon herself to do such a stupid thing? She should have left well alone. All she had achieved was a renewal of that poor man's torment, something for which, however much she tried, she could never excuse herself.

Flo eyed her sharply when she walked through the door several hours later. 'You've been gone almost all day. I hope yer trip was worth it?'

Ally paled. 'No,' she whispered. 'It wasn't worth it.'

'The butcher you went to see was no good then?'

'No, he was not at all the type we are looking for.' She forced a smile. 'If you don't mind I think I'll retire straight to bed, I really am very tired.' She was tired but the truth was she could not face Flo after what she had done. And more worrying was the fact that, should Flo ever find out, the consequences would not bear thinking about.

Flo eyed her quizzically. Interviewing a possible employee surely could not be that exhausting? And why, she thought, had it taken Ally nearly all day? There was something going on here, but she was not able to dwell on it any further as she received a summons to attend to one of the apprentices who was feeling sick, and by the time she had seen to him she had forgotten all about it.

★ ★ ★

It was several days later when Flo was hanging out a pile of wet washing, preoccupied with thoughts of whether it would dry or not before the rain came, when she saw a figure standing before her and froze rigid.

'Hello, Flo.'

Shocked to the core by her unexpected visitor, she dropped the pile of clean washing in a puddle and all she could say was: 'Oh, look what yer've made me do.'

Whipping off his cap, Malcolm Carpenter smiled tenderly at the woman whose loss he had mourned for the past fourteen years. 'Never mind the washing, Flo. You and I need to talk. I'll deal with this while you go and fetch your coat.'

'But . . .'

'No buts, Flo. Just do as you are told.'

Later that morning a man and a woman walked through the doors of Listerman and Fossett. The woman held back, pretending to browse. The man marched across the floor, and although Jack was busy advising a customer, demanded his attention.

'You there,' he called, snapping his fingers, 'tell me where I can find Miss Listerman?'

Jack's eyes narrowed. He did not like rudeness in any shape or form. 'And who might be enquiring after her?'

A card was thrust at him. 'Hurry up, I haven't got all day.'

Jack's first reaction to Lionel Williamson-Brown was one of dislike and immediate concern as to why Ally's ex-fiancé, a man who had thrown her aside on learning of her grave financial predicament, should turn up out of the blue demanding to see her. But as much as Jack wanted to throw the man bodily out, he knew he had no right to stop him from seeing Ally. He turned and called across to Albert.

'Please take this . . . gentleman through to Miss Listerman's office.'

'Right yer are, Mr Fossett. I'll be with him in a jiffy.'

Jack watched intently as Albert led Lionel around the back of the counter. He made a striking figure with his dark good looks and immaculate attire. A sickening fear rose within Jack. Had this man come to reclaim Ally?

He felt a sharp nudge in the ribs.

'You were telling me about these new-fangled carpet sweepers?'

'Eh! Oh, Mrs Riddle, I do apologise. Now where was I . . .'

Ally was deep in discussion of their finances with Mr Trumper when the office door's opening momentarily distracted her. When she realised who was entering her jaw dropped in disbelief.

Lionel strode over to her, took her hands and gripped them tightly. 'Albertina! Oh, Albertina, how good it is to see you.'

She snatched them away. 'What are you doing here?' she demanded.

He flashed a glance at Mr Trumper. 'Leave us. Miss Listerman and I need to talk in private.'

'Stay where you are, Mr Trumper. Mr Williamson-Brown is the one who is leaving. Please go, Lionel. I have nothing to say to you.'

His dark eyes flashed. 'I'm not going anywhere until you hear what I have to say.'

Ally clenched her fists. She was unprepared for a confrontation with the man she had once loved and fear rose within her as to whether she could handle it. She had no idea what Lionel could possibly want with her, but whatever it was, he could be charming and persuasive and she knew she was no match for him. Well, she had not been in the past. But he would soon realise that it was a new Albertina Victoriana Listerman he was dealing with now. Taking a deep breath she turned to her clerk. 'Take a five-minute break, Mr Trumper. Go and get yourself a cup of tea.'

He rose hesitantly. He did not like this young man's attitude and was deeply concerned for his employer, who was obviously upset by the sudden arrival. He liked Miss Listerman. In all his years of working he had never felt so happy in a job. 'Will yer be all right, Miss Listerman?'

'Yes, thank you.'

As soon as her clerk had left she looked at Lionel, her eyes icy. 'You had better make it quick, Lionel, I am very busy. If it's money . . .'

'Ally,' he interrupted, 'I have not come here for a loan, if that's what you think.'

'Well, what have you come for?'

'You.'

'Me!' she gasped. 'Well, you can forget that. Any feelings I had for you died the night you turned your back on me. Without your help I have made a life for myself, and it does not and never will include you.'

He made to embrace her.

She recoiled. 'Do not touch me.'

He flinched. 'Ally, please hear me out. The way I acted that night was wrong. But you have to appreciate, my mother had just told me of our financial status. I was shocked. Can you imagine how I felt?'

'How can you ask me such a question?'

'I'm sorry, I phrased that badly. I should have said you of all people would know how I felt. Well, I just couldn't take it in. I wasn't thinking straight. And you know how forceful my mother is.'

Ally lips tightened. 'I know only too well, Lionel.'

'Please will you let me finish?'

'All right, I'll listen to the rest of this fairy tale and then you can leave.'

'This is no fairy tale, Ally.' He sighed heavily. 'It was not long after you left that I came to my senses and told Mother I was going after you. Our financial predicament did not matter to me. I could under no circumstances live without you. Believe me, Ally, I did my best to find you. It was a filthy night. Do you remember?'

250

That fateful night was one she would never forget. Regardless she remained silent.

'Well,' he continued, 'I got soaked to the skin. I caught a bad chill and was terribly ill. But as soon as I was well enough I began my search again. But you had disappeared, Ally. No one had seen or heard anything of you.'

'So you gave up and got yourself engaged to Felicity Burginshaw.'

He scowled deeply. 'Who told you that lie?'

'Are you saying you did not become engaged to her?'

'No, I did not. How could I when I still loved you? I did see her for a while, but it was only to please Mother, and for a short time I worked for her father though that did not work out. He expected me to start right at the bottom and work my way up, learning the business. Cheek of the man! Expecting *me* to do that.'

I do not want to hear this, she thought. Please, Lionel, just go away.

He could sense her resistance and despite her struggles grabbed her, embracing her tightly and putting his lips against her ear. 'Do not say you don't love me any more, Ally. You do, I know you do. We were meant for each other.'

She struggled against him. 'Let me go, Lionel. I may have loved you once but I don't now.'

'No,' he cried, 'I will not believe that. You are just trying to punish me. I love you. Without you I am nothing. I have had the most dreadful time. The creditors caught up with us and we were forced out of the house. We lost everything. Mother had to beg a relative to take her in. It is all so terrible for her. I too was at my wit's end. I tried everything to get a job, then a miracle happened. I was approached with an offer of employment so advantageous I could not refuse. I now live in London. My work takes me all over the country and I am remunerated most handsomely. I have been promised a partnership soon and when that happens I will be able to support us both in the manner to which we are accustomed. Think of it. We can have a large house and servants, anything you want.'

She succeeded in pulling away from him. 'I have everything I want here, Lionel, I do not need your support. And I do not care where your job takes you. Nor am I interested in your partnership. I do wish you well, though. Now, I have listened to what you had to say, will you please leave?'

His dark brows met angrily. 'No, Ally, I will not. You are shocked by my reappearance, I know that's all it is. You made yourself believe you did not love me any more because you thought I had abandoned you. You need time. I will give you that time. Will you dine with me one evening?'

'No.'

'Ally, what harm can it do? I have told you I will give you time and I will. Do not make me suffer any more. This time without you has been purgatory for me. I beg of you, please accept? Please?'

She turned from him and shut her eyes, aware of the hurt she appeared to be causing him. She sighed. He was right. What harm could come from such a simple thing as having dinner with him? All the same she was very reluctant to agree.

'Say you will?'

She sighed. 'All right, Lionel, all right. I will dine with you.' She watched his eyes light up with delight, and fear that he would think their romance was starting all over again filled her. 'Just so long as you realise that it's as friends and no more?'

'I am prepared to wait for you, Ally. You are worth waiting for.' He leaned forward, kissing her lightly on the cheek. 'Does Friday suit you?'

She nodded.

'Friday it is. Until then, my sweet.'

He turned from her and rushed from the room. She knew his hurried departure was for fear she would change her mind.

Immediately he'd left, Mr Trumper hesitantly poked his head around the door.

'Everything all right, Miss Listerman?'

She eyed him blankly. 'Er . . . yes, thank you. Now where were we?'

Jack spotted Lizzie Green just as he finished helping Mrs Riddle. He hesitated for a moment before walking across to her. 'Hello, Miss Green. Is there anything I can help you with?'

She looked embarrassed. 'Well . . . actually . . . I was just . . . looking for something for my father's birthday. Can you recommend anything?'

'Oh, let me see. We do stock several men's personal items such as collar studs and garters but nothing that I think is quite appropriate for a birthday present for your father. Oh, just a minute, what about gold cuff links?'

'You stock jewellery?' she asked, impressed.

'Yes, not an over large selection at this present time but there might be something that takes your fancy. Come, let me show you what we have.'

She inspected a platinum and diamond tie pin and a pair of gold cuff links. 'These are exquisite, Jack. How much are they?'

He told her the price.

'Are you sure? That is so reasonable for what these are.'

'That is what the jeweller priced them at.'

'I'll take the cuff links. And if you'll put the tie pin aside, I will call back for that later.'

He smiled. 'It would be my pleasure. Anything else you need?'

'No . . . well, there was something else. I . . . well, I just wanted to apologise, Jack, for my father's behaviour on the night you left his employment. This is very embarrassing for me but, you see, he had got it into his head that I had set my heart on you and . . . well, he thought you

252

felt the same way about me so he decided to hurry things along. I am sorry, Jack.'

'It's all forgotten, Miss Green. I shouldn't concern yourself about it any longer. Your father actually did me a favour. His actions helped to bring all this about in a way.'

'They did?' She sighed with relief. 'Some good came out of it then?'

She gazed up into his handsome face. Oh, Jack Fossett, she thought. If only you knew how deeply I care for you. How many times I have paced outside this shop, willing myself to come in. You do not realise this, Jack, but I am going to marry you, if it takes me a lifetime. 'So we are still friends?' she pressed.

'What?' Jack's thoughts had momentarily strayed to the meeting between Ally and her ex-fiancé. The man had been with her for nearly twenty minutes. What could he possibly have to say to her that would take so long? 'I'm sorry, what did you say?'

'I asked if we were still friends?'

'Friends? Oh, yes, of course. Shall I get these wrapped for you?'

'Please. But before you do,' she said, tentatively laying a hand on his arm, 'my parents are having a few people round on Friday night. It's all very informal and I know Dad would like to make amends to you. Will you come, Jack?'

Before he could answer, Lionel Williamson-Brown walked jauntily past. Frowning, Jack stared after him. The man looked pleased with himself and Jack wondered why.

Lionel suddenly stopped, turned and called over to him: 'You there, tell Miss Listerman I will call for her at eight sharp on Friday.'

Without waiting for any response he strode through the door.

'So will you, Jack?'

'Sorry. Will I what?'

'Come to dinner on Friday?'

Deeply distracted, he nodded. 'Yes, all right.'

A warm glow filled Lizzie and she smiled in delight.

After Mr Trumper and Miss Beam had left for the day Ally sat for a while in the dimness of the office, lost in her own thoughts. She felt she should be happy about Lionel's return and convinced by his plausible excuses. But she wasn't. And neither was she looking forward to her dinner engagement with him. But she had agreed, albeit under extreme pressure, so she would have to honour her promise.

She let herself into the house in the yard. A delicious-smelling aroma greeted her. Her eyes fell on the table which was neatly laid then settled on Flo who was bustling around looking very pleased with herself.

'You look happy, Flo. And whatever you are cooking smells good. Special occasion, is it?'

Flo stopped what she was doing and smiled. 'Yes, I am happy. And yes, it is a special occasion. A very special occasion.' She addressed Eric and Emily. 'You two, go and get washed and changed.'

'Do we have to, Ma?' they both wailed.

'I've worked all day,' Eric grumbled. 'Anyway what's wrong with the clothes I have on? You don't usually mek me change.'

'Tonight yer do. Now stop back chatting and do as I ask. You ain't too big yet to feel my hand across your backside. Oi, and I'm warning yer, yer'd both better be on yer best behaviour tonight or you'll not live ter regret it. I want no more of yer back chat, Eric. And you, Emily, no feeding Sal off yer plate. Are yer both listening?'

'Yes, Ma.'

'Good, then off you go and hurry up about it. Oh, and Emily, wear your green dress. You look pretty in that.'

Emily skipped out happily. She liked her green dress.

'Can I do anything for you, Flo?' asked Ally.

She shook her head. 'No, it's all under control. I just want you all to sit back and enjoy it.' She grimaced. 'Have yer seen our Jack?'

Ally, still wondering when she was going to be told exactly what the special occasion was, replied, 'No. He must be still in the shop.'

'Bloody typical. The one night I want everything to be just right, he decides to be late. Do you know what's up with him?'

'What do you mean?'

'I caught a glimpse of him a while ago and he looked like doom itself.' Flo eyed Ally critically. 'Come to that, you don't look too happy yourself. What's the matter with you both? You ain't had a row, have yer?'

'No, we haven't. I haven't seen Jack all day.'

'Oh! Well, what's up with you then?'

'I do not have a clue what you are talking about,' she lied. 'I am quite all right, thank you.'

'Have it yer own way, but I happen to think different. I suppose you'll tell me when you've the mind. Oh, here's Jack now. Where you bin 'til this time?'

'Working, Ma. Why? Oh, summat smells good. And what's with the table? Is royalty coming?'

Flo rubbed her hands together. 'Now yer both here, I can tell you. We are having a guest for dinner. A very special guest. Malcolm Carpenter,' she announced.

Ally nearly choked. 'Is that the . . . er . . . man you were once engaged to?'

'Yes, it is,' replied Jack. 'I was only a lad but I remember I thought a lot of him.' He frowned at Flo quizzically. 'How did . . .'

'It's a long story, Jack,' she cut in. 'Too long to go into now 'cos he'll be here soon. He's sold his shop and was going to travel a bit but then he heard Listerman and Fossett were on the look-out for a butcher. I tell you what, people seem to know what we're doing before we do but for once

I'd like to thank the person who invented gossip. Hearing the name Fossett, Malcolm made some enquiries and found out it was me and you, Jack. He came to see me this morning and we had a really long talk. The upshot is we've put everything right and . . .' she smiled, '. . . if things work out, we just might get married. Not yet,' she added. 'But in time.'

'Oh, Ma,' Jack cried. 'Oh, I'm so pleased for you.'

Ally sighed with relief. Obviously Malcolm had not divulged to Flo her own part in this. He was an honourable man. 'So am I, Flo.' She threw her arms around her friend and embraced her warmly. 'It's about time you had someone to share your life with.'

'You say you put everything right, Ma?' Jack asked. 'Did you . . . er . . . tell Malcolm everything?'

'Yes, I did. I told him all that had happened since the last time I saw him. When I told him about the children, he cried and said he understands completely why I did what I did. He asked a lot about you, Jack. He loved you like his son. In some ways, despite my reasons, I see that what I did to him was cruel. I have a lot of making up to do. And, Ally, I hope yer don't mind but I told him all about you. How you came to us and how all this began. I felt if we were to go on properly, I had to be honest.'

'And you did right, Flo. I have done nothing to be ashamed of.'

'Did you tell him about the job, Ma?' asked Jack.

'Oh, you,' she scolded. 'At a time like this, all you can think of is work. You can tell him yourself over dinner.'

The meal was a resounding success. Flo's delicious food was praised highly and Jack joked that being able to cook as well as this Flo should open her own eating establishment. Ally said he should not poke fun at such an idea and they should seriously consider setting aside an area at some stage in the future to cater for weary customers. Jack eventually turned the conversation around to the butcher's shop and Malcolm expressed an interest in coming to work for them, so long as Flo was happy with the arrangement. The smile that lit her attractive face gave him his answer.

And Sal was fed under the table, but it was not the children scolded for being the culprits, it was a red-faced Malcolm.

Ally knew as she witnessed the loving exchanges pass between Malcolm and Flo that their marriage would be sooner rather than later and that she would have to plan a move out of the house in the yard. After all, newlyweds could not be expected to begin married life with a lodger in tow, no matter how dear that lodger was to them. When the time came, no matter how sad she was, parting under these circumstances was something she would not mind. And besides, she thought, she was almost twenty-three, old enough and wise enough now to be taking care of herself.

Chapter Thirty-Four

Many months later, a preoccupied Ally strolled aimlessly along the corridors. She had much on her mind and wasn't aware of the route she was taking. It was well after closing time and the whole building, after the hustle and bustle of the day, seemed ghostly and empty. But Ally was not conscious of any of this. Her mind was filled with thoughts of Lionel.

Her relationship with him was a strange one. Despite his attentiveness whenever they met, those meetings were erratic. His excuse was always that business took up much of his time. He was, he told her, building a future for them both and she should be understanding. She was understanding, knew very well what long hours had to be worked in order to achieve set goals. But she didn't know if she wanted her future to be with him.

It was almost a year since their first dinner together which had not gone at all as she had expected. She had steeled herself to withstand pressure, expected him to demand she resume their engagement, but he hadn't. He had been gentle, cautious, and with these unexpected tactics had begun to win her over, despite herself.

During this time she had also witnessed, to her inward grief, a closeness developing between Jack and Lizzie Green. To ease her torment she had turned to Lionel. That had been wrong of her, she knew. But even now, deep down, she had to admit that she would give anything to have Jack facing her across the table gazing lovingly into her eyes instead of Lionel; have his arms embrace her instead of Lionel's; have him kiss her instead of Lionel. What was wrong with her? She had loved Lionel once, why could those feelings not return? That would ease so much of her pain. But no matter how long she waited, she knew she would never love Lionel the way she loved Jack. It was impossible. Jack possessed qualities Lionel never would; had touched a part of her that Lionel never had or would, no matter how he appeared to have changed now he had got himself a job and was far away from his domineering mother.

Somehow, though she did not know how, she had to get used to the idea that Jack would never belong to her. It was Lionel who loved her, Lionel who wanted her, Lionel who was working hard in order to marry her, despite the fact that Listerman and Fossett was making enough now to provide for them. When they married, Lionel had told her, it would be

256

his finances that provided for their needs, not hers. His sentiments had surprised her, but what had shocked her was the realisation that she really did not want him to become involved in her business. And yet she was considering marriage to him . . . why was everything so difficult and confused?

She stopped walking suddenly and glanced around, wondering where she was. Then she realised she was close by the room Roy Arnold used as his workshop. The flame from a lighted gas lamp inside flickered against the glass in the door. She smiled. Roy did take his work seriously. He seemed to work dreadfully long hours for a man not so young in years any more. But then, business had expanded so rapidly for him she supposed he had no choice, although he had now employed two experienced assistants to help ease his workload. If things continued as they were, he would have to employ some more.

There was now a counter devoted entirely to exclusive Roy Arnold jewellery and including a selection of watches and clocks. The counter was proving very popular and their initial gamble had paid off handsomely.

She should not disturb him, she thought. The only odd characteristic Roy Arnold displayed was his insistence on not being disturbed, complaining bitterly that it caused a lapse in his concentration and if a piece was ruined it could prove a costly business.

She hesitated just before the door. As she was here, she would brave his annoyance and pay a visit, she decided. She liked Roy Arnold. As Flo had said, he was such a sweet old man. And it had been a long time since she had been inside this room. It was also soothing to watch a craftsman at work. Maybe he would allow her to stay and watch for a while.

She made to tap lightly on the door when it opened and the man who had been in her thoughts minutes before walked out, closing it hurriedly behind him.

Frozen in shock, they both stared at each other.

'Ally . . . er . . . what are you doing here?'

'I am quite entitled to be here, Lionel. It is my shop. What are *you* doing here?'

'Er . . . business. I came to see Roy about a bit of business.'

'I didn't realise you knew him?'

'I don't. On my travels I heard of someone wanting some jewellery and knew of Roy through your dealings with him. I decided to tell him, that's all.'

'Oh, I see.' She gazed at him quizzically. 'You told me you were going to be in London all week?'

His eyes flashed. 'What is all this, Ally? I don't appreciate your accusations. Don't you trust me?'

'Lionel,' she said lightly, 'I only queried your presence here. I made no accusations and it's not a matter of trust.'

His gaze softened. 'I'm sorry. I'm just tired.' He took her in his arms. 'My diversion here wasn't just to see Roy.'

'Oh?'

'You know it wasn't. I thought I could take you to dinner. I plan to catch the night coach to London. That gives us four hours.'

'Will you always be working from London?'

'Wouldn't you like to live there? If I remember correctly you always liked to visit the capital.'

'Visit, Lionel. Living there would be a different matter. Besides, I have the shop. I could not manage it if I was living in London.'

'Oh, Ally, stop being silly. You started all this to make a living. You won't have to do it when we are married.'

An icy fear suddenly flashed through her at the thought and she wondered why she should react that way when she should be overjoyed at the prospect.

'Come on, let's go and eat. I'm starving,' he said.

'I can't, Lionel. I have accepted an invitation to eat with Flo and her husband Malcolm this evening.'

'You'd turn me down for them? Ally, really. I know all you've told me about them, but after all . . .'

'After all, Lionel?'

'They are hardly our type. All right, so the Fossetts helped you out when you needed it, but you have repaid them. I think you are mad to have made them partners.'

She disentangled herself from his arms, glaring up at him furiously. 'How dare you speak of my friends in such a manner? If this is the way you feel, maybe we should put a stop to our association right now.'

'Hey, calm down. I am entitled to my opinion.'

'Yes, you are, but even so . . .'

'All right, I apologise. I'm tired. I've had a long day. Let's forget what I said. I suppose I'll get used to your choice of friends, given time.' He smiled down at her, eyes tender. 'Now are you coming with me or not?'

'I've already told you my plans for this evening and I will not hurt Flo's feelings. I would have accepted your invitation if I could have warned her earlier but as it is she will already have cooked for me.' He was angry and she knew it. 'I will see you on Saturday as we planned. Are we still going to the theatre?'

His pout reminded Ally of a spoiled child's.

'I have the tickets,' he snapped. 'They did not come cheap so I would be obliged if you did not change your mind.'

'Oh, Lionel, don't be childish. I'll be ready and waiting.'

She reached up and kissed him lightly on his cheek.

He grabbed hold of her. 'Is that all I get?' he said, bending to kiss her demandingly. She did not respond as willingly as he'd expected and he pulled away from her, frowning. 'I see. I am being punished, am I?'

'Don't be silly, Lionel. Like you, I am tired. But I must admit, I am still very upset by what you said.'

'Oh, Ally, really. I apologised and asked you to forget it.' He shrugged his shoulders. 'I'd better go. Are you at least going to see me out?'

'I was just going to pay my respects to Roy, since I am here.'

He hurriedly cupped her elbow with his hand and began to steer her back down the corridor. 'I shouldn't disturb him at the moment, Ally. He wasn't pleased when I appeared, despite my putting some business his way. He's a funny fellow in that respect, isn't he? Still, I suppose with the talent he's got, we shouldn't really object.'

Malcolm flung his arms around Flo and hugged her tightly. 'Happy, Mrs Carpenter?'

'Mmm, so, so,' she replied, hiding a smile. 'I'd be happier if you'd let me get on with dishing up this dinner.'

'Sod the dinner, Flo. Just give us a cuddle.'

So she did.

'Now will you get out of me way?'

He laughed. 'You're a hard woman, Flo Carpenter. Mean with it, too.' He rolled up his sleeves. 'Come on, gel. What can I do to help?'

'Nothing, just sit down. The others will be here in a minute.'

'Is Ally coming?'

'Yes.' Flo sighed heavily. 'Oh, yer know, Malcolm, I don't like her living all alone in that house. It was good of her to move out and give us this, and what she's moved into is a nice enough place and I know she has that housekeeper person doing for her, but I can't help feeling she's lonely.'

Malcolm eyed his beloved wife questioningly. 'But she has the business and plenty of visitors, and she's still seeing that Lionel fella, so how can she be lonely?'

Flo shrugged her shoulders as she placed warmed plates on the table. 'I dunno, I just get the feeling she ain't happy, that's all.'

He paused, thoughtfully. 'I don't know why but I don't really like that fella's manner. He's too condescending for my liking.'

'Well, he's gentry, so what can you expect?'

'Flo, Ally's gentry, and so is that friend of hers, Bella, and you like Bella well enough.'

'Yes, she's all right, I suppose. But Ally's a different kind of gentry. A one off. I try, yer know, Malcolm, but I still don't trust 'em. Except Ally and maybe Bella, of course.'

'Flo, I thought we had discussed this. I thought you had agreed to forget about what happened. You cannot judge everyone by that experience.'

'I know, I know, and I try hard not to, but sometimes it all comes back. Forgetting something like that ain't easy, yer know, Malcolm, no matter how many years pass. Anyway, you promised we would never talk about it and you know I'd hate anyone to overhear. You are the only one who knows about all that. I trusted you with it all those years ago, felt it only right I should tell you, being's we were gonna be wed, and you promised not to tell anyone. I still hold you to that.'

'I know, my love, I know. Stop worrying yourself. I haven't told a living soul. The devil himself wouldn't drag it from me.'

She smiled affectionately. 'I do love you, Malcolm.'

'I know you do.' He sighed distractedly. 'What about Jack, Flo?'

'Get down, Sal. You'll have yer dinner soon.' She eyed her husband sharply. 'What about Jack?'

'He's not happy either.'

'Of course he is. He's seeing a lot of Lizzie. I'd say he's growing quite attached to her. I think an engagement is likely soon.'

He eyed her searchingly. 'That's what you'd like, Flo, isn't it?'

She frowned. 'And what's that supposed ter mean?'

'You know well enough. An engagement between him and Lizzie would put a stop to the threat of him and Ally getting together.'

'Him and Ally! There's nothing going on there, I can assure yer.'

'Flo, that isn't true and you know it. Those two love each other. It's as plain as daylight.' He rose from the table and gathered his wife to him. 'I've a feeling something you said has put a stop to it coming together. Am I right, Flo?'

'No,' she lied. Then her shoulders sagged. 'Well, I might have voiced me opinion to Jack. And I don't regret it neither! Look, Malcolm, I've grown to love Ally like a daughter, I'd trust her with me life, but when all's said and done she's gentry. Her and Jack were born different sides of the tracks. It wouldn't work between 'em. I've tried to change me mind on that, Malcolm, I really have. I knew something was developing a long time ago but I thought it'd all stopped.'

He shook his head. 'Might appear so, Flo, but I'd stake me life it hasn't.'

She sighed heavily. 'For a man you see a lot, don't yer?'

'With people I really care about, yes. Ally and Jack have been good to me, Flo. They have both made me feel so much a part of things. And look how much responsibility they have trusted me with. Who else would have given me the chance to manage not only the meat department but the foodstuffs too? They didn't have to, Flo. I would still have married you.'

'Don't decry yourself, Malcolm. You were the best person for the job.'

'I like to think so. But I'd have been quite happy just running the meat section without anything else. I know you might have had a say in it, but when all's said and done you're just one of three. They trusted me and I'm grateful to them. Now, during a working day I spend a lot of time with Jack and Ally. I see the way each looks at the other, secret like.'

'What do yer mean?'

'Flo, you know perfectly well. The only way I know how to describe it is with longing.'

'Oh, Malcolm,' she said emotionally. 'You make me feel so bad. But I can't relent. I can't give me encouragement to something I feel wouldn't work in the long run. It's the hurt it'd all cause.'

'What about the hurt that's being caused now, Flo? By keeping two people apart that should rightly be together. I don't know what you said to Jack but he'd never go against you. He loves you too much. But we are talking of two grown people, Flo. Shouldn't you let them work matters out themselves? Try, Flo. Try hard to forget your grudge towards the gentry that's stopping you giving your blessing . . . Oh, hello, Ally,' he said, flustered, as the door opened and she walked in. Releasing Flo, he scanned Ally's face. 'Is there summat the matter? You look peeved?'

'Do I? I'm fine, really. Just a little tired.' She kissed Malcolm in greeting then repeated the action with Flo. 'Something smells good.'

'So it should. I've spent all afternoon cooking it. Steak and kidney pudding with nice thick gravy. So sit yourself down, I was just about to dish up. I was beginning to worry yer weren't coming as time wore on.'

'I apologise, Flo. I got a little waylaid.' She sat down at the table. 'Is it just the three of us eating tonight?'

'Yes, just us,' Flo said, placing a piping hot pudding bowl in the centre of the table. 'I did think of asking Roy but he's refused every other time I've offered so I thought better of it. Eric's rushed in and rushed out again. He's going to the music hall with his mates. Emily has been invited over to a friend's house and . . .' she flashed a glance at Malcolm as she dug a serving spoon into the bowl '. . . Jack's gone over to Lizzie's.'

Ally hoped they did not notice her dismay. 'This looks delicious,' she said lightly as Flo placed her dinner before her.

Chapter Thirty-Five

'Come on,' Lionel urged Ally. 'I need a drink and if we don't hurry we won't be served.'

Ally sighed. 'Lionel, don't be so impatient. The interlude lasts half an hour. Plenty of time for two drinks, should you wish. Please excuse me,' she said, smiling as she eased herself by a large woman blocking the aisle and hurried to catch up with Lionel. She caught up with him in the refreshments area.

'What would you like to drink, Ally?' he asked, clicking his fingers to attract a harassed waiter. The bar was filling quickly and all of the seats had already been taken.

'A dry sherry, please.'

'A dry sherry and a double whisky. And make it quick.'

She frowned at his rudeness. 'Lionel, what on earth is wrong with you?'

'Nothing.' In fact, there was a lot on Lionel's mind but the last person he could discuss his troubles with was Ally, for so many reasons. He did not need to wonder how she would react if she learned half of his business and how it affected her. He grimaced. This job was proving to be far more than he had ever anticipated. He was getting in out of his depth but his boss had assured him he was perfect for the job and was proving his worth. Instinct told Lionel he should get out now while the going was good but the money he was being paid far outweighed his qualms. Plus there was the promise of greater things to come. He had no choice but to stick with it. His employment record meant he had few other options open to him.

Ally studied Lionel's handsome face as he gulped his drink. He was lying, she knew. The man before her had much on his mind but obviously did not want to discuss business matters with her. All through the performance he had fidgeted in his seat and she could tell he had hardly taken in any of the music, something she herself had looked forward to. She was not a great follower of opera but Dame Nellie Melba's visit to the De Montfort Hall in Leicester was a rare occasion and not to be missed. Tickets had been hard to come by and very expensive. It was a shame, she thought, that Lionel was not enjoying it.

Her eyes strayed around the crowd. By the looks of it she was not the only one enjoying her evening.

She automatically stepped forward to let several people pass and as she did so her eyes met Jack's. For several long seconds they stared at each other.

'Er . . . Jack, how nice to see you,' she finally said, unnerved by his scrutiny which she put down to surprise at their unexpected encounter.

'You too, Ally,' he replied, then nodded a greeting at Lionel. 'Lionel.'

He scowled, annoyed. The likes of Jack Fossett had no right to address him by his Christian name. Fossett had obviously forgotten his place.

'I did not realise you were coming to see this performance?' said Ally.

'Neither did I 'til late this afternoon. Lizzie's father got hold of the tickets.' He had been given no choice about accompanying her. She had told him so tearfully how much trouble her father had gone to to get the tickets and how much he had paid for them. The very least Jack could do was attend.

Ally's eyes darted to the woman hanging on Jack's arm. She forced a smile. 'Hello, Miss Green. Are you enjoying the performance?'

'Oh, very much so.' Lizzie's reply was a mite curt. The last person she had expected to bump into was Albertina Listerman, and despite the fact that Ally had her own handsome escort, the exchange of looks that had passed between Jack and Ally had been obvious to Lizzie. So that was it, she thought, dismayed. That was why Jack was so reluctant to further their relationship. He was in love with his partner, and if Lizzie was not very much mistaken his partner felt the same. Her heart ached painfully. She would have to do something about this state of affairs. Jack was the most important person in her life and she would not let go of him easily. She clung possessively to his arm, smiling sweetly at Ally. 'Jack is enjoying it too.' She gazed at him adoringly. 'Aren't you, Jack?'

Before he could reply Lionel spoke. 'I should not have thought opera was to your taste, Fossett. I would have said that music hall was more your line.'

'Lionel,' Ally reproved, deeply embarrassed.

Jack shrugged his shoulders nonchalantly. 'You would probably be surprised by my tastes, Lionel, operetta in particular. *The Merry Widow* is a particular favourite of mine. It has probably escaped your notice but the year is 1911 and we common folk know a bit more about things nowadays. We have been given some rights – not many, but some. Did you know that some of us can even read now?' He turned to Lizzie. 'If you've finished your drink, we ought to be getting back to our seats. I don't want to miss anything.' Ally was still staring at Jack, surprised and amused by his response, when he inclined his head to her. ''Bye, Ally.' He flashed an icy glance at her companion. 'Lionel.'

'Insolent swine,' he hissed harshly as Jack and Lizzie were swallowed up in the crowd. 'You see what I mean, Ally? Out of the goodness of your heart you made him a partner and now he treats you as an equal. He should be flogged!'

'Lionel,' she erupted, 'you asked for all he gave you. Jack has as much right to be here as we have.' The last thing she felt like was a confrontation in the middle of the splendid De Montfort Hall before several hundred witnesses, and definitely not with Lionel in his present mood. 'Now can we please return to our seats and enjoy the rest of the performance?'

But Ally did not enjoy herself. All her mind's eye could see was Jack and Lizzie Green, and the way Lizzie had looked so adoringly at him. She had to admit that they made a good couple. Lizzie was an attractive woman and came across as very pleasant. Although it distressed her greatly to think it, the announcement of a marriage between them would surely be made soon.

As for Ally herself and Lionel . . . After his outburst tonight she knew without doubt that marriage between them would never work. She had always known it, right from Lionel's reappearance, but had been swept along by his persuasive charm. She was too far removed from him now. Over the last three years her whole perception of life and of people had changed drastically. Not so Lionel's. Tonight's outburst had finally brought home to her his true nature and she had not liked what she had witnessed.

She would have to tell him her decision. Not tonight, though. Lionel was in no mood to take in what she had to say. She would have to pick her moment but would do it soon, feeling it best for both concerned to get it over with.

Across in the cheaper seats, Jack too was deep in thought, Dame Nellie Melba's singing going over his head. All he could picture was Ally, looking stunning in a dark blue velvet gown. Their unexpected encounter had upset him. He knew, of course, that she was seeing Lionel, but why? He wasn't worthy of her. The man was arrogant and a total bore. Jack had never taken to him; there was something about Lionel he did not quite trust, and after his display tonight he thought even less of him. Jack's eyes narrowed. Lionel Williamson-Brown was lucky not to have received a good punch for what he had said. Another man in Jack's position, spoken to so patronisingly, would have done just that. But not Jack Fossett. He would not give the likes of Lionel the satisfaction.

His brow was deeply furrowed. He just hoped Ally did not decide to marry this man. She would, in his opinion, be making a grave mistake. Jack sighed heavily. The thought of her with any man, let alone Lionel, still cut him to the quick and tonight's unexpected meeting had spoilt his whole evening.

The only thing he was glad of at this moment was that he had attended night school. At least his perseverance on that score had paid off, affording him the ability to retaliate to Lionel's comments far more articulately than would previously have been possible.

He felt Lizzie squeeze his arm.

'You all right, Jack?' she whispered.

He nodded. 'Yeah. Yeah, I'm on top of the world,' he lied.

Chapter Thirty-Six

'Are you going to have another cake, Ally?'

She eyed the delicately iced petits fours on the cake stand. The Grand Hotel served the most delicious teas for miles around. Bella and she had feasted on wafer thin slices of freshly baked bread, butter and strawberry jam, plus a choice of cakes from the two-tier stand, washed down by two pots of Earl Grey tea. All this had been served by very polite, very stiff, waiters. She hid a smile. Flo would have described the waiters as penguins with broom handles up their shirts.

'Oh . . . I'd better not, thank you, Bella. I have had three already. I feel positively greedy, and if I don't watch out I'll grow fat.'

'With a figure like yours, Ally, that is one thing you do not have to worry about. I hate you for being able to eat anything you like and not putting on an ounce. I only have to look at food and it's already sitting on my hips.'

Ally laughed. 'Oh, you are adorable, Bella, and we all love you, whatever your size. Especially Maximilian, if I am not mistaken.'

Bella smiled secretively. 'You do like him, don't you, darling?'

'I love him, Bella. I took to him the first time you introduced us,' she answered with deep sincerity. 'But,' she added, 'whether I like him or not is hardly important. It is how you feel. You love him, don't you?'

'Yes, I do. But you are wrong, it is very important to me that you should like my . . .' she paused to achieve the desired effect '. . . future husband!'

Ally looked stunned then beamed in delight. 'Really, Bella? You are going to be married?'

She nodded happily. 'Yes, I am,' she said excitedly. 'We have fixed a date, April the ninth, and I want you as my bridesmaid. And guess what?' she cried, clapping her hands in excitement. 'We are going to America for our honeymoon.'

'America! Oh, Bella, how thrilling.'

'Isn't it just? Maximilian, the darling, has booked tickets for the maiden voyage of the *Titanic*. That is why we've decided to hold the wedding so soon. The voyage is the chance of a lifetime.'

'The *Titanic*! Oh, Bella, you are a lucky girl. I have seen pictures of that splendid new liner. It looks positively out of this world. Oh, and

America! Bella, that's one place I have always longed to go, especially since we started up the shop. America is so advanced where shopping is concerned. Promise me you will visit all the shops, Bella, and make as many notes as you can and report . . .'

'Hey, hey, just a minute, Ally,' she cut in, eyes twinkling. 'The trip will be my honeymoon, remember, not a working expedition.'

Ally laughed. 'Yes, of course. But all the same,' she coaxed, 'just visit one or two for me. When do you sail?'

'After the ceremony we will travel to Southampton. The boat is scheduled to leave on the twelfth.'

'Oh, Bella, I am so pleased for you. Marriage to Maximilian, and America! How heavenly. Although I have to say I did not realise matters had gone this far between you and Max.'

'Well, Ally, you have been so busy in the shop, and what with Lionel back on the scene, you haven't had much time for me.'

Ally eyed her dear friend, ashamed. 'Oh, Bella, how can you ever forgive me?'

'It's all right, darling, I do understand, really.'

Ally looked searchingly at her. 'You do not like Lionel, do you?'

Bella answered without hesitation, 'No. Despite his excuses for the night he turned his back on you, and his insistence he searched high and low for you, don't ask me why but somehow I don't believe him. And, regardless, I do not feel he is right for you.'

'Neither do I.'

Bella looked surprised. 'You don't? Oh, Ally, I *am* pleased. Oh!' She clasped her hand to her mouth. 'I did not mean to . . .'

'It's all right, Bella. I decided a while ago to break things off, but it hasn't been possible.' Ally shrugged her shoulders. 'Firstly, I do not see very much of him. Once or maybe twice a week, that's all. Lionel seems to be very tied up in this mystery job of his. And secondly, whenever I try to broach the subject, he quickly guesses what is coming, turns on the charm and changes the subject. I am no match for that charm, Bella. It very quickly erodes my resolve to get matters sorted out. But only I can do it, I know that.'

'The sooner the better, Ally.'

'I know. I am supposed to be seeing him tonight and have made up my mind that whatever happens I will make sure I tell him. I do not enjoy his company the way I should any longer and it is quite distressing to know that he believes we are going to marry.'

'Well, I am sorry to say this, but I am glad you are not marrying him.' Bella screwed up her face thoughtfully. 'Lately there is something about Lionel I just cannot fathom . . .'

'Yes, I know what you mean. He is very . . .'

'Very what?'

'I would say nervous about something.'

'Mmm, yes. The few occasions I have met him with you, I would say that about sums him up. Any idea of what, though?'

'Not a clue. He tells me nothing. He is so secretive, and quite apart from anything else that's not a basis on which to build a marriage.' She sighed. 'I could be being a little uncharitable, though. Lionel has great difficulty with the fact that I work. Women, according to Lionel and his like, do not work, and certainly business is not something to be discussed with them.'

'Ally, you know what I feel about Lionel, but yes, I do think you are being unfair. Until three years ago you would never have expected him to discuss business with you. We women are not supposed to take an interest in anything of that nature.' She picked up her tea cup. 'Business,' she said matter-of-factly, 'does not interest me in the slightest.'

Ally opened her mouth to chastise Bella. She felt she should be taking an interest in matters other than social. But she quickly realised Bella was right. Until recent years her own attitude would have mirrored her friend's because she had not known any better.

Bella was staring at her quizzically. Finally she asked, 'Is there anyone else, Ally?'

Her eyebrows rose in surprise. 'Anyone else? In my life, you mean? No, of course not. Who would there be?'

Thoughtfully, Bella studied her tea cup. Despite the denial, she knew there was someone else in Ally's life. So she was still trying to cover up her true feelings for Jack Fossett? Oh, Ally, thought Bella sadly.

Over the last eighteen months, as Bella had come to know the Fossetts better, she had changed her mind completely over the prospect of a relationship between her very dearest friend and Jack. Mixing with these people had afforded her, just as it had Ally, an insight into their way of life, and just like Ally her findings had astonished her.

Working-class people were most definitely not the lowest form of life, as her peers had led her to believe. The majority were hard-working, loyal, faithful people. Most of those who landed up the wrong side of the law did so trying to supplement the pittance of a wage her own class paid their employees, their misdemeanours carried out solely to survive.

Max, her future intended, was one of the new breed of gentry. He realised that without a loyal workforce, one adequately paid for work done in decent surroundings, society as they knew it could ultimately be jeopardised. There was an ever present unrest which had to be stemmed before it was too late. Old school masters needed to be educated in modern ways of thinking. Max was at this very minute attending a meeting with his father, to try to work out how to bring about better working conditions for their employees. His father was quite formidable, his ideas set firmly in the past, and Max had a struggle on his hands. But Bella had faith in his abilities and felt that sooner or later he would win through and begin the process of gradual change that many knew was needed.

Her thoughts came back to her friend. The better she had grown to know Jack Fossett, the better she had grown to like him. It was a shame that Jack and Ally could not somehow be brought together. But that was obviously not going to happen, especially in light of the fact that Ally herself denied having any romantic inclinations towards him, and that Jack seemed to be seeing a lot of his former employer's daughter.

Still, thought Bella optimistically, Ally was a beautiful woman, in nature and in looks, and Bella knew there was someone somewhere for her. The love of a good man was the only thing missing from Ally's life. But there was plenty of time, once she had sorted out Lionel and buried any feelings she had for Jack Fossett. There were many men who would fall head over heels for her once they knew she was available. Bella's eyes lit mischievously. She for one would start spreading the word. Max had plenty of eligible friends. As soon as they returned from honeymoon they would hold a party, and who knew what would happen?

'Oh, have another cake, Ally, for goodness' sake, or I'll finish them myself. Then I'll never get into my wedding dress and it will be all your fault.

Ally smiled. 'Oh, all right. But just to please you.' Besides, she thought ruefully, she would need all the energy she could get if she was going to have a showdown with Lionel. That thought was not one she relished.

Chapter Thirty-Seven

'I will not listen to this, Ally!'

Lionel paced the room, his expression thunderous.

'Lionel, please, don't make this any harder than it already is.'

He spun to face her. 'Harder than it is?' He wagged a finger at her. 'Ally, you could not be doing this to me at a worse time. I have enough on my mind without this.'

'What do you mean by that remark, Lionel? What is happening to you at the moment that is so bad?'

'Besides your rejection of me, you mean? Nothing. There's nothing.'

She sighed. 'You see, you don't even talk to me. I know nothing of your life.'

He held up his arms. 'Just what is it you want to know? Come on, Ally. What?' he shouted.

'Stop it, Lionel. There is no need for this display of anger.'

'Isn't there? You expect me to be calm, do you? Just accept your rejection of me and walk away. Well, I won't, I tell you. I love you, I can't live without you.'

'Yes, you can, Lionel. We may have loved each other once but we have both changed. Grown away from each other.'

'You may have grown away from me, but I haven't from you.' His eyes narrowed alarmingly. 'I know what's happened. It's those people you've been mixing with. They have done this to you. Changed you, as you say.'

'Yes, they have, Lionel,' she said softly.

He sneered at her. 'So scrubbing floors, eating in the kitchen, serving behind a counter, doing your own washing – all that has made you a better person, has it?'

Ally sighed despairingly. 'I think you had better go, Lionel.'

'That would be easy for you, wouldn't it? If I just left.' He leaped over to her and grabbed her by the shoulders, pulling her close. 'Don't think I don't know who's really behind all this. It's that Fossett fellow. Come on, admit it.' He shoved her away. 'You're mad, Ally, to give me up for the likes of him. You settle for him and he'll drag you down to his level. Heed what I say.'

Her face tightened angrily. 'Lionel, how dare you? Jack Fossett is a decent man. I will not have you speak of him like that.'

'Huh, it's as I thought.'

'No, it's not as you thought. There is nothing going on between me and Jack Fossett, and there never has been. He is my partner and nothing more. And you know for a fact he is regularly seeing Elizabeth Green. I have no doubt you will read of their engagement very shortly in the newspapers.' She paused for breath and her face softened. 'Lionel, believe me, I never wanted us to part on such bad terms but we have said all there is to say, so please go before either of us says something we will regret.'

To her dismay his face puckered and he started to cry. 'Ally, please don't do this to me, please! I beg you to reconsider. I will do anything you want. Just tell me what it is?'

She swallowed hard to rid herself of the lump in her throat. Witnessing Lionel's apparent distress was upsetting her greatly. She did not enjoy being the cause of his misery. But she had resolved to finalise matters between them once and for all and to back down now, just to please Lionel, would only result in a life of purgatory for them both.

'Lionel, I am sorry. I do not feel enough for you to warrant continuing this relationship.'

Wiping his eyes, he stared at her, stunned. 'You really mean it, Ally?' he whispered.

She nodded. 'Yes, Lionel. Yes, I do.'

'Then . . . then I suppose there is nothing else for me to say.'

'No, there is not.'

She watched, filled with emotion, as he headed out of the door. Several moments passed before she heard the front door slam shut. Leaning back against a wall, a sob caught in the back of her throat. Covering her face with her hands, she wept.

Chapter Thirty-Eight

Jack entered the newly refurbished haberdashery department and smiled in satisfaction. This had been solely Ally's undertaking and she had done a superb job.

Shelving behind the long length of the dark wooden counter was filled to brimming with an assortment of fabrics, from exotics to plain everyday cotton twill, curtain fabric and upholstery stuffs. Something for every pocket. Rows of small drawers held a vast array of assorted buttons, trimmings and elastics, paper patterns and pins. Smiling staff served an ever present line of customers.

He stood at a discreet distance and studied with interest Kathleen Milligan, a new recruit, as she served a customer with a length of fabric. When she had finished and the customer had left, he walked over to her.

'Have you a moment, Miss Milligan?'

'Why, yes, certainly, Mr Fossett.'

She hurried around the counter, patting her mousy hair and smoothing her pale green and white uniform dress – a more friendly-looking uniform, Ally had decided, than the usual austere black and white which made the wearer look so formidable. With large pale blue eyes Kathleen stared up at Jack.

All of the hand picked staff of Listerman and Fossett enjoyed their conditions of employment and the generous remuneration they received. In return they were loyal and faithful and knew without doubt they were amongst the fortunate few in a country with thousands of underpaid, overworked shopworkers.

The older men on the staff liked Flo's humour and wished their wives could cook as well as she did, much preferring to pay the small amount charged each dinnertime to eat the meals Flo supervised in the small staff canteen rather than go home, and also wishing their wives looked half as good as she did for her age.

The young men lusted secretly after Ally but knew a cultured woman such as she was well out of their league. Nevertheless, much to Ally's amusement, they would hurry to open doors, readily offer to fetch and carry for her, or just gaze at her whenever she passed by.

The female staff, young and old, simply adored Jack Fossett. Kathleen Milligan was no exception.

'Yes, Mr Fossett?' she said coyly.

He smiled warmly at her before he proceeded, picking his words carefully. He felt strongly that the way to get the best out of staff was to praise more than was strictly necessary and only chastise in private when required. 'Miss Milligan, I congratulate you on the way you handled your customer. It was first class. But I just happened to hear her ask for Chinese silk.'

'Oh, yes, that's right, she did. We ain't got none, Mr Fossett. But she were quite happy with the Japanese silk she bought.'

'Yes, I could see that. A very nice piece of fabric and exactly right for her requirements. But did you know that we are expecting a shipment of the Chinese in very shortly? Next week, in fact.'

'No, I didn't.'

'Well, a good assistant always knows her stock, what is on order and when it's due to arrive. So it might be a good idea just to check with your supervisor next time. If a customer comes in in future and we do not have what they want on the shelf, ask them if they would like us either to place a special order for them or put whatever they require aside when it arrives. You see, Miss Milligan, that customer might have seemed to have gone away happy, but in truth she wanted Chinese silk. We did run the risk of losing her custom to another store.'

Kathleen looked confused. 'But there ain't another shop in Leicester that sells the Chinese, Mr Fossett.'

'Yes, I am quite aware of that fact. Miss Milligan, you are missing the point. If you had given her all our options she would have been even more pleased with our service. She may have waited for the Chinese to come in or have done as she did, settle for the Japanese. But she would also have told all her friends how obliging Listerman and Fossett's are. Remember nothing is too much trouble for our customers and you won't go far wrong.'

'Oh, I see. Yes, Mr Fossett, yes indeed.'

'Thank you, Miss Milligan. By the way, I shall be telling Miss Fathersham, your supervisor, how pleased we are with you. Well done.' He smiled as he made to turn then stopped. 'I do think your new hair style suits you,' he said, before he resumed his rounds.

Kathleen stared after him, mouth gaping. Fancy Mr Fossett noticing she had had a new hair cut. Well, fancy indeed. And him such a busy man.

'If the wind changes your face'll stay like that. You look like a fish.'

'Cheeky bugger you are, Eric Fossett! Get back to yer own department,' she hissed, stalking back behind the counter.

Next Jack wandered slowly through the hardware department, stopping to chat to several customers and also the staff, asking how they were, if they had any problems, and then repeating the process in more depth with the supervisors. Everything settled to his satisfaction, he was about to proceed through to see Malcolm in Provisions and Meat before returning to his small office and tackling a mountain of work, when he spotted Ally arriving at the jewellery counter. He hesitated for a moment before he walked across to her.

'Buying anything special?'

'Oh, Jack,' she exclaimed. 'You startled me. Well, I am ashamed to admit that with being so busy with the alterations and coping with everything else, I have not taken the time for a while to see how the jewellery counter is progressing.' She scanned her eyes across the display cases inside a small glass-topped counter. 'There are several nice pieces here.'

Jack did not say anything. Never having had much, if anything, to do with jewellery, he would not know a good piece from a not so good one.

'Actually,' said Ally, 'while I am here, I may as well look for something special for Bella. Her wedding is only days away and I have not had the chance to buy her anything yet. "Something old, something new, something borrowed, something blue",' she quoted. 'Well, the something new could be a piece of jewellery from me. A necklace maybe.'

'That's a nice gesture, Ally. Has anything taken your fancy?'

'One or two pieces actually. That locket,' she said, pointing. 'It's rather pretty. But maybe a bit ostentatious for what I had in mind.'

'Mmmm, it is,' Jack agreed, not having a clue what ostentatious meant. 'It's a bit gaudy too.'

She looked at him then hid her mirth, realising that Jack was not aware that ostentatious meant gaudy. Remarks like this were just one of the many things that endeared him to her. Oh, dear, dear, Jack, she thought, then pulled herself up. It was no good lapsing into those kinds of thoughts. All they succeeded in achieving was making her feel unhappy that Jack would never be hers. 'What do you think of the brooch?' she asked in a clipped voice.

'Which one?' he said, moving right beside her in order to get a better view.

His closeness sent a thrill through her. Her whole being sensed the nearness of him so acutely she shuddered violently.

He eyed her sharply. 'Are you all right?'

She turned her head and gazed directly into the face of the man she adored, his own so close she could feel the heat of his breath. And that look in his eyes . . . why, oh why, did he look at her like that when she knew he had no interest in her other than as a friend?

She forced herself to take a sideways step. 'I'm fine,' she snapped, dragging her attention back to the brooch. 'That brooch. The one with the . . . Oh.'

'Ally, what's wrong?'

She frowned hard. 'That's strange. I thought Mr Arnold made all his own jewellery? Was rather proud of the fact.'

274

'So he does?'

'But if I am not mistaken, that piece, and that, and that, are quite old.'

'Does it matter?'

'I suppose not, but our arrangement with Mr Arnold was for his own craftsmanship, not someone else's.'

'But does it matter, Ally? The man pays his rent regularly for the counter space and workshop, and we receive a percentage of what is sold. It was all your idea, Ally.'

'Yes, I know, and I suppose it has worked out rather well. The jewellery counter has brought in custom for the other departments. Although when we expand upstairs, he will have to move out of his workshop.' She smiled. 'He is rather a sweet old man and I'm glad we have given him this opportunity. Mind you, I find his insistence on isolation rather disconcerting. I understand the need of a craftsman for peace and quiet but I feel he takes it to extremes.'

'There nowt funnier than folk.'

'I beg your pardon?'

Jack grinned. 'Nothing, Ally.'

She glanced across the display cases again. 'Oh, I don't think jewellery is what I'm after for Bella. Luggage, maybe. She would appreciate a nice piece of new luggage for her trip on the *Titanic*. You know, that's something we should think of selling ourselves. Most people at some stage in their lives need a piece of luggage, and women are always changing their handbags. Jack, what are you looking at?'

'Eh? Oh, that man . . . don't look, Ally, he'll see that we're watching him.'

'What is he doing?'

'Nothing, that's just it. He was just leaving this counter when I arrived. It's a wonder you didn't see him. Now he's lurking near that pillar by the door. He looks suspiciously like a shoplifter to me. Ally, I said don't look. Oh, he's seen you now so he's off,' Jack grunted, annoyed.

'I'm sorry, I couldn't help it. I was intrigued to see what he looked like.'

'You women. Born nosy, the lot of you. Mind you, I suppose I should feel lucky it was you and not Ma. She would have marched up to him and demanded to know what he was up to.'

'And quite right too,' said Ally. 'I suggest you do that the next time you see him. Have you warned all the assistants about shoplifters?'

'Yes, of course. You know as well as I do that they are forever being asked to keep their eyes peeled for potential thieves. And it isn't always the most likely people who are the culprits. I did not like having to have that old lady with the false bottom to her basket arrested last week, but I had no choice.'

'It's all part of being shopkeepers, isn't it, Jack? But, like you, it's the bit I least like.' Ally suddenly caught a glimpse of the large clock on the wall. 'Oh, my goodness, look at the time. I am expecting a man from the tax office to call shortly, and I do so dislike dealing with matters of taxation. I am so fortunate to have Mr Trumper as my senior clerk. That man has taught me so much and is so patient and has never yet made me feel the slightest bit inadequate. I honestly do not know how we would manage without him, Miss Beam and the other two new clerks. Really, Jack, I feel a bit of a fraud being supposedly in charge of the office.'

'Ally, you do much better than you think you do. You handled most of the paperwork when we first got going.'

'Yes, but that was such a small amount compared to what is entailed now. Besides, you used to help me.'

'We did it together. Anyway, imagine what it will be like when we open up the next floor and start selling ladies' wear, and now the luggage you've set your heart on.'

Ally shuddered. 'Don't start worrying me any more than I am now. I really must go. 'Bye, Jack,' she said, hurrying away.

As he made to walk away an object caught his eye. It was a very handsome engraved silver cigarette case. Flo's husband Malcolm had his birthday soon, and it would make a nice present. What was even nicer, he thought, was the fact that he now had enough money to consider buying such an object when previously he could only have admired it through a shop window.

'What price the cigarette case, Mr Capstick?'

The assistant, a middle-aged, balding man, black-suited, his waistcoat straining over his portly middle, scuttled across to Jack. 'I have no idea on that, Mr Fossett. It wasn't priced when it came down this morning along with other items to replenish the trays. I was going to ask Mr Arnold when he came tonight for the till receipts. It is a nice piece, isn't it, Mr Fossett? Early nineteenth century, I'd say. Previous owners must have had money to afford a nice piece like that,' he said enviously.

'You know about jewellery? Oh, of course you would,' muttered Jack, feeling embarrassed at asking the obvious. He had not had much to do with Mr Capstick, as he was not a direct employee of theirs, so decided it would be good relations to have a general chit-chat with the man. 'What is your opinion of all the jewellery sold here?'

'Oh, very nice indeed, Mr Fossett. It's all a pleasure to handle. The customers like it too. Although, if I may say so, sir, it's my opinion that Mr Arnold sells it too cheaply. My previous employment was with Green's in Market Place. Jewellers of repute they are, sir, but I was tempted by the good wage Mr Arnold offered.'

'Do you like working for him?'

'Oh, yes, sir. Though I hardly see him, to be honest. In my last place the boss was always breathing down me neck. I made a good move in coming here. Although I do find the set up a bit strange, if you'll pardon my saying so?'

Jack smiled. 'We are all, Mr Capstick, entitled to our own opinion. Never be afraid to speak out in front of me.'

'Oh, right you are, sir. Can I show you anything else?'

'No, thank you. It's the case I'm interested in. When you see Mr Arnold tonight, enquire after the price for me, please.' He made to walk away then stopped. 'By the way, Mr Capstick, have you noticed a strange-looking character hanging about?'

'Strange-looking character? No, can't say as I have, sir. Oh, unless you mean the man in the long raincoat with his hat pulled down?'

'That's him.'

'He was here this morning. Just before you and Miss Listerman arrived. Browsing, he was.'

'Just browsing?'

'Said he wanted something for his wife, but he never bought anything. He didn't seem too strange to me. I could tell you so many stories about customers and what they get up to.'

'I bet you could.' Jack laughed. He had encountered many strange customers himself in his time.

'Well, I say he didn't *act* funny,' mused Mr Capstick. 'Apart, that is, from asking what the set up was here? I thought it odd that he should be interested.'

'And what did you tell him?'

'The truth, sir. What else would I say? I said that Mr Arnold rented a workshop where he and his assistants crafted the items for sale from this counter, which he rented from yourselves. I also mentioned, I think, that I was employed by Mr Arnold. Did I do wrong, Mr Fossett?'

'No, of course you didn't. I don't need to remind you to keep your eyes peeled for shoplifters, do I?'

'No, you don't, sir.'

'Thank you, Mr Capstick.'

Jack walked away thoughtfully. People did not ask questions for the sake of it. So what was the man's intention in asking after the arrangements here? And why was he hiding behind the pillar watching . . . watching what? As he wandered back to his office, Jack pondered deeply. Then the truth dawned. It was another shopowner who had heard how well the jewellery was selling and was after poaching Roy Arnold. Jack had better sound out the jeweller and see what he had to say about it. It would be a blow to lose the jewellery counter now it was beginning to do so well. They might not be able to find anyone else who possessed a talent for jewellery like Roy Arnold. Or who would consider accepting the arrangement they had with him.

Jack was surprised on trying the door to the workshop to find it was locked. He knocked impatiently. It was several minutes before it opened just enough for Roy to poke his head out.

'Oh, it's you, Mr Fossett. Nothing wrong, I hope?'

'No, not that I know of. I thought we might have a chat.'

'A chat! What about?'

'Er . . . well, this is a bit awkward. But you weren't thinking of leaving us, were you?'

Roy shot out of the door, closing it firmly behind him. 'Do you mind if we talk out here? My assistants are working on some new designs. Peace and quiet, you understand. Now what did you mean by asking if I'm thinking of leaving?'

Despite Arnold's giving his reason for doing so, Jack thought it very rude of the man to keep him standing in the deserted, dimly lit corridor, but regardless suddenly felt stupid, now he was faced with it, for wondering about the jewellery concession. Maybe the strange man's questions were just idle gossip after all. Although that still did not explain his hiding behind the pillar in such a suspicious manner. Jack shrugged his shoulders. 'It's probably nothing. It doesn't matter.'

'It mattered enough for you to come and disturb me, Mr Fossett.'

'Yes, it did at the time. Oh, well, I might as well mention it. A man has been asking questions on the set up . . . arrangements . . . we have with you and I just got to thinking that it maybe was another shopowner about to make you an offer, that's all.'

'Asking questions, you say?' The older man's eyes narrowed. 'And what did you tell him?' His tone was abrupt.

Jack frowned. Had that been a flicker of fear he saw in Roy Arnold's eyes? 'It wasn't me who spoke to him, it was Capstick, your assistant. He told him the truth.' Jack frowned, puzzled. 'You seem upset.'

'Upset? Oh, no, not at all. Thank you for telling me, Mr Fossett. Thank you very much.'

'So . . . have you been approached?'

'Approached? No, indeed not.' Roy Arnold smiled. 'I would never consider leaving without discussing it first with you and Miss Listerman, so please don't worry. Now, I must get back. I can't leave my assistants long on their own. Mistakes cost so much to rectify in time and money. Excuse me, Mr Fossett.'

Before Jack could utter another word, Roy Arnold had shot back inside his workshop and the door was firmly closed.

Well, he thought, peeved. Ally and Flo thought this old man sweet . . . that was not how Jack would describe him after such a display of bad manners. 'Oh, blast,' he uttered, remembering he had forgotten to ask the price of the cigarette case. He made to knock on the door again, then thought better of it. Capstick could deal with the matter. Besides, after Roy's rudeness he had gone off the idea of giving Ma's husband the cigarette case. I wonder, thought Jack, as he strode back down the corridor, if Malcolm would prefer a piece of luggage?

278

Chapter Thirty-Nine

Jack was busy in his office early the next morning when an urgent knock sounded on his door. Reluctantly he raised his eyes from some paper-work. He had spent so much time on his rounds of the shop the previous day that he had got behind with his orders and knew only too well that such slackness could cause grave problems. The ordering of the stock was something he usually strove hard to keep abreast of. Shortages could result in lost custom.

'Come in,' he called. 'Why, good morning, Mr Capstick,' he said, surprised. 'Oh, I take it you've come to tell me the price of the cigarette case?' The one he had changed his mind about though he may as well find out how much it was since Mr Capstick had gone to the trouble.

'Er . . . no, I haven't, sir.'

'You haven't. Oh!' Jack eyed him sharply. 'Are you all right, Mr Capstick?'

'No, Mr Fossett, I'm not. I'm very worried.'

'About what?'

'Well, I came in as usual this morning, and it's all gone.'

Jack grimaced. 'What on earth are you babbling about? I don't understand?'

'The jewellery.'

Jack sprang up from his chair. 'You mean, we've had a robbery?'

'Well . . . er . . .' Mr Capstick said in confusion. 'I don't rightly know, sir. Yer see, Mr Arnold's gone an' all.'

'What?'

'Cleared out, Mr Fossett. His workroom's empty. When I saw the state of the counter, I ran straight to Mr Arnold to tell him and that is when I discovered the workroom. There's nowt left. Not even a matchstick.'

Jack sank down, totally confused. 'This doesn't make sense.' He grimaced at Mr Capstick. 'You're not making this up?'

'Oh, no, Mr Fossett. Why would I do such a thing?'

'Come on,' ordered Jack. 'You'd better show me.'

'And you and Ma thought he was a sweet old man?' Jack fumed. 'Sweet old men do not leave their benefactors high and dry without a word of explanation.'

279

'So we were wrong about him,' snapped Flo. 'Don't tell me you ain't made any mistakes in yer life, Jack Fossett?'

'Oh, I'm sorry, Ma, Ally. I didn't mean to take my temper out on you both. It's just that he's left us in a bit of a mess. People have been coming in all morning enquiring about the jewellery and I don't know what to tell the staff to say to them.'

'Do you think he has gone to another shop?' Ally asked.

'I don't know what to think. All sorts of thoughts are running through my mind at the moment. I'll tell you both something for nothing: we'll not take pity on another as we did on Roy Arnold.'

'What are we going to do about Mr Capstick? The poor man is beside himself. Can we find him something, Jack?' Ally asked.

He nodded. 'Yes, I'll slot him in somewhere. I like Mr Capstick. But no more jewellery. Apart from us not having the finance to buy enough to run our own counter, I don't care if I never set eyes on another piece of jewellery for the rest of my life.'

Ally and Flo flashed a glance at each other and both hid their amusement, though realising this situation was far from amusing.

Ally rose. 'I have to be going, Jack. I have arranged to see Nelly Bramble and her grandfather. It's a social visit as much as business. But either way, I don't want to let them down when they're expecting me. Have we finished here?'

'Well, there's not much left ter say, is there, Jack? I've got all the apprentices' bedding to be washed and dried, plus a hundred other things to do. I really need to get off as well,' Flo told him.

'Yes, we've finished. Oh, er . . . does either of you think we need to inform the police?'

'Why should we?' asked Flo. 'It's not as though he took owt belonging to us, is it?'

'Jack has a point, Flo. It might be wise just to keep ourselves straight. The police probably won't be at all interested. They have barely enough time to investigate real cases as it is. But this is all such a mystery, I feel informing the police might be a wise precaution,' Ally declared.

Jack decided it best to tell the staff the truth about the business with Roy Arnold but told them they were to inform any customers who enquired that Mr Arnold had decided to retire rather suddenly. Listerman and Fossett extended their apologies for any inconvenience this had caused. There was not really much else they could do.

Jack was still undecided as to whether to inform the police. It was not really a police matter, he thought. He was still pondering when of all people Sergeant English walked through the doors. English looked preoccupied and grave. A worried Jack altered his course to intercept him.

'Were you looking for me, Sergeant English?'

'Oh, morning, Mr Fossett. Looking for you? Not particularly. Should I be?'

'I thought maybe you were.'

'It's garters I'm after.'

'Garters?'

'Yeah. Mine are all threadbare and Mrs English has threatened to throw 'em out. So I have to get some new 'uns 'cos it's against Police Regulations not to wear 'em. You do sell 'em?'

'Oh, er, yes. Men's hosiery. Down the steps between hardware and haberdashery.'

Sergeant English eyed Jack sternly. 'You look like a man with something on his mind. And you obviously thought I'd come to interview you on some matter. Has something happened I should know about?'

'Something has happened, but I'm not sure if it's worth bothering you with. I don't really think it's police business . . . Oh, look, I might as well now you're here. Have you heard of Roy Arnold?'

Not a muscle on Sergeant English's stolid features twitched as he stood and thought for a moment. 'Can't rightly say the name rings a bell at this precise moment. That's not to say it doesn't, of course.' He glanced slowly around at the milling throng of shoppers. 'This isn't the place to talk. Come down to the station and speak to my inspector.'

'I don't think that's necessary, Sergeant.'

Sergeant English took his arm and guided him towards the double entrance doors. 'Let us be the judge of that, sir.'

Chapter Forty

Later that afternoon Ally was busy answering correspondence when the door to her office burst open and Bella rushed in.

'Bella!' Ally smiled. 'What a lovely surprise. I'll order some tea.' She suddenly realised her friend was extremely upset. 'Darling, what on earth is wrong?'

Bella plonked herself down on a chair in front of Ally's desk. Stripping off her gloves, she flapped them across her knee. 'Just everything,' she wailed. 'The wedding's off.'

'What?'

'Well, not off exactly. Max wants to postpone it. Oh, it really is so thoughtless of him.'

'But why?'

'Something to do with a march he's got himself involved in. Oh, Ally, what am I going to do? All the preparations have been finalised and the invitations have been sent out. And the trip to America . . . If we postpone the wedding, we won't be able to go.' She unclipped her handbag, delved inside and withdrew a long envelope, smacking it angrily against the desk. 'These tickets are like gold. People are paying a fortune for them.'

'Bella, what on earth are you doing carrying them around in your handbag? What if you should lose them?'

'What does it matter?'

'Oh, Bella. Take a deep breath and tell me properly what has happened?'

She sighed heavily. 'Max came to me this morning and announced that he was taking part in a march. It's all to do with working conditions and pay and such like. The march starts from up north somewhere, I'm afraid I didn't take much notice, then passes through all the major towns before heading off for London. Max said thousands will be taking part. He was sorry it would interrupt our plans but regardless felt he had to go. But why, Ally? Why should Max's involvement make any difference?'

'He's the son of an employer, Bella. His involvement is the kind of presence that's needed for the powers that be to sit up and take notice.'

'Oh, not you as well, Ally. Have you been talking to him?'

'Yes, we have talked. He's very committed, Bella. I admire him for it. He has met great opposition, especially from his father.'

Bella tightened her lips. 'This obviously means more to him than our wedding. Maybe it's a good thing it has happened then.'

Ally saw tears fill her eyes. She jumped up from her seat and raced round, placing her arm on her friend's shoulder. 'Bella, Max has asked that the wedding be postponed. He has not cancelled it completely. This means a lot to him. You will have to be understanding about it or risk losing him. You both love each other dearly, so what difference will a couple of weeks make?'

'I want to be married to him now, Ally. A couple of weeks seems a lifetime. Oh, dear, this is so distressing for me. I was so angry with him and we had the most dreadful argument. He left without saying goodbye. He will be away on this march for three or four weeks and I shall not see him during that time.'

'Well, go with him.'

'What? I cannot possibly walk all that way.'

Ally smiled. 'No, maybe not. I don't think I could either. That's why I admire these men, Bella. Most have hardly the boot leather to withstand a walk of such a distance, let alone food in their stomachs. But they are committed to their cause. Just like Max.'

Bella sniffed. 'I wish I knew more about it.'

'Well, since this is so close to Max's heart, maybe you should take more of an interest?' She stared at her friend thoughtfully. 'Maybe it is too much to expect you to take part in the march but there is nothing to stop you from catching a train or taking a coach to a town en route and meeting up with Max there. You could put matters right with him then.'

Bella looked at Ally through watery eyes. 'Do you think I should?'

'Most certainly. Give him your support, Bella.'

She hurriedly dabbed her eyes. 'I will then. I'll go, Ally. You're right, Max needs my support. It's the least I can do. I hope I'm not too late. He was very angry with me . . .'

'It's not too late, Bella.'

'Oh, I hope you are right.' She stood up. 'I'll go now.'

'Haven't you time for some tea first?'

'No, thank you, Ally. I have so much to do.'

She pulled on her gloves and kissed Ally on her cheek. 'Thank you for making me see sense. In future I will make sure I involve myself in everything Max does. Oh, Ally, I do love you. You are indeed the best friend any woman could wish for.'

Ally blushed. 'I feel the same about you.'

'Wish me luck.'

'You don't need it, Bella.'

Ally watched with a smile as Bella headed off for the door. 'Oh,' she cried, turning and snatching up the envelope her friend had left on her desk. 'The tickets. You've forgotten them.'

Hand poised on the door knob, Bella half turned. 'Oh, er . . . they are no good to me now, Ally.'

'But you could trade them in. Go another time.'

'Maybe . . . oh, I haven't the time.' Her eyes suddenly lit up. 'Ally, you take them. You go.'

'Me? I couldn't possibly.'

'Why not? You said yourself you would love to travel to America and see all the shops for yourself.'

Oh, the thought was a wonderful one! 'But I can't, Bella, I haven't the time either.'

'Ally, I am in such a dreadful rush. I want to sort out the arrangements for meeting Max. Just do what you want with the tickets. Whatever you decide, you have my blessing.'

With that she was gone.

Ally stared at the envelope she was holding for several long moments. In her hand she held the chance of a lifetime but it would not be fair to take advantage of Bella's misfortune. Besides, she thought, what joy would she have in travelling alone? She walked around her desk and reached for her handbag, putting the envelope inside. She would try to get a refund for Bella and Max. They could then rearrange their trip. With tickets being so sought after, she would have no trouble.

She suddenly felt very tired and gazed distractedly out of the window. It was barely three o'clock but due to the heavy sky already growing dark. A longing to go home and curl up in front of the fire suddenly filled her. It wouldn't hurt for once.

Ringing a bell on her desk, she waited until Mr Trumper appeared.

'I am going home, Mr Trumper. I feel we have all worked hard for such a long time we deserve the rest of the afternoon off. That includes you and the rest of the office staff.'

Mr Trumper's face was a picture. 'Really, Miss Listerman?'

'Really, Mr Trumper. Now off you all go.'

Gathering up her belongings, she left her office before she could change her mind.

Chapter Forty-One

'I know you think I'm silly, Malcolm, but I'm telling you, our Jack is worried and he's bin that way since he came back from the police station two days ago.'

'I don't think you're silly at all, Flo. I happen to agree with you.'

'You do?'

'Yes. Although I'd say he's troubled rather than worried. But regardless, he's trying to act as though nothing's the matter. You know, his mood doesn't make sense. He claims the police weren't interested one iota but . . . oh, now I'm being silly.'

'Go on, Malcolm. Spit out what yer were gonna say?'

'It was nothing, Flo, really. I'm just making something out of nowt. If Jack has something on his mind then it'll all come out in the wash when he's good and ready.' Malcolm sighed. 'Ally's not her usual self either, is she?'

'Oh, I know what's to do there. It's Lionel. She's finished with him, thank God. Like you, my old love, I never took to him. It's guilt that gel's suffering from. I expect Lionel's convinced her that without her he'll die of a broken heart and she's feeling the burden of the guilt he's heaped on her. She'll soon shake it off, she's a sensible girl at heart. I'll have a word with her when I get the chance.'

'Does . . . er . . . Ally's finishing with Lionel worry you at all, Flo?'

She flashed a warning glance in his direction. 'Don't start on all that, Malcolm, please. As far as I'm aware Lizzie is keeping Jack well occupied at the present. Besides, Bella's intended is very well connected, which in turn means Ally will be too busy meeting plenty of her own sort to be hankering after our Jack.'

Malcolm relaxed back in his chair and shook out his evening paper, deciding it was best to drop the subject though it worried him that Flo still refused to accept what was staring her in the face. He realised she was muttering to herself and lowered his paper.

'What was that you said, me darlin'? I never caught it proper.'

Flo fidgeted uncomfortably in her chair. 'I can't get used to sitting around in the evening with nowt to do. All me life I've bin used to being that busy I just collapsed into bed. Now, what with all the help Ally insists I have, the work's finished come evening. I feel like a fish out of water sitting doing nowt and I certainly don't collapse shattered into bed no more.'

Malcolm's eyes twinkled. 'And for that I'm grateful.'

'Mucky beggar,' she laughed. 'All the same, Malcolm, all this sitting around gives me too much time to think. I'm worried about Emily now.'

'She's in bed, ain't she?'

'Yes, you kissed her goodnight, remember? It's when she's awake she worries me. This new posh school she goes to . . . I thought it was supposed to mek her a lady. Some lady she's turning out ter be! Oh, I grant yer, she speaks nicer and knows how to dress for any occasion. And she curtseys without falling over, though God knows what good that's gonna do her. It ain't very likely she's ever gonna be in the presence of royalty, now is it? Little madam she is, though. I caught her astride one of the outbuilding roofs before dinner, playing conkers with a lad from down the road. And she was winning!'

Malcolm laughed. 'Flo, she's only thirteen. She's still a kid. She's plenty of time to become a lady. Leave her be.'

Flo folded her arms under her shapely bosom. 'I suppose yer right,' she reluctantly agreed.

'What about Eric?'

'What about him?' she demanded. 'What's wrong with him?'

'Nothing that I know of. It's just that you've been through everyone else, I just thought Eric was next.'

'Oh, you!' she cried, grabbing up a pillow she was leaning on and throwing it at him.

He ducked, laughing. 'Flo, do the ironing,' he ordered.

Her eyes lit up. 'Do you mind? There is a bit that needs doing.'

'If it makes you happy to do something and stops you worrying, then I don't mind at all.'

She jumped up, hurriedly collected the flat iron from the cupboard and settled it on the coals to heat. She looked across at her husband and smiled. 'I do love you,' she whispered.

Malcolm lowered the paper. 'Sorry, what was that?'

She laughed. 'You heard.'

Across town Jack was not enjoying his evening much. He had thought the meeting would help take his mind off matters, create a welcome diversion, but that had not happened. It was a pleasant crowd that had gathered to attend the bi-monthly meeting of the Grocers' Association and Jack usually enjoyed catching up with all the news of the trade, despite the fact the other members were a bit wary of him. Listerman and Fossett was fast becoming a force to be reckoned with in the retail trade, and there was besides the fact that Jack, albeit with his partners, was such a young age to have achieved more than it had taken many of them a lifetime to attain. But then, they muttered jealously amongst themselves, it was the building that gave him the edge. They themselves could have done as well as Jack and his partners if they had had that prime site at their disposal.

Jack mingled aimlessly, expressing the right words here and there until he thought it safe to leave. He would be glad to get to bed. He was a man carrying a great burden, one he could under no circumstances share with anyone, and sleep was the only time he was released from its weight. That was when he did not have nightmares concerning it.

He strolled over to Sidney Green and pulled him aside. 'I'm going to make my excuses, Mr Green, so I'll say goodnight.'

'Oh, er . . . just a minute, lad. I'd like a word.'

Jack bristled. He detested Sidney Green's insistence on still addressing him that way. He made Jack feel like his young employee. 'If it's a quick one.'

'I'll make it as quick as I can.' Flushed from several large whiskies, Sidney squared his large body and puffed out his broad chest. 'I'd just like to know when you're going to make an honest woman of my Lizzie?'

Jack's back stiffened. 'Are you talking of marriage between Lizzie and myself?'

'Oh, come on now, lad. What else would I be talking of? You've been courting her now for over a year. Plenty of time, don't yer reckon, to get used to the idea and set a date?'

Jack groaned. This was the last thing he felt like contending with, but it did not seem he had much choice. 'Mr Green . . .'

'Sidney, lad. I think it's about time yer called me Sidney.'

'As you wish, Sidney.' He took a deep breath. 'Lizzie and I are just friends. We enjoy each other's company. But that's all it is, Mr . . . Sidney.'

'Wadda yer mean, just friends? You've been regularly to my house, ate at my table, escorted Lizzie on numerous occasions. Listen, lad, that's courting in my book. Besides, our Lizzie's set her heart on yer. She thinks . . . Listen here, lad. I don't appreciate you trifling with her affections.'

'That I haven't,' Jack erupted. 'Let me assure you, Lizzie is well aware of the situation. I have accepted invitations from her on the basis of friendship and nothing more. Look, your daughter is a lovely woman. She's good company and I have a great regard for her. But I keep telling you, it's nothing more. And I most definitely have not trifled, as you put it, with her affections. I told you once before, I will not be pushed into marriage to please you, Lizzie or anyone. I hope I have made myself clear? Maybe in the circumstances it might be better if I didn't see Lizzie even as a friend for the time being, because obviously our friendship is being taken for more than it is. Now I'll wish you goodnight.'

Sidney, drink getting the better of him, grabbed Jack's arm and roughly yanked him back. 'Now you look here, lad, I ain't taking this twaddle. You've led my Lizzie to believe marriage was in the offing and I'm gonna make sure you honour that.' His face darkened thunderously. 'You've got above yerself, lad, now you've got that shop and you're hobnobbing with the likes of the Listermans and their kind. Well, I know yer roots, son. When I took you on, yer trousers were that threadbare you could see yer arse through 'em. The likes of us were good enough for you then. But not now, eh?'

Jack shrugged himself free, stepping backwards. 'You're making a fool of yourself, Mr Green.'

'I'm meking a fool of meself, eh?' Eyes ablaze, he pushed his face into Jack's. 'The fool is you! Set yer sights on better things now, ain't yer? Albertina Listerman, perhaps. Let me tell yer, lad, the likes of her ain't gonna settle for you. You might think yer Mr High and Mighty but yer'll never escape yer roots. When it comes down to it, yer as common as muck and in truth even my Lizzie is too good for yer.'

'That's enough,' Jack hissed. 'I'll not stay and listen to your drunken ramblings and I certainly won't take lying down any insinuations against my partner, Miss Listerman. 'Cos that's all she is – my partner. Now get yourself off home and to bed, man, before you say anything else you'll regret. But I'll leave you with a thought. Without your interference, come time, something more just might have developed between me and Lizzie. Now we'll never know, will we? Goodnight, Mr Green, and I hope you sleep well.'

Aware that every eye in the room was on him, Jack raised his head, turned and strode from the room.

He made to hail a hansom cab then changed his mind. A good walk might help clear his headache. Digging his hands deep into his pockets, he lowered his head and strode forward. As he walked deep sadness filled him. He liked Lizzie, had enjoyed her company, would miss her in a way. In some respects she had helped to keep his mind off Ally. But he felt no guilt for that. In no way had he led Lizzie to believe their friendship was anything more than it was. In truth she had done all the running. He should maybe have seen the way matters were heading. Maybe for that at least he should feel guilty.

He paused at a kerb and glanced around, then realised with a shock that in his preoccupied state he had arrived at the end of the road where Ally now lived.

In the darkness of the late evening he looked down the row of fine three-storey dwellings. In a house in the middle of that row was the woman he loved. A vision of her rose before him and fear filled his being. He fought a desire to run to her now, hammer down her door and warn her of the danger she could be facing. But he could not do that. He was under oath. He should not even be in the area. His presence here could jeopardise everything. If he should be spotted, he himself could be in severe trouble. But that thought did not worry him. All he could think of was Ally.

He stood frozen, fighting deep emotions, terrifying thoughts racing through his brain. He almost yelped in shock when a shadowy figure emerged from the hedge to one side of him.

'Go home, sir,' a deep voice commanded.

'But surely I can . . .'

'Sir. Go home.'

He eyed the huge man before him for several long moments before, resigned, he bent his head, hunched his shoulders against the bitter wind and forced his steps to lead him homewards.

Chapter Forty-Two

The book Ally was reading held no interest for her. She felt nervous, on edge. There was no reason for it and she did not understand why she should feel this way. She closed the book. She had left the office early to relax her mind and body but had not succeeded.

Before she had dismissed Mrs Vincent for the evening, the housekeeper had banked up the fire and prepared her a tray. As yet the food remained untouched. Employing Mrs Vincent had made her feel slightly guilty, since she was capable enough of caring for herself. But apart from the fact that middle-aged Mrs Vincent had desperately needed a job, Ally was fully aware she could not look after the house by herself as well as give the business all the attention it deserved. And she did like Mrs Vincent who reminded her a little of Flo: motherly, always fussing and scolding, and not afraid to speak her mind.

A feeling of loneliness flooded through Ally and for a fleeting instant she wished the housekeeper were still around. It would have been nice to have had a chat with her, listen to tales of her boisterous grandchildren and the capers they got up to. Ally smiled wistfully, wondering if she would ever herself become a grandmother like Mrs Vincent and delight in all they did.

Uncurling her legs from beneath her, she rose and headed for the deep bay window, pulling the curtain aside slightly to stare out. It was only just after five but as dark as midnight and the wind was picking up. Strangely for the normally busy street it appeared deserted; most of the residents, she assumed, were inside their own houses, having hurried home out of the bitter winter cold.

She returned to her chair again, perched on the edge, reached for the poker and rearranged several coals. Then sat for a moment, mesmerised, as flames spurted upwards, hissing and crackling.

Replacing the poker, she sat back. She suddenly knew what was wrong with her. She was missing the Fossetts. In fact, she was missing them badly. Her life had not been the same since the day she had left them to come to this house. For a moment she sat and pictured them all: Flo, Malcolm, Emily, Eric and Jack, all sitting around the table, talking and laughing as they ate their evening meal. Soon, Ally thought, there would be another at that table, laughing, talking, helping Flo to clear away:

Lizzie. Lizzie would sit in the chair that she herself had vacated.

Oh, Ally, Ally, she silently scolded herself. You have to stop this. Clinging on to something you never had in the first place is doing you no good.

Her ears suddenly pricked and she listened hard. There was someone in the kitchen. Mrs Vincent? Maybe the woman had forgotten something and returned. She rose. Another noise. Her head jerked upwards and she looked at the ceiling. It was not someone in the kitchen, they were upstairs.

Retrieving the poker, she tiptoed for the door, heart thumping painfully. As quietly as possible she turned the handle, pulled the door open and stepped into the entrance hall. It was large, its floor tiled black and white, wide stairs sweeping upwards from it. She reached for the gas mantle and turned it up to its fullest. Light flooded down. She stood for a moment and listened again. There was nothing now and for a moment she wondered if she had imagined the noises. Regardless, though, she knew she would not be able to relax until she had checked around just to make sure.

She padded softly up the stairs, the thick Wilton carpet warm under her feet. She stood on the landing and glanced the length of it. She frowned. Her own bedroom door was slightly ajar and she could have sworn she had closed it after changing out of her work clothes two hours earlier.

Heart beating rapidly, she tiptoed to the door and pushed it fully open. Light from the passageway eerily illuminated the interior, sending long shadows bouncing off the walls. Taking a deep breath, she ventured inside.

The room was empty. She chided herself. She had, after all, imagined it. She turned – and caught sight of the figure crouched behind the door. Before she could scream at the shock of discovery, the figure leaped out and grabbed her, a hand clamping her mouth.

'Ally, don't scream,' a whispered voice urged. 'Please, don't scream.'

A voice she recognised. Wide-eyed, she stared up as his hand was slowly withdrawn from her mouth.

'Lionel?' she uttered. 'What are you doing here? And why are you . . .'

'Don't ask questions, Ally.'

'But, Lionel . . .'

'Please, Ally. I can't answer. Have you anything for me to eat?'

She stared at him, stunned. He looked dreadful. Unwashed, unkempt. And that look on his face . . . it was a haunted expression. The man before her was desperate.

'Lionel, whatever is the matter?'

'Ally, I can't tell you. It is best you do not know.' He took hold of her shoulders. 'Tell me, have you any idea where Roy Arnold has gone?' His voice was urgent, pleading.

'Roy Arnold!' she exclaimed. 'Roy Arnold? Lionel, is he the reason for your condition? What is going on?'

His grip on her shoulders tightened and he shook her. 'Ally, just tell me, do you know where he is? Have you any idea where I can find him?'

'No. No, I don't.'

'Oh, God,' he groaned in despair.

As she stared up into his ashen face acute fear rushed through her. Just what was it that Lionel had become involved in? And what had Roy Arnold to do with it all?

He released his grip on her, rushed towards the window, pulled the curtain aside and tentatively peeked out.

'Who are you looking for, Lionel?'

He let the curtain drop. 'No one,' he blurted, and turned to face her, running a shaking hand over the stubble on his chin. 'I have to go. It isn't safe. I shouldn't have come.'

She gasped at his words. 'Not safe? What do you mean? What isn't safe?' Anger filled her suddenly. 'Lionel, don't do this to me. You have broken into my house. Babbled incomprehensibly about things I do not understand. You have worried me senseless and yet you will not tell me what it's all about. I want to know, Lionel. I can't help you if you won't enlighten me.'

He took hold of her shoulders and stared into her face. 'At this moment, Ally, there is only one person who can really help me – and he is the last person I can turn to.' Fear filled his face. 'Ally,' he whispered. 'Oh, Ally, why did I ever get involved in all this?' Then the fear in his face was replaced by panic. 'I have to go. Have you any money?'

'A few pounds I keep here to pay the household bills.'

'That will do.'

'It's in the kitchen, in a pot – a blue one – on the shelf.'

'Thank you, Ally.' He leaned over and kissed her cheek. 'Remember, whatever happens, I will always love you.'

'What do you mean, whatever happens? Lionel? LIONEL!'

But he was gone.

She stood transfixed for several long moments until she heard the faint click of the back door as it shut. She took several steps until her legs came up against the edge of her bed and she slowly sank down. Head bent, she clasped her hands tightly, thoughts producing all manner of explanations for Lionel's behaviour. But none made sense.

She rose and made her way out of her bedroom and down the stairs. She stood and looked into her sitting room and noticed that the plate of sandwiches on the tray was empty. She went down the corridor and into the kitchen at the back of the house. The blue pot stood on the table. It too was empty. She made to return to the sitting room, to sit before the fire and gather her thoughts, when she realised the back door was still unlocked. She went over to secure it, not relishing the thought of any more unexpected visitors; the one she had had was more than enough for her. As she threw across the bolts and turned the key she noticed a scrap of paper on the floor. She picked it up and was about to throw it in the waste bucket when she noticed it had writing on it. Moving across to the gas mantle, she smoothed it out and peered hard.

From what she could decipher it appeared to be some form of address but the light from the mantle was flickering too much and hindering her sight. She went across to the table, struck a match from the box kept on a shelf and lit the lamp, turning the flame to its fullest. Holding the piece of paper next to the glass stem, she tried again.

There was no name, just an address. It looked like 38 Catherine's Wharf, Tobacco Road, E something.

She frowned. She did not know any such address in Leicester. There were wharves down by the canal, but none to her knowledge by that name. She frowned thoughtfully. E? What on earth did that initial stand for? Then it struck her. Of course! Tobacco Road was a famous dock area in London, E stood for the East End. The address was 38 Catherine's Wharf, East End, London. Her brows knotted. Whose address could it possibly be? It must be something to do with Lionel who had dropped it in his haste to get out. He would have been stuffing the money and sandwiches into his pockets, obviously in desperate trouble. Could this address have something to do with that? Her eyes suddenly flashed as a thought struck. Could this have anything to do with Roy Arnold? He came from London. Was this an old address for him? Lionel was desperate to know his whereabouts. Or maybe there was a simpler explanation for it all. This address was Lionel's safe place. It was where he was heading now in order to hide from whatever was troubling him.

Anxiously gnawing her bottom lip, she again stared at the piece of paper in her hand. Lionel needed help. In his desperate time of trouble, with this information before her, she could not ignore it. She had loved him once. For old times' sake, her conscience left her no choice but to try to do something for him.

She raised her eyes to the clock ticking merrily away on the wall. It was eighteen minutes past six. There would be another train leaving for London that took the mail from the Great Central Railway Station. If she hurried she could catch it.

The train journey seemed to go on forever as they slowly puffed their way through towns and cities and vast dark areas of the English countryside. It was well after twelve by the time they pulled into St Pancras Station. Despite the lateness of the hour, Ally was surprised when she alighted on to the long freezing platform to see so many people still milling around. Porters were offloading the Royal Mail wagon of its postal cargo; other freight included milk churns and livestock. Her handful of travelling companions hurried ahead to the cab rank.

So preoccupied was she with her deep concern for Lionel she did not notice a man in a mackintosh, hat pulled well down, following a discreet distance behind.

The cab she took was a motorised one, its driver smart in a black uniform and cap. He stared at her in surprise when she gave the address.

'You sure, miss? 'Tis a good way and . . . well, pardon me for saying, but it ain't the kind of place for a lady like yourself to be visiting any time, let alone this hour of night.'

'Please, driver, just take me there. And hurry,' she urged. She was far too tired and worried to be conducting a time-consuming argument with this well-intentioned man.

'Suit yourself, miss.'

Again the journey seemed to take an age. The car chugged along streets filled with rows and rows of grimy grey terraces, then past wealthier dwellings, and finally turned down a short narrow lane which led on to a wide mud track lined to one side with sheds and dilapidated warehouses on the river side. The car pulled to a halt and the driver turned in his seat to face her.

'This is it, miss.'

She gazed out of the window. It was almost pitch black but she could just about make out the old three-storey shipping office they had stopped outside. It appeared to be completely deserted.

She handed him the fare. 'Thank you.'

'Do you want me to wait?'

She paused for a moment, wondering if Lionel would have arrived yet and if he had how long it would take her to persuade him to come back with her. If his state of panic had worsened since earlier this evening it would be too long, she thought, to warrant keeping the driver hanging around on such a bitter night. 'No, thank you,' she said, alighting.

The car pulled away. She stared up at the building then walked over to try the door. It was locked. Maybe, she thought, there was a way in around the back. As she skirted the building, over the sounds of the night river – boats' hooters, dogs barking, a distant hum of voices across the other side – she heard the crunching of wheels against the mud track. She stared around but could not see any sign of a horse-drawn carriage or motorised vehicle's headlights. There was the muffled sound of a door closing then the soft tread of footsteps. Then silence. Her heart raced wildly. The driver was right. It was no area to be in at this time of night. For a fleeting moment she wished wholeheartedly she had never come, then remembered Lionel's plight and his desperate need for help.

Picking up her skirt, she hurriedly felt her way around the side of the building and on towards the back. She stood and stared slowly upwards. All was in darkness. Her gaze reached the top of the building. Light from an oil lamp was flickering in a window right in the corner on the top floor. Lionel must have caught the same train as her, she thought, and she was surprised she hadn't seen him. A door leading into the building was just to the right of her. She headed for it and tried the handle. It opened and before her was a flight of iron stairs.

Slowly she climbed onward and upward. In the silence of the building the soft tread of her leather-soled shoes against the metal of the stairs seemed to bounce deafeningly off the walls. She finally reached the top and a long dark corridor with several doors leading off it faced her. A light shone from under the door at the very end. Taking several deep breaths, she walked slowly towards it. Reaching it, she tapped lightly.

'Lionel,' she called. 'Lionel, it's Albertina. I've come to help you.' She listened. She thought she could hear movement inside. She called louder, in a reassuring voice: 'It's only me, Lionel. I'm on my own. Don't be afraid, I've come to help you. Whatever it is that's troubling you, I am sure we can somehow sort it out.' She reached for the door knob, turned it and stepped through.

Standing just inside the threshold, she glanced hurriedly around then frowned. At the other side of the room was a faded wing-backed chair, a desk on which stood an oil lamp and an open suitcase. To the side of the desk, against the wall, stood an empty wooden cabinet, the doors of which were wide open. A metal barrel by the cabinet was three-quarters full of discarded paper. The room seemed to be devoid of anyone but herself.

Intrigued, she made her way over to the desk, turned the case around and looked down into it. She gasped in shock. 'Oh, Lionel,' she groaned, having great difficulty believing what her own eyes were seeing. The case was almost full of jewellery and gold coins. Diamonds, emeralds, rubies and many other precious stones shone from necklaces, rings, brooches and pins; there were also sovereigns, half-sovereigns and gold crowns, all appearing to wink wickedly at her in the light cast by the oil lamp. Hand clamped to her mouth, she walked slowly around the desk and sank down in the chair. 'Oh, Lionel,' she groaned again. 'What on earth have you got yourself into?'

'Yes, what indeed?'

Her head jerked as the door clicked to and a large figure loomed. It took several steps towards her.

'You should always check behind the door, Albertina, my dear, when breaking into premises. You never know who might be hiding.'

The sight of the man lumbering towards her froze her rigid. 'Ahhhh!' she screamed.

'Oh, stop the dramatics, Albertina. I have never been able to abide emotional women and I'm not about to start now.' The man reached the desk, placed his large hands on top and leaned over. His face was grotesquely fat, features almost obliterated by folds of skin. 'Lost your voice, my dear? Aren't you going to say how nice it is to see me?' He laughed, a low menacing sound. 'Well, of course you wouldn't, would you? You never did like me. Or me you for that matter.'

'But . . .' she cried. 'But you're . . .'

'Dead?' he interrupted. 'Not me, as you can see. Only the poor unfortunate soul who resembled me.'

Ally stared in stupefied terror at her half-brother and remembered the mangled remains she had thought were his and had had buried as such. Suddenly deep loathing and hatred for this man filled her. 'You killed my parents,' she shouted accusingly.

Tobias Listerman sneered mockingly. 'Most unfortunate but unavoidable. What would you have done, eh, if you'd been about to lose your inheritance?'

'I . . . I . . . would never resort to murder.'

'Oh, it isn't so bad. Quite easy, in fact. Well, it is for me.'

'You bastard!' she spat.

'My, my, such language, Albertina. Well, it's very apparent what sort of low life you have been mixing with.' His eyes narrowed menacingly. 'And I should watch that temper, my girl, because I have one too and I'm not nice when I lose mine – as several have found to their cost.'

She shrank back against the chair, her loathing and hatred rapidly overwhelmed by sheer terror under his threatening glare.

'What brought you here?' he demanded. 'How was it you found this place?' He held up his hand. 'Don't bother explaining. It's of no consequence now. As soon as I have burned this lot,' he said, pointing to the metal barrel, 'I shall be out of here.' His eyes darkened warningly. 'You shouldn't have come. I'm not ready for you yet. I was quite content to sit back and wait until you'd built up the business. Because the better you did, the more it was worth to me.' His voice lowered dangerously. 'But in the end I couldn't let you keep it. By rights it is mine. I have had everything else. That is all that remains. Still, maybe it is good you are here. It will save me a lot of trouble later.'

'What . . . what do you mean?'

He suddenly whirled round and stared across at the door. 'What was that?' His large frame spun back towards her. 'I heard you say you came alone?'

'I . . . I . . . did.'

'You'd better have done,' he warned.

He made for the door and yanked it open, peering down the dark length of corridor. Nodding, he slammed it shut and walked back to the desk, large body wobbling as he moved.

He perched with difficulty on the edge of the desk. 'I was surprised to learn that you had reopened the shop.'

'You . . . you were not worried about . . .' She swallowed hard. 'The discovery of . . . of the bodies?'

'No, why should I be? I am dead, remember. It was inevitable they would be found at some time. Upset you, did it? Oh, dear. I suppose I should apologise for that. But then, why should I? They deserved to die, about to cut me off like that. I was his first-born. His son. He told me he was going to disinherit me, which meant you would have got everything. Well, my dear, I couldn't allow that, so I made sure you didn't.'

Momentarily her fear left her as hatred for this man flooded in. 'You are mad, insane!'

'Do you think so? I think not. What I have done took careful planning. A madman could not devise the plans I have executed successfully.'

'Mr Bailey was right about you. He said you were evil.'

'Him?' Tobias then smiled. 'Did he tell you everything?'

'All that he knew. Is . . . is it all true?' she demanded.

'What do you think?'

She eyed him in disgust. 'How can you live with yourself?'

'Oh, quite easily, my dear. Quite easily.'

Blind panic raced through her then. She knew without doubt that her half-brother was capable of anything. Her immediate thought now was just what did he propose to do to her? She gulped, scared witless by terrible thoughts of what was to come, and her eyes darted around for a possible means of escape.

'Don't bother, my dear. You are going nowhere until I decide what to do with you. And don't think of trying to make a run for the door. I might be large, but I'm still very agile. You'll never make it.' He leaned over and slammed shut the lid of the case. 'That was all destined for Listerman and Fossett.' He tutted disdainfully. 'Though why on earth you had to add the "Fossett" is beyond me. Lowers the tone somewhat.'

She was staring at him. 'Listerman and Fossett? You mean, the jewellery was destined for my shop? But whatever for?'

He guffawed loudly. 'My goodness, child, have you not guessed yet? To be reworked, of course. Melted down, reset, refashioned. Roy Arnold did me proud. He's the best craftsman I have in my employ.'

'Roy Arnold?' she gasped. 'He works for you?'

Tobias laughed again. 'He certainly does. You'd never know that he's the crookedest jeweller in the trade. I'm lucky to have him. He was the one who tipped me off that the police were on our trail.' He eyed her mockingly. 'And I bet you thought he was a sweet old man? Oh, dear, dear, Albertina. What a lot you have to learn. In case you have not realised, I am what is known in the trade as a fence. I handle dubiously acquired precious objects. You see, my dear, when I had gone through all the family money I found myself in the dreadful position of having to work for my living and didn't much relish that thought. What kind of job could I do that would suit my needs and bring in the kind of remuneration I required? Then the idea came to me. I had sold jewellery before. Good jewellery, like your mother's, sold in the right quarters, brings in quite a nice sum. So I thought, why not? Before long I had built up a lucrative business. I have craftsmen in workshops all across the country and unlimited outlets for sales.'

Her mind whirled frantically. 'Lionel!' she cried. 'Where does he come into all this?'

'That fool! He was my courier. My last one got himself killed rather unexpectedly. Lionel took over from him, transporting the goods back and forth. I gather you were expecting to find him here tonight? Well, I'm sorry to disappoint you, this is the last place he would come. If he has any sense he will have gone to ground for quite a long while. If he hasn't, it is of no consequence as nothing he says can be traced back to me. I am very careful to cover my tracks. When I offered him the job, I made it very clear I would have no further personal dealings with him, all his contacts would be made through Roy Arnold. That is why he rekindled your romance. He needed an excuse to call upon Listerman and Fossett. He surprised me. He certainly did a good job. I paid him well, though.' Tobias smirked. 'Or promised him I would . . . eventually. The fool believed me. I made sure he was paid just enough to keep his appetite whetted.'

He rose abruptly. 'I shall take great pleasure in selling the shop, then my revenge against my father will be complete. I did so enjoy getting rid of his money, it was such fun! I have amassed my own fortune now which the sale of the shop will enlarge. In a day or so I plan to move my operations abroad. The police will not think to look for me there. France maybe or Switzerland. The châteaux are quite comfortable and the climate much pleasanter than England's.' His eyes glinted wickedly. 'And there is an ample supply of excellent wine and accommodating women.'

She could not believe his callousness. 'You . . . you will never get my shop,' she blurted.

'And why ever not?' he asked sarcastically.

'Because I have partners. They will stop you.'

He grinned condescendingly. 'Albertina, how stupid do you think I am? You may have partners but there is no record of that arrangement ever being legalised. You are a very silly girl, you know. Having deeds of partnership drawn up was the first thing you should have done. You do realise there are a great many unscrupulous people about? Such as myself.'

She gulped. Legalising their partnership had never entered her head. She, Jack and Flo had had a verbal agreement, marked by a handshake. She had thought that good enough. 'But . . . but you still can't claim it. The authorities would be alerted straight away. You are a wanted man.'

'Tobias Listerman is a wanted man, Albertina, my dear, not me. You do not really think I still use that name, do you? I'll let you into a secret – I have many aliases.' He leaned over the side of the desk and grabbed a small attaché case which she had not noticed before, opened it and withdrew a long envelope. He took out a folded piece of paper which he put on the desk and pushed towards her. 'Read it,' he ordered.

Heart pounding painfully, she snatched it up and opened it out. 'It's a marriage certificate,' she proclaimed. 'But . . . it has my name on it?' She raised her eyes to his, confused. 'I don't understand . . . it's dated on my twenty-first birthday. And just who is Michael St Mortimer?'

'Have you not guessed? Me.'

'What!'

'We are married, you and I. Under one of my aliases, of course. It is surprising what you can get people to do for enough money, but the certificate is well worth the price I paid for it. In due course I will claim my rights as your husband. Of course, I will be living abroad. A very friendly solicitor I know will be working on my behalf. I can see you are quite shocked by all this, my dear. Well, don't worry. I will tell those who need to know what a devoted loving wife you were and how much your death distressed me.'

'No!' she screamed. 'I will not let you do this.'

She leaped up from the chair, brandishing the certificate, and flattened herself against the wall.

Standing before the desk, eyes narrowed menacingly, Tobias told her: 'Do not be stupid, Albertina.'

'Come near me,' she cried, 'and I will rip it up.'

'Go ahead and rip it up, you stupid little fool! I can get another. I can get as many as I want.'

Before she knew what was happening he'd used his huge bulk to push the desk towards her and it was pinning her against the wall, the edge pressed so tight against her thighs she could feel it digging right through her clothes and into her skin.

He lunged forward, one large hand grabbing her throat, and as he slowly squeezed his eyes shone bright with pleasure.

'No, Tobias,' she rasped, eyes frantic. 'No.'

A sudden commotion erupted behind him. Tobias, hand still gripping Ally's throat, swung round. 'What the . . .'

'Let her go,' a voice ordered. 'I said, let her go. The game's up for you, Mr Listerman.'

Eyes bulging in fury, Tobias lurched back to face her. 'You bitch! You lied.'

With the speed of an athlete he released his hold on her, shot around the desk, heaved it forward and wrenched her out from behind it. He pulled her in front of him, one arm tight across her chest, then dragged her over to the window. With one heave the sash shot up.

'Come any closer and I'll throw her out!' he threatened. 'I'm warning you, stay back.'

The three policemen standing just inside the door froze momentarily, sizing up the situation.

Ally shut her eyes. She knew he would do it. Her half-brother's threat was no idle one. Her mind raced wildly. She did not want to die. Not at the hands of her mad half-brother. He had already bloodied his hands enough with the Listermans. She was already weakened by his strangle-hold on her throat and now immobilised by the force of his huge arm around her chest. There was only one thing she could do. She just prayed it would work, because she was not going to give up her life without a fight. She raised her leg and kicked back with her heel as hard as she could against his shin. Just as she had hoped, the shock of her unexpected retaliation made him fractionally loosen his hold on her. Bending her head, she bit deep into his hand, drawing blood.

He yelped in shock and pain, and automatically his hand swung back to come down hard across the side of her head. The blow sent her crashing to the floor.

The policemen dived forward.

Tobias froze. He knew without doubt the game was up for him. 'No!' he screamed. 'You'll not have the pleasure of hanging me.' He made a dive for the window and, as he heaved himself through it, cried: 'I will see you in hell, Albertina!'

The dull thud that followed seconds later echoed hollowly in the silent room.

Chapter Forty-Three

'Ally, please, please don't do this.'

Malcolm Carpenter looked into the tragically drawn face of the young woman of whom he had grown so fond. She was huddled in a chair, shivering despite the roaring fire. He was sitting opposite, begging her to change her mind.

For the last week, Ally had shut herself away at home. The only person allowed in the house was Mrs Vincent, and only to see to Ally's urgent requirements. Malcolm had managed to slip in unnoticed when the housekeeper had left the door ajar whilst taking a hurried trip to the washhouse.

'Ally, please,' he beseeched again. 'Please change yer mind?'

'I can't, Malcolm, so please don't ask me.'

He sighed. 'But America, Ally? It's the other side of the world.'

She gave a brief smile. 'Yes, it is a fair distance. But I need to get away.'

'But that far?'

'Well, it seems a shame to waste the tickets. With all that has happened I have not found the time to do anything with them. As she could not go herself, Bella gave the tickets to me to use as I wished.'

'Will yer come back?' he asked tentatively.

'That depends, Malcolm, on many things.'

'Oh, Ally,' he groaned. 'We'll miss yer. We'll all miss yer so badly. Especially Jack. I wish you would agree to see him. He's beside himself, Ally. Convinced you think he knowingly put you in danger.'

'Malcolm, please, please tell Jack I do not hold him responsible. The police have very thoroughly explained exactly what went on, and the predicament they were in. They told me how Jack was placed under oath not to breathe a word of their operation for fear of jeopardising it. I know now they had been trailing the gang of jewel thieves for months, and the people behind the fencing side. It was . . .' the name was so difficult for her to say '. . . Tobias they knew nothing of. They knew there had to be a mastermind behind it all, but had never been able to discover who it was. They just knew whoever it was, was a very clever man.' She wrung her hands despairingly. 'They had thought it would be Lionel who would lead them to him eventually, or possibly Roy Arnold. They told me they followed Lionel to my house then kept someone outside in case he should return. The policeman, lucky for me, was just following a hunch when he decided to see where I was going.' Her eyes filled with tears. 'I was only going to help Lionel, or so I thought. I never expected . . . never . . .'

'Ally, this is all so upsetting for you.'

She wiped her eyes with her handkerchief. 'Yes, it is. It pains me deeply to think of Lionel in jail. And all the others. Twenty they caught altogether, including Roy Arnold.'

'Greed, Ally. It was greed that put them in jail. Don't be too sorry for them.'

'Yes, it was, and Lionel will pay for his greed for the rest of his life, but the blame lies entirely with Tobias. It was he who enticed Lionel into taking a job as his courier.' Her head drooped, voice falling to a hushed whisper. 'I still have trouble accepting all that Tobias did. He must have been mad.'

Evil to the core, thought Malcolm. The only surprise was that such a man could have been related at all to such a lovely young woman as Ally. 'Look, my love, you have to put all this behind you. It's finished, over. Your half-brother is dead. But you don't have to go away to the other side of the world to do that.'

She lifted her head and smiled wanly at him. 'Yes, I do, Malcolm. And you will not change my mind so please don't waste your time trying.'

He sighed. 'All right, Ally, I'll respect yer decision. But please, if yer can't bring yerself to do nowt else, please just speak to Jack before you go. The man . . .'

'No,' she interrupted. 'I don't think that would be wise.'

At this moment, in her low state of mind, she would give anything to see Jack, to fall into his arms, to feel the comfort of his strength envelop her. But it would do her no good. After a long struggle with her conscience she had made up her mind that the only way forward for her was to start a new life. What faced her in America she had no idea; she barely wanted to think further than catching the boat. She had some money, enough maybe to start up a small shop of her own in a tiny back-of-beyond town somewhere where no one knew her or of her connections with her murdering half-brother. Earlier that morning she had despatched the spare ticket to the offices of Thomas Cook and Son, and also informed them she would not be requiring the return journey allocation.

She wanted to put everything behind her when she started her new life and that included Jack.

She rose, walked to a side table and picked up an envelope which she handed to Malcolm.

'What is it?' he asked.

'Please give it to Flo. It's a legal document conferring equal ownership of the shop and the buildings on Jack and herself.'

He gasped. 'What! Ally, you can't do this.'

'I can and I have. Please give it to Flo with my love. Now if you do not mind, Malcolm, I have to leave in a few minutes. The boat sails early tomorrow morning and I have to journey to Southampton.'

He knew any more pleading with her would be useless. He rose, threw his arms around her and hugged her tightly. 'Take care, me duck.'

She fought to stifle the tears that threatened.

'You too, Malcolm. You too.'

'You will write, won't yer?'

She did not reply.

Chapter Forty-Four

Flo was rocking backwards and forwards in her chair, weeping softly. All this was too much for her. Not only was Ally, the young woman to whom she had grown so attached, refusing to see her, but Jack, her beloved Jack, was prowling around like a man possessed, driving himself mad. And deep down she knew this state of affairs was all her doing.

Jack loved Ally, loved the very soul of her, and it was only his promise to Flo herself that was stopping him from going to her now. She tightened her arms around herself and rocked even harder. It was her own deep-seated hatred of the gentry that was the cause of all this.

She raised her head. 'Lord,' she pleaded, 'oh, Lord, I've never held much store by Yer but You've helped me before. Please help me now. Please tell me what ter do? Please, I beg Yer?'

She turned as the door burst open and Jack came in.

'Ma, I can't go on,' he cried, raking a hand through his dishevelled thatch of hair, face drawn and ashen from lack of sleep and a tormented struggle with his conscience. 'I'm sorry, Ma, but I have to break my promise to you. She might not want me but I have to try.' He strode towards her, kneeled down and grabbed her hands. 'Ma, please understand I have to do this? I have to tell Ally how I feel.'

Tears swept uncontrollably down her cheeks. 'Oh, Jack, Jack, will yer ever forgive me?'

'Forgive yer? Ma, I understand your worry. Ally and me, well, it might not work. But . . .'

'Not for that, Jack. Not for standing in yer way with Ally.'

'Forgive you for what, then?'

'For . . . for lying?'

'Lying? About what?'

'About . . . Oh, Jack, about yer very existence.' She grabbed hold of his hand, gripping so tightly her knuckles shone white. 'Yer know I love yer, Jack? I love you more than anything.'

'I know that, Ma,' he said, confused.

'But would you, if yer'd have known . . .'

He frowned. 'Known what?'

Her bottom lip trembled. She had to tell him. She had to or knew she would never find peace again. 'I'm yer mam, Jack,' she blurted out. 'Yer proper mam.'

His mouth dropped open, eyes widened in shock.

She shrank back in horror. 'Please don't look at me like that, Jack? I was afraid this'd happen. I knew you'd hate me, be disgusted by it all.'

'Ma, Ma,' he cried, gathering her shaking body to him. 'I think I knew. I think I've always known. And you're wrong, I'm not ashamed. I am proud. I love you, Ma,' he whispered, voice husky with emotion.

'You don't hate me?'

He pulled away, looked her straight in the eye and whispered tenderly, 'I could never hate you, Ma. Never.'

'Oh, Jack,' she cried. 'Jack, oh, Jack.'

For several long minutes, locked in each other's arms, they sobbed together.

Finally he asked, 'It's to do with the gentry, isn't it, Ma?'

Choking, she nodded. 'I was attacked by a guest of the Squire's late one night as I returned to me mam and dad's cottage after work. I was only eleven, Jack, and scared witless. I never mentioned it to nobody. It was me mam who guessed I was pregnant. It was her who dragged the story from me. I'd never seen me dad so mad. When me mam broke the news he grabbed his coat and marched straight to the house. Squire Belldon laughed. He laughed, Jack. Called me dad a liar, said it must have been a farm labourer I was giving me favours to. Me dad went for him.' She sobbed at the memory.

'The rest you know,' she whispered. 'But do you understand now, Jack, why I was so against any relationship between you and Ally? I hated the gentry so much and, stupidly, tarred Ally with the same brush. I was wrong, Jack, so very very wrong.'

'Oh, Ma, Ma,' he uttered.

'You don't hate me?'

'No, Ma, of course not.'

She grabbed hold of his hands again. 'A better son I could never have wished for.'

'And me no better Ma.'

'That was a wise thing you just did, my love.'

Flo's eyes darted across to her beloved husband standing in the doorway. 'Oh, Malcolm, you heard?'

'Not all but enough to know what were going on. I'm proud of you, gel.' He looked down at Jack. 'I managed to see Ally. Crept in when the housekeeper's back was turned.'

Jack sprang to his feet. 'You talked to her? Made her see sense?' His eyes darted over Malcolm's shoulder towards the door. 'You did bring her back with you?'

'No, son.' He handed Jack the envelope. 'She asked me to give you this.'

Jack snatched it, ripped it open, and hurriedly read. 'Oh, no, no,' he groaned. 'Ma, she's going away. Ally's going away. She's given us the shop. Split it legally between us. I don't want it, Ma. Without Ally, it doesn't mean anything.'

Flo jumped up. 'Then go to her, son. Tell her you love her. Tell her what you've just told us. And tell her it's my fault you kept your feelings hidden.'

'And you'd better hurry, Jack,' Malcolm urged. 'She left on a train about half an hour ago, heading for Southampton.'

Chapter Forty-Five

'Driver, will you hurry? I'll pay you extra. Anything. Just get me to the docks before that boat leaves.'

'The *Titanic*, sir? Fine boat. Never seen one like it. Magnificent, it is. Huge. Wait 'til you see it, sir, you won't believe it.'

Jack was not hearing one word of the driver's well-intentioned prattle. All his thoughts were concentrated on his urgent need to arrive at the docks before the ship sailed. If it left before he got there he feared he would never see Ally again.

'Can't you go any faster?' he demanded.

'I'm going as fast as I can. If you don't mind my saying, sir, you shouldn't have cut yer journey so fine. Time and tide wait for no man. Come on, Bertha,' he addressed the tired old horse. 'Gee up there.'

The driver had barely pulled the carriage to a halt before Jack had jumped out, slapped a note in his hand and run off.

'Oh, thank yer, gov'ner,' the driver shouted, delighted. 'A fiver. Well, I never.'

Ally leaned against the ship's rail and scanned her eyes over the thronged dock, wishing she herself could feel the excitement so obvious in all her fellow travellers. The *Titanic* was indeed a splendid ship. Majestic, she thought, would be a better way to describe it. Her cabin was luxury indeed, fitted out with everything she would require on her journey, and stewards stood by to obey their clients' requests.

The dock below was teeming with people, several brass bands, fairs, and a regiment from a nearby army barracks all adding their weight to the pomp and ceremony of it all.

Streamers and balloons blew high on the wind. Ally caught hold of a streamer and twiddled the coloured paper absently between her fingers, smiling distractedly at a lady next to her who remarked what a wonderful occasion it was. Were they not indeed lucky to be travelling on this magnificent ship's maiden voyage? And what a story it was going to be to tell their grandchildren.

Soon, Ally thought, as the first call sounded for visitors to leave the boat, she would be sailing away forever from these shores, leaving behind all she held dear. But she must not think of that. Her future was what she had to concentrate on now.

Jack dodged through the crowd of cheering people blocking his route to the ship's gangway. He had heard the call for well-wishers to disembark and his heart had leaped frantically. He had only minutes in which to try to stop the love of his life sailing away forever.

He finally pushed through to the bottom of the gangway sloping up to the deck.

A uniformed man raised his hand. 'Sorry, sir, no one else is allowed on board. The ship will be sailing in just under ten minutes.'

'But I have to,' pleaded Jack. 'There's someone I must find.'

'Sorry, sir.'

Jack had no time to plead his cause. Without further ado he unceremoniously pushed the man aside and belted up the gangway, the resulting barrage of shouts and calls going unheeded. He did not stop at the top either, just pushed straight past the welcoming party and ran down the deck, eyes darting frantically, calling loudly: 'Ally, where are you? Ally. ALLY!'

The second call for visitors to leave came over the speaker. Ally sighed. Her heart was not in these jollifications at all. Better, she decided, that she went below to her cabin and watched the shore recede through her porthole window. Nodding a goodbye to the couple pushed right up against her, she manoeuvred herself through the crowd at the rail's edge. It thinned and she found she could walk quite freely. She had reached the stairs leading to the floor below and was just about to descend when she heard her name being called in the distance, and the voice sounded so familiar, just like Jack's.

She frowned. She must have been mistaken. She had made no acquaintances as yet who would address her by name. Foot raised in midair she heard her name called again, louder this time. She drew back her foot and turned. She could see a head bobbing up and down behind the crowd. Her mouth dropped open in shock.

'Jack!' she exclaimed.

He arrived breathless, grabbed hold of her arm and yanked her towards him. 'Oh, Ally, I thought I'd never find you. I can't let you go, not without hearing me out. I love you, Ally,' he shouted frantically. 'I love you, I love you! I don't want the shop. If you don't come back I'll have it sold and send you the money – and I mean that. Now the boat is leaving any minute. We have to get off.'

She stared up at him, dumbstruck. 'But I can't . . .'

'You can, Ally. I'll not let you leave, I can't let you leave.' He pulled hard on her arm, propelling her forward, and ran with her the length of the deck.

'Jack,' she cried, 'stop! I can't possibly get off. My luggage . . .'

'Stuff your luggage, Ally. You can wire ahead,' he shouted above the noise of the crowd. 'Get it sent back.'

With all the strength she could muster she pulled him to a dead halt. 'Jack, why? Why, if you felt like this about me, have you not said anything before?'

He grabbed hold of her shoulders. 'There's no time now to explain. Just believe me, Ally, when I say that I love you. That I've loved you since the first moment I saw you, covered in all that mud. The thought of living the rest of my life without you is . . . well, I might as well cut my own throat.'

'But Lizzie,' she whispered. 'What about Lizzie?'

'There was never anything more than friendship between us, Ally.'

'Got yer!'

Jack leaped inches from the deck in fright as a hand grabbed his shoulder and without further ado he was frogmarched back towards the gangway.

'Jack!' Ally screamed. 'Officer, just a minute . . .'

'Ally,' Jack shouted. 'Do you love me, Ally? Do yer?'

Her answer came without hesitation. 'Yes, Jack, yes.'

'Then come with me now.' Poised at the top of the gangway, he glared at the officer restraining him. 'Can't you just give me a minute?'

'We ain't got a minute, sir, the boat is ready to sail. You shouldn't be on board at all. We can have you prosecuted, you know.'

'Then prosecute me,' he hissed, pushing the officer out of his way once again. Ally arrived breathlessly by his side and he grabbed her shoulders. For a fleeting moment he saw the hesitation in her eyes and knew the reason for it was that, after all she had gone through, all she had suffered, she could not quite believe in his declaration. But there was no time left for persuasion. 'I'll toss yer for it, Ally,' he cried, almost ripping his inside pocket in his urgency and yanking out his battered wallet. The sixpence in his hand, he looked deep into her eyes. 'Is it a deal?' he demanded.

'Show me that sixpence,' she ordered.

'Oh, Ally, don't you trust me?'

'It isn't that,' she uttered.

'There isn't time.'

'Show me first or I'll not agree. My life has already been decided on the outcome of that sixpence and I just want to see it before I agree again.'

The ship's hooter sounded. Jack handed her the coin and she hurriedly examined it.

'I told you, Ally. It's just an ordinary sixpence. Now, you took a gamble twice before, have you the nerve to try one more time?'

She nodded.

The sixpence rose, they both watched it fall. Jack caught it expertly and flicked it over. His fingers traced its outline. 'Heads you come with me, Ally. Tails you sail off to America. Agreed?'

The hooter sounded again. The clanking of the huge mooring chains being cast off their buoys crashed against the stone dock.

'Sir,' the officer demanded, 'you have to leave now.'

'Well?' he repeated.

She nodded.

Jack smiled as he lifted his hand and they both looked down.

'It's heads,' he shouted jubilantly.

'Thank God,' she whispered.

Hand in hand as he raced her down the gangway the grin that split Jack's face was a pleasure to behold. He looked like a man who had just been given the universe. But a man who held a secret too, one he would never divulge, especially to the woman he adored.

The sixpence had a flaw that only he knew of. It was undetectable to the human eye unless viewed through a magnifying glass. But Jack's fingers knew exactly where to search for the tiny nick just to the side of the sovereign's head.

LEAP

LEAP

MAKING THE JUMP
TO TAKE NETBALL TO
THE TOP OF THE WORLD

GEVA MENTOR

WITH ABI SMITH

CORONET

First published in Great Britain in 2019 by Coronet
An Imprint of Hodder & Stoughton
An Hachette UK company

1

Copyright © Geva Mentor 2019

The right of Geva Mentor to be identified as the
Author of the Work has been asserted by her in accordance
with the Copyright, Designs and Patents Act 1988.

A CIP catalogue record for this title is available from the British Library

Hardback ISBN 9781529353372

Typeset in Minion Pro by
Palimpsest Book Production Ltd, Falkirk, Stirlingshire

Printed and bound in Great Britain by Clays Ltd, Elcograf S.p.A.

Hodder & Stoughton policy is to use papers that are natural, renewable
and recyclable products and made from wood grown in sustainable forests.
The logging and manufacturing processes are expected to conform to the
environmental regulations of the country of origin.

Hodder & Stoughton Ltd
Carmelite House
50 Victoria Embankment
London EC4Y 0DZ

www.hodder.co.uk

To all the unique people, who dare to
be different, continually pay it forward
and whose innuendos are top notch!

CONTENTS

PROLOGUE

'While I'm loath to make comparisons between great athletes, to give you some idea of her influence and standing in women's sporting circles, Geva is to netball as Roger Federer is to tennis.'

Jenny Sinclair, managing editor, *Netball Scoop*

'A BOOK? Really, Mum? Me, write a book?'

'Think about it, Geev, you've had one hell of a year, 2018 has been a rollercoaster of a ride. The stuff that has happened this year alone would be enough to write about – three awards, two trophies, one divorce . . .'

The word hung in the air as she looked at me. 'What I mean is, why not tell people everything. Everything that thirty years of being involved in sport has culminated in – this incredible professional year on court coinciding with a heartbreaking personal one off court. Be honest and show folks what hard work and dedication and sacrifice looks like. Sing it from the rooftops, so women and men, girls and boys can see what can be achieved with a positive attitude and self-belief. It's just a suggestion. But you should do it.'

Mum was right. Like mums normally are. The year 2018 had been one of incredible highs and some heartbreaking lows. And the more I thought about it, the more her idea didn't seem so crazy. I had recently become an ambassador for the JAN Trust, empowering Black, African, Minority and Ethnic women (BAME) in communities to achieve their full potential. A book was on a bigger scale but it would have the same message: that my experience might benefit others. That the path I have trodden might well resonate with someone and then someone else and the legacy of hard work and commitment and focus would continue.

I do receive lots of wonderful messages from young girls and women telling me I inspire them and I am their idol and, as lovely as it is to hear, I can't get my head round that concept at all. An idol? Me? Are they sure?! I have never really had an idol so I can't really fathom that.

'You're such an inspiration, I want to be just like you, I love watching you play,' they say. And 'My daughter really looks up to you, she wants to be just like you.' I don't know how to reply or what to say. It's easy when they ask me for playing tips or advice; my response to those sorts of questions come very easily – but not when I am called an inspiration. How would you respond? I feel like a phoney sometimes as I don't always eat healthily, I don't always feel like training and I can be quite stubborn. But perhaps that is what makes me relatable and normal. An inspiration? I'm just me. Geva Mentor. But I suppose in a sense it is quite reassuring that what I am doing is making a bit of a difference, having a positive impact on people. I'm just going about my normal business, I'm just playing netball. Netball has been my business for nearly twenty years, so you could say I have shown commitment to it for sure. I have dedicated myself to it, yes; but I didn't set out to. Not in the beginning. I often say netball found me, I didn't find it – there was a heap of other things I was doing before netball came into my life.

Before I moved to Australia to improve my game.

Before I got signed up for the England senior squad.

Before I got picked for the England under-twenty-one squad.

Before I got scouted for the England under-seventeen team.

Before playing for a county, a club, a school . . .

Back in the beginning netball was probably the furthest thing from my mind.

'What would you be doing if you weren't a netballer?' I get asked that A LOT. Probably every interview I have ever done, people ask me that.

What did I want to be when I was growing up? I struggle to answer that, even to this day. I think I just used to make things up when I would get asked those questions in interviews for TV or magazines. Or I'd say whatever popped into my mind at that moment.

I never really had any professional objectives, I never had a set career path. When I was younger I think my 'plan', such as it was, was just to be healthy and happy and enjoy whatever I decided to do. I don't know if that makes me a bit different as it means I'm not driven in terms of wanting a certain career path – or maybe it is a positive as it means I have been able to just go with the flow. Don't get me wrong, that doesn't mean I haven't given things 100 per cent, but I'm a firm believer that if you enjoy what you are doing you'll put more into it. Rather than having a rigid plan, I have seen opportunities as they arise and taken them if I felt like it. I never set out to play netball, it was never on my radar; it was a case of just giving it a go. A bit like going to Australia. A bit like being a university student now, later in life, as I know now that I like working with kids, inspiring the next generation. And I have worked out where I feel most settled, where I best fit in. In a team, working as a team. So you see, I really, really struggle with the questions, What do you want to be when you grow up? and What would you be doing if you weren't a netballer? I guess what

I'm trying to say is, it's OK to not know. Sometimes you just have to take a leap of faith.

Aah, that word. Leap. The title of my book.

The word conjures up so many images, doesn't it? You've probably not thought too much about it, but to me that word means a great deal. I have taken leaps of faith throughout my life and my career. Sometimes I have found that to be my only mode of transport. Of course, I leap a lot in the literal sense too – I leap to take intercepts, block shots, to defend my post, to win games as that is what I do, that is my job. But I have found my life to have been a series of opportunities and challenges and I have leapt into the unknown on many occasions. I have worked bloody hard, but I have never lost the belief that everything will work out in the end. You have to have that belief, take that leap sometimes. Trust me, keep reading. You'll see what I mean . . .

1 SPRINGING INTO ACTION

*'It was written in the stars, Geva Kate (G.K.), and little
did I know she would be playing GK for England.'*

Yvonne Mentor, mum

I PEEKED over the top of the green curtain; the solid green
base of it was meant to act as a privacy shield but I was
tall enough, if I stood on my tiptoes, to see above and
through the netting part of the curtain. I curled my fingers
round the netting and pressed my face up against the strings.
The springs of the trampoline beds were making a rhyth-
mical noise and the trampolinists bounced gracefully. I
watched in awe. They looked like they were flying, bounding
and leaping all over the place and having so much fun. I
had been doing gymnastics for a few weeks now and every
week I heard the noise of the trampolines and wished I was
the other side of the big green curtain. Everyone looked so
happy over there, everyone was smiling, chatting and having
a laugh. This is what I should be doing. I wanted to be over

that side of the curtain too. The funny thing was my mum was on that side – she was one of the trampolining instructors, coaching the athletes as they took turns on the trampolines. My mind was made up. Gymnastics was fun, don't get me wrong; it had given me a good understanding of core stability and discipline, but I had given it a go and now I wanted to try something else.

I was only ten years old but already the thought of trampolining was what I had my heart set on. Forget gymnastics . . . rocking up to train in shorts and a T-shirt? Yes please! I was a bit of a tomboy so this was extra-appealing. Bouncing high in the air and feeling a sense of weightlessness and freedom is hard to describe. I could often bounce high enough to peer over the balcony and see what was going on in the café, where I would check how long the line was for the Slush Puppie machine. That was a post-training treat I had negotiated with Mum!

I still get a little buzz now when I see a trampoline. The urge to jump on one is strong; however, I know people would freak out because of the risk of injury! I do have to be careful nowadays, although I reckon I could get on and do a few bounces – just maybe not the double somersaults. Although to be fair, I'm definitely not as fearless now as the ten-year-old me was. The ten-year-old me joined the trampolining classes the following week and although Mum wasn't my coach, we were now the same side of the curtain, both having fun.

* * *

Mum was pretty good at getting me to try different sports, and trampolining was no different. She didn't mind about gymnastics; she knew I had given it a go. She was a county tennis and squash player and so would take me down to the tennis courts for a hit-about. Sport was all around her when she was growing up and so it was natural for her to surround me with sports and activities. Her father was an athlete, her grandfather was a sailor and she was into tennis. So I loved anything sporty. And she was nearly in the Olympics too – well, sort of. Before I was born she was into windsurfing big time and, in the early eighties, it was awarded Olympic status. A couple of the other GB potentials went to Australia for their warm-weather winter training but Mum couldn't afford that, so she went to St Lucia instead after being offered a deal. And it was a good thing she did too as she met my dad there! It's so funny when she tells the story. She was twenty-three years old at the time and apparently didn't have time for boys until she saw my dad, Gregory, early on her first morning, coming out of the ocean. She had flown in the night before and couldn't sleep so went for an early morning run on the beach. He was working for the local hotel and would supply them with fresh fish he had caught with his spear gun. He emerged from the ocean, spear in one hand and catch in the other, dripping wet, a very tall, very muscly black man, and Mum was struck by love at first sight. He apparently was too as he spotted her – an athletic white woman training on the beach with a big smile – and, as the sun came up, they started talking. Mum says they talked so long that the fish he had caught spoiled in the sun and he was unable to sell them to the hotel. Dad says it was the best catch ever, too, but Mum was worth it. Mum says that was crap as she was his best catch ever! Mum never did much windsurfing training after that; she phoned my grandma and told her she was staying in the Caribbean for a few weeks longer and the rest, as they say, is history. My brother and I definitely take after our dad in terms of figure – he is very tall and athletic and has very long legs. Mum says she is bloody pleased we have both inherited his physique and not her short, dumpy legs – although she does point out that as she has a low centre of gravity she doesn't topple over very often. So there you have it.

Looking at them, you probably couldn't get two more different people: Dad, who is over six foot tall, a dark-skinned man-mountain, and Mum, an only child from a white English middle-class family. But it was love.

They got married in St Lucia and spent the first few years of married life, before I was born, enjoying a wonderful, free-spirit type of existence in the Caribbean. Mum says she remembers lying on the beach, pregnant with me, listening to an old-fashioned radio after a busy day of windsurfing. She knew she had to come back over to England to have me as back in the eighties there were problems with children being born out of the country to an English parent – potentially they might not be recognised as GB nationals. She was convinced I was going to be a girl, apparently; there were no names chosen for if I was a boy but she heard on the radio, on that warm Caribbean afternoon, an Indian opera singer who was visiting the island and performing. On that small, crackling radio, Mum thought they announced her name as Geva. She fell in love with the name. It was only years later that she discovered the opera singer was of Sri Lankan descent and her name was spelled and pronounced 'Jeeva', which means 'life'. Mum's spelling, Geva, is meant to be spoken with a hard 'G' and in this form it's a Hebrew name that means 'hill', so not quite the same romantic sense! But Mum stuck with her original spelling and pronunciation when she registered my birth in the UK. She had to repeat herself many times and spell out my name, to the amusement of the registrar. Thankfully, my middle name is fairly simple: Kate, after my dad's mum, who was known as Miss Kate on St Lucia. I use the name Kate when I am ordering takeaways or making restaurant bookings as I have found it less confusing for people taking the booking. Otherwise people mishear my name as 'Diva', 'Gina' etc. Mum is convinced that on the day I was born, back on 17 September 1984, it was foretold in the stars that I, Geva Kate, would eventually play goalkeeper, GK. There was no other position for me! I love her thinking and I love thinking that the stars maybe somehow did align and I have this spooky connection. Who knows? She and I are firm believers that everything happens for a reason. Sometimes you can't see the bigger picture but things happen and they happen for a good reason. And you always have to make the best of situations; you have to keep positive and believe that things will have a way of working out for the best in the end. I hadn't always thought like that but after going through some of the more frustrating and hurtful moments of my life, I definitely do. I've come out stronger as a person.

So, there you have it. I am often asked about my background and I say I was made in St Lucia and born in England. Apparently the midwife was shocked at how long I was when I was born. 'And she's still coming out!' she told Mum. I was 59 cm long so it probably was a bit of a shock! Rather annoyingly, my brother Raoul, who was born eight years later, was only 57 cm long when he was born. And now he is six foot eleven inches tall and I am only six foot two – but I do tease him that it doesn't matter how tall he gets, I know where he is ticklish and I will always be able to take him down!

Dad left the Caribbean and came over with Mum to England to be a proper family and when they set up home in Bournemouth, on the south coast of England, you could probably count the number of black people there on one hand. Did he come across any racism or prejudice? Most likely yes, not that he ever made a big deal out of it; his resilience was admirable. My mum's family took a while to accept the marriage. My granny was fine but my grandad took a little while to accept that his precious little girl had brought home a black man. He did come round and it wasn't a major problem; I think the attitudes of his generation were just different back then. Growing up, I never had an issue with race, with being the colour that I am. I never saw myself as something different. I don't recall ever being a victim of racism when I was growing up. I was completely fine at school even though at primary school I was one of only five kids who were black, mixed race or Asian. I never really saw my skin colour or my hair being different as a negative thing. I certainly didn't feel different. On reflection I think sport certainly gave me that respect from my peers: the fact was that I was one of the fastest runners at primary school; I could beat all the boys and people always wanted me on their team!

With Mum and Dad both being so sporty and athletic, it probably wouldn't have been too much of a shock that their children enjoyed being active too. I get most of my competitiveness from Mum but probably most of my athleticism from Dad. When they both came over to the UK to have me, he continued his sporting aspirations and played cricket, moving up to county level before getting into boxing and bodybuilding. It was always an interesting time when he was bodybuilding as he wasn't always in the best of moods before a competition. Bodybuilders have to fast to make their muscles pop out, it's crazy! And Dad would do an egg diet beforehand and get moody and snappy and you'd always know when he was like that and just be like, 'Oh, Dad's preparing for a competition.

Normal!' Although you'd know not to wind him up around that time – we'd know not to ask silly questions to annoy him!

Mum and Dad didn't want to be far from the ocean and we all lived in a house in Chessel Avenue in Bournemouth, which is literally a five-minute walk from the beach. Dad loves the water and I remember being very little and going down to the sea on his shoulders and staying there while he waded out. Some things haven't changed and when I am back in the UK we will still head down to the beach and go in the sea, whatever the weather and whatever the temperature. We will go in on Christmas Day, New Year's Day, whenever. It is the best feeling ever and I love it. You get a sense of your existence as soon as the cold water shocks your body but then you become accustomed to the sensation and you're treated to views of the beautiful coast-line, the Isle of Wight to your left and the Purbecks to the right.

I was an only child for eight years before Raoul, my brother, came along. Probably, for those first eight years, I was Dad's precious little girl. I say that because I remember one day, I must have been four or five years old, wandering out to where he was working in the garage. I spooked a stray cat that was sitting on the top shelf at the entrance of the garage and it jumped down in fright and scratched me. I still remember how cross and how distraught my dad was that this cat had 'scared his beautiful girl'!

We weren't ever allowed cats or any other pet growing

up; Mum liked dogs but Dad had grown up with the ideology that dogs were working animals and therefore never allowed in the house. So we never had one. Mum didn't like caged animals either, so we weren't allowed anything like gerbils or hamsters; the only pets we were allowed were fish. We got a couple of goldfish once and, although they were supposed to belong to my brother and me, I took ownership of them and thought of them as mine as I was the one who looked after them, fed them and cleaned the tank. Then one day I came home and noticed the tank was empty. 'Where's Bart? Where's Homer?' I asked, rather surprised and panicky. It turned out that my little brother had thought they were getting too hot and so decided to put them in the freezer. He was very careful, he said, he used the net and took them out very carefully. 'What do you mean they got hot?!' I fumed. Yeah, they were in the freezer. That was the end of Bart and Homer. As angry and upset I was at the time, I can look back now and see the good intentions of my then five-year-old brother!

I like the fact that there is a big age gap between me and Raoul; being the older sibling, I can remember a lot of what he got up to when he was younger – all the mischief – and I will have no qualms about sharing it all with, say, the guests at his wedding one day when I give a best woman speech! We are that close; he was a part of my entourage when I got married. He is my rock and from the moment he was born I felt such a protective bond with him. And that might have had something to do with the fact that I was there when he was born and I remember it well. Mum was happy for me to be there. I had been to her antenatal classes with her and we have such an open and honest relationship and always have done; nothing is a shock or taboo for me. She never hid anything from me or refused to talk about anything and I guess that is partly why I am so chilled now. I could have asked her anything and she would have answered me truthfully – whether it was about sex or where babies come from, alcohol, anything I heard at school or in passing. I could always go to her and she would answer truthfully. This relationship with my mum also allowed my parents to openly discuss with me how things weren't going well between them when I was five years old, although that trial separation didn't last long and only a few years later I was told I was getting a little brother!

On the day Raoul was born, I had no idea how exactly he was coming out, if that makes sense. Obviously I knew he was coming out of Mum but I had no concept of exactly how and I never made the connection between Mum's body and what my body might do one day. At the age of eight, I just watched what was happening, with no great under-standing other than that Mum was in pain and discomfort. We were in the hospital and Mum was lying on the bed and I was on the left side of her, Dad on the right side, up by her head. I remember they couldn't find Raoul's heartbeat and they stuck this massive pin-type thing up her, basically to pinprick his head to see if he had a heartbeat. Luckily, he did. Then the next thing I remember is him suddenly being there and lying on the table. Dad cut the umbilical cord and I was the first person to hold him. As I went to pick him up he peed on me and I know I thought that was disgusting! And then he did it again. 'Eurghh!' I said, as Dad celebrated the fact that 'it' worked! It's funny what little snippets you remember, isn't it? I know it was the middle of the day as well – I wasn't at school as it was the Easter holidays – and I know Dad's best friends were outside too. They were there to support him and I heard them giving him a bit of grief and joking with him. Little did I know at the time that one of the guys, Lawrence Dimham, would be asked to be Raoul's godfather and would end up living in Melbourne, Australia, not far from where I am based now! He and his family are all so incredibly supportive of me. It's brilliant to have them so close.

There wasn't any jealousy or worry that I would have to share Mum and Dad's attention with my new brother. I just felt pure excitement. In a way, I felt like a second mother to Raoul. My personality had pretty much formed, even at that young age, and I loved helping and nurturing him. I still love sharing and I love supporting people and I have always got most of my enjoyment and pleasure from looking after those around me. Even though I didn't realise it when I was young, I already liked to be with other people and have company rather than do things as an individual. I am quite comfortable in my own space and with my own company but I thrive on being part of a team.

My relationship with Raoul has gone from being like a second mother to him, to big sister, to friend, and now he is my rock. We support each other but he really is my champion. He totally gets me. He knows when I'm down, he knows what to say or what to do. He is at the heart of some of the decisions I've made in my netball career. I would pay more attention to the clubs who would offer to support and look after Raoul than those who would just offer me a good deal. Family was, and is, so important to me. My brother, my parents, my grandparents.

Mum had strong female role models when she was growing up. Her mum's mum, Evelyn, was a publican in Stepney, east London and her father's mother, Winifred, was landed gentry, but they were both suffragettes in the 1920s. So although my two great-grandmothers were at opposite ends of the social spectrum and their paths would never have crossed, both of them understood the importance of empowering women. Mum definitely had that instilled in her and it was natural for her to pass it on to me, too.

I was extremely close to my grandad, my mum's dad, growing up and when my grandma passed away when I was five years old, I became even more besotted with him. Dan Dan, I called him. I don't know why but the name stuck and the whole family ended up calling him that.

Dan Dan's real name was David Reeves and he was an

athlete himself, a 440-yard runner, as it was in those days (400 metres now). He was also a keen sailor and loved being on the water (a trait I have inherited), and I remember going down to the boatyard with him and him tinkering away on his boats. My love of sailing and boats developed from Dan Dan, although we didn't really go out on the water, we'd just get the boats ready for winter and he'd talk to me and tell me stories and then he'd take me home and make me bacon sarnies. It's funny what sticks around in your memory . . . I also remember that he would always give me a Werther's Original, which seemed like the best thing ever as I wasn't allowed those at any other time! He would spoil me rotten and I'd sit on his knee while he sang songs about an old lady riding to Banbury Cross.

As I got older we kept up our solid connection. When I walked home from school I would often call in to his house on my way. I am so pleased Dan Dan managed to see me play netball for England. He passed away over ten years ago but he saw me wear my England dress and he'd always ask me how I was getting on. He said he knew I would do well. If I tried my best, if I worked hard, it would all pay off. When he got very frail and ill towards the end I made sure I went to see him every day in his care home. It was so tough, seeing someone you love so much slip away and not be the person you want them still to be. He had given so much to me and taught me so much. I do miss him still.

Mum won't forgive England Netball for the fact that they neglected to present me with my first England cap, as she had arranged for Dan Dan to come to Wembley and watch me receive it. He was using a wheelchair then, very old and frail, and they had assured her I would be presented with it after this game. I should point out that this wasn't my first England game – for some reason I didn't receive my first England cap for a couple of years and it was something Mum had to keep chasing and chasing. I might let her tell you this story. I warn you, she pulls no punches!

'One thing that pisses me off is that Geva never received her first England cap. England Netball never gave it to her after she played her debut game. Yes, she gained it while away in New Zealand, but when I watched other players come and get theirs and the tremendous fuss that was made over them and Geva has only just received hers, eighteen years later! I spoke to them on so many occasions to ask them when they would present it to her and when they told me it was going to be awarded after a game at Wembley, I arranged for my dad, who was in a wheelchair, to come too. Getting to Wembley isn't easy, it's a long way from Bournemouth as well as travelling with a frail, elderly man, but I knew it would all be worth it. Dan Dan was so proud of Geva and it was going to be such a special moment. But they forgot. Nothing. No fanfare, no presentation – the game finished and that was it. My dad died a little time after that and so he never got to see his granddaughter presented with it. I will never forgive England Netball for that.'

* * *

Growing up surrounded by different sports was brilliant and I loved having access to them all. I wanted to try everything. I guess I was what you'd call naturally sporty. It wasn't that I wasn't academic as well, but doing sports, playing games, being active, that is what I loved. Mum signed me up to ballet lessons, then there was gymnastics, and then I found trampolining and that was that. Although before I started trampolining properly, I was asked to make up the numbers for the swimming team at my primary school, King's Park. The school was entered into a swimming gala and the teachers knew I was pretty sporty, so they asked if I wouldn't mind joining the team. We ended up doing so well and winning so many of the races that Mum was approached to see if I wanted to join the local competitive swimming club. They were impressed with what they saw when I swam, but she turned them down and I know that for a while she thought about how she never did discover if I could have been any good or not, and wondered if she'd made the right decision.

She told me a few years later the reason she had declined was because she couldn't bear the thought of getting up at 5 a.m., driving me to a pool, sitting by the side in the humidity and then driving home again. I remember telling her after she picked me up from a netball training session, that I had seen a group of cold, wet swimmers waiting around for their parents to pick them up and that they looked miserable and I would never want to do swimming. So I think that eased her guilty conscience a bit! It's true though, I am pleased I never went down that route. Being mixed race, having the hair that I have, I don't think it would have withstood that regular exposure to chlorine – my hair gets so dry! Swimming was just something I did a couple of times at primary school and I don't know whether I was amazingly good or just good for my age group. We won a few races but I couldn't tell you if that was me being especially talented or just that I didn't come up against lots of strong swimmers. Early mornings aren't a problem for me now but back when I was nine or ten years old, eurgh! I think Mum would have struggled to get me out of bed on those cold, dark winter mornings.

I come across a lot of swimmers now and I know what a gruelling training programme they have. Perhaps Mum knew it wasn't going to be right for me and she made the right decision. But that isn't to say I don't respect swimmers – or any athletes for that matter – who put their heart and soul into a sport. I get asked a lot in interviews who my 'idols' are and it's a bloody tricky question as, quite honestly, I admire so many people from all walks of life. Of course, the likes of Roger Federer, Serena Williams and Steph Curry are pretty high up, as are the athletes who I've watched still achieving their goals in their late thirties and forties and older, like Jo Pavey, Tom Brady and Kelly Holmes.

Before you think that my mum might be one of those 'pushy mums', making me do all these sports and trying all these things, she was – but only because I wanted to!

I never showed any interest in anything else. It wasn't like I wanted to go to the library all the time, otherwise she would have taken me. She did encourage me to try things other than sport on several occasions but they didn't work out. Music was one of them; she got me into the violin. I think I started playing the recorder at primary school (and yes, I think I can still play the start of 'When The Saints Go Marching In'), and then when I moved up to secondary school I saw all the kids turning up carrying these cool cello bags or violin cases and flute cases. I was like, 'I want to carry one of those!' Around that time there was a musician called Vanessa-Mae, who made playing the violin look so effortless and so cool as she played to really funky backing tracks. And I was like, 'That is me! I can do that!' So, I tried. I was desperate to get to the stage where you wiggle the strings really fast and your head and shoulders move in effortless rhythm. Do you know what I mean? I'm not exactly sounding like a top-class musician, am I?! Needless to say, I never made it to that stage. I was horrendous. Not just bad, really bad. I loved it, that was the thing, I really loved it and I don't think I was tone deaf, I just think perhaps I wasn't a natural. I probably needed to work harder on it or perhaps have picked it up earlier, before Vanessa-Mae made it look cool. Mum banned me from practising in the house, it was that bad. 'Worse than a group of cats all meowing,' she said, and made me play at the bottom of the garden. It probably got a bit too cold for me to carry on and I probably realised I was making a horrific noise rather than music and so I put the violin down. And never looked back. That's as far as my musical career goes! Trampolining, however, now that is another story . . .

2 A SWAN IN FLIGHT

'Those who don't jump will never fly.'

Leena Ahmad Alsmashat

S IGNING up to trampolining at ten years old was the
start of my competitive career in that sport. I was a
quick learner, I can't remember how many times a week I
would train in the beginning but I think I was probably
going to the sports hall three times a week. I would work
with my first coach, Jane Chapman. She had coached two
junior World Champions so she knew her stuff.

Raoul was only two or three years old at the time I started
and while Mum and I were practising, he'd be toddling
around getting into mischief. He was a right terror. The
sports centre had a wide staircase and there was a nice
water fountain feature right in the middle. It wasn't a
wishing fountain per se but people had got into the habit
of throwing their pennies into it and one time my trouble-
some toddler brother went around scooping up all the

coins. That wasn't the worst of it; another time he was caught standing at the side of the fountain, trying to pee into it! And then there was the time he pushed the fire alarm button and we all had to evacuate the building. It's a wonder we didn't get banned from the sports centre completely and that would have been the end of my trampolining career! I have so many memories from my trampolining days. I remember once I was going to my first music concert straight after training and I rushed to the changing rooms to get ready. I came out looking pretty cool, I thought, in my denim miniskirt and strappy vest top, but Mum wasn't impressed and made me change into something less revealing. I was not happy. I was on my way to see Peter Andre!

I was fearless from that first moment I climbed up on a trampoline and started jumping. I just went for it. To be the best, to reach the top level, you need to have this element and I think, especially when you are doing it for the first time, you just need to have no fear. Be 100 per cent into each bounce without holding back. Nowadays is a different story. I get on a trampoline and think, 'Ooh, this could go wrong if I try this move,' but back then, when I was younger, I was unafraid and that is something the coaches liked in me. I had been playing various different sports for a while by then, so I already knew how to hold myself, how to put my body in the right alignment. I loved being around the group of people there, the coaches and the other kids. It was so much fun. And the more I practised, the more I enjoyed it, and I started to learn some routines. Don't get me wrong, I wasn't rocking up each week just to bounce, learn some moves and then go home again. There has to be a purpose to what I am doing. I have to have a goal to reach, a point, as it were, to what I am doing, and so one thing led to another and I started entering competitions at weekends. I had a new coach now, Rosie Bascombe, and together with Mum we'd often travel around the country competing.

I had started secondary school by now and I was tall. I was five foot ten by the time I was twelve years old and I was still growing. My height wasn't ever something I worried about. My dad was tall, my brother was tall, so it was just normal to me. I wasn't ever teased about it, certainly. Even in primary school, where I guess I could have become self-conscious about it, because of all the sporty things I was doing my height always worked to my advantage. Especially in swimming, gymnastics and now trampolining. It was all about having the right body alignment, so I would always stand with my shoulders back and stand tall. You'd get better marks the better your posture and your extension – it shows strength. Why on earth would I try to hide my height? Standing tall is so important; how you carry yourself shows what inner strength you have. I see it so often with young girls now. They have that hunched-over look, they bend down, they are conscious of their height, and I'm like, you know what, shoulders back, stand tall, be proud of who you are and the height you are! Take confidence in your height. The only time I think I made an issue of my height was when I was about fifteen or sixteen years old and I had started playing netball properly. I had probably been six foot for about a year by then but I kept telling people I was 'five foot eleven inches'. It wasn't anything to do with shame or embarrassment, I think I'd just read that a lot of models were five foot eleven and it sounded so much cooler to be the same height as the supermodels. I was actually part of an Yves Saint Laurent campaign when I was younger. They were looking for tall, athletic, strong-looking women to be part of a 'Pink Amazon' theme and I went to London for the weekend, strutted around in six-inch platform heels, and then came home. Modelling definitely wasn't as cool as it sounded. I was going to stick to sport!

Mum reminded me recently of the time when I had started playing for England and I suddenly wasn't the tallest any more and so from that point on I made sure I got my height correct to the last inch! I was six foot two inches and proud. It gave me more of a presence. The taller you are, the more intimidating you are for the opposition. I think that is one of the reasons I found myself in a defensive position on a netball court; I liked the idea of being the last tall hurdle that attackers had to face. I was the last line of defence and so I wanted to stand tall and stand strong. I find it funny when I see the height some people have recorded themselves as, making themselves taller than they are. It happens a lot in netball and I'm like, really? You think you're that tall?!

So, back to the trampolines and one thing led to another and I started competing at weekends for a new club, Ringwood and Bournemouth, in various different competitions in our area. I was travelling around with Mum and Rosie and we would start moving further and further afield as the competitions and events came up. I was never able to control my nerves however. It became a big issue for me. Nowadays, I get nervous before a big game but I have found ways of dealing with it. I take myself away, I close my eyes, I nap . . . I allow myself to be distant until the moment I need to focus. Back then, in my trampolining days, I think my nerves became all-encompassing. I couldn't eat the day before a competition and I couldn't eat on the day either, so I would turn up to this big event running on empty. Then as soon as I had competed I would eat and everything would be back to normal again. I was trampolining for about five years in total and I just remember the nerves I used to feel; they still haunt me to this day.

When you compete in tramp first everyone performs the same set routine all at the same time, all on different trampolines. Then you do a routine that you have put together yourself. It's called a VOL – a voluntary routine. You have to add certain moves such as a twist, one move that has you landing on your front or your back and one move that has you doing more than one rotation. And you can put those moves in any order with seven other linking moves, so each VOL is ten moves in total. Then you are scored and if you rank in the top ten, you do your VOL routine again. That is when it gets the most intense. The whole arena goes quiet and it is just you performing, just your springs going, the whole place watching you. I just remember the sound the springs made as I was bouncing, knowing that all eyes were on me, everyone was looking. So many times I would crash out and land on the end decks or through the springs on the side. I couldn't handle it. I couldn't cope with the pressure of this individual sport; I was not cut out for it. When it's an individual sport, it affects you and you alone, and the nerves really did affect my performances. Your senses are so alert when you climb up on to a trampoline; you hear the murmurs of the people watching in the crowd, you hear every creak of the apparatus, every sound of the springs as you take your position, your heart beating, your own breathing, the sound of the springs. There is a panel of judges watching you – Are they whispering? What are they thinking? They are waiting for you to begin. You start counting yourself down into the routine in your head, then the moment comes and you rotate your arms to get them into the best position to commence your routine. You perform your first bounce and start your first manoeuvre but as soon as you are doing that you are aware of what has to come next; you have to prepare to move seamlessly into the next one, so you never really think about one move completely as you are always moving on, in your head, to the next one. There is such a heightened sense of sound, and yet everything is so eerily quiet at the same time. You need to try to think about your alignment, to not over-rotate each move, to keep your toes pointed, your arms extended and what move comes next, rather than worry about who is watching, what they are thinking or whispering.

And it isn't without its dangers either. I became a junior national champion and reached number four in the country at under-thirteen level, but I took some serious knocks along the way too. Getting back on the trampoline after a fall or injury is much like getting back on a bike or horse when you have fallen off. You have to keep going, you can't let that injury or that accident define you. But they do knock the confidence and I remember getting a corker of a black eye when I had just started secondary school – I think I was in year seven or eight – and feeling so embarrassed. I couldn't open my eye for a whole week; it was swollen shut and black and blue, and I looked like I had been in a fight. Not ideal when you've just started secondary school and have become more self-conscious. It was a silly accident as well.

I was at a training session in the sports hall and practising a new move. I was rehearsing a double somersault off my back and I came into the trampoline at the wrong angle and so my feet ricocheted back up to my knees, which in turn ricocheted back up to my face and I ended up fracturing my cheekbone. Luckily, the sports hall was just across the road from the Royal Bournemouth Hospital, so we just walked over the road to casualty. They didn't seem that surprised to see me there; it seems it was quite a common occurrence for trampolinists training over the road to end up in A&E at some point! All the doctors and nurses were always so amazing when we went.

The odd minor injury coupled with the fact that I was still struggling to get over my nerves were probably a bit of an indicator for me. Mum said I looked like a swan in flight when I was up in the air but she also encouraged me to keep playing other sports during my trampolining years. Either she didn't want me to funnel all my energy into it or she knew that it probably wasn't going to be my defining sport. I suppose the final indicator, the realisation that my trampolining life was coming to an end, happened a year or two after my first accident. I was training at a different venue and I was working on another new move – a forward double somersault with a half twist. Anyway, I'm not sure if I blacked out or the sun blinded me through one of the skylights, but I ended up landing on the back of my neck on my trampoline before being flung onto another trampoline and then falling to the floor. It was pretty horrific, and I was put in a neck brace in A&E straight away. I had concussion and I was badly bruised and knocked but thankfully there was no permanent damage. Funnily enough, it didn't scare me or put me off trampolining – I probably would have climbed right back on the next day if I could – but Mum took control. I was still only just a teenager and I think the decision was, quite rightly, taken out of my hands. She sat me down and we had a conversation about what she thought. 'You are starting to grow taller and taller and it's harder to keep shapes and keep balance,' she said. 'You are growing out of your body a bit, Gee.'

Mum was just saying what I knew deep down – I wasn't cut out for this sport, not really. I used to crash out so many times as I had to bounce a lot higher than the others to get my limbs round each move, coupled with the fact that when I was competing I couldn't handle the pressure. So, with all this and together with the accident, I decided to call it a day. But I hadn't wasted my five years on the tramp. If anything, it helped shape the athlete I am today. It taught me some key ideas – about discipline, planning, preparation, timekeeping and work ethic – but it also taught me about myself as a sportsperson and the environment I work best in. This individual sport just wasn't the right place for me to succeed.

I did well in the odd competition but most of the time my nerves got the better of me. I was doing the odd bit of athletics too, the hurdles, during this time and whenever I used to compete, I was so nervous I couldn't eat all day. And now? Nerves are a funny thing. I suppose this was my first indicator that nerves are a real and common thing and part of the sport. But now I control them, they don't control me. I am part of a team now, so I have a bigger purpose than myself and that is my focus. I still get very nervous, don't get me wrong. I'll be in the England changing rooms and while some of the other girls are dancing around or singing, you'll often find me lying down, having a sleep or a doze. People might think I'm quite nonchalant and switched off but I am actually just lying there, listening to classical music, trying to chill out and not think too much. That is where my nerves still come into play; but as soon as I step onto that netball court and that whistle goes, they are gone. I am energised by them and I am in focus mode.

I guess sport helps us identify who we are as people as well. Are you an introvert? An extrovert? Do you prefer and thrive and perform better playing as part of a team? I know I do. I am not an individual sportsperson but I know athletes, swimmers for example, who do succeed by focusing on themselves and pushing themselves. It doesn't matter who you are, it's just about identifying it and using it to your advantage. So you might thrive in an office environment with a room full of co-workers, or you might prefer to be working by yourself. Or you might worry about letting a team down because, say, you have always had a psychological battle about being a weak link, and yet you are unstoppable when you work as an individual. Trampolining taught me that I wasn't an extrovert, I wasn't a confident bouncer who had an inbuilt belief in myself and my ability to perform as a soloist. I am a team player. And so I concentrated on the sport I spent most lunchtimes and breaktimes playing: basketball.

A lot of people see me now and they think 'basketball' rather than 'netball', because basketball is much more well known. I am trying to turn the tide on that way of thinking; it would be great for people to think 'netball' as they would of a world-famous sport – because it is! – but it's funny how people always assume basketball first. I did play basketball for a while before the netball court called. I had started playing a few years into my trampolining years, just at lunchtimes at my secondary school, and I loved every second. My secondary school, St Peter's Catholic school in Bournemouth, was a great school. I would rock up to the sports hall and join in with the boys playing basketball. It was, back then, more of a sport played by a collective mix from the school, some sporty types, some nerds and me, the only girl. Or, more accurately, me, the tall, mixed-race girl who could kick arse on the basketball court. I was in year seven when I first joined and I probably came across as more confident than I felt. To begin with I probably tried a bit too hard to fit in and impress them and they probably thought, 'Who the hell is this?!' They just wanted to have fun and relax at lunchtimes and then there was me, ultra-competitive! But as they got to know me and I got to know them, I relaxed and they realised I was actually all right. Then we would play the odd game and they realised I was pretty OK and invited me to join the team. I felt at home in a team situation, playing and working together as one side. I think I played on the team for the whole of year eight and playing against boys I would use my height to my full advantage. I would want to be intimidating and I definitely thought I was pretty cool. There was no girls' team at the school but I loved playing on the boys' team. And they were great fun and were happy for me to be on the team too. But other schools we came up against in matches weren't so happy. I was in year nine when I was told I couldn't play any more. Apparently word had got round that St Peter's had a girl on their team and the other schools started to complain. It was such a shame; we were unstoppable when we played, we beat most of the schools we came up against, and I am sure that is one of the reasons they complained – they didn't like being beaten by a school with a girl on their side! I am still really good friends with two of the guys I played with all those years ago. We became known as the Three Amigos: me, Laurent Rossi and Matt Ahan. They were brilliant basketball players and I love that we are all still in contact. We were probably a very unlikely trio back then; Laurent had bright red hair, Matt was highly intelligent, and then there was me, the six-foot gangly one. I didn't want to give up on basketball, even though playing for the school team wasn't an option any more, but I felt the sport had taught me about what I enjoyed most – being part of a side. Basketball is obviously a team sport but there are elements of it that are very individual. There are just one or two people who can win or lose a game for you and I would get nervous playing under this pressure. I would stress if it was down to me taking a free throw or taking a shot and would often pass it off to one of my team mates. 'What if I miss?' was becoming a thought that would enter my head frequently, and so, slowly, even this team sport started feeling more like an individual game. I realised jumping for the rebound and passing it on was my way of not losing it mentally on court. I was well on my way to finding my niche, to finding the right sport, but I wasn't there quite yet.

I still wanted to play basketball matches, though, so when I had to stop competing at school, Mum took me to a sports centre that she had seen was advertising for players for a well-established team in the area.

'This could be just what you need after trampolining,' she told me, and I agreed. And so we went into the sports centre. We didn't want to get in the way, so we stayed at the back. And we stood and watched. And waited. And waited some more. There was a training session happening, we understood that, but at no point did anyone approach us or signal for us to come forward. OK, we thought, they are obviously very focused in their training, we will wait until the end of the session. And at no point, in the hour we sat and waited, did anyone approach us or signal to acknowledge our presence. We were completely ignored. Mum was fed up by now and so when the session was over we went over to the coach to speak to them. Mum explained that I was interested in playing and joining the squad, how I had been playing matches at school, but they were not the slightest bit interested in having me on the team or in training. They did not give us the time of day. Now bear in mind, I was around thirteen or fourteen at the time, I was five foot eleven inches going on six foot, looking athletic and keen, and I didn't even get a chance to show them what I could do! At the very least you would think they might ask me to join in a session to see me play and give me a try. But no. And we just ended up turning round and walking out. It was pure rejection. Mum tried her best to lift my confidence as we walked out. She was furious. As a coach herself, she couldn't understand their lack of interest. And the strangest thing? We had watched them play a game and they were obviously short of players. It would have been an ideal time for the coach to get me to step in and see how I would fit in to the side. To this day I have no idea what happened. Mum probably took it to heart more than I did but she made sure I didn't feel rejected and so I knew it wasn't anything I had done wrong.

'It's all right, if they don't want you, there will be some-where else that does,' she kept saying. However much she was fuming inside, she was so positive, she never let me believe it was my fault. Still it makes no sense to me, even now. If nothing else, it seems like a bit of a waste . . . I do a bit of coaching now and if I saw someone like that, someone like me back then, walk in to a training session, I'd say, 'Right, let's have you play here, let's see what you've got. No pressure, just give it a go.'

But everything happens for a reason. It was their loss and it was a turning point for me. I find it funny to think about how different my life could have been if I had been given a chance that day. With my height and skill, perhaps I could be playing professional basketball in America right now, instead of being based in Australia and playing netball.

I guess this was my fork in the road. I could have been sent on the path to the left but instead it was closed to me, which meant I turned right. I was on the correct path, I just didn't know it yet.

3 TAKING THE REINS

'No hour of life is wasted that is spent in the saddle.'
Winston Churchill

'THERE is something we need to talk to you about, sit down.' Mum and Dad both looked very serious and for a fleeting moment I had to think hard . . . had I done something wrong? No, no, I don't think so. School was going OK, I was doing OK . . . I don't think this is about me. And I was right. It wasn't actually much of a surprise when they made it official that they were going to be splitting up. At fourteen years old, I wasn't stupid, I knew things weren't great between them. Raoul was probably too young to understand properly, but I was fine with it all. And that is all credit to Mum and Dad as they kept things very amicable. In all honesty, they probably get on better now than they did when they were married. Dad has now remarried and has two other daughters, which means Raoul and I have two half-sisters! I take my hat off to Mum – she had the foresight to see that at the end of the day, it is all about the children and some things don't go to plan but the children will end up being the grown-ups one day and what you instil in them now will help them when they are older. There was no animosity. We have had them stay over with us and we have spent Christmas with them in Holland where they live – Dad, his wife, his ex-wife and all his children. It's pretty incredible really, isn't it? It has taught me so much about relationships and life and how to look at the bigger picture. No one had died, everyone was OK. Dad was happy. He didn't shut us out of his life. The only thing that I think I was a little annoyed about was Dad never told us that he was going to get remarried. I think he thought we'd be too upset and so he just got married out in St Lucia and then told me and Raoul afterwards. He was nervous telling us, thinking we might be quite upset, but I told him, 'I'm the opposite, Dad, I would have loved to have been part of it!' So there you have it. The split wasn't a big thing and I saw them both and neither of them were upset at what had happened. Mum was always probably more influential in my younger years anyway and that hasn't changed. Dad would do shift work and do a lot of nights and we didn't really see a great deal of him during the week, so it wasn't really a massive adjustment.

I think the world of my dad and I have a huge amount of respect for him. I still see him when I can and I have a good relationship with him. He had quite an old-fashioned upbringing in that women were seen more as 'homemakers' but I think seeing Mum and me be so independent, successful and confident has softened him over the years. He has seen how hard I have worked to get where I am and he knows it hasn't been easy and he is proud of me. And I guess as we have got older, I have been the mediator between Mum and Dad – if they have any little disagreements I'm the one sorting it out, speaking to both of them. I love them both and I want them both to be happy, to continually respect each other and, most importantly, play a prominent part in my life.

It scares my dad how much like my mum I am. Before I moved to Australia I'd answer the phone when he called from Holland and he'd think it was Mum. We sound the same, although I do admit I have a slight Aussie twang now, but our sayings were and are the same and other than to look at us, you would never know! But I have got some traits from my dad too: I like to be more reserved in a group scenario, quiet almost, and will sit and assess a situation and not make any rash decisions, whereas my mum will be the talkative storyteller and never shies away from giving her opinion. Dad and I are both very cautious about our surroundings and sensitive to others, whereas Mum will drop people in it – she doesn't suffer fools and she doesn't hold back on her dislike for a lot of things. I guess what I am saying is, life isn't perfect. Things don't always work out the way you think or want them to. And I have the best relationship with my two sisters. I appreciate the small things a lot more with them around. I like just spending time with them, watching them grow up. Things aren't always going to be rosy but you have to make the most of it, ride out the tough times; and having that support crew around you who love you for you? That level of unconditional support is immeasurable.

Our house was never the kind that was empty and quiet. We had five bedrooms and Mum had decided to offer the spare rooms to foreign exchange students who needed somewhere to stay. There was a school just down the road, so it was ideal for them, and Mum was adamant that it was good for me and Raoul too. So we had an extended family.

Growing up in our big house with all sorts of different people was one of Mum's most fun and influential ideas. She was keen on us interacting with people from all over the world. She loved to travel, she loved to talk to anyone and everyone, and she liked to show off the area of Dorset we lived in. It was a real treat growing up meeting individuals from different backgrounds and different cultures, and we have kept in contact with some of them over the years and forged strong friendships; we've even spent Christmases with former students. They would stay in our home and be part of the family, eating breakfast and dinner with us and just being around. Mum wanted Raoul and me to be exposed to different characters from all walks of life; she was teaching us, from a young age, that differences are what define us and should be celebrated. Subconsciously, we learned not to judge people on where they came from, but just to accept them as the norm and get on with it. And hearing their stories about their travels and where they lived probably encouraged us to go out and see the world, to not be scared about visiting different places and learning new things.

Mum's love of travelling and her real sense of adventure have definitely stood me in good stead for all my travelling now with netball. When I was seven years old, I went to Iceland for three weeks by myself. Yep, all by myself! Mum put me on the plane and I travelled as an unaccompanied minor, with one of those necklaces that had all my tickets and passports and information attached. I had to carry that round my neck all the time. I don't know if you can even do that any more?! So I had no fear or worries about leaving home or being homesick; it was something I was used to from an early age. I was staying with a really good friend of Mum's who had a daughter the same age as me. I don't really remember much about that trip so I am guessing it didn't scar me for life travelling by myself so young.

I was quite independent and grown-up for my age and I was fearless when it came to horses. When Mum gets asked that question, 'What would Geva be if she wasn't a netballer?', she says I should have been a horse whisperer. I have a connection to them I can't explain. I was probably riding bareback when I was four or five years old. There is a photo of me riding alone on the beach in St Lucia. Dad had a couple of horses and would take me out for a ride, him holding the horse on a lead rein and me just riding bareback on the sand. That connection was always there, even as I got older. My godmother, Angi, had a 200-acre farm in the New Forest and Mum and I used to visit her a lot. Mum would sit and have a cuppa and chat for ages and I would go off and be with the horses. If ever they needed to find me I would be in the paddock, sitting on the horses, talking to the horses. I just loved that; it was just a nice way for me to get lost in my own thoughts, be at peace with nature. As soon as I started spending time with the horses, I felt calm. And I would relax.

When I was twelve years old I wanted my own horse but I was persuaded by Mum to have a pony on loan to begin with, and keep it at Angi's farm. The idea was that I would appreciate how much work went into having a horse – the expense, the time, the upkeep, the daily mucking out, the grooming, the regular riding. So I got loaned a twenty-five-year-old pony called Max from a lady called Mrs Cox. Mrs Cox said if I could handle old Max, who was blind in one eye and a bit of a character, I could handle any horse. Angi agreed to let me keep him in her stables and, to help me, she would put him out every morning and I would have to bring him in every night, groom and feed him and muck him out. Mum had to drive me there every day as the road was too unsafe for me to ride my bike, and it didn't take long to work out that this was never going to be a permanent arrangement. Going up there seven days a week took up a lot of time and both Mum and I realised having a horse was a nice idea but it wasn't very practical at this stage in my life. One Saturday morning we took Max out for a hack on a route that involved me riding him on a small country road for a short bit of the journey. Mum was walking next to me and Max when he suddenly bolted. Now I was a good rider but he was a strong-willed, stubborn old horse and he didn't want to stop! I tried turning him to his blind side but he kept on cantering sideways down the road and I just thought to myself, 'I've got to leap off, I just need to leap . . .' I tried to keep hold of the reins as I did so, but they ran through my hands and I was pulled forward, onto my tummy, and I let go. I could hear Mum shouting behind me and when she caught up, I think she was relieved to see I wasn't lying dead in a ditch! But I was in pieces: 'I've lost Max, he's gone, Mum!' I cried. I think her reply was something along the lines of, 'Sod Max! Are you OK?!' I was only twelve years old, so I suppose it was a bit terrifying for her. Max turned up back at the stables later that day looking very pleased with himself. But it didn't put me off horses and I kept helping and volunteering at Mrs Cox's stables.

One time I took out about five or six paying customers for an hour-long hack and I was on the lead horse (whose name was Commander, funnily enough), a beautiful pure-bred Arab, with the others following. We were on our way home and just before you got back to the stables there was a nice spot for a bit of a canter. So I signalled to the group that we would have a canter again, as we had done several times during the hack. We had just broken into a canter when a bird suddenly flew out of a bush and spooked all the horses. My horse went from a startled canter to a gallop and I struggled to slow him down. When I finally did, I turned round and saw that none of the other riders were on their horses! 'Oh crap,' I thought. 'Please don't have let anyone have broken any bones, I don't want to lose my job!' Not that I got paid for it, but I didn't want to be told I couldn't take people out any more. Thankfully, no one was injured. I collected all the horses from the cattle grid gate further down the route, where they'd all headed – horses are smart animals and they knew their way home – and got everyone mounted again, and everyone survived to tell the tale! I think they all enjoyed the excitement of that ride; they told me they had a great time. And yes, I was allowed to continue taking out people on hacks. These things do happen, you can't control a bird spooking a horse; it is about how you react and control the situation. I then spent the following two summer holidays in New Zealand with our cousins, who owned a ranch in Waitomo, on the North Island. I would work with the horses on the ranch, taking tourists who were staying at the nearby youth hostel for hacks across the terrain. There was no health and safety or English-style hacks of the kind where the group leader would ride out first and the others would follow in a line. We were just cantering and galloping over the beautiful terrain and it was utterly brilliant. And no one fell off that I can remember! It's not that I'm not allowed to ride horses now, but I do have to be careful as my sport is now my income and I can't afford to get injured before, during or after netball season. I guarantee one day I'll have some stables myself, with a few horses grazing happily.

Horses, and people from all walks of life, both played quite a big part in my childhood. The people who stayed with us didn't always progress to being friends for life though; we had so many different characters stay and some were just plain weird! There was a Greek guy, who was old and fat and hairy and who I once saw wearing nothing but these horrible white Y-fronts. I was leaving my room to head downstairs and caught him on the landing, coming from the bathroom back to his room. He was just sauntering around in his pants! I was mortified. I still have that unsightly image in my head to this day!

And I remember once we had a Spanish lad stay. He must have been about a year younger than me, fourteen or fifteen at the time, and he seemed very spoilt, always complaining. He was quite rude to Raoul and me on occasion. We got fed up of his attitude, so one day we decided to play a prank on him. One of the bedrooms at the front of the house has a window that overhangs the front door and when he came home from school we dropped a water balloon from the window all over him. It was summer, in our defence, and it wasn't like the water was ice cold, but he didn't see the funny side and cried. Mum was not happy and told us off, then explained that he had a lot of problems at home and we needed to understand his sometimes naughty behaviour was a result of frustration over his family life. 'Never judge a book by its cover' is a favourite saying of hers and I think I understood its significance for the first time then. And yes, it was probably a little mean, thinking about it now – but also it was only water! Toughen up! Raoul and I would always be spending time together and occasionally getting up to mischief, and I would forget that he is actually a fair bit younger than me. For example, I loved horror films (I still do). One evening I had invited some friends over and we watched *It*. I didn't notice Raoul, whose bedroom is next to mine, sneaking in to watch it too. He is to this day absolutely terrified of clowns. No joke – he is six foot eleven inches, a big muscly guy, and he's absolutely petrified of them. Whether it is a toy or a picture of one. I have scarred the poor boy for life!

I had a fun and adventurous childhood and things that might have had an effect on me growing up – my race or being tall – never did. I had differences all around me and was taught respect for everyone. I suppose sport has only intensified that ideology; people don't see my different hair or the colour of my skin, they see a person, my contribution to a team, my skill on court. I am judged by my ability. As an adult, I am probably more aware of my skin colour than when I was a child. I find myself more attuned to these things. I will go into a room and immediately be aware if I am the only person there with a tan. I am so conscious of it now that, if I am asked to be a guest speaker or if I'm just attending an event, I will look around the room and just scan and see if there is anyone of a different nationality or colour or appearance. I don't know why it is a thing for me now, but I think as an adult you are aware of what happens in the world, of the racism, the prejudice that can happen. People probably see me for me, they don't see me as mixed race or a braided-hair six-foot chick, and in netball there has never been any occasion on which I have felt threatened or intimidated by being mixed race.

I think the one and only time I was aware of any sort of racist comment was when I took my driving test for the first time. I was coming off the dual carriageway and I came off into the right-hand lane instead of the left-hand lane as I had someone coming up on the inside of me. My examiner said I had two minors and that major fail. 'In this country we drive on the left-hand side of the road,' he said. I didn't think anything of it at the time but I was upset about failing and I got in the car and told Mum what happened. She made me repeat what he said word for word and we ended up putting in an official complaint about him. I think we heard, about a month or so later, that there had been lots of complaints against him and he had his licence as a driving examiner revoked and had to go on a course to reapply for his job. But that is probably the only time I felt under attack for the colour of my skin. I am lucky, I guess, but I do feel I have escaped it because of sport too. People get behind you, they respect you for doing what you do. If you try a sport and you are not very good at it – whether it's running a 100-metre race or playing football or hitting a tennis ball – you have enormous respect for people who can do those things. When someone comes along and excels at something you know is tough, there is an appreciation, a respect, and you want to be around them. People don't see the colour of my skin, they see what I have achieved. Sport has given me the strength to be who I am and be respected among my peers.

So, you get the gist that sport was my thing. School-wise, I probably wasn't the most academic. Something has to give though, right? I loved St Peter's school. Mum was never big on making sure we got all the top marks; she always put more emphasis on us being healthy and happy and well-rounded kids. She never wanted us to follow a trend or do something just because everyone else was doing it. She made sure we knew the importance of standing up for ourselves and making sure we never judged anyone by what they looked like or where they came from. If you're brought up with these ideologies, you accept them quite naturally. And we did.

I was quite a social person and I had a lot of friends. I wasn't ever part of just a small clique; I could join any friendship group and get on with everyone, whether it was the arty lot or the music guys or the sporty lot.

I could move between different groups probably easier than others. I found it easy to mix with the boys – I wasn't a girly girl, let's put it that way, although I could quite happily hang out with girls. I was probably more of a tomboy. I found I could spend time with the boys and be more relaxed. I could just sit there with them and we wouldn't always have to make conversation or anything. I suppose I could just chill with them partly because of my interest in sport.

I didn't enjoy studying. I'm very practical and hands-on and I learn better that way than listening to someone talking to me or reading to me. I used to love geography, going away and doing projects and researching different countries. I loved languages, I found maths quite hard, and history was probably a subject that grew on me. And spelling? I wasn't great at that either – in fact, I would say I was atrocious . . . did I spell that right? So I probably wasn't the most academic but I did have a good work ethic. I tried!

A lot of what you learn and how you learn and how much you want to learn comes down to teachers. I had some great geography teachers and PE teachers who completely inspired me. I know what a difference a good teacher can make, so I am putting my money where my mouth is and I'm doing a Bachelor of Education Primary degree. I'm in my third year and trying to fit in all the study and practical sessions too. I've done a bit of coaching too; I've come across some pretty rubbish coaches and I thought to myself, how are these kids going to be inspired by you? There are ways of encouraging and making learning fun and that is what will help kids learn, at the end of the day.

PE was great at school too; the whole faculty was

awesome. Viv Hawkins was one of the PE teachers who helped me out when I started to play a bit of netball. She was always incredibly encouraging and I learned a lot from her. I guess this is where my journey as a goalkeeper really began, at secondary school, having finished trampolining and been snubbed at basketball. I think there were a few times I played netball at primary school but it wasn't like anything happened after that. Then, I think it was towards the end of year seven, or the beginning of year eight, my friend Caroline Marshall called me over to the netball court in the playground one breaktime. 'Can you join us, Geva? Just stand here and wave your arms and look scary . . .'

4 WHEN NETBALL FOUND ME

'The bird dares to break the shell, then the shell breaks open and the bird can fly openly. This is the simplest principle of success. You dream, you dare and you fly.'

Israelmore Ayivor

I F basketball showed me how little it cared, netball welcomed me with open arms. There is no other way of describing it. Trampolining taught me that I needed to be part of a team, basketball taught me that I was close, close to finding the 'one', and on that gravel netball court one breaktime, I did indeed. Or netball found me.

I joined Caroline and my friends and every time they played, I played. It probably wasn't until the end of year eight, when I had played a few tournaments at school, that I started to get noticed. Two of the coaches at Bournemouth Juniors, a local club, had seen me play and asked if I wanted to join the team. Jacqui Berry, also known as the 'Godmother of Bournemouth Netball', and Pam Croft were both hugely encouraging when I joined, although I think the best thing about that was it was basically the same players we had in the school team so I was playing with my mates both at school and afterwards! There were a few extras from the other schools around too and we were pretty good, I thought. I was friends with Nina Quick, the goal attack from school, and Rachel Finan, a centre. Then there were girls who played for the club as a team but went to different schools, so when we played them in school tournaments we became almost enemies. That is how we saw it anyway. I would say 'rivals' but when you are young and take everything so seriously, 'enemies' sounds better! At school I always got picked to play first; I was a 'starter'. But when I played for the club, yes, I was tall but I wasn't the only tall girl there. There were three teams in the club, Bournemouth A, B and C, and for some reason I got moved to the older age group, up from C to B. It was around this time Mum spotted that Team Bath had a development programme in place that was run by Lyn Gunson, a former New Zealand Silver Ferns player. She was the coach and together with Waimarama Taumaunu, another New Zealander who had been newly appointed as England Netball's Performance Director, was on the lookout for future England stars. Mum, who hadn't had a clue about netball to begin with but was beginning to see there I had potential, was adamant I had to attend the open day at the university. I was only fourteen years old and she took me out of school to see what Bath University and Lyn Gunson had to offer. Can you imagine doing that now? Mum put so much emphasis on getting a good life balance – it wasn't all about good grades. I can't imagine my headteacher, Mr McCaffrey, being able to stop her even if he'd wanted to. Which he didn't, but more on my amazing school support a bit later. So while Mum had to sit through a lecture on nutrition and sports at the university, Lyn took me off to see what I could do on the court with a ball. I enjoyed the day and I think I made an impression but, most importantly, I knew this was what I wanted to do. I had found my sport, I had found my place, I knew I had to give it my absolute all. I was still playing for Bournemouth B team when I was invited to play for Dorset in an under-fourteens county tournament. It was in Gosport and the nature of these tournaments was that you went off in your little groups, said bye to the parents or whoever brought you, played for most of the morning, had a break for lunch, and then played again. You'd play probably ten-, twelve- or fifteen-minute games. Little did I know there were some England scouts who had come along to see what the south-west teams had to offer. It was at this tournament that two important things happened: firstly, Mum realised that I was actually quite good at this netball game and, secondly, I was T-IDed. Talent Identified. Spotted. Mum told me on the way home that she was sitting up in the back of the court watching the games and, whenever I played, some of the comments she could hear were, 'Who is this amazing goalkeeper?', 'Where has she come from?' 'What is her background?'

Mum, a short, white woman, was the perfect spy! No one knew she was related to me, the gangly mixed-race GK, and so she sat quite happily hearing wonderful things about me and feeling very smug. She could only be a spy for those early days though; now she is all over bloody social media and commenting on everything and I'm like, 'Mum! Enough!' She told one interviewer on TV years later that she gets so nervous watching me play matches she wets herself. I was mortified, I can't tell you the embarrassment. But she has also gone from being someone who never really liked netball as she never really experienced it at school ('Of all the sports, Geva!') to knowing all there is to know about the game. Considering she was so incredibly sporty, netball, she said, wasn't something she really 'got'. And now she is my absolute champion and gets so caught up in the games she wets herself!

At that match she was asked to give in my club details and the next thing I knew, I was invited to play in an opening ceremony for a brand-new sports complex that was opening in Bournemouth. It was called the Sir David English Sports Centre and I was put into the Dorset Seniors team, who were playing against some of the under-twenty-one England squad, by Liz Scott, a Bournemouth Sports Development Officer.

There were two netball courts at the centre and I can't tell you much about the match itself, other than I just remember feeling so incredibly nervous. There was a balcony where the crowd would look down and watch you and it was full of people. This was the first time I felt a little bit of pressure. There was expectation. Already people were asking why I had been brought in to play; was I good enough to be there? People were intrigued. I wasn't technically old enough for the senior side and I was set to be playing against some very decent players who were well on their way to making the England senior squad. I was fourteen years old and everyone seemed older and bigger and more experienced than me. And if England selectors were watching, what would they think? The worst thing about that match was the watching and waiting. The anticipation. I just wanted to get out on court to see what it was like, to see if I could keep up with the speed of the girls, whether I could get any intercepts or turn over any balls. I look back to those days and think how much my mindset has changed.

I started as goalkeeper and there is no other place on court I will ever want to play, but at the beginning it was all about me. I wanted to go out on that court and be the best I could be. Now I want to go on court and of course still be the best I can, but I am so focused on finding the right teammate to do that with. My goal defence. It is so crucial to be able to work together, to think what the other person is thinking, to shut down the attacking end. Now, it is about getting the best out of my goal defence and adapting my game to suit them so we become a strong defensive unit. I have played with some amazing GDs in my career: Billy Bowers at Team Bath, Sonia Mkoloma at Surrey Storm and England, Mo'onia Gerrard at Thunderbirds, Bianca

Chatfield at Vixens, Karla Pretorius at Lightning; but back then, I wasn't experienced enough in the game to appreciate how vital that was in a team, in a match. I was focused on myself, on making sure I shut down my player, making sure they didn't shoot. It was all about me. But that is youth and inexperience and pure rawness talking. I had come across from the individuality of trampolining and I was still learning the values of a team sport. One good player on the team isn't going to win you a game; you have to work together. So I sat and watched the first three quarters and then they brought me on in the final quarter. Dorset had lost the first three quarters and, as it turned out, had lost the match overall, but in that final quarter, the quarter I played in, we won. I am not saying I made all the difference, but I like to think I made a good impact and I was pleased that I made a difference to the team. I can't remember the actual score but I remember the mood afterwards. Everyone was so positive. One of the local newspapers was there, I think it was the *Bournemouth Echo*, and I was taken onto court for a photo. I had my weird hair back then; I used to have my fringe – well, two bits of hair that looked like antennae – that I would curl down and then I would keep all my frizzy, fuzzy hair tied back behind.

And hair idol or not, there were some pretty important England selectors watching that game and the next thing I knew I was sent a letter asking me along to try out for selection in the under-seventeen England team. The excitement was mixed in with a bit of naivety, I think: this was exciting but what did it mean? What would happen if I was chosen? Mum was probably thinking, 'Oh Jeez, where do I have to drive this girl to now?!' but for me, it was all about the next stage. Of course this was cool but what would I be doing at trials? What was next? Would I still be able to go horse-riding at the weekends?

It's pretty insane, looking back at it now. I was a fresh-faced fourteen-year-old who was fairly new to the game, and I was about to try out for the under-seventeen England netball team. The trials were up at Bath University one weekend and were split into two days. The first day was all about fitness testing, some ball skills and drills, and then the second day was all about match play.

One of the assistant coaches who is with us in the England camp now remembers me clearly from the first time she saw me at trials. Her name is Colette Thomson and she used to play for England herself. One of the fitness tests you had to do was throw a ball against a target on the wall for thirty seconds and see how many passes you could achieve. It was about quick, accurate, strong passes. Colette watched me as I came in and she said she was surprised that I had been put so close to the wall. Because I was so tall for my age, I should have been put at the five-metre mark, but because they had classified me due to my age, I was much closer. A lot of the testing I was smashing because of my height. And I had the strength and ability of some of the older girls but because I was younger, I had to be in the younger age group for testing. I was fourteen, in year nine, but looked and competed as if I was a lot older, which makes a difference.

It's hard to remember exactly how I felt about that weekend. I would have been nervous, like I was with most things, as I put such high expectations upon myself. Like in most new situations, I found it daunting meeting people I didn't know and being in new surroundings. Would people like me? Would I make friends? Most of the other girls knew each other from previous teams and I recognised a few familiar faces too. They were all nice and friendly. But in terms of nerves about what I was doing and what it meant – playing for England – I didn't have any. I love doing new things, I love challenging myself. Mum had signed me up for loads of things when I was younger and this was no different; I just had to go for it. It wasn't like I went that weekend thinking, 'I must get in the England team, my life will be over if I don't.' I approached it how I approach most things – by giving them my best shot and seeing what happens. Little did I know Mum had made friends with Eva Cookey, the mother of Pam Cookey who I was to play with in the England squad until she retired a few years ago. And there was another girl I met there too, Jade Clarke, who is still in the senior squad with me now and is the most-capped England player. But back then we were just three young girls hoping to impress selectors with our netball. Mum told me at lunchtime that she and Eva were chatting over a cuppa and how much they had in common. This process was new to both of them and they discussed how little they knew about netball and how neither of them had any previous interest or involvement in it. Mum was pleased she had found someone to pass the time with – it was a long weekend! – and they soon realised Pam and I were the two youngest girls there, with Pam just two weeks older than me.

After lunch things became quite brutal when the selection process kicked in. We were in the sports hall, with all the parents watching from the balcony, and suddenly we were split into two groups. Mum and Eva both said they initially thought we had been put in the 'thanks but no thanks' group and would be able to go home, but they were wrong. Our group was told we were wanted to stay and continue for the rest of the day and the other group were sent home. There were tears, girls grabbing their coats and storming out, some angry, most upset. That was the end of their trials. But Pam and I were still there. We were so excited but it felt wrong to make a big deal of it while the other girls were so distraught. 'I'm OK,' I thought to myself, 'I'm tired, but I'm OK, I'm still here!' So poor old Mum and Eva had to stay for another few hours with the other parents, while Pam and I went back for more training. Mum has often said to me that you can tell a lot about a player from their parents. Mum's mum and dad gave her free rein to pursue her tennis career and it paid off, but she played against so many kids whose parents, with no knowledge of the sport at all, would be on the edge of the court trying to coach or educate them. She saw so many kids dropping by the wayside because they got fed up of their parents trying to live their lives through them, and so I think from that moment Mum knew when to step up and when to step back. She told me that she had always believed in me and had the belief that, if I enjoyed what I was doing, she should just let me get on with it. As soon as that stops, you have to walk away. It seems so simple but watching some of the reactions from the parents of the girls who were rejected – they were angry and cross – you think, 'Hang on, who is more upset by the rejection?!'

It was a long day and by the end of it, when it was time to face the final cut, I don't think I was nervous about selection at all, I just remember being exhausted! From the sixty girls who started the weekend, forty had been sent home. Now it was just us, the final twenty, and we were going to see who would make the squad of twelve.

The protocol of how they announce a squad has varied greatly in my years for England. Sometimes you are given a letter, sometimes you get a phone call; it depended on the coaching team at the time and how they did things. This was my first experience of the process and, rather than be overwhelmed by it all, I just wanted to know one way or the other. We were all sitting cross-legged on the sports-hall floor, ready to hear our fate. Then in they came, the line of selectors, ready to deliver the news. 'We have seen such fantastic talent this weekend, well done everyone.' This was the start of the motivational speech. 'For those of you who have missed out, this isn't the end of the line,' and then they talked about girls who they wanted to put into a development programme and some they wanted to keep an eye on but who weren't quite ready yet. And then it was time to cut to the chase. 'We will call out the names of people in alphabetical order who have been selected. Please then come up and get your envelope. Congratulations.'

Pam and I sat there waiting and trying to work out if they had gone past our letter in the alphabet. Well, I did – Pam didn't have long to wait with the surname of Cookey. When she got her letter she stood over to the side with the other successful girls with a big grin on her face. I don't think I was concentrating on any name other than mine. I closed my eyes and willed myself to hear that familiar word . . . and then I did. 'Mentor,' they said and I leapt up to get my envelope. It was only then that I looked round to see who the other girls were, standing up next to me with their letters. We had all given it our all this weekend and had all gone through the same experience and now I would be seeing a lot more of my teammates! The letter you got was such a bog-standard letter – it was typed out and then after the word 'Dear' someone had handwritten the names. It was only when I opened the envelope and saw my name that the surreal nature of it sank in. I had made the England under-seventeen squad! Oh my gosh, I had made the England squad!! Mum says she was a little bemused by it all really but I remember that the car journey home, which took us an hour and forty minutes, whizzed by in what seemed like ten minutes because we were so excited! We couldn't stop talking about the weekend and the pure elation we both felt. Mum was delighted, I knew she was. She was so chuffed that – after trying gymnastics, swimming, trampolining, basketball – I could now settle into a sport I seemed destined to play.

Needless to say, when I got home there were lots of phone calls to make! All I wanted to do was sit down and rest and Mum was like, 'Geva, come and speak to Dan Dan,' or, 'Your godparents are on the phone, Geva, come and tell them the news.' Her levels of excitement far surpassed mine at that point, I was just so tired. And I had school the next day!

There wasn't time to sit back and reflect on what had happened that weekend. Everything seemed to move very quickly from the moment of being TalentIDed to playing my first game for the under-seventeen squad. Our first competition was called FENA and it was against Ireland, Scotland and Wales. We were playing in Manchester at the Velodrome, which was still being built for the 2002 Commonwealth Games. The day my England kit came through was the proudest day of my life! It was a second-hand kit from the senior squad but I was just so excited. I was only fourteen and had been playing netball for just over two years and I was representing my country – it was just all so nuts! I look at young girls now coming through the younger squads and rising through the ranks and I don't always pay them much attention or think too much about them. Then I have to remind myself that this was me once, that it meant so much to me then, that it meant so much to my family, just as it does now to the girls forging their own path through England Netball. Mum had arranged a photoshoot with me wearing my England kit, and still has the photo up in her living room. It is, unfortunately, hideous! But I was the proudest teenager you could imagine. The worst part of the kit was the red blazer, which had massive shoulder pads. I am posing on a chair, leaning on the back of it with my hands folded neatly in front and gazing off into the distance with a big smile on my face. It is so cringeworthy! But the fact it is still hanging up in my mum's living room shows how much it meant to the family.

The England under-seventeen experience is a bit of a blur. One of my teammates lived in Southampton and Mum would drive us both up to Manchester for training and matches. I remember one journey when we picked her up and she was buzzing with excitement. Mum and I assumed it was because she was going to represent her country at netball but she was so energised, she told us, because one of her good mates at school had just signed a record deal and she was so happy for him. We were impressed. 'Who is it?' we asked; her excitement was quite contagious. 'His name is Craig David,' she said. Ha!

I was on the team but I was probably third or even fourth goalkeeper in line. There was one girl who I would watch and just think she was amazing. They would call her Velcro fingers and she would just pull in intercepts from everywhere. 'I want to be brilliant just like you,' I thought to myself. 'I want to be able to rip balls in like you, I want to be that sort of defender.'

I did get my chance to show them what I could do too. I got the opportunity to play in every game. I was never a starter – this is when a team, at the beginning of the match, starts with their strong 'starting seven', their best players – but I played a quarter if not a half in every match. They were easy games at the time; Scotland, Wales and Ireland weren't as strong as they perhaps are now and we would win every match by about fifty or sixty goals if not more. Having that time on court meant that I definitely felt I had contributed to the team. I was part of something so cool. It's a spine-tingling moment when you stand on court and watch the England flag being unfolded and held up and then sing the national anthem. I know I have used the word 'surreal' before but it really was! This was just a normal weekend, I would be going back to school on Monday, and yet here I was now, singing 'God Save The Queen'! And that was pretty amazing.

I was fearless on court and yet, in assembly at school that following week, I was so embarrassed. The headteacher, Mr McCaffrey, announced that 'Our year nine sports star, Geva Mentor, represented the under-seventeen England Netball team at the weekend' and I had to walk up on stage as everybody clapped. Our assemblies were held in a theatre and I was so petrified of tripping down the stairs in front of the whole school, or walking up with my skirt tucked into my tights or something. That was fear. Not stepping onto a netball court at fourteen, against bigger, older, more experienced girls. Mr McCaffrey, apart from when he got cross when I came into school with braids and extensions in my hair a year later (something about it not being practical; Mum argued with him about how in Caribbean culture it was a way of taming Afro hair), was the most supportive headteacher I could have asked for. It wasn't like I was going around bragging about it; everyone at the school showed an interest, and so if anyone asked I would tell them. The level of support the school gave me really stepped up after that first tournament, when I started having to leave early two or three times a week for training. One of my PE teachers, David Dunne, who coached the rugby team, was especially encouraging.

You'll have to excuse me if the following account goes past in a bit of a blur, as it certainly did for me. The FENA games were early in 1999, around February time. I didn't realise but at those games was the England Senior Coach at the time, Julie Hoornweg. Lyn Gunson, her assistant who had seen me briefly in Bath, agreed that age shouldn't matter and, knowing I was 'one to watch', sent Waimarama Taumaunu to come and watch me play in a county match. I was playing for Dorset County and the match was against Surrey County but we were only the warm-up game as, after we played, the England under-twenty-one side were scheduled to play the under-twenty-one Jamaica side. Waimarama Taumaunu came early to watch our match and liked what she saw. I was shaking up the game; I was young and fearless and making a big impression against girls who were a lot older. I believe my naivety actually stood me in good stead as well – I didn't overthink things, I just played. Liz Broomfield had got my mum and my PE teacher, Viv Hawkins, tickets to that game and she went over to Mum afterwards. 'Geva is going places,' she said, and both Mum and Viv told me afterwards how they were bursting with pride. It was after this that I was invited to come and train with the under-twenty-one England squad, who were taking part in the World Youth Cup the following year. So we went up to Cardiff and met with the squad, who were all a lot bigger and a lot older than me, and I felt totally out of my depth. But I knew I had been asked to train with the side for a reason and so I just went for it. I met one of my best goal defence partners there, Sonia Mkoloma, who was also to become my best friend off court and would be maid of honour at my wedding years later.

Now, prior to me, fresh-faced and having only recently turned fifteen, training with the under-twenty-ones, England Netball had quite a rigid training and playing set of rules. If you were under seventeen, you played under-seventeen, if you were under twenty-one, you played for the under-twenty-ones. If you were over twenty-one and considered good enough, you went into the senior squad. That is how it worked until Julie, an Australian with her own set of ideas, together with the performance team of Lyn Gunson and Waimarama Taumaunu, changed the

England set-up. They didn't believe age should be a barrier. If you were good enough to play in the senior side, whether you were ten years old or forty years old, you were in the team. And so it was that, after that very brief training session with the under-twenty-ones, Mum got a phone call on Wednesday morning inviting me to come to Loughborough and trial for the England senior squad.

I remember Mum being in such an excited panic as we had to make a quick decision. Was I happy to drop everything, leave school that afternoon, and travel up to Loughborough with Raoul in tow? My reaction? Of course I had to do it; there was no question. And so Mum drove us all up.

Try-outs for the England senior squad were very much like the under-seventeen selection process. They were conducted over two days, with the first day devoted to fitness testing and the second day all about match play. We went into the Sir David Wallace Sports Hall at Loughborough University on that second day to play our games and there was a balcony filled with all the selectors, the coaches, members of the England staff looking down to watch. And instead of being nervous, I felt completely at home. I had no worries in the world. I think Mum's words were ringing through my head – when we were driving up to Loughborough she told me something that her coach had told her when she was playing county squash: you fight for everything, you run down absolutely everything from the off and you stay like that until the dying seconds. You get inside your opponent's head and in those final moments of a game, when they are starting to crumble from having you constantly chipping away at them, you win the game. It isn't just about winning a quarter, it's fighting until the last second and not letting up on your opponent for a single second.

When it came to that match-play day, I played fearlessly and committed to everything. I was young, I was happy to run out of the circle and do flying intercepts and if that meant I would knock someone down accidentally I did, although more because I was Bambi-esque and didn't have full control of my limbs. Obviously I would pull the other player back up again! But I played like I had no fear. I think the selectors must have liked what they saw – this young goalkeeper wasn't afraid of stepping away from the post and coming out of the circle, which wasn't the norm at the time. I let my play do the talking and at those trials in October 1999 they selected me, fifteen-year-old Geva, to form part of their England senior squad. In the space of a year I had gone from getting a place in the under-seventeen squad to playing in an international tournament, to training with the under-twenty-one squad, then getting invited for selection with the England senior team, and finally to being offered a place not just within the England squad but as part of their team of twelve. It had been one hell of a year!

5 EARNING MY STRIPES

'Patience is not simply the ability to wait – it's how we behave while we're waiting.' Joyce Meyer

I F 1999 was a whirlwind of excitement on court, 2000 was going to be a year of watching and learning from the sidelines.

I had been picked for the England seniors and there was a test series in England against Australia that was going to be my first taste of international netball at a senior level with the squad. Australia were the team to beat back then; we knew they would beat us easily, by thirty or forty goals, but the test series was important as you don't improve unless you play against the best. I was so excited just to be part of the squad for those test matches that I don't think I minded that I didn't actually play. The whole experience was about exposure and learning and I'm certainly someone who gains a lot from sometimes sitting back and watching at first.

For all of those three test matches against Australia, being played in England, I sat on the bench and I think I was OK with that. I say that – obviously I would have wanted to get out there and play; I was eager and young and I might not have fully understood what being part of a squad meant back then. It was a rite of passage. You don't just come into the squad and get a game, you have to show you are part of the team. I'm a firm believer now that it isn't just about exposing people to court time, it is letting them earn their position. And that doesn't always come easily. You have to challenge those on the court who are playing in your position and you have to fight to get on; it's what I've come to know is healthy competition. You can't just be handed your caps. It is a valuable lesson you learn that you have to ride the bench, you have to keep it warm, so to speak, and that is an important part of being a netballer and being part of a team. My thoughts were along the lines of, 'I can still make sure I am giving feedback or coaching points to the girls as they come off. I can still tell them what I can see, what is happening on court to improve their game and improve the team performance.' Finding the confidence to give helpful advice to my peers, who were all senior to me, was definitely a daunting experience but an important lesson; if I was confident in what I was saying I shouldn't feel self-conscious.

Sitting on that bench builds character: you learn to contribute, you learn from those around you, you learn to encourage and interact and bide your time. I was OK to be on the bench as I was ecstatic to be in the senior squad. I appreciated what the players were doing, and if they were better than me then they should be the ones on court. We were a team. Of course, Mum wasn't quite so understanding at the time. Her little girl had made the England team and she didn't understand why I wasn't getting a game!

Every test match that series she had brought different members of the family to travel up and watch me play. At the first match she had everyone hold up a piece of paper that would spell out my name, but they were never able to hold them up as I stayed on the bench the whole time. In the second test she came with her friend Pat Mathie and her daughter, Leanne, and things looked promising in the third quarter when the GD, Amanda Newton, was injured and they thought that would be it – I'd be on. But no. In the third test Mum came with six of her cousins and they ended up sitting next to Jill Neville, Tracey Neville's mum. Tracey was playing at the time but, of course, I stayed on the bench in that final match too.

Mum decided to ask Lyn Gunson after that third match why Julie wouldn't bring me on for the last quarter, especially as we were being so badly beaten that it wasn't like it would have mattered to the overall result. And Lyn's answer was simple. It was easy to make the squad of twelve, the difficult part was getting on court. And when you do, you need to make sure you are a starting contender. She also told Mum that the Australian side we were playing were a rough, tough, take-no-prisoners side and she wanted me to experience that game from courtside. She was also watching how I reacted to the game and what motivation I brought to the other players. She knew it was important, Mum now understood its importance, and I definitely feel it taught me something – I was still a vital part of the squad, even if I wasn't on court with the team.

I learned some big lessons that first year, about staying focused and staying positive and knowing that my time would come. It's an important thing to remember when you aren't playing, either through deselection or injury; you just have to bide your time. You're always going to have moments in life where you don't think you are where you should be but you have to have patience. This is something netball has taught me and I guess it applies to any work environment. You didn't get the promotion or someone else got picked for a work project over you, or you feel like you are just going through the motions without ever getting notice. Patience, resilience. Keep doing what you are doing – which you are doing perfectly well – and the opportunities will come. I see so many girls coming through the England set-up, gunning for court time and despondent when they aren't picked, without seeing the advantages of spending time on the bench and learning how to read the game. It's all about self-belief.

* * *

In September 2000 I turned sixteen. 'Forget the piercings, everyone is getting a piercing, G, be a bit different!' Mum was right. I wasn't that fussed about getting more than one hole in my ears but I did want to do something to mark turning sixteen and to commemorate the fact that I was part of the England squad. But what?

And then she came back from the dentist with an idea. Pete Gilfedder, who is also a close family friend as well as a great dentist, had showed her a tooth jewel, a new idea from Scandinavia that required the dentist to glue a sparkly jewel on to a tooth. Mum was convinced that these 'twinkles' were so individual, unique and cool that they summed me up perfectly! Plus she was told they weren't meant to last long so, in Mum's eyes, a perfect solution! I chose a dolphin as I think they are amazing creatures – they seem so free and graceful – plus I've always had an infatuation with the sea, probably from living so close to it. It made sense. Mum was right, it was a nice treat to celebrate a brilliant year. My first one lasted a couple of years, although they are only meant to last a year or so; I lost it after it came out when I bit into an apple. The second one lasted a bit longer but I don't know where that went; I think I might have swallowed it, so we all know where that ended up! And the one I have now has lasted for yonks and I forget that it is even there. People who I have known for ages don't always spot it. Even the other day, a girl who I've been playing against for years was like, 'Oh gosh, I never knew you had a dolphin on your tooth!' My brother thought it was so cool he went and got a scorpion. I quite like the fact that we both have one. It's like our little shared sibling sparkle.

The following year, I was selected again to join the England senior squad as they embarked on a tour of New Zealand and Australia. It was a seven-week tour and I was in the middle of revising for my GCSEs. The school were brilliant; I was to take lots of revision material out with me so I had plenty to work with. Travelling to another country with eleven other girls to represent the country at netball was a pretty unique experience. I wasn't homesick as I had been away before when I was much younger, but I was still relatively young and so I did appreciate having our amazing welfare lady, Margaret Palmer, with us. She was like a second mum to me and took me under her wing and having her there was a comfort; I could concentrate on netball and not be missing Mum and Raoul too much. I knew that this might be the series I would get some court time and I was preparing myself for that. We played a couple of games in Australia to begin with and then moved to New Zealand, where we would be facing the formidable Silver Ferns team. I remained on the bench in that first match but I was conditioned to the idea that this was good for me, this was OK, I was still part of everything that was going on. I had started to read the games really well and made sure that I gave constructive feedback to girls as they came on and off. We moved to a venue in the city of Palmerston North for the second match and things started off the same as any other match day. We would do what is called a 'captain's run' in the morning, when the captain would take us through a warm-up and a few drills. It was our opportunity to familiarise ourselves with the court and the arena as a whole. We wouldn't be back until the evening for the game, so it was important to see and experience the surroundings first. When I say arena, that's a bit misleading – it was like a big farmyard shed or an aeroplane hangar. It was no big fancy venue, it was cold, and there were fold-up chairs round the side and a makeshift court right in the middle. But this was New Zealand and they loved their netball and so we all knew the crowd would be bloody vocal! At the start of the captain's run we got into a huddle and we all put our hands in the middle. Something didn't feel right to me. 'Where's Chioma?' I said, looking round. She was one of the girls on the team and she wasn't here . . . we had basically hopped on the two buses that morning without checking we were all on board! We had to get someone to call the hotel and go back and collect Chioma and bring her to the court. I remember it well, it was quite funny in the end but, for a split second, a bit of a panic! The main reason I remember details like this from that day was that this was to be my first match; I would get my first cap for England on that day, 11 July 2001. I can't remember exactly how the announcement for the starting seven was done that day. This lack of specifics probably reflects the way I am: I just take things in my stride as they happen. It varies from game to game and from coach to coach. You some-times get told the night before, sometimes it is in the morning on the day of the match, and sometimes it is when you are in the changing rooms an hour or so before you are about to go on court. I can't remember, that first time, when exactly I was told I would be part of the starting seven. But what I can remember from my first cap was the line-up before the game, standing there, arm in arm, singing the national anthem with my teammates. Before we started to sing, there was lots of whispering from the line: 'Look!' came the whisper, 'the All Blacks!' and we all turned to see the New Zealand rugby team coming in to watch. Apparently one of the players was dating one of the Silver Ferns players, Anna Rowberry, and so the whole team had come to watch the game. It was very surreal as they are like rock stars in New Zealand! Then the national anthem kicked in and we all got serious. After singing you head to your position on court ready for the umpire's whistle, but just before that, in this sport, the first thing you do is greet your opposition player. This is the person who, for the next fifteen minutes, you will be trying your utmost to upset and disrupt. Some players do a quick high-five or a handshake. But I knew who I was up against, a legend in netball, and back then one of the most capped international players of all time: Irene van Dyk. Irene was born in South Africa and moved to New Zealand in 2000, the year I was earning my stripes. She was a dominant force for the Silver Ferns for many years and is regarded as one of the best goal shooters in the world. Even though she was such an icon I wasn't intimidated or frightened about coming up against her. When I went over to greet her she just put out her arms and pulled me in for a giant hug. Then she kissed me on the cheek. Well, I wasn't expecting that! And then all of a sudden the whistle went and the ball got thrown into the circle and I came across with an outside hand and managed to get a tip, my outside mid-courter collected it and we went down the other end. Then it was our centre pass, then it was their centre pass, and then the ball came down our end and I ran out and got a deflection, which I gathered to intercept, just outside the circle. And then the ball went down our end and I don't think we scored – I remember in those England days, our goals percentage was a lot lower as we struggled to convert most times – and then the ball came back down to us defenders again.

I can't remember if I stayed on for the whole thing but I remember those first couple of minutes of the first match I ever played for the England senior squad, nearly twenty years ago. I was playing elite international netball against one of the best players in the world and I did my job. I am a goalkeeper, I am the last line of defence, my job is to disrupt the opposition's attack end and I did just that. I got my hands to the ball, I turned it over for the team. I think we went on to lose by about thirty-six goals but it wasn't quite one of the forty-goals losses that we had had before. And the next game, they started with me again and we only lost by twenty-two goals . . . I know it is still a loss but you've got to find the positives – the margin was decreasing! I gained my first cap in rural New Zealand against the world number-one shooter, against the Silver Ferns team, who were number two in the world and, I have to say, it was pretty cool.

I had the realisation that I was properly part of the team now. There was no official cap, medal or certificate, just a card from my team and some flowers, but that was special as it confirmed all the training, all the time I had spent on the sidelines, and now I really felt I was part of the twelve-woman squad. It was an incredible feeling for a sixteen-year-old!

Unfortunately, until you get on court and experience that first taste of elite netball, you don't truly feel like you are contributing and what part you play in the team. No matter how inclusive your teammates are, it is very difficult in netball as there are the seven or eight who are always on court and then there are the four or five girls who are always on the bench. Those of you on the bench start to form a sort of 'clique' – no, that's the wrong word . . . you form a bond. You form a bond because you go through an exhilarating adrenaline-filled experience for anything from fifteen to sixty minutes. It is difficult not playing. I've been there, I know. While everyone who has just come off court does their cool-downs, you have to go on and do drills, shuttles, all sorts of training as everyone is exiting the stadium. You have to push yourself to fatigue to keep the training load the same as the ones who have played. It almost feels like a punishment. It's obviously not but it's the last thing you want to do as, although you weren't physically out there, you've just gone through the emotions of the game and it feels like you were playing and you're exhausted. So as much as being on the bench is part of the learning, it is difficult. I knew and appreciated what it was like for the girls on the bench who don't necessarily get on to court and I know how important it is to make sure they still feel part of the team. It's funny how for me, after my match with Irene, I felt: 'Yes, I am contributing to this team now.' Contributing in a way I thought I was better at, through playing, not coaching.

I had ticked all the other boxes and this was the final one: I was on court and playing, which at the end of the day was what we were here to do. The buzz the next day, after my first match, was amazing. We went to Queenstown, if I remember rightly, and the scenery was just breathtaking. They love their netball in New Zealand and the local paper wanted to do a story on me. Apparently the youngest netballer playing for her country was news! I say this because netball didn't have any real profile in the UK at the time. A photographer came out and took some pictures of me while the rest of the girls were getting ready inside for a court session. We went outside and I had a backdrop of the Remarkables, a beautiful mountain range. And the photographer set me up for some leaping shots, so there I am jumping, posing, being photographed in this stunning country for a newspaper that wants to tell everyone how I played on court. I had never experienced any sort of media interest before then and, I have to say, it was pretty cool! And then the next day or the day after there was an article in the paper and a really nice photo. I bought a few copies and I sent the article to Mum as I knew how much she wanted to have been there for my first game. But not only were the flights expensive, it was a long tour and Raoul was still in school. We talked a lot on the phone so that was cool, and although it was sad not to have Mum and Raoul there I was able to fill them in on everything that happened. And on how I was probably just as excited that the All Blacks came to watch our game as I was at getting my first cap! I still have the photos and the article from the paper too; I have kept it in a scrapbook. I've also kept a 'cap' book, a record of all the games I have played for England. I record the date, where we played, the score, the starting seven and the girls in the team. I am the only one keeping a record, I think, but when I retire and get presented with a nice red, leather-bound cap book, I will get someone to write up all the details beautifully.

Travelling with eleven other girls meant that you didn't ever get the chance to really feel homesick or lonely. There was always someone to chat to or do something with. It was a bit like having a netball family. All of the girls wanted to make the most of visiting New Zealand, so they would plan sightseeing excursions around our training and matches to make the most of being over here. This, however, did not apply to me. I had to study for my GCSEs, so while the others went off for their fun adventures I was a good girl and took myself off to the physio room, where a little desk had been set up for me to revise. Glamorous, eh?! But it was one of the stipulations of me being allowed to join the team on tour – I wasn't allowed not to complete my GCSEs. And I did have special dispensation for some of the exams. I didn't have to sit many; for a lot of my subjects, grades were taken from previous assignments and classwork. I think I only took two or three exams in the end. I did OK in them – well, maths wasn't great but the rest of the subjects were Cs or above with an A* for PE. And you'd bloody well think so considering my involvement in and understanding of sport! All in all my GCSE results were not bad for someone trying to train, play at the elite level, study and still be a teenager all at the same time!

I didn't just come back home with my first England match experience under my belt, I somehow managed to come home with a fridge-freezer too! Every time we went to play for New Zealand – and I gathered this right from the first tour – their hospitality was pretty awesome. After every game, you have your recovery session and then normally have a dinner. I remember going up to a conference room after the final game. It was a chance for both teams to chat and then the captains would do their speeches. This time they had arranged for a fun game to be played and they wanted everyone to join in. They had set up this big washing machine, a top-loading one, in the room and the competition was that you had to 'shoot' a netball into it. Every time you got a ball in you would go through to the next round and it was only a bit of fun but everyone got into the spirit of things. So it was England versus New Zealand again and this time there was no one on the bench – the team physios, the coaches, the doctors, everyone tried to launch the ball into the washing machine. Now, I am not sure if I've mentioned this but there is a good reason I am goalkeeper and not goal shooter. I'm the twelfth shooter in line on the team and, honestly, I am OK with that. I knew from the moment I started playing netball that I was a defender. I haven't ever wanted to play in any other position other than defence; it is where I am, it is who I am. Each person on the team fits into their role and I have always had a defensive mindset. I started off as goal defence at school because that's kind of where I just got put. When I moved up divisions and played for better teams and better opposition they moved me back to goal-keeper as I was quite tall and I was able to handle the taller shooters.

You sometimes come across defenders who have been given a go at shooting by their coach – Ama Agbeze is a classic example; she was a goal defence, moved to a shooter and then back to defender – but I am pleased to say that has never happened to me. I am quite happy where I am. I have played some training games where you rotate through the positions but I bottle it when it comes to shooting. You see, everyone on the team has different personality traits, which is why they fit into their positions. What you are like on court is very much a reflection of how you are in life. Defenders? You tend to find us quite laid-back, quite chilled. We won't take life too seriously, we like to have a bit of fun. Midis – the mid-court players – they are the engines of the team. They will go, go and go again. They are the real workhorses of the side, and they are often the bubbly, big personalities of the team. And then you have the shooters, who tend to be known as the princesses of the team. If the ball doesn't feel right to them they'll want to change it. If the ball doesn't feel right to us we're just like, 'Oh well, who cares, let's get on with it!'

Shooters can be very high-maintenance and like everything to be a certain way. But I won't knock that trait as when the pressure is on they're the ones who have to put the ball in the ring. I guess you have to be a bit like that because it sometimes comes down to the finest detail about whether you are going to make that shot or not – how the ball comes off your fingers, how your body positioning is, what happens around you. You have to have that attention to detail as a shooter, you have to have that picky mentality. They are also a bit cocky and a bit arrogant but they are playing in an under-pressure position – all eyes are on them, the crowd are on the edge of their seats, they have just one final shot of the game to win a match . . . so of course they need that self-belief that they are going to make the shot. They really do have nerves of steel but, in essence, they're definitely a different breed to the rest of us – says every defender!

So, back to how terrible I am at shooting. I expect the majority of the people in that room thought that Irene van Dyk would be the one heading home with a new fridge-freezer, so no one was taking it too seriously. Everyone seemed to be doing a netball-type shot into the washing machine so I went for the underarm, between-your-legs type lob instead. And it went in! I was chuffed not to be out first time and so waiting for another go. There were still a handful of people on each side and I went round again and I got it in again! Then it was only me and a New Zealand physio left in the competition. She lined up like before, the washing machine a good five metres away. She took her shot and missed and I took my shot and got it in. Just like that, I had won! It was completely surreal and no one in the room, including me, would have ever predicted it.

I rang Mum afterwards and was like, 'Mum! I've just won a fridge-freezer!', to which her reaction was something like, 'Where's that going to go then, Geva?' She didn't get the excitement at all at the time, but it is still in her house, this big stainless steel Fisher & Paykel fridge-freezer, on the upstairs landing, and I know she has found it useful for all the students to use. I got asked after I had won it whether I wanted the doors to open to the left or to the right and I was like, 'Erm, I'm sixteen years old, I have no bloody idea!'

It was quite cool to think that all this was happening while I was still at school. My GCSEs done, I was now studying for A levels – and playing for England. As well as my headteacher giving me the best support at school, my PE teacher, Patrick Lucas, was the most encouraging person I have ever met. He was an ex-London Irish rugby player who had had to stop playing for them in the nineties after a serious injury. We just hit it off straight away. He had motivated me quite early on and helped me follow the training schedule that England Netball had put together for me. It was quite an intense programme and he didn't let me just 'tick off' each section, he really made sure I did it with extra intensity, extra passion, extra quality. He also made up some drills for me; he wanted to push me to see the benefits of training hard and training well. I learned a lot from him and he understood me too. He had a real understanding of what it meant to play at an elite level. He gave me the advice that he had been given when he was playing rugby, which was always to look out for myself. 'No one is going to look after your body but you,' he said, 'you are literally just a plate of meat and you need to make sure you look after yourself because if you get injured, don't think there won't be ten other girls ready to step in and take your place.' It was sound advice that I probably didn't appreciate at the time but as I get older I certainly do. I helped him one summer with a rugby clinic he ran, and worked with the rugby schoolboys on ball-handling, as rugby and netball have lots of transferable skills when it comes to handling and spatial awareness. He knew that playing these rugby games would only improve my skills on the netball court.

But even though I was benefiting from having such a dedicated trainer, I decided at Christmas that I needed to put myself in the best possible position of being selected for the England team for the Commonwealth Games the following year. They were being held in Manchester and although I had a good chance of being in the squad, it was never a forgone conclusion. I had to show how serious I was about being part of the team and that meant joining the training sessions with England coach Lyn Gunson in Bath. And so I did just that: Mum would drive me up to Bath twice or even three times a week. Raoul would join us on occasion and we'd just sit back and play silly games while Mum spent the best part of her week driving. She would never complain about it either and I didn't appreciate how tiring driving could be until I learned to drive and made that journey myself a bit later.

The training sessions were quite nerve-wracking, if I am totally honest. I was nervous, never sure of what they would involve. My skill level wasn't as polished as it is now and I was so focused on trying to do my best, not drop balls, not be the weak link. I was training with girls who all had a bit of experience behind them but they were all nice and encouraging to me. There was a school we used to train at, Monkton Coombe, which was really dark and dingy. The sessions were tough – I am happy to admit I found them quite intense – but it was fun. I used to treat myself to something from the vending machines afterwards as a treat. Like a little reward for the challenging sessions! But at no point did I think I couldn't do this. There was never any doubt about me continuing, or any thinking, 'Yeah, this isn't really for me after all.' I have never felt like I couldn't accomplish something or go through with something when I put my mind to it and focus. And I was focused.

Of course, there are always some things that have to give and that was stuff back at St Peter's. If everyone else was talking about the end-of-year graduation prom, for example, what they were going to wear, who'd be going with who, I would just sit and listen knowing that I was going to miss that. But then again, I still thought what I was doing was pretty cool. I was going along to high-performance training, England training; the prestige of that outweighed school social events for me and although it did suck to miss out, it's all part of the sacrifice that young athletes often speak about.

And leaving school at lunchtime while everyone still had an afternoon of lessons to come was always quite cool. Waving to my mates as I left. 'Where you going, Geva?' was the normal shout. 'Gotta go England training!' would be my grinning response. I felt like I gained a lot of respect from other pupils and teachers as it was unheard of at the school, a pupil playing for England, so in a sense I was probably treated a bit like a star. It made me blush, and I like to think I was usually quite modest, but if not Mum would bring me right down to earth. She definitely kept me grounded. 'You're a small fish in a big pond' was her favourite saying. And she was right. Yeah, it was cool, I had played for England. So what?! Now I had to crack on and prove I deserved a place on the team. So I had no chance of feeling too smug for too long! The training was also no place for bragging. Lyn's training sessions were full on and I had it hammered into me every time: 'Do not cut corners, Geva!' It was her favourite thing to say but it sank in – there was no substitute for hard work and practice.

After about three months it was clear that driving up and down to training so many times a week wasn't the most time-effective way, and so it was agreed that I would stay up in Bath for the week instead. Mum would drive me up to Bath on a Sunday evening and I'd stay with Lyn for the week until Mum collected me on the Friday morning. I would then go straight into school and hand in all the coursework I had done that week and get more work from the teachers for the following week. I was studying for my A levels, living away from home, and training three times a day for England Netball selection.

I probably didn't much appreciate my teachers at the time but, bloody hell, when I look back at the preparation and time they gave me, I am beyond grateful. They would often stay late after school and meet me in the detention room with all the so-called naughty kids to go through work that I had missed and stuff I was going to miss the following week. So not only did they make sure I had all the right material and study sheets, they would have had to prepare what they were teaching the following week in class in order to give it to me the Friday before. Credit to those teachers – Mike Spackman, thank you!

My time in Bath wasn't that fun, to be honest. I was staying with the coach, after all, and you can imagine how on edge that would make you. I was young, I wasn't at home, and I didn't feel I could relax. Home should be a place where you can switch off and forget about training or netball, which is a bit hard to do when you are living with the England Netball coach! However uncomfortable I might have felt, Lyn's comments had the best intentions. She wanted to make me a better athlete, a better student, a better person . . . I just didn't fully appreciate it as a teenager!

So my week would pretty much run like this: Monday to Thursday I would train early in the mornings, then when I had finished I would go to the library and do some school-work. Then there would be more training in the afternoon before I would head back to Lyn's house and study some more in the evening. She lived at the bottom of this really steep hill, Claverton Down, and she used to tell me that if I wanted a lift up the hill for training I would have to be ready to leave at 4.30 a.m. Or I could walk it and get an extra hour in bed and get away with leaving at 5.30 a.m. So some mornings I would try to get a lift; it meant a horribly early start but at least I didn't have to climb what seemed like Everest with a backpack full of books and training gear. Other mornings I was like, 'Screw it, I can cope with the walk, I want another hour in bed!' But oh my goodness, that walk. I used to come up with some ingenious ways to get up the hill in my head while I was stomping up it with what seemed like the heaviest bag in the world. I could stick out my thumb and try to hitchhike, or if I'd had a skateboard I could have tied a rope round a car's bumper and got pulled up! Anything to take my mind off walking up the hill! So that was a pretty intense time but I knew it would ultimately be worth it. If working hard meant I could secure a place in the Commonwealth Games for later that year, I would do all that I could.

And in June that year, I was named one of the twelve in the squad. All the hard work had paid off.

6 COMING OF AGE AT THE COMMONWEALTH GAMES

'We have picked the people who are playing the best netball in the country at the moment.'

Waimarama Taumaunu,
England Netball Performance Director

WHEN I first got into the England squad, netball was Lottery-funded and one of the programmes we had was called Sporting Champions. The idea was that elite athletes or well-known local or national sporting heroes would go out and visit kids in schools and sports clubs and community centres to tell them their story. Sometimes I think children believe you wake up in an England kit and don't always see that we started off just like them with only ambition and dreams, so it was great to chat to lots of different children about our pathway and give advice or motivation for theirs. I would talk about my netball training, what I would go through day to day, how I got into the sport, what other sports I enjoyed doing. I loved being involved in this campaign; this was exactly what I enjoyed most, motivating and enthusing the younger generation. I was still only young myself and so I think I made a real connection with the majority of the kids I had the pleasure to meet. I was happy to travel all over the south coast and even caught a ferry over to the Isle of Wight one day to speak to children at a school over there. I enjoyed sharing my story. What I did was bigger than just me, and if I could inspire people or give them a glimpse of all the things I did, that was cool. Not that I was expecting them to take everything on board but at the end of the day it might give them some insight, it might help them find a way, help them on their journey. Sometimes hearing from someone who has done everything you want to do and has turned out OK does help, whether they would ultimately go down the sporting path like me or whether I just gave them ideas about how to balance things at school or maintain relationships with friends.

I was no public speaker, though, and at the time I didn't have my story down; I just spoke from the heart about things I had experienced, difficulties I had come across, the exciting people I had met. Kids seem to get that. I have a lot of time for youngsters; it's probably why I decided to start studying for a teaching degree. I would always go back to my old school when I had the chance and help out in a PE lesson or something. It was nice to give something back. The point I think I am trying to make is that while I was living and breathing netball and focusing on my career and on playing for England, there was a whole new generation about to embark on the same thoughts and decisions and possibilities that I had faced and I thought it was important to show them the same encouragement and support that I got.

The announcement that I had made the squad for the 2002 Commonwealth Games in Manchester came in June. After training us hard in Bath for the previous five months, Lyn took the England team on an intensive seven-match ten-day tour in Australia. Timing-wise for the team, it was perfect to get some good match practice in against the reigning champions as well as two of the top National League teams.

I had been playing netball for Team Bath since I started training and living with Lyn. It was one of the top premiership teams in the South West. Before that I had been with Team Surrey and before that East Dorset Counties. After my first game with the senior England side I was told I had to play for a higher division than the one I was in with Bournemouth, in my home county. We were playing in Division Five and thrashing anyone who came up against us. England Netball told me I had to be playing in Division One or Two and no lower. One of the ladies on the England team, Lyn Carpenter, was playing for Surrey at the time and she took me under her wing a bit and encouraged me to join Surrey, which I did for a season. It was a bit of a trek, travelling to Epsom once a week, and I don't know if I just didn't enjoy it because of the journey or if I just didn't like it, but I didn't think long about joining Team Bath – it helped that my friend Pam Cookey was also part of the team – and Gloucestershire was to be my new county team. I later moved over to HNC, Hucclecote Netball Club, with Gloucestershire, as they were in Division One. Everything was just slowly finding its place, everything went into some sort of order without being too overwhelming for me or my family.

Team Bath actually had three players selected to form part of a 'development squad', a team that would be available in the training camp two weeks prior to the Games. It was their job to provide competition for the teams who would be playing in the Games and were looking for final match-play opportunities. The development squad also acted as training partners for the England team and it was great to see some teammates and girls from other clubs having that opportunity to play against the best in the world before the big event.

There was a real buzz in Manchester leading up to the Games. We were there prior to the opening ceremony and I remember wandering around the city, checking out the shops, as we mostly did in our free time during camp. On a rare afternoon off from training, I was out and about with Amanda Newton, Sonia Mkoloma and a few other girls when we bumped into Tracey Neville's brother. Tracey is my current England coach and was one of my teammates back then, and it was her older brother Gary we saw, the famous Manchester United footballer. Tracey is from a great sporty family; as well as Gary there is her twin Phil, who is also a former Premier League and England footballer. Gary is particularly close to one of his former teammates, David Beckham, and both lads are very well-known in the area, having played football for Manchester United and England. That afternoon we hadn't officially entered the athletes' village yet and we just wanted to leave the hotel and stretch our legs a bit and get some fresh air. So there we were, just wandering around the shops, and we bumped into Gary. We started chatting about the upcoming Games and he asked us how we were feeling. He was very chatty and interested in what we thought our chances were. And to be honest, I think we were a bit bemused that he would just wander around and not get hounded by a million fans.

'I'm normally all right,' he said, 'but this one over here,' pointing to David Beckham, 'stands out like a sore thumb!' And we all turned and there was David, less than two metres away, in a bright red cap and bright red trainers. It was so funny. There was no way he wasn't going to get noticed, he was like a beacon! But he was equally friendly and encouraging and it was a surreal but cool moment for us. Gary and Phil were very supportive of their sister and Gary would often come along to international matches to cheer Tracey on, bringing his pal David on more than a few occasions.

And then it was time to experience my first Commonwealth Games. The first of five Games, as it would turn out, but at the time I had never experienced anything like it before and it was beyond exciting. Manchester had been preparing for this for a couple of years and the atmosphere was unreal; there was a real thrill about playing on home turf and the anticipation was high. England had won a bronze medal at the previous games in Kuala Lumpur four years ago and half the team playing this year had been part of that squad, including Tracey. Pam and I were in the team and there was a bit of a buzz about us, two seventeen-year-old girls hoping to make an impact. I remember seeing an interview with Waimarama Taumaunu when she was asked about the squad, which mixed the experienced girls with us newbies. 'We have picked the people who are playing the best netball in the country at the moment,' she said, and I was proud that that included me! I really felt part of the squad and I knew I would be getting some action on court even though I wouldn't be part of the starting seven. I was probably the third of four defenders in line but that would mean some court time. England Netball would normally work tournaments by having a strong starting seven play for at least half the game before they would bring on fresh legs and rest the top players for after the group stages, when the serious business really began. It gave everyone a good amount of court time and you weren't tiring out all your starting seven. We had Canada, Sri Lanka, Wales and New Zealand in our group and we felt all would be easy wins except the world number-two team, the Silver Ferns.

My godmother and Mum's best friend Jackie lives in North Wales so Mum stayed over with her and did the commute in to see our games. She was there for the whole thing, and it was great as she actually got to see me play for England this time!

The opening ceremony was on 25 July and our first game was the following day against Canada. We then faced Sri Lanka on 27 July, Wales on the 28th and New Zealand on the 29th.

The athletes' village, where all the athletes in the Games slept and ate and prepared, was just unbelievable. Someone once described it as the best all-inclusive holiday you can ever go on and that was exactly what it felt like. Everything was free, so you'd walk around and there'd be little food stalls and vending machines and you could just help your-self to stuff. And then in the main food hall there were different stalls set up with food from all over the world. So you took your pick as to what national cuisine you fancied – Indian, Asian, British, Italian . . . it was just mind-blowing.

People call the Commonwealth Games the 'friendly games' and you can see why. Everyone is very happy and sociable and giving lots of smiles – at least before the compe-titions start. You pass nations who are playing in other events and wave and say; 'Hi! How are you?' But when you spot another netballing team, you try to get your game face on and give them a serious look. I should point out, however, that nowadays I have either played or am still playing with girls from other countries, so not only do I stop and say hello, I'm usually there for a good half an hour having a natter!

Being part of Team England was pretty incredible. You weren't just this tight-knit netball family any more; there was a huge extended family here ready and waiting to encourage and support and cheer you on. You were more than a netball team, you were part of Team England and you were wearing the kit with pride. Whenever you walked around and spotted someone else with the same gear you gave a little head-nod, a smile, an acknowledgement of this powerhouse you were now part of. It was one of the most memorable things I took from the Games, that feeling of being appreciated as an athlete by other athletes in this amazing family. And being on home soil gave Team England an extra boost; this was our territory, we walked around with an extra air of confidence. This was home to us. Good luck to everyone else. That isn't to say that walking around among some of the most iconic sporting heroes you have seen on the TV at the Olympics wasn't mind-blowing. It was incredible to think you could bump into a world-famous athlete in the same food hall or wandering around the village. That feeling doesn't go either; each Commonwealth Games is the same, the same appreciation that you are in the presence of athletes at the top of their game in their chosen sport, and it is truly memorable. I would love to see netball recognised as an Olympic sport – to bring it to a bigger audience, put it on a bigger stage, would be phenomenal. I know it probably won't happen in my playing career but perhaps it will in my lifetime. I think the major problem is that there are too many sports already part of the Olympics and it's only really played by women. At the 2000 Sydney Olympics there was talk of it being included as Australia were the world champions, but the other three big Olympic nations, America, Russia and China, didn't play it at an elite level and until they do it is unlikely to be included. Any athlete would love their sport to be in the Olympics so it is frustrating. But for the time being, the Commonwealth Games was proving to be a magical experience.

Team England headquarters were very impressive; we had our own little apartment complex. There was a main entrance area as you walked in and then each sport had their own little apartments and sections. There was a guy on the reception who would send you in the right direction for laundry or for the massage rooms. He sat behind a big desk and forgive my youthfulness but I remember that on that desk was a massive vase. I thought there were sweets in it at first and it was only when I went right up for a look at what sort of sweets that I realised it was full of colourful condoms! 'Right, OK,' I thought. 'That is why it's called the friendly games!' It wasn't embarrassing, it was more just so funny that there was this ginormous vase in the Team England reception for everyone to see and help themselves from! And in the second week of the Games, in the vending machines that had previously been giving out Gatorade, soft drinks and water there were now bottles of beer. I was shocked! I would like to say here that the other Games I have been to haven't been anything like this. There was no massive vase of johnnies on display; if you wanted protection you had to ask for it. It does seem weird, doesn't it, like something from the seventies! It wasn't something I told Mum – she didn't need to know there was free beer and contraception!

There was another surreal moment for me when the Queen came to visit the athletes' village during the competition. I am a huge fan of hers and the royal family; in fact, I have a bit of an obsession with the monarchy, and so seeing her in real life was a massive deal for me. As I am sure it would be for anyone! Word went round that she was there and that she was in the food hall and then, of course, everyone in the village wanted to try to get to see her and it was a massive scramble. I managed to get within about five metres of her and to see her in person was so exciting. She was tiny. She only had a few delegates with her and she was looking and smiling at everyone. Her being there was an extra-magical moment. I think I have become more of a royalist since living in Australia because they absolutely adore the royal family over there. I love the history, I love the traditions; I find it all so fascinating and so you can imagine my pure excitement of being just a few feet away from the Queen of England!

But back to the Games themselves. England had a bit of expectation around them; we had won bronze four years ago, would we be able to match that or go one or two better with the home crowd behind us? Sadly not. We performed as expected in the group stages, beating Wales, Canada and

Sri Lanka quite comfortably before losing to New Zealand, which meant we finished second in our group. We then had to compete in the play-offs between the four teams that finished second and third in the two groups. We played South Africa, who had come third in their group, and Jamaica played Wales, who had finished third in our group. We managed to hold our own against South Africa, the SPAR Proteas, beating them 55–40. And then it was time for the semi-finals. The mood in the team was positive but we were up against Australia, the reigning champions, and we lost by nearly ten goals. We ended up losing in the bronze medal play-off against Jamaica too, by two goals. That was hard. We were so close yet not quite there. Although we came away from those Commonwealth Games with nothing, I had a mind full of incredible memories. It might have been youthful ignorance or determination or a fire in my belly but I vowed that this wasn't going to be my only Commonwealth Championship. I was seventeen years old and hungry for better results.

We were back in Australia and New Zealand later that year on another tour and test-match series. It stands out in my memory because we met with the England rugby team while we were in New Zealand. It was the year before they won the World Cup and it was just so cool meeting the likes of Jonny Wilkinson and Martin Johnson. I have a great deal of respect for rugby players, maybe in part thanks to my PE teacher Patrick but also due to the incredible pressure they put on their bodies and how they just knuckle down and get on with their games. They have a job to do and they do it. The England rugby team is a bit like the netball team; there is a bit of national interest in it but nothing on the same level as football. I think this works well for us and them – we both just get on with things. We have a job to do, we want to do it well. I was on a netball court in England the following year playing a match when it was announced that England had won the rugby World Cup. There was a massive cheer as the news came over the tannoy! Then we just carried on, buoyed by the victory.

The year 2003 was a big one for the England rugby team in the World Cup but would we have the same result in our World Championship? It was being held in Kingston in Jamaica for ten days from 10 July. I had the small matter of completing my A levels first, however, and – as always – it wasn't straightforward for me. I was with the England squad on a test series in New Zealand when I was due to sit my exams and so while all my mates were back home in England, all sitting round nervously together in the sports hall, I was in New Zealand sitting nervously with six or seven strangers from all over the world, all doing their own exams, in a small classroom at the university.

It was all very expertly done; the school had posted the sealed envelope with my exam in and the envelope was opened in front of me to show it hadn't been tampered with. I only did two A levels, geography and sports studies, not the more usual three. I did originally start with three but I had to drop one in the second year. It was too much trying to fit in study and travelling and training and something had to give. So on this day, all the other girls on the team were out sightseeing or shopping or having lunch somewhere and there was me, sitting in a strange classroom about to sit my A level exams. But I did it, and I am pleased I did.

England Netball took the build-up to the World Championships very seriously. They wanted us to be as prepared as we possibly could be as we were playing in Jamaica in July, in extremely hot conditions. It was decided that we should train at the University of Hertfordshire in Hatfield as they had a heat chamber we could use. They had exercise bikes in the heat chamber and so we'd take it in turns, in groups of about five or six, to go in, use the bikes and do passes against the wall before swapping over. We did heaps of work in that heat chamber, making sure we did all we could to prepare ourselves for the climate of Jamaica. We took it very seriously and when we went home after the training we were advised to use our local saunas too so we could keep ourselves acclimatised. I went along to the David Lloyd gym round the corner from Mum's house and used the sauna. I took with me a list of exercises they had given us – ten squats, ten sit-ups, fast-feet running on the spot – all designed to lift our heart rates in a humid environment.

And the coaches kept drumming into us about keeping ourselves hydrated; we must keep drinking all the time. England Netball even invested in these ice vests for us to wear. They were a bit like buoyancy aids but they were full of ice packs, and you'd put them over your dress. They would help to cool down our body temperature and the aim was to put them on between quarters.

When it came to flying out to Jamaica you could say we felt pretty prepared for the temperature and how our bodies would cope with playing in the heat. We weren't exactly smug but we felt like we had done our homework and it wouldn't be our surroundings that would let us down. You can imagine our faces when we turned up at the sports arena for our first match and it was bloody freezing because of the air-conditioning! Seriously, what a waste of time all that intense heat training had been! We actually found it quite funny – we were expecting it to be an oven and we end up freezing our tits off! It sort of summed up England Netball at that point. I shared a room with Sonia Mkoloma, who was GD to my GK. The first night a bloody fruitbat somehow got into our room and we couldn't get it out! I can laugh about it now, but it was traumatic at the time and neither of us got any sleep.

It was another disappointing championship for us as we came fourth. Having made it through our group stages, we played against South Africa in the quarter-finals and Sonia and I were working well as a defensive partnership, turning over the ball and sending it back down the other end, but our error rate as a team was high, simple passing and catching mistakes or missed shots. It was so frustrating; we had our hearts set on the semi-finals and playing against Australia and we were struggling to get the finish. Australia, New Zealand, England and Jamaica were considered the top four teams in the world and the other three seemed to be doing what was expected of them but we were struggling. I remember distinctly one passage of play, in the final quarter of that game. The scores were neck and neck – well, South Africa might have been up by one goal – and Sonia and I had managed to turn over the ball and send it back down our end. Someone threw it to our goal shooter and it went right through her hands and off the back line. That's the thing with shooters, when a game goes right they take all the glory but when it goes wrong, the finger of blame is pointed directly at them. Sonia pounded the ground with both hands, shouting her head off in frustration. It was a frustration I felt too, of course, but we had to keep our heads in the moment and keep providing opportunities. Sonia and I were a formidable team and eager to show that we were potential starters for the team. We had been working on our defence partnership once a week in Brunel before this championship and I remember saying to her as she took her annoyance out on the court, 'It's OK, Sonia, we can get it back, it's our game.' You have to have that belief, that fighting-to-the-end spirit, especially as a defender, because quite often games are lost in the final quarter, in those dying moments as the players start to lose momentum. Sonia and I were both fighting for every second, as were all the girls on court at the time, and I just needed to remind her of this. 'Just be cool, this is what we love to do, we love to turn over the ball.'

It didn't help that the lights went off in that game as well. You couldn't make it up. Jamaica were playing Australia on the other court and I think the rumour was that someone had done this on purpose to help the Jamaicans. We don't know if it was planned or not but the lights went off for a period of time and when they finally came back on – they were on a generator so it took a good five minutes for it to all kick back in again – there was a dispute over where play should start again. It was all a bit controversial but we ended up winning by the skin of our teeth – but then went on to lose against Australia 37–45 in the semi-final. That led us to face the host nation in the bronze medal match and I ended up coming on in the third or fourth quarter as their goal shooter was just destroying us. I was pleased to have got on court but we ended up losing that match too. We just weren't quite firing on all cylinders yet, we weren't clicking as a team. I remember watching Australia and New Zealand play each other in the final and it was an epic battle. The Silver Ferns centre got sent off for too many contacts or too many offsides and was off the court for about two minutes. The score was neck and neck at that point and when she came back on, she stole some balls and New Zealand ended up winning. It was such an amazing game to watch. This was the level I wanted to play at. It was phenomenal to watch those girls in action; I was in awe.

After the World Cup disappointment I took part in some county matches with Gloucestershire and test matches in Loughborough. I was preparing for the 2005 World Youth Cup, which is basically the same as the World Cup but for the under-twenty-one squad. Having played for the senior squad in the World Cup, I was now scheduled to play for the under-twenty-ones too and get familiar with my team-mates. I was nineteen years old and netball had taken over my life completely. I had finished my studies, I was doing a bit of work for Dorset's Sports Council as a sports rep coach and it all fitted in nicely around training.

Each year I would have to try out for the England squad. They often say it's hard to make the squad, harder to make the team, and even harder to make the court, and it's true. Each time you go in front of the selectors it is around my birthday in September. And again, it would involve a day of fitness testing and a day of match play. All the selectors are out and making notes and watching. I think I got to a point where I looked at it as a nice way of catching up with everybody. We would often say to ourselves, 'Why are we even doing this? The coaches know who they want to pick half the time, they know what combination they want, why do they want to burn us out for the weekend?' But it is a rite of passage; they make us do it and we do. I have never taken it for granted and definitely in the early days I was very grateful for the opportunities that came my way. I was never complacent that I was being selected and some friends of mine weren't. Girls I had got to know at different competitions or test matches, who were in the team and then the next moment weren't. I have been very fortunate not to have ever gone through deselection with the England team at trials. My time of not being allowed to play for England was going to come in a few years but I was never not selected through ability. I worked bloody hard to stay in that team and I am pleased that although I was still young, my maturity and passion to play for England was clear to see. It did become difficult when the try-outs were moved around the country – sometimes they were in Sheffield, sometimes they were in Loughborough, and you'd travel up with a group of girls all hoping to get a place on the squad. And then of course England Netball went through different stages of letting us know who they had selected – sometimes you stood up and were told, other times you got a letter and you could choose to open that letter there and then or later on.

I remember once, driving back from try-outs with five of us crammed into the car, we started opening letters on the way and only two of us had been selected. It is the most awkward feeling because obviously you are completely elated that you are part of Team England but you feel for the person sitting in the car next to you who has gone through exactly the same things – busted their arse just like you – to prove they deserve a place and not been selected. In those early years of being part of the selection process I think the coaches saw some potential in me and wanted to keep me around. I was a quick and eager learner and I was a team player and, although I wasn't having much on-court time still, I was contributing to the team.

And so it was that I stayed as part of the senior squad and the under-twenty-one squad and after a tough three- or four-week tour with the seniors in Australia, I then met up with the under-twenty-ones, who had come out to Oz to prepare for the World Youth Cup in 2005.

They were headed to the AIS, the Australian Institute of Sport, to play against the Australian under-twenty-ones. I was exhausted and feeling very run down from coming off one tour and going straight into another one. It always seems to be a thing with me that after every tour I get a bit poorly and suffer. It's amazing what performing does to you; it keeps you going all the way through and then literally a week or two after a test series I'll get a cold for a couple of days. I was really run down when we were at the AIS and I picked up a chest infection. It got to the point that the physios were having to bang me on the back to clear the mucus from my chest. I used to come off at the end of each quarter and they'd be banging my back around to give me a bit of a breather and then I'd run back on again. All of this was at the side of the court and it got to the point where they were knocking my back and freeing up my mucus so much that I started to cough some of it up. I then had to have a spittoon at the side of the court, which was disgusting, but it meant I could carry on playing! I'd like to say I got a lot of sympathy from my teammates but I think they found it quite funny. It also didn't help that one of my teammates, Naida Hutchinson, had an uncanny knack for doing impressions and impersonations of the umpires and she had us all in stitches that game, which for me wasn't great as it set me off coughing again!

7 GETTING THE JOB DONE

'Somewhere behind the athlete you've become and the hours of practice and the coaches who have pushed you is a little girl who fell in love with the game and never looked back. Play for her.' Mia Hamm

MIGHT have been suffering during the preparation, but I was firing on all cylinders by the time I joined the under-twenty-one squad on a plane heading to the 2005 World Youth Cup. It was being held in Fort Lauderdale in Florida and the best thing was that my mum and Raoul flew out to watch me play. They were staying with a friend from Bournemouth, Vicky Simmonds, who now lived in Fort Lauderdale.

America wasn't the most obvious place to hold a big netball tournament as they hadn't really heard of the sport and I think people were confused when they saw us walking around as a team. We often got comments like, 'Oh, you're here to play basketball? No? Volleyball?' The World Youth

Cup is the pinnacle of netball competition for emerging players and features twenty countries competing across the five INF (International Netball Federation) regions: Africa, the Americas, Asia, Europe and Oceania.

Whether I had an extra fire in my belly having come away disappointed from the World Championships in Jamaica two years before I'm not sure, but my mentality was strong – we could do this! And we started off our campaign in that frame of mind, winning our group stages. We played Jamaica in the semi-finals. I was a starter for the under-twenty-ones and sometimes I would be swapped in as goal defence. We managed to beat Jamaica in the semis, winning 52–48, and I was about to enter my first gold medal finals match with an England dress on. I can't speak for any of the other girls but in my experience when you are faced with a gold medal final, you have to have the desire to win, to go for gold. I know I did but it still burns me to this day that when it came to that match, playing New Zealand for a gold medal, we didn't do ourselves justice. It seemed a lot of the girls in the squad were content with the fact that they had already come away with – at the very least – a silver medal. I genuinely felt that when we went out on court in the first quarter it was all there for the taking, the whole tournament, and we just didn't take it. I couldn't help but feel that the girls didn't feel they could win gold. The mood was different; everyone had been so prepared and focused for the semi-final match and when we won it the whole squad just seemed to relax and not have the same care about going into a gold medal final. We should have been even more focused! Everyone stayed up that little bit later the night before, there was a little more messing around and carefree attitude than before. I couldn't fathom that; perhaps it was because we weren't used to competing at the very top, or maybe I had an increased air of maturity, having been in the seniors and knowing what getting to a final would mean, and the under-twenty-ones didn't have that same hunger. Rather than think, 'Sweet, we have propelled ourselves to silver, let's propel ourselves all the way,' the mentality seemed to be more, 'Cool, we've got a silver medal!' I got moved from goalkeeper to goal defence in that final quarter and we ended up losing by four goals.

It's funny but I still feel the same frustration I felt then and this was nearly fifteen years ago! So we ended up with a silver medal and the best thing about the tournament was having Mum and Raoul with me and us all taking a little holiday afterwards. We went to Disney World and Universal Studios and all the usual tourist hotspots. It was nice to slip away and have a bit of a distraction. It just didn't sit well with me, that attitude, and although I didn't vent to my teammates I had a chance to chat it out with Mum and Raoul. And then it was time to make the most of our holiday and some much-needed family time!

When we came back to England after America it was all about preparing for the Commonwealth Games, which were being held in Melbourne in March the following year. I am pretty sure we had another series tour out there in preparation before the Games themselves. Barring the 2018 Games when we took the gold medal (I have to mention this at least a few times!), the 2006 Melbourne Games were probably my favourite. I was named in the twelve-woman squad and although I was still one of the youngest, I was already one of the most capped. It was a great feeling. I think I commented in one newspaper interview that it meant I didn't have to carry the netball bags any more! And it was an awesome Games in terms of its surroundings and vibe and the sun was out and it felt like everyone was buzzing. All the tickets to the netball matches were sold out in the initial ballot as the sport was so popular, so we felt really important! I was twenty-one years old now and I feel I had matured a little bit since my last Games. We made it through our group stages fairly easily, losing to New Zealand, who were also in our group. We played really well too. I was getting a bit more court time and things were going well. Sonia and I were like partners in crime; we worked as a solid unit and our slightly different defensive style was getting us noticed. The *New Zealand Herald* wrote: 'while defenders of similar height and stature often grapple with speed and control, Mentor and Mkoloma seem to whip their tentacles out and connect with the ball at lightning speed'. It was true, we both knew we had our height and we had our timing and we know we can do it, which is why we go for it. I suppose I have to thank trampolining for that. Being friends with Sonia on and off the court certainly helped too and I think having Lyn and

Waimarama, a former defensive player, helped us work on our game. Waimarama was quite scary, don't get me wrong – you made sure you listened to her, that's for sure. But she was a former Silver Ferns player and we benefited from having her on our side.

We lost out to Australia in the quarter-finals by eight goals and were due to face Jamaica in the bronze-medal play-offs. It was a goal-for-goal match and we were determined not to lose out in the same way as at the previous Games. We stayed focused and strong and ended up winning 53–52. We got bronze! And it was a gorgeous medal too. Some of them can be quite plain but this one felt and looked beautiful.

After the Games Rachel Dunn, who was our goal shooter, and I decided to go travelling around Australia for a bit. I think I probably fell in love with the country on our travels. Normally when you come over for a series or a tournament you don't get much chance to sightsee other than in the area you are playing. Rachel and I decided we wanted to fit in as much as we could and so we backpacked in style. We used contacts we had made from being in the country before and we went to Sydney, Alice Springs, Uluru, the Whitsundays . . . it was such an adventure. It was great to really explore the country without the pressure of sport. Being a shooter, Rachel is quite tall too and people would stop us and ask if we were netballers. We said that yes, we were, and explained that we had just played in the Com Games and people were so interested and wanted to talk to us. Nothing like when I was in Florida the year before! And even in England, you can travel around and people don't really pick up on who you are.

It was still two years away from me making the move to Australia but I think that stint travelling and exploring with Rachel was my first indication that I was falling in love with the country. But back to England we went and back to training for the World Championships, which were going to be held in Auckland, New Zealand in 2007.

I was very excited that Mum and Raoul were coming out to watch the World Cup. I missed Raoul a fair bit when I was away at tournaments and it was great to know he and Mum were watching. I owe a lot to Raoul; he often kept me company when I was travelling up to Bath for training two or three times a week. I could drive now, so Mum didn't have to make the journey, but I would get lonely and I could sometimes persuade him, in exchange for a KFC Twister on the way home, to come up and back to training with me. I remember almost pleading with him to come with me and saying that I would make it worth his while. It's still a thing for me now; any long drive I have to do I will almost always beg Raoul to join me if he can. I'm not needy, I just appreciate the company! While I trained, he would shoot some hoops or something at the side of the court or just entertain himself and then I would get him the KFC I'd promised. He would then be supposed to try to keep me awake on the way home, although most of the time he would end up falling asleep himself – which didn't

Mum and Raoul are massively important to me; the relationship I have with them is like no other and it is stronger than any other relationship I will ever have.

I think the world of my dad and I have a huge amount of respect for him, here we are on holiday in Minorca.

'Can you join us, Geva? Just stand there and wave your arms and look scary . . .'
Where my netball career began at St Peter's School in Bournemouth.

I didn't think long about joining Team Bath and ended up playing
with them for ten years winning the Super League three times.

My first Commonwealth Games in Manchester in 2002 was unlike anything I had ever experienced before, the atmosphere was unreal.

My move to Adelaide in 2008 caused a bit of a stir, but it was the best thing I could have done for my netball.

The 2010 Commonwealth Games in Delhi was certainly an interesting experience.

Thunderbirds won the ANZ Championship in 2010 and it was
a great way to round off my time in Adelaide.

My trip to Bali to chill out during a bye week soon turned into a
much bigger drama – 'The Bali Four' were pulled apart by the media
and it was the beginning of the end of my time in Adelaide.

I moved to play with the Melbourne Vixens in 2010 and was elated to win the premiership in 2014.

Kadeen Corbin blamed herself for our loss against the Silver Ferns at the 2014 Commonwealth Games, but one mistake doesn't make a loss and we win together, we lose together, we hurt together. We ride the emotions – the highs and the lows – as a team.

We won a bronze medal at the 2015 World Cup, which was the hardest and most emotional competition any of us had been involved with.

My name had been put forward to be the flag bearer at the 2018 Commonwealth Games, in the end the flag was carried by the triathlete Alastair Brownlee, but he was mobbed by netball players the whole time!

There aren't many moments in my life that I can remember in such vivid detail but I can honestly say, that Commonwealth Games on the Gold Coast when we were tied with Australia until the final few seconds of the game – I think I will have that moment tucked away somewhere safe in my mind for ever.

The gold medal presentation was a bit of a blur but I remember as soon as the England flag went up we were all in floods of tears.

Me and my Lightning team mates dressed in our national kits: England, Australia, NZ and South Africa – netball forges true friendships all around the world.

Moving to Collingwood Magpies has been great for me professionally and personally, I met Mason who plays for the AFL team.

My wonderful mum is my biggest supporter, she's been there for me throughout my whole career and our relationship is the most important thing in the world.

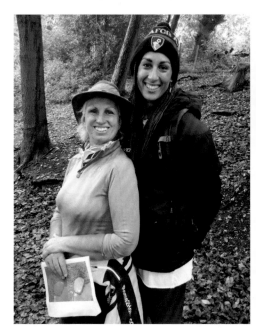

Netball is a sport that demonstrates dedication, teamwork, skill and perseverance. It's a game that shows nerves of steel and wills to win and it's a game I'm so proud to be part of.

matter; having the company was all I needed. It seemed a fair trade and I liked having him with me. Well, most of the time, but not when he puked everywhere in my car when we were probably about fifteen minutes away from home! He'd looked a little off since we'd left Bath and I asked him if he was all right. He looked at me, looked at the road, looked at me again and vomited everywhere. And I mean *everywhere* – the footwell, the gearstick, the handbrake, all over me, all over the dashboard. I couldn't really get that cross with him as I was the one who had wanted him there, but he could have done a nice tidy pile of sick! I had to have the car completely valeted after that and I even had a special lemon car bomb exploded in it afterwards, but I still couldn't get rid of the smell for about a month!

During the World Championships I don't think he was that interested in watching many of the games, but I was getting more court time and my mum was there at every match. She gets really nervous about watching me play so she started to develop this habit, which she is now well known for. She would watch the first two quarters and then walk out of the stadium; she couldn't watch the remainder of the game. When we lost out to Australia in the semifinals and faced Jamaica in the bronze medal play-offs again, it was too much for her. She had seen the relationship England had with Jamaica over the years and didn't think it was fair. Bless my mum, sport isn't fair and that was as much for her to learn as me, I suppose. To her it seemed that they would come through and steal the medals right at the end of the match, which is why she couldn't watch the final quarter. I would like to say that the bronze-medal play-off was different this time round but they snatched victory again, by one goal. It was heartbreaking but character-building and like with most tournaments, we had lots to take and learn from it. There was one funny thing that happened in that tournament – I say funny, but at the time we were a little panicked (I was definitely stressed, I hate being late). Sonia and I almost missed a complete training session. We were sharing a room and were running late to catch the team bus that was going to take us to the training venue. We got downstairs just as the bus was pulling away and chased it, banging on the sides and back for it to stop. It was so funny as we could see the girls on there chatting away and not having a clue what was happening outside! We couldn't get anyone's attention and the bus drove off. It was like in the movies, the bus driving off into the sunset and us looking at each other with a look of 'What the . . .?!' on our faces. But there we were, left behind. We actually saw Kath Harby-Williams, an Australian player, walking along the pavement on her way to the venue and we were like, 'Eeek! We've just been left behind!' She just shook her head, laughed at us, and continued on her way. We ran back to the hotel reception and got them to call a taxi for us and we headed after the bus. Thankfully, when you get to a practice venue people strap themselves up and the shooters go and shoot a few goals to warm up before the coach calls everyone over to commence the session. We strapped ourselves up in the taxi so that when we arrived, albeit a little frazzled, we made it in time before they wondered where the hell we were!

Mum decided that a road trip around New Zealand was what we all needed and she hired a wicked camper van as our very own tour bus. She picked me up from the team hotel, her driving, my brother in the middle and me next to him. I needed to forget another disappointing tournament and Mum knew this would help. She has always been there to pick up the pieces. She was also good at giving me a reality check and when we stopped at our first campsite and woke up the next day to the most beautiful scenery and dolphins playing in the bay below, I did think to myself, netball? It's just a game. As frustrated as I felt – as much as that feeling of hurt engulfed my mind – I found perspective. I was resilient. I had fight in me. Life goes on; you grow, you learn and you keep going. There is life outside of the sport. When you are in that bubble of post-match frustration it is very hard to get on with things but then you do and you realise, actually, things are OK. You can be thankful for where you are and the opportunities you have experienced.

It hurts when I lose. I don't get angry or lose my temper, I just ache with hurt. In my heart I know we should have done much better, so a lot of it is self-pity mixed in with frustration. And it can be hard to deal with. Immediately after a game, you try to do exactly the same things you'd do if you had won. Everyone knew that we weren't unfortunate; we lost. And that is the important thing in sport, you can't beat around the bush. Either we played shit or we allowed the opposition to get on top of us, or we didn't execute when it mattered. You have to be open and honest about what went wrong or you will never improve. It is never bad luck, there are some unlucky calls perhaps but I'm a firm believer that you make your own luck. So we do break it down in the debriefing room and we look at the game and we then pick up where our areas of concern are. Maybe it was our centre pass conversion rate or our shot-to-goal percentage, or maybe we didn't turn over enough balls in defence . . . we really make sure we all know the areas we didn't nail so we know that these are areas to target and work on next time. However raw you feel after a defeat, you have to keep it practical. You have to try to keep emotion out of it. It does help to try to be precise and have a focus. It is emotional, of course it is. You wouldn't be human if you didn't feel anything, and those emotions, for me, are the motivation. They are the drive to make the changes and put in the extra hours and keep pushing for a win. One of the obvious things with team sports is that it's very easy to blame your team-mates and dissect their performance as well as yours – and yes, it can be frustrating when a teammate who you know is capable of great things doesn't perform. But we've all been there, we've all had bad days at the office. The annoyance comes when they can't recognise that they have underper-formed, because the first step in improving is recognition.

You've got all of these things coming into your head after a game and that is the hardest thing with a team sport. Obviously it is great when you're winning but sometimes winning masks the cracks and when you are losing you see things more clearly. I often think you can learn more from your losses than your wins. Don't get me wrong, I hate to lose, but I can see the bigger picture.

I guess that is the intriguing part of sport – you can really identify people's characters, how they deal with things, when you watch them lose. I actually like looking at the behaviours of the teams or individuals that lose. I think the reactions they initially display are a true reflection of what it means to them but, more importantly, how they'll learn from it. I look at how they support the team, how they strive to rectify or improve their game. And that is the important bit. You have to keep the same sort of mannerisms and behaviour whether you win or lose. And then you identify the areas that need to improve. And if you recognise that there is never a 'perfect' game, there is always room for improvement, you'll continually make yourself a better player.

All the teams I have been involved with are pretty good like that; there is no one that is delusional with what has happened after a match. Whether they are at fault individually or as a unit. I like to be around everyone after a loss and keep the focus positive. 'OK, it's done. Let's look at the bigger picture.' I keep things level-headed and I keep plugging the fact that everything happens for a reason. It wasn't our time and, as crap as it is, that is the way it is.

I try to be supportive and talk about the effort everyone has put in and it's only afterwards, when I step away and see my mum and my brother and have time to deal with it and reflect, that I probably think about my own performance, think about the lost opportunities, and that is when my frustrations kick in.

Years later, in the 2014 Commonwealth Games, this mental approach helped us deal with a horrible loss. Yes, you can isolate particular things that happened in a game – like a bad pass or a missed shot – but you can't put the loss down to just that. We all have things that happen throughout a game but it just so happened that at a critical moment in our last-round game against the Silver Ferns, one teammate, Kadeen Corbin, who was GA, made a terrible pass that got intercepted by Laura Langman, the Ferns centre, and the ball whizzed down their shooting end. I couldn't stop it and they scored to equalise and then scored again – we lost the game by one goal after having control for fifty-nine minutes and thirty seconds. We were all gutted and of course there was a mixture of emotions – frustration, anger, sadness. I guess Kadeen felt it was all her fault but the blame can't be placed just on her shoulders. One mistake doesn't make a loss. I knew she was hurting after the game and I made sure I went up to her and consoled her. She was in tears. We were all upset but we were realistic as well – netball is a team sport. We win together, we lose together, we hurt together. We ride the emotions – the highs and the lows – as a team.

But back to 2008. Actually, let me take you back to a phone call that Mum and I were in on in September 2007, a phone call with the Adelaide Thunderbirds CEO, their head coach Jane Woodlands-Thompson and netball guru Todd Miller. There was going to be a new premier league starting in Australia and New Zealand that would be contested between five teams from Australia and five teams from New Zealand. There would be sixty-nine matches held annually, played over seventeen weeks, and Todd wanted the Thunderbirds, one of the five Australian teams, to sign me. He had spotted me before the World Championships and knew that if Adelaide Thunderbirds waited until after that tournament, I would be receiving offers from most – if not all – of the teams. I was twenty-three years old and I was about to embark on the biggest move of my career.

Signing with the Adelaide Thunderbirds wasn't a spur-of-the-moment decision. I had lots of conversations with Mum and we both realised that this was one hell of an opportunity. This brand-new league was starting up, the timing seemed right, I wasn't studying and, ultimately, we both knew that playing with some of the best netballers in the world was only going to improve my game. The ANZ Championship, which was named after the main sponsor, ANZ Bank, was going to be good for me and good for my career. There really wasn't a downside to it. Adelaide had obviously seen me on the international scene and now I knew they wanted me, we began discussions about a contract. My first proper elite netball contract. There were five of us in the end, five

England players who accepted invitations to play in the world's first professional netball league: me, England vice-captain Karen Atkinson, Ama, Sonia and Tamsin Greenway. England Netball's director, Nigel Holl, saw the advantage of such an opportunity from the word go and he told the *Daily Express* that this move was only ever going to benefit English Netball, saying, 'It is a huge compliment to these English players and recognises the progress that the English game has made. When they return with advanced skills, training ideas and having experienced another level of domestic competition week in week out, their input will be crucial to the national squad.' All positive, right? You might wonder why I am putting this in but you will see how the attitudes changed over the next couple of years – and not only changed, but became so narrow-minded that my international career was put in jeopardy.

We worked out a deal for Raoul to fly over to do a six-month school exchange in Adelaide. Mum knew how much it would mean to me to have Raoul with me as I started playing for a brand-new team, in a brand-new league, living in a new country. So I did it; we made the move over. Mum had travelled to Adelaide in the late seventies and she remembered it having a similar feel to Bournemouth. She thought moving to a great rural city would be a good first step into Aussie life for me. I would live out there for five months of the year, a couple of months pre-season, and then three months of the actual season, before coming back to England. It was all quite exciting at the time; the main thing was that I got a salary, but also I could ask for things from the team and it would just happen. 'I need a car.' 'Yep, no problem!' This was a whole new way of life. I could make a career out of playing this sport now and it was pretty cool. I saw it as a natural progression for my netball game.

I signed a two-year contract and had a couple of amazing years in Adelaide. I rented a place in the suburb of Glenelg the first year and my boyfriend at the time, Luke Yeates, came over from England to stay. He was a sailing instructor and I had met him at the Southampton Boat Show, which Mum and I would always go along to as a birthday treat for me as it was held in September. My love of sailing always increased tenfold after these visits and this time I'd bought my Hobie Cat, a fifteen-foot sailing catamaran. Mum joked that as well as a boat I got an instructor as a package deal – I wasn't complaining! So Luke, Raoul and I lived a bit of a happy family existence for a while. It was pretty cool; I'd come home after training and cook dinner and we'd all eat together. They were such simple things but it meant a lot to me. I have always lived by myself or with family; I would never opt for a team house. You do get girls who rent a house with their teammates but I love having my own space and being able to come home and not have to talk about netball. It's OK not to live and breathe your sport – in fact, I think it's key to keeping you sane and letting your mind rest. Getting that work–life balance is essential, whether you are playing sport at an elite level or reaching your target in an office; you need to be able to come home and switch off. It is an important element of my game and it means I am able to go in fresh the next day. Your home is your domain and an area where you should be able to be comfortable and be at one with yourself.

It was nice to have an escape and I started making friends locally, not just in the netball circle, which was important too. I even joined a local sewing group when Mo'onia Gerrard and I saw an advert for a 'knit and natter' session after training one day. It was full of local pensioners who would put the world to rights while they knitted and we ended up going for several weeks. It was very therapeutic and inspirational listening to these women talk. Mum came out to visit too and stayed in my little apartment. She loved it, and I loved hosting her for a change!

In the netball league back in England I had had talks with England Netball about cementing the strong partnership Sonia and I had when we represented the country, and we decided it was a good idea for us to both sign for the same team. I had been with Team Bath for ten years now and we had won the Superleague three times, but it was time to move on. Sonia and I signed to Surrey Storm and we got paid £15 for each quarter we played. In that first season we came first in the league, which earned us a bonus of around £100 each. Hey, it was something! So that is how my life was looking: I would be in Australia for five months, playing for Thunderbirds for three of those, before returning to play for England and for Surrey Storm with Sonia when I was back home.

At the beginning of 2009 Sue Hawkins, a former national player for Australia, took over as England coach and in an interview with a sports website, she told a reporter that she considered Sonia and me to be the strongest aspect of the England team. We were known as the M&Ms and were a force to be reckoned with. 'We have the strongest combinations in defence of anywhere in the world with Sonia Mkoloma and Geva Mentor,' she said. 'England didn't perform to their highest level at the World Championships, you just have to look to the last quarter, that is something we have been addressing. As a team they will be really looking to step out every quarter and be on top every quarter.' I liked Sue straight away. She had a no-nonsense approach and she was getting the team focused on a part of the game that I knew was important – fighting until the very last second of a match. We had a very successful series with her against Jamaica at the start of 2009, winning the series 3–0, and coming from our one-goal defeat in the World Championships this really helped. We were ranked fourth in the world to Jamaica's third and it felt good to get that win under our belt.

In 2010 I signed a new three-year contract with Adelaide Thunderbirds and this was the year we went on to win the ANZ Championship, my first ever ANZ title. We had got close in 2008 and 2009 and then in 2010 we managed to earn ourselves a place in the grand final. Our home venue changed from the Priceline Stadium, with a seating capacity of 3,200, to the Adelaide Entertainment Centre, which had a seating capacity of over 11,000. The roar of the crowd was deafening and it made the whole final so thrilling, I didn't want it to end! We defeated the Waikato Bay of Plenty Magic side from New Zealand by ten goals and it was a great way to start my new-season signing. My first premiership title!

But 2010 was also to be my last year with Adelaide. The rules of the competition changed, perhaps because we'd won, and now the league would only allow one main import per team. We had signed a Jamaican player, Carla Borrego, as a new shooter earlier that year and the club chose her as their main import, which meant if I wanted to carry on playing for Thunderbirds I had to drop down and play in the league below.

I was initially shocked and then sad, whereas Mum was fuming when she found out what was happening and flew over to take part in one of the meetings. Basically, Thunderbirds still wanted me but they had offered the position to play in the ANZ league to Carla and I was dropped to play in the state league, the league below. I might get the opportunity to play with the top team but not compete with them – the team I had just won the championship with! When the realisation of it all set in, I was stunned. I had come over to play top netball, and I had been playing just that the last couple of years. I didn't want to take a step down. But I had already signed a new three-year contract and I didn't know what I could do. Mum certainly did though; she wasn't going to accept any bullshit and had a meeting with the head coach Jane Woodlands-Thompson and the CEO. She came out and told me straight that I had to get out. She took matters into her own hands and spoke to one of the other Australian teams in the ANZ Championship, the Vixens. The coach was none other than Julie Hoornweg, the England coach I had been guided by in the very beginning, and when Mum contacted her and explained the situation, her response was simple. 'We'll have Geva. Whatever happens, we'll have her.'

Julie told Mum that if the crap hit the fan, the Vixens would support me. And by that point, it was most definitely getting serious. Thunderbirds had threatened court action; they were going to sue me for breach of contract. But Mum and I organised our own management team and they argued that Thunderbirds too were in breach of contract. The contract I had signed stipulated that I should be playing in the ANZ Championship and not a state league, so they could take me to court but equally I could take them! They did indeed try. My managers, Allison Tranquilli, an ex-basketballer for Australia, and Mel Jones, who was an Australian cricketer, had set up a firm and were ready to fight my corner. Adelaide were putting a 'restraint of trade' defence against me, citing that I couldn't go and play for anyone else. But they were blown out of the water in the ensuing legal battle and I was released from my contract.

Mum had also approached Kate Palmer, the CEO of Netball Australia, to alert her to the situation and she was horrified. She was shocked at the way Thunderbirds were acting and she wanted me to find other imports to see if they were going through the same problems after the rule change. Netball Australia had no understanding of what was going on at some of these clubs. And in a nutshell, that is how I ended up going to Vixens.

It was a sad end to my time with Adelaide. Although that third year wasn't the smoothest with all the issues off court, winning, like I mentioned before, can mask a lot of cracks. Jane hadn't exactly been a supportive coach to me or a few of my teammates before we won the championship in 2010. In that season we had a few bad defeats and one that sparked everything off happened after we had a 'bye' week. The club had given us the weekend 'off' – no game was scheduled, plus we had the whole week before that weekend off too. It gave us the chance to have a bit of a break mentally and physically and it split up the season. After playing against West Coast Fever in Perth, four of us from the team decided to go to Bali. We thought a couple of days of massages and chilling out would be perfect, then we'd come back all refreshed and ready for training the next week and a game the week after. So we checked we were OK to do that, which we were, and we went across to Bali, which was just a three-hour flight from Perth. We had a great time; it was nice to chill out and relax with the girls.

What I didn't know at the time but have learned since is

that Bali is quite a party destination for Australians. Lots of Aussies go over there to get drunk and party. Yes, you can hire out villas and have a nice tranquil time – like we did! – but most of the time people would go out there to get drunk. I don't drink, and we spent our days on the beach getting massages and just chilling. It was a lovely, relaxing break that helped us recharge. We came back to a normal training week and then we flew up to Sydney for an away game.

Sydney Swifts had always been a bit of a nemesis for us – the Victoria and NSW interstate games were always quite intense – and on that day we got beaten badly. Admittedly we didn't play well as a team; it was one of those games where everyone was 'off', but it didn't help that Jane made a few odd coaching decisions. She moved a few people into different positions and we ended up getting beaten by ten or fifteen goals. That is a horrible loss in these championships. And the next day it was reported in the papers that the game had been lost due to 'The Bali Four'. The press had somehow decided we had been on a boozy trip to Bali and been distracted, and basically blamed the loss on the four of us who went away. 'The Bali Four' label came from an incident a couple of years before about a group of drug dealers who were sent to prison after a drugs bust and had been labelled 'The Bali Ten'. So for some reason, because we had lost a netball match, we were being likened to a gang of hardened criminals!

We were pulled apart by the media and Jane grilled us

one by one over our 'antics' in Bali. The whole ordeal was blown way out of proportion and was nasty. One of the girls who came with us was quite young and it really knocked her confidence. Whenever the team went out to take part in netball clinics or appearances, people assumed that we were doing community service. It was pretty incredible that all that was going on off court and yet we were still able to get our act together as a team and win the competition. But it wasn't just me (and the rest of us who went to Bali) who left the team after that. There was a mass exodus. I think Jane mishandled this incident but there's no doubting her success over the years. She is now in charge of the Women's Development Programme at Magpies, the team I am currently playing for and I will be professional and civil when I see her but I won't forget what happened.

It was my first taste of negative press. The problem I had was that the story was just complete crap; it just wasn't true. I could understand the negative story if we had done all or any of that but we hadn't and yet no one was listening to our side of the story. I was glad to be leaving Adelaide; it turned out to be the best move I would make. And while all this was going on in Australia, things weren't looking so good for me in the England camp either . . .

8 FROM THUNDERBIRD TO VIXEN AND BEYOND!

'The most dangerous phrase in the English language is: "We've always done it this way".'　　　Grace Hopper

You think you can only handle so much, you think there must be a limit to it. But then again, they do say it never rains but it pours, and I felt as if I was standing in a torrential downpour. While all that was happening with Adelaide, there were whisperings that all was not well in the England camp. Anna Mayes, who was the assistant national coach to head coach Sue Hawkins, wasn't happy about players playing in Australia and still representing England. When the England squad for the Commonwealth Games in Delhi, which was going to be held in October 2010, was announced, to say it was a closely fought selection would be an understatement. Anna didn't want me or Sonia on the team, not because of who we were but because of what we were doing. She didn't think we were showing commitment to England and she didn't see how playing in the ANZ in Australia, in this new dimension of professional sport, would serve my ability as a player for England. Her vision for the England team was that players playing out in New Zealand and Australia should not be part of it.

It was such a blinkered approach. Why should I not play in Australia, in the best league in the world, and also be part of the England team? She couldn't see that one would benefit the other and thought I should have to choose one or the other. But she was only assistant coach at the time, and my teammates made their feelings very clear. Sonia and I needed to be part of the squad at the Commonwealth Games, that was the overriding opinion in the team. 'They are the best defenders we have,' was their argument, 'we need them.' Sue Hawkins took their opinions on board and Sonia and I were selected but it was the start of something that was only going to escalate further. For now, though, we joined the girls and went to Delhi to get on with the job in hand.

This was my third Commonwealth Games and it was the first time that the Games had been held in India. Going to Delhi was an interesting experience; there was abject poverty and yet you'd also see majestic places like the Taj Mahal. There was a bit of controversy over the fact that the athletes' village hadn't been finished and the rooms weren't quite ready for us – little things like the light sockets weren't installed properly and some walls hadn't been painted. And the plumbing was a little dubious; I think one of the netball rooms had a blocked toilet, which is never a good thing when you have a lot of athletes wanting to use it (those nerves often get the better of us!) But apart from that, I loved every minute. Team England had two apartment blocks and England Netball were across two floors of one of them. We had the women's and men's hockey team on our floors, which was cool. Meeting up with familiar faces and people from other countries from past Games gave us a sense of ease and familiarity. As always, the food halls and the games room were enjoyable places to hang out; it was where you'd find lots of athletes chilling, mingling, switching off and having fun. Kit-swapping had become a big thing and during the first week you walk around and check out the different countries and see what kit they're wearing, see what you like the look of. Canada normally have the best garments; they have really nice hoodies and T-shirts. And then in the second week you swap and exchange kit if you want, although you have to be good at haggling! 'I'll give you my T-shirt if you give me your hoodie,' that sort of thing. It's a great way to get mementoes from each tournament and it's all a bit of fun. I was never up for it, I was too precious about the kit I had, even if it didn't fit or it wasn't the greatest. But I always liked going around with the girls who would be swapping. It was hilarious to watch, this bartering between nations over a T-shirt! The only kit I suppose I ever thought I should get was something from the St Lucia team, something from my dad's home country. In my most recent Games on the Gold

Coast I finally swapped something and managed to get some shorts from St Lucia. I was super-chuffed about that.

It's good to see the same athletes each Games. In the team sports especially, which don't have the same turnover as individual sports, you often get to meet up again with the same people. We became quite close to the hockey lot and the basketball team. And then you'd end up following them in the competition and throughout the year to see how they were getting on. There were a couple of boxers I first met in Manchester who we got quite friendly with: Paul Smith and, at the following Games, his younger brother, Steve, and then at these Games in Delhi, another brother, Callum Smith. That was pretty cool; what a family!

We got through our group stages with ease, beating South Africa, Barbados, the Cook Islands and Papua New Guinea before losing to New Zealand to come second in our group. We then faced Australia in the semi-finals and lost 45–51. Sonia and I were part of the starting seven now; we were number one and number two in the defensive unit and we did our jobs. We were quite an intimidating duo to the opposition and that is why our teammates wanted us in the team – they knew we would cause trouble for the shooters. But in the last quarter they took me off. It was a bizarre decision as I am the sort of player who grinds down the opposition. I come into play in those last crucial moments. This match felt like I was getting my mojo, I was starting to read play, get my hand to the ball, get the intercepts, and it felt like everything was slowing down around me and I could predict the ball's movement. I really felt like I was getting into my rhythm – and then Anna decided to take me off. I was surprised, but beyond that I didn't think anything of it. I think I just thought OK, that decision has been made for good reason, it was obviously the best thing for the team at the time. And then Australia just took over and they rolled us. It was bitterly disappointing; we thought we had that match from the starting whistle. It wasn't until after the game, when a few people said to me, 'Why did they take you off?', that I started to question the decision. Mum said it too. She wasn't happy about it; she knew my style, she knew the final quarter is where I come good, I fight it out. So I guess it started to weigh on my mind and I started to question it. We ended up facing Jamaica in the bronze medal play-off again, but this time we didn't buckle under pressure. We went out and fought for bronze and ended up winning quite comfortably (70–47) against what had always been our 'bogie team'.

When I flew back to Australia at the end of 2010, I wasn't an Adelaide Thunderbird any more, I was with the Melbourne Vixens. I was lucky that the coach was Julie Hoornweg, my first England coach, who'd scouted me all those years ago. We met up a couple of times to chat as she wanted to check I was OK after everything that had happened with Adelaide. She had given me her support as soon as the trouble began and I was grateful, but I knew she wouldn't want to put me on the team without scoping me out first. She hadn't seen me play for a while so I did some training with the team and she liked what she saw. I moved to Melbourne at the beginning of 2011 and started the new year with a new team.

The Vixens already had a goalkeeper, Bianca Chatfield, and a goal defender, Julie Corletto, who were both in the Australian Diamonds set-up. It didn't put me in the best position when I joined; it wasn't like the club needed strong defenders when the two already on the team were playing for the Diamonds! This probably got back to Anna in England too. But I couldn't think about that now. I had a new club to focus on. Julie put me in the team as wing defence. Yes, you heard right, wing defence. I am sure there are a couple of photos of me out there playing with a WD on my dress! I had one practice game as a wing defence, which I remember very clearly. We were playing in Bendigo, a regional town in Victoria, and they had me start as WD, Julie as GD and Bianca as GK. I don't think I made it to the end of that first quarter before the coach called 'time' and moved Bianca to GD and Julie to WD and me back to goalkeeper. And from that game onwards we never looked back. I managed to hold down the GK bib, Julie played a very good WD and Bianca started to solidify her position as GD. I felt a bit bad; basically I had come in and pushed these girls out of their normal positions to make way for me! But in doing so they have then excelled at their new posts and everything has just worked. And it's worked a bloody sight better than having me as WD! I think I spent my time running around like a headless chicken. Wing attacks are so speedy and, although I could just about get away with using my arms and my reaching range, trying to keep up with these girls was just . . . well, I was a fish out of water, that's for sure. I felt a lot more at home when I put the GK bib back on.

The situation with England Netball still wasn't great. I just couldn't see the reasoning as to why they weren't happy with what I was doing. I've forgotten that period – I must have blanked it from my memory. It was an emotional time. I was also struggling with a herniated disc in my back that was pushing on my sciatic nerve. It felt like a knife was running all up and down my hamstring, into my calf and then back up again. I had it all throughout the Com Games in Delhi but with the right treatment and medication I managed to get through the matches.

I went on an antidepressant drug because it was meant to be good for nerves, I had two epidurals, I had a nerve root sleeve injection, which is where they put a needle near where the nerve leaves the spine and then inject a long-acting steroid and a long-acting anaesthetic into it. I looked a little bit like the penguin Mumble in *Happy Feet* when he returns to his family with the antennae in his back. But nothing really touched it and so I just got on with it and, over time, it just sort of cleared itself up. Well, I could perhaps put it down to something – or someone – else but more on that later.

I was back in the squad for the 2011 World Netball Championships in Singapore, although things between Anna and me still weren't great. I felt I was getting the blame for the fact that English netball players had been given this opportunity! I remember saying in a BBC interview after the competition that it would be beneficial for the England squad if more home-grown players joined me in the ANZ league. I was quoted as saying, 'Obviously England need to step it up, so if we get more English girls playing over here and strengthen our Superleague in the UK too that would help. The ANZ league is the top domestic competition that I can play in so I will really improve my netball.' It probably didn't help the situation but it was true; I didn't want anyone to be scared of girls going out to hone their skills and then using those skills wearing an England dress. Sue Hawkins was still the coach and the team were feeling confident, Sonia and I were confident in our defensive unit and the whole team had an air of expectation about them. We wanted to get better than a bronze; we wanted to show everyone what we were capable of. The pool matches, usually a chance for the starting seven to do a couple of quarters and then fresh legs to take over, allowing us to stay rested for the next stages, were completely crazy. We had two young defenders in the squad that competition, Eboni Beckford-Chambers and Stacey Francis, and then Sonia and me as the two experienced defenders. But instead of playing Sonia and me together for half a match, getting us used to playing together, they played us in different combinations; they had me playing with Stacey and Sonia playing with Eboni. It really bothered me. Why wasn't I being given any match practice with Sonia, the starting GD? It was so frustrating. It felt like we didn't get any quarters together at all. And then I started overthinking and stressing myself out: what if I'm not the starting GK any more? I would have to work harder. But then if I AM the starting GK, I don't feel like I have been given enough time to gel again with Sonia. All these little niggles started getting to me and it's the last thing you need in a tournament because it's a complete waste of energy. And in the end, after playing all the lead-up games in different combinations, we then faced New Zealand in the semi-finals and Sonia and I were back together in the starting seven. I was like, 'What the hell?!' What was the point of all that mixing?! By then we hadn't played together for months, we hadn't had a build-up together in this tournament and now you are expecting us to click for the semi-final? It was terrible coaching if you ask me. Sonia and I were good enough players to make it work – we had had years together and we knew each other well – but we still lost, and I don't necessarily think it was from the defensive end. The coaching wasn't great, the atmosphere wasn't great, the environment wasn't great. I got a cold sore because of the stress and ended up with a massive fat lip because I tried to treat it with medication. The last couple of games everyone was asking me if I was all right as it looked like I had been punched in the mouth! It was turning out to be the worst tournament ever. We ended up playing Jamaica again in the bronze-medal play-offs and I was so wound up inside by everything at that point. I was fired up and I wanted to win. I wasn't going to let this bronze medal go; this competition had to be good for something! I was on a mission. I remember saying to Sonia, 'Right, let's just get this done.' In my mind no one was going to get in the way and we ended up winning fairly easily. I remember standing on the podium after collecting our medals and everyone was obviously so excited and I was just numb. Why were we happy with bronze again? Why weren't we fighting? We had a team that was good enough to really make a mark on the championship, and I felt that with a different approach we could have challenged for a better medal.

Yes, we came away with something but I had this dissatisfied taste in my mouth. It felt like a waste. The new girls on the squad were happy with a medal but I knew deep down that we were better than that. I had this real yearning for a better medal and it felt like a chance had been wasted. I did make sure I didn't just think this; I wanted to talk about it afterwards with the coaches so they understood why I didn't think we were strategically sound. In the debrief after the semi-finals, I said just that: 'You can't expect a starting seven combination to fire in the finals if you don't give it a chance in the early rounds. It just won't work.'

Now, you see that happen in all the top competitions. You may not be on together for the full game or even half the game but at least you have your starting seven on for a quarter or two throughout the different games or pool matches. That bronze medal match, on 10 July 2011, was to be my last England game for over fourteen months.

Anna Mayes took over from Maggie Jackson, who had taken over from Sue Hawkins as head coach after the World Championships. Maggie had stepped in when Sue had to resign for personal reasons. Now Anna was taking over from Maggie and I was being punished for wanting to improve my netball game in another country. I had been officially dropped from the England team.

9 NO LONGER A ROSE

'How dare they?! They are national selectors. It is their job to make decisions and not sit on the sodding fence!'

Yvonne Mentor

NETBALL works on a four-year cycle. You have the Commonwealth Games in the third year, the World Championships the following year (year four) and the two years prior are spent preparing again for those big tournaments in a series of test matches. At the end of July 2011 I had no idea that I wouldn't be putting on an England dress for nearly a year and a half.

I was back in Melbourne in August and preparing for my second season with the Vixens. It was good exposure being in Melbourne. They love their netball. Adelaide is a small city but living in Victoria and playing for a Melbourne team meant I was exposed to a lot more opportunities. We went out into the community and I developed a real love of coaching and working with youngsters and kids across the multicultural spectrum. It was similar to my early days on the England team when we had the Sporting Champions programme. I loved chatting to the kids and meeting lots of different people, making appearances at lots of different venues. I formed some partnerships with Netball Australia and I used my profile of playing with Melbourne Vixens to be able to actually get out in the community. I was able to explore and be involved in another side of netball.

Mum and Raoul joined me for Christmas in 2011. I had a little place in Melbourne and Mum wanted to be around at the start of 2012 for the Aussie Open tennis tournament, which was being held in Olympic Boulevard, Melbourne Park. I think she was also a little worried about me; she knew that things weren't great with England Netball and I was still finding my feet a bit with Vixens, so she flew out to see me. When I joined Vixens I became good friends with some of the players from the Melbourne Tigers, the basketball team. I remember one evening, in those dull days between Christmas and New Year, I convinced Raoul to come out for the evening to just 'hang out' with these guys. Raoul liked playing a bit of basketball so I thought it would be good for him. I suppose I was a bit of a chaperone. I wasn't dressed up, I was just hanging out with my brother; I didn't need to doll myself up. And that is when I met my future husband, Lachlan. He was out with some of his cricket buddies and we got chatting by the bar. I was in a T-shirt and jeans and felt a bit of a scruff but there is no way I could have predicted I would meet a guy that I would get on so well with on a relaxed night out with my brother. We hit it off and at the end of the night we exchanged numbers.

Our first proper date was at a rooftop cinema. We had planned to meet on the corner of Bourke and Swan Streets, a busy spot in Melbourne, a big intersection with lots of foot traffic because the Bourke Street mall and shops begin there. Not only was I not sure what corner he would be on, I wasn't sure if I would recognise him or not! I wasn't paying much attention to his looks the night we met, I just remembered him being tall. Luckily, we found each other – well, he found me. I'd been smiling at all the tall men who walked past just in case! The date went well. We started by having a drink at a bar and a couple of people came up to me to ask if I was a tennis player, probably because the Aussie Open was about to start. I think Lachy liked this, the fact that I stood out and appeared to be 'somebody'. We then moved to the rooftop of the bar and watched a movie under the night sky. That bit was romantic, even though the film wasn't – *Trainspotting*. I didn't mind. It was a classic, even though probably not ideal for a first date!

The next day Mum, Raoul and I were meant to be going to the Aussie Open, and I'd said to Lachy on our date, 'If you want to come down tomorrow you're welcome to.' And indeed he did. He ended up meeting Mum the day after we had our first date and Mum, bless her, who bloody loves tennis, gave up her seat for the men's doubles match so he could sit with me. But she could see the sparks, she said.

She was happy for me if I liked him, and at first there wasn't much not to like. I won't lie, I was flattered by his attention. He was tall, he was handsome and charming and when you spend so much time working, training and playing with women you don't always get much chance to meet men. Especially outside of the netball world. We had similar interests in sports and we got on well and it was nice that Raoul and Mum got to meet him before she went back to the UK. So I started my 2012 season with Vixens with a new boyfriend and it was at that point that I decided to stay out in Australia permanently. Lachy's mum had a vacant apartment in Melbourne as she was mostly based in another city, Geelong, so as it came to the end of my season and everything was going well between us, I ended up moving in with him. It was the next stage of our relationship.

After the ANZ season finished in July, I was due to start a new job that had been organised with the Vixens in August. Back in April I had been invited to attend the trials for England, which would be happening in July and would decide the squad for the next nine months. I rang Mum in a bit of a panic. I wanted to be at trials but I knew I couldn't commit to the first test series with the team in Jamaica in September as I would be working. Mum told me that she didn't bring any of her children up to not be upfront and honest and simply said, 'Geva, just tell them you have too much stuff happening in Oz, you won't be available for the Jamaica series but you would be available for all other England commitments.' So I rang England Netball and explained the situation – that I was so eager to go for trials but I wouldn't be available for the test series in Jamaica. I even asked them if they still wanted me to come for the selection process, knowing I wouldn't be available for one test. They told me on that call that they understood and yes, they still wanted me to try out. I made a point of checking that they understood my decision and I got them to confirm I was still requested for trials, as I pay for my own flights back to the UK and they aren't cheap! Having that confirmation meant it wasn't going to be a wasted trip, I thought, and I flew back to the UK after the season with Vixens finished and attended the trials at Hatfield.

At the end of the first weekend I was called into an office and there were six people all sitting round a table. There was the selection panel, which included Colette Thomson (the coach who saw me at my very first under-seventeen try-outs) and Anna Mayes. Colette was also the assistant coach for England and I know that this next moment was a professional decision and I'm sure nothing personal. They asked me if I would make myself available for the Jamaica series in September. I again explained that this wasn't possible and that I had already spoken to people at England Netball about it and had it confirmed that it wasn't a problem. But they decided to put it to a vote: if I couldn't make myself available for the whole of the season – including Jamaica, Australia, New Zealand and then the series in Australia again – I wasn't going to make the squad. My stomach just dropped. I remember that feeling to this day.

I have to be honest, I think the majority of people on the selection panel were in favour of me being selected, but then Colette Thomson spoke. She couldn't agree to it. She was from the old-school brigade I guess, the one that says you have to do it exactly this way, the right way. No ifs, no buts. And I wasn't doing it the right way and so it was a no. There was no compromise, no leeway. I was looking at her thinking, 'Who are you to have this totally black and white opinion and sway everyone else in this room?' I thought I had built up a really good relationship with Colette as she was one of my coaches when I played under-seventeens and assistant coach when I was in the under-twenty-ones. She knew how much playing for England meant to me. As I said, she is still involved with the team and I am of course respectful to her and professional. To her, it wasn't an emotional decision, it was a case of applying the standards she believed in. And while I respect that, it was hard to take. I don't think I'll ever forget her decision. So it went to a vote and in the end two selectors sided with me and said yes, while Colette and another selector said no. Two selectors abstained from the vote, which meant the final decision went to Anna. She told me that she had to set an example and that her decision was no. I wasn't going to be on the team for the next year.

I was in floods of tears when I spoke to Mum later that evening. I was so frustrated and cross with myself. I thought I should have just lied, not mentioned I wouldn't be available and then just pulled a sicky before the Jamaica series wasn't perfect, but I was fooling myself in always trying to see the good in our relationship and trying to change it, which just wasn't ever going to work.

I find it a struggle to talk about the fact that I was once married to him, but I suppose over time it will stop being this big failure in my mind and I can move on. I am happy to be out of that relationship and of course I want nothing but the best for Lachy, but the whole experience knocked my self-confidence. My self-esteem took a dive and it took a long time for my self-worth to start to recover. I didn't think anyone would want me, I didn't think any man would want my 'history'. It's funny, isn't it, how we completely doubt ourselves and our worth whether someone we love didn't love us back or because what started well just went wrong, or because we just weren't ever right for each other. For some reason we feel it's our fault, that we've failed. I thought I was an all-right person and yet now I believe the person I thought I was in love with didn't love me and that still hurts. I have become harder as time has moved on, less easily impressed, although I still am who I am and I know, when it comes to relationships, I give it my all and I do everything in my power for that person. I just hope, that someone will love me for me, will bring out the best in me, will look at me like there is no one else in the entire world. My heart might have been broken but I still believe in true love, I still want 'for ever' with someone.

* * *

and said I was too ill to fly. But I knew deep down that wasn't the answer. I was honest and it cost me my place on the team.

Mum was absolutely livid about the vote. Not about Colette or Anna or the selectors who voted, but the ones who abstained. 'How dare they?!' she shouted. 'They are national selectors. It is their job to make decisions and not sit on the sodding fence!'

I have no memory of what happened to England in the Jamaica series; I was still so hurt and, sadly, I probably didn't care. I flew back heartbroken to Melbourne, to my flat, to Lachy, to Vixens. In October, England flew out to Australia and then New Zealand to compete in a seven-week test series. I decided that the only way to prove my passion for England was to open the lines of communication. It was a bit like being back on the bench again; I could still help the team and give advice even if I wasn't playing.

I found out that some of their practice sessions were being held on courts that had a very hard playing surface (they should be sprung), which could lead to injuries due to the impact. I rang England Netball and suggested other venues. It was really tough, though: I was literally just round the corner from where the first test was being held and I was at home twiddling my thumbs. I was sending messages, pacing around the living room, and just wanted to scream, 'Use me!' I was fit, I'd been training, I was there, I was ready! But instead they flew out a new player from the UK. I haven't heard of her since but that didn't stop it hurting at the time. I couldn't understand why they would fly a less experienced girl halfway round the world to play in a position that I could play and was more experienced at playing than her. But I kept making contact, I sent more messages, I kept trying to keep the lines of communication open and positive. For example, I remember mentioning to Anna that as I had been playing against a lot of the Diamonds for the past four years I knew them pretty well and I could perhaps provide information that would help her and the coaching team.

When the team flew to New Zealand for that leg of the series, Pam Cookey, the goal shooter, was allowed to fly home as she had work commitments. Netball isn't a professional sport in the UK like it is in Australia, and all the girls playing in the league in England also have full- or part-time jobs.

That was it. I couldn't believe it. Talk about double standards. Mum now gives this example to all the parents she meets. She has very little faith in England Netball and she will never forgive them for the way they treated me. She tells all the parents to focus on putting their daughters' best interests first and to question everything they are told by England Netball. I was actually quite naive about a lot of this at the time, although I like to think that things have improved nowadays. You can see why Mum is so passionate about it; she only had my welfare in mind and hated to see me being treated unfairly.

When Australia went over to the UK at the start of 2013,

they lost the three-match test series 3–0. This was a great result for England – the ten-time world champions beaten at Wembley. The mood was one of pure celebration and some of the players were backflipping down the court. It was a wake-up call for Australia not to underestimate England, but it was obvious to those in the netball world that Australia hadn't taken over their strongest side. One of the reasons was that this tour takes place in the Australia off-season, so a lot of the girls were being rested or weren't quite match-fit. I don't think Australia will make that mistake again.

I was really happy for the girls winning so comfortably. At the end of the day, if Australia want to bring an under-strength side to face England so be it. England can only play who the Aussies put out and it was a tremendous boost to the team knowing that we could beat a team of Australians 3–0. I think my only concern was that we had the potential to get carried away and complacent. I knew it wouldn't always be that easy, I knew there were some big guns they didn't play, and those big guns brought with them a lot of experience. I rang Anna and congratulated her and the team. All the time I was trying to show enthusiasm; I didn't want to be forgotten or cast aside. I was determined to show Anna that even though I wasn't playing, I was still hungry for that England dress. It still meant so much to me. And I knew I had so much to give my country. And the talking and the constant communicating and messaging must have helped. Eventually I found myself sitting down with the selection panel again. They could see that this was obviously something that I wanted to keep doing. I wanted to play in Australia to improve my game and they slowly started to see the benefits and finally started making it work. Suddenly we were talking about planning schedules and when I would be flying back and how it could work with me living and playing in Oz. Timing-wise, I guess I was quite lucky. Throughout this period I had never missed a big tournament; I hadn't missed the Commonwealth Games or the World Championships. And I never gave up on England. I never accepted that being dropped was the end. That would have been easy. I could have just stayed with Vixens and enjoyed a career in Australia without worrying about playing for England ever again. But I wasn't ready to not be a Rose – I wanted to see England in that number-one spot.

All this time I hadn't been playing with England I was enjoying my time with the Vixens. It gave me a real purpose and it was great for the team when we made the final at the end of the season in 2013. We ended up losing to Waikato Bay of Plenty Magic, which was hard, but quite a talking point in the championship as it was the first time a New Zealand side had ever won the ANZ.

My first game back in the England squad was on 25 September 2013. Exactly 450 days since I had been banned. I was picked to play in a test series against South Africa that was being held at Wembley. England Netball didn't make a song and dance about my being absent and then suddenly back in the squad, although a few commentators picked up on my return to court. We always play three matches in a test series but I didn't get to play in the first or make the starting seven in the second. I came on in the third or fourth quarter of that match. In the third match I was a starter and I have pretty much stayed in that position ever since. So was the first-match snub to teach me a lesson? Was putting me on late in the game in the second match to spite me? Was the underlying message, 'Look, Geva, you can't just waltz back on to court straight away like nothing has happened'? OK, I could cope with that. Seeing Anna again and being back in the squad wasn't weird. I never had anything personal against her, I just found her approach so narrow-minded. We have always had a pretty good relationship and while I was banned I was always trying to keep in contact and so when I eventually came back on the team, it wasn't this massive thing. I'd been absent from playing but I hadn't let them forget me, and so there was no bad blood. I was pleased to be able to show how much I could contribute to the team on court as well as off it. My biggest bugbear over the whole thing revolved around Colette being there. She didn't have the final say but she had the biggest impact.

Coming back into the squad and being back among the girls again was bloody brilliant. I was back with players I'd known since a young age – having laughs, having jokes, striving towards the same goal, which was all I wanted. The girls were intrigued about what it was like playing out in Australia, especially the media aspect of the game. All the games in ANZ are televised as netball is such a big sport out there and the girls wanted to know what it was like, being part of netball when it had such elevated status. The Australian leagues were the pinnacle of netball and, after I came back, a lot of the English girls started aspiring to get contracts out in Australia and New Zealand. That wasn't the big deal now that it had been and I had made it possible. It wasn't easy for me to stick to my guns and not come running back to the English league as soon as the mood changed in the England camp, but I kept focused on what was best for my game. I could have easily relented and come back to play for an English club, but would my netball improve? Doubtful. Would it have been of any benefit? Probably not. I am pleased it has worked out the way it has. It's nice for girls to be able, if they have that opportunity, to go out and play in the Australian league, the premier league for netball in the world. To know that if they get an offer from an Australian side, they can accept it without fear of consequence. They know that if they are good enough, they can still represent their country. The important point is, they have a choice. I have been called a trailblazer and a pioneer but, to be honest, I am just glad others are able to have that opportunity.

Life was good in Melbourne. Things with Lachy were going OK. He would often come to games at the weekend if it didn't clash with his cricket matches. The Vixens were building momentum in the 2014 season. Bianca Chatfield and I were forming a good connection as GK and GD and we made it into the final that season. We didn't want a repeat of the previous season and on 22 June we ended up beating the Queensland Firebirds to win the title. It was the second time Vixens had won the premiership, but the first time was long before I joined the team and I was so pleased to be involved in this second victory. No, forget that – I was elated! I left Melbourne for England on a high, knowing that I wanted to achieve the same result with England in this year's Commonwealth Games. I was fed up with bronze, I wanted a different colour!

Lachy had managed to get permission from the school where he was a PE teacher to come over for the Games, which were being held in Glasgow that year. It was good to have him there. It would be the first time he would see me play at a major tournament and he had been with me when the England ban was in place, so he knew how much it meant to me. Mum, Raoul and lots of my friends and family had travelled up too and I was excited to share the experience of a major tournament with everyone.

I felt the England team had a real chance this year. Playing in Australia had done exactly what I wanted it to do; we as players didn't put the Silver Ferns and Diamonds on pedestals any more. I had been playing with them and against them week in and week out and I had learned from them and gained confidence. And I knew now that they were human, after all; they had strengths and weaknesses just like us. I was more battle-hardened too. I was ready to fight! The BBC wanted to hear my thoughts on our chances and I remember being really upbeat and positive and saying: 'We have been talking the talk for many years but now I'd like to think this is the year we can walk the walk and show the world what England are all about.'

This was my fourth Games and it never loses its excitement. The athletes walking around the village, the likes of Usain Bolt and people like that giving the place an extra vibe. Team England were buzzing. I felt like we were in good form and I personally felt in good form. We had lost Pam Cookey due to an anterior cruciate ligament injury and we had a couple of debuts in the team, but we felt OK about the balance. We pottered along throughout the tournament, changed a few combinations and kept things nice and fresh.

We went up against Australia in our final Group B match and we came out fighting. We were fired up, we were ready, we knew we could compete against the top teams and now it was time to show it. The game against Australia was goal-for-goal and I think we had the momentum throughout. Australia made some changes and mixed up some of the positions to mess with us mentally. There was one girl who normally plays GK or GD and they put her in at WD to hound Serena Guthrie, who was WA for us. It was obvious their coach had told her to come in and bulldoze Serena; she had no intention of going for the ball, it was just about roughing up Serena and getting in her face. Losing to Australia hurt. We were 100 per cent in that game but then in the last few seconds Jo Harten's missed shot, the shot that would have won it for us, just came back down and the Diamonds went on to score, and won 49–48. We just couldn't finish it. Player errors and coaching decisions were to blame. And it made us more determined than ever to hit hard against New Zealand, who we were facing next in the semi-final.

The night before that match Anna insisted that we all make an appearance on the BBC's Commonwealth Games show. She wanted the whole team to go and do our bit of netball PR. It was going to be a very late night for the whole team and we'd probably only get a couple of minutes of airtime and, to be honest, I was dead against it. Eboni and I made our objections and said we didn't think it was appropriate for the team, who were playing in an important match the next day, to be up all night filming a BBC show. It shouldn't be how we prepared for a big match, the team should be rested and ready, we argued, but we were overruled.

The game was tough. We were matching the Silver Ferns goal for goal and you could probably say that the momentum was in England's favour for the majority of the game. In the final quarter two things happened that I thought altered our flow. Our GD, who had been on all game, was changed in the last five minutes. It was a weird decision. Not that the replacement was bad but when you have someone who has been grinding down the GA from the starting whistle and was dominating that circle, taking nine or ten rebounds and hustling the shooters, replacing her in the dying moments with someone who hadn't built up that 'presence' seemed like a very odd decision to me.

The score was level right up until the last seconds of the game and it was our centre pass. We took the ball, we moved it around court, we sent it into our goal third so our shooters were ready. And then just outside the circle, Kadeen Corbin, who was playing goal shooter, threw the ball away. She made a bad pass and threw it – quite literally – straight into the Silver Ferns centre. There was barely twenty seconds left to play and then all of a sudden the ball was whizzing down to us and they scored. They had won 35–34 in those final few seconds. We had lost. We had thrown away our chance to play for a gold medal. It was a wasted chance. We didn't need to tell ourselves that it was a glorious failure and that we had given as good as we got. We were better and we knew it; we just didn't seem to have it in us to prove it.

Everyone was distraught. This was my fourth Games and this defeat really hurt. Corbin was inconsolable. I went up to her at the end. She was in tears and she obviously felt completely to blame. She was crying and I started to well up too, but I put my arm round her to show her that we were a team. It shouldn't come down to those single moments. We have all had those 'one moments' in a sixty-minute game where we should have thrown a better pass or we should have got this ball or made that interception. But her tears were for the fact her mistake occurred in that last thirty seconds when we should have scored and won. That was really tough for her, and us.

Which led us into the Jamaica game. Yes, we were going to face Jamaica in the bronze medal play-off AGAIN. I'd like to say that losing by so little to New Zealand and Australia before that spurred us on to not leave the Games empty-handed but we didn't have any fight left. We were broken by this point; we'd had our hearts ripped to pieces against Australia and then ripped out losing to New Zealand, and when it came to the Jamaica game, we literally got rolled by them. They came into that match aggressive, fired up and ready and we were still hurting and deflated mentally. Everything we tried wasn't working, the umpiring wasn't the greatest, the combinations we had practised over and over weren't working. Mum walked out at half-time; she couldn't watch any more. We ended up losing by over ten goals. I had a black eye and fat lip after the match because the Jamaican goal shooter was swinging her elbows around every time she got the ball and I got too close and bore the brunt of it. It looked like I had been in a rugby game! When it was all over, Mum came to give me a hug. There were no words spoken between us, I just let her safe arms envelop me while I sobbed.

It was a horrible way to end the Games, the Games that we had hoped would be ours. We all went to the warm-down court afterwards and just sat there in silence. In utter dejection. We were all thinking the same thing, that this was going to take us a while to get over. This one really hurt. There is a convention in these competitions for our coach and management team to want us to remain behind and watch the final. It was torture. None of us wanted to watch the gold medal match knowing it should have been us on court. It seemed very unfair making us come out and sit among everybody to watch that game. We had to sit through the medal ceremony too. It left a really nasty taste at the end of our Commonwealth Games campaign, which had been ours for the taking. We had the team, we had the game plan . . . it was just horrible. I knew we wouldn't be looking ahead to the 2018 Com Games just yet. We were too busy licking our wounds.

10 WHAT DOESN'T BREAK YOU . . .

'It's OK if you fall down and lose your spark. Just make sure that when you get back up, you rise as the whole damn fire.'
                                                    Colette Werden

THE defeat at the Commonwealth Games was made slightly more palatable by going on holiday with Lachy for my thirtieth birthday in September. It was a holiday I had organised myself, which I normally did, and we went to Croatia and then Lanzarote. Unbeknown to me, Lanzarote was where he had planned on proposing and he told me afterwards, after he had done the deed, that he'd been walking around all day with the ring in his pocket but there were lots of rowdy people and it wasn't appropriate. In the end he proposed that evening, on our hotel balcony. I was due to have a big birthday party when we got back to Melbourne but he told me he had arranged it all with his mum to turn it into an engagement party instead. I had never really had a birthday party as I've always been travelling or playing – I never got to properly celebrate my eighteenth or twenty-first. So I thought I would really go to town for my thirtieth and booked a venue and entertainment . . . but it wasn't to be. It got turned into an engagement party and I just accepted that and laughed it off. If you are happy in a relationship, if you are with the man you want to spend the rest of your life with, this sort of thing might not matter. I think that's when my doubts first started, which was ironic as I now had a ring on my finger and, if anything, this was the thing I should have been the most sure about.

What I do know is that we got married on 20 December 2015, in Torquay, Victoria, Australia and we are now legally divorced, as of 5 November 2018. The relationship started off OK; I met him at a time in my life when I wanted a significant other to share it with. So I think when I met him, it was a bit of a relief; I had found someone, I was going to be all right.

Sonia, my English teammate who I had known for years and knew me better than most people, was my maid of honour and my two half-sisters, Inez and Noor, who came over from the Netherlands, were my flower girls. As a nice gesture I asked Lachy's sister Rachel to be a bridesmaid too. I had thought that he would ask Raoul to be in his groom's party but he didn't ask him so I had my brother in my bridal party as well. I had quite an entourage and he had a couple of his mates. Everything had already been organised for the wedding to take place in Australia and that was down to his parents. I'd wanted to get married in Hawaii or somewhere; I think I felt it should be a halfway point that both families could get to. But I was happy to go with the flow and convince mine to come to Australia. After all, I had been trying to get my dad over to this side of the world for years. Mum and many members of my family were there. I knew they'd spent a lot of money on flights and accommodation to come to the wedding for me and I think I felt a little guilty, as I was having serious doubts.

It wasn't a massive wedding; we had about eighty guests in total, and I wanted it to be laid-back and relaxed, so we had it on a nice golf course by the beach. We had an evening of canapés – I didn't want a poncy three-course set meal, I just wanted people to enjoy the scenery and for it to be casual. Dad gave me away and I was absolutely bawling my eyes out when I walked down the aisle. We had had a rehearsal the day before and the weather had been blisteringly hot, over forty degrees. Lachy couldn't make the rehearsal because he was due to play in a cricket match, although it ended up being cancelled due to the heat.

The wedding day itself was really emotional. We had planned to have the ceremony outside originally, but only an hour or so beforehand, the weather turned and there was a storm with gale-force winds and torrential rain! Everything had to be moved indoors and Lachy and everyone else who was there, a few friends and family who'd turned up early including some dear friends of ours, the

Caldwell family, just knuckled down to help and got everything inside and set up. I was so grateful to them all. So I walked down the aisle with my dad. I was emotional as I felt a bit out of control, given the weather, but there wasn't anything I could do so I had to let that go. And I was emotional because of the day. I don't normally display my emotions so openly but I was properly crying as Dad and I made our way down the aisle. And when I got to Lachy, I think I sort of hoped he would be emotional too. Look a little teary-eyed or something. But there was nothing. When someone I love is upset I know I always start to well up a bit just because they are crying, but from him there was nothing. OK, I thought, some men just don't show emotions, I get that.

Emotionless he might have been but he was also a very intelligent man, so I never felt I was ever going to win an argument because he always had all the answers. I like to stick to my guns if what I believe in is true and fair, and I can be stubborn about it, and he wouldn't ever give up or back down, so there was no point in us going to battle. It wasn't pleasant and I'm not a great one for confrontation; I just want to solve things and move on. And if things in our relationship weren't great before the wedding, they definitely weren't great after the wedding. Everyone says that the best bit of your relationship is the honeymoon period but it wasn't for me. Being on the road, travelling with netball, does take a lot of commitment and a lot of your time and you need to be with someone who not only understands but appreciates this. I guess we didn't really have the quality time together we needed before we got married to see if we were suited. The thing that baffles me is that he knew I was a netballer, he knew the commitments and sacrifices that had to be made to play this sport at the elite level, but he seemed to want someone who was going to be around when he got back from work, a wife first and foremost.

He also couldn't get his head round the fact that it wasn't going to be for ever, that I wasn't going to be playing at this level for the rest of my life. I was constantly telling him and reassuring him that in years to come I would be able to spend more time with him, more time at home. I ended up feeling very guilty for being a netballer.

To begin with, I think he was a bit swept away having a girlfriend who was in the public eye. Remember how big netball is in Australia. He has enjoyed being part of my netballing life in that sense, coming along to the nice events, doing the nice things. It was the little, everyday things that added up and chipped away at me. There were so many little things that I thought he did because they were best for our relationship, but perhaps I was just naive.

The biggest indicator, the big red flag for me that our marriage was never going to work, was the fact he didn't seem to understand my relationship with my mum and my brother. Mum and Raoul are massively important to me; the relationship I have with them is like no other and it is stronger than any other relationship I will ever have. So the fact that Lachy seemed not only not to like them but that it felt to me that he showed them so little respect, was what got to me the most. I understand that not all husbands have to like their mother-in-law or brother- or sisters-in-law and that's OK. It wasn't like they were living next door to us either; we were on the other side of the world for heaven's sake!

There is a good reason for me including all of this and it's not to air my dirty laundry in public or make you feel sorry for me. I know, too, that there are always two sides to every story and that Lachy has his good qualities. And it doesn't matter what people see for sixty minutes on a netball court – a fearless, confident, dominating goal-keeper, perhaps. I never let my personal life affect my netball but it would probably have come as a bit of a shock to those who know 'me on court' to see the other me. The one whose confidence was low, who was struggling, who wasn't sure where this relationship was headed. I was lucky I had netball to concentrate on. If I am totally honest I have tried to blank a lot of what happened from my mind. So I've asked Mum to contribute to this bit. She saw everything from a mum's point of view, of course, and is biased, but hopefully it will give you a good idea of the emotions I was dealing with.

'Geva was hitting thirty and wanted someone to build a life with, start a family with . . . Because of her sport and her lifestyle, she wasn't meeting guys. Lachy was the only one *who really showed any interest. A lot of guys were intimidated by her; they didn't feel they could approach her. Patrick Lucas, her PE teacher, said there were guys at his rugby clinic who would have the hots for her when she helped out but were too terrified to talk to her. Lachy was the first one who really made the effort and he came along at the right time, when Geva was getting nearer to thirty. She always told me she wanted to start a family in her early thirties and I think there was a strong element of not wanting to let go of this guy. A "Could he be the one? Full steam ahead!" mentality. Geva's personality changed when she was with him, without question. We had a conversation before the wedding and she questioned whether she was doing the right thing. She actually asked me, "Mum, should I be doing this?" and I said, "No. I don't think you should."*

'When Lachy brought Geva home to meet his mum for the first time she was everything Sue ever wanted in a daughter-in-law. She adored Geva – Sue was also a horse-rider and a netball nut and Lachy had brought home an ideal woman. It was like he thought "Geva will tick all the boxes for Mum, she will love her."

Whenever I went over to visit them or they would travel over to the UK – like for the Com Games in 2014 – we were always putting in so much effort to make him feel welcome and part of the family. But it didn't feel like he made as much effort with us. He just wanted to spend time with Geva.

Geva is so calm in an argument; she doesn't raise her voice easily. She would be trying to keep things calm, not adding to the argument by shouting and I honestly believe that probably infuriated him.

They did work on things and try to sort their relationship out, but to no avail. Lachy is very eloquent and a real charmer, and Geva somehow always ended up feeling like things were her fault. As her mum it was hard to watch.

'In 2017, Geva was captain of Sunshine Coast Lightning and they played in the grand finals. That was a Sunday, and they won! And yet I had her on the phone to me in tears on the Monday morning as he had completely and utterly burst her bubble. Instead of being out there, enjoying the celebrations, she was sobbing on the end of the phone, a complete wreck. I don't even know what he said to her but that was it for me. When I was over there at the beginning of 2018 I told her enough was enough, she needed to get out of this relationship. And she knew it too.'

So there you have it. In a nutshell, my wedding, my relationship and my divorce. It's probably best to get it all out in the open. Getting married to Lachy will always be my biggest regret and it embarrasses me that it happened. I am embarrassed because I never want to fail at anything in life but this I definitely did. I am embarrassed to tell people I was once married. I find it hard as I project such a strong, level-headed persona on court and yet I find myself, even now, getting emotional about that part of my life. When two people aren't right for each other, no amount of trying to make it work will solve anything. It does take two, I

But back to netball. After our disappointing Com Games, we were preparing for the Netball World Cup in 2015, which was being held in Sydney. It was a tough time for a lot of the girls and it took us a while to pick ourselves up again. It didn't help that England Netball decided to sack Anna Mayes as our coach. It just didn't go down well with the players, the way it was done. Whatever had happened between Anna and me in the past, I respected her as a coach and I think England Netball dumping her was a harsh and unfair call. Yes, we had a disappointing Games, but if anything it showed how close we were to causing a major upset. They appointed as head coach Tracey Neville, my former teammate, who had been assisting Anna for the past couple of years.

Tracey came in and in all honesty it felt like a bull in a china shop. She hadn't built up that rapport with the players, something that was part of Anna's coaching style – working with each individual, focusing on their strengths and weaknesses on court and their nerves and confidence off court. I think it took a while for the players to start to believe in what she was doing and settle themselves again. When she first came in, she was very headstrong and managed to piss off a lot of players and staff. She wanted to put her stamp on the team; she started running all these new programmes and changing routines and she was quite dominant. Being strong-minded isn't a bad thing in itself, though, as she sticks to her guns and you know where you stand with her! She has softened over the years and she has grown in confidence in the role too.

So, at the end of 2014 we had a new coach and a new challenge – to forget the mistakes of the Com Games and concentrate on kicking arse in the 2015 World Cup.

I'm not lying when I say that 2014 had its fair share of highs and lows, but one of the biggest highs for me was receiving my hundredth cap for England in December. A month before that momentous occasion I had been voted number-one netball player in the *Guardian*'s annual world top ten rankings. The panel of judges were big names in the world of netball, consisting of former national and international players, ex-England coaches and current coaches from other countries, TV pundits from the UK, Australia and New Zealand, university sports professors . . . it was an extensive and prestigious list and I was honoured to have been voted number one. I was also the only England player on the list. I couldn't believe I was now getting this recognition and this accolade, having missed out on playing for my country for nearly a year and a half.

My hundredth cap for England also came after completing my hundredth game in the ANZ Championship. I became the first import player to have reached such a milestone in the trans-Tasman competition, and ironically my hundredth game was against my former team, Thunderbirds, in Adelaide. It was such a cool situation; I don't think I ever thought when I first signed up for the league that I would be playing out there for so long! But Australia wasn't just where I was playing netball and improving my game. I was making great friends too, having great experiences and finding myself feeling more at home here than in England. I was really enjoying my time with Vixens. Having the right relationship with my goal defence, as I had with Sonia in England, was so important to me. I had it now with Bianca, the Vixens captain, too. It was definitely a combination we didn't have to work too hard at – it just clicked.

On 14 December 2014 I was to receive my hundredth England cap and I was hoping things would go a bit smoother than when I was due to receive my very first cap all those years ago. But this is England Netball we are talking about and nothing ever goes to plan! There was a bit of a debacle over the match as we were meant to be playing Malawi in a three-match series in Liverpool, but there was an issue with the team getting their visas, or something with their governing body, and they ended up not being able to make the flight over in time for the first game. But the series still went ahead and the Welsh national team stepped in and took their place for that match.

So there you have it. I got my hundredth cap against Wales and, without sounding big-headed, it meant we were pretty much guaranteed a win as the ranking difference between the two teams was quite substantial, so everything was a little bit more relaxed. But the best thing was that I was able to lead the team out on court. That honour normally falls to the captain but this time it was me and I was allowed to have my two half-sisters walk out either side of me too! Inez was only ten years old and Noor was eight and they were just my little mini-me's. They wore T-shirts that had 'Mentor' and '100' printed on the backs and it was the best feeling in the world to be able to walk out with them.

It was announced to the stadium why I was leading the team out and we got a massive round of applause and standing ovation as we came out. I loved having my sisters be part of that moment. I knew how cool it would be for them and I loved that not all eyes were on me – I hate being the centre of attention! Yes, of course it was great to have reached such an important milestone, but I'm not good when the spotlight is on me. I like to hide at the back normally! But I accepted that this was going to be one hell of an experience for Inez and Noor, and I was happy thinking it was a cool thing for them rather than a big thing for me.

Mum and Dad were both in the crowd and that in itself was quite special as it's not often I get all the family to a game. They watched as their children stood on court and sang the national anthem and got a standing ovation. I'm pretty sure they were bursting with pride! When Inez and Noor went back to Holland and into school, they told all their friends and teachers about it; they had TV clips to show and they were able to talk about me and netball, a sport that isn't very well known to the Dutch.

After the game I received a bunch of flowers but I think that was because I was named player of the match. I didn't get anything for my hundredth cap, other than that experience. Mum and I had organised everything that day because we didn't want to leave anything down to England Netball. Jade Clarke celebrated her hundredth cap at the Glasgow

Commonwealth Games and England Netball didn't do anything to mark it at all, so the rest of the girls and I made it special for her and made a fuss of her that game. In my case, I have only just managed to get my little medallion for my very first cap, for goodness sake, so I expect I will be a lot older when I finally get something for my hundredth cap – if anything at all! I did make sure all the girls signed my dress, though, and I have it framed. All the girls on the team had decorated the changing rooms as a surprise for me; there was a big '100' banner over my locker area and balloons and banners everywhere. It was a bit of a mess! Dad hadn't been to any of my games in Australia yet and only one or two in the UK, so it was great to have him there at such a momentous game. Inez and Noor are adamant that he needs to bring them over and watch the World Cup this year, which would be so cool. They haven't seen me play at a major event yet, so to have them there would be the icing on the cake.

The start of 2015 was just as magical as the end of 2014. I was back in Melbourne and driving to training with Vixens when I got a call from Tracey.

'Geva, I'm looking towards the World Cup . . . I want to offer you the captaincy role.'

And I would like to say my reply was dignified but I think I was more like, 'Oh . . . oh! SHIT! What?! Really?!'

'Will you take it?' she said.

'I'd be honoured!' I said. I think I was still in shock. 'I'm not used to being handed this sort of thing . . . is it something the players want?' I asked.

'To be honest, Geva, this is something I want,' said Tracey. 'I think you are the right person to lead the team.'

And that was that! It was a short phone call but what a life-changing moment. Me, England captain! Of course right away I wanted to ring Mum. I had no idea what time it was over there but I knew she wouldn't care.

When the announcement was made, it was like I was royalty or something. When I told people I was captain of the England netball team I was put on a bit of a pedestal. I think people still refer to me as captain of England now, and I feel a bit bad and I always correct them. 'No, not me any more!' I say. But it's quite funny, I suppose. And flattering!

Having been given the nod, it was all systems go and as I was based in Melbourne, a lot of the communicating with the England squad was done over the telephone or with Skype calls. I would be talking to everyone in the UK, everyone who played their part in the team – the staff, nutritionists, psychologists, the CEO, the personal trainers, members of the board. And I would sort everything out with Tracey, talking through and agreeing ideas and routines and everything with her. She likes her captain to have lots of involvement with the planning, the training and preparation. She likes to bounce ideas off the captain and you end up making quite a few decisions and having lots of control. I don't mind that as I am a control freak and I like to know a little about everything so I can see what's happening. This was important to me; as with whatever I do I want to give it all of my time, energy and commitment. But because I was on the other side of the world it did mean I had lots of 5 a.m. alarm wake-ups in order to speak to people and sort stuff out. I definitely had no idea being captain was so intense. It wasn't just leading the team out onto court on the day and chatting to players between quarters – it was like a full-time job! There is no accurate role description for it – you are always managing this or negotiating that or giving your opinion on something else. And you have a squad of twenty-four you are looking after, not just twelve. So that's a lot of people with a lot of individual concerns to deal with!

The World Cup came round and we headed off to Sydney. I remember we stayed in the Pullman Hotel for a week before our first game. Tracey's parents were flying over from England. They were due to arrive on the Wednesday and our first game was on the Friday. We got a phone call Wednesday evening saying that Tracey's dad had been taken into hospital; he had come off the flight very unwell and had had a heart attack and was on a life-support machine. Tracey's brothers got flown over to Sydney and although as captain I was aware of what was happening, the rest of the team didn't know anything was wrong. I spoke to them on Thursday, before our game the next day, and explained the situation. The leadership team, the assistant coach and I made sure we were organised and had planned everything, making sure the team was ready for the first game so Tracey could just concentrate on her family.

And on that Friday afternoon, we played. Tracey was there for the game in body but not in spirit. They had turned her dad's life-support machine off that morning. It was a very emotional game. It was a very emotional World Cup. Her mum and her brothers stayed on for a while afterwards because they wanted to support her. I knew she would be flying her dad's body back to the UK after the World Cup was over and I just felt so sad for her.

It was the most heartbreaking time we had ever had as a team. We knew what we had to do, we knew the task at hand and we were, to a certain extent, able to stick to that. We were making sure Tracey had distractions, that things were positive and upbeat in the team, but it was hard. It was incredibly draining for the whole group as everyone just felt such sadness for Tracey and her family. In that World Cup we played some of the toughest games we had ever played. Sonia, my best buddy, my GD partner in crime, was still in the team and as far as the pool games went, we did OK, but we played against New Zealand in the semi-finals and they beat us easily. I think it was probably by ten goals or so. We just weren't in the same contest. So that left us with Jamaica in the bronze medal play-offs. I had been here countless times before and, to be honest, I didn't see us mentally winning it. The game started to go the way I had predicted; we were just plodding along, everything was a battle. Jamaica had the momentum and the upper hand through most of the first two or three quarters. And then I remember they brought Sonia on as GD. And no word of a lie, she came on, she was very vocal and she made such a difference to the team performance. Her intercepts and turnovers and freshness just lifted the team completely and suddenly we were off and away! We ended up winning quite comfortably in the end, 66–44, and it was a great finish to what was the hardest and most emotional competition any of us had been involved in. We had won a medal for Tracey and for her dad.

Amid all this, Pam and I were honoured to be invited to a special event to tell us we had been inducted into the English Netball Hall of Fame. It was organised by the England Netball Supporters Club and it gave fans who had travelled down under a chance to meet us and the team. It was so surreal, I was being inducted into the Hall of Fame, but poor old mum who had travelled to Sydney to watch me play hadn't been given an invite! She and Eva heard about it, though, and gatecrashed! Their daughters had over two hundred England caps to their names and this was a momentous occasion – there was no way they were going to miss the evening celebration.

After the World Cup there was a bit of a break for us. Tracey chose different captains for different series matches, and the captaincy changed hands a few times and then I think they decided they wanted someone who was based in the UK. I understood that; there was a lot going on there and the schedules were tight. Tracey had developed the

England programme so that the people playing out in Australia and New Zealand would come back two weeks before an international, train in the training camp and then go into test series mode, or Commonwealth Games mode or World Cup mode, depending on what was happening. That is the point when Ama Agbeze took over the reins as captain and she did a great job. But it definitely took its toll on her, as it has on captains before. I think we netball players can do a lot better in the way we support our captains, as a team and as a bigger organisation. There is a lot of work involved and we rely on them a lot. Mum calls captaining a poisoned chalice and she advised me that if I was ever offered it again I should think long and hard before I took it!

Life with the Vixens in 2015 had gone from high to low. We had won the year before with Bianca Chatfield as our captain, but this year we got the premiership curse. The year 2016 didn't start off much better for us; I think we ended up at the end of the season bumming out in third or fourth position. Simone McKinnis, a very good former Diamonds wing defence, had been the coach when Julie Hoornweg left in 2014 but it felt like there was a lot of change in the air. The league was changing too.

The ANZ Championship saw netball become a semi-professional sport in Australia and New Zealand, which meant increased media coverage and player salaries. Netball Australia were looking to create a bigger, nationally exclusive league with significantly improved broadcasting and media deals. It still had the same teams from Australia involved, but three new teams joined the league too. New Zealand formed their own successor league, the ANZ Premiership, which is contested by six teams based in New Zealand.

At the beginning of the season that year, I had a conversation with Vixens that started something like this: 'Geva, you're getting on a bit . . .'

I was thirty-two years old. I had a few wear-and-tear problems with my knees and the previous year I'd had a scope on my left knee, which is basically just a clean-out because I had lots of floating fragments. Now my right knee needed a good clean-out too. Instead of the swelling staying in the front of my knee, it 'pulled' round to the back of my knee and I developed a Baker's cyst, a large swelling at the back of my knee.

I used to go into a clinic every four or five weeks to have surgery to get my knee aspirated. I had to lie on my tummy and they would find the bulging bit and put a needle in to suck out the fluid in the back of my knee. There was no anaesthetic involved. Sometimes there was a little bit of puffiness at the front too, so they would suck that out as well. Mum was with me once when I was having it done. She couldn't handle it at all. I think the doctors were worried about her – she was turning green! There was a big difference for her between me describing it and her actually seeing it happen – I think she felt bad that I was being put in so much pain on a regular basis. But the treatment has always worked brilliantly and I feel so good afterwards! I can move my knees with no aches or pains. I can't thank the Olympic Park Team enough for all the care they've given me.

I also had platelet-rich plasma (PRP) treatment, which acts as an anti-inflammatory. In a nutshell, doctors would take out some of my blood, spin it, and then put the white blood cells back. I had this for most of 2016 and, again, it wasn't pleasant but the results were worth it.

I suppose, in a sense, the Vixens were looking at the bigger picture. They were being honest with me and I did appreciate that. I was getting old in their eyes and I'd had a few injuries, a few niggles. They told me that they'd like to keep me around, maybe on a year-long contract, but that they saw me in more of a 'mentoring' role. They wanted me to focus my attention on girls who were up and coming and needed someone to nurture them.

Now don't get me wrong, I am not opposed to helping others in the team – I like that, I enjoy that and I think it is a good way to push both of us for a playing position. I had already spent time mentoring and nurturing some of the younger girls like Emily Mannix and Jo Weston (they are both now Diamonds players) and guiding them through the game. But I didn't want to do just that because I didn't feel like I was done playing yet. I was still very competitive – I am still competitive! It was two years to the next Commonwealth Games and I wanted to play in it. I needed to carry on getting court time and playing at a top level. What they were offering was a defence-coach position, which meant reduced court time and a reduction in salary.

But then along came rugby. I was approached by Melbourne Storm, the National Rugby League team in Melbourne, to help them with a video-advert campaign. Rugby union and rugby league struggle to get the attendance that netball, AFL and soccer get, so I was called upon, along with a guy called Nick Maxwell, the Collingwood FC premiership captain, and Molly Meldrum, a well-known Australian musician, to persuade people that whatever 'code' you came from, meaning what area of Melbourne, you could still support Melbourne Storm. It was great fun to be part of the ad and it had such a good, fun vibe to it. It wasn't long after the ad that the team got in contact with me again; Melbourne Storm NRL club had put in for a licence to start up their own netball team, and together with the University of the Sunshine Coast they formed the Sunshine Coast Lightning. The formation of the team came about as the league changed from ANZ to the new Suncorp Super Netball league and I was asked, did I want to be involved in this brand-new team? They had recruited Noeline Taurua, known as Noels, who was a New Zealand coach and assistant coach for the Silver Ferns. And it was like they had just spoken the magic words.

I had heard some great things about Noeline being an amazing coach who had a very holistic approach. So I was very intrigued. She called me and I remember we talked for over an hour – about everything apart from netball! The biggest thing that sold it for me was that the team she was putting together on the Sunshine Coast would be a collection of people with the best stats – most deflections, most pick-ups, high percentage of shots, and the ones with the best netball traits that together would make a great team. Combined with the fact that the people she had in mind were players she believed would all mix well personality-wise, it was sounding like a very healthy, strong and exciting team that I definitely wanted to be part of. To cut a long story short, I loved everything she was saying. I think in the end it was probably quite a tough decision to leave Vixens, because they had been good to me and I had a good relationship with Simone. But then again, I didn't want to stay with them and not play elite netball. I still had a fire in my belly to win and now I was ready for something new and completely different.

I moved to the Sunshine Coast in November 2016 and it meant leaving Lachlan behind in Melbourne. That was good. This move probably couldn't have come at a much better time for me; I needed to get away. I think we both needed some time apart. Besides, his school was in Melbourne and he was teaching full-time, so he couldn't have moved away that easily. I don't think Vixens knew how bad the marriage was, to be honest, and I wonder if they might have made more of an effort with me if they had. I think initially they didn't think I would leave the club as it meant leaving my husband behind, so potentially they might have put forward a better offer. But it didn't matter. I had my heart set on a new start, a new team and a new challenge.

11 GEVA AND THE SEVEN DWARFS

'There are far, far better things ahead than any we leave behind.'

C. S. Lewis

WHEN I first moved to Lightning, Noeline told us she had selected a skeleton of a team. She went for experience across the court with a strong person at the attacking end, a strong mid-quarter and a strong defender. The mid-quarter was from New Zealand, Laura Langman. She still holds the title for the most capped player for the Silver Ferns, a record previously held by Irene van Dyk. Making up the attacking end, Noeline had recruited Caitlin Bassett, who is the current Australian Diamonds captain. I had faced Caitlin on many occasions – we have battled it out against each other in the goal circle countless times before – so it was quite cool to think she was on my team now! She was ready for a change too, and after years of playing against each other we'd be putting on the same dresses and fighting for the same result. Well, as Lightning teammates that is; I knew the rivalry would come back next time I met her in my Roses dress!

I'm a naturally organised person, so when I arrived I took on the role of setting a few things up and helping everyone out. Laura, Caitlin and I formed a bit of a leadership group and both Laura and I thought the natural choice would be to select Bass as captain. She and I were both very supportive of this; we told Noels the same thing: she was a big star in Australia and a phenomenal player and we would be happy for her to lead us in this competition. Even the media were making hints, running stories about her being made captain, and whenever other teams were interviewed about this new Lightning team, they assumed that Bass would be in charge, even though nothing had formally been announced. But then our players got wind of what was going on and they wanted to have their say on who should be their captain. So Noeline set up a vote.

It was a new club so there needed to be a lot of new procedures put in place, including this one. They decided to split the vote so that the players' vote would account for 50 per cent of the vote and the other 50 per cent would come from the staff – the CEO, the coach and assistant coach. The top three names ended up being Bass, myself and Laura. Noeline then wanted to interview us for the position, so we each had to prepare a presentation about why we would make a good captain. It was the most terrifying thing I'd ever had to do! I think I had one or two sleepless nights in the lead-up to it and I don't know why; it wasn't like I had a strong desire to be captain, but I suppose, like with anything I do, I wanted to do a good job. But the more I prepped, the more nervous I got and I realised I did want this captaincy role, the role I wasn't initially fussed about! Everything was fine when I was in the interview. I think all the stressing out beforehand was because I was worried that I wouldn't present myself well. But in the end it went well. I told the panel all the things I would personally bring to the role and I think I conveyed the most important message – that it would be a massive honour to lead the team. The next day I got a call from Noeline congratulating me on being captain! It was an incredible feeling. I had been voted for by my teammates, the coaches, the staff and the CEO and that made it even more special. It gave me the confidence to lead and be myself, knowing that the team had that faith and trust in me. It highlights the one thing we don't do as well as an England side – in our set-up it is just the coach who chooses the captain. And that isn't to say our captain isn't great, but as a captain, it's an incredible feeling to know you have also had the nod of approval from your teammates.

I got flown to Sydney the next day, as the league had put on a launch day and were bringing in all the captains from the eight different teams. We took part in TV interviews and had photos, there were lots of speeches and it was all quite a fun way to mark the start of the season.

The funniest thing for me was that all the other captains

there that year were middies (mid-court players) and all of a certain height. Then I rock up as the new Lightning captain, all six foot two inches of me, and I think the waiting photographers quickly realised how funny this would look and started calling us Geva and the Seven Dwarfs! There are some great photos out there of that.

Mainly I remember being just so excited and honoured and ready to get my teeth into this new challenge. All the other captains were very supportive of me and congratulated me, which was brilliant. Although I do remember one of them asking me why my dress looked so different from the others as it was just a very plain dress with the logo of the club, a lightning strike, on the front and back. The difference was that we didn't have any sponsors yet as we were a brand-new team and no one wanted to take a chance on us. Sponsors don't like taking a risk and would prefer to stick with the more established teams. We didn't even have any offices or anything to begin with; we had a temporary room at the university, one or two staff members, coaches and players and that was pretty much it. We had to build up everything from scratch. All credit to Lightning, they did manage to recruit some of the best people in their fields, from Kurt and Greg, our physios, to Mark, our strength and conditioning coach, to Anthony, the whizz behind the camera, and Kellie, our nutritionist. We were fortunate enough to be able to use the facilities at the university and also some of their staff to cover some roles. But otherwise, no one really paid us much attention. I don't think anyone would have predicted that this new team, built from scratch, with limited resources, no sponsors and a novice English captain, would ever win the premiership. We felt underestimated, a new team in a league of established teams with lots of money behind them.

Our first game saw us up against our state rivals, the Queensland Firebirds, who had been very successful in previous years. We ended up getting a draw for our first game and that was a good outcome.

People often ask me if heckling or sledging happens in netball. There is no space for booing in netball in my mind; it shouldn't happen. I understand that crowds get emotional and overexcited and carried away but it's unacceptable when you are targeting an individual player. But does it happen? Of course it does. The first season we played as Lightning we went across to Perth to play against Fever. Bass had previously played for the club; she was their top goal-scorer and had played as a junior before moving her way up through the club to the top level. And then she moved clubs and came to us. When she went out against Fever in that first game, she was booed the moment her foot stepped on to that court. I was shocked. It was horrible for her. I can't remember exactly what was shouted but there was just lots of jeering and booing and taunting. I wasn't going to stand for it and when I was interviewed at the end – as both captains are – I absolutely laid into the crowd. I told them how disappointed I was in them and how disrespectful they were in their behaviour towards this girl who had given them so much netball over the years.

Netball is not a place where we want or tolerate heckling, booing, sledging – leave it to us players on court. I got on my soapbox as I felt very passionate about it and I made sure everyone knew how cross I was. I was also very protective of Bass, who took it all very well, considering. She is a tough cookie and very thick-skinned. But I was reeling. The behaviour of the crowd hurt me and I was upset for her. Normally after a game I make sure I spend a lot of time with the spectators, and I will go around and sign autographs and take photos, but I made a point of not doing it that time as I was furious about the way they'd treated one of my own. Bass actually got player of the match that game, which was awesome – and a big two-fingers-up at the crowd!

I'm not saying that we are so precious we can't cope with a bit of heckling, but it's just not needed in our sport. Of course we do get hecklers. They tend to flock around the goalposts and attack the shooters, saying nasty things when they miss a shot. But the majority of the crowd are pretty good at telling these few to shut up or calling for security so they can be removed. Shooters are more sensitive souls and they have enough things to block out already when they're making a shot, never mind someone calling 'Miss!' as the ball is about to leave their fingers.

Now, when it comes to heckling on court, there are some particular players in this league who will drop comments during play. They'll stand round the circle edge and they'll be like, 'Oh, umpire, can't you see that?' or 'Did you see her pushing?!' or 'Good pass!' when the ball goes off the back line. I don't say anything myself; defenders don't really say anything unless we are shouting out encouragement. The ones who do it tend to be the middies and, to be honest with you, I don't know how they have the energy to throw cheeky comments about – they obviously aren't working hard enough!

We had got off to a good start in the league and after a few wins we started to get noticed a bit more, which meant most weeks we had to hand our dresses back to add to the growing number of sponsor logos we were accumulating. They bought into our club and wanted to be part of our team, and by the end of the season we were full! The thing that I enjoyed most about our team was that we really did create it from scratch – we had devised our own values and culture and built a foundation for the years to come. It was the first national team the Sunny Coast had and that meant everyone got behind us too; we had a great community feel.

I remember the first time we played my old side, the Melbourne Vixens, they travelled to our home court and although we didn't start well and were down at half-time, we ended up winning. In my book that is always good because you always want to be able to beat the team you've just moved from! It's a satisfying feeling. You want to feel like you have proved something to yourself, you are moving forward in your game, you are bettering yourself. We lost a few games, we won a few more – the ones we won were important ones, sentimental ones, and as the season progressed we were looking pretty good and sitting in a strong position on the ladder.

The Giants, based in Sydney, were another new team and they ended up being our rivals. Unfortunately for them they lost their captain Kim Green to injury, which left a huge hole in the team. She was an amazing sportswoman and a few years later, when England won gold at the Commonwealth Games, she made sure she went and found Mum in the crowd and gave her a big hug. She told Mum that I deserved every moment of that victory, which, as an Australian and having just witnessed her country lose, was an incredibly generous thing for her to say.

On the couple of occasions we had previously met the Giants, the matches had been a real battle. We'd be going goal-for-goal in each game, which made it so tense yet thrilling.

We had a good season, improving with every game, which was our motto – to be better than the week before. We finished the regular season in a strong position in the table, sitting second, which meant we got into the finals. It was the start of a crazy couple of weeks for us and we travelled to Melbourne to play Vixens on their home court. They finished top of the table ahead of us. We came from behind to win the match by one goal, which meant we faced a home grand final against Giants. You just want to hit another level come finals and that is what it felt like we did. It's hard to pinpoint exactly why it all went right (if I could I would bottle it!) but everything just worked, everything clicked. We hit our stride and no one could touch us. We talked about that in our mindfulness and psychology sessions – what that feeling is like when everyone is on the same page. And to have a team of individuals, all in sync – it was a feeling you can't really describe. Everything slows down around you and you are just grinding away all together. We ended up winning by seventeen goals, which was incredible. To finish the season off like that, well, like it was a fairy tale!

We were a new team, we had taken a risk, we had come together as a lot of individuals from different states, different backgrounds, different countries, and we had managed to make it work against all odds and in a competition that, at the start, probably hadn't really accepted us properly. We won the premiership in our inaugural season. I hope one day someone makes a film about this team and this journey. It would be a blockbuster!

Karla Pretorius, a phenomenal South African player, was my goal defence and we just 'got' each other right away. I thrive off my connection with Karla, and I love how much she has developed her game and grown in confidence. I am proud to watch her when she plays with South Africa. Yes, it's to England's detriment, but at the end of the day she is a great player and a great person off court, and I want her to do well.

I took the role of captain very seriously but I didn't try to be someone I'm not. I like to have fun and I also like to make sure all the girls on the team feel valued and to lead by example. I was keen to have an environment where everyone felt they could have a voice, but also had enough trust in me to know I would make the right decisions. I wasn't perfect but I like to think I did an OK job.

Throwing myself into the new team and captaincy was what I needed. Being apart from Lachy due to my netball commitments was a blessing. Things felt better between us when we were apart.

It's funny to think that although in my industry I have to be strong and confident and a positive leader, I can feel the opposite in my personal life. I often felt sad, empty and deflated by our relationship and the negative environment it created. In a sporting context, I would stand up for what I believed in, I would be strong, I would be confident; and yet in my own home with my own husband those behaviours were absent.

You don't realise at the time how weak you have become, you just accept it. It was what it was. Now I think to myself, what was I thinking? It is hard for an athlete to admit failure and what you learn in a professional capacity – to play to win – you bring to your personal life too. I didn't want to 'fail' at my marriage and so I did a lot of things because I thought it would somehow make everything better. I went along with the wedding because I had planned it and it was at a time in my life when I thought this was what I should be doing. I have learned now that it is OK to say no, it is OK to rock the boat and not worry if that upsets other people, and it's OK to admit defeat sometimes, although that is hard for an athlete to accept! I have to remind myself that I am a strong, independent woman first and foremost and that I need to trust my gut more and stop trying to please others. Life is too short; you have to give everything your all, yes, but you also have to accept when it just isn't working. I think we both knew that our marriage wasn't working and it was over, but neither of us wanted to acknowledge it.

Things got worse when my brother, who was playing basketball locally in Melbourne, hurt his foot. His visa was coming to an end and he had just arranged for a new one to go and work in New Zealand for the next two years. He flew over to New Zealand and looked to base himself there, but his foot didn't get any better. He turned out to be suffering from a Lisfranc fracture. I said to him, 'Right, we need to get this sorted,' and I flew him to the Sunshine Coast to be treated by the Lightning medical team, which is something I would do for any member of my family or any close friend who needed it. The team were amazing and helped devise an action plan for his recovery. A few scans showed that he had to have quite a major operation on his foot, with a twelve-month recovery period. He is a tall, solid lad and needed time to heal so he could move around before he even thought about playing sport again, so he stayed with me. Lachlan didn't seem to understand that I would always help and support my family, just like I would his, and all I wanted him to do was to get that and be part of it.

Having my brother around was a huge comfort as Lachy and I were arguing a lot – I was in tears most nights while I was talking to him. I said to him that I was happy to pay for some of Raoul's surgery and medical costs up front and my family would pay us back. 'I have an Australian bank account,' I said, 'I earn money too.' And that was the hardest thing. I earned that money and I am entitled to spend it how I want to. I don't go out shopping, I don't fritter it away. I spend money on what I need. Money caused us endless issues and arguments on the phone each evening and it was so draining. And meanwhile I was trying to manage and lead a team, make sure I was still training and performing and doing my studies too. The grand final when we won the season was on a Sunday and I was on a complete high. Until I spoke to him. I rang my mum on Monday in tears.

If my personal life was torturing me, in a sense you could say my netball life was saving me. I came away at the end of the Suncorp Super Netball season and straight into a Quad Series with England. We finished third, which we were pleased with, behind the big hitters Australia and New Zealand but above South Africa. We also competed in a Fast5 competition, which is a bit like Twenty20 in cricket; it's a five-player match and each quarter only lasts six minutes. The competition is held over three days and the first two days you play in a round-robin format. Then the four highest-scoring teams play in a finals day. It's fun, it's fast, and we seemed to adapt to its rampant pace easily. We ended up beating Jamaica in the final and it topped off not only a successful tournament for us but an extremely fun one. There was lots of dancing and singing and I played with my hair in bunches! It just finished off the winning streak for me that year. Well, not quite, as it turned out. I received an invitation to attend the Netball Australia awards; I had been nominated in two categories, Player of the Year and Best Goal Keeper. My professional fairytale year was about to get even more magical.

It is very bizarre as an English international to be invited to the Netball Australia awards. Although I am dual nationality, having received my citizenship on Australia Day in 2016, I still felt a little bit of an intruder. That year they were also celebrating the twenty-five-year history of Netball Australia; all their previous playing dresses were displayed in frames and it felt extra special. The awards were held at the town hall in Melbourne and just to be there and be acknowledged was pretty awesome. It was quite humbling to be among people in and from Australia with them celebrating me, an international.

Sitting round the table representing Sunshine Coast Lightning were myself, Lachy, Bass, who had been named Diamonds captain again, our coach Noeline and her husband, our CEO Danielle Smith and her partner.

When the Coach of the Year award nominations were read out, I think everyone in that room – and certainly everyone on our table – expected Noels to be the winner. Absolutely, 100 per cent, no contest, hands down, she should have won it. But she didn't. I don't know what Netball Australia were thinking. Maybe they didn't want to acknowledge her performance because she was from New Zealand? Whatever the reason, it left a nasty taste in our mouths. Everyone could see that it should have been her. And yet they gave it to the Vixens' coach, Simone, who had previously played for Australia and was a product of the Australia coaching pathway. Not to take anything away from her, but it did not seem fair or right.

When the Suncorp Super Netball Best Player of the Year award came up I think I was still a little aggrieved for Noeline and I'm pretty sure I didn't think I would ever win. I knew I'd had a good year and people had mentioned that I was a strong contender, but I still didn't think it would be me. And then the presenter, Pete Lazer, announced my name! I hadn't planned a speech, so I just winged it and I was lucky enough that Pete knew netball and me well enough that when he handed the mic over I felt comfortable enough to just speak from the heart and say whatever came into my mind. I was still in complete shock, but I thanked a lot of people and I acknowledged a lot of people – although I probably forgot to thank and acknowledge a whole lot more! I think I got a laugh too when I held up the award and said, 'This is for the over-thirties!' We had been a little deflated after Noeline missed out on her award, so this definitely picked up the mood and gave us something to celebrate. And when I won Best Goalkeeper of the Year too it just topped off a pretty unbelievable night.

When I first moved up to Sunshine Coast I was living with a lady who I knew through a friend of a friend of Mum's – good old Mum is great when it comes to chatting to the right people. I then moved into another place a bit closer to the beach that I found on a site called flatmates. com. Wayne Buxley owned a four-bedroom house and needed a lodger. He was also English and he had moved to Adelaide, then to Melbourne, and then made his way up to the Sunshine Coast, just like me. It was like I was destined to be his lodger! He was a trainee pilot so he was away a lot, so it was a perfect living arrangement. I lived with him from 2017 to 2018. Lachy and Wayne didn't have much in common – but Wayne and my brother got on brilliantly well. Wayne witnessed several tearful phone calls between myself and Lachy but he was always good at offering support without interfering. I remember after another tearful argument with Lachy. Wayne tried to boost my confidence a little. 'Lach's got a racehorse, not a pony, with you, Geev, he should bloody look after you like one.' It made me laugh!

Sharing a house was good for a while but after about a year I decided it was time to get a little place for myself and start to settle. I was really loving the Sunshine Coast; I loved the community feel of the place and I had made some wonderful friends. Everyone was so welcoming and I felt so embraced by the locals. In a strange twist of fate I made friends with an ex-England player, Chrissie Browne, who had been axed from the netball team in 1999. She and her clan made me feel like part of their family. She helped me set up Netty Girls, an initiative that involved visiting primary schools in the neighbourhood and running netball workshops. I was so happy when I found my own little place near Birtinya, overlooking the waterways. It was so nice to feel like I had set up a home. Having somewhere that was home has been the most important thing for me throughout my years of playing and travelling back and forth between the UK and Australia.

At the beginning of 2018, Lachy decided to go on a sabbatical from work and come up to stay with me. We hadn't had a good Christmas and then I had the Quad Series in the UK in January, during which I was away for about a month, and we didn't speak for the entire time. It was a bit of a relief to have that break, to be honest. When I got back we had a discussion. We agreed that it wasn't working and basically decided to call it a day, and kind of lived like housemates for a couple of months. I was conscious of him having all this time off work and I didn't want him to waste it, so I suggested he book himself a trip away. He had always wanted to go to Japan so I tried to encourage him to do that. But he is one of those people who isn't always comfortable doing things by himself and prefers to have someone with him. He did go to Japan for three weeks and, again, we didn't really speak in that time. When he got back he packed up his stuff, went to stay with his brother for a bit, and then went back to Melbourne. Our marriage was over and the divorce proceedings would be starting soon.

12 GOING FOR GOLD

'If you don't see yourself as a winner, then you cannot perform as a winner.'
                                                        Zig Ziglar

THE Commonwealth Games 2018. My fifth Games. It felt like it was going to be a home Games for me, as it was being held on the Gold Coast, which was only a couple of hours' drive south from me, also on Australia's east coast. It also meant that when Mum flew in from the UK and my brother came over from New Zealand, they were able to stay with me and then get to the Games relatively easily. Mum got herself a little Airbnb place and was all set up to come and watch every match. I think she knew I might need a little extra support this year and it was good to have her and Raoul nearby.

Our England manager, Paul Dring, flew over a couple of months before the Games to check out the athletes' village and do a bit of a recce. He called me and asked me if I wanted to join him and some of the other Team England management group and my response was, 'Of course I bloody well do!'

I jumped in the car right after training, drove down through Brisbane, and met him on the Gold Coast. It was really cool to be able to walk around the village without any of the other athletes there, like a 'behind-the-scenes' look. The purpose of me being there was to help Paul write his report from a player's perspective, so he could report back to the team. A month or so later, when I was back in England at the training camp, he gave his presentation to the team and talked about the accommodation and the set-up and the different areas and I was able to contribute. I also had my uses – in some of the rooms you could ask for bed extensions for taller athletes, so all the managers had asked me to lie down on the beds to give them a visual guide to bed length. It was quite amusing, me having a little lie-down as we toured round all the beds!

To say England Netball's campaign got off to a strange start is probably an understatement. First of all, we had a training camp in Sydney to attend. We were all meant to meet there for a week before the Games but things were a little controversial for me as Lightning, who I was in pre-season training with at the time, had a three-day camp in New Zealand for all their players. England were to fly over the team members who were not aligned with a Suncorp Super Netball team and weren't already in Australia, and we SSN players were told to join the team a day after they landed. Lightning and I tried to negotiate whether I could do a day and a half in New Zealand with the team, as I was captain and would normally have a lot of input into our pre-season camp, and then come and join the England girls a day late. The coaches, Tracey and Noeline, ended up at a stalemate. Neither were prepared to budge, and in the end it was decided that I would just go straight to Sydney to the England camp and forget New Zealand. I'm not sure how it was resolved but Tracey is headstrong and you don't want to cross Noeline, so I'm sure it was interesting!

Rather frustratingly, the week in Sydney ended up being the biggest waste of time. We didn't get going until day three or four as we had to wait for some of the girls to get over jet lag. Then there wasn't much time for training; I think we had just a couple of gym sessions before heading straight into some practice matches. These were against two other teams in the Suncorp Super Netball League, the GWS from Sydney and the Sydney Swifts, both of whom are extremely good and who I'd obviously come up against in the season. A couple of the English girls who played for those teams in the league were allowed to play for them rather than be in the England team, which didn't seem right to me; surely the whole team should have been training and playing together from the start? And we got our arses well and truly kicked. We lost by about thirty goals one day and thirty-five goals the next.

Talk about deflated. England, the national team, about to compete at the Commonwealth Games, and we had lost to two Australian club sides. It was demoralising to say the least. It completely broke us. I called Tracey out after the second game and a thirty-five goal loss while everyone was sat in a circle cooling down. I had had enough and I asked her, in front of everyone, 'What is going on?!' I was just furious. 'This isn't helping us,' I said, 'what is the point of getting some of our girls to play against us? What do we get out of this? This is about us as a team, us as a team trying to prepare for the Coms!'

The girls were silent, Tracey was silent. I continued. 'Tracey, we need to train together. We need to go through a bit of a game-plan, have some structure, then we can go out and play. Not just come away from all our different club sides and just automatically think we can gel as the England team!'

My rant was over. I think she was a bit taken back by it all. She tried to respond but then realised she had no leg to stand on and said she would speak to Ama, our captain. This was unlike me – I am normally a lot more tactful – but this was my fifth Games and it meant so much to me. When I spoke up to our coach in front of the whole team I was hoping that I was speaking on behalf of everyone; I thought I had a pretty good idea that we all felt the same. I had talked to some of the girls after our first practice match and some of them were in tears. They were doubting their ability, their self-confidence was knocked. While I was addressing Tracey I also spoke directly to the group. I remember asking, 'Guys, if you don't agree with me, speak up, please.' But they were all nodding and saying, 'No we do, we agree.'

Ama, our captain, came up to me afterwards and was very grateful. We ended up having a bit of a joke about it all and someone said, 'Wouldn't it be funny if after all this, losing in our practice games to a club team by thirty-five goals, we end up winning the gold medal!' Oh how we laughed! What a joke. And that was the end of that.

We had one more practice game lined up for the next day and this time we made sure we had an hour's training session all together before we played. It made such a difference – we came out and we played really well. We had a bit more of a boost when Chelsea Pitman's parents treated us all to a boat ride round Sydney Harbour. It was a bit of light relief after a fairly emotional and stressful few days and we loved it! We got our England kit while we were in the Sydney camp too. The dresses were a bloody nightmare as they didn't fit at all and it looked like we were wearing sacks! If you look good, you feel good, you play good. No one wants to go out on court looking like they are wearing ill-fitting gear – what does that say about the team? That we can't even sort out our kit?! The rest of the kit was fine but our match dresses were unwearable.

We got a seamstress on to it, and she pinned and stitched and added more material to the length and made all the alterations that had to be made. I basically needed two dresses sewn together as mine was like a swimsuit made for a toddler – far too short and tight! Because she took them away to work on, we didn't end up getting them back until the morning of our first match. I'd like to say this was a one-off, but there seems to be a problem with our dresses every time. I don't think I've ever had one World Cup or Com Games where we haven't had issues with them. It is beyond ridiculous. At the Commonwealth Games in Manchester the dresses were so awful that Mum called in her trampolining friend who used to design and make my leotards to alter them all. I genuinely think the designers seem to forget we are tall, athletic women or something. We always need to have extra length added and we are female so we always need to have a bit of shape for our hips. Some of our trousers have sometimes been like ankle-swingers or come up to mid-shin. You would have thought that they had got the gist by now – we are netballers, we are tall!

So that was our week's camp in Sydney and it was horrible and demoralising but we were England, we get on with it.

It was time to move to Brisbane for another holding camp with Team England. It was there that we had arranged to play Lightning. But that match got cancelled, I think because of what had happened beforehand with me in the New Zealand camp. To this day it seems to me there is still a little bit of angst between Noels and Tracey, although they're totally professional about it as they see each other quite often as coaches of their national sides!

So we were in Brisbane, in the holding camp. The basketball team were there, and the athletics guys and girls were there, and it was brilliant. Team England had such a vibe! The camp was right in the middle of Brisbane and as we walked around there was such a sense of excitement in the air. We carried on training hard and it was much more positive; it was just what we needed. We needed that time as a team. We were there for five or six days and then it was time to head an hour south to Gold Coast and be checked into the village. You get to select who you want to share rooms with and I was sharing with Eboni, the goal defence, who I get on really well with and who has similar routines to me. This is important as you need to be with someone you'll be comfortable with in tight quarters for an intense and pressured period of time. There were two apartments, with three bedrooms in each apartment and two beds in each room. The village had a good vibe to it as always. I had been before so I didn't have to spend a few days finding my way around – I knew where things all were. I hit the swimming pool as soon as we arrived. The complex was as cool as I remembered. Being here in the holding camp beforehand was good as we had chance to make friends and form bonds with other athletes; when you get to the village everything is so super-huge, you'd struggle to get to know people properly. I met up with lots of people from Team England who I recognised and had made friends with previously, along with other nations. And I know lots of people who play for New Zealand and South Africa and Australia too, obviously, so

I think this year I was bumping into lots of old faces – friends and foes! The best bit about the build-up to the Com Games is the last few days leading up to the opening ceremony. Everyone is relaxed and full of expectation and there is almost no pressure. I suppose there is a bit of sussing each other out, checking out the competition, but on the whole it is more about just enjoying ourselves. Then after the opening ceremony – bang! That's when all our competitive natures kick in.

There is always a voting poll for who they want Team England to have as a flag-bearer. Because this was my fifth Com Games, I was a bit of a front-runner for the honour. There were a few other athletes in contention, though, one of them being Alistair Brownlee. 'Well,' I thought, 'of course, if I'm going up against Alistair I'm never going to get the job!' But our manager Paul took it very seriously and he ended up printing off these little flyers with pictures of me, at all the different Com Games I'd been to, with the message 'Vote Geva!' He put them all round the hotel and tried to persuade all the managers in Team England to vote for me. He tried to get the basketball vote, the boxing vote . . . he was a man on a mission! The way it works is that in each sport the team discuss it and decide who they want – third preference, second preference and first – and the managers have the casting vote.

Anyway, despite the hearty campaign from my manager, Alistair ended up winning it. And rightly so – he is a great athlete and obviously a big name. The funny thing was, when it came to the opening ceremony, I'm quite embarrassed to say we literally mobbed Alistair as he came out! When you walk out on to the track for the first time at the ceremony you are all meant to be in lanes, but then as you walk out a bit further there is a bit of a scrum and a scuffle to get to the front and get to the cameras so everyone can be seen by their loved ones around the world. Every one of my England Netball teammates had the front patch on lockdown and we swarmed round Alistair like bees round a honeypot. There is the poor bloke, trying to carry the flag and wave, and he's basically being mobbed by twelve netballers! I was literally right next to him – I probably touched the flagpole I was that close – and I remember my mum saying afterwards, 'Jeez, Geva, you couldn't hold the flag but you couldn't have got much closer if you tried!' On camera and in all the photos the netball girls were front and centre and poor Alistair looked very bemused surrounded by this bevy of beauties!

Our first game was the day after the opening ceremony. We got presented with our dresses the morning of the match and they were perfect, thank goodness, and everyone was feeling positive and ready to perform. We started our campaign well; our first game was against Scotland and we won comfortably, 74–28. We then played Malawi, which was a little bit tougher, but we still won by thirty goals.

We felt at that point that everything was going well – the training that we had in between was really upbeat, our preparation was on track, we did our homework, we did our analysis . . . everything was working. And working well.

Then we had a bit of a test against Uganda. This is important to mention as we were doing well, we were on track for a comfortable win, and then they took me and Jo off to give us a rest and rotate some of the combinations. And then Uganda started coming back at us and we were totally unprepared! They have quite a good shooter and so they put me back on to put pressure on her and we did end up winning but only just, by about six goals. It was really close and this was still the group stages and we really didn't want to lose any matches. We had a tough draw; we had to work through the smaller-threat countries before we faced the biggest one in our pool, New Zealand. Although we had beaten them earlier in the year in the Quad Series at the Copper Box in London, we had never beaten them in a major tournament before, either a World Cup or Com Games. And yet beat them we did, by just under ten goals. It was so significant that people started to take note of us: 'OK, here are England now, top of their group, they have talked the talk, now they are walking the walk, they have come to play!' was pretty much the mood. And we had. We weren't here to mess around or make up numbers or come in third or fourth – we wanted to do well.

We are such a tight unit during a competition. We know what we are about and we don't let the media or anyone distract us. Everyone was on the same page. No one was overexcited that we had beaten New Zealand. It was good but we didn't really celebrate that win, we were more like, 'OK, yep, that's a tick in the box – next!'

I know that previously we had turned up and were a bit like, 'OMG, we are playing the Silver Ferns!', whereas now we were thinking, this is just another team, this is just another pool game, this is just the next step. There was no mental block to playing the Silver Ferns any more. Myself and a fair few other girls including Serena, Ama and Jo Harten, who had joined the Suncorp Super Netball league, were playing against girls we had trained with and played with week in week out and I think that helped. In fact, I know it helped; I knew there was no massive gap in ability any more. We didn't put them on a pedestal like we used to. I ran with them, I jumped with them, I threw with them. They are players and we are players. Tough games are not won in the first quarter; it is about grinding it down, it is about sticking it out. It's about knowing that momentum swings do happen, and whereas before that momentum would go against Team England and we would freeze, now we knew it was about the long game. We could get it back, we just had to keep going.

It was at this point in the competition that Tania, our assistant coach from Australia, had a brainwave. She had been with Thunderbirds when I played there and on occasion, to make me practise against the tallest of opponents, she had brought in Raoul as my training partner. When she heard that Raoul was here on the Gold Coast she called him in and set up some training practice for me to go against my six-foot-eleven brother. He took no prisoners and Eboni and I trained our socks off against him, knowing that we could use this opportunity to see how we could work against someone of his height. I can't tell you how cool it was having him there and being part of it all. He was our secret weapon!

Next up was Jamaica. It was the semi-final in a new venue and I felt like the crowd were probably more behind Jamaica than us. And it was a bloody tough game – we were down by seven goals at one point. I was up against Jhaniele, who is just a woman-mountain. She's an incredible athlete, not only tall at six feet six inches, but she can jump, she can shoot, she is very sturdy and she is hard to move. And trying to get the ball off her is very difficult, particularly when it's placed right in her hands. So that was the game. It was a tough first quarter and then, maybe in the second quarter, they managed to steam ahead. At half-time we were down but we just kept ploughing on and managed to keep ourselves in contention. And then we got down to the fourth quarter and I don't really know what happened but we managed to turn over enough balls to keep us going and everyone was doing their jobs – the shooters were managing to score, the mid-courters were bringing it down, and we were defending. We ended up, with seconds to go, with Jo having the ball in hand. She took a long shot, scored, and we won by one goal.

And it was at precisely that point when we all thought, 'This is it.'

Before, we had all been in teams where we had been a little complacent at this stage. We'd have been happy thinking, 'Hell, yeah! We are coming home with a medal!' We had never focused on getting gold, it was more, 'Well, at least we have something.' But now we meant business. Ama, Jo, Jade, Serena, Kadeen, Helen Housby and Eboni; we had all been at Glasgow four years ago, we were ready.

The end of that game signalled the battle cry, if you like. We were in it to win now. Nothing else would do. There is footage of me doing the most girly jump on the transverse line after that game. I was jumping around and skipping up and down because I was so excited – I knew we just had to get ourselves to this position to be unstoppable. This was our time.

Don't get me wrong, there were several times during the Jamaica game when we were losing and I was like, 'Shit, here we go again . . . back to the same old, same old.' But that thought didn't stay in my mind for long. I knew if we just kept going, kept chipping away collectively as a team, if we just kept working and working and chipping and chipping we could do it. There were no drastic coaching decisions made by us but there were some changes down the other end that worked in our favour. Tracey out-coached the Jamaican coach Arleene Findlay and it set us up for the final.

I remember Eboni and me going back to our bedroom after that match knowing we needed to get some sleep. But we were so hyped up – it is very hard to come down and start to chill out after a game, particularly a game that has just set you up into the final! As we were lying there – it was probably gone eleven now – we kept saying to each other, 'I can't sleep, can you? No!' We knew we needed to sleep, we knew we needed to get a good rest – especially as it was an early game the next day. Sorry, it was an early gold-medal final the next day!

Eventually we did get to sleep and the next day it was down to business. We arrived at the venue and the Jamaica and New Zealand games had already started. Jamaica were all over it and I remember feeling sorry for New Zealand. They were going to come away from the Com Games with nothing; it was going to be their worst ever performance. But I couldn't dwell on that. In our changing rooms we had a good vibe. Of course, there were lots of nerves too. I can only speak for myself but as soon as I take to the court, those nerves go and you forget about all the people watching and what it all means, and at the end of the day it's just about trying to do your job.

Initially, in the changing rooms, everyone is left to their own devices. People prepare for a game in different ways so it's important to let them get themselves ready. We focus, we calm ourselves, we strap up our ankles, we listen to one more song on our headphones, we repeat one more mantra in our head. Then Tracey speaks to us. It's normally short and I'd like to say it is always to the point but some of the most memorable coach chats from her have involved some wacky metaphor! I remember once she was speaking to us about how we needed a strong performance. 'A house is strong, you mustn't let anyone up the garden path,' she said, and then finished off by saying something like how we had to put a roof on that house. I'm confused trying to explain it! Most of the time we got the gist though, and actually some of her team chats eased our nerves because they were so random and got a few giggles and smiles. And then the captain talks. Tracey and all the coaching staff leave the room and so it is just all the players and the captain, Ama. Ama always does something for us beforehand – whether it is giving us gifts or playing a silly game or doing some singing, there is always something she has planned that brings us together. This time she had some bits of paper with different letters on and we all had to put them together. She wanted us to put the bits of paper up on the wall and it ended up spelling out the sentence: 'This is us, why not now?'

Ama's message was motivating and it was a great way of momentarily forgetting about the enormity of what we were going to face. And then we stepped out on court and that was it. The biggest thing for me was that I knew it wouldn't be as hard as playing against Jamaica. Jamaica was a tough bloody game and they have always been our bogey team. I think I sort of knew that nothing would be as tough as that game. And of course I knew the Australian players fairly well. I knew the combination I was coming up against – hell, I knew the goal shooter I was coming up against; I had just won a premiership with her. It was my teammate

Caitlin Bassett. She was the Diamonds captain, a good friend and someone I knew very well. They mixed the goal attack around as well and at one point the GA who came on was the GA for Lightning so I was playing against a combination I train against week in, week out.

I had forgotten about a training session that Noeline had put on at the beginning of the year. As Caitlin and I greeted each other on court, the memory flashed back into my head. Noels had organised some sessions for just Bass and myself, one-on-one in the circle. She knew we both were trying to better ourselves for Lightning and when she set us up on that training court we knew it was going to be one hell of a battle!

The thing between Bass and me was that we didn't hold back. We knew that if we made each other better here, in training as teammates, we'd both be even better in the Com Games. It was all about challenging ourselves to find new ways to beat each other in training, knowing that we'd most probably meet each other in Com Games at some point and we'd go head-to-head where there was no holding back. We laid bare our strength and weaknesses in training because when it came to a game that mattered, we both had to find a way to be the better player.

To the final. I was reading the ball, I was connecting well with my GD and outside defenders, I was getting my fingertips on balls, I was getting turnovers and intercepts. We were clicking as a unit. We did the usual, we played our normal game. Eboni started at GD and then switched up at half-time and Ama came on. The momentum was swinging both ways; it was goal for goal all the way through. It was an exciting game all right, not just for the crowd watching in the stadium but for all the people watching on TV. This was one of the last sports to have its medal-decider matches, so anyone who tuned in hoping to catch a last bit of action from the Com Games was in for a treat! The problem with having played in the game, not watched it, is that things are all muddled into one in my memory. I don't remember what happened our end, I just remember that I think we were down by about four goals in the last quarter. And then we brought ourselves back level . . . and then those final few seconds.

'Really, Geev? Netball? Really?!' A flashback of my mum's voice came into my head, clear and crisp as if it was yesterday, as I watched what was happening down the other end of the court. I was right up to my third-line, I was leaning forward as far as I could and I could barely breathe with excitement. We were level with Australia now: the score was 51–51. The seconds were ticking by, the ball had just been down our end and all I could think about was that conversation I had had with my mum years ago and the confused look she gave me when I told her about this new sport I had fallen in love with.

I watched Jo, our champion goal shooter, as she took her shot. The ball rose into the air . . . and missed the goal. This was it now. It was over. And then Helen got the rebound

. . . Oh! Yes! We have another shot at goal! She missed. The klaxon had sounded, there was no time left to go – Then the whistle blew. Obstruction called! What? I couldn't hear the roar of the crowd or the screams from the spectators over the thumping in my chest. Time seemed to stand still.

And then another voice came into my head: 'We need you to make up numbers, Gee, can you stand at the back and wave your arms around and jump a bit?' My best friend from school. The conversation we had years ago, the reason I was here, the reason I was standing, barely able to breathe, as I watched Helen take the shot to goal that was to win us gold in Australia, against Australia.

It all seemed to be happening in slow motion as the ball went up, went over and . . . fell cleanly through the net. Goal! My brain needed time to process what had happened . . . the goal. The shot went in. OK, we'd won, right? We had won? No . . . I looked up to the scoreboard, was that right, was I reading it right? Fifty-two England . . . we'd won, we'd won, WE'D BLOODY WON! Hell, yeah! A shiver of pure adrenaline, excitement, euphoria . . . call it what you will, it felt like there was electricity running through me and I exploded into a scream of pure joy.

There aren't many moments in my life that I can remember in such vivid detail but I can honestly say, that Commonwealth Games on the Gold Coast when we were tied with Australia until the final few seconds of the game – I think I will have that moment tucked away somewhere safe in my mind for ever. And when I'm old and grey and can't remember what day it is, I will close my eyes and hear with crystal clarity the squeaks of my trainers on that polished court, the way the ball felt in my fingertips, the smell of my newly made England dress and the joy of knowing that after years and years of training and playing and competing and losing, we had struck gold.

I ran to my teammates. We were jumping and hugging. There were hugs and tears then there were people running on court from all over and there were pile-ons, and it was just a moment I wouldn't ever forget. When you have all that celebrating together on court, you forget all the people in the crowd. I was lying on the floor and everyone was on top of me screaming and shouting and crying and I turned my head to look at the crowd. I wanted to celebrate with our fans too. And when I got up I saw my brother and my mum hugging and Mum just had the biggest, proudest smile on her face. It was the first time she had stayed for an entire game in a big competition. It was a momentous occasion in many ways! I did say to her afterwards that I was surprised she stayed in for this one and she just said to me, 'You know what, I was just content you guys had got yourself in a position to contend. You had given yourselves a chance for a gold medal and you gave the Aussies a contest they will never forget!' She believed we could do it, and that was the difference. That belief. We had it too. It's just such a euphoric moment. You get flashbacks of when you first played the game, and previous games and training, and then, finally, you get that feeling that you have managed to achieve something that you have wanted for so long.

Whenever I watch a game on TV, and it doesn't matter what sport it is, any team game, I always like to watch the footage of the winning team and the losing team. I like to see how different players deal with the emotions and their reactions to either winning or losing. And I did that then on court. I knew what losing was like, I've been there.

All the time the game is going on, you are in battle mode. For sixty minutes it is you against them. But when that final whistle goes, that's it and there is nothing but respect for the other team – in this case, the losing team. I went around court and saw my past teammates, my current team-mates, my good friends, and I wanted to shake all of their hands. It is something you do in netball to finish the game off and it's about respecting your opponents because you recognise the heart and soul they put into the game, just as you did. Then you go back to your team and celebrate. It could have gone either way and that is what made it so emotional. I've been in games before and you've been up by five or six or ten goals and you know it's in the bag. But that game, no one knew. There was tremendous heartbreak for the Aussies because they lost it in that final few seconds, and tremendous excitement for us because we won it in those dying few seconds.

The crowd were on the edge of their seats right until the end, but once that final whistle went the Australian fans went very quiet and left very quickly! I remember being a bit shocked. I knew everyone had been hoping for an England vs Australia final ever since we beat Jamaica; they were gunning for it as it was a guaranteed medal for them. And gold at that; they pretty much thought it was theirs for the taking. 'Come on, guys, just appreciate the game!' I thought, but the fans were too upset to stay. They were in shock. And so were we! The medal presentation was a bit of a blur but I remember as soon as the England flag went up we were all in floods of tears. The England team were the last to walk out for the presentation; the Jamaicans came out first, happy and dancing in third place. Then the Australian team walked out sombrely before we made our way excitedly to the podium. Mum said she overheard someone describing the Australian team walk-out as looking like they were going to work on Monday morning and ours as looking like we were leaving work on Friday afternoon!

By the time we got back to the changing rooms we were a little bit giddy with adrenaline and excitement. There was more laughing and tears and joking and someone said, 'Remember our conversation in Sydney?!' From a team in despair after a thirty-five-goal loss to a club side to beating the world number-one netball team! Our CEO Jo Adams came in and congratulated us and she said, 'Oh my God, is there anything I can get for you girls? You don't know what you've just done for netball, for England Netball, please tell me if there is something I can do for you!' And I was the cheeky one in the corner and shouted out, 'BONUS!' And then everyone shouted at the same time, 'BONUS!' We don't get paid much as athletes; we get £1,000 for playing in the Com Games, we get nothing else for finishing with a medal or winning it. I think in the end she gave everyone an extra £2,000 each, which was amazing. OK, it's nothing in terms of what footballers get but, still, it was something else to celebrate!

Jo told us that the gold medal had made her job and her team's job a lot easier. It meant they could secure for England Netball some future funding. We had known for three or four years that Sport England had said they would stop all funding for England Netball in 2019, so that wasn't a shock for us. The shock came when Sport England decided to reverse that decision and continue the funding until 2022. This was the only time that they had changed their minds. So what we had achieved just then, and over the past year, helped everyone notice us. England Netball had proved they were worth the investment and to have Sports England turn a decision round, for the first time in history, and say, 'You know what, we are going to stick around and continue supporting you, we can see what brilliant work you do. We want to see more success with England Netball and we know that can happen' – well, that was probably worth more than any gold medal.

When I read about the number of women taking up netball now my heart swells with pride. There has been a 44 per cent increase in participation in the twelve months since we won gold and it is the UK's number-one female participation sport. What a legacy that is, what a time to be involved in the game, knowing that future generations of girls have a sport that has such a positive and powerful impact. The netball court is our safe space and our chance to get together and show what a formidable force a team of women can be.

13 THE ROCK
OF THE ROSES

*'At the end of the day, it's a game of netball, no one has
died.'*
                                    Noeline Taurua

LACHLAN had come to see some of our Com Games; in
fact, he even came to the grand final. It was a bit weird
afterwards. I went up to him and thanked him for being
there but it was very awkward. There was no love any more,
but no real hatred or anger either, it was just a very weird
feeling. Mum, give her her dues, made sure she involved
him with our family and friends at the event but he didn't
want a part of that. He didn't want to sit with any of them
and I'm sad to say it did put a bit of a damper on our
victory. I think I was affected by him being there more than
I thought I would be. He drove back to the Sunshine Coast
that night and that was it. I think I only saw him once more
after that. I can't tell you for certain why he came to the
Games. Perhaps he felt some sort of strange obligation to
be there? He loved going to sporting events and, as a PE

teacher, loved watching rugby, gymnastics and athletics, so he probably didn't want to give up a ticket. He knew a lot of the Australian netball girls when I played with them in the league and probably, like most Australians, expected them to win. I can't say I am sorry to have disappointed him.

After the final, I went to New Zealand for a week with my brother and it was just what the doctor ordered. Noels had given me the week off as a chance to take a break and get myself fresh again for the start of the new Suncorp Super Netball season. Raoul and I spent the week horse-riding with our cousins, spending some quality time together, chilling. It was just perfect and I felt so refreshed afterwards.

Bizarrely, though, I found myself really missing my England team. Half of the squad were now playing out in the league for Australian teams while the other half were still involved in the English Netball Superleague. The ones who were in Oz managed a bit of a break, did some travelling, took a week or so to chill, while the other six – Jade, Beth, Jodie, Eboni, Kadeen and Natalie – flew back to the UK.

They got a huge welcome when they arrived back in London; there were flowers for them, lots of media interest. Lots of fans who had set their alarms to watch us in the final were there cheering for them. It was unreal! It was brilliant to see those girls being in the papers and on the internet and you'd turn round and BBC Sport would be interviewing them and then Sky Sports were interviewing them – they were everywhere! Then there was us, left in Australia feeling a bit left out, back to business with pre-season training with no one making a fuss of us!

I really wanted us to be all together, I guess. It had been such an intense couple of weeks and we had gone through so much. I normally quite like the break afterwards, but this time I missed them.

And the girls in England were all being treated like stars (rightly so, of course). They had invites to this, invites to that – they got asked to go to the BAFTAs! Everyone wanted to speak to them, to have photos with them. They said it was incredible. There was so much interest from the media too – they were on breakfast TV, lunchtime shows, radio shows, they did newspaper interviews . . . and meanwhile back in Australia, well, I probably don't need to say it was the exact opposite!

The biggest problem was obviously that we had beaten Australia on their home turf. No one could give a crap about congratulating us! I went back home to the Sunny Coast and my beautiful medal just sat there in my bedroom. The girls back in the UK were wearing their medals out all the time, in every interview they did, when they did appearances at schools, when they visited community centres or did talks at the local netball clubs – I was honestly a little envious; I wanted to wear my medal too and show it off at all these events! It was definitely a tale of two teams. There wasn't much that came of it all for those of us who were playing out in Australia. I even said to my management company, 'Surely this is the perfect opportunity to be creating more revenue for me with some sort of sponsorship deal or something? Surely someone wants to jump on the bandwagon, this doesn't come around often and, in my case, it's been twenty years in the making!' but there was just nothing.

Anyway, there was no time to dwell. I had the next season with Lightning to focus on, and as Noeline had given me that one week off to recharge I was left with only one week to train with the team before the season started. Two weeks since we won the Commonwealth Games and it was time to be back in action in the league. I hit the ground running and, as I was captain again, I had to fly to Sydney for official launch day with the captains of the other league teams. At one point, when the microphone came to me, I was asked, 'As reigning premiers, do the Lightning have what it takes to get another win and be back-to-back champions?' There was definitely an air of increased rivalry between the teams – we were the hunted this year and everyone wanted to bring us down.

I do remember there being quite a sting from the Australian head coach, Lisa Alexander, who was quoted as saying that the inclusion of international players in the Australian domestic league wasn't having a positive impact on the national team. 'I can't say it any other way, I'm the national coach and this [English players in Super Netball] has clearly assisted them to win this gold medal. That's our high-performance system working for another country.' Ouch! But how funny. All those years ago when I was not allowed to play in the Australian league and represent England because England didn't think it was right. But I knew deep down that it was only going to benefit my career and my netball ability. And now Australia are cross that we have become too good!

As Lightning were reigning champions, I wanted to lead us off to a great start again. Our first game was against Giants, who we had beaten in the grand final at the end of last season. It was a tricky game for us; everyone was touting it as the 'grand final rematch', and we lost. It wasn't a heavy loss, there was just a three-goal difference, but everyone was probably a bit flat to begin with. Our attacking end featured Caitlin Bassett and Steph Wood – the Australian Diamond combination – and they were coming off the defeat from Com Games. And myself and Karla, who had played in the defensive circle, had also been through the hype of the Games so I don't know if that played a bit of a part too. I think we were all just a little bit knackered.

It was a tough game to kick off the league and our next two games were equally tight and resulted in us losing. We didn't panic. We had to keep our circle quite tight, we had to keep each other focused as in the community there were a few mumbles. People were now touting us as 'one-hit wonders'. And there was definitely a bit of angst. We were 0–3 down at the start of the 2018 season but losing by small margins (I think it was 2–2 goals or something like that). So it wasn't an ideal start, but we didn't give up. We tried to keep everything very tight and very positive. We also had a great performance analyst, Anthony Bedford, who was able to give us a plan for what it would take to still make the top four. Having a plan like that, having evidence in front of us that all was not lost, helped boost our confidence and reassured us that we were still on track.

There is such a fantastic community vibe on the Sunshine Coast but it is a group of small towns and, while they really got behind us and the success we had in 2017, there was an air of doubt creeping in after those first few defeats. We had a brilliant media following on the coast, which meant that every loss was played out across the radio and TV, and as the losses clocked up, it was very important to us to stay quite positive and realistic in our comments. We got some wins and we kept ourselves in contention and things took on a more positive stance in the community – everyone started to have faith in us again!

We hit a bit of a rocky patch when Noeline lost her father. She went back to New Zealand for a couple of weeks, as she was to lead the funeral ceremonies and they went on for a week because her father was fairly high up in the Maori community. That was tough for the whole team. Our manager also lost her ex-husband who she was still very close to, and of course my marriage was broken and I was going through the process of divorce proceedings, so you could say we had a few serious personal problems in the team. But what we managed to do well as a team was enjoy each other's company and have fun and leave whatever was going on personally at the door. 'At the end of the day, it's a game of netball, we're not going to die out there,' was Noels's favourite quote to us. We just needed to appreciate what we had, appreciate life, and realise that at the end of the day it's just a game.

Halfway through the season and there was talk about girls signing up for next year and who would be staying on in the club. I made sure that all the girls were getting things they had been promised, that everyone was happy with what they were doing. I wanted to ensure that we could look after each individual player and their personal circum-stances. Then it came to me talking to my manager and the CEO. They said, 'You're not getting any younger. We were going to offer you a one-year contract but, after talking to your manager, we will give you two.' I was taken aback. I ask you, is that any way to make a player feel valued? Feel wanted? Let alone the fact that I had captained their side to victory in their debut season and this season we were picking ourselves up nicely? I was pretty shocked and slightly sad. I would have thought the conversation could have gone something like this: 'We appreciate everything you have done for the club, Geva. You have backed it up with performance and, taking into consideration your age, we'd like to offer you a two-year deal.' Now to me, that's fair. I was also aware that Noels was under contract with

Lightning for one more year and I would want at least another two. Would I want to play under another coach if she wasn't there for my second year?

I started to look around. I think I thought perhaps it was time to move out of my comfort zone. Try to bring something else to my game, surround myself with new people, push myself a bit – all these things were going through my mind as the season continued. I was genuinely knocked a bit after that first conversation with the CEO. I guess I was probably a bit slower the first couple of games into the season, but I think we all were. We were all a bit lethargic, particularly the internationals who had played in the Com Games. But as the season progressed, I found my rhythm again and Karla and I ended up being a great defensive combination, with me getting the most deflections that year and ending up high on the list for the most defensive rebounds and intercepts. It showed that I had found my form, that I was still strong. I put all thoughts about a move to the back of my mind; there were no decisions that had to be made until the end of the season and I wanted to be able to focus on what I was doing now as captain.

The season was still going OK for us, but the big blessing came with a new rule that was brought in, the bonus point rule. In essence it was this – when you win, you get five points, but the new rules meant you could also get a point for every quarter you won throughout the game. Basically you were rewarded even if you lost a match. We were against it. This was changing the sport, the whole thing, we said.

Whereas before you'd go through a netball game like this: find your feet in the first and second quarter, the third quarter would be your championship quarter, and the fourth quarter you bring home the win. Now, you are wanting to win every bloody quarter because there is a point up for grabs! In fairness, it made the competition quite exciting and, after initially being so dead against it, we found that it actually worked out well for us. We had won pretty much the most quarters against every team, so even though we lost matches we were still getting points, which was putting us in contention for a final-four spot on the table. It pissed a lot of people off because we lost more games but had more points. You, as the losing team, could still get three points and the winning team five points. There wasn't much in it. Each team started to cheer on drawn quarters where neither team got any points.

We played Vixens in Melbourne and beat them, which secured us fourth spot on the table. We had a shocker in one of our quarters; we could have ended up finishing third, which meant we could have hosted the final, but we ended up finishing fourth and we had to go down to Brisbane and play the Firebirds, who'd finished third, in the knockout final. Straight after the Vixens game I came off and I was asked about what I thought about our next game, against the Firebirds. I was quite honest. I hadn't thought too much about what I was going to say, so when they asked me about it, I said it would be a great contest, that the team had some real firepower across the court and that there was a great state rivalry growing between our two teams. The match was set to be a cracker, I said. As the journalist quizzed me some more, I got a bit more heated and continued the interview by saying I found it very disrespectful that the Firebirds hadn't acknowledged us as another team in Queensland. We were teams from the same state and yet we were largely ignored. We were providing another pathway for girls to come into elite netball . . . I think I started to rant.

These feelings had been building up all season; as captain I am obviously privy to quite a lot of information, and I felt that some of the decisions that the Firebirds made were a deliberate dig at us and that they wanted us to play second fiddle to them. They had their season launch in Mooloolaba, which is our home town on the Sunshine Coast. They had their clinics up around there, our home area, and they had a slogan that said, 'Queensland is a one-team state'. I just found it so disrespectful and I decided not to hold my tongue any more and just speak quite fairly and honestly. We all felt that we weren't getting any respect from our fellow Queensland teams and it just put even more fire in our bellies to win. Enough was enough.

It was just funny as it got picked up massively in the media as this big story and they said that I had issued a 'war-cry!' The next day the CEO of Netball Queensland, Catherine Clark, felt she had to issue a public response, something meaningless like, 'If Geva wants to sit down and discuss things . . .' That was even funnier. Our CEO pulled me into the office and was not happy. She told me quite frankly, 'This is not how we operate, Geva!' But I wasn't backing down. 'To be honest, Danielle,' I replied, 'I am standing up for this team, something we should have done a long time ago.' Yes, I was on my soapbox, but I'd had some really nice messages from Melbourne Storm, the NRL team in Melbourne and our owners, as well as the University of the Sunshine Coast. They backed me up 100 per cent; they were happy to get more people fired up over netball, more bums on seats – although they did also say to me that I had to back it up next week when we played Firebirds in the semi-final! Still, I had support from the right people and that's what mattered.

The week before this monumental match was tough. There was a lot of media interest, lots of reporters wanting more comments from me to fuel the fire even more. We travelled down to Brisbane, to the Firebirds' home ground, and straight away we knew it was going to be a feisty atmosphere. Eighty per cent of the spectators were Firebird fans – it was their home turf, after all.

They had this beer tent right behind the posts that had a whole load of drunks in shouting 'Queensland! Firebirds!' every time our shooters were down that end. But you know what? Our fans, our minimal 20 per cent share of the spectators, completely and utterly blew away the whole stadium. They overpowered the Firebird supporters and everyone was amazed at this level of noise and support from such a small group and it was just brilliant. Our fans were the eighth player in that match and they got us over the line. We ended up winning that match by one goal, 57–56, after being down earlier in the last quarter and it was just crazy. That was the hardest game of the final three games we played but it gave us such momentum as a team. I had 'talked the talk', as it were, and we definitely showed the opposition that they needed to show us some respect. That win gave us strength as a team and it was the crowd that won it for us. We were so thankful to them. We made sure that in every interview afterwards we thanked them and praised them. So many of them decided that if we won the week after they would fly to Perth for the grand final! But first we had another hurdle in the way and a job to do, which was to head to Sydney and play in the semi-final against the Giants. It was a tough game against them – they had a couple of girls who were retiring at the end of the season and were playing with a lot of heart – but we just hit the ground running and we felt a little bit unstoppable. It turned out we were! We won. We beat the Giants in Sydney to book us a ticket through to our second grand final and to have the opportunity to defend our title. After a fairly slow and unthreatening start to the season, in only our second season as a club here we were again, in our second consecutive grand final.

Lightning were happy for me to delay my decision about signing a new contract until after the final. I needed to give that all my focus and concentration and I appreciated the leeway. The final was a tough, well-fought battle with West

Coast Fever and one hell of a win – for us! We had won back-to-back titles in our two-year history and it was just the most magical, crazy and exciting end to the season. I was physically and emotionally exhausted and I think I was ready for a change.

After the grand final we had a week before we had our farewell gala dinner and I still hadn't decided about where I was going to go. The gala dinner was on the Friday and I told Lightning that I'd take the weekend to think things over. We had achieved something so special as a team and there was a big part of me that thought, 'Do I want to stay and keep that momentum going?' Equally, if we had lost the final, I might have had a burning urge to stay behind and rectify things, chasing that title win again. So that weekend, knowing I had to give my decision on Monday, was full of honest conversations with Mum and my manager. I was sought after, which was nice; there were a few teams interested in me. It was a case of working out what would be best for me and for now. I started to put myself a little higher up the list now; I was starting to put plans in place for my life once my elite playing career was over. First and foremost I wanted to make sure I finished my university degree. I am so passionate about teaching. I want to be able to give something back, to make a difference. I have seen how great coaches and great teachers can make a difference in a child's life and I have seen how poor ones can kill a dream before it has even started. I want to use what I have learned in my playing career and make sure I am the sort of teacher who can ignite a passion in a child. It will be incredible to inspire students to learn, to push themselves, to have a dream and go for it. With teaching, you have the potential to shape young people's minds, the potential to show them the world we live in and provide them with tools so they can go out into that world and flourish. I like the idea of working as a team in a school, in a faculty with like-minded teachers in an environment where we are all striving towards the same goal: to provide a great education for the next generation. And I guess, from a personal point of view, I want to be able to be the first person in my immediate family to get a university degree. I know I won't be playing elite netball for ever, so teaching will be my next challenge and, like with everything I do, I want to feel fulfilled and do that to the best of my ability.

Leaving Lightning was an unbelievably tough decision and not one single factor was the cause of me leaving. I loved the community, I loved the beaches, the lifestyle, I loved walking into the local shops and people wanting to talk to me and hug me. After my move became public knowledge I was in the post office and two ladies came over to me and gave me a hug and said they were going to miss me. A guy came and shook my hand. They made you feel like little rock stars – everyone knew who you were, they always wanted to talk or say well done, or tell you what they thought about how a particular game went. I will definitely miss that sense of support from the Sunshine

Coast community as they were a massive reason behind our success.

But I wanted a change and a new challenge. In leading the team to two successive victories I felt like I had done all that was asked of me by the club. I had also just been named Goal Keeper of the Year again at the Netball Australia awards evening. I remember going out with the whole team for brunch and Bass and another player, Kelsey, told us all that they would be moving on. I hadn't signed anywhere else yet but I was seriously considering things. It was quite an emotional catch-up as we had gone through a lot together, but I think we all appreciated that we needed to focus on us as individuals now and things were pulling us in different directions for a variety of reasons.

So, where to go? I have always gone to teams where I feel I have something to offer, where I can develop that team in some way. I take the greatest reward in bringing a team together, pushing them forward, making a difference. I had made another decision during the season and changed management, moving from TLA; they had been great but – perhaps because they had a growing amount of talent on their books and I was quite isolated on the Sunshine Coast – I wasn't getting a lot of action. We parted company on good terms and I put my playing career in Trent Tavoletti's capable hands. I'd actually had a fair bit to do with him over the last couple of years, as he helped make sure any English girls who were playing down under got fair contracts and he had used me as a sounding board. Trent came back to me and was embarrassed by the offer that Lightning had put on the table compared to what he was getting from elsewhere and, in the end, we narrowed it down to two clubs. And my final decision went in favour of Collingwood Magpies in Melbourne.

The important thing for me was that I wasn't leaving Lightning on a bad note. I still respect the team and the coaches and I am proud to have been part of the inaugural set-up and to have brought them success two years running. I don't know what it will be like going back there and playing my first game against them, but so far I've felt nothing but love and support from the community.

It was time to put myself first. I'd had a pretty shit time in my personal life for the past eighteen months or so, but on the flip side I'd probably had the best eighteen months of my netball life. Winning back-to-back Premierships, the Com Games, being named Best Player in the World twice. As the shit was hitting the fan in my personal life, as my marriage came to an end, I'd been able to focus on my game and play the best netball I have ever played. Maybe having nothing to look forward to in my life except netball, nothing to focus on but putting my heart and soul into the court, was the reason for this success. Some players lose a bit of focus once they become married because there is something else to think about: their husband, children . . . I am not saying that doesn't happen to sportsmen as well, but it has been my experience of playing with women who start a family. I had nothing, so I put everything into my netball. There is probably a message somewhere here, something like, shit does happen but that doesn't mean everything is shit. You can't always let failure in one small part of your life overshadow the great things you have achieved and will achieve. Sometimes the failures help to shape you to be the person you are now, and failing in one area doesn't mean you give up on everything. There aren't many things I regret in my life but, yes, getting married is one. I will probably always regret it as deep down I knew it wasn't the right decision for me and I should have stopped the relationship sooner. I am sad that I wasted all those years with someone who in the end didn't make me happy. So I focus now on making myself happy.

Having gone with my gut, I left Sunny Coast and moved back down to Melbourne, to a fresh start, a new club. I love it there. I have a good friendship base, plus my brother is there with his godfather and family. Everything had fallen back into place after me being in limbo for months, perhaps even years. I now have a place to call home again. The fact that I can live with my brother without angst is amazing; he is my rock. And work is amazing too. It was fantastic to come to Collingwood. You can rock up there at seven in the morning and you've got the training all under one roof whether it's on court, in the gym, altitude training, recovery or the track outside. And you have all the physicians, physios, welfare staff, nutritional experts – anyone you could possibly want. It is an amazing set-up.

Collingwood have been around for 127 years, first as a football club and the netball club was formed in 2017. They are the club that everyone loves to hate. I think back in the day they were very arrogant, very vocal, very big-headed, and it was all about winning. But that culture has shifted in the past couple of years and they are making changes. Their mantra 'Humble in victory, gracious in defeat' is helping them focus on the right attitude. And the people who work there are good people. I haven't grown up with the AFL or Aussie Rules culture of just being involved in one team your whole life, but people here have and they are passionate about Collingwood, even if that passion is sometimes misdirected. I was looking forward to coming to the club and joining the netball team.

I knew a bit of their history too. Over the last two years the team had bought so many different players they pretty much had most of the Australian Diamonds line-up. Everyone picked them as the 'dream team' in that first year of the Suncorp Super Netball League set-up. But they came in fourth that year and didn't make finals the following year. It's that classic saying: they are a 'team of champions rather than a champion team'. I don't necessarily want to come in and play for the best club, the club at the top; I want to come in and work hard, work on bringing the team success and hitting milestones together. We'll focus on short-term challenges first, like winning the derby battle against the other team in Melbourne (my old team, Vixens) and then perhaps focus on finishing in the top four. I am not saying I can change everything myself but I will keep my professional standards high, let my play do the talking and, more importantly, relax and enjoy playing. We have a road to travel as a team and it's important to remember why we play – we enjoy the game. The focus needs to go back on that rather than on getting wins all the time. We have to remember that we are not going to be doing this for ever – some of us might have another ten years, some of us might retire in a year – but netball will continue long after we are gone and forgotten so it's important to enjoy the moment. Right now we have a common goal. We know it will be bloody hard work and some things might not go to plan, but we can keep putting our best foot forward and keep having fun while we are doing it.

Joining Magpies has brought about a new start for me professionally and personally. Funnily enough, before joining Magpies was ever a thought in my mind, I met a guy who plays for the football club there, and his story is pretty similar to mine. He is American and had just completed a mechanical engineering degree when he got scouted and asked to try out for AFL. He came over, they liked him, and he's been involved with the club for the last four years. He is six foot eleven, the same height as my brother, and we have been dating for the last six or seven months. In the early days when there was talk of me joining the club he wanted to make sure the decision to move to Magpies wasn't anything to do with him. I reassured him that it wasn't, that it was all about me and what was best for me professionally. But I won't lie, it has worked out quite nicely that we are at the same club! We go in to work in the mornings together, we see each other during the day. We are both new to the country but we both love Australia. Yes, he has met my mum. The final test will be Dad but for now it's pretty cool getting to know someone new, being able to open myself up emotionally again. Don't get me wrong, it is daunting and my self-confidence is taking time to build up again, but we are taking things nice and slowly. I'm happy. And that is all I can ask for.

14 AND THE WINNERS ARE . . .

'Just play. Have fun. Enjoy the game.' Michael Jordan

THE end of 2018 was still so full on with travel plans, work plans, international duties – and retrieving some of my belongings. To cut a long story short, my ex-husband still has a lot of my personal stuff, things that are of no monetary value or use to him but that are sentimental items and mean a lot to me. I was due to head off on my travels, for some much-needed R&R in America and Canada and then some netball work in Singapore. Then I would be heading back to the UK for a couple of awards evenings and England training camps.

But before that, after the season had finished, I also squeezed in a trip with Raoul to Thursday Island, which is located north of Queensland. We took small planes, drove bumpy roads, and even flew out in a helicopter to meet the locals and deliver coaching sessions. It was a great way to explore more of this beautiful country, to inspire and hopefully empower the locals, and for us to appreciate the history and culture and achievements of Aboriginal Australians and Torres Strait Islanders across the country. Raoul and I loved it.

I was back in Melbourne for a few days before I flew out to begin my travel adventures in America. My holiday was broken up with a visit to Singapore, where I was running a netball clinic with Netball Singapore. I love these clinics; it's a chance to meet and run sessions for young players and their coaches and it's quite rare that I find the time to be able to deliver such sessions, although I'd love to do more. Then it was time to fly back to England and I was able to spend a night in Bournemouth before I was due to attend my first event as a gold medal winner at the *Sunday Times* Sportswomen of the Year Awards.

The ceremony was held at the News UK offices in London Bridge and I was excited – not only would I be catching up with the girls, but I had brought along my new man and I wanted to show him the cool landmarks of London. When we arrived at the venue his first comment was one of shock: 'Why is it so small?! Is this the right room?' He couldn't get over that if this was celebrating the top women players in sport why wasn't it full to the brim. At Collingwood, we go to awards as a club and the rooms are filled with hundreds of people – ten people or more sit round each massive table, and there are probably over sixty tables. This event had roughly thirty tables in total, with six or eight people on each. 'If this is meant to be the best of British . . .' he said, looking at me, smiling.

It was great to be able to go there, though; although I call Australia home now, I'm still very proud to represent England and it was exciting to have been nominated in the Team of the Year category, alongside the British wheelchair basketball team, Chelsea Football Club and Team GB's 4x100-metre relay team. I was there with our captain Ama Agbeze, Jo Harten, Helen Housby and Tracey, plus our CEO Jo Adams, and it was a real honour to be in that room. Being based in Australia, I miss so much of what is happening in British sport. You just get Australian athletes and Australian sport shoved down your neck, you don't get to see much of what is happening in the rest of the world. So it was brilliant to see and hear so much about what was happening in women's sports in the UK.

It was incredible, the list of triumphs and successes that were talked about that evening. It might have been an intimate event in size, but it certainly packed a punch in showcasing the achievements of women's sport. There were a lot of people I wanted to see. Mum told me that she had put forward a nomination in the Inspiration category for her good friend Pat Mathie, who had come to watch me play when I first got picked for the England squad. She is an amazing woman who has done so much for sport where we lived when I was growing up. Her kids used to trampoline with us and she had set up a gymnastics club down in Bournemouth twenty-five years ago. It was brilliant to see her. And there was another woman, Georgia Hall, who won the Women's Golf Open as a junior. She is also a Bournemouth girl and I was very excited to meet her. You see, I'm not just England proud, I'm Bournemouth proud – you can take the girl out of Bournemouth but not Bournemouth out of the girl. Yes, I actually own one of those T-shirts!

The room was full of amazing sports stars, faces that you had seen on TV or in the papers, and I was a bit like, 'OMG, is that who I think it is?' Jessica Ennis-Hill was there, Dina Asher-Smith . . . and everyone looked so beautiful! I guess it is a nice change for us athletes – you're normally in your sports kit, hair pinned back, doing your job, so getting the chance to dress up was fun. Why not go to town! When it was announced we had won in our category we all went up on stage and I think we eclipsed the backdrop, being so tall and there being so many of us! That award meant a lot as it was voted by the *Sunday Times* readers, which meant that people were enjoying netball, they were enjoying what we were doing. We heard that night that six months after we had won gold at the Commonwealth, a survey commissioned by England Netball showed that over 130,000 adult women had started playing netball. And 77 per cent of adults who watched us at the Games said the Roses are an inspiration to young girls. Hearing those statistics is just mind-blowing. It makes our game feel so special – to inspire so many girls and adults alike is phenomenal. How can anything ever top that? Forget any medal or trophy or anything else: getting people active, getting more boys and girls on court, is our biggest achievement.

The Uganda series was coming up in December. I had been approached about taking the captaincy role for it a month or so before, as Ama was out with a knee injury. Of course, I was honoured to have been asked but I explained that I was struggling with personal matters and I actually needed special consideration to be excused from this series. I had so much stuff going on at home with my ex, getting my stuff back, trying to find a place to live in Melbourne, pack up my apartment and belongings on the Sunshine Coast and to relocate them to Melbourne in my car. My mind was all over the place. I didn't want to be captain unless I could give it my complete, undivided attention and effort. Tracey was initially not OK with the situation and I found this hard because I didn't want to leave my team in the lurch; however, I needed to get everything sorted. In the end we came to an understanding and Tracey gave me special consideration to miss that series. In turning down the captaincy role I potentially gave up the chance to lead England in the 2019 World Cup. Is it going to be a decision I regret? I don't think so. I can't do something without giving it my all and it wouldn't have been fair to do the job half-heartedly.

I trained with Collingwood for three weeks and then came back to England for Christmas. Having been out in Oz right after the Com Games and not able to be part of the team celebrations in England, I was really determined to attend the BBC Sports Personality of the Year Award and join all my teammates and revel in being nominated. We had been nominated for Team of the Year and Greatest Sporting Moment of the Year and whether we won or not, this was an opportunity I didn't want to miss.

I flew from Melbourne into Birmingham, where the awards were being held. I had been loaned a car by one of Mum's friends, Steve Hendy. He always gives me a set of wheels whenever I am in the UK and is an avid supporter of our sport. Mum drove the car up all the way from Bournemouth to Birmingham, picked me up from the airport and took me to the Holiday Inn she had booked just round the corner from the NEC. I had done a bit of online shopping before I left Australia and ordered three or four dresses from Dorothy Perkins and Boohoo, hoping that one of them would fit me (there is always a risk in ordering online when you aren't exactly a conventional body shape or height!). Thankfully, one of the dresses – just the one though! – was perfect. I spoke to some of the other girls from the team, who were in Loughborough getting ready for the awards. They were all having their hair and make-up done professionally before a coach would drive them down and I would meet them at the venue. I couldn't believe it – they were having professional make-up done and there was me who doesn't really wear make-up struggling to whack something on my own face!

I didn't have a lot of time to worry about it as Mum wanted to leave early so I could get there in plenty of time to soak up the atmosphere and enjoy the evening. The problem was, the traffic was bad, it was chucking it down with rain, and she got a bit lost. Instead of going left at a roundabout she ended up going all the way round and then out again and got herself in a bit of a tizz. I really wasn't worried about the detour, but she was very upset. 'No, Geva, it's not all right! I wanted to make this evening perfect for you!' Luckily one of us is less dramatic! I still arrived in plenty of time and met Tracey there. I was so pleased to see her – you know what it's like when you get to a party and you scan the room to try to see a familiar or friendly face, knowing there is strength in numbers!

The best thing about finding Tracey when I arrived was that I didn't have to walk the red carpet by myself. Talk about being a fish out of water! We both were and, I kid you not, the red carpet at these awards is like the one you see on TV at the Oscars. It was wide and long and there were TV camera crews, press, photographers all lined up along one side. The backdrop had all the sponsors' logos on it and Tracey and I started walking along, but we kept getting shouted at to stop and pose. It was so funny. We were like, how do we stand? What do I do with my legs? What should I do with my arms? We stood there trying to not look awkward and the photographers were just shouting at us to look this way and that way. I had one of my hands on my hip and was trying my hardest to pose effectively but how do you do that? No one teaches you that! I pull the worst face when I'm on the netball court but I don't care, I think screw it, it is what it is! But on the red carpet I just don't have a clue whether I should pout/smoulder/game-face it, so I just smiled and hoped for the best. I remember looking back at some of those photos of Tracey and me on the red carpet and it looks like we are holding hands! Our legs looked good though – we nailed the pose!

After a few minutes you are sort of ushered on as more personalities arrive and we thought we had made it to the end of the red carpet without being called across for a TV interview but then, at the last moment, someone grabbed us. A lady came over and asked if we'd spare a moment for a chat and we ended up speaking on TV, although I can't remember what the programme was. I was so jet-lagged and bewildered by this whole experience, I have no idea what I said! We finally made it to the end of the red carpet and went inside. The other girls were all late leaving Loughborough and didn't have time to enjoy that red-carpet experience, unfortunately – or maybe fortunately, considering the level of stress it can cause!

I probably spent the whole evening in a state of mouth-open excitement. When Tracey and I first walked in we met Billie Jean King and had a photo with her. Well, that was after we'd spent about five minutes saying to each other, 'Is it her? Is it her? Shall we go and say hi?!' Talk about setting the standard for the evening! The other girls met us before we all walked round to the stadium and it was just pure nuts. All these people are sat looking gorgeous and glamorous in this massive room and you want to look at everyone but not be obviously looking at everyone either. We have played in arenas like that, so the size itself isn't daunting – the daunting thing is trying to walk in heels when you are wearing a nice dress! We all ended up walking along the front row, right by the stage. We passed Lewis Hamilton and his family and Jessica Ennis-Hill, and then all of a sudden you notice all these cricketers and footballers and athletes who you have seen and supported on the TV and they are now just a few feet away. All the time we were all trying to be cool; I'd smile at people as we walked to our seats and I remember trying to see if I could spot Alistair Brownlee, but he wasn't there. We had a lot of people smile and watch us as we made our entrance, which, if you think about it, isn't that unusual as we were quite a sight to behold! Not only are we all so bloody tall, we've all worn heels and we are like these glamorous Amazonian women. Plus when we move, we move as one, so we made quite a noticeable entrance. So we were smiling at people, these super-athlete-stars, and they were smiling back and we were just having fun and soaking up the atmosphere and enjoying the company. We took our seats and the evening just turned out to be a really cool stage show with music and awards and interviews. We noticed that every time they were announcing the nominations for an award, someone from the TV team would alert the winners, who would then go backstage. Then when it was announced they had won they would come on stage for the interviews and to collect their gong. When it came to the Team of the Year award, we were a little, 'Oh we are still sat here, it can't be us . . . that's a pity.'

And then they announced we had won, and beaten the likes of the England football team. We were completely and utterly genuinely shocked! We couldn't believe it! I am sure I just shouted, 'Whattt?!' as I turned round to check I had heard right. Then we all had to slide out of our rows of seats, checking we hadn't got our dresses tucked in anywhere they shouldn't be, and then the next battle is you have to walk up the stairs in your heels! We all walked up as the auditorium just kept applauding and it was just an incredible feeling. To stand on the stage and look out at all the people who were clapping and then remember you are on live TV and there are thousands of people watching at home – it was beyond exciting. I don't think any one of us stopped smiling the whole time we were on stage and, fair play to Ama, she spoke beautifully on behalf of us all.

And then the strangest thing happened, Gabby Logan, the co-host, came over to us on stage and told us to wait. It was time for the Greatest Sporting Moment of the Year award. They started showing footage of the other nominated 'moments' and then it came to us and they showed in full the moment Helen scored the goal that was to win us Commonwealth gold. And the next thing we knew we had won that as well! The looks on our faces probably showed that we weren't expecting that award either; it was just the most amazing feeling and an amazing night. Greatest Sporting Moment is voted for by the public, which meant the world to us. It felt that our sport was being embraced by the country, and not only that, our most amazing moment was the voting public's most amazing moment as well. Winning that award felt like we had given our sport a whole new audience, and to be up on stage with the biggest names in the sporting world watching us and the fans at home supporting us, to be up there representing our country in a sport that was now getting the recognition it deserved – all in all it was an extraordinary night.

We went backstage after winning our second award as it had come to the end of the night and they were announcing the actual BBC Sports Personality Award. Then we got to stand on stage again with all the runners-up and winners and that was brilliant! We wanted photos, lots of photos, and netballers are so bossy (something that Harry Kane and Lewis Hamilton found out quite quickly!) – we organised everyone on stage for a series of shots.

I am a massive fan of Formula One so meeting Lewis was an insane moment for me! I made sure I wangled my way to the front and I had to touch him, so I put my hand on his shoulder . . . how corny am I?! But he was so cool, he didn't mind and the girls knew I was so happy to be within touching distance of him. Jo Harten and some of the other girls are massive football fans so they pretty much did the same with Harry Kane – it wasn't just me being embarrassing!

After the live show you all go back to where you first congregated in this big room and now they had filled it with food trucks with every conceivable type of food you could want to eat. There are lots of bars around the room too and everyone who came out of the auditorium was now ready to party! Everywhere you looked there were athletes of the most incredible calibre. Sporting stars in their prime, retired athletes, Olympians, Paralympians: the room was filled with legends. You feel very small and insignificant among all of them, knowing what they have done and achieved and worked hard to do, and will work hard carrying on doing. And what was more incredible was that so many of them came over to us and wanted to congratulate us! A lot of them told us that they had set alarms to watch our game at five in the morning and that was just mind-blowing.

We were a bit star-struck as all these big sports stars came over and then they would start chatting and we'd realise they were just normal like us. We had a great time! Stuart Broad the cricketer was one of the first over and spoke to us for ages, and then the CEO of Amazon UK came up and had a long chat. We spoke to the hockey girls, boxers, gymnasts. It wasn't just sportspeople; the Weasley brothers from the *Harry Potter* films, actors James and Oliver Phelps, came over to us and had a chat, which was super-cool. And I don't watch it but apparently there is a *Love Island* TV show or something in the UK? There were three of them there, a girl and two guys, and apparently they were the three that everyone loved. Only the London girls in our team knew who they were; I had no idea!

An hour or so into the evening a live band started and Clare Balding and all the hosts were first up on the dancefloor and started shouting over to us, 'Come on, girls!' And before we knew it they were dragging us on to the dancefloor like overexcited relatives at a wedding reception. It was so much fun! Apparently these awards are renowned for having a great after-party and this one certainly didn't disappoint. Everyone let their hair down and drank and ate whatever they wanted. Sometimes it can be hard to go to an awards evening when you are the only athlete or part of a small group of athletes there. You feel everyone is judging you on what you eat and whether you drink or not. But there was no judging here. Everyone was the same, everyone had the same appreciation for how bloody hard it was being an elite sportsman or sportswoman and we all just let our hair down. And took our shoes off! We aren't made for heels, us netballers, so our heels were off probably within the first hour and we were wandering around barefoot – we had no shame!

The next day we all had to be in camp for England training. Spirits were definitely high all that week as we reminisced about that night. This was the last camp of 2018 and the end of an incredible year for the England netball team. A week later it was Christmas and so I went back to Mum's and we drove over to Holland to share the festivities with my brother, Dad and his family. It must be very hard for my mum and my dad's new wife and my hat goes off to both of them for the way they are able to accommodate us all with no angst or bad feelings. I have a lot of respect for that, the way they are content just to see all the children together. Myself and Raoul, Inez and Noor – we all get on so well. We love our dad and we love our mums and that quality time we spend together is so special. I appreciate it every time it happens because I know it can't be easy but it is done for our benefit. Those moments with family, that special bond we have . . . whenever I am finding things tough or get lonely, I remember that contentment I have when I am around my family. And one day, when I have a family of my own, it will become even more special.

The year 2018 was pretty amazing all things considered and it wasn't like I was aiming for anything in particular, I was just going about my business and whatever I was doing, I tried to do it well. There was something even more special about 2018 and I knew what it was at the beginning of December, but I wasn't allowed to mention it to anyone until the official announcement came through at the end of the month: I was to be awarded a CBE in the queen's New Year Honours list!

This is something I am struggling to get my head round. I still can't quite believe it. I am still in shock when people mention it and congratulate me – I know I probably sound like an authentic Aussie when I say something is 'unreal' but blimey, this was as unreal as it got!

I got the phone call when I was in Australia, a couple of days before I flew back to England. It was a call from the British Deputy High Commissioner in Canberra and the conversation (as I remember it because, let's be honest, it isn't an everyday sort of conversation and I was a bit blown away!) went like this: 'Geva, because of your services to netball, we'd like to present you with this CBE if you would accept it.' Of course, I said, 'Wow! Yes, please, thank you, yes thank you!'

She then continued to tell me that this was top secret and I wasn't allowed to tell my family until the announce-ment had been made public. Well, surely that is code for 'You can tell your mum!' I was actually at my boyfriend's place at the time and after I finished the conversation I was quite obviously in a state of shock. I had to tell someone! I told him, which was pretty safe as it turned out, because he didn't have a clue what a CBE was or why it was so special. He is American and he didn't give a crap, to put it nicely! I'm OK, I thought, I haven't broken any rules – he's not going to tell anyone. It literally went in one ear and out the other. The secret would be safe. But there was no way I wasn't going to tell Mum! So I rang her, and God knows what time it was in the morning, I think it must have been around 4 a.m., but she answered the phone right away. When I told her she pretty much lost the plot; her voice went up a couple of octaves and she was just so excited.

What I didn't realise at the time was that she had put in the application nominating me. She had been contacting people, from both across the netball spectrum and the charities I was involved with. She contacted England Netball for a reference but they told her they were thinking of putting forward some of the team themselves, including me. They wanted Mum to hand over all the letters and emails she had received in support of my application as they thought it would be better coming from a national governing body, but Mum decided against it. And it is thanks to her that I have been awarded my Commander of the British Empire award, as not a single other England netballer made the honours list.

Once I had got Mum to calm down I did try to hammer home that she had to keep this to herself and that I was breaking the rules by telling her. I did worry about her telling everyone as she gets so bloody excited about everything, but she did well and kept it to herself. And so did I. And as the end of December got closer we kept thinking, they must announce this soon. And then I started getting emails from Radio Solent and BBC South Today congratulating me and I knew that, at last, the good news was out. The Deputy High Commissioner had told me that it would be going to the media twelve hours before the official announcement so I knew that, now the likes of the BBC were contacting me, it was only a matter of hours before everyone knew!

* * *

When I woke up in the morning I had so many messages and texts from people in Australia and around the world. It was crazy. So I put out my 'thank you' post on social media and tried to respond to as many messages as I could. It still hasn't really sunk in; I still don't believe I am someone deserving of such an accolade. How can I be? I just do what I do, I play netball. I found all the attention and kind words and tributes overwhelming . . . Was it all real? I imagine that when I go to the palace, I will still think it's not real! I really hope that the Queen is there. Can you imagine how amazing that would be?! I adore the royal family. I am going to be in my element! And of course, I will take my mum and dad with me if I can. I would take everyone if I could, but we'll just have to wait and see. I might have to keep an eye on Mum if the Queen is there. I think I'll have to muzzle her – she's bound to say something she shouldn't or will go up and try to hug her or something!

EPILOGUE

'I don't know where I'm going from here but I promise it won't be boring.'
David Bowie

MET an old teammate, Johanna Haynes, from my Dorset Junior days recently after playing for England at the Copper Box arena at the beginning of 2019. It was a real blast from the past; it seemed like only yesterday that Jo and I, fresh-faced youngsters, were playing together and now here she was watching me play with her seven-year-old daughter Harriet. Harriet was really into netball, she told me, and was playing at school, and I was struck by a sudden instinctual longing in my heart. Mother and daughter, watching netball together and playing netball together . . . wouldn't that be wonderful? Maybe that will be me in ten years' time, taking my own daughter to an England match, telling her how I used to do it in my day or showing her a trick or two on court.

Remember I mentioned the questions I am asked most

as an athlete? There is a new one doing the rounds just now – where do I see myself in ten years' time? – and that is precisely the image that comes to mind. We all dream about the future but generally don't give a picture to those dreams, and yet I saw Jo and Harriet and felt that actually, bringing children into the world, bringing a new generation into netball, sounds like a pretty cool dream. I know from experience that things don't always go to plan and you have to be open to change and not be too rigid in your planning. Ultimately I hope that in ten years' time I will be happy and I will be something I am proud of and making others proud – being the best daughter, best sister, best friend I can be. Teacher? Wife? Mother? Who knows, but I want to be happy with life because, at the end of the day, it's too short and all we actually eventually end up being is simply a memory for someone. I want to do my best to be a good one! My answer to the question at the moment is quite practical: 'still walking,' is my first response! My ankles are bloody terrible; I have no ligaments left in them now and I joke with the physios and say I just rely on my tendons (the tissue that connects muscle to bone). I suppose because I've had issues with my back and my knees, my ankles wanted a little bit of attention too. But I'll do what I have always done with my ankles – strap the hell out of them and carry on.

Travelling is also getting to be a factor in my life. I class Australia as my home and I miss it when I leave. I always feel unsettled flying over to the UK and excited about returning to Australia which makes me think I have found home. I have been travelling since I was very young, from Bournemouth to Bath, to training to trials, to this part of the country to that part . . . to Australia, to New Zealand . . . to all the amazing places I have been to with my netball. So perhaps in ten years' time I would like to be properly settled and answerable to just myself. Having been involved in netball from the age of sixteen means that I have been 'organised' all that time; all the decisions about training, where to train, how to train, have been made for me. All the decisions about where I need to be before a season starts, timings for this, checking in with someone, asking permission to do something or go somewhere . . . My whole life has been organised for me. Perhaps having control of my own diary might be nice in ten years. I want to be my own boss. As an athlete you are to a certain extent; you can control what you eat, how you train, the effort and intensity that you put in, and yet you are still under some sort of control. You are still answerable to someone because if you don't put in the effort and watch what you eat and you don't train and don't perform you have to explain why. I am older now and I probably work a bit harder in all the aspects of the game that I slacked in as a younger athlete.

I suspect a lot of people will probably retire after the World Cup in 2019. I'm not sure where I am at personally; I always thought maybe I would because I thought I would be married and possibly looking at starting a family, and I would concentrate on club netball and retire from the international scene. But now I am just going to see what happens. I definitely want a bit of a break after the World Cup; whether that means I have a break for a year or a couple of months I don't know yet. I definitely want to keep playing netball as long as I am still contributing to the team, as long as I still feel like I am an asset to a club and to my teammates. I want to do that for as long as possible.

In the short term I just want success at the World Cup, pure and simple. Australia are gunning for us now. We beat them in the dying seconds of a game that had their name all over it and that is their driving force, that is the fire in their belly. They want to come to our country and steal that medal back on our soil. People have realised we don't just talk the talk, we can put our money where our mouth is, but we are very conscious of trying not to get ahead of ourselves. That is something that we are reminded about as a team constantly – from the coach to the captain to the players – this isn't going to be easy. The World Cup won't be handed to us. We have put ourselves up there and now we have a big target on our back. All the other teams and countries playing want to win the World Cup and they want us to lose.

I am personally cautious about the New Zealand side. They have Noeline at the helm now, and Laura Langman as their captain. Along with Jamaica, they have some real firepower that hasn't been seen on the international scene for a while. It is setting up to be a fantastic World Cup and I really hope each team goes out there firing on all cylinders and giving it their all. If that is the case there will be some fantastic games for the fans. And I hope even more fans will get caught up in the excitement and edge-of-your-seat thrills that our game can provide. I was told just the other day by a lady who watched us play on TV at the beginning of the year that her son, who had never watched a netball game before, was glued to the telly. He told her that he thought it was better than football! How cool is that? Let's get that going, let's get everyone involved and behind us – boys, girls, mums, dads, grannies, uncles – enjoying the show. Because it is a show – a show that demonstrates dedication, teamwork, skill and perseverance. It's a game that shows nerves of steel and wills to win.

It's a game I'm bloody proud to be part of.

ACKNOWLEDGEMENTS

I WOULD like to dedicate this book to all those folk who have featured in my life thus far. From Lyn Gunson who spotted something in me in the early days, to Julie Hoornweg who had the balls to elevate me into the senior squad Noeline, you've showed me great empathy and put the fire back in my belly. My teachers from St Peter's, in particular Viv Hawkins and Patrick Lucas, who enlightened me with the balance of elite sport and education.

My oldest friends Vicky and Pete Simmonds, 'the twins' who know me better than most. To all my teammates that make me a better version of myself. Mo'onia Gerrard and Sonia Mkoloma, my besties who just get me.

To old love that has given me strength to stay true to myself and new love that has provided me with hope. To Mason, you 'leapt' forward with inspiration when I needed it most and I look forward to returning the favour one day.

I would not be half the person I am today if not for many of my family members. All those cousins in England and St. Lucia, my cheeky Auntie Nina, my little sisters Inez and Noor, my inspiring dad, Greg and my rock of a brother Raoul. They have ALL contributed to my life offering support, encouragement, many hours of laughter and loads of hugs.

And last but not least, the most heartfelt thanks to my mum, Yvonne. You are my best critic and my strongest supporter. You saw something in me worth believing in long before I believed in myself. You are emotional but a rock, impatient and yet patient, tired but you never stop, calm amid the chaos but most of all, you are simply bloody wonderful Mum.

PHOTOGRAPHIC ACKNOWLEDGEMENTS

THE author and publisher would like to thank the following for permission to reproduce photographs:

Quinn Rooney/Getty Images, Matt King/Stringer/Getty Images, Scott Barbour/Getty Images, Nigel Owen/Action Plus/Getty Images, Michael Dodge/Getty Images

Other photographs are from private collections.

Every reasonable effort has been made to trace the copyright holders, but if there are any errors or omissions, Hodder & Stoughton will be pleased to insert the appropriate acknowledgement in any subsequent printings or editions.